"Park's gripping debut novel, an unconventional love story, unfolds in KKK–controlled Cattahatchie County, Mississippi, during a violent 1969 civil rights struggle. ... the author's ability to turn a phrase, capturing, in a few words time, place and atmosphere, is a joy. Solid character portrayals, personal melodrama, a murder mystery, and unrestrained violence propel this page-turner to its explosive conclusion. ... an addictive read with some final surprises." --*Kirkus Reviews*

"Louis Hillary Park is one of those rare authors who spins an intelligent story driven by complex, believable characters with heartbeats a reader can hear." – *New York Times bestselling author John Ramsey Miller, author of THE LAST DAY.*

"All That The River Holds pulls readers in and keeps them turning pages with not only a continuous flow of action and mystery, but with characters so deep and well-crafted that you simply want to stay within their world." – *Eliot Klienberg, journalist & author*

ALL THAT THE RIVER HOLDS

A Novel of Mystery, Suspense and Passion

LOUIS HILLARY PARK

authorHOUSE®

AuthorHouse™
1663 Liberty Drive
Bloomington, IN 47403
www.authorhouse.com
Phone: 1 (800) 839-8640

Published by AuthorHouse 11/06/2019

ISBN: 978-1-7283-3141-6 (sc)
ISBN: 978-1-7283-3140-9 (hc)
ISBN: 978-1-7283-3139-3 (e)

Library of Congress Control Number: 2019916148

Print information available on the last page.

FROM DESIRE STREET BOOKS
NEW ORLEANS, LOUISIANA

In this reinvention of his acclaimed debut novel, Louis Hillary Park, an award-winning journalist with deep roots in the Deep South, tells the story of Holly Lee Carter, a young, beautiful photo-journalist left paralyzed while covering the Vietnam War. When she inherits her family newspaper, she reluctantly leaves Los Angeles and returns to Cattahatchie County -- "the last of its kind, even in Mississippi." As Holly fights to keep the newspaper afloat and out of the hands of the Ku Klux Klan, she comes to believe that her father's death was no accident. Returning home in a wheelchair, Holly must deal with her own fears, insecurities, frustrations and the reawakening of powerful, long-dormant desires.

A surprising friendship develops between Holly and Cutter Carlucci, an 18-year-old high school football star with a chip on his shoulder about "cripples" and a vicious Klansman father. Living on his own, with all his belongings stowed in his old Jeep, Cutter is mature far beyond his years. With the county school system under a desegregation order and a new all-white academy set to open, "the best football player anybody in (the county) ever saw up close" will have to make a decision that will shape not only his future but that of his sister and mother - and perhaps cost him his life.

When the sheriff is murdered and churches and crosses are burned, the county is ready to explode; and does when the Klan's most fearsome, deadly and unstoppable bomb-maker arrives in town.

This book is a work of fiction. DeLong, Mississippi and Cattahatchie County, Mississippi, are fictional locales. All of the characters, situations and events depicted in this book are the product of the author's imagination, other than historic events, which are used fictitiously.

The Lord does not look at the things man looks at.
Man looks at the outward appearance but the Lord looks at the heart.

1 Samuel 16:7

This book is dedicated to my wife, Joyce,
who has taught me the meaning of grace and dignity and committed love.
Thank you for your faith in God and your faith in me.

PROLOGUE

Life is full of so many small pieces, moments and days in shades of color that when gathered form a whole like stained glass in a chapel window. So, it's sometimes difficult to pick out the piece that, taken away, would have changed the entire picture of one's life.

Such is not the case for me.

Looking back from the distance of five decades and stops all over the Far East, I can pinpoint the year, the summer, the month, the day – July 6, 1969 – when my life changed forever.

It was the day that Holly Lee Carter came home.

It was in the summer before my senior year in high school. The summer of my eighteenth year. And for me, my best friend Cutter, and our little two-stoplight town of DeLong, Mississippi, nothing ever really would be the same.

It was the summer I killed a man.

At least I think I did.

I hope I did.

• 	Nathan Wallace

PART I

CHAPTER 1

Mississippi, July 1969

Vietnam killed my older brother in the fall of '66. By the following autumn, Momma had grieved herself into the ground. Since then, Daddy had been drinking hard and daily, trying to follow them down into the black soil of our Cattahatchie County farm south of DeLong.

At the open kitchen window, I lowered my coffee cup and drew in a long breath, wanting to hold within me the dark, cool minutes just ahead of morning when the world is at its quietest and crops stand in their orderly moonlit rows like acres of green, freshly washed crystal. Daddy's deep, drunken snoring soured the moment and my stomach. He snored when sober, but the potent red-corn whiskey lowered the tone until it became a rasp, capable of grinding away my best moods and making rough even the most pleasant mornings. Alone in the kitchen that had been so well used and loved by my mother, Denise Wallace – "Neesie" to her friends, and they included nearly everyone in Cattahatchie County – I told myself I shouldn't let myself get worked up … again.

Moments ahead of first light I pushed through the screen door and let it slam. On the front porch I listened as the ring of the door spring died away, buried in the noise from Daddy's bedroom. No awakening. No concern that maybe an intruder was endangering the comfortable home he'd built on land handed down from his grandfather. The farm was in near ruin, but he didn't care. He didn't even change cadence.

It made good sense for a farmer with two sons to hint of splitting the land between them. The policy made considerably easier the task of keeping both interested during the tedium of plowing and other repetitive, mechanical chores that made up the bulk of farm life. And I'm sure I would have gotten a decent share of our 520 acres. But from early on it was obvious Steve, who was my senior by eight years, was a born farmer. After Steve, my mother had had a hard time getting pregnant and carrying a child – there were three miscarriages – so I was a born surprise. Steve had our father's touch, unwilling as was, in the fields and I had our mother's love for books, and world events and history. He was stout and handsome,

1

in a wind-burned unpretty way, and had an ability that was little short of magic to urge a sturdy bean plant or a cotton stalk out of the soil. What magic I made was in spiral notebooks, writing on both sides of each page until the books were filled with stories set anywhere other than a farm.

Steve quietly encouraged me the only way he knew how — with his hands, building the large bookcases that covered one entire wall of my room. Sometimes when I was missing him the most, I ran my hand along the shelves and could almost feel his sweat and see the smile he wore as confidently as his Army fatigues. *How could he be dead?* Still, my writing was seen as nothing solid. Not a bean plant or a cornstalk, like the green legions that stood at attention at the edge of my headlights as I bounced toward the highway. Back in the spring, Daddy had managed enough sober days to guide me and some part-time laborers in getting the seeds into the ground. Then about the middle of May he began a solid drunk and dumped the whole farm in my lap. There was no other lap to drop it in. Certainly not Steve's. After my brother leaped from a helicopter onto a land mine, he lived for thirteen days with both legs and most of his pelvis blown away. Then he stopped.

When the half of Steve that remained was returned to us ten days later, Brother MacAllister, the minister of First Denomination Church where mother had been a member for forty-odd years, stood beneath the large oak tree set alone in the middle of our acreage. Like a massive umbrella, the ancient tree overspread and shaded the Wallace family cemetery. Over stones that dated back to the 1820s, Brother MacAllister intoned – "It's better that the Lord took Steve to sit at His right hand rather than leave him to *cra-a-awl* this earth. The Lord spared Steve that humiliation. Now let us kneel here on this good ground Steve so loved – took so much from, gave so much to – and give God thanks for the merciful sleep He granted your Steve."

But Mama didn't kneel and she didn't give thanks, and she never went back to First Denomination. She figured, I think, that if God was all that merciful, He would have had Steve hop off that Cobra gunship about a foot to the right. But it's funny how things work out. A little more than two and a half years later years later and heading into my senior year, I was all but engaged to Brother Charles Everett MacAllister's youngest daughter, Patti. Everyone, except her folks and me, called her "PattiWac" – because it rhymed with Mac and because she could be a bit – well, "wacky" would be the kindest word.

By the time I reached the intersection of Highway 27, the last of Saturday night's quarter moon was as white as my Sunday shirt and set off in a blue-black belt that was tightening on the western horizon. I looked south, then north, then south again. Highway 27 was the main artery of travel and commerce through Cattahatchie County, running as it did all the way from the shrimp boat docks of the Mississippi Gulf Coast, through several hundred miles and dozens of small towns like DeLong and deep into Tennessee. On most days it was thick with traffic – pickups loaded with vegetables for sale on DeLong's town square, eighteen-wheelers roaring through and people in their used cars headed for jobs in New Albany or Tupelo. But this was Sunday morning and in the far distance I saw only two sets of headlights cutting through the day's first pink-purple light. Sunday was the one day that most of the county let itself sleep until it was time to rise for church. But I hadn't slept in because I knew my best friend, Cutter, would just now be winding down from another Saturday's worth of work at a Tennessee juke joint called The Gin.

Slapping the long neck of the floor shifter into first, I swung north off the gravel of Pleasant Ridge Road and onto the damp, gray pavement that loosely followed the contours of the Cattahatchie River's east bank and the railroad tracks that ran beside it. Next stop, DeLong and the Cotton Café.

DeLong was the county seat and the largest town within 40 miles. Population 1,991. An active set of fall births and a moderate number of autumn deaths at the old-folks home would send DeLong brimming over 2,000 before the next decade arrived in January. It was something to shoot for. Something – anything – in a little place like DeLong was better than nothing. We already had plenty of nothing.

Had it not been for perpetually bald tires and a suspension that was irreparably warped – accounting for the tires, I could have dropped my hands from the wheel and let the experienced old Chevy find its own way to the café on River Street. The Cotton, after all, was a tradition ingrained in the county's farmers, merchants, lawyers, cops and kids who daily moved through its booths and tables on a schedule as regular as factory shifts. Miss Winona St. Julian, a small, bent black woman from across the river, had cooked for three or more generations – depending on how prolific the family. She had stayed on through two changes of ownership, four husbands and a pair of world wars. Her breakfast biscuits, fried chicken lunches and chicken-fried steak suppers were what really kept people coming back.

C hanging gears, I was eager to cover the 8.7 miles between the highway intersection and The Cotton. Cutter probably would beat me to the café, be at our usual Sunday morning spot at the counter, drinking black coffee from behind even blacker aviator shades. He was always a step ahead or a flash quicker. Not just of me, but of every teenager straining the reins of manhood at Cattahatchie High School.

At six-foot-three, two-hundred-and-thirty-two pounds, Cutter Carlucci would have been a blue-chip, nationally sought-after college running back/linebacker prospect had he played anywhere except at a little high school in Mississippi's smallest sports division. But it wasn't just his size. Dodge McDowell, who played right guard, and Gary Vernon, the left tackle, were bigger. Truck Jamison, our center, was two hundred and fifteen. But that was all just grunt-and-push muscle. Cutter had an extraordinary mix of pure speed, lateral agility and something Coach Pearce called "football vision" – the ability to see running lanes before the holes opened. Defensively, he was a brutal linebacker who played every down with that quality of barely tempered insanity that coaches admire above all others. "Reckless abandon," they call it.

Driving four miles south of DeLong I was eager to hear from Cutter what adventures had transpired the previous night in his oh-so-exciting and independent life. At least, that's how his life seemed to me heading into our senior year. Cutter had left home almost four years earlier, and between farm, construction or mechanicing jobs worked as a bouncer, bartender and waiter at a notorious roadhouse just above the Tennessee line. The Gin was famous – or infamous, depending on how hard you thumped your Bible – and the closest place within 20 miles of bone-dry DeLong to legally get a cold beer. Of course, some of Cattahatchie County's more enterprising bootleggers made rounds as regularly as milkmen. Dodge McDowell's dad, "Shootin' Sam," stopped by my house twice a week delivering gasoline-colored home-brew in pint-sized Mason jars. Daddy left cash money for him under a loose brick on the porch steps.

With all that on my mind, and my eight-track player blaring The Stones' *Beggar's Banquet* from the four speakers behind my seats, I didn't hear or see the two vehicles racing up behind me until they practically were on my bumper. Their lights exploded in my rearview mirrors. I felt my chest tighten, my eyes widen and I had to fight my instinct to hit the brake. If I had, the big, four-door convertible would have plowed right into me. Instead, it shot into the passing lane as a green Ford sedan tried to cut it off. Both cars went by me doing what had to be close to a hundred. It happened so fast, I didn't get a look at either of the drivers, but I knew I wanted to see who was racing this time of the morning so I floored my old truck and got it all the way up to sixty. I couldn't come close to catching them, but maybe I could watch from a distance. It was the first Lincoln Continental convertible I'd ever seen up close. Even for the couple of seconds it took to blow past me.

When I rounded a curve into a long straightaway that led to the Yancy Creek bridge south of the fairgrounds, I saw the sedan banging door to door with the baby blue Lincoln, trying to push it into the ditch – and succeeding. Two wheels were off on the shoulder and – *ohh, shhhit!* – the concrete bridge abutment was coming up. Fast!

Turning my face half away, I was prepared to see the convertible shatter against the end of the bridge – metal and limbs flying in all directions, propelled by a fireball. At the last instant the cars separated. The Lincoln disappeared into the wide ditch on the right as the driver of the green sedan shot across the bridge without ever touching the brakes.

A few moments later, I slid to a stop at the foot of the bridge and ran around to the edge of the road, expecting to see the car upside down and torn apart. Maybe even burning. But the driver hadn't let the nose climb up the steep bank, where it would have snagged and rolled. Instead, he – *no she!* – had held it in the flat of the ditch, letting the water, mud and thick stand of cattails slow the big convertible like a safety net. The water from Yancy Creek flowed just under the front bumper.

Quickly, I hustled down the ditch bank and came up on the back of the car.

A little white ball of fur leaped over the shoulder of the black woman in the front passenger seat and onto the luggage that was scattered in back. It began to yap.

"Easy," I said as the little dog barked and snapped and bared its black gums. "I don't mean anyone any harm. I saw what happened. I wanted to see if anyone was hurt. If I can help."

Still gripping the steering wheel and staring straight ahead the white woman in the driver's seat said, "Charlie, *régler après à moi.*"

The dog gave me one more hard look then hopped over into the front seat and lay down. I pulled my feet through muck to the front door.

"Whatever you told it, that dog sure seems to mind," I said, but the woman with the long auburn hair and Wayfarers didn't respond. I looked her over and there was plenty to see – lots of curves even under a tie-dyed T-shirt and pair of well-worn Tuff-Nut overalls. Especially as she drew in one deep breath after another, her chest rising and falling. The pretty black woman with the big Afro and pullover blouse was holding her hand over her mouth as if she might throw up. Then I saw it. The hand control beside the driver's knee. I had never seen one up close before, but I knew what it was – that it allowed someone without use of their legs to control the brakes and the gas. I glanced into the back seat and saw the handles of a wheelchair sticking up from a pile of luggage that had slid atop it. The woman behind the wheel was Holly Lee Carter, my new boss at the county's twice-weekly newspaper.

"Miss Carter, my name's Nate Wallace. I work part-time for *The Current-Leader*. Are you –?"

"Nate Wallace, yes. You write high school sports," she said without looking at me.

"Yes, ma'am. Miss Carter, should I go get an ambulance or a doctor or somethin'?" I tried again, and the questions finally seemed to bring her into the moment and loosen her grip on the wheel. "Are you two okay?"

She flexed her fingers then ran her hands along her thighs. She still hadn't looked at me. "I think so. Eve, are you all right?"

The woman nodded but didn't remove her hand from her mouth.

It was then that we heard another vehicle on the bridge, and it crossed everyone's mind at the same moment that the men in the sedan had come back. "They had a gun," gasped the black woman, real fear in her eyes. "I saw it!"

My heart started to race. If they had one now and decided to use it, it would be like shooting fish in a barrel. Easier, really. I exhaled an audible sigh of relief when Cutter leaned over the rail. Flustered and embarrassed by my own fear, I swallowed and tried to force my voice to be steady. With limited success, I asked, "What are you doing here?"

"I went by the Cotton and you weren't there. I thought one of those may-pop tires you ride around on might have seen its day," he said. "I expected to find *you* in the ditch. What'cha got?"

"Two men in a green Ford ran these ladies off the road," I told him. "Nearly ran 'em into the end of the bridge."

Cutter pulled off his Ray-Bans for a better look. His eyes were so light blue that they were nearly clear. From our bottom-of-the-ditch angle it seemed you could look straight through the back of his head and up into the morning sky.

"I didn't see a car on this stretch."

"You think we're making it up?" demanded the black woman, her voice quivering with anger and a residue of pure fear.

"Nope. You ladies clearly had a run-in with somebody. I expect your green Ford turned off on Buena Vista Road. That's why I didn't see it," he said. "Are y'all hurt?"

"No broken bones," said Miss Carter, pulling off her sunglasses to take a look at the man twenty feet above her. Her eyes were the same sunlit green as the wet fields that spread out around us. Hair the color of smoked copper framed a face that still was beautiful but no longer the carefree face of the wild eighteen-year-old girl she'd been when, an hour after her graduation from Cattahatchie High, she pointed her Corvette toward California and took off. It was stuff of small town legend. I was only seven when she left, though I remembered her from around town but most especially from the night she won the Miss Cattahatchie County Pageant. What I mostly remembered was the way she sang and how tall she was. How she towered over the other girls that night in the floodlights of the fairgrounds rodeo arena. Now, from what the whole town had heard, she couldn't walk or even stand up. Glancing again at the wheelchair folded behind her seat, I guessed it must be so. But sitting at the wheel of that Lincoln convertible with her dusky features, long tanned arms and sturdy shoulders, she looked plenty healthy to me.

"You're Cutter Carlucci," said Miss Carter in the same husky speaking voice she'd already had at my age. I remembered that, too. In fact, a lot about Holly Lee Carter was coming back. "I've seen your picture in *The Current-Leader*."

"Cutter," he said, not angrily but firmly. "Just Cutter'll do. I've seen yours, too – Miz Carter."

"Your mother was my homeroom teacher my junior year. How –"

"That was a long time ago."

Holly took the hint and changed the subject. "This is my friend, Eve Howard."

Cutter nodded – "Miz Howard."

I did the same, then told Miss Carter, "I'm real sorry about your dad."

She pulled those bright, field green eyes away from Cutter and turned them toward me, though she seemed focused on something past me. Thomas Lanier Carter III had drowned one chill, rainy March night when he missed a sharp turn onto the Old Iron Bridge at the foot of Blue Mountain. His car went into the Cattahatchie

River, which at that time of year always runs high and brutally fast, engorged with spring rain. Except for the pinging of the engine and the splash of a fish jumping in the creek we all were silent for several long moments. Maybe she was in some sort of shock from what had just happened, and almost happened, or maybe she was simply thinking about how to respond. Although father and daughter shared a passion for journalism – he as an editorial writer with statewide influence and she as an award-winning war photographer for the *Los Angeles Chronicle* – everyone knew there was no love lost between them. In fact, as far as anyone I talked to knew, they had not spoken in years and she did not return for his funeral. That's why it was so shocking when a lawyer from Greenwood showed up in DeLong with a will that left controlling interest of the newspaper to her instead of her brother Tom IV. "Four," as he was often called as if he were merely an appendage to T.L. III, had spent most of his thirty-five years working for his daunting and demanding father. Everyone – most especially Tom's wife Mary Nell – thought Tom would inherit the newspaper and the family's century-old country house, Wolf's Run, but under the terms of Mr. Carter's surprise will, Tom got neither.

Finally Miss Carter's gaze shifted and she focused on me. "Thank you, Nate. That's kind of you. I know my father could be tough to work for, but he ran a good newspaper. That's probably what should be on his tombstone." And that's all she had to say on the subject. Then she drew in a deep breath as she took in the situation, let it out and said, "So … The good news is, we didn't hit the bridge."

"The bad news is, you're stuck in that ditch," said Cutter, looking things over. "If that soft-top limo of yours'll crank, I might be able to winch you out with my Jeep. It's a lot of weight and a lot mud, but I'll try."

Miss Carter turned the key once, twice – on the third turn the big eight-cylinder caught. Within five minutes Cutter had the Jeep swung around and a cable secured to the Continental's frame.

"Nate, you climb on out and run the winch," he said. "I'm gonna stay here and see if I can't rock the back a little. Get us some traction. Just make sure, if we can't winch this big ol' thing out of this ditch, we don't winch my Jeep into it."

Cutter went to the driver's door. "Can anybody drive this car?"

"Sure. The floor pedals work."

"Then maybe your friend should do this. I don't want to get run over."

"I've driven this car nearly every day for the last three years," Miss Carter told him. "And over the last three days, I've driven it most of the way here from L.A. I assure you, I'm capable of backing it out of this ditch without inflicting any fatal injuries."

He looked her over skeptically but said, "Aw'right, then. You go forward when I say. Backwards when I say. And *stop* when I say. And be careful. If it catches, it'll probably want to fishtail."

Holly Lee Carter saluted – "Aye, Aye, Captain."

Cutter smirked and moved to the back quarter panel and gave me the sign to wind the winch. He put all of his weight over the right rear tire. Two minutes of rocking the car forward-and-back, forward-and-back seemed to be doing no good. Then the muck let go of the Lincoln with a sucking sound and Cutter pushed out of the way, muddy from his shoulders to his work boots.

"Yea!" cheered Eve Howard, waving both arms over her head. Miss Carter kept her focus on backing the big and now battered Lincoln out of the ditch while I reversed the Jeep and kept the winch cable tight.

Cutter watched our progress. After a few moments he seemed satisfied, and he turned and walked down to the creek. He peeled off his black T-shirt with The Gin logo on the front, washed it in the shallow stream and used it to get the mud off his arms and face. He rinsed it again and pulled it back on. When Cutter climbed out of the ditch, the T-shirt clung to his chest and abdomen and made his upper body look as if was forged from black steel plate. His arms, neck and face could have been smelted from bronze and his short black hair shined like wet coal. As always, his Levi's fit like they were sewn on.

About 50 yards down the highway, I gave the winch cable some slack, crawled under the Lincoln and freed the hook. I wound it back onto the spool mounted on the Jeep's front bumper. When I walked back next to the car, I saw Miss Carter and her friend share a look as Cutter came toward us on the road. I had been around Cutter and girls – and not just girls, but *women* – enough that I'd seen the look many times. When he got almost to the car, the spell broke and Miss Carter began digging in her purse.

"Look guys, we really appreciate this," she said, pulling out two bills. "If you two hadn't stopped, there's no telling how long we'd have been down there."

"It looks like you swapped some paint with that Ford, but otherwise this big ol' tank fared pretty well," I said as I took the twenty she offered. "Riley Pressman does good body work if you want to get the dings smoothed out and get this side of the car repainted."

"Thank you, Nate," she said, extending her hand toward Cutter.

He turned away.

"I don't want your money," he said, getting into the Jeep. "I only did what I'd do for anybody I found off in a ditch. But, Miss Carter, we don't need any more of your kind in this town."

"Cutter!" I said, shocked, at least by his directness. He cranked it and pulled up beside us. "Maybe you should take this for what it was – a warning – and high-tail it back to California before you end up in even worse shape than you are now."

Before anyone could speak, Cutter threw the Jeep in gear, barked the tires and headed toward DeLong. For several moments we stared after him, saying nothing and listening as the gears changed.

"Nice guy, huh?" grunted Eve Howard.

"He usually is," I said. "He just has a real blind spot."

"For what? White folks with black friends?"

"No. For, uh, for –"

"Cripples?" Miss Carter asked softly.

I looked at her, at the handles of the wheelchair poking up behind the car seat, and back at her. I started not to answer, then considered lying, but decided there was no point denying the obvious to my new boss. "Yes, ma'am," was all I said. It was all I needed to say.

CHAPTER 2

In DeLong, Highway 27 swung slightly east, away from the Cattahatchie, and kept to a shallow valley. Sitting on a long ridge to the east were DeLong's elementary and middle schools, and the county's only high school — for white kids, that is. Behind it, the big antebellum and Victorian houses of Hill Street looked down on the rest of town, including the plateau directly above the river where the courthouse stood, surrounded by faded brick storefronts.

I took one turn around the square to see if any of our friends were sleeping it off a Saturday night drunk in the parking lot beside the Rebel Theater. None were, which was unusual. I turned down the hill at Commerce Street and went the one block to River Street, where The Cotton Café overlooked the Cattahatchie. A string of cotton warehouses painted green or red, tin grain silos and the depot for Weathers-McLain Trucking Company lined the other side of the river and mostly screened "Roseville" from view by the town's white residents. There the unpaved streets nearly were devoid of trees, cut for building material and burned for firewood long ago. But from spring to late fall, the place was overflowing with wild roses of every type and color, planted there in the 1890s by the women of the DeLong Garden Club in an effort to "brighten the lives of the unfortunate." While the plants had added lively hues to the mostly dilapidated neighborhood, over the decades they had bred and mixed and tangled to create a sea of thorns on nearly any plot of land larger than a gravesite. Nonetheless, black residents maintained their small businesses, clapboard churches, low-slung schools and street after row of shotgun-style houses. All were roofed in tin that was rusting away in myriad shades of weather-worn decrepitude. And for most of us — that is to say, those of us born with white skin — Roseville nearly was as distant as the spot on the moon where Apollo XI was scheduled to land later in the month.

As soon as I turned my truck onto River Street I knew something was up, and that it probably wasn't good. Sheriff Floyd Johnson's unmarked cruiser, its red dash light flashing, was parked behind a row of Cadillacs, Buicks and new pickups.

I parked and got out of my old truck and stomped as much mud as I could off my only pair of good shoes. The twenty Miss Carter gave me would have to go for a new pair of oxblood penny loafers at Handley's Department Store up on the square.

As it was, I'd have to hustle back home and get my tennis shoes and some clean socks. Patti and the rest of the MacAllisters would not look favorably on tennis shoes in the grand sanctuary of First Denomination, but after my Good Samaritan efforts it was tennis shoes, work boots or barefoot.

Stomping around some more I noticed that one of the vehicles was the spotless Chevy pickup former Governor Weathers had been driving around town for the last eleven months. Weathers had a deal with Kamp Motors. Each August, he got the very first pickup of the new model year that came onto the lot. And always in white, with a red interior.

"The ol' Guv, he thinks he's keepin' the common touch by drivin' a pickup around town," Daddy once said. "Ever'body knows he does his Memphis business and visits his fancy Delta planter friends in a chauffeur-driven Rolls. But that's like puttin' a dirt clod in a velvet sack. It's still just a dirt clod."

W hen I pushed through the double glass doors into the air-conditioned comfort of The Cotton Café, it was as if someone had found the volume knob on the room and turned it down to a whisper. A hand or two raised to wave in my direction, and another few heads nodded my way, but no one spoke, not wanting to break the quiet that let them hear the bits of raised voices coming from the restaurant's side room.

Paula Simpson walked to the end of the counter. "Mornin', Nate," said Paula, whose family owned the café. She was in the same Cattahatchie High class with me and Cutter. On Sunday mornings, she worked the counter so her parents could sleep in one day a week.

"What's goin' on? How come everybody's bein' so quiet?"

"Big confab goin' on in the Rotary Club Room," she told me. "From what it sounds like, the Klan was out doin' their dirt last night. They burned a cross out by Willy Slater's Grocery."

"Klan, huh?" I said, wondering if some of the Klux could have been in the car that ran Miss Carter off the road.

"Yep. Seems like the hotter this summer gets, the busier and meaner they get."

"There must be two or three county supervisor cars out there. The mayor's Caddy. Seems like a big meetin' for –"

"The cross burnin' wasn't the worst of it," said Gary Williams, who was working on a plate of bacon and buttered grits on the stool closest to us. "I heard they shot up a bunch of houses out at Pickens Ferry, up on the Moccasin Slough."

"Is that right?"

"My cousin, Phil Ward – you know, he's a dispatcher down at the jail?" Gary went on as I nodded. "He talked to his daddy, Uncle Claude, this morning. And Uncle Claude told Aunt Ezzie, who told momma, that Sheriff Johnson came back to the jail hoppin' mad. That he called a whole covey of our civic leaders and told them they could meet here or in a jail cell."

"You think he's actually got something on 'em?" I asked. Gary shrugged.

"Nate, you want coffee?" asked Paula, who played the flute in the CHS band.

"Sure. Have you seen Cutter?"

"Only in my dreams," she said, sighing theatrically. "But your stools are open. Say, Nate, how come Cutter don't date nobody from around these parts?"

It was a question I got on a fairly regular basis and my answer was always the same. I shrugged. "I guess he hasn't found anybody around here he likes that way."

Paula leaned forward propping her elbows on the counter as she looked directly into my eyes. The top three buttons of her uniform top were open. I fought with limited success to keep my gaze from tumbling into the deep valley of her cleavage.

"If Cutter would give me half a chance, I bet I could make him like me," she said, and I felt the warmth rising in my neck and spreading into my cheeks. "I'd do anything," she said, running her tongue slowly around her lips. I felt a warmth and a stirring begin in the front of my pants. "Anything."

Paula Simpson held my gaze and I realized I'd stopped breathing. "Miss Paula, could I get some coffee, please?" called John-Ned Renfro from down the counter.

"Sure thing, Mr. Renfro," said Paula over her shoulder as she straightened. Then to me, "You tell Cutter I said that. Okay?"

I took a breath and cleared my throat. "Yep," I croaked, lifting the coffee cup to my lips as Paula turned away. I hoped she didn't notice that my hands were trembling.

Except for the clatter of plates and the sizzle of bacon frying, the main room of The Cotton remained quiet as the ten or so early Sunday morning regulars strained to hear what was going on behind the folding panels that closed off the back part of the dining area. We caught a word here or there from a raised voice, but mostly it was just a rumble. Like the time Daddy took me and Steve camping and canoeing up in Arkansas. You could hear the sound of rapids around a bend in the river before you ever saw them, and you knew there was trouble ahead. In DeLong, we'd been hearing the rumblings for a long time. I thought of what I'd just heard and what I'd seen this morning out on the highway and wondered if we finally were rounding the bend toward something dangerous and inescapable.

Floyd Johnson had been my father's boss when they were on the Memphis police force after World War II. Daddy had spent most of four years in Europe as a paratrooper with the famous 101st Airborne, and when he came back he had no desire to settle again on the farm. So, he got on with the Memphis P.D. and Lieutenant Johnson, who also had family roots in Cattahatchie County, took the young officer under his wing. Daddy proved to be a skilled and able officer, and quickly rose to the rank of detective sergeant. But Momma hated the city. She wanted to be back closer to "her people" in Cattahatchie County. When Grandpa Wallace's health failed in

'52 and he could no longer handle the farm, Momma talked Daddy into moving back and taking it over. So, my father watched the detective shows flicker across our black-and-white TV screen, regret in his eyes but never on his lips, because Momma was happy. More than anything else in this world, that's what had mattered most to Billy Wallace. I think that hurt Daddy as much as Steve's death itself. The day the grim-faced Army sergeant turned into our driveway, the light went out of Momma's eyes and no matter his best efforts, Daddy never was able to make it shine again.

I sniffled and wiped my nose with a napkin. Why I was thinking about that, I wasn't sure. Sometimes thoughts of Momma and Steve, and by extension Daddy, just came on me that way.

In any case, when Captain Johnson retired from the Memphis police in '61, he moved back to Cattahatchie County. He opened a bait shop and boat dock on the river south of town. When Sheriff Moore decided not to run again in '65, Floyd Johnson defeated Governor Weathers' hand-picked candidate, Highway Patrol Sergeant J.D. Benoit, by sixty-one votes.

Sheriff Johnson had developed a reputation for relatively fair treatment for poor white folks and even blacks, but he wasn't naive. Thanks to systematic intimidation by the Klan and government officials high and low, less than three percent of the county's black population voted. The power in the county resided on Hill Street and out at Weathers' Chalmette Plantation, and it was all white.

The phone rang on the wall behind the counter. Paula picked it up, listened for a moment and said, "I'll tell him right away."

She went to the sliding panel and cracked it open. "Sheriff, Doctor Garner just called. He said the little Hayes girl is ready to go."

"Thank you, Paula," said the sheriff as he came out, pushing open the partition.

Inside the room were a dozen of the county's most prominent citizens, including Tom Carter and Brother MacAllister, my future daddy-in-law, I hoped.

"Sheriff, where do you think you're going?" demanded Frank Powell, the president of the county board of supervisors.

"I'm going to lead the ambulance to Memphis."

"May I remind you that you're not authorized to take a county vehicle across state lines unless you're in hot pursuit," said County Prosecutor Jimmy Epps.

Floyd Johnson had been a frequent visitor in our home until Daddy took to drink so bad that we no longer had visitors. Sheriff Johnson was normally an even-tempered man, but his cheeks were flushed now, and I could see he was fighting to keep control. The sheriff took a deep breath and reset his gray fedora. "Funny, Jimmy, you didn't mention that last year," he said, "when your mother had her stroke, and I cleared the way right to the emergency room doors of Baptist Hospital."

Mr. Thomas cleared his throat. "Well, that was –"

"A white woman from a prominent family," said the sheriff. "I know. But let me tell you gentlemen something. I've looked the other way while your bunch has marched around in your bed sheets and burned your crosses, because that's the way it's always been here. But I'm warning you, settin' fire to those two colored churches last month and now this? Shooting into occupied homes with automatic weapons?

"It's only pure, dumb luck your thugs didn't kill somebody up there at Pickens' Ferry. As it is, Dr. Garner says Roy Hayes' little girl may lose her sight from the flying glass. If she does, I intend to put somebody's ass in Parchman Prison. And it may be more than one.

"Mr. Bradshaw … Mr. Handley … *Governor* Weathers," he said, fixing each man with his gaze, "you better get those hooded clowns under control. If you don't, I will."

S heriff Johnson reset his hat and then went out the front door. He never broke stride on his way to the unmarked cruiser. From where I sat at the counter, I could see that several of the men in the room were red-faced. A couple started to speak, but Governor Weathers cut them off.

"Now's not the time," he said sharply in his hill-country baritone. "And this sho' as hell ain't the place. We'll let the High Sheriff cool down a bit before reconvening and deciding how to *pro*-ceed. Good day, gentlemen."

The men who'd been summoned to the café's back room headed out. Suddenly, Brother Mac was standing over me, looking at my shoes. "Nathan, I hope you're not planning to come to church like that."

"Uhh, no, sir," I told him, standing. "I was going to go home and –"

"Those shoes are ruined and you smell like river muck. What have you been up to?"

I hated to tell him the truth. Tom IV was a deacon at First Denomination and his wife, Mary Nell, taught the Young Teen Girls Sunday school class. As far as Brother Mac and his flock were concerned, Holly Lee Carter had stolen the newspaper from Tom. Even talk that "integrationist race-mixers" were behind Mr. Carter's will. There was a rumor that J.L. Burke, the carpetbagging U.S. Attorney for the Northern District of Mississippi, and Reverend Ronald Clemmer, the much-despised vice president of a Negro voting rights organization called the National Coalition for Justice, had gone to California to hatch the scheme with Miss Carter. But if she reported the morning's high-speed bumping and grinding to the sheriff, the whole town would know the details soon enough.

"Miss Carter," I said. "She's back. Somebody ran her off in the ditch down by Yancy Creek."

"Huh!" he snorted. "Holly Lee Carter is a well-known harlot and consumer of spirits. When she was a mere girl she eschewed our choir so she could stay out all night, singing in roadhouses and juke joints. I would proffer that it is a great deal more likely that she was simply imbibing alcohol and ran off in the ditch."

I started to tell him I'd seen the whole thing, but there was no point.

"Still, I suppose I can't chastise you for being a Good Samaritan. Especially considering her invalid condition."

Invalid condition?

I thought of the curves under Holly Lee Carter's overalls, those eyes and the way she'd handled that big car in the ditch, but there was nothing to be gained by sharing my observations. Brother Mac was going on – "In fact, Nate, I continue to have deep reservations about you staying on at *The Current-Leader*. Satan can take on many guises, and that of a Jezebel can be among his most dangerous."

"Yes, sir. I know! But like you say, she is an, an invalid now. And I promise, I'm gonna be on my guard every minute," I reassured. "Anyway, I'm just a part-time sportswriter. I report to Mr. Rainy, the sports editor. I hardly ever even spoke to Mr. Carter. I'm sure it'll be the same with her."

"We'll see, Nathan. But I can't have doubts about someone with whom my daughter is keeping company," he told me, the threat less than subtle. "Now you better get on home and change your shoes. Shall we go?"

I wanted to say no, that I was waiting on Cutter, but he was another line on Brother Mac's long list of the unworthy. So, I got up and followed along. When we walked out the front door, Cutter was angling the Jeep into a parking spot across the street. I found a little bit of nerve and said, "Brother Mac, I need to talk to Cutter for a minute."

He looked down his nose in the direction of the Jeep. "Very well, but I expect you to be in your Sunday school room on time."

"Yes, sir. I –"

"And, Nathan, don't forget, goal posts are no substitute for the cross."

"Nope. No, sir. I sure won't forget."

How could I? I wondered. It was one of C.E. MacAllister's favorite catch phrases.

"This whole town's just too football crazy," he said, working an old saw. "Cattahatchie County has put that boy on a pedestal, like an idol, like a golden calf. But you mark my word, his feet are made of clay, and one of these days they'll crumble."

Cutter already was a sore subject between me and Patti and her daddy. When I made no response, Brother Mac headed for his new Mercury and drove away. I crossed the street. "Where've you been?"

"I pulled down Convict Road and changed clothes behind that big stand of oaks. What was Brother Daddy doing here of a Sunday mornin'?" he asked, teasing me about my would-be daddy-in-law.

Cutter propped against the Jeep and listened as I related, like the good reporter I hoped to someday be, everything I'd seen and heard inside the café. Every ugly and exciting and worrisome detail. As was his way, Cutter let me talk, taking it all in and saying nothing.

"So, what do you think?" I prodded as Cutter walked to the back of the Jeep and began unlocking the metal footlocker bolted into the bed.

"I think you need new shoes."

"Shoes? I'm not talking about shoes. What do you think about what the Klux're up to? You think it was them that run Miss Carter off the road?"

"I don't think about it one way or another. Mainly, I think it's not my fight," he said, keying the trunk's padlock and sliding it out of the eyelet. "I'm not a politician or preacher. And I'm not a policeman. I'm just a guy who plays football and tends a little bar."

"But —"

He pushed up the trunk lid and pulled free from an elastic strap a set of new black cowboy boots with white stitching and silver toe caps. "Here," he said, handing them to me. "They're too small for me. But you might get some wear out of 'em. I'd planned to pass 'em on the next time you dropped by camp, but it looks like you could use 'em now."

"Wow!" I sighed, smelling the fresh leather. "Where'd they come from?"

"I stopped in the Cone & Cream the other night for a milkshake, and they were on the seat when I came out."

Such unexpected and unrequested offerings had become part of his life. And though I knew he understood it at some level the way the town – the whole county, really – had adopted him since he left home, he never grew comfortable with the odd way in which his Jeep often was treated like a four-wheeled shrine by football-worshipping pilgrims. Their gifts usually had more significance to the giver than to Cutter, but he accepted them in the spirit of kindness and solemnity with which they were offered.

A watch, waterproof.

Pies of all sorts, and cakes with every flavor of frosting. A box of rubbers, 200 count.

A mask and snorkel. Boxes of shotgun shells.

Ablack-trimmed wallet with "Cutter #13" sculpted into the tan hide.

Pocket knives were popular.

Bushels of butter beans and black-eyed peas.

Several hand-made fishing lures and a number that weren't.

Gallon cans stacked with fresh peaches.

Watermelons appeared so regularly we'd taken to calling them "Jeep eggs." We didn't call the steaks anything but "great" each time a Styrofoam ice chest showed up loaded with T-bones, top sirloins and rib-eyes.

Bottles of good bonded liquor, a limitless amount of homebrew and cases of beer appeared to help wash down the meals. Six-packs of Coke came, too.

Several Bibles.

Four pages from a Baptist hymnal.

A worn-out collar for a dog named Jess.

Tickets to various college sports events and Memphis concerts.

A nice ratchet set.

Then there were the rolls of cash that sometimes materialized under the seats.

All of it was left more or less anonymously, except for lingerie that often had a phone number written in the crotch or cup.

And there were more odds and ends that Cutter mostly passed along to teammates. I worked out as a scrawny third-string wide receiver on a Cattahatchie Wolves team that had only two real strings. On football Friday nights, all I ever caught was the clipboard Coach Pearce tossed my way. But I was Cutter's best friend.

In any case, he could keep only so much tribute. Everything he owned had to fit into the old Jeep he'd rebuilt from the ground up. And it did.

On the back bumper, I sat and slipped off my ruined penny loafers. Cutter tossed me a pair of white athletic socks.

"You comin' out to the camp tonight?" he asked. "Me and Dodge are gonna throw some steaks on the fire."

"Sounds good. I'd love to. But me and Patti have practice for the youth choir until eight. I'm hopin' Brother Daddy'll let us go ridin' around for a while after."

"Out Palmer Road? To that little cutback behind Josh Knowles' barn?"

I felt my cheeks flush a little pink. "If I'm lucky," I said as I pulled the second boot on and stood. "Nice! These are beauties. Thanks."

"I'm glad to see somebody get some use –"

Cutter snapped the phrase off in mid-sentence like an icicle breaking under its own weight. His lips tightened and his gaze was as easy to follow as a strand of cold barbed wire. Cutter's father, Tony Carlucci, was turning onto River Street. He was in the passenger seat of a green Ford sedan driven by Highway Patrolman J.D. Benoit.

The car slowed to a crawl before approaching in the narrow street. My friend's body tensed then uncoiled in the same way it did right before kickoff. Cutter stepped to the driver's side of the Jeep and popped his shotgun from its dashboard mount, chambered a round and laid it across the seats.

"Nate, step back," he said, but I was frozen in my new boots.

"They're probably just looking for Weathers," I offered, my voice suddenly brittle with a charge of nervous adrenalin.

Benoit was the ex-governor's state-provided bodyguard and Cutter's father ran the machine shop that took care of all the trucks, tractors and various other pieces of motorized equipment on Weathers' sprawling farm west of town. He and Weathers had been war buddies down on the Gulf Coast where Tony was sent to recuperate after losing his leg when his B-17 bomber was shot down over Holland. At least, that was the story told by the former prizefighter and street thug raised here and there but mostly near the Philadelphia docks up north in Pennsylvania. Cecil Weathers had been a major in charge of a supply depot in Gulfport, and rumor had it that Carlucci and Weathers did some shady dealing with the New Orleans mob involving spare parts that should have gone to the war effort in Europe. Nothing was ever proven, and in 1946 Tony arrived in DeLong on the heels of Weathers and a young and trusting nurse's aide named Jennifer Ambrose Cutter. Tony went to work supervising Chalmette's big machine shop and, some said, as an enforcer of Weathers' will among the dozens of black sharecroppers and poor white sawmill and gin workers who earned a living on the big farm. It was a meager living to be sure, and Weathers intended to make sure it stayed that way. Less for them, more for him, and for old Senator DeLong, while he was still alive, which he wasn't for long after Weathers returned from his military service. In '47, a starry-eyed, I-know-I-can-redeem-him Jennifer Cutter defied her family's most strident objections and eloped to Memphis to become Mrs. Anthony J. Carlucci. Now the son produced by that union stared into the car as his father and Benoit slowly passed by.

"Don't stop," Cutter warned Benoit, his hand on the twelve-gauge in the Jeep.

This was a battle that had been brewing since the first punch Cutter ever could remember seeing his barrel-chested, hammer-handed father deliver to Cutter's 105-pound mother. He told me once, his eyes bright with moonshine, that it had been a right hook and that he'd heard his mother's rib crack. By Cutter's recollection, that was at least a decade and a half ago.

Tony stared straight ahead, refusing to look his son's way. Benoit sneered and thumped his cigarette butt at Cutter's feet. But he didn't stop.

Cutter warily followed the sedan's progress along River Street until it turned right onto Commerce, allowing us a view of the passenger side. I shook my head as the adrenaline stiffness drained out of my muscles. Their arrogance was at once astonishing and unsurprising, driving the vehicle through the middle of town, its side dented and scraped and streaked with baby blue paint. They thought they were invincible, untouchable – protected by Weathers' vast wealth and political clout, and embraced by the Invisible Empire of the Klan. The truth I had learned growing up in Cattahatchie County, the truth I knew in that moment was that they probably were right.

CHAPTER 3

Holly Lee Carter crossed the old iron bridge north of DeLong without slowing down any more than the sharp curve and steep hill on the west side demanded. It was the spot on Blue Mountain Road where her father's car had gone into the river. But she couldn't allow herself to think about that now. She kept her eyes straight ahead, glad to be getting close to Wolf's Run. It was the place where she had spent many happy weekends and summer days before finally moving in with her grandmother a few weeks shy of her fifteenth birthday. Even during the pain, anger, confusion and chaos of Holly's high school years, Wolf's Run was a refuge because Meemaw Lois filled it with so much music, life … and love.

No longer the rich, reckless girl in the white Corvette, Holly took the turns carefully on the unrailed switchback road that climbed the face of Blue Mountain in a double S. Her muscles ached with fatigue and her arms were like weights on the big steering wheel and the hand controls, but her pulse still was strumming in her neck after the near disastrous encounter on the highway.

By the standards of California and many other places with a more craggy geography, Blue Mountain would not be a mountain at all – more like a big hill. But at 746 feet, it was the second highest point in Mississippi. It was called Blue Mountain because of the gas released by the tens of thousands of pines that grew on and around it. When the setting sun struck the gas just right, it created a blue halo over the mountain. On a plateau 300-and-some-odd-feet above the river, Wolf's Run was cupped in the palm of two enormous limestone hands gloved in wild grape and kudzu vine.

Holly turned off the gravel road between two leaning brick posts that anchored a wooden fence badly in need of whitewashing. Under a canopy of big pines, maples, oaks and pecans trees, the driveway sloped down to a U-shaped clapboard house with a steep tin roof and a wrap-around porch. There were long rust stains here and there on the roof and the whole place needed fresh paint. Off to one side was a brick building that served as a garage and past it a dilapidated greenhouse. Many of the panes were broken out of the glass walls and roof, and what plants remained were running wild.

Charlie was standing up in Eve's lap and looking around. "It needs some work, but it is beautiful," said Eve. "I might even call it idyllic if I didn't know it was built by slaves. Maybe even my own blood."

"It is what it is, Eve. You knew that when you asked if you could come with me and help. Don't start in on me now," said Holly. "I've got enough on my mind without you layin' on the old-Southern-family guilt trip."

Eve looked at her teacher, mentor and friend. "Yez'zum, Miz Holly. I'z mighty sorry, Miz Holly."

"Stop it!" Holly said more sharply than she intended. Her nerves and Eve's were frayed and sparking like electrical wire scraped down to the copper by three days on the road and the two-man welcoming committee that had fallen in behind them at the county line.

Eve opened the door and stepped out, arching her back and stretching. Charlie hopped down into the pea gravel and began sniffing everything in sight. "I guess we're both still shook up about what happened out on the road," offered Eve. "You drove most of the night. You have to be exhausted."

"I guess I am, but that's not it."

"So clue me in?"

"What do you see?" asked Holly but didn't wait for a reply. "More precisely, what don't you see?" Eve looked around, shrugged. "You don't see any ramps up to the house or any of the walkways I asked Tom to have installed in the yard."

Eve slumped back into the car seat. "Shit," she sighed. Then put into words what Holly was trying not to think about. "It's almost like he didn't expect you to get here," she said. "When you called your brother from San Antonio, I heard you tell him we were going to drive all night. That we'd be here early this morning.

"That's why you didn't want to report what happened to the police, isn't it?"

"No," she said but there was little conviction in her voice. "Tom could have casually mentioned it to any number of people, and before you know it, everyone in town would have known. Or it could have just been bad luck. A white woman and black woman traveling together in a big car at night? Or almost night. It would have been enough for a couple of Ku Klux liquored up and looking for an excuse for meanness."

Eve groaned. "You don't really believe that, do you?"

For the first time since the green sedan fell in behind them during the last minutes of the night, Holly looked rattled. Her chin quivered, she sobbed and a tear slipped from behind her sunglasses. "I have to believe it," Holly told her. "The Carlucci kid is right. I'm *not* wanted here. Not by anyone. Least of all, my brother. I guess I'd hoped –" Holly wiped her nose on the sleeve of her T-shirt. She looked at her shaking hands and then at Eve. "Damn, girl! We nearly got killed out there!"

Eve reached across the seat and rested a hand on her friend's shoulder. "But we didn't," she comforted, gently kneading Holly's taut muscles. "You were great! You kept your cool. Not even one of your good ol' boy stock car racers could have done better."

Holly laughed softly, sniffing back more tears. "They're not necessarily my good ol' boys."

"Sure they are," said Eve. "This whole cracker world is yours."

"Not anymore."

"We'll see," said Eve, looking around at the grounds and the house. "Anyway, we're here. Now all we have to do is figure out how to get you inside. Those steps are steep. I doubt I can get you up them in your chair."

"I know," said Holly, putting the car in gear and wheeling around the gravel circle that surrounded a disused fountain and planting area in front of the house. "When Grandma Lois was alive, this spot was filled with flowers. She started them in the greenhouse and then moved them here."

"I'm sure it was beautiful."

"Back then Wolf's Run was so full of life," said Holly as she stopped with the driver's door as close to the front steps as she could get it. "Grandma Lois was amazing. She could play piano and organ. There was always music in the air.

"At one time or another, Lois Carter was president of every woman's civic or church group in the county. So people were always in and out of the house. She was like sunlight in a bottle. Everyone wanted to be around her. And she loved this place so much."

"I can see why," agreed Eve. "But – you know, I never thought to ask – why is it called Wolf's Run?"

Holly swung her door open and Eve came around. "Get me under my arms, and ease me down. Okay?"

Eve came around and hooked her arms under Holly's. "Ready. One, two …"

"Three," they said together as Eve lifted Holly off the seat and sat her in the driveway next to the steps. Holly propped on her hands and Charlie ran over to lie in the tiny gravel beside her. She stroked Charlie's head. After a moment, the little dog rolled onto its back and offered its pink-and-black belly in an act of pure love, complete submission and absolute trust. Holly scratched it and Charlie actually seemed to smile.

"Let me get your chair set up on the porch," said Eve, swinging open the dented back door of the Lincoln convertible. Eve shoved the displaced luggage out of the way and propped a guitar case against the back fender. Holly studied the scabs of green that streaked the Lincoln's baby blue paint job and eyed a variety of dents, but said nothing. The car still ran; the doors still opened. A few dents and scraped paint were the least of her worries. She bit her lip. No matter how Holly tried to play it off to Eve, or to herself, it was true, they'd nearly been killed.

Eve unfolded the wheelchair on the porch and placed a special cushion in the seat as Holly tried to refocus, tried to push that dreadful reality from the front of her thoughts. "It's called Wolf's Run," she said, "because when the first Carters in these parts built a rough cabin on this plateau in the eighteen-twenties, there were loads of black bear, fox, deer, bobcat and wolves all through these hills. There was a trail – well, there still is a trail, very steep and narrow, that leads down the cliff face to the river.

"Packs of wolves used to come running through here on the way to that trail, and the name stuck."

"Makes sense. Chair's ready."

Holly reached behind her and lifted her hips onto the first step, then the next and the next.

"So are there still wolves around here?" asked Eve as she held open the screen door to the porch.

"Only at the high school. The mighty CHS Wolves," Holly told her. "As far as the real thing, unfortunately, wolves and the rest of the big game – bear, panther and such – were hunted out by the 1930s."

Holly lifted her hips onto the porch, her long legs trailing, the heels of her leather moccasins dragging. She rested on her arms, looking at the sprawl of yard rising up to the road. A breeze stirred the leaves of the nearby pecan trees as Charlie scampered onto the porch and began a thorough investigation.

"I swore I would never come crawling back to DeLong. Never! But look at me now."

Eve eyed her with hands on hips. "Girl, you're not crawling. You're … You're … You're butt walking. There's a difference."

Holly smiled at her friend, aide and protégé, glad to have Eve and her sense of humor nearby. "Now I remember why I asked you to come on this adventure, this mission, this odyssey, this – fool's errand? I just hope I haven't gotten you into something that – well, that –"

"Holly, I'm not a child. I've been a big girl for a while now. I came here for you, yes. But you know I came for my own reasons, too. As much as I may hate it, my roots are somewhere here in Mississippi," she told her. "So let's stop going over it. I'm here and I'm staying.

"This Podunk, redneck burg should be a piece of cake. I mean, hell, you survived Vietnam."

"Barely," said Holly, again feeling concern about Eve's L.A. privileged naiveté. But privileged or not, when the Holly's pain had gotten so bad that she could no longer lift herself out of bed and into her wheelchair, Eve, her star student, had moved in for three weeks to help. Holly did not know what she would have done without her. And she loved her for it, but nothing in Eve's Malibu upbringing could prepare her for how deep passions ran here on any subjected connected to race. After the morning's high-speed ambush, Holly wasn't sure at all that Cattahatchie County would be more hospitability than the bloody rice paddies and napalm-blackened jungles of Southeast

Asia where she'd almost died. Almost. But there was no point fretting about that now. They were here. She was home. Or at least back in Mississippi.

Holly forced a smile that was a lot more confident and optimistic than she felt. "Okay," she said. "I give up. So, big girl, help me get my big butt into my chair before I end up with a row of splinters in my backside."

CHAPTER 4

Once inside, Holly felt almost like a little girl again. Pushing over the wide oak floorboards in her wheelchair, she was about the height she was when she went running through the house at age eight or so. Countertops, cabinets, furniture, a multitude of pictures, the fireplace mantels, even the beds were as she remembered them at that age. The twelve-foot ceilings, coupled with exhaustion, made her feel as small and fragile as she had back then. The year her mother left.

"It's in a lot better shape inside than it is out," observed Eve.

"Yes, my father was living here until he – until the accident," Holly told her. "He moved out here from town after Meemaw Lois died a few years ago. While I was in Vietnam. By the time I got word –" Holly sniffled, shook her head. "Another funeral I missed." Eve started to say something. They both had known that Holly's return to Mississippi would be emotional, but the near-death experience out on the highway had pumped up the effect. But Holly pushed on – "Anyway, Daddy was kind of a neat freak. Everything in its place. Everything shipshape. Plus, Tom told me Daddy had a housekeeper out here three days a week."

"Colored help?" jabbed Eve, unable to help herself.

"I suspect so," replied Holly without taking the bait.

Holly had chosen Grandma Lois' bedroom because it was the only one in the house with a bathroom large enough that she could maneuver her wheelchair. It also had a massive claw-foot tub in which her grandmother would take her bubble baths surrounded by candles, the voice of Frank Sinatra or Nat King Cole crooning from a nearby record player. Sometimes she'd pull Holly in with her. Clothes and all. Holly smiled at the memory as she ran her hand along the edge of the tub. But of more importance now, the tub was of a height that would allow Holly to easily transfer into it from her wheelchair. Those were the sort of practical considerations that had become a part of Holly's everyday life, even moment-to-moment thinking since Ia Drang.

Grandma Lois' bedroom also held the largest share of good memories. Memories of snuggling together under blankets in the big four-poster bed and watching snow fall on winter mornings. Sitting together in front of the fireplace as corn kernels popped inside a metal basket. Propping with her guitar on the sill of the open eight-foot windows on summer nights and quietly picking out chords while her grandmother reclined in a La-Z-Boy reading her Bible, or one of the many wonderful authors she loved, and with whom she helped Holly fall in love. Grandma Lois knew Holly had a wild and angry side, but never judged or condemned, unlike many in town who gossiped about Holly and occasionally dared to whisper their complaints and concerns in Lois Carter's ear.

Grandma Carter's standard response was, "I know that Holly's heart is strong and gentle and faithful. And that's all I need to know."

To Holly, she would say, "We all have our share of rough roads to go down. Sometimes those roads lead through dark places in this world. And dark places in our heart. That's so we can appreciate the light. I know the Lord will lead you back in his own good time, in his own good way."

Holly often thought about "dark roads" when she thought of her runaway mother.

Veronique Dupre of New Orleans and Grandma Lois had been very close. It shocked and hurt Lois Carter terribly when "Miss Vee" disappeared. In fact, Holly's grandmother had kept in place at Wolf's Run a large portrait of her daughter-in-law. As Holly's body began to show its curves, her lips gained their full shape and her hair took on a glow like that of smoldering fire, the resemblance between the woman in the picture and her daughter became striking – almost eerie. After a time, Holly had come to accept that her very appearance was painful to her father. When she was fourteen she'd tried changing her hair style, cutting it short and dying it blonde. Thinking, perhaps, if she didn't look so much like her mother, then ... but T.L. Carter only ridiculed her effort. So, it was better if they saw each other as little as possible. That's when she left the house in DeLong and moved, full time, to Wolf's Run. T.L. Carter did not object. It was the last sad blow to a teenage girl's relationship with her already distant father.

Through the long series of French doors that formed the interior hallway of the house, Holly saw Eve standing on the porch that wrapped around the slate-covered courtyard. She pushed through an open set of doors.

"Malibu's got nothing on this," Eve said without looking Holly's way. "This is some view!"

From the porch they could see for miles down and across the Cattahatchie Valley. Holly's eyes followed the golden-brown curve of the river sparkling in the morning light and the emerald quilt of the summer crops that spread away from its steep banks. To the east were the Tennessee & Gulf Railroad tracks and Highway 27, and beyond that a long row of green, thickly wooded hills.

"I'd almost forgotten how beautiful it is," said Holly, resting her arms on the railing as Charlie explored the porch. "At night, off in the distance, you can see the glow from town. But there's not much man-made light out this way, so the stars are amazing. And the moon? Sometimes it looks as if it'll fill the entire valley."

Holly smiled at the memory, then slowly let her eyes refocus closer in. The two arms of Wolf's Run embraced a large stone fountain that was clogged with leaves from the previous fall. Perhaps several previous falls. The same was true of the thirty-foot-long pool near the patio's edge. It was one of only three in-ground swimming pools in the county. Lois Carter had it put in during the late forties after she began suffering with arthritis in her knees and ankles. Now its walls were stained black with algae and only a few swampy inches of green water stank in the deep end.

"It would be nice to have dinner over there on the edge, by the pool," said Eve.

"It will be nice as soon as I can get a pool service from Memphis to come down here and clean out that mosquito pit," said Holly. "Daddy wasn't a swimmer. Besides, knowing the kind of hours he kept at the paper, he probably didn't do much more than sleep here.

"The pool is something else I asked Tom to please call about," she told Eve, both hurt and angry by the way in which her brother had apparently ignored her simple requests. And if he had sent those thugs after her … *No!* … She wasn't going to let her mind go there.

"Is your room all right?"

"It's great. It's just, well, not quite like I pictured it."

"Not like in *Gone with the Wind*, huh? Well, Wolf's Run really is a glorified hunting lodge that's been added onto for the last hundred and thirty years," said Holly. "To get the 'Tara effect,' you've got to visit the top of Hill Street in DeLong or go out to Governor Weathers' fiefdom, Chalmette Plantation. Ex-Governor Weathers, I should say."

Eve walked around the porch and propped on the rail next to Holly. "Well, Wolf's Run may not have the big white columns, but it's certainly a mansion compared to some of the places we saw on the road. Like that place we passed on the right, before we got to the river. Rusty tin roof. Hasn't been painted in my lifetime. The whole place leans. To think that people have to live that way just because of the color of their skin," Eve said angrily, shaking her head. "I just – I guess I don't understand you people."

"Eve, I love you as a friend. But growing up in Malibu with both your parents in TV – well, it allows you to make some pretty easy assumptions."

"What's that supposed to mean?"

"Look, there is no doubt that a lot of black folks here – for a lack of education or jobs or opportunity – live in deplorable conditions. But, sadly, there's plenty of poverty here to go around. Don't assume it's limited to black people. For instance, that house you're talking about is the one Cutter Carlucci grew up in."

Eve stared at her. "You're kidding! Mr. Mean-and-Handsome?"

"Yes. Although it could have been different for the Carluccis. Their poverty is of their own making. Or, at least, the making of Cutter's father, Tony," Holly explained. "That old farmhouse and hundreds of acres around it were Jennifer Cutter's inheritance from the Ambrose side of her family. In this part of the world, that much land is worth a small fortune. Unfortunately, Tony Carlucci is a drunk and a womanizer. And a gambler. Not to mention a wife-beater. Anyway, to pay for his habits, Tony has been selling off the Ambrose acreage here and there since I was a girl."

Eve cocked her head to one side. "How do you possibly know all that?"

Holly thought of Meemaw Lois. "A very wise woman once told me, 'At one time or another in Cattahatchie County we've all seen each other's underwear hanging out on the clothes line. Holes and all. There are no secrets here, only lies we live with'."

Eve studied Holly for a moment. "What lies are you living with?"

Holly drew in a long breath as she looked out onto the disused courtyard and the valley, and then at the old house surrounding her. "I wish I knew," she said. Then, pivoting her wheelchair – "Come on. Let me show you the rest of the house."

There was a formal dining room with a twelve-place table hewn from one of the giant maples that once had adorned Blue Mountain. Overhead was a chandelier imported from Germany that still sported real candles. Grandma Carter's dinner parties were legendary from Memphis to Tupelo and from Oxford over to Iuka, and invitations were much sought-after. Into the late 1940s and for a hundred years before, candidates for governor and senator, and even a handful of would-be presidents, had dined at that table while seeking the blessing of *The Current-Leader*, Holly explained.

"This was my room," she said as they reached the corner where the north wing almost pushed up against the limestone ridge. She opened the door and felt her breath catch. The room was empty except for three cardboard boxes lined up under the window that faced onto the front yard. The wallpaper, which had been a sunny yellow with pink-and-baby-blue flowers of indeterminate genus, was whitewashed over. Dozens of large white drops and hundreds of smaller drips speckled the heart pine floor and roller marks stained the tongue-in-groove ceiling. Holly pushed over the threshold and looked at the large white shoe prints scattered here and there.

"Size twelves. Looks like Daddy didn't waste any time erasing me from Wolf's Run after Meemaw died and he moved up here," she said, studying the room. "He didn't even bother with a drop cloth."

Holly flipped open the lid of one of the boxes and on top was an eight-by-ten photo of her dancing with a young man at some long-forgotten party. He was in tails and she was wearing a strapless white formal, with white gloves that stretched above her elbows. Her high heels made her slightly taller than her date. She recognized the ballroom at the Peabody Hotel in Memphis, but there had been so many parties and dates, and so many lovely formals. She turned and opened the door in the corner.

Her closet once had been filled with them. Now it was empty. Nothing of the girl she had been remained.

Eve felt for her friend. Their emotions already were raw from what had happened on the road. She said, "People change. Don't forget, in the end your father wanted you to have this place and the newspaper."

"Yes, well, it's yet to be seen whether that was Daddy's final gift to me, or his final punishment," said Holly, crossing the room and pushing past Eve and into the hall.

Holly pushed past the doors to several guest rooms and a shared bath but didn't bother to look inside. This stroll – no this *roll*, she reminded herself – down memory lane quickly was becoming more painful and wearisome than she was ready to deal with. Whatever reserves of adrenaline she'd had were tapped dry playing demolition derby with the Ford. All she wanted to do was to climb into Grandma Lois's bed and sleep ... sleep until she felt strong again. Until she felt able to face Tom and Mary Nell and the many *Current-Leader* employees who would see her as a usurper. Until she was ready to deal with the redneck politicians, advertisers and so-called "good ol' boys" who would resent a woman running the county's only newspaper. Until she felt strong enough to face others who would figure that since her legs were paralyzed, her brain also must be impaired. And still others, like Cutter Carlucci, who would assume that because she used a wheelchair she would be an angry, manipulative sympathy junkie – like his father.

Near the end of the hall, Holly grabbed a set of brass handles and pushed open a set of double doors.

"This is the library," she said pushing into the home's largest room. A catacomb of bookshelves and picture nooks flowed away from a sprawling fieldstone fireplace and wrapped around three walls, from the room's floor to the edge of its eighteen-foot ceiling. The head of a snarling wolf was mounted over the fireplace. Several deer heads and that of a boar and black bear looked down as well. The furniture was dark and heavy, a testament to leather and testosterone and an earlier way of life. There was a felt-top card table in the center of the room. At one end was an antique billiard table and behind that a ten-slot gun case fully loaded with shotguns and rifles. At the other end of the long room, a window at least ten-feet wide arched from floor to ceiling. A chess table with jade pieces ornately carved in an Asian style sat in front of the window along with two chairs. A large telescope stood to one side.

"Wow! This is – impressive," said Eve, crossing past the sofa to the window. She checked the panoramic view of the valley. The room almost hung over the bluff and Eve took a quick step back. "Impressive, even if a tad spooky," she added, motioning to the animal heads.

"They take a little getting used to. I used to have names for all of them," said Holly. "That's Ben the Bear. And there's Tusker, the boar."

"And the wolf?"

"Vixen."

"How do you know it's a female?"

Holly shrugged. "I don't. It's just how I imagined her as a kid."

Eve crossed the room and rolled a ball the length of the billiard table. It silently kissed the rail and stopped. "Nice. Now I see how you became such a pool shark."

Holly pushed over and ran her hand along the perfect surface. "The lessons Meemaw Lois taught me on this table kept me from going hungry more than once when I first got to L.A. She was cutthroat when came to her *billy-yards*."

Holly smiled vaguely at the memory but Eve saw that her friend's eyes were fixed on one of the few empty spots on the room's walls. The space to the right of the fireplace was about three feet by four feet. "Is something wrong?"

"My mother's portrait," Holly told her. "That's where it always hung."

"You've told me that your parents' split wasn't exactly on friendly terms. When your dad moved back up here, he probably took it down. Or burned it."

Holly seemed lost in thought, then – "You'd think that. But no. In one of Daddy's last letters to me he wrote that he could hear 'a cold spring rain pecking at the library window.' That he was sitting beside this fireplace, looking at mother's portrait and wondering how different all our lives might be had she not – not …"

Eve could see how hard this was on Holly and she didn't let the moment linger. "Maybe your brother took it," she suggested.

Holly bit her lip. It was a natural thing to say for someone who did not know Tom. If anyone held more resentment for Veronique Carter than her jilted husband, it was her son. In the late 1940s and early '50s, runaway wives and divorce were uncommon and frowned upon, especially in the Bible Belt South. Meemaw Lois had protected Holly from the worst of the gossip, but as a teenager and then university student, Tom was forced to deal with the full weight of the social stigma. Had Mary Nell Poindexter, of the grand ol' Vicksburg Poindexters, not gotten pregnant while she and Tom were dating, she never would have married into "a family with a history of instability" – as she often reminded her husband. "But I shouldn't be surprised. Newspaper printers are little better than tradespeople."

Holly smiled at the memory in spite of herself. Mary Nell's pretentious ways would be comical if they weren't so hurtful to Tom.

Lies we live with, thought Holly as she pushed over to the wall. She touched the spot on the dark wood paneling where the portrait had hung. Like her mother, it was simply gone.

"I guess I'll add this to my list of things to ask Tom about," she said, not wanting to get into the serpentine intricacies of Carter family dynamics. Then, "Come on. Let's get unpacked. I'm dying for a bath," she said as she pushed close behind the huge sofa on the way to the door. A crunching sound under her left tire caused her to stop, pivot. "Damn! What was that?"

Eve and Holly saw a circular piece of glass now fractured into dozens of pieces. "Go through that door over there," said Holly, pointing to a corner of the room. "That hall connects to the bedroom my father was using. There's a bathroom and closet on the right. There might be a broom and dust pan in one of them."

While Eve searched, Holly studied the bright fragments against the hardwood floor. The glass from a small picture frame, maybe? But it seemed too thick for that. Maybe part of a broken whiskey glass?

"Found them," said Eve, returning. She squatted beside Holly and swept the fragments into a dust pan and headed for the waste basket she saw beside the door.

"No, wait!" said Holly as Eve prepared to dump the pan. "I saw some envelopes in the desk there by the window. Put it in one of those." Eve cocked her hip and stared at her friend. "I beg your pardon?"

"Please."

"Why?"

"I don't know." It was the truth, and the only answer Holly had. "But, please, just humor me."

"Okay," said Eve, crossing the room. She pulled an envelope from a cubbyhole next to the typewriter on a secretary built into the wall. "But my brother is right. White women *are* crazy!"

"He should know," said Holly. "He's married to one."

"Amen!"

CHAPTER 5

Most people would say Cutter and I grew up rough, just tumbling toward manhood with little direction or notion of when or where our wheels would stop. Like many of the 31 teenagers who played Wolves football during our previous 13-1 season, we spent the summer between our junior and senior years in the fields each weekday, and more, working hard in the relentless sun. At night we ringed our tubs with the day's sticky remnants, then picked up our dates and ringed the town square with our pickups and second- and third-hand cars.

At the center of the square was the three-story Cattahatchie County Courthouse. It was by far the largest public building in town, and we orbited it as regularly as planets able to turn at right angles around a yellow-brick sun. Circled it until we were dizzy, then parked on River Street and watched the river run, and commerce flow and the in-out tide of people through the doors of The Cotton Café. Some went in for Cokes and burgers before walking up the hill to the Rebel Theater on the square. We all went parking, and on weekends many of us went north, some twenty miles, just across the Tennessee line, to roadhouses on the main highways and whorehouses down dusty, unlit back roads.

Cutter, Dodge McDowell and I shared a problem in common, and perhaps it was what bonded our odd trio. We were without homes.

For me and Dodge there were structures – beams, brick and wood. Beds to call our own and soft places to put our heads. But to one degree or another, we already were making our decisions about which way to turn in life, for better or worse. Our parents had lost their interest, their will, their freedom, their minds or their lives – or some combination thereof. But since the smoke and lead and ear-ringing echo of a shotgun blast punctuated a final falling-out with his father, the only consistent roof Cutter had over his head was the tent he kept in his Jeep. Dozens of families in football-mad Cattahatchie County gladly, gleefully, would have taken Cutter into their homes, but he preferred keeping to himself – sleeping wherever the wheels of his Jeep stopped turning on any given night. His favorite place was a cleft in the rock of Blue Mountain. The spot was known locally as The Well.

Located off Blue Mountain Road, The Well was an artesian spring that boiled up cold from a limestone shelf hanging over the river a couple hundred yards north of the Old Iron Bridge. The spot, which was shaped like a set of huge stone jaws, would have been the most popular parking place in Cattahatchie County had it not been located at the end of a narrow, heavily rutted dirt road that snaked desperately along the river's edge where the bank fell away thirty feet into the water. Poor, most often drunken judgment allowed the Cattahatchie to claim a car or two annually. But for those of us who chanced The Well often, it was a refuge as secure as a fortress – guarded, as it was, on three sides by the river, the current holding the rock outcrop in the crook of its twisted elbow. It was further screened by a curtain of languid willows and low, thorny brush that gave way around the rocky platform where Cutter made his camp. At the center of the space, the spring boiled in frosty silence, stewing slowly in the teardrop-shaped pool before streaming away and tumbling over a cut in the stone lip. Depending on the time of the year and the depth of the Cattahatchie, the small waterfall formed a perfect, if horrifically bracing shower.

S ummer twilight had just crossed over into full darkness when I rattled my pickup in behind Cutter's Jeep. It was a miserably hot, nearly liquid July night. I'd been to a prayer meeting and practice for the youth choir at First Denomination. I couldn't sing a lick, but it was another excuse to spend time with my girlfriend, Patti. Dodge McDowell and Cutter were propped by a low fire built to the side of The Well. Their hair and shorts were still wet from plunges into spring, to cool off and to retrieve beer tossed in for chilling, which the crystal water accomplished nicely as it held at a constant forty-five degrees.

I looked down at two tin plates from Cutter's mess kit. All that was left was the T-bones from what looked to have been – three? no, four steaks – and the skins of four potatoes baked in the coals.

"They must have been good," I said.

"They were," said Dodge, who produced a long, slow belch to punctuate his culinary appraisal.

"We're out of bakin' potatoes but there're two more steaks over there in that ice chest," said Cutter. "Throw one on the fire."

"Thanks. I will. Between gettin' my ass off the tractor and to church on time, I didn't get a chance to eat," I said, and lifted out a thick-sliced steak. I squatted and laid the meat on the metal grate resting atop a natural fire pit in the rock. I poked at the fire and added some wood. "You should have heard Brother Mac tonight. Preachin' about DeLong being infiltrated by whores and race-mixers. Miss Carter comin' back to town sure has him wound up."

"Nate, you cain't hardly tolerate Brother Mac as it is," said Dodge. "How you reckon you're gonna live with him as your preacher-in-law?"

I sat and pulled off the boots Cutter had given me and started unbuttoning my shirt.

"It'll be different when me'n Patti go off to college. We won't be home much.

I'm gonna get my journalism degree and she's gonna make a teacher. When we're finished, we're not comin' back to Cattahatchie County. There're good papers in New *Or*-leans and Miam-uh. Heck, maybe we'll even go north. Maybe I'll even get a job with the, by god, *New York Times*."

"I wouldn't count on it," said Dodge. "Haven't you ever noticed how all of Patti's sisters live within a long walk or a short car ride of Brother Daddy?"

I ignored the question as I stood and undid my belt. "Dodge, how come you don't like Patti?"

"'Cause she's a snotty, two-faced little kiss-ass, and she treats you like cow shit."

Cutter saw me gritting my teeth. "Don't pull any punches there, Dodge, just 'cause she's Nate's girlfriend," he offered.

I dropped my pants, folded them and laid them with the rest of my other clothes. A big mosquito immediately nailed me in the shoulder. I smacked it and myself with a loud pop as my steak started to sizzle in the grill. "You don't know her," I told him.

"No, Nate. You're the one who don't know her."

I'd had enough. "Go to hell," I told him. Dodge only chuckled. "Patti loves me and I love her, and as soon as we can, we're getting' married and gettin' the hell out of here. She knows I'm not stayin' in DeLong, fuckin' Miss'ssippi."

"Her sister Melody promised to love, honor and obey Ray Wilbanks. He's got him a good job offer at the shipyards down on the coast. Good money. But Melody won't go. Don't want to leave daddy. I hear they're about to bust up over it."

"You're a liar!" I snapped and instantly regretted it. Dodge McDowell might be a bootlegger's son and beer hall tough, but he was as honest in his word and his promises as the day was long. Dodge sat up on his sleeping bag and looked at me, hard. Neither he nor any of his clan were given to let an insult pass unchallenged. I swallowed hard, knowing that if Dodge sprang to his feet he likely could break me into several pieces before even Cutter could stop him. The steak spit and sizzled above the fire as I stood there in my Jockeys glancing around, wondering which way to run. Jumping into the river and taking my chances with water moccasins and night-hunting gators would be a healthier decision than tangling with Dodge if he were actually angry.

"Hey, Dodge, come on," said Cutter, trying to distract the big lineman. "It doesn't do any harm for Nate to dream. And he might as well dream big. For him and PattiWac. I mean, wouldn't it be something if he really did make a writer for the, by god, *New York Times*? We could all say we knew you back when."

Dodge grunted and lay down, cupping his hands behind his head. "Yeah, back when he was a scrawny pencil dick who ran off at the mouth too much. If you're gonna make a writer, Nate, you need to be more careful how you choose your words."

The fear that had been thumping in my chest a moment earlier drained away. I was aware that I'd dodged a bullet – or more accurately, a fist that would have landed like a nine-pound hammer. I knew better than to demand an apology from Dodge, but I wasn't going to offer him one. The moment dragged on.

"Nate, are you gonna get us some beer or just stand there lookin' pretty?" asked Cutter, nodding toward the cold, silent boil of The Well.

I stepped off the rocky edge.

A n almost electrical shock crackled through my nerves as I passed down into the spring, my balls darting like quick, round fish in search of the warm bay behind my pelvis. Inside the earth I gasped but held it inside myself, every part of me tingling, throbbing with the liquid fire of total sensation that comes just before the numbing.

Once inside, The Well was a world unto itself with its own atmosphere, and geography and twisted physics.

During daytime expeditions, the water felt so pure and weightless that it seemed not to be water at all, but the barely liquefied air of a blue-white winter morning. And suddenly you could fly. It was so clear that it did not bend light in brittle angles, it merely melted it into pastels and added texture. Yet when seen through the full twenty-six feet of water, the light was never the same. It could pour into the mouth of The Well and swim there like liquid gold in a white porcelain bowl, or float on the surface in an animated jigsaw of colors, a cathedral window onto the summer sky.

At night, The Well lurked. A black, open mouth leading to a throat that some swore constricted and changed in the darkness. Tightened to swallow them. Despite the knowledge that The Well's flow was up and out, some shaken "divers" emerged certain that there was a current pushing them down. That the water took on weight and the slushy heft of black, crystalline mud. Over the years some people had become so disoriented that they bolted sideways or even down in a frenzied try at coming up. The rock walls were ridged and unforgiving, and though no one in our generation had drowned, there had been some close calls – stitches, broken bones and the direction of several noses forever changed. But for those of us who regularly tossed in beer by the case and made a game of who could bring up the most cans, The Well was not a pit constricted by claustrophobia. It was a challenge and a test, and there was care to be taken. For me, at least, it was a door into space – the space between my ears. In the minute-like seconds and hour-like minutes of floating downward it was like being adrift in the vast blackness beyond the earth. I imagined it was how the astronauts felt when they walked in space. Weightless, yet in control at the edge of danger with a mission to accomplish. Every sense alive and tingling. Every moment dreamlike. The moon their scarred lighthouse, just as for our veteran corps of night divers it was the compass point that guided us safely up.

"Five!" I yelled as I broke the surface, gulping air, arms up-stretched, holding two cans in each hand. Another was stuffed in the front of my underpants. "Five!"

B y the time the big steak had filled my belly, Dodge was snoring. Cutter was lying on his side, propped on an elbow with a *National Geographic* in front of him, reading by the light of a kerosene lantern. "Everybody's on pins and needles at the paper," I said by way of conversation. "Miss Carter is supposed to make her grand entrance tomorrow morning. She told Jimmy Fuller and his dad that she expected the ramps and such to be done at the office by seven a.m. even if they had to work all night."

Cutter turned a page. "I reckon she plans to pay 'em, doesn't she?"

"Sure. But that's not the point. She's already had them bustin' their tails puttin' in ramps and fixin' up stuff at Wolf's Run since Monday," I told him. "I didn't think so down there on the road the other mornin', but now? She does come off as mighty high-handed.

"I heard she read Mr. Tom the riot act about not having things ready for her when she got here. Cussed him worse than a red-headed stepchild, from what Miss Mary Nell told Patti's momma. Used language no Christian woman should use. And this afternoon she made Mr. Tom move out of the publisher's office and into a little room down the hall. Wouldn't even let him go back to the general manager's office downstairs. The room she put him in ain't much bigger than a closet." I shook my head in long slow movement, exaggerated by the three beers I'd consumed in rapid succession. "Why do you suppose she came back anyway?"

Cutter studied a diagram of the lunar-lander, the Apollo space capsule and the huge Saturn V rocket that was supposed to propel them and three astronauts to the moon later in the month. "It doesn't seem to me to take too much supposin'," he said without looking up. "If somebody left you a newspaper and a house like Wolf's Run, wouldn't you come back?"

I tried to make my mind focus. "Yeah, I guess I would," I conceded. "But it's all mighty curious, the way her daddy changed his will just a few weeks before he died."

"Maybe she talked him into changin' it by makin' him feel sorry for her," Cutter suggested with no enthusiasm for conversation. "A cripple'll do that, you know? Work you that way. 'Ohhh, po'r me! Po'r, po'r me!' I saw it a thousand times with Tony and my mother. Until he beat the sense out of her."

Cutter could be right. It could be that simple but – "A lot of people think there's more to it than that," I said. "I heard through Brother Mac that Governor Weathers is havin' that Greenwood lawyer looked into. The one who drew up the will. The word is, he's known to do work for the colored crowd. And one of the partners in his law firm is a Jew."

"And?"

"And … Mr. Carter goes off in the river. So, that U.S. Attorney, Burke, and that colored preacher and their bunch see a chance to steal the paper out from under Mr. Tom, so he can't speak up against the race-mixers. They get that Greenwood lawyer to dummy-up a phony will."

Cutter looked up at me where I was propped against a log. "I hope you and Patti do hurry up and go off to college because you're soundin' more like Brother Mac every day."

"Just because he's wrong about you, doesn't mean he's wrong about everything."

"The problem is," said Cutter, "Brother Mac doesn't think he's wrong about *any*thing. From God's lips to his mouth, to hear him tell it."

"Well, he sure does pray and read his Bible a lot."

"Good for him," said Cutter returning to the *National Geographic*. The subject of Brother Dr. C.E. MacAllister and the whole First Denomination crowd was a sore one with Cutter. Even though he and his sister Rose carried in their veins the intermingled blood of some of the county's oldest families, the black hair, full lips and olive skin they gained from their father had made them targets early in their lives. Even their name. To the best of my reckoning, Carlucci was the only one in the county directory that ended in a vowel. But all that changed when a pee-wee league coach handed Cutter a football and the whole town discovered he could run faster and harder with it than any kid they'd ever seen. Now, if anyone had anything bad to say about Cutter, they mostly kept it to themselves or to a whisper. Everyone except Brother Mac.

It was time to change the subject. I took a sip from a very cold can of Miller, and I had just enough of a buzz on to let my curiosity turn into words. "How come you never date anybody from the high school?"

At first, I didn't think he was going to answer, which was not unusual. If Cutter thought a question silly or intrusive, he felt no obligation to respond. Then to my surprise he said, "I like having time to myself and a place where I can be alone. I don't want a bunch of little girls showin' up out here. Nor their daddies with shotguns."

"You don't seem to worry much about husbands with shotguns."

Cutter grunted. "Most husbands with cheatin' wives have 'em because they're not men enough keep 'em. They're sure not men enough to take me. But I watch my step."

"You could have *anybody* at CHS. Paula Simpson pretty much told me Sunday at The Cotton that she'd give it up for you in heartbeat. And she wanted me to tell you so."

Cutter actually seemed to consider that offer for a moment, then said, "Paula's a fine lookin' girl. Sweet, too. But I don't want somebody followin' me up and down the halls at school. Or askin' me where I'm goin' after practice? Or why I haven't called her in two or three days? Or who's that girl I was talkin' to outside the theater? Or wherever. It's just not worth it. I'd rather be with somebody who's got somethin' going on in her life besides me."

For a couple of minutes I sat in fairly stunned silence. Cutter always was judicious about revealing the parameters of his private life, even to his friends. Even to me. *Why doesn't Cutter date anyone at Cattahatchie High?* Paula wasn't the first wonder.

He'd just given me the most direct answer I'd ever gotten from him on the subject. Funny how different people could be, I thought. Even best friends. I wanted Patti to think about me night and day. I wanted her with me every moment she could be. I wanted our lives to be completely entwined. I wanted Patti to moon over me the same way so many women – young and considerably older -- mooned over Cutter. Of course, Cutter could have been the model for Michelangelo's David while some company might hire me for an ad about zit cream. I understood that. It didn't make me jealous. It just made me … wishful, sometimes. So I let it drop along with my verbal intermission. Whenever I had a few beers in me, I needed conversation nearly as badly as air.

"Is that a good one?" I asked about the *National Geographic* Cutter was reading.

"Nah. Not a single naked Indonesian in the whole thing."

"Why do you pretend that you only look at the pictures?" I blurted, letting tumble out another question I'd wondered about for a while. I knew that Cutter actually read everything he could get his hands on concerning science, math, mechanics and architecture, and a novel here and there. He had three or four library cards and was a frequent borrower, but not in Cattahatchie County or nearby towns. "I mean, you could make straight As but –"

"What is this, Nate? Twenty questions?" Cutter asked, a little testily. He was not one to engage in what he considered meaningless conversation, especially about himself. But he looked over at Dodge and listened for several moments to his snoring as if weighing something. Then he returned his eyes to me and said, "Because smart kids scare coaches."

The answer caught me off guard. "What do you mean?"

"Coaches may say they like smart players, but that's bullcrap. The only things they really care about are size and speed, and having somebody who will do *exactly* what they're told. The last thing a coach wants is a kid who's smart enough to ask, 'Why?'"

"I guess," was the most intelligent response I could come up with. I'd never thought about it. But Cutter had. I suspected he had thought about an awful lot of things I'd never thought about. Had to think about them just to survive.

Cutter slipped his long, powerful legs out of his sleeping bag and stood, dressed in black-and-red CHS gym shorts and a snug white T-shirt that glowed against his skin. We all expected those legs to make him a star at Ole Miss – the University of Mississippi – and maybe carry him all the way to pro ball.

When he walked over to the edge of the stone outcrop, I followed. He took his penis in hand and pissed into the river below. I eyed the huge expanse of stars above us and the moon climbing over the eastern hills. Its pale glow illuminated the mile or so of cotton stalks between the river and the Old Ambrose Place. All the bottom land in that direction for as far as I could see should have belonged to Cutter one day. Now the worn-out old farmhouse was only a dark silhouette against crops that would profit someone else. The only light came from Cutter's sister's room at the northwest corner. I knew Rose slept with it on because no matter when I awoke during a stay at The Well, it was always there – pale and gray through dingy glass, but always on. I knew it was some sort of a signal to Cutter. What exactly the light meant I wasn't sure, but I was afraid of what might happen if it ever went out. A fish jumped in the river nearby trying for one of the hundreds of lightning bugs floating above the water. Somewhere past the Old Iron Bridge an alligator grunted deep and long. My best friend tucked himself back into his shorts and paid them no attention. I aimed drunkenly at one of the passing bugs, missed, then finished and did the same as Cutter studied the inheritance that was no longer his. In the moonlight the muscles of his chest and shoulders, his high cheek bones and the hard ridge of his jawline looked as if they could have been cut from the same stone upon which we stood.

"Nate, I didn't make this world. I didn't conjure up DeLong, Miss'ssippi. I surely didn't ask to be born into the family I was born into," he said quietly, his voice mixing with the murmur of the river below. "But things are what they are. Until I sign a scholarship somewhere, and some big booster with a fat wallet slips me the money to get my momma and sister out of DeLong, I'm going to give them what they expect. What they want. A dumb jock with nothing on his mind except the next game."

I tried to think of something to say, but my thoughts were foggy with alcohol and knocked a little off kilter by the way Cutter had opened up to me. Now he kept his eyes on the house across the dark fields, a sad place wrapped in a chain of shadows.

"Football is all I've got," he said. "Without it, I'm just the son of a crazy woman and a drunken, mean, dago cripple."

CHAPTER 6

Some three miles away and three-hundred feet higher up, Holly Lee Carter lay on her stomach between fresh, sun-dried cotton sheets – twelve-hundred count. Meemaw Lois had, indeed, enjoyed her small luxuries. A ceiling fan turned over the bed dulling the sounds of crickets and night birds through the tall windows that were open to the screened porch. Wolf's Run had never been air-conditioned, though there were now window units in the bedroom her father had occupied next to the library and in the guest room that Eve was using. But on her more open side of the house, Meemaw Lois preferred the natural cooling that came from the way the walls of rock to the east and west created a funnel that captured whatever small breeze was stirring thirty stories above the valley floor and, too, whatever cool vapors the summer river might give up even in the dead heat of July and August.

Holly ran her lightly calloused fingers slowly down the mahogany neck of her prized 1952 Martin D-28 that lay next to her in the bed. The guitar – with its top of Sitka spruce and sides and back of Brazilian rosewood – had been a gift from Meemaw Lois on her twelfth birthday. It had opened up the world of music to Holly and allowed her to become confident in herself beyond just the early curves she was developing, which was all anyone seemed to notice. When she was bolted into a Stryker frame and airlifted out of Da Nang in November of '65 with other survivors of the Battle of Ia Drang the only thing she asked for was that guitar. Screw her cameras and the rest of it, but that Martin "Dreadnaught" was irreplaceable. They had left Mississippi together and been through some chancy scrapes in some hard parts of the world. Now here they were, back in DeLong. "Dee" still delivered the same gorgeous tones it always had when she smoothly fingered the frets. Holly sighed. "But I'm not the same girl," she said into the pillow and rolled restlessly onto her back, anxious about the day ahead. The sudden movement sent her legs into spasms, the long muscles bucking as they stiffened. She gritted her teeth, clinched her fists. Though she could not feel the actual contractions in her legs, they jarred her all the way up through her back and into her shoulders. Shoulders made muscular by the daily lifting of herself in and out of her chair, plus miles of laps done religiously in the pool at the community college where she he taught photo-journalism, and planned to do so again.

After about ten seconds the spasms subsided, though such events always felt more like ten minutes, especially when they came in public. Her legs had a mind of their own now, disconnected from her thoughts and will. It was all about positioning them correctly, in a way they liked. Holly looked down. Under the sheet she could see they had crossed at the ankles when she'd rolled over. They never liked that. She reached under the sheet and lifted her left leg off her right and endured another few seconds of spasming before they settled. She lay back on the pillows, her neck damp with perspiration, her breathing ragged. She took in several deep breaths and her nostrils filled with the mingled scents of the fresh-cut pine that had been used to build the ramp up to the kitchen door and down from the interior gallery to the big patio, and of the heavy dose of chlorine that permeated the newly scrubbed pool. Holly would not be able to swim in it for another two or three days. Her body craved the exercise and her spirit longed for the minutes of freedom that the water's buoyancy gave her. Even if her legs no longer were really hers, at least they were not a clumsy drag on her in a pool.

Holly let out a long breath. "What in the hell am doing here?" she asked the shadows in the room, and for the hundredth time since trading paint with that green sedan on Sunday morning whether she'd done the right thing coming back to DeLong. Right for her? Right for Tommy? Right for anyone?

If only the lawyer Burke and Reverend Clemmer had shown up in her hospital room a couple of hours later, it would have been done. Over with. She'd still be in Los Angeles, in her bungalow above the ocean. Maybe not happy. Maybe not content, as if she'd ever been. But at least comfortable and secure in her home, and accepted and respected by students and her peers at the college.

Holly placed her hand on her forehead and stared at the tongue-in-groove ceiling nine feet above her, replaying again in her mind the events that had brought her back to Mississippi.

H olly remembered waking as she was being snatched upward, her face rising in a dizzy trajectory toward two uncovered fluorescent lights on the ceiling of the hospital room she'd already been confined in for ten long days. One of the lights flickered like a flare dying in the night jungle. She tried to get her bearings, tried to shake herself from a dream of fire and noise and blood-spattered elephant grass. She blinked, blinked as the contraption that held her spun to vertical.

"Fuck!" she gasped, her startled heart thudding against her ribs, as she tumbled forward, falling, spinning inside the Ferris-wheel-like Stryker frame that held her body rigid from head to foot. Fast. *Too fast!* Holly wanted to scream but the lambskin straps cinched across her chin and forehead held her face so snugly that she could not really open her jaw. She gritted her teeth and scrunched her eyes, praying for the spinning to stop, but it didn't until the whole five-foot-ten-inches of her was past horizontal and her brain was trying to fly out the top of her head. She gagged on the bile thrown into her throat before she finally felt herself settling back to even keel. Face down. Now it felt like the full weight of her brain was resting on the back of her eyes. They throbbed as she opened them again and tried to focus. Her arms slipped from their straps and dangled below her. She watched a salty drop of perspiration — or was it a tear? – trickle to the end of her nose and tumble free. It fell and fell until it splashed soundlessly onto the hospital floor.

Holly recognized the aide's scrawny in-turned ankles, grotesque in sagging white hospital hose. "Nora," gasped Holly, "you bitch!"

The aide made no response, only chuckled meanly as she released the pins that had held the back panel of the frame that Eve Howard called "The Stryker Sandwich."

"Only, you're the white bread in the middle," she'd joked.

Holly worked her arms and fingers and hoped she wouldn't vomit. "Damn you!"

Nora Harper put the piece aside for later when Holly would be flipped again onto her back, all in an effort negate bed sores and keep her spinal column as immobile as possible as she recovered from the surgery that she hoped would end or at least ease the terrible bouts of pain she had frequently endured since taking two bullets in her back during the worst of the fighting in the Ia Drang Valley. More than six-hundred North Vietnamese Regulars and seventy-nine Americans died there. She'd nearly made it an even eighty.

"I've never done anything to you," said Holly, hating the sound of her usually husky voice sounding so fractured and fragile, almost pleading. "Why do you treat me this way?"

The ugly, ostrich-like woman leaned close to Holly's ear and hissed, "Because I can, bitch. I despise changing your piss bag and sponge-bathing your dead ass and your big tits. I hate the way you talk. Miss Way Down South in Dixie. I hate everything about you."

Holly wanted to scream. At Nora Harper, yes, but mostly at her own terrible helplessness. She swallowed and summoned her courage and tried to make her voice sound firm. "If you ever do that to me again, I swear I'll report you," she told the aide. "I'll get you fired if it's the last thing I do."

Nora Harper grunted in Holly's ear, unimpressed. "If you report me, it will be the last thing you do on this earth," she growled. "I got friends on the night shift. A lot of bad shit can happen in the middle of night. Shit people don't recover from."

Holly fought the angry tears she felt welling in her eyes, ashamed of how frightened she was, how frightened she had to be of this awful woman. At that moment, Nurse Frederick tapped on the almost closed door, pushed it open as the aide straightened and began to stroke Holly's back.

"What's going on?" asked Rhonda Frederick.

Nora Harper smiled with her nicotine-stained teeth. "Oh, I'm just giving our star patient some extra TLC," she lied. "I just turned her and that makes her queasy sometimes."

Holly thought of the endless, lonely minutes, the still quiet that came over the orthopedic ward between midnight and dawn and said nothing.

"More august visitors for you today," said the nurse. "I thought you might want to freshen up a bit before they come down."

"Is it the same men who came the other day?"

"I don't know," said Rhonda Frederick, who often spent her breaks with Holly. They'd become friends of a sort in the days since her surgery. Her brother was a West Point grad serving in Vietnam. "The administrator's secretary didn't say. But they must be bigwigs or Mr. Chandler wouldn't be walking them down. So Nora let's get this room ship shape." Nurse Frederick crossed the room. "And let's open these drapes. It's dark as a dungeon in here."

While the floor nurse looked on, Aide N. Harper efficiently took the half full urine collection bag from its hook and placed it on the frame between the patient's calves, covered her from waist to foot with a yellow hospital blanket and handed Holly a warm, damp washcloth. Holly scrubbed the places on her face she could reach, then ran it over her neck and up and down her long arms. Rhonda took the cloth.

"Is my butt covered?" she asked the nurse, unable to feel the material on her hips or legs and not trusting the spiteful aide to care about her modesty.

"Yes, you're fine," said Rhonda Frederick. "Nora, nice job tidying up. I think you can go now. Please take that bag of garbage with you."

Holly heard Nora Harper leave and considered telling the head nurse, her new friend about Harper's cruelty but thought again about the long nights she still had ahead of her and of who the woman's friends might be, and what they might do. She felt helpless and angry, but mostly ashamed. Still shaken, she swallowed those emotions, as she'd had to learn to swallow so much since Vietnam, and remained silent.

"I've got to get back to the nurse's station, but your visitors should be down soon."

"That's fine, Rhonda," said Holly. "Thank you."

She saw Rhonda Frederick shift on her immaculate white nursing shoes then felt a kiss on the back of her head and a gentle pat of her shoulder. She wanted to weep.

As Holly waited, she wondered anxiously if Haughton Wellingham III, her brother's attorney and a Mississippi state senator, had returned to renege on the generous seven-figure offer that Tom had made a few days earlier for the fifty-one percent of the family's newspaper that their father had inexplicably left to her. She had lived in L.A. long enough to learn that no deal was really done until you had the cash in hand. Or least a certified check.

"Awwww, Miz Holly, I do hate to see you sufferin' so many trials," Mr. Wellingham had crooned in his melodic, cotton-soft drawl as she lay on her back in the Stryker frame. An associate so young he still had pimples had unloaded a massive bouquet of roses into the arms of an aide. "But you are a treasure. Just as gawjus as the night you won the Miss Cattahatchie County crown.

"That was nineteen-and-fifty-eight. Eleven years but I remember it like it was yesterday. For your talent you sang *Faded Love*. Marvelous! It gave me goose flesh," he'd gone on, then sighed dramatically. "And my gracious, you just haven't changed a tad. It's truly an amazement."

Haven't changed?

It had been a straight-out lie and so enormous under the circumstances that Holly remembered having to fight the urge to laugh, or perhaps to cry. Yet it was the sort of genteel shading of the truth for kindness's sake that she missed about the very Deep South.

Not everyone has been so kind. Certainly not her brother.

On the day T.L. Carter died, Tom had tried to reach her at her home in Pacific Palisades then at the community college in Malibu. College officials had referred him to the Los Angeles hospital where Holly was recovering from the dangerous operation she'd put off for too long. Obviously, her father had not told Tom that she was having surgery, though he knew. Since her evacuation from Vietnam, Holly and her father had begun to correspond here and there and occasionally worked their way through stiff, formal telephone conversations on birthdays and at Christmas. She always asked about Tom and assumed her father had told him that they had reconnected, at least tangentially. But, knowing her father, maybe not.

No, there was no way she could come home for their father's funeral, she had told Tom. Holly explained that she'd just had surgery and would be immobilized in the frame for several weeks and it would be at least a month after that before she would be strong enough to travel.

Silence.

"Tom, it's not like I timed this surgery so I couldn't come home for Daddy's funeral," she finally had said. But her brother was having none of it. He said, "Aw'right, I guess we'll just have to go on without you. Just like we always have."

Starting with the seven-year age difference, Holly and Tom had never been close, but he now was the only significant family she had and the words had stung. Yet in a strange way, they had made Holly smile. In many ways, Tom IV was every inch T.L. Carter's son.

A few minutes later, Nurse Frederick tapped on the door. "Your visitors are here." "Show them into the royal bed chamber," Holly had said, regaining some of her bravado, false or otherwise.

As soon as they were close enough to see their shoes and pant legs, she knew Wellingham had not returned. One wore brown pinstripe trousers that hung perfectly over a set of expensive, perhaps handmade brown wingtips. The other had on faded jeans that bunched atop hard-used work boots.

"Miz Carter?" said wingtips, the drawl definitely Southern but not from Mississippi. Maybe the Carolinas, the soft tidal flats of the Low Country rounding the vowels.

"None other."

Both sets of feet shifted with indecision.

"There's a blanket and some pillows in the closet over there. You can spread them on the floor and stretch out," she told the men. More awkward shifting. "Look, whoever you are, I'm not going to have a conversation with your feet. Either get comfortable where I can talk to you face to face or come back in about four hours when they flip this pancake."

"I'm sorry," said wingtips, squatting beside her. "Of course. How rude of us."

Holly shifted her eyes — the only part of her face she could easily move — and saw brown hair and a square jaw. "I'm J.L. Burke," he said, extending his hand. Holly took it. It was strong but soft. "I'm the United States Attorney for the Northern District of Mississippi." Work boots was spreading the blanket, throwing down pillows. "This is Reverend Ronald Clemmer of the National Coalition for Justice."

"Call me Ronnie, please," said Clemmer, extending his hand – a nice hand that did harder work than simply turning pages in a Bible. Though sturdy, Clemmer was not a big man. Maybe one-hundred-and-sixty pounds, including his tight Afro and granny glasses – *a la* John Lennon. "We're based out of Ohio."

Burke took off his suit jacket and hung it over a chair back.

"Okay. I know what the NCJ is. And I think I know what a U.S. Attorney does," said Holly, as the men positioned themselves shoulder to shoulder on the blanket. On the sleeve of his monogramed white shirt Burke wore gold cufflinks with a white inset of the Department of Justice seal. "The big question is, what are you two doing getting cozy on my floor?"

"You're as sharp and down to business as Gerald Yards said you'd be," offered Clemmer.

Gerry Yards was chief of photography for the *Los Angeles Chronicle*. He'd been Holly's boss, her mentor, her lover – briefly – and still was her friend. On more than one occasion since she was flown back stateside, he'd asked her to be Mrs. Yards, but Holly thought that was mostly guilt talking. Guilt for taking her with him into a war zone. She'd only been twenty-three when they landed in Saigon. Guilt because she was a woman, and a woman's place ... but they both knew being a woman had nothing to do with what had happened. If it hadn't been her, it would have been some other young photog who climbed onto that chopper bound for Ia Drang Valley. Like the GIs, reporters and photographers take their chances in the mud and blood when the bullets start flying and the mortars start blowing big gouges from the earth. A camera and press credentials didn't mean diddly-squat. She knew it. Gerry knew it, but he couldn't let go of the guilt. They still enjoyed a melancholy friendship and the occasional good bottle or two of California chardonnay on the back deck of her home, watching the cars pass below on the Pacific Coast Highway in waves nearly as ceaseless as those of the ocean beyond.

"Sounds like you two have been making the rounds," said Holly. "Now what can I do for you?"

The men looked at each other, deciding who should take the lead. Reverend Clemmer started. "It's about your father's newspaper. *The Current-Leader*."

"What about it?"

The men shared another glance. "We've come to ask you not to sell it," said Burke. "At least not to your brother and the people who are financing him."

Holly looked from Burke to Clemmer and back and didn't hesitate. "I'm sorry, gentlemen, you're too late. I signed the papers this morning," she said, motioning to a large brown envelope on the seat of her wheelchair parked in the corner. "Nurse Frederick is going to mail it for me when she goes off duty."

Clemmer's brown eyes brightened, unfazed. "That doesn't mean anything, Miss Carter. As long as you haven't mailed the documents, you can just tear them up."

She had fixed him with her eyes. "Why would I want to do that? My father was a wonderful journalist, but he was a lousy businessman. Considering *The Current-Leader* is in very shaky financial shape, Tom has made me quite a generous offer."

"How do you think he can afford such a generous offer?" asked Burke.

"He has backers. So what?"

"Do you know who they are?" asked Clemmer.

"No. Tom says they'll be silent partners. He'll remain publisher and the paper will stay in the family. Just as it has been for a-hundred-and-thirty years."

Burke reached over, unsnapped an expensive briefcase and withdrew a single sheet of paper. He handed it to Holly. There were five names. All were prominent Cattahatchie County citizens. All were major advertisers. They were men she knew to be sometime poker buddies, occasional allies but most often enemies of her father. All but one had expressed in one way or another an interest in "knowing her better" before she left Cattahatchie County, even though she'd been barely eighteen. But it was the final name that had caused the breath to tighten in Holly's chest -- Cecil Weathers. Though no sound came out, Holly's lips formed the words – "Son-of-a-bitch."

Holly knew Weathers to be a conniving backwoods politician who'd married into the DeLong family and over time gained control of sprawling Chalmette Plantation, which had been in his wife's family since the early nineteenth century.

He'd been elected to various state offices throughout the 1930s, '40s and '50s on a "segregation then, segregation now, segregation forever" platform. As governor in 1962, he'd sworn no black would ever set foot in a Mississippi university "except as a janitor." It had taken a troop of U.S. Marshals and a show of force by the Army's 82nd Airborne Division to prove him wrong. Four people died and dozens more were injured in the three days of rioting that Gov. Weathers instigated.

For reasons unknown, T.L. Carter never had taken on Weathers in print. At least not in a serious way. A bee sting here, a pin prick there. That was all. In private, they detested each other. *How could Tom take that racist Neanderthal on as a partner?* Holly fumed inwardly, then steadied herself. "How do you know this?"

"We have our sources," said Burke.

"You're going to have to do better than that. What kind of sources?"

"All I can say is that it came up as part of the FBI's effort to monitor Klan activity," he told her.

Holly hesitated. It was no secret to anyone who grew up in DeLong that Weathers pulled the strings in the Kattahatchie Klavern of the so-called Invisible Empire of the Ku Klux Klan. She knew Tom always had held Dixiecrat segregationist views – egged on by Mary Nell – *but to go into business with that pompous, backward megalomaniac?*

Holly clinched her jaw to keep from cursing. Cursing Tom and Weathers, and cursing the timing of these men on the floor beneath her. Another two hours and the sales contract would have been in the mail. Within a week, there would be a seven-figure check in her mailbox. Much of it would go to hospital bills, old and new. But it also would pay off the mortgage on her little house above the ocean. Then it would be all hers. A safe place, completely modified so that even in a wheelchair Holly would need no one's help to get to every inch of it. There would be enough left over to convert the garage into a photo studio where she could augment her teaching salary doing family portraits, portfolio stuff and maybe some advertising shots. Not glamorous. Not the stuff of Pulitzer Prizes. Not like covering a war. But it would help put gas in her car to fuel her all-night drives, and keep her in wine and cheese and strawberries, and big bowls of buttered popcorn – her secret passion.

"Miss Carter, if you mail those documents, you'll be signing your father's legacy over to the Klan," pressed Clemmer.

Holly didn't want to deal with this bombshell. After a twelve-year roller coaster of reckless behavior that finally had landed her in a wheelchair, she simply wanted to be able to live quietly, comfortably – without pain, or at least without so much of it. All she wanted was her cameras, her little dog and sunsets that melted into the Pacific. She said, "You know, Reverend Clemmer, *The Current-Leader* always has maintained a white news only policy. And Daddy never directly took on Weathers or his crowd. We fought about it more than once."

"That's true," said Burke. "But I had the pleasure of meeting with your father several times. He was a pragmatist, not a racist."

Clemmer smirked at that and Holly saw derision, even disdain cross his lips. He shunted it aside, though, and said, "In any case, while *The Current-Leader* may never have come out openly against the segregationists, it never supported them. Your father's editorials always emphasized that there was a political process in place and that violence on either side was unacceptable."

"By Mississippi standards, that nearly made your father a Bobby Kennedy Democrat," said Burke. "Do you think T.L. Carter would want Weathers in control of the paper he put forty years of his life into?"

Holly was so angry with Tom, and with herself, that she felt the same bile rising in her throat that she had when the aide had carelessly spun her onto her chest. Maybe she had known deep down that Tom would get in bed with men like Weathers as soon as their father died. Maybe that's why she hadn't asked about his backers. She hadn't wanted to know. She'd been afraid to know. Now she forced a steadiness into her voice that she didn't feel. "I'll talk to my brother, but this is a family matter. I'm sorry."

"You're wrong, Miss Carter. This is *not* just a family matter," pressed Reverend Clemmer. "A federal judge has ordered Cattahatchie schools and other public facilities integrated by September. With local elections coming up this fall, the NCJ is planning the county's first-ever black voter registration drive over the summer."

Holly wished she could turn away, run away, but the metal frame felt as if it were tightening around her. Her head hurt, her stomach was queasy and her breasts ached under her weight. Said Burke, "With Cattahatchie his home county, Weathers has used all his wealth and political power to keep it segregated. It's the last county of its kind, even in Mississippi."

"A lot of the old-time Klan crazies see this as their last stand," Clemmer went on. "Weathers already owns the county's only radio station. If he controls the newspaper, too, there'll be no voice of reason or moderation. Things could get very ugly, very fast."

Burke could see they had shaken Holly Lee Carter, and he moved in with the precision of a seasoned prosecutor playing to the jury. "Miss Carter, your father had a big plaque on the wall behind his desk – 'A newspaper is the conscience of a community.' What sort of conscience do you think *The Current-Leader* will be for DeLong if its soul is mortgaged to Weathers?"

Holly wasn't looking at Burke or Clemmer. She was gripping the steel frame, looking through them, into her past and her future.

"What am I supposed to do?" she asked. "Refuse to sell my half? Let the paper go into bankruptcy? Because without some new financing, that's where it's headed. And Weathers and his cronies will get it anyway, at a fire-sale price."

Burke had been waiting for the right opening. "We've found another group willing to purchase your fifty-one percent. Not at the inflated price that Weathers' bunch is offering, but a fair price. Well into the mid six figures."

"Cattahatchie County people?" asked Holly.

"No. No one in that part of the state is willing to go up against Weathers," explained Burke. "One man is from Kentucky, and two are from Indiana."

"What about Tom? Would he remain publisher?"

Burke and Clemmer shared a look. "The men we're talking about certainly would try to work with Tom," said the U.S. Attorney. "But their views are more, well, forward thinking. If they couldn't come to an understanding on *The Current-Leader's* editorial policy they, well, they might have to go a different direction."

Tom had worked at *The Current-Leader* since he was old enough to run copy from their father's desk to the hot lead typesetters in the backshop, and had spent his entire adult life trying to keep it solvent as the company's vice president and general manager. More than that, ever since their mother abandoned the family – disappearing when Holly was eight and her brother was fifteen – Tom had been her father's verbal punching bag. Some of the assaults at the dinner table, in the newspaper office or even on a public street were so vicious and degrading that a leather strap or brass knuckles almost would have been kinder. Tom took it stoically, but Holly would hear him crying when she passed his door. At first, she tried to go in and comfort him – or share comfort as children physically abandoned by their mother and emotionally abandoned by their father. But Tom always would shut the door and shut her out. After a time, he took to locking it.

"No. No way," said Holly. "No, gentlemen, I'm sorry. I won't – I *can't* do that to my brother. *The Current-Leader* is Tom's birthright. Lord knows, he's earned it."

Clemmer tried, "Please, Miss Carter –"

"No!" she interrupted sharply. "The answer is no. I won't help you steal *The Current-Leader* from Tom. Now please go."

There was nothing in Holly Lee Carter's eyes or the tight set of her lips that allowed for further discussion. J.L. Burke and Ron Clemmer rolled off the pillows. Clemmer picked up the blanket, folded it and returned it and the pillows to the closet.

"Thank you for your time, Miss Carter," said Burke.

Holly watched wingtips and work boots head for the door. She said nothing, inwardly furious with Tom. She shifted her eyes to the envelope with her future inside of it, and Tom's. Tears of frustration burned her eyes.

"Miss Carter, there is one other alternative," Reverend Clemmer said from the door.

"Please leave," she said, sensing what was coming. "I've heard all I want to hear."

"You could go back and run the paper yourself," he persisted.

Holly laughed. "Forget it, Reverend," she said, quickly wiping her eyes with the backs of her hands. "I have a life here. I have a house where I don't need legs to get around. I can see the ocean from my porch. I have flowers I can take care of and a little dog that loves me. I have a job, and students who respect me. Most of all,

I have nice neighbors and friends at the college who have never seen me without a wheelchair. They don't look at me with pity, remembering who I used to be."

The silence hung deep and long between them. They could hear the sound of nursing shoes squeaking on the floor and the elevator doors opening and closing down the hall. The pastor's eyes moved around the dimly lit room as he searched for words to change Holly Lee Carter's mind. Then they stopped on a table in the corner. "I see you keep a Bible close," he said. "Before you mail that envelope, would you pray about it?"

Holly drew in a long breath and let it out. "Reverend, I pray every day to be a little better person than I was the day before. To stay on a good path, to walk in the light," she told him, then grunted. "But you know what? I don't need to pray about this. I'm not going to betray my brother, and I'm never going back to DeLong."

After several moments, Holly saw Clemmer's work boots turn to go. She didn't intend to speak, but she heard herself say, "Be careful, Reverend. Cattahatchie County can be a dangerous place. It's covered with steep hills and thick woods. The swamps are wide and the rivers are deep. There are a lot of unmarked graves. Most are filled with people who look like you."

Ronald Clemmer shifted at the edge of Holly's sight. "Thank you, Miss Carter," he said after a moment. "I'll remember that. I don't want to die in Mississippi."

"Neither do I, Reverend Clemmer," said Holly. "Neither do I."

CHAPTER 7

T he early light poured onto the yellow brick of the Cattahatchie County
Courthouse as Holly and Eve – and Charlie, too – turned the old beat-up
Lincoln onto the town square in DeLong.

"My goodness," sighed Holly, "it hasn't changed a bit. If it weren't for the cars,
I'd think it was 1959."

Indeed, DeLong, Mississippi had changed little since the last big surge of civic
pride when the majority of the plank storefronts were replaced by mostly two-story
brick structures in the 1920s. Wood sidewalks were replaced with cement. The town
square was paved in the '30s but even into the '50s many of the town's residential
streets were hard-packed red clay. Drugstores, clothing stores, appliance stores,
hardware stores, grocers, barbers, beauticians, jewelers and an ice cream parlor
faced the courthouse. The President Jefferson Davis Hotel was the only three-story
building on the square, and though the rooms had mostly gone to seed, the lobby
and dining room hung on to a worn elegance. The Rebel Theater occupied all of
one corner, the marquee announcing Paul Newman in *Cool Hand Luke*, which had
debuted in L.A. two years earlier.

Eve laughed, and smiled the same TV-star perfect smile as her mother, actress
Carol Howard.

"What's so funny?"

"You know that TV show *Time Tunnel*?"

"Yes."

"I think we're in it," said Eve. "Or maybe *Lost in Space*."

"I'm just glad you didn't say *The Beverly Hillbillies*," said Holly, smiling.

"Ohhh, I was headed that way."

"Once you're here a while, you'll find out it's just another soap opera. Like most
small towns."

"I hope I'm not here that long," said Eve, almost to herself, an undertone of
anger imbued in every word as it had been since Sunday. Then to Holly, "I hope
neither one of us is."

Holly forced a smile but said nothing. She made a second trip around the
square, waving as she passed the truck farmers who dropped their tailgates beside

the courthouse each morning. Fresh from the fields were vegetables and fruit of every kind – sweet corn, okra, snap beans, peaches and strawberries, and tomatoes so big, firm and delicious they could be sliced up and served on a plate like red steak. What wasn't locally grown, the men bought off the railroad dock, queuing up by four a.m. to determine who got first crack at the crates as they were unloaded from Tennessee & Gulf boxcars.

Cattahatchie Current-Leader was painted at the top of the red brick building that squarely faced the front doors of the courthouse. That was no accident. When Holly's grandfather erected the building there in the 1890s, he wrote that it would be "the eyes of the community watching its government at work." And so it had been. A fair, consistent, even progressive voice, at least for the white community, through depressions and wars and good times. There were so many old hurts and hates between Holly and her father, and many of their battles had been fought inside those walls, but she could not look at the building now without feeling a powerful sense of pride in what *The Current-Leader* had meant to Cattahatchie County for more than a century.

Holly turned off the square and down the steep hill that led to the river and the newspaper's parking lot. "The carpenters weren't able to widen the hall from the front lobby," she told Eve. "Those walls help support the second floor, so we'll have to use the back door and take the freight elevator up."

"Now you're getting a taste of how my people feel," Eve quipped.

"Touché," agreed Holly as she stopped the car beside the zigzag ramp. The air was fragrant with the clean scent of fresh-cut pine. Holly looked at her watch. "Six-twenty. Good. Miss Frances opens the front door at 7 a.m. This first day, I just want to get in the building and make sure I can get around without any embarrassing hassles."

"Understood, Madam Publisher. So, let's do it," said Eve, stepping out. "That means you too, Charlie."

The Current-Leader building really was three stories, though only two were visible on the square. The first, more like a basement, was set deep into the hill upon which the square and courthouse sat. Past the loading dock and metal doors, a big room held the press, the five-hundred-pound rolls of paper that the machine devoured and the fifty-five-gallon drums of ink that made the stories and pictures come to life.

Using a set of keys Tom reluctantly had sent her, Holly unlocked the door and pushed through … into her newspaper. The sweet, woodsy scent of paper mixed with machine oil and ink filled her nostrils. She had not been in a newspaper office in more than three years, and almost had forgotten how much she loved the smell. It smelled like *now!* Like energy about to be unleashed, like history caught in that moment before it slipped away into the past.

Without even looking, she reached for the switch and turned on the long rack of overhead lights.

"There they are," she said, motioning to the set of Goss presses that T.L. had mortgaged *The Current-Leader* to purchase in 1966, converting the paper from an out-of-date Linotype system to offset, just like the big boys. "They're what's killing us," she told Eve. "The paper isn't getting enough use out of them to make them pay for themselves. That's got to change."

The freight elevator clanged and rattled and groaned. It automatically stopped at the first floor where the advertising and circulation departments were located. At the front desk, Mrs. Frances Ragland, who had been with *The Current-Leader* for over fifty years, controlled access to the interior of the building with the tenacity of a centurion guarding the gates of Rome. "Miss Frances" took in classified ads, birth announcements and death notices, and wrote one of the paper's most popular community news/gossip columns.

On the second floor were the composing room and the newsroom. There was plenty of clearance between the tall angled tables where strips of film were pasted onto white, news-page-sized cardboard to create the image that later would be photographed by a giant camera, transferred to a metal plate and finally stretched onto one of the press's steel cylinders. The newsroom, however, was like a maze thrown together by a madman. Piled high with papers, open phone books and eight-by-ten photos, desks were pushed into corners and into any cubbyhole where there was room for a telephone and a typewriter.

Several spots were a tight squeeze for Holly's wheels, but she loved it. Even empty, the room felt busy. The walls seeming to hold within them the echoes of ringing phones and clattering typewriters. As she passed Ridge Bellafont's darkroom she smelled the developing chemicals. They were more intoxicating to her than the best weed she'd ever smoked.

The newspaper had only four full-time reporters and a sports editor, but several of the community correspondents and part-timers had desks in the office, a jealously guarded perk. They all reported to C. Michael Morton, the newspaper's eager, young managing editor.

It had been quite a show yesterday in the newsroom, Holly's chief source had told her. Tom packing up his possessions from the publisher's office, carrying them to a small windowless room down the hall. He'd declined to return to the general manager's office downstairs.

"Oh, my, it was like a movie, *The Good Son Wronged*," photographer Ridge Bellafont told Holly and Eve over a delicious dinner of chicken piccata he prepared in the kitchen at Wolf's Run. "It was absolutely dramatic. He was carrying this small cardboard box and his chin was a'quaverin'.

"You'd have thought he was walking to the gallows. I was dying to make a photographic record of the tragedy, but feared for my life should I go to clickin'."

Holly nearly fell from her chair laughing, not at Tom but at Ridge's way of telling a story. In conversation, he could make the folding of a dishcloth sound interesting, turn it into an event. He never had been able to translate that wonderful humor into words on paper, but in the crystal dew on a single cotton stalk, the rolling hillscape of northern Cattahatchie County or the deep sun-blistered ruts at the corner of a farmer's eye, Ridge could see a photo. First in his mind's eye, then through the lens of his camera and finally onto paper in the darkroom. "Magic!" Holly had enthused the first time Ridge let her watch him dip a piece of photographic paper into the developing bath and coax an image into being. She had been only four then, but Holly never had lost the sense of alchemy she'd felt that first time with Ridge, or the sense of peace and accomplishment that came to her when working alone in the dim red light of a darkroom.

W hat wasn't funny, however, was Tom's attitude or that of his wife, Mary Nell. When the phone finally had been answered late Sunday afternoon at Tom's house in town, Mary Nell had said, "Ohhh, honey, don't be angry with Tommy about Wolf's Run. He asked me to oversee the renovations, but it's such a beautiful old place I just couldn't bear to see it torn asunder."

"'Torn asunder?' What are you talking about? All I asked for was a ramp up to the exterior porch by the kitchen door and one from the interior porch to the courtyard. And a wooden sidewalk out to the garage."

"Yes, well, even though Wolf's Run is more a cottage than a classical antebellum manse – such as Wilmont Place, where my people reside – it does have some wonderful architectural lines. I said to Tommy, 'Why, Holly, has been through *sooo* much, she just isn't thinking straight. There is simply no way she'll want to distract from the country elegance of Wolf's Run with … *ramps.*'"

Holly had felt the heat in her face and had forced herself to take a deep breath. "Mary Nell, Wolf's Run has been changed many times over the years," she had reminded her as calmly as she could manage. "At one time, the kitchen was in the building that now is the garage. There was no indoor plumbing or electricity, and there certainly was no swimming pool. Which, by the way, no one cleaned."

"Darling, I called several swimming pool services in Memphis. To come down to DeLong? My goodness! You'd have thought I asked them to travel to the back side of the moon. Their fees were simply exorbitant, and I told them so."

Holly had been so angry that she was afraid to speak. "Sweetie, are you there? Are you all right?"

"Mary Nell, may I please talk to Tom?"

"Why of course you may," she'd practically bubbled with artificial sweetness like the foam at the top of a shaken diet soda. "He's ever so eager to talk to you. But, honey, I trust you're not going to alter Wolf's Run too much. I mean, surely there must be places where someone in your – well, condition – would be more comfortable."

"Mary Nell, Wolf's Run is my home, and I intend to be perfectly comfortable right here for as long as I remain in DeLong," she'd said from the desk phone in the library. "But don't worry. I don't intend to replace all the furniture with hospital beds. When I go back to California, the house will still be livable for normal people."

"Oh, good! I'm so glad. ... Tommy, dear! Your sister is on the line."

As Holly waited, she absently ran her finger over the outside of the envelope containing the glass she'd crushed under the hard rubber of her wheel. She could hear the voices of her niece and nephew, playing perhaps in the back yard of the three-story Victorian on Jackson Street where Holly had spent her early years. Finally, Tom had picked up the phone. Pleasantries were brief. Like most of the town, by now he probably knew about the incident on the highway – even if he hadn't planned it, but he didn't ask and she didn't give him the satisfaction of telling him how close she'd come to the bridge abutment at Yancy Creek.

"None of the changes I asked for at Wolf's Run were done," she had said. "But I assume you took care of things at the paper."

"Well, actually, you see, we had some questions about the specifications –"

"Damn it, Tom!" she had cursed, then closed her eyes as she fought to rein in her exasperation. "I don't intend to have to crawl or be carried into my own place of business." She'd heard one of Tom's sarcastic snorts at the other end of the line. "I'm sorry, Tom, I didn't mean that like it sounded. Daddy left the paper to both of us."

"A little more to you than me," he'd reminded coldly. "And that makes all the difference. Doesn't it, Sister?"

Now as Holly sat outside the double doors leading to the publisher's office, she knew that Tom was right. Whether she wanted it that way or not. It was all going to be on her. She was going to have to try to stabilize the paper financially while walking the fine line between practicality and the social and political issues that were boiling just beneath the surface of the town. Tom was going to be of no help. In fact, he likely would hinder her in whatever small, mean ways that he could. After what happened Sunday, Holly knew he might even be dangerous, but without absolute proof it was something she wouldn't allow herself to dwell on.

On the exhale of a deep breath, Holly opened the big doors and pushed into what had been T.L. Carter's office for thirty-five years. She stopped in the middle of the big room and took it in as Eve spotted the coffeemaker on a table by the door to the office's private bathroom.

"Thank goodness! I need more caffeine," said Eve. "I'll make a pot."

Charlie crossed the worn Oriental rug, hurried past the conference table and leaped onto the leather sofa pressed against a wall of glazed brick. She marched up and down the cushions twice to get the lay of the piece then settled against an arm by a large window.

"Glad to see you're making yourself at home," Holly told the little dog, which gave her a quick yap in response.

The first thing Holly noticed was that the hardwood floor tilted toward the four eight-foot-high windows in the front of the room. Not much, but a little. On her feet, in high heels and hose or tennis shoes and dungarees, she'd never felt the small angle in the hardwood. Now she had to hold onto the steel grab-rims on the outside of her tires to keep her chair from rolling toward the balcony that overhung the sidewalk and looked onto the town square. Ornate wrought iron rails guarded the porch's edge, as they did on many such second-floor sitting areas around the square, a nod to the French influence that once rode the river north, up from Louisiana. On election nights and when a jury was out on a big trial, the lawyers, accountants and doctors who occupied most of the upstairs offices moved chairs outside to take the breeze and wait for news while discreetly sipping their after-work highballs.

Holly rolled over next to one of the windows and looked out. Always it was this balcony where the loud speakers were set up. Her father and his father before him took microphone in hand to read election returns to the farmers and townsmen gathered on the square to spit tobacco, speculate and barter with the hill people for quilts, firewood and moonshine. Wives spread blankets beneath the big oaks that shaded the courthouse and unpacked picnic basket suppers of fried chicken, cornbread and sweet potatoes while black fiddlers, guitar pickers and vendors passed among them. Holly's earliest memory of her father was not a toy he'd bought her or a playtime moment at the house on Jackson Street. No, she was four and T.L. Carter was standing on that porch, his seersucker suit pants braced by red suspenders over a white shirt, the back wet with sweat, the sleeves rolled above his elbows. He was holding up a paper and crying and smiling at the same time. The headline read:

JAPS SURRENDER; WWII ENDS
Fathers, husbands, sons coming home

Holly felt her eyes welling and pushed away from the window. The last thing she wanted was for her makeup to start running before she saw Tom or the staff. She knew the day, and several to follow, likely would be emotional. She had grown up in this building as much as at the Jackson Street house or Wolf's Run. Many of the longtime employees had treated her as a surrogate daughter, especially after her mother disappeared and her father changed, hardened by anger and disappointment. On top of the homecoming would be the wheelchair. It would not be easy on Miss Becky in classifieds, Miss Frances at the front desk, "Shorty" Rodgers in composing or Frank Hodges, the paper's advertising director, to see her in the chair. It wasn't going to be easy on Holly either. In all their eyes she would have to watch their image of the girl she'd been disintegrate into the truth of the woman she was now. It was a truth that Holly had mostly come to accept. But that didn't mean her heart wouldn't ache, if only for a moment, each time the sadness and pity in their eyes forced her to relive that moment in the Honolulu hospital when the doctors told her she'd never walk again.

CHAPTER 8

Gospel music was something Holly Lee Carter remembered fondly about her upbringing at First Denomination Church. Even if it was just about the only thing. She loved the omnipresent four-part harmonies, the raucous rattling of the soprano piano keys and the uncomplicated spirituality of the music played there – and by WHCI, DeLong's only radio station.

"The sweet gospel sounds of WHCI" were interrupted hourly by local news, farm price reports and sports – mostly taken right out of the pages of *The Current-Leader* -- and editorials by the station's owner, former Governor Cecil Weathers. The station carried Brother MacAllister's sermons live on Sunday mornings and replayed them daily at 10 a.m. and 10 p.m.

It was early Friday afternoon and Holly had heard Weathers' latest editorial about ten times since returning from California. It urged all "morally upright" citizens of Cattahatchie County to support the new private school that was to open in September on a piece of property donated by Weathers. He walked a fine line when it came to inciting violence – "It would be better if God utterly destroyed the public school system of this nation than have it turned over to *Nee*-groes and those who seek to create a mongrelized mud race. ..."

She wheeled around the publisher's desk, turned off the radio and put on the turntable one of the record albums she'd brought with her. Bob Dylan's *Sitting on a Barbed Wire Fence* sing-songed through the speakers. Holly smiled at the appropriateness of the tune as she pushed over to the conference room table. She again flipped through a copy of the most recent edition of *The Current-Leader* – July 11, 1969. At the bottom of page one was a story announcing that she was back and would assume the title of editor-in-chief, and that Tom Carter would remain as the paper's general manager. It didn't mention the publishership.

Holly looked at the plaque behind her father's desk – *A newspaper is the conscience of a community*. And as far as she had run, the truth was, DeLong still was her community, her home. She pivoted her chair and rolled next to one of the four big windows, all open to catch what little air was moving outside. Her roots went as deep in the Mississippi soil as the oaks on the courthouse lawn. In fact, deeper, since her ancestors had helped plant some of the very trees that now were thick and mighty.

Outside on the busy square women with hair as solid as combat helmets leaned over tailgates in their high heels, purses on their arms, squeezing huge, red, ripe tomatoes. Some actually wore white gloves. It was like looking at a postcard mailed from DeLong in 1959. So little had changed since she'd left, especially compared to California. Holly scanned the men in overalls and work khakis and off-the-rack suits, studied the women walking in and out of the courthouse, the bank, and the drug store. Not one of them in pants. Heaven forbid, jeans! Walking, stopping in front of the big window at Handley's Department Store, in two's and three's, and walking on. No tennis shoes, not even sandals. Low pumps or high heels. Some laughing as they walked into the lobby of The Jeff Davis Hotel or walked under the marquee of the Rebel Theater.

Holly ran her hands over her skirt, over legs sheathed in pantyhose that her thighs and hips couldn't feel. Her calves were thinning and there was nothing she could do about it. If she didn't take care to keep her feet positioned correctly on the chair's pedals, they flopped at odd angles. Her feet remained pretty, maybe prettier than ever since they suffered almost no daily scuffing. She studied the pale coral nail polish on toes peeking from the brown, open-front pumps. All of those women on the square walking … some carrying babies … walking … some girls she'd gone to high school with leading children ready for first grade or more … walking … others buying dinner or running errands or going to work or planning for the hour when the kids are put to bed and the lights are off, and their husbands come to them and … and … Holly drew in her breath … all of them *walking!*

In her throat, Holly felt a sob or a scream welling up but she choked it down, whatever it was, and pivoted hard away from the window – fighting not to focus on what she'd lost. On what her headlong rush toward some illusion of absolute independence had cost her before it came to a halt with the suddenness of a .762-millimeter slug traveling at 2,346 feet per second. Her legs had gone out from under her as if severed by some great scythe. Even as she hit the ground hard, she was rolling trying to tear off her green army T-shirt – her back on fire, sure she must have been smoked with a blast of napalm that she'd neither heard nor seen. But when she got the shirt over her head she saw only blood and the holes … *the holes!* … the holes the slugs had cut through the shirt and into her.

Holly shook off the memory and pushed behind her father's desk – her desk, at least for now – and locked the chair's brakes. With a shaking hand she slipped her reading glasses onto her nose and picked up her pen. She had work to do. Thank God.

A few minutes later through the open doors to the hall and nearby stairs, Holly heard Tom's voice.

"Yep, it's small but it'll do for me," she heard him say, no doubt referring to the nearby office he'd wedged himself into. "Bein' in that chair and all, Holly needs the space and the privacy," he went on, as if she required almost continuous medical treatment. "It's really amazing that she's held up as well as she has considering the *severity* of her condition."

Tom knew nothing about Holly's "condition." He had returned few of her calls from Los Angeles, and during Thursday's cold fifteen-minute meeting, he'd asked nothing about her health or Vietnam, her time in California or what her life was like in a wheelchair. Holly had tried to draw him out with talk of his children – Georgette, thirteen, and Thomas Lanier Carter V, ten – and even with polite questions about Mary Nell, clubs and church, but his response had been negligible. In the end, she'd gotten down to business, wanting to lay out her preliminary plans for the paper, get his ideas and meld them with hers, if possible. But, "No, thanks," he'd told her. "I'd just as soon find out with the rest of the employees."

Only thirty-five, Tom looked at least ten years older. His firm, athletic frame was gone; his brown eyes were flat and lifeless. The spare tire around his middle was somewhere between truck and tractor size, a double chin hung from beneath his jaw and the capillaries of his cheeks and nose broke red across his face like the fissures of a smashed windshield. They provided the only color to his otherwise pallid skin. If anyone looked in need of continuous medical care, it was Tom.

"Let's see if she's up to talking with you," she heard Tom say. "Holly?"

"Yes!" she replied, more sharply than she intended.

"There are some folks here who'd like to see you," he said, stepping into the office.

The words, "Do they have an appointment?" formed in her mind but not on her lips. She knew that wasn't how things were done in DeLong, for the most part. People often simply stopped by, and her father somehow found the time to chat about kids, fishing or farming before letting them share, in their own time, what they'd come about. Holly never had that gift of small talk, and it was one of the reasons she'd become a photographer and not a reporter. She preferred letting her pictures do the talking, but, "All right, Tom," she said. "Please show them in."

As Holly wheeled around the desk, she did her best to disguise her shock and dismay as Charlie hopped down from the sofa and began to greet them. There were eleven mostly middle-aged businessmen who represented the newspaper's largest advertisers – Handley's Department Store, Grisham Supermarket, Kamp Motorcars and The Rebel Theater among them. Brother C.E. MacAllister was next. The last through the door was Cecil Weathers, who owned the Cattahatchie Valley Bank, among other things. He was flanked by his Mississippi Highway Patrol body guard, Sgt. J.D. Benoit, and state Senator Haughton Wellingham.

"Oh, Miss Holly," Wellingham sang as he extended his hand. "It's so good to see you up and on your – err, well, up and around. When I saw you in that terrible contraption in Los Angeles, I feared so for your health."

"Thank you for your concern, Mr. Wellingham. It took a couple of months of hard work in rehab, but I have my strength back now and I feel great. The surgery relieved much of the pain I'd been dealing with since – uhm, since Vietnam," she said. "Charlie, *le silence de ve et règle.*"

The little dog went to a corner of the room and lay down under a side table where Holly had placed her food and water dishes. "Well, gentlemen, I have to confess that you've caught me a bit off guard," said Holly. "I wasn't expecting this august delegation."

"Nonsense," said Weathers, a round-faced man, five-ten or so, of medium build in his sixties with thinning hair dyed shoe-polish black above a long forehead. His critics described him as "the bulldog of segregation," and that was apt both physically and philosophically. He had full lips below a puggish nose that separated large dark eyes. His ears were small and lay flat against the side of his head. When on the political stump, he favored off-the-rack suits in various shades of white, from bone to cream. Today he was wearing a gray, vested suit, probably tailored for him in New Orleans, or maybe Dallas. Below hand-sewn French shirt cuffs his nails were manicured but his hands remained the beefy mitts of a pig-farmer's son. "We're all family here. You dig deep enough, and all our roots are intertwined. Common blood.

"We just wanted to come by and welcome you back to the community and hear *all* your plans to rejuvenate this grand ol' newspaper," he went on, and without invitation settled into a chair at one end of the conference table. Haughton Wellingham sat at the governor's right hand and Charles MacAllister at his left. The others found positions at the table or around the room. Sgt. Benoit closed the office doors and stationed himself in front of them. Holly was becoming more furious by the moment at the high-handed gall of Cecil Weathers and with Tom, who likely set up this ambush. She forced herself to remain calm.

"Well, I appreciate your concern about my health, and *The Currrent-Leader* family appreciates, as always, your continued advertising support," she said. "But as far as my – as *our* plans for the newspaper, I'm afraid there is very little I can tell you. But I can say that Tom and I are going to be looking at ways to improve the appearance of the paper and increase circulation to give you the best possible return on your advertising dollar."

"Do you plan to increase your ad rates?" asked Walter Kamp, owner of the county's largest automobile dealership.

"We haven't increased our rates in almost three years," she said, having spent the last two months studying the paper's recent history. "Some small increase probably is warranted, but our rates will remain far below those of the Tupelo and Memphis dailies."

There was some grumbling but Milton Handley spoke up. "*The Current-Leader* always has been a valuable advertising tool. But it can only remain so if it continues to reflect our community values."

"Our white community," added Walter Kamp.

"The talk is you've already hired a colored reporter," said Clifton Reese, who owned the Rebel Theater.

Holly drew her hands together, giving herself a moment to find a diplomatic response. She knew she had to be careful. "If that's 'the talk,' I hope you all will help me set it straight. There's no truth to it."

"What about the Negro girl you've been seen with?" asked Handley.

"Eve Howard is a talented photography student who is working on a book while assisting me with my personal – while working with me as my personal assistant."

"Like a nurse, you mean?" asked Wilbur Grisham.

Holly drew in her breath and her pride as she thought again of all the women walking ... walking around the square below. "Yes, sir. That's what I mean," she said, without further explanation. Negro nurses caring for elderly or infeebled white folk was a tradition. It was acceptable, and no threat to DeLong's tightly woven social fabric. Holly felt ashamed of relegating Eve, her friend, to the role of body servant in the eyes of these men, but the answer was truthful as far as it went. This was no political science class or Philosophy 101, she told herself. These men could keep the paper afloat or sink it.

"What about the paper's whites-only news policy?" asked Governor Weathers. "Will you keep it in place?"

Holly knew she had to carefully choose her words. "Gentlemen, I've been in this office less than two days. Before I make any changes, I intend to carefully study the needs of this community."

"Then let us be blunt, Miss Carter," said Milton Handley, meeting her eyes. "What this community does not need, and will not tolerate is a rag carryin' nigg'ah news and advocatin' for race-mixers. Is that understood?"

Holly drew in a breath and returned his fierce gaze with one of steady determination. Then, "You've made your position quite clear," she said, flattening her hands on the table and pushing away from it. "Gentlemen, thank you for coming. Tom and I certainly will take your feelings into consideration when making our decisions about *The Current-Leader*'s future. But at the moment, we're on deadline for our weekend edition. So, if you'll excuse me."

"Very well," said Governor Weathers, standing. "Tom, thank you for your kind invitation to share our thoughts with you and your sister."

Tom Carter smiled and nodded. Holly was almost surprised he didn't bow.

CHAPTER 9

From my desk next to that of Sports Editor Clete Rainy, I saw the doors open to the publisher's office and watched the men file out and down the stairs. Brother Daddy and I made eye contact but he kept his thoughts focused on a higher plane and did not acknowledge me. The newsroom, which had been buzzing about the meeting, fell silent. Just as a few fingers were beginning to fall again on typewriter keys, Miss Carter pushed into the hall, her purse in her lap and her little dog trailing behind. She wheeled into the tiny office Tom Carter was using. With her chair inside, the door could not be shut, but she was so angry she didn't care.

"Tom, you're my brother, and I love you," those nearby heard her say. "But don't you ever pull a stunt like that on me again."

"Why, sister, I don't have a clue what you mean. But whatever you say, Holly. You're the boss."

It took Miss Carter three attempts to back her wheelchair out into the narrow hall and get it pointed toward the freight elevator in the composing room. By that time Ridge Bellafont and Eve Howard were out of the darkroom. Eve hurried after her boss, stepping into the elevator just before the big doors rattled shut.

"What happened? What did those men want?"

"I don't want to talk about it now," Holly told her. "I'll fill you in later. I just need to go for a drive and clear my head."

"Let me grab my purse and I'll go with you?"

"No! I mean, no thanks."

The elevator doors opened in the pressroom where the two-man crew was preparing the big machines to print the weekend edition starting at ten o'clcock. Eve followed Holly onto the loading dock.

"Girl, are you sure it's smart for you to be out on the road by yourself?'

"Despite what people around here may think, I'm not an invalid."

"Hey, come on! You know that's not what I meant."

Holly stopped at the bottom of the new ramp. "I know. I'm sorry. But I doubt the Klan would try anything in broad daylight, and I *really* need to be alone for a little while," she said. "Besides, they've already delivered their message for today. And I sat there and took it."

Eight miles east of DeLong on the Dumas Road, the Continental convertible dropped over a steep hill and into a long bottom. Cotton fields, cut by three creeks, spread away from the pavement. The air was whipping through Holly's auburn hair and a Rolling Stones eight-track was roaring in her ears. The louder the better. The less able she was to hear Milton Handley's words ... and her weak response to them.

She was barely aware of the dark blue Dodge coming toward her, but even before it went by, the red lights on the dash and behind the grill were flashing. "*Ohhh, shhhit!*" Holly groaned as she looked down at the speedometer. Eighty-four.

The last time she'd been on the Dumas Road, she might have floored it and kept going. Her '56 Corvette had outrun more than one police car in its day. But that 'Vette was gone and so was the girl who drove it. Holly looked for a place to pull over on the narrow shoulder and watched in the rearview mirror as the unmarked cruiser turned around.

Two minutes later an older gentleman in a white short-sleeved shirt and khaki pants stepped from the Dodge and set a fedora on his head. He left the red lights flashing as he approached, giving the bruised convertible and woman behind the wheel a long once-over. He studied the wheelchair folded behind the front seat.

Holly held out her California driver's license and the registration. He motioned it away and rested his hand casually on the hilt of his revolver. "I don't know how fast you were going, Miss Carter, but I know it was too danged fast for this stretch of road," he said. "If you don't care if you kill yourself, that's between you and your maker. But if you plow into a family pullin' out of one of these side roads, that's something different. And I assure you, if you live, it'll be between you and me and the state of Miss'ssippi. I don't care whether you're in a wheelchair or not."

Holly held up her hands in surrender. "I'm sorry. You're absolutely right. I guess I was letting off steam but –" she shook her head. The excuse sounded weak even to her.

The man studied Holly with neither pity nor lust. It felt to Holly more like fatherly interest, perhaps even amusement. "I don't think we've met. I'm Sheriff Johnson," he said, extending his hand. "I moved back to DeLong in the fall of '59. I believe you'd already escaped to the West Coast."

Holly smiled, instantly liking the man. "Escaped? That's a very – uhm? – perceptive way to put it."

"You're not the first teenager ever to want to spread your wings and fly the coop. I did it myself back in the twenties. I did six years in the Navy before hooking up with the Memphis police. But ol' Cattahatchie County? I guess it called us both home," he said, taking a step back to look at the scrapes and green paint still evident on the

Lincoln. "From what I hear, you had a pretty rough welcome last Sunday. You should have come by and filed a complaint."

"And said what?" she asked. "That two hooded men driving a Ford sedan that's as common as dirt ran us off the road? And, by the way, it didn't have a tag.

"We weren't hurt, thank God. It had been a long drive from L.A., and all I wanted to do was get out to Wolf's Run."

The sheriff nodded but said, "You still should have put it on the record. You never can tell, I might run across a green Ford with a strip of baby blue across the doors."

"No you won't. I'll guarantee you that car was rolled into some river or lake, or torched at the end of some dirt road before noon on Sunday," she said as Sheriff Johnson gave her a look of quizzical respect. "I rode with the night cops writers at the *L.A. Chronicle* for three years while I was working part-time and going to college," she explained. "I kept my ears open when the detectives talked."

He changed the subject. "Is everything out at Wolf's Run aw'right?"

"Pretty much," she said, not sure how far Johnson could be trusted. But the fact that he'd run against Weathers' hand-picked candidate for sheriff and won spoke well of the man. So, she cracked the door open. "The only thing – well, my mother's portrait was missing from the library. It was there right before Daddy died. He mentioned it in a let- ter. Now nobody knows where it is."

"By nobody you mean Tom?"

"Yes."

"And nothing else appears to be missing?"

"No. Not that I can tell."

The sheriff drew air into his cheeks and slowly let it out. "Well, your father left Wolf's Run and all its contents to you. If anyone removed anything without your permission, it's theft. If you want to come by the office and file a report, I'll go over to Tom's place and have a talk with him."

"No, no. Of course not," Holly quickly told him. "It's just strange. I suppose I'm more curious than anything else."

"Is there anything else you're curious about?" asked Sheriff Johnson.

Holly tilted her head to one side as if trying to hear him better. Was Floyd Johnson inviting her to question him about her father's death? Holly thought again of her mother's missing portrait and of the piece of glass she'd run over in the library. She wasn't certain what it was, though over the last five days, she developed a good and perhaps troubling guess. That was all it was, though -- a guess and she didn't intend to share it until she was sure. Still, there was something else that had bothered her since the first time she'd heard about her father's accident.

"It was a bad, rainy night, the night Daddy died, right?"

"Yes'um. And cold."

"Well, where was Daddy going?" she asked. "It seems like if he had a meeting in town or even a card game out at the country club, he'd have stayed at the office." Sheriff Johnson adjusted the thick black gun belt on his hips as he listened. "He kept a change of clothes at the paper. He had his own bathroom and shower. Of course, he could have gone home with no intention of coming back out, and gotten a phone call that –"

"Nope. We checked that," he told her. "Your father left the office early that Tuesday the 25th. Just after three o'clock. He was afraid he was coming down with a cold. He wanted to get home and get some of the chicken soup in him that Miss Frances had brought him. There were no calls into or out of Wolf's Run."

Holly thought about that. "Then that makes even less sense. Daddy must have been sick as a dog if he left the office early on a night when the paper is put out."

"No. According to Miss Frances, T.L. only had the sniffles," the sheriff told her. "But he was already nervous about flying. So, he wanted to make sure he wasn't down with a cold."

"Flying?" asked Holly. "What are you talking about? My father was never on an airplane in his life."

Floyd Johnson started to speak then reassessed his words. The mysteries within families never ceased to amaze him. "So, no one told you?" he asked gently.

"Told me what?"

"Miss Carter, your father was scheduled to be on a 10:25 flight out of Memphis on Thursday morning. He was going to Los Angeles. He intended to be at your bedside when you woke up from your operation. He wanted to surprise you."

Holly twisted her hands on the steering wheel as an old truck roared past loaded with pine logs. She stared off into the long cotton-filled hollow between two sets of low hills. Twice she started to speak, but couldn't manage it. Patience was one of Floyd Johnson's virtues and Holly was grateful he let her take her time.

Finally, "No. No one told me," she said, clearing her throat. Then, "Sheriff, would you mind if we got together and went over the accident report, autopsy and such?"

"No, ma'am, I wouldn't mind that at all," he said. "I'll have those files pulled from the county records office. My wife and I are going down to the coast this weekend to attend our granddaughter's wedding. We won't be back until late Monday. How does Tuesday, nine a.m. sharp sound to you?"

"That'll be fine. In fact, it'll give me time to check on something I've been curious about."

"What's that?"

"I'd rather not say until I'm sure."

"You know, Miss Carter, if your father's death wasn't an accident, there'll be someone out there who won't appreciate you askin' questions."

"Don't worry, Sheriff. I'll be discreet."

Floyd Johnson chuckled. "Miss Carter, you *have* been away a long time. If either one of us start pickin' at your father's case, it'll be like tossin' a brick in a very small pond. The ripples'll go every which way."

"Maybe you're right. Maybe we shouldn't meet at the paper."

"And if you come to my office, it'll be the talk of the town before noon."

"How about I buy you a cup of coffee out at Wolf's Run?"

"Aw'right, that sounds good," he said, touching the brim of his fedora. "In the meantime, young woman, slow it down. Please!"

CHAPTER 10

"What are you so blue about this early in the morning?" Cutter asked over a plate of biscuits smothered in white gravy speckled with spicy brown sausage. Miss Winona St. Julian's sawmill gravy was famous, and the only place to get it was at The Cotton Café.

It was just past first light on Sunday and low river fog hung among the warehouses across the Cattahatchie River. The mist made them look like movie sets painted on soft canvas rather than the tough plank-and-nail reality of commerce in our little corner of the world.

Cutter was just off work at The Gin. "You and Patti on the outs?"

"No, not really," I told him between mouthfuls of pancakes. "Not exactly, that is."

"That clarifies it."

"The thing is, I went over to the MacAllisters' last night to watch TV with Patti – you know, just hang out, eat some of her momma's chicken. Well, Brother Mac wouldn't let up about Miss Carter and the paper. He wanted to know everything I saw, everything I heard. He grilled me like a murder suspect," I explained, putting down my fork. "Ever since it got out that Miss Carter was coming back to run the paper, he's been hinting that 'the righteous should have no truck with a woman of such obvious immorality.' Meaning I should quit the paper."

"Well, you do have more than enough farm work to do," Cutter said reasonably.

"The farm? Fuck the farm!" I said more loudly than I meant to – loud enough that several regulars glanced up from their plates. I lowered my voice. "If Daddy wants to be a farmer, he can sober up and be one. Or at least help. But I was born to write. It's like I have this whole huge reservoir of words and thoughts built up inside me. The paper is like my spillway to let them out. At least some of them. If that gets cut off – well, I, I –"

"Might get all green and slimy inside?"

"Cutter, this is no joke."

Paula Simpson came over and cleared our plates, her body pressed as snuggly against the seams of her pink-and-white uniform as the coffee against the walls of the glass pot. "More coffee?"

"None for me," I told her.

"Could I get a cup to go?"

"How big a cup you want, Cutter? I've got some big ones."

Cutter let a smile play at the right corner of his mouth. "I'll take the biggest you've got."

"Sure thing, Cutter. You know you can have all you want, any time you want."

Cutter stood as he said, "I'll keep it in mind."

Paula filled a Styrofoam cup and smiled at Cutter as we paid for our breakfasts. We went outside and propped against his Jeep. I went on – "I'm not like you, Cutter. I'm not gonna have women fallin' all over me wherever I go. Patti is a knockout. She's even a cheerleader! And I love her and I'm lucky to have her. If I lose her …." I shook my head, the fog cool and damp on my neck and bare arms.

Cutter blew on the black surface of his extra large coffee. "Nate, you sell yourself way too short. You always have. PattiWac is the one who's lucky to have you. You're the only thing keepin' the cork in her bottle."

It was then that the baby-blue Lincoln turned onto River Street. "Speak of the she devil," said Cutter, smiling. I groaned.

Holly Lee Carter pulled into the only available parking place next to where Cutter and I were standing. She was wearing those Tuff-Nutt overalls again. And doing it very well. Her hair hung loose on the shoulders of a green Army jacket bearing the blue- and-yellow insignia of the U.S. 7th Cavalry. She pulled Janis Joplin's *Cheap Thrills* from the tape player and dropped it on the seat as Charlie perched on the passenger door and sniffed at us.

"Good morn —" Miss Carter started but her words were overtaken by a long yawn. She covered her mouth then said, "Pardon me." She stretched her arms over her head, her hands balled into fists. "Good morning."

"Mornin'," I said, patting Charlie's curly hair. Cutter nodded, but said nothing.

"It seems like the three of us meeting at dawn on Sunday mornings is turning into a habit. We'll have to be careful or people will talk," she teased.

"People are talking already," said Cutter.

"Really? What are they saying?"

Cutter looked off toward the river. "This'n'that."

"Wow! That's a big subject," she said. Then to me, "Nate, I called in a takeout order. Would you mind running in and checking on it? Just tell them to put it on my tab."

I glanced at Cutter, dipped my head. "Sure," I said and went through the glass doors, leaving Cutter and Miss Carter alone on the misty street. Inside, people were, indeed, talking and craning their necks to get a better look.

"That was one of the first things I did when I got back – set up a tab at The Cotton," Miss Carter was saying by way of conversation. "No one can fry up a chicken or make a pan of cornbread like Miss Winona. She's a bona fide culinary legend."

Cutter was someone who felt no need to fill even the most awkward silences with the sound of his own voice. He could stare a frog off a flat rock and never utter a word.

"You know, out in L.A. they call this kind of cooking 'soul food.' I think that's true. I know it feeds my soul. Unfortunately, it also feeds my hips," she went on, smiling, but Cutter only sipped his coffee. Then, more seriously – "Cutter, I can understand why you might have a, well, distaste for people with disabilities. For people who use it as an excuse to –"

"Look, Miss Carter, the way I hear it, you've got a lot bigger problems than worryin' about what I think," he interrupted. "If I were you, I'd keep my mind steady focused on dealin' with those things." Cutter climbed into his Jeep and turned the key. "But since you sent Nate to step-and-fetch your breakfast, if it's not too much trouble, would you tell him I'll be at The Well after four? In case he cares to drop by."

"The Well, huh? That's a beautiful spot. I made a lot of memories there. And a few of them are even good," she told him, smiling. Cutter did his best to look past her. "Did you know I held the record for two straight years?"

"The record?"

"You know what I mean. For how long you can stay under. Two-minutes-eighteen-seconds," she told him. "Bobby Freeman finally broke it, I think. He was on the Tupelo swim team."

Cutter dropped the shifter into reverse. "Good day to you, Miss Carter."

Two sausage-biscuit meals were in a paper sack on the back floorboard when Holly Lee Carter turned west onto Blue Mountain Road, crossing the railroad tracks. The gravel cut twisted through fields of cotton, soybeans and some corn, and past the Old Ambrose Place, where Cutter had grown up. Ahead, the fog curled above the river like a thick, white snake keeping close to the hills before exposing itself on the open floor of the Cattahatchie Valley. Holly eased back on the hand control and stopped the car on the heavy plank flooring of the Old Iron Bridge. In the early morning dew, the rust stains leaking from the rivets looked like blood. Sunlight was yet to dip into the fissure cut next to the limestone face of Blue Mountain, and under Holly the river ran black and deep. This was the spot where her father's car had gone in.

It was easy to see how it could happen. Just past the bridge and the rutted lane leading to The Well, the gravel road rose sharply and curved. Coming at night from Wolf's Run, in the rain, T.L. Carter's Oldsmobile quickly would have picked up momentum and with only a little too much speed it would overshoot the turn, miss the bridge and go right off into the river – swollen then by spring rains and spiked with debris.

T.L. Carter did not know how to swim. More than once he'd told his water-loving daughter that he had no use for it as "I do not intend to make a spectacle of myself by bathing in public."

There was no sense brooding now. Still, Holly wished there had been a little more time. Through letters and phone calls, for the first time in their lives, she and T.L. were getting to know each other – starting to accept each other's flaws, fears, hopes and regrets. Filled with drugs and sandwiched tight in the Stryker-like frame, it had been a struggle even to cry when Tom called with the news. But cry she had, and longer and deeper than she would have supposed she might in that situation. Crying not for the father she'd lost, but the father Holly hoped T.L. might finally become – and the daughter she wanted to be.

Now here she was back in DeLong, at the very spot where he'd died. Or was it? Holly couldn't shake what Sheriff Johnson had told her about T.L. resting up for a trip to California. "To be at my bedside when I woke up," she whispered, exhaling a long sigh as she stared at the unprotected shoulder at the west end of the bridge. No guard rail, just a berm of soft earth.

The new will … the increase in Klan violence … the trip to L.A. … the accident … the missing painting of her mother.

It all was probably only coincidence, Holly told herself, but it's a *lot* of coincidence. And it sounded as if Sheriff Johnson thought the same thing.

CHAPTER 11

One of Wolf's Run's most favorable features was that the limestone bluffs rising on either side of the plateau kept the house and courtyard mostly in shade except for a couple of hours on either side of noon. That meant that without air-conditioning, the house stayed reasonably cool even on the hottest days. And now that the pool had been scrubbed, acid-washed and refilled, the wrought-iron patio table at the edge of the bluff was a beautiful spot for breakfast or dinner.

Eve put a silver coffee service on the table and Holly placed a tray of cookies, doughnuts and fresh fruit beside it. Sheriff Johnson probably had eaten breakfast several hours earlier, but they could snack. Holly was both eager for and anxious about the conversation.

"Okay, you're set," said Eve, looking at her watch. It was almost nine a.m. Tuesday morning. "I'm going to take a shower."

Holly watched her friend walk away, up the steps to the west wing and disappear into the house.

Eve had borrowed the car Sunday afternoon to go to a voting rights rally at Pickens' Ferry A.M.E. Church, where Reverend Clemmer and the National Coalition for Justice volunteers were making their headquarters. She returned with the news that Roy Hayes' little girl, Cynthia, had indeed lost her eyesight in the Klan attack a week earlier.

"That would be front-page news in a lot of papers," Eve had pointed out. Holly could only respond with silence, and the tension between them had been growing since.

Shaking off those thoughts, Holly sipped her coffee, glad to have a few minutes to review the notes in her steno pad from two calls she'd made on Monday, and a meeting with Dr. Marvin Gilbert, DeLong's only optometrist and one of her father's oldest friends.

The first call had been to the attorney in Greenwood, down in Leflore County at the edge of the flat, fertile alluvial plain known simply as The Delta. His name was James J. Emmerich.

"Your father came to me as a referral from Gilroy Baddin, whom, as I'm sure

71

you know, owns the newspaper here," Emmerich told her. "The other witness to the will was Conrad DePew, a local planter and circuit judge."

"Now you say Daddy was emphatic about keeping the will a secret?"

"Absolutely," said Emmerich. "Until he chose to reveal it, or his death."

"And why was that?"

"I couldn't tell you. But he was very clear on that point."

"Is it possible either Mr. Baddin or Mr. DePew violated my father's confidence?"

"Miss Carter, when you've been an attorney for thirty-five years, you come to realize that very few things are *im*-possible when it comes to relationships among members of our species. But in this case, I'd find it very difficult to imagine," he said. "These are men of excellent reputation. And from what I could surmise, they and your father were old and dear friends. Fraternity brothers at Tulane, I think."

"Yes, that sounds right," Holly agreed. "Did my father tell you why he came a hundred and fifty miles to execute a new will?"

James J. Emmerich was silent for a moment. Then, "Not in so many words. But I would postulate that he feared that the legal community in Cattahatchie County and nearby environs has been – shall we say, compromised? – by political influence. I think he was concerned that many of the attorneys there might not take their oath of confidentiality seriously enough."

"Last question," she'd said, "Did he tell you why he was changing the will? Why he was leaving controlling interest to me?"

"No. I'm sorry, Miss Carter. He did not."

*S*o, she thought as she speared a piece of cantaloupe, *if someone wanted Daddy out of the way, he surely would assume the newspaper would fall into Tom's hands.*

Holly flipped to the next page.

*O*ld Man" John Pierce, who had run the DeLong Funeral Home for more than half a century, was not so affable or forthcoming. When she asked about the disposition of her father's effects, he took immediate umbrage. "If you're implying some impropriety on our part, young woman, I won't have it."

"No, sir. Not at all. I'm simply trying to do due diligence as the executor of my father's estate," Holly had assured him.

"I don't see why you're pestering me," he said. "Why don't you ask your brother? I turned everything over to him and Miss Mary Nell."

"No, sir. I need an official inventory of my father's effects as they were delivered to you."

"Hold, please," he said and the line had gone silent. Several minutes later he spoke again. "Very well. I have it. But it's rather short."

"That's all right, could you –?"

"Young woman, you realize, of course, that Mr. Carter's body was not recovered until five days after the accident," he interrupted. "It was discovered by two fishermen over in the edge of Lafayette County. The autopsy was performed there, so DeLong Funeral Home workers were not the first to handle the remains or Mr. Carter's effects. If there are any items missing, I suggest you call Dr. Phelps in Oxford."

"Thank you, I –"

"I'll have a copy made and left for you at the front desk. Good-bye, Miss –"

"One more question, please, Mr. Pierce. Was my father buried with his glasses on?"

Holly heard Mr. Pierce draw in a ragged breath. "Ahh, how could I have forgotten? You were not present for your father's funeral," he said, twisting the blade of guilt in her side. "So, you would not know that it was a closed-casket ceremony."

"Be that as it may, Mr. Pierce ..."

"I was present when my staff sealed the casket. The answer is no, he was not."

H olly opened the file folder next to her plate. There was a Delong Funeral Home letterhead at the top of a typed page briefly listing all of the items recovered with her father's body – or at least those conveyed to Mr. Pierce's establishment. She read it again and it was about what anyone would expect under such circumstances. Two socks (one black, one brown), but only one brown leather wingtip shoe; brown suit pants and a white shirt; one brown belt; one pair of red suspenders; the remnants of one suit vest, brown; one pair boxer shorts; one white T-shirt; one black tri-fold wallet containing six dollars and various photographs.

More notable in Holly's eyes was what was not listed.

In many ways, T.L. Carter was quite old fashioned. He practically put on a tie to get up in the middle of the night and go to the bathroom. The gold watch he'd been given when he retired as president of the Mississippi Newspaper Association was absent. But more glaring than anything else was that no raincoat, not even a suit coat, was recovered.

If he went home early that afternoon trying to hold off a cold, Holly reasoned, *it made no sense for him to go out in a cold rain that night in nothing but a vest and shirt sleeves. Of course the currents of the river and myriad snags along the bank could have pulled those items of clothing off him. Still ...*

T he final set of notes regarded her visit to Dr. Marvin Gilbert's office.
 Three generations of Gilberts had been taking care of the eyes of Cattahatchie County for almost eighty years, including Holly's. Though she saw perfectly at long and medium distances, she had worn reading glasses since childhood.

After the usual formalities of re-acquaintance following a decade of absence, and the perfunctory compliments about how good she looked, how young and healthy, came the all-too-typical moment of silence when the person took in the wheelchair – really took it in – and let their eyes drift down her legs. Holly had come to think of it as "the broken-china moment." But Dr. Gilbert quickly freed himself from the familiar spell, saying, "I'm sorry I couldn't see you this morning. I was simply jammed. I do believe this whole county is going blind. It's good for business, but – well, Holly, what can I do for you? Do you need new glasses?"

"No. I need to speak to you about a private matter," she said. Dr. Gilbert's receptionist, Susan Hodges, shuffled papers and worked hard at pretending disinterest. Susan had graduated from CHS two years ahead of Holly.

"Of course, come on back to my office," he said, and Holly followed the tall, stork-framed doctor down the narrow hall, barely able to make the sharp turn into his cramped quarters. He pushed a chair older than Holly out of the way and made room in front of his desk, then sat down.

"Dr. Gilbert, when was the last time you talked to my father?"

"T.L. and I had lunch together a week to the day before the accident – across the street at The Jeff Davis. His death was a terrible shock."

"Did he seem particularly worried about anything?"

"Other than your upcoming back surgery, no."

"He mentioned that? And his plans to fly to Los Angeles?"

"Yes. He was nervous about flying, but he was quite excited about seeing you. Such a shame," said Dr.Gilbert, his eyes losing focus for a moment, then settling again on Holly. "Did the surgery go well?"

"Yes, very. Thank you."

"Is there any chance it will allow you to, to uh –?"

"Walk? No, sir. I'm afraid this is – well, quite permanent. But the surgery did alleviate a lot of pain, and I'm grateful for that," she told him. "Now, beyond any concerns about me, did he seem particularly worried or upset?"

The optometrist studied the woman in front of him and his own recollection. "Well … T.L. was agitated about Weathers and his bunch, but then he always was. Still, he was beside himself at the notion that DeLong's place in history might be as 'the last battleground of segregation.' Which at this point seems a wholly valid concern."

Holly reached behind her and freed the purse straps that were wrapped around one handle of her chair. She took out a white business-size envelope and handed it to the doctor. "What's this?" he asked.

"That's what I want you to tell me." Marvin Gilbert felt the exterior of the envelope. "Careful," she said. "You might cut yourself."

He put down the envelope in the center of his desk calendar, and leaned back in his chair. "Where did you get this? This whatever it is?"

"Again, doctor, for the moment I'd rather not say. But I'd like for you to examine the contents and tell whatever you can about it."

A slender finger played at the corner of Dr. Gilbert's narrow lips. "All right, Holly. I'll help, if I can."

"Thank you, Doctor. Also, how many pairs of glasses did you make for my father in his most recent prescription and frame style?"

"As always, two. One to wear and a spare."

"Did he still keep the spare in the glove compartment of his car?"

"To the best of my knowledge," said Marvin Gilbert. "As you know, your father's eyesight was quite poor. He was always fearful of being off somewhere and losing or breaking his glasses. He knew he couldn't drive without them."

"Certainly not on a pitch-black, rainy night," Holly added.

"Certainly not," agreed Dr. Gilbert. "Holly, where are you going with this?"

"Probably nowhere. But before I say anything more, I'd appreciate it if you could help me satisfy my curiosity."

"Very well. I'll get back to you as soon as possible."

"Thank you, Dr. Gilbert," she'd said.

The optometrist had stood and come around the desk. As he reached for the door knob, he and Holly had heard low-healed pumps clicking away on the tile. They looked at each other. "Welcome home," he said.

Holly bit deep into a large, delicious strawberry purchased from one of the county's many roadside vendors selling from their tailgates. The area was famous for them. She looked at her watch – 9:08. Sheriff Johnson probably was simply running late.

At 9:20, Holly dabbed a napkin at the corner of her mouth and pushed up the new ramp into the house. From the living room windows, she could see the circle in front of the house and all the way up to the road. She pushed back to the kitchen and took hold of the phone, but decided against calling. After all, Floyd Johnson was the sheriff. Any number of emergencies could have come up; and if she called looking for him, it would only rev up the talk her Monday inquiries probably already had generated.

Holly placed the receiver back on the hook and startled when it instantly rang. It sounded as loud as a siren in the quiet house. The voice on the other end of the line was excited, almost gleeful. "Miss Carter, it looks like we've got our lead story for tomorrow. And it's a big one! It sure is," enthused C. Michael Morton, *The Current-Leader*'s young managing editor. "I sent two reporters and Ridge Bellafont out there."

"Calm down, Michael," said Holly. "Sent them out where?"

"Out to Sheriff Johnson's house on Buena Vista Road," he said. "Haven't you heard?"

Holly suddenly felt the pit of her stomach drop out. "No. Tell me."

"It looks like somebody planted a bomb in the sheriff's car. He got in it this morning to come to work and *ka-boom!*"

"Is he –?"

"Oh, yeah. Very," said Morton. "Ridge called from down the road at Kyle Renfro's house. He says the car was blown to bits, along with half the house."

"Mrs. Johnson?" Holly managed.

"She was in the back bedroom. She's all right."

Holly thought of the nice, steady, likable man she'd met on the Dumas Road less than four days ago. "At least you got to see your granddaughter get married," Holly said to herself.

"What's that, Miss Carter?" asked Morton. "I didn't catch that. Something about a granddaughter?"

Holly forced herself to don the hat of editor-in-chief. "Nothing. It was nothing," she said. "I'll be there in twenty minutes."

CHAPTER 12

E ve Howard stood in the door to the publisher's office holding a page proof. It was just after sunset Friday night and the mid-July heat was stifling, even with the ceiling fans turning overhead and the big windows open onto the balcony and the square. And open, too, at the back of the building to catch whatever breeze was stirring along with the river's current.

Holly looked up from her desk "Which page is that?"

"Five."

"How many pages do we still have out?"

Eve was staring at the page in her hands. "Six. No, Mr. Rodgers said seven. I think. I'll have to check."

"May I see that proof?"

Eve crossed the room and laid the page in front of Holly. Most of Wednesday's paper had been about the murder of Sheriff Johnson. Most of Saturday's paper would be about the investigation and funeral arrangements. The headline at the top of the page read:

Ex-Gov. blames 'outside agitators' for sheriff's death
By Randall Murphy
Staff Writer

Flanked by four state legislators and three of five county supervisors, former Mississippi Governor Cecil Weathers rose before a crowd of more than three hundred gathered at the site for the new Riverview Academy and accused "outside agitators" of orchestrating the Tuesday car-bomb murder of Sheriff Floyd Johnson.

"We've all heard of them. Seen them on our televisions. In their black leather jackets and funny little foreign caps. Some people are afraid to name them because it is no longer fashionable to call a spade a spade," Weathers told the crowd Thursday night. "But I'm not afraid. I'll name them! They call themselves The Black Panthers, and these Negro thugs will stop at nothing to see that the social and moral fabric of this nation is torn to shreds.

"We know that they have killed police officers in Oakland, California, and Chicago, Illinois. And now they've brought their murderous ways here by killing one of the best and most decent lawmen in Mississippi, my dear friend, Floyd Johnson," continued the former governor.

"Holly, I just can't believe you're running this racist shit," said Eve.

"I'm burying this 'shit,' as you call it, on page five," she said.

"Well, la-de-dah, page five? I guess that makes you a candidate for some sort of social justice award?"

Holly straightened in her wheelchair and took off her reading glasses. Her shoulders ached from hours at that desk reading stories and checking pages. She rubbed her eyes and ran her hand down her neck where a sheen of perspiration glowed. The editor of *The Current-Leader* said, "Whether I like it or not, when the ex-governor of this state, flanked by members of the county board of supervisors and the state legislature, speaks to three hundred people, it's news. By all rights, front-page news."

"What about the two hundred people who came to Pickens' Ferry Church last Sunday for that voting rights rally?" asked Eve. "I have pictures. Mr. Rodgers says there's a hole we need to fill on page three."

"Stop it, Eve."

"Why? You don't think it's news? Or maybe you don't think black folks qualify as people?"

Holly felt a bolt of heat rush up her neck and into her cheeks as she pushed around her desk, intending to face young Eve Howard. Instead, she forced herself to turn away, stopping beside one of the large open windows. She stared out at the courthouse, letting the flash of anger cool. After a moment, "Eve, when you agreed to come to DeLong with me – practically begged to come here with me, I told you that I want to make changes in this newspaper," she said. "Especially in the way news from our black community is handled. But I warned you, that I was *not* returning to DeLong as some sort of political crusader. My first responsibility is to stabilize this newspaper financially, so that I *can* keep it out of the hands of people like Weathers. And if that means that I have to hold off for a time integrating the pages of this paper, then that's just the way it is."

Holly felt her friend's eyes fixing her. "Then tell me, when is the time going to be right? How many more black families are going to have to have their homes or businesses shot up? How many more black churches have to burn? How many more little black children have to be blinded? Or worse?" she demanded. "What's it going to take?"

"If you'll read my editorial, it calls for calm and a cooling off of the rhetoric by–"

"That's not enough," said Eve.

Holly pushed away from the window and returned to her desk. "I'm sorry, Eve," she said as she reset the glasses on her nose and picked up the page proof. "I guess I'm no Martin Luther King."

"No," said Eve. "I guess you're not."

L ess than a minute later the editor's private line rang – "Holly Lee Carter," she said. "I'm not much of a hunter, but with the shutters open and your office lit up like that, I could put a deer slug right into your ear," said the voice.

Holly felt her heart suddenly thump in her chest as she looked out the second-floor window onto the quiet square. Those going to The Rebel Theater already were inside, chuckling at Michelle Lee and Dean Jones in *Herbie The Love Bug*. Then the soft Carolina drawl registered. She hoped her relieved sigh wasn't audible.

"Nice to hear from you, Mr. Burke," she said. "Where are you?"

"Third floor. Corner room. The Jefferson Davis Hotel," he told her. "With a 30.06 and a scope, I could take the side of your head off."

She took off her glasses and squinted across the square, but the third floor room was dark. "Do you have a scope or a 30.06 with you?"

"No."

"Good."

"Seriously, Miss Carter, you should be more careful. At least close the shades."

"It's hot as Hell in here. Daddy never bothered to have this place air-conditioned," she said feeling the dampness under her arms and along her collarbone. "Besides, don't you think you're being a little paranoid?"

"Being a little paranoid is a lot better than being a little dead. Just ask Sheriff Johnson."

"That's not funny."

"It's not meant to be."

The editor of *The Current-Leader* and the U.S. Attorney had talked several times before her return to DeLong, and a couple of times since. It was part of a pact they'd made. If Holly came back and ran the paper to keep it away from Weathers, Burke agreed to keep her abreast of things as best he could without endangering any ongoing investigations or prosecutions. Burke worked closely with the FBI and controlled his own force of federal marshals. Next to U.S. District Judge Oren Mulberry, who had ordered the desegregation of Cattahatchie schools and public offices by September 2, J.L. Burke probably was the most powerful and most hated man in north Mississippi.

"Seriously, Holly, if the Klan is willing to take out a county sheriff," he went on, "then they won't think twice about a newspaper editor."

"The Klan? Haven't you heard? It was the Black Panthers."

"Yeah, right."

"Besides, they sent me their message the first day I got here. Out on the road. Why should they come after me now? I'm toeing the Ku Klux line. I'm still running a segregated newspaper," she said, resting her elbow on her desk and holding her forehead in her hand.

"Is that what that exchange with Miss Howard was about?"

"I don't appreciate having a Peeping Tom."

"You look tired."

Holly sat back and ran her fingers through her hair. "I am. And I still have a newspaper to finish putting out tonight. So, if this is a social call –"

"It's not," said Burke. "I've got a scoop for you, though you can't attribute it to me."

"Sources close to the investigation?"

"That'll do."

"All right," said Holly, opening a steno pad. "What've you got?"

The U.S. Attorney told her that on the previous Thursday an informant spotted a man buying gas at a country store in eastern Cattahatchie County whom the FBI believes to be Robert Bedford McBride of Jasper, Alabama. McBride was a former Army Ranger and demolitions expert who served in Europe during World War II and later Korea.

"He's known in Klan circles as 'Dynamite Bob' and is one of the main reasons why Birmingham, Alabama got its nickname – 'Bombingham'," Burke went on. "In fact, we've always liked him for that 1963 church bombing there."

"The one that killed the four little black girls?"

"That's the one," said Burke. "We think he's responsible for at least sixteen bombings from Richmond, Virginia to Houston, Texas, since 1955, resulting in more than fourteen deaths and dozens of injuries. More recently, we think he engineered a series of break-ins at four military armories. Everything from M-16s and ammunition to hand grenades and C-4 plastic explosives were taken.

"McBride is smart and mean and Klan to the core. We've arrested him four times but never been able to make anything stick. We do our best to keep track of him, but when he wants to be, he's a ghost. About six weeks ago, he dropped completely off the radar."

"And you think he killed Sheriff Johnson?"

"We can place him in Cattahatchie County within a few days of the murder and he certainly has the requisite skills and mindset," said Burke. "So, yes, Bob McBride certainly would be our leading candidate. We also think he's helped plan the recent string of church arsons and attacks in black communities in the county."

"And the motive for killing Sheriff Johnson?"

"Multiple motives. The sheriff had refused to break up the voting rights rallies or the NCJ encampment up at Pickens' Ferry. He'd also made it clear that unless it was overturned on appeal, he would enforce Judge Mulberry's integration order," Burke told her. "And just two weeks ago he had a run-in with Weathers and his cronies at The Cotton Café."

"Yes. I heard about that," said Holly absently, wondering if another motive should be added to the list? That the sheriff had pulled her father's file from county records. Was someone worried that Floyd Johnson was about to start asking new questions about T.L. Carter's death? Maybe, maybe not. It wasn't time to talk about that. Not yet. After all, what did she have? Nothing but an empty spot on the library wall where her mother's portrait had hung, and a feeling. Holly refocused on the moment, asked, "How much of this can I use? Can I call McBride 'the prime suspect'?"

"No. But you certainly can say he's wanted by multiple law enforcement agencies for questioning in the matter," said Burke. "As for the rest of it – well, you can use all the background. And I'm sending a marshal over right now with mug shots and description of the vehicle he was driving. He's probably long since switched cars, but who knows?

"We think he's moving from one Klan safe house to another along the Tennessee-Mississippi line. Hopefully someone has seen him in transit. Maybe we'll get lucky."

"Aren't you afraid this will spook him?"

"Spooking McBride is the best thing that could happen. That he'll bolt, and we'll run him down two or three months from now on some empty stretch of highway in Utah or Montana," said the U.S. Attorney. "But Bob McBride operated behind German lines for nearly fourteen months during World War II. Spook? No, Bob McBride won't spook. He's a true believer in The Cause, as they call it. He'll stay here until we catch him or his mission is completed, however he defines it."

"You almost sound as if you admire him."

Burke grunted. "Admire him? I despise him and all he stands for. But I don't underestimate him."

Holly sat back in her chair, saying nothing, letting that thought settle in. "Then I wish you luck, Mr. Burke," she said. "I think you'll need it with J.D. Benoit occupying the sheriff's office. I doubt you're going to get a lot of cooperation from the locals.

"You've heard, I'm sure, that the county board of supervisors voted this morning to recommend to Governor Broderick that Benoit be appointed to fill the position until the November elections. In fact, Benoit's already bragging that Broderick is coming here Wednesday to personally administer the oath of office and get an update on the investigation into the bombing."

"Yes, I heard. Weathers controls the supervisors. It was a forgone conclusion."

Holly laughed sarcastically. "Under the circumstances, you sound pretty nonchalant about having Cecil Weathers' bodyguard as sheriff. That's like having not just the fox, but a wolf, guarding the henhouse, isn't it?"

Now it was Burke's turn to be silent, to measure his words. "Miss Carter, it's a long time from now until Wednesday," he told her.

Holly thought about that for a beat. "Would you care to elaborate?"

"No. But a word to the wise is sufficient," he said. "If I were you, I wouldn't put my Tuesday night paper to bed until you've heard from me."

Burke stared through his binoculars as a smile spread across Holly Lee Carter's face. Even from all the way across the square, it was like sunlight.

PART II

CHAPTER 1

On Saturday I awoke to a golden blade of sunshine cutting across the bookcases that my brother Steve had built for me before Vietnam. From the depth of my pillow, the worn spines of books by Twain, Fitzgerald, Steinbeck and Eudora Welty glowed on the shelves like jewels touched by morning light ... morning light!

I bolted up in the bed and looked at my clock – 7:34. I should have been up two hours ago.

Quickly I hurried into the bathroom to relieve my bladder, brush my teeth and wash up. It wasn't until I was back in my room and was dressing that I noticed the curious smell of coffee laced with the scent of bacon frying. It had been a month of Sundays and then some since anyone made breakfast at my house except me. Daddy was lifting strips of bacon from a black iron skillet when I entered the kitchen. He poured some of the bacon grease into a Mason jar and put the skillet back on the stove, then began cracking eggs into it.

"Sit down," he said. "Eggs'll be ready in a minute."

"I must have forgotten to set the alarm. I'm sorry," I said, though why I was apologizing to Billy Wallace I wasn't sure. He hadn't seen more than a dozen sunrises in the last two years.

"I shut it off," he said as he scrambled the eggs. "I figured you could use a break."

The man at the stove looked like my father – barefoot, worn jeans, a white T-shirt and denim work shirt open down the front. His whiskers were thick and mostly white, and his sandy blonde hair was disheveled. But all I could think about was that 1950s movie, *Invasion of the Body Snatchers*. In it, aliens kidnap humans and put them in giant pea pods, and when they emerge they look the same but they're compliant zombies.

I poured myself a cup of coffee as Daddy said, "In fact, I dropped by Elmo Washington's place yesterday. He and his boys are lookin' to pick up some extra work. I told 'em you could use some help startin' Monday mornin'."

"So, I can't handle the farm? Is that what you're sayin'?"

I'd been angry for months that I had next to no help on the place, and now when Daddy was providing with me with three willing bodies, I took it as an insult. It was stupid, but there it was.

"I'm sayin' that this farm is too big for any one person to handle. Even if that person loved farmin', and you don't," he said, dumping a big yellow pile of eggs onto a plate. "Sit down and eat."

He fixed himself a plate and sat down with me. His right hand trembled when he lifted his coffee cup, so he steadied it with the other. "Nate, I know I've been pretty sorry the last couple of years. Pretty worthless," he said. "You've done a good job under rough circumstances. I'm proud of you."

The words tugged at something inside me and caused the corners of my mouth to twitch.

"The truth is, I hate farmin' too," he told me. "When I got back from fightin' the Hitler's bunch, I swore I'd never put my butt on another tractor seat. And wouldn't have if it wasn't for your Grandpa Vernon gettin' sick and your momma missin' her people as much as she did. Then Steve took to plowin' and plantin' like a duck to water and I suppose I felt like I was buildin' a legacy for him. And for you, in a different way. So we could afford to send you off to college wherever you wanted to go. It made it tolerable.

"But when Steve was killed and Neesie grieved herself to death –" Billy Wallace shook his head. "There just didn't seem to be any point. To keepin' up the farm or anything else."

I dropped my fork and it clattered on the plate. "Then why the hell have you made me work like a dog the last two years?"

Billy Wallace swallowed a mouthful of eggs. "I don't have a good answer for that, Nate. Except that when you own a piece of land like this, that's what you do. And I supposed you might come to like it."

"Well, I don't."

"I know that. It wasn't fair to you."

The words my father was speaking should have sounded sweet to my ears, but I had so much resentment built up inside me that they simply sizzled on my eardrums like water on a hot griddle. I studied him suspiciously.

"If you don't mind me askin', what's the cause of this miraculous turnaround?"

Billy Wallace rubbed his whiskers, sighed. "I can't tell you the number of times over the last two years I said to myself things like, 'Come the first of the month I'll sober up. … Come plantin' time I'll put the bottle away. … Come Monday, I'm gonna turn over a new leaf. … Tomorrow I'm pourin' it out.'

"Then, finally, I'd say, 'Just one more drink, then I'll be done with it.' But there was always just one more drink."

"So, what changed?"

Daddy stood and poured himself another cup of stout black coffee. "You know that Floyd Johnson was my boss, my teacher – my best friend when I was on Memphis

P.D.," he said. I nodded. Of course, I knew. "I'm sure Floyd thought he'd have another day or another hour – another minute to deal with worldly affairs. Then he turned the key in his patrol car and time ran out.

"We just don't know, Nate, how many days or minutes, or even seconds, are allotted for us on this earth. I've wasted most of the last two years swimmin' in self-pity," he said. "Floyd was as good a man as I've ever known. I wish I could give him a little of that time I wasted. But, of course, I can't. At least not in that way. All I can do is pull myself out of this cesspool I've been in, and not waste any more of whatever life I have left."

I suppose some sons would have jumped to their feet, shouted *hallelujah, praise God!* and hugged their daddy's neck. I did none of that. It wasn't so much that I didn't believe him, it was simply that my father had separated himself so completely from me over the last twenty-four or so months that it just didn't seem to matter. It was like having a conversation with a stranger.

After several long, awkward moments, I managed, "That's good, Daddy. I'm glad for you."

"The funeral is at eleven. I better get cleaned up. Myrtle Johnson asked me to be a pallbearer."

My brows arched, surprised. "I didn't know."

"Thought maybe we could ride out to New Hope together."

I wasn't ready to go anywhere with Billy Wallace, besides – "Brother Mac has a carload of ministers riding with him. So, I'm picking Patti up."

"How are things with you and her?" Daddy asked as if he'd only this morning returned from a long trip that afforded him no mail or phone calls.

"They're good. Real good," I told him. "We can't wait to get away together to college."

Even as he was trying to make peace with me and himself, I knew I was sticking the knife in his side and twisting it. Saying, in essence, that I could hardly wait to get out from under his roof and away from him and this farm. But if he was wounded by my response, he didn't show it.

"Aw'right, son. I guess I'll just see you out there," he said and headed down the hall to the bathroom for his first shave in two weeks.

CHAPTER 2

Had Sheriff Johnson's funeral been held in DeLong in the sanctuary of First Denomination Church, as Brother Mac and other county officials had wanted, it might have been the biggest in years. Maybe even bigger than T.L. Carter's service back in April. But Mrs. Johnson was adamant that she wanted no part of a show funeral at First Denomination. Though she and the sheriff had not been regular church-goers over the last several years, mostly due to her emphysema, he had grown up in New Hope Community. If he had a church home, New Hope was it. The church's floor and beams and joists pre-dated the Civil War. A new clapboard shell had been put on around the turn of the century and a new tin roof sometime in the 1940s. But the building seated only about ninety people and air-conditioning had never been installed. The massive oaks that surrounded New Hope Church and stood sentinel in the adjoining cemetery provided good shade, but with the temperature at ninety-three it didn't help much.

Highway patrolmen directed most mourners into a nearby pasture that had its share of dips and chuck holes. We were at the far end of one of the last rows since we were near the tail of the mourner caravan. Patti had insisted we slip off down a side road, park and smoke a joint before we got to the church.

"Funerals are so depressing," she said and took the baggie from her purse and rolled a fatty. She licked the edge of the Top paper like a pro and fired it up. I didn't like pot and I didn't like her smoking it, but whenever I tried to talk to her about it she said it was the only thing that calmed her nerves.

"All the MacAllister women are high strung. We can't fuckin' help it," she'd say. "Momma has her nerve pills, and I have this. What's the difference?"

"Well, one's legal and one isn't," I said for the fiftieth time. Knowing I was just wasting my time. Knowing I was just inviting abuse. "There're cops all over the place out this way today. If we get caught with this stuff, it could completely screw our chances of getting any scholarship money. Hell, we could end up in jail with the amount of stuff you've got in that bag. Where'd you get all that?"

"None of your damn business," she snapped. Patti always was particularly edgy right before she mellowed out. It was a cycle to which I was accustomed, and knew she really didn't mean the ugly things she often said. Two hours from now she'd be apologizing, maybe even crying, and letting me push up her bra. But in the moment, the barbs could cut.

"Here," she said, holding the big joint out to me, her voice strained as she held the smoke in her lungs. As usual, she insisted I join her, and I coughed my way through a couple of hits to keep the peace. I admit that Patti's blonde hair, gray eyes, hefty chest and motor-driven hips blinded me to a lot of her faults, but this wasn't one of them. I knew she couldn't care less if I smoked, except that by her calculations if she involved me in her crime, I was less likely to tell. I thought the pot was a phase she'd grow out of, and that as she matured in college away from Brother Daddy her sharp tongue and prickly attitudes would soften.

"Sometimes, Nate, you're such a pussy," she said, exhaling the last of the smoke out the truck window and applying fresh dabs of perfume behind her ears and at her wrists. "Let's go."

From the backside of the pasture, the walk up the gravel road to the small dirt churchyard where only family members and dignitaries were allowed to park was long, hot and particularly perilous for women in their Sunday go-to-meetin' heels. The pot had done little to take the edge off Patti's mood. She cursed the gravel, her hose, her shoes, the heat and Mrs. Johnson for refusing Brother Mac's "most generous invitation" to hold the sheriff's funeral at First Denomination. She held out her hand. "Give me some Dentyne."

Patti knew I always kept it handy to disguise the pot on our breath, at least for the casual momma or daddy we might encounter. How well it would work with every kind of law enforcement officer prowling around – from FBI agents to sheriffs and their deputies and even auxiliaries – I didn't know. What I did know was that if cops searched under the seat of my truck, we were screwed. What was worse, I knew Patti would ball and whimper and cry out to Jesus, and tell with utter sincerity whatever lie worked in the moment, and blame me for all of it. That was who she was. How she was. But not how she always had to be, I told myself. Not if I could get her out of DeLong and away with me.

When we reached the churchyard and Patti saw that we'd have to stand at the back of the circle of mourners ten deep around the outside of the sanctuary, she cursed me for getting us there so late.

"We'll be able to hear," I said. "See, they've got loudspeakers set up."

"Hear? What the fuck do I care about hearing some barely literate redneck stumble through a sermon that my father could deliver twice as well in his sleep?" she asked. "But they've got ceiling fans inside. I'm melting like a damn popsicle on a car hood."

Then she spotted Miss Carter, sitting in her scraped-up Lincoln convertible next to the cemetery fence. She was wearing a sleeveless black dress, black lace scarf and Wayfarers. "What do you suppose that bitch wants here?"

"To pay her respects, I imagine. Like everyone else."

"Huh," Patti snorted. "That woman shouldn't be allowed anywhere near a church until she repents. The way she stole the paper from Mr. Tom and Miss Mary Nell. After all the years of hard work he put in. It's a shame and it ought to be a crime. Her ass ought to be in jail, wheelchair or not. I can't believe you're still working for her. Daddy don't like it one little bit."

"I don't work for *her*," I tried. "I work for the paper. She just happens to be running it right now."

"She's no good. She's never been any good," Patti went on as if I hadn't spoken. "My brother-in-law, Tommy, went to high school with her. Says she'd spread her legs for any man who could get it up. But God was watchin'. God saw. And God punished her. Put her in that chair so no man'll ever want her again. Got what she deserved, if you ask me."

There was a part of me that wanted to inform Patti that no one had asked her. But those would have been fightin' words, for sure. I let it pass and two minutes later the black DeLong Funeral Home hearse stopped in front of the old church.

Holly Lee Carter pulled a handkerchief from her black purse and patted the perspiration shining along her collarbone as she watched Mrs. Johnson make her way inside with one of her sons at her elbow. Old Man Pierce took his time organizing the pallbearers who had arrived in two sheriff's cars. Daddy was wearing his black suit, one of only two he owned. He'd lost so much weight it looked as if he'd borrowed it from the closet of a much bigger man. I saw he had his tie tight to his collar, but the shirt was still loose around his neck and already discolored with perspiration. As he passed close with the casket he smelled of the Aqua Velva on his face and the grain alcohol seeping out of his pores.

In my ear Patti whispered, "I hope your daddy doesn't have the shakes so bad he drops the por' ol' sheriff." Then she giggled. The muscles in my arm twitched and wanted to slap her. I might have had the same thought, but Billy Wallace was still my daddy. I tightened my fist so hard that my nails cut into my palm.

To the side of Holly Lee Carter and slightly behind her, a man cleared his throat. She twisted in the car seat. A young sheriff's deputy was standing there.

"Hi! Can I help you?" she asked. When he hesitated, she said, "I have permission to park here. I talked to –"

"Oh, I know!" he said stepping forward a bit so that she didn't have to crane around. "That's fine. You're fine." The young officer's hair was so blonde that it was almost white; his eyes were the blue of soft denim and he still seemed to be hanging onto a layer of baby fat at – what? – twenty-three or twenty-four. "Hon-, Honestly, I came to ask if I could help you?"

"Help me?" she asked, pulling off her sunglasses. "Help me how, Officer – ?"

"Deputy. Deputy John-Thomas Hinton," he said, pointing to the gold nametag above his badge. "My sister, Shirley, graduated with you in '59."

"Of course! How is Shirley?"

"Doin' pretty good. She's got two little'uns. Me'n the rest of the family spoil 'em like crazy, but – well, her husband, Charlie Jumper from over Booneville way, he got killed in Vietnam."

"Oh, I am sorry."

Deputy Hinton looked away then back. "I tried to enlist, but I tore up my knee playin' high school ball, and they wouldn't take me."

"Count yourself lucky."

"We all heard about what happened to you over there. You were in some of the worst of it. Ia Drang back in'65. With the 7th Air Cav." When Holly said nothing, he went on, his eyes moving between her and the wheelchair folded behind the front seat. "Anyway, I just wanted to say I'm sorry how it turned out. I mean, about, uh –"

"Don't be," said Holly, launching into her standard answer. "I'm one of the lucky ones. I came back alive." And even as she said it, thought the same thing she always thought but never uttered … *At least half of me did* …

"Shirley took me with her to the fair the night you won the Miss Cattahatchie County Pageant," Deputy Hinton continued. "I was only in the eighth grade, but I won't ever forget. When you sang, *Faded Love*. Wow! I get chills just thinkin' about it."

Holly felt a warm flush at the base of her neck. "It was a lot of fun," she said as he continued to look her over as if she were some exotic cat. "So…?"

"Oh! So, I thought maybe you needed some help. I mean, getting in your wheelchair or whatever. I could put you in it."

Holly finally was recognizing the signs of a crush, apparently long held – and hung onto now despite her changed circumstances. "That's very sweet of you, John-Thomas, but I've gotten pretty good at that over the last four years."

"I could even carry you inside if you want," he said, a little too enthusiastically. "I'm plenty stout."

"I'm sure you are. But really, I'm fine right here. Thank you."

John-Thomas Hinton's soft blue eyes looked crestfallen. "Well, aw'right, then. Maybe I'll see you around town."

Suddenly, something crossed Holly's mind – "Oh, John-Thomas, you might be able to help me with one thing."

"Sure!" he enthused. "Whatcha need?"

"I was supposed to meet with Sheriff Johnson when he got back from the coast regarding my father's accident. Just to tie up some loose ends."

"For insurance? That sort of thing?"

"Something like that, yes," she told him. "Anyway, he was going to have the file pulled from the county records. I was wondering –?"

Deputy Hinton already was shaking his head. "I think you may be outta luck there. I was in the office when Sheriff Johnson came by Saturday morning. He picked up some files from his desk and took them with him. I imagine he planned to study them over the weekend. "I'll look around, but if I had to guess about it, I'd say they were in his car on Tuesday morning."

Holly bit her lip. "That's what I was afraid of."

"But I was there that night. At the bridge. I helped with the investigation."

The family and pallbearers still were arranging themselves inside the church. Holly hadn't expected this opportunity and she didn't want to let it pass. "Well, then, I was wondering, was there any indication that the brakes failed? Or that Daddy was going too fast?"

"After the car was pulled out of the river, we had a mechanic go over it. As far as he could tell, there was nothing wrong with the car," the deputy told her. "And speed wasn't a real factor from what we could see. It appeared that your dad just kinda of lost track of where he was in the rain. There were no skid marks at all. Of course, with all that rain, it'd be mighty hard to tell. But Rose Marie Carlucci – Tony's girl, Cutter's sister – saw the whole thing. She said –"

Holly snatched the sunglasses off her face. "Wait a minute," she said, pushing herself up straighter in the seat and fixing Deputy Hinton with her eyes. "Rose Marie Carlucci saw the accident?"

"Yes, Ma'am," he confirmed. "Her brother, Cutter, was there, too. But not 'till later."

"That wasn't in the paper," Holly said, sounding more exasperated than she intended, but not as exasperated as she felt. "Sheriff Johnson didn't tell me that. No one told me that."

The young deputy saw the quick flash of green fire in Holly Carter's eyes, in her tone. "I'm sorry, I didn't mean to –"

"No, it's fine. You didn't do anything wrong," Holly assured him. "But why haven't I heard this before now."

The deputy shrugged. "It was no particular secret," he told her. "But the sheriff didn't give it to the paper because the girl's a minor and she just confirmed what we could see for ourselves. Plus, well, you've been gone a long while. Rose is a little simple-minded."

Holly looked at him. "I haven't been gone that long," she said. "Mrs. Carlucci was my homeroom teacher my junior year. She was my math teacher for two years. Rose Marie was very shy, but she wasn't retarded."

The deputy thought about that for a moment. "Maybe I used the wrong word," he said. "She's not retarded. But she stutters real bad, and she's a little, well, off." Holly looked at him. His cheeks were flushed. "Of course, livin' under the same roof with that asshole – sorry, pardon my language – with Tony Carlucci would drive anybody a little crazy."

What was unspoken between them was that they both knew Tony Carlucci had driven his wife, Jennifer, more than a little crazy.

"What, exactly, did Rose Marie see?"

"I'm sorry, Miss Holly. I wasn't there when Sheriff Johnson interviewed her. She was pretty upset. It all would have been in the reports."

"The reports that Sheriff Johnson had with him in his patrol car."

Holly meant the comment as a statement, not a question, but the young deputy answered it anyway. "That'd be my guess."

T.L. Carter's daughter mulled over the new information at the same time trying to think of anything else she might ask while she had the chance. "John-Thomas, you didn't find a raincoat or a suit coat in the car or the river, did you?"

"No. But if Mr. Carter had one on, he probably threw it off getting out of the car. Or it could have been swept out of the car by the river. The windshield was smashed and the driver's side window was open. The current in that bend was as fierce as I've ever seen it."

Holly thought about that for a moment. "The driver's window was open? On a cold, rainy night like that? Not broken out?"

"That's right. In a situation like that, it's almost impossible to open a car door until the vehicle is full of water. If I was doin' the figurin', I'd figure your daddy rolled down the window to try to equalize the pressure and open the door."

"Makes sense," said Holly, slipping her Wayfarers back on and already thinking about how to approach Rose Marie Carlucci. Considering the ancient enmity between her and Tony and the recent friction between her and Cutter, that wasn't going to be easy. Whether Mrs. Carlucci was in any condition to help, she had no idea.

From inside the church and through the loudspeakers a choir began and attendees were asked to join in *Standing on the Promises*.

"Thanks, John-Thomas," said Holly as she began tapping her fingers on the steering wheel to the old time gospel beat. "You've been a big help."

T he service lasted an hour and a half, and by the end of it we all looked and felt as wilted as the white gladioluses beside the pulpit. The fans stirred the air in the church but it had to be at least a hundred degrees inside that tin-roofed sweatbox. I was glad to be outside but Patti kept complaining about her feet and how hot it was. Finally, the family marched down the steps behind a nearly empty casket draped in a Mississippi state flag, the stars-and-bars of the Confederacy prominent in the upper left-hand corner. About fifty mourners went down to the gravesite, but most of us headed to our cars. The lucky ones had air-conditioning.

Dr. Marvin Gilbert got his wife situated in their gold Chrysler Imperial, started the engine, put the air on high and excused himself. He crossed under the oaks shading the small parking area to where Holly was watching the graveside service.

"Am I intruding?" he asked, mopping his face with a monogrammed linen handkerchief.

"No, doctor. Not at all," she said, removing her sunglasses. "I was just waiting for the traffic to thin a bit so that the car doesn't fill up with dust."

"I'm sorry I haven't gotten back to you this week on that matter we discussed, but it's – well, it's been a difficult few days for everyone," he told her. "Floyd was my wife's second cousin. She wanted to go down to the graveside, but it's far too hot for her."

"Oh, I didn't know they were related. I'm sorry."

"In any case, yesterday I got around to piecing together those shards of glass you brought to me," he said. Holly held her breath for a quick moment as she waited, not sure what she wanted to hear. "As I'm sure you suspected, it was a lens from your father's most recent glasses." He paused, considering. "I want to ask, where did you find it?"

"For now, I'd rather not say. And I'd prefer that you not share this information with anyone."

"All right, Holly," he agreed, straightening. "But promise me, you'll be careful. We've had enough funerals around here recently."

"I promise, Doctor," she assured him, even as both knew careful might not be good enough.

CHAPTER 3

Blue Mountain Road dropped suddenly down the face of the hill in a long, steep S. Near the bottom, Holly had to dramatically slow the big convertible to make the turn onto the bridge. That on a clear, bright summer afternoon. On a wet, slick night, T.L. Carter would have had to slow his four-door Oldsmobile to a crawl. A little too much speed and it would have been easy for her father to overshoot the turn in the darkness.

"So, why don't I believe it?" Holly asked herself again as she finished driving the route for the third time and parked beside the bridge on the narrow cut of road that led to The Well. Fish jumped in the brown, gentle current and a breeze fanned stalks of cotton and soybeans that spread for miles to the east away from the river. The crops paused at the railroad tracks and Highway 27, then picked up again and ran all the way to the eastern hills.

The road beside the bridge was a familiar one to her. As a teenager, she and friends often had found refuge at The Well. They would dive deep into the spring's maw to retrieve beers and shiny flasks of whiskey then swim off the chill in the warm summer waters of the Cattahatchie, ignoring the danger of water moccasins and gators. Even though there was a pool at Wolf's Run, there was more danger, more thrills and more privacy at The Well.

With Charlie next to her, Holly lay her head back on the seat piecing together the apparent sequence of events.

T.L. Carter went home early that rainy Tuesday afternoon. … At some point, his glasses were damaged and he lost a lens. He would have had to go out to his car, probably parked in the carriage house, to get his spare pair; otherwise he wouldn't even have been able to function around the house. … There was nothing on his schedule and there were no phone calls in or out of Wolf's Run, but at about 8:30 he left the house, maybe without a raincoat or even a suit coat, even though he was trying to hold off a cold. … Not even a tie, which was very atypical of T.L. Carter III. … Wearing his spare glasses he would have negotiated the S of the hillside road as he had done hundreds of times and yet he failed to make the turn at the bridge – or even try, apparently.

... Could he have been distracted by something? Maybe a deer or raccoon running across the road? she wondered. *Or simply overconfident that he could handle the turn in the wet conditions?*

Holly stared up at the clouds sailing languidly in the July sky. To the west, from behind the mountain, there was a rumble of distant thunder. She tried to think like the detectives she'd ridden with in L.A.

... So, then the car goes into the river. ... The windshield probably was intact when the car went into the river, she figured. *But Daddy, who could not swim, has the presence of mind in the utter blackness of that freezing water to roll down his window to try to escape? ... He surely wouldn't have been driving on a night like that with the window down. ... And at that point, while fighting for his life in the raging current, he, in theory, could have shed his raincoat, suit coat – even tie? – and lost his pocket watch and so on.*

Holly straightened in the seat. There was nothing in the scenario that was impossible, she told herself. "But there sure is a lot that's improbable," she said aloud.

Now, with Sheriff Johnson dead and her father's file probably destroyed, the events of that night would have to be reinvestigated from scratch. She took a small day planner from her purse and wrote a note in the square for Monday, July 21: "Call Dr. Phelps in Oxford. Get copy of autopsy report." But Holly knew that the first step was right in front of her, about a mile across the bean fields at the Old Ambrose Place. She put the car in gear. She knew she needed to talk to Rose Marie Carlucci.

As Holly approached the turnoff to the paint-faded, dog trot house that represented all that remained of Jennifer Ambrose's once considerable inheritance, she eyed the dilapidated structure and the surroundings. She'd seen Tony Carlucci driving around town in an old white pickup with a missing tailgate. It wasn't present, or at least it was not parked in the dirt yard in front of the house. She turned down the pocked lane that ran between two barbed wire fences, fighting the urge to jam on the brakes and back out of there as quickly as she could. The eleven-year-old memory came rushing back more powerfully than she had expected it might, jangling her nerves and unsettling her stomach more with every turn of the Lincoln's big whitewalls.

It was 1958 and she'd just done a couple of songs with the house band at The Gin. She was alone in the backstage hallway when Tony stepped from the shadows and pulled her into a janitor's closet. Holly remembered thinking, with the unlimited confidence of a youth, that she knew how to handle men like Tony Carlucci. For an instant she was more angry than scared, and the slap she had delivered sounded like thunder in the small tin room, but it had barely slowed him. He slammed her into the wall, smiling with bloody teeth before he threw his weight against her and jammed his lips onto hers. She tasted his blood and beer-soured spittle in her mouth. She twisted her face away and tried to scream but he grabbed her breast so ferociously that it squeezed the air from her lungs. He pivoted on his real leg and used his weight to drive her to the gritty floor, all two-hundred-and-sixty pounds landing atop her. The world went black for a moment before she saw stars flying every which way around the bare bulb hanging from the ceiling. The nicotine browned into Tony's fingers filled her lungs, his meaty hand covering her mouth as he shoved his other hand up her dress, a dirty nail tearing her hose, cutting the inside of her thigh as his thick fingers found their way past her slip and her garters.

Tony Carlucci had stuck his tongue into Holly's ear, then whispered, "You think your pussy is solid gold? That it drips honey? Just because of your grandma and her fancy house and fancy ways?" He grunted a laugh as corrosive as battery acid. "You're just another little dick-tease. And when I'm done borin' you out, not even a nigger'll have you."

Rage and adrenaline and, yes, fear, too, had roared through Holly's veins as Tony pushed aside her satin underpants. She instantly gathered all her strength and bucked against Tony's weight as she twisted her head and bit fiercely into the webbing between his thumb and forefinger. She tasted his salt sweat and testosterone in her mouth, and then blood, and when he jerked his hand away cursing her, she screamed as loud as she had ever screamed. But the sound was suddenly cut off as he dropped his bloody hand onto her throat and squeezed.

If the band hadn't decided to take a break after one more song, there was no telling what might have happened. No, that wasn't true. She had seen it in the wildness of his blood-fractured eyes. He would have raped her, then killed her. Or, hell, vice versa. It would not have mattered. But the guys in the band had heard her scream as they headed for the kitchen and cold beers on the back deck between sets. They pulled him off of her, but he beat the crap out of three of them before a Tennessee highway patrolman, who happened to be in the club, heard the commotion and put a .357 to the back of Tony's head and cocked the hammer.

Holly didn't press charges. The courts weren't interested in the goin's on at state-line roadhouses unless a corpse had to be explained, and the reach of Tony's buddy and boss, Cecil Weathers, easily extended into the Tennessee counties that bordered Cattahatchie. Plus, the Carters could do without what would be seen as another "family scandal" by people who already saw Holly's general behavior as scandalous.

Now after spending many nights riding with L.A. cops, a summer smoke jumping for a prize-winning photo essay capturing wilderness firefighters and spending many weeks in Vietnam, Holly knew she could handle herself much better than she had a decade earlier, even without her legs. Besides, she told herself, dragging a paralyzed woman out of her car and attacking her in the front yard of his house within sight of his daughter and a public road probably was a stretch even for a worthless bastard like Tony Carlucci.

At the end of the dirt lane, a flower bed fit into a massive and worn-worthless tractor tire creating a circular turning area in front of the old house. Behind a nicked and rusted screen, Jennifer Ambrose Cutter was bent over a quilting frame on the side porch. She had been Holly's homeroom teacher at CHS until one February morning in 1958. She had come to school as usual, chatted amiably with fellow teachers at the front desk, went to her classroom, removed her top coat and began writing algebra equations on the blackboard in nothing but her low-heeled pumps.

Holly had been sitting in the third seat in the second row. Every place that normally would have been covered by a teacher's modest clothing was crisscrossed with scars, bruises and burn marks. Some old, some new. Some very new. Holly remembered the tears of pity and outrage that had scorched her cheeks as the girl beside her lost her breakfast on the black-and-white tile floor. Holly remembered how shaky her knees were when she pushed up from her desk. No one else moved as she walked to the coat rack, then to Jennifer Carlucci. She placed the coat around her teacher's bruised, boney shoulders and then drew her into a long, long embrace.

Mrs. Carlucci never had been heard to speak in a derogatory fashion about the father of her children. Whatever the problems of their marriage, she'd kept them all inside that house and inside herself, until she just couldn't do it any longer. Though she could not bear to speak it, she exposed it in a wordless cry for help. In the end, it made little difference. The Cutter and Ambrose clans had long since disowned Miss Jenny for marrying and then staying with Tony Carlucci; and Cecil Weathers had made what little investigation there was to abuse go away. School officials were more shocked and concerned about the impact of Jennifer Carlucci's nudity on the children than on what caused it. After six months in the state mental hospital at Whitfield, one of Weathers' cronies on the bench placed Miss Jenny back in Tony's hands as her legal guardian.

To the best of Holly's knowledge, the bright, talented, big-hearted teacher with the amazing blue eyes had not spoken or written a word aside from mathematical formulas since that morning of Holly's junior year. Through winter and summer she sat on that porch making quilts with the geometric precision of a rag-box Einstein. Quilts Tony sold as fast as his wife could make them. If she understood or cared, she didn't show it. She merely started another quilt.

Still, Holly stopped the Lincoln as close to the porch as she could. She put it in park and called, "Miss Jenny! Hello, Miss Jenny. It's Lee Carter. Holly Lee Carter. I recently moved back. I'm living just up the road at Wolf's Run." But Jennifer Carlucci continued her rocking and stitching, as her lips calculated and figured and recalculated numbers that had meaning only for her.

Rose Marie Carlucci emerged from the house and came down the foot-worn, swayback steps from the front porch carrying a large tin bucket. She looked for a moment at the big car, then began watering the colorful rose bushes that grew inside the planter.

"Sh-Sh-She don't talk," said Rose Marie.

"I know. But I thought I'd try."

"Tr-try all you want. But sh-she don't talk."

"Okay. Rose, do you know who I am?"

"Y-Y-Yes'um. Y-Y-You own the n-newspaper," she said. "I-I can r-read. I r-read it every-everytime somebody br-brings me one. But I-I-I just g-go by M-Marie now. D-D-Daddy says I-I'm t-t-too ugly to be c-c-called Rose."

Holly had to fight a sudden quivering in her lips and a hot, dampness in her eyes. The last time she had seen Rose Marie Carlucci, the girl had been a big-eyed eight-year-old carrying a stuffed panda bear doll down the sawdust midway at the county fair. If memory served, Cutter had won it for her, throwing baseballs at milk jugs. Miss Jenny was sharing a swirl of pink-and-white cotton candy with her children when Holly stopped to say hello. Rose was shy with huge brown eyes, long brown hair and large, dark features – bearing no resemblance to the Cutter or Ambrose sides of the family. She'd had a slight stutter even then. Now her eyes were just as huge in her face, but she had grown tall for a girl and broad-shouldered like her brother. Holly could see that Rose was shapely and full-figured, but the teenager was doing everything she could to hide it under baggy overalls, a loose T-shirt and work boots. Her hair was tied up and stuffed under an old straw sunhat. And her stutter was worse, so much worse.

"I think you're beautiful and so are your roses," said Holly, wanting to say something nice. There were pink, red, white and yellow roses growing in a bright, healthy profusion at the center of the otherwise tired and ill-cared-for property. "You must take wonderful care of them."

"Th-Th ... Thank ... you," Rose Marie managed. "Cu-Cu-Cutter br- brought me a, a book."

"A book on roses? About caring for them?"

The teenager nodded, smiling at the rainbow blossoming amid the decay of the surroundings. "'R-Roses for a, a Rose,' he-he said."

There was no sense in putting it off, thought Holly, knowing it might be difficult to get another chance. Besides, it was all she could do to keep tears from her eyes.

"Rose, I came to ask you about the night my father died."

The girl's smile faded.

"You saw it? You saw what happened? Yes?"

Rose nodded but offered nothing more.

"Y-Y-You *shhhh*-ould go."

"Rose, I'm just trying to understand what happened that night," Holly persisted. "I understand you saw the whole thing. I was –"

"Y-You should g-go! D-D-Daddy don't like you."

"I know, but this will only take –"

From the long open hall of the house, Holly saw a screen door swing open.

Tony Carlucci let it slam behind him as he leaned on a nicked and scarred set of under-the-arm crutches. He swung his one leg forward followed by his crutches until he was propped at the edge of the porch in a strap T-shirt and his boxer shorts, the gnarled remainder of his thigh poking from the left leg opening. *His truck must be in the barn,* thought Holly.

"Well, if it's not the high-and-mighty Miss Cattahatchie County herself, come to call in her big, fancy car," he said. "Welcome to our humble house. It's no Wolf's Run, but we call it home."

For all his meanness of spirit and ugliness of soul, Tony Carlucci had been a handsome man a decade ago. Six-foot tall with coal black hair and an olive complexion paired with a chest as broad and hard as a keg of nails. He still had the short, thick, tattooed arms of a boxer who enjoyed working in close, but now his middle was much broader than his chest, and the whiskers on this chin and cheeks were the color of dirty dishwater. His hair still was black, though there was less of it except what was sprouting from his ears and nostrils.

Memories of that night at The Gin came again. Holly fought to keep her disgust and revulsion, and a twinge of fear, in check. "Mr. Carlucci, I came to ask Rose about the night my father died."

"Well, well. So Holly Lee Carter finally wants something from por old crippled Tony. How does it feel to have people stare at you with nothing but pity? The same as I saw in your eyes plenty of nights at The Gin."

Holly knew she should bite her tongue, but such had never been her nature. "If I looked at you that way, it had nothing to do with your leg."

"Kiss my fuckin' ass," he snarled. "Rose had to answer the sheriff's questions, but you're no kind of law. She's weak in the head and she don't have to talk to you.

"Rose, get in the house!" he barked.

The girl gripped the watering can in her arms like a tin shield. "T-T-Talk to C-C-Cutter," said Rose.

"Shut up, girl! Get in the house like I told you."

Rose Marie turned and hurried up the steps and past her father into the deep shadows of the hall.

From his vantage point on the porch, Tony Carlucci looked down into the convertible. Holly felt his eyes fix on her wheelchair, then on her. It felt like someone was rolling dirty marbles over her skin.

"Thought you were too good for me, didn't you? A one-legged dago mechanic," he said and spit into the dirt yard. He wiped his mouth with the back of his huge hand. "Well, just look at you now. Draggin' that *fine* ass of yours around and loading in and out of a rollin' chair, as dead as a sack of flour in a wheelbarrow." Holly gripped the car's wheel. "I bet you *wish* you could feel my hand between your legs now, don't you?"

Slowly she met the man's angry, lustful, spiteful gaze. "Honestly, Tony, I'd rather be paralyzed."

A red rage suddenly boiled up under the olive skin on the broad surfaces of Tony Carlucci's unshaven face, and he began to curse. Holly pushed her Wayfarers onto her nose and Charlie stood in the seat and yapped a feisty reply. As she pulled away, Holly heard a crutch clatter off the car's trunk.

"*Bitch!*" he yelled after her. 'You worthless *crippled* bitch!"

CHAPTER 4

T he Gin was an intersection of sorts – geographically and culturally – in our small part of the world.

Just across the Tennessee line at the northern terminus of Two-Mile Bridge, it was within a rock's throw of the Cattahatchie River and on the banks of Moccasin Slough, which sprawled westward across twenty swampy miles. Before the Cattahatchie, and its mother, the Tennessee River, were dammed in the 1930s for flood control and electric power, Moccassin Gin #1 was one of the biggest cotton gins in the South. From September through November, it ran twenty-four hours a day, seven days a week. For decades, barges and mule-drawn cotton wagons brought the bright, white fiber there by the tens of tons to be cleaned and separated. Flatbed trucks and rail cars waited at the other end to haul away the burlap-wrapped bales. But the damming of the rivers and the construction of low-slung bridges for car and truck traffic eliminated the barges and small riverboats that had worked the Cattahatchie. Smaller gins sprang up and massive Moccasin #1 was no longer practical to operate.

By the time Gilbert Clanton, whose family owned the property, returned from four years in Europe during World War II, it was nothing but a huge, barn-like tin shell. But Gil Clanton saw the possibility for a supper club and music hall like he'd seen in England. For years The Gin struggled, until he heard a sound that was being called "rockabilly" and fell in love with it. Before long, unknowns such as Carl Perkins, Johnny Cash, Jerry Lee Lewis, Ray Charles and even Elvis Presley were playing The Gin and singing what came to be called "rock'n'roll" – and everyone wanted to hear it. Blacks and whites, and all shades in between. All of their money was green, and Gil Clanton expanded and improved the restaurant until it was famous from Memphis to Birmingham for its steaks and ribs and Cattahatchie catfish. Added were a dock and a screened deck that hung over the slough, and a "colored balcony" that wrapped around a dance floor the size of a basketball court. To the side was a big room with eight pool tables, and through a semi-secret door was a room where poker and blackjack were dealt every day but Sunday.

With so many black singers and bands regularly performing at The Gin, the color barrier inside the building pretty quickly broke down even in the early 1950s.

By the last night Holly spent there in May of '59, The Gin was as integrated as any club in the South. That's not to say there wasn't tension, especially as the Civil Rights Movement began to make headlines, but that was where a bulky staff of no-nonsense bouncers came in handy.

Still, it created a stir when a young white woman in a wheelchair and an attractive black woman in jeans, sandals and a rainbow dashiki came in. The place was packed and cigarette smoke as thick as L.A. smog hung in the high wooden rafters.

"I think I see a table," said Eve.

They worked their way to it, a row off the dance floor, as peanut shells crunched under Holly's wheels. The band was on a break.

"How's this?"

"It's … It's fine," said Holly as if she'd heard the question from a distance across the din of voices and a kaleidoscope of memories inside the large tin room. The stage she'd often stood on looked the same, as did the dance floor scattered with sawdust. How many times had her high heels tapped on that hardwood? How many times had her tennis shoes left their mark? How many times had she felt the fine warm tingle of sawdust under her stockings or bare feet?

She looked toward the balcony and saw a mix of black and white faces, and smiled when she saw that a hoop was still in position at one end of the dance floor. On Sunday afternoons when the club was closed, employees and their friends often played pickup basketball games on the freshly swept hardwood. Holly had loved those games, and developed a reputation for being unafraid to take it to the hoop even against the biggest guys from the kitchen or the roadies just passing through. She'd lost a tooth that way, but she'd spit out the blood, wiped her mouth and kept playing.

"Do you see him?" asked Eve.

"No," said Holly.

"How do you know Mr. Mean-and-Gorgeous is even working?"

"It's Saturday night."

At six-three or four, Cutter Carlucci would be a hard guy to miss, but in the moving, shifting crowd of three hundred or more he could be anywhere – working the outdoor deck or the balcony. When the waitress came to the table, Holly asked for him.

"He's around here somewhere," she said.

"If you see him, could you send him over?"

The young waitress eyed Holly and then Eve with a mix of suspicion and curiosity. "I haven't seen you around here before. Are you a friend of his?"

Eve and Holly shared a glance. "I wouldn't go quite that far. Acquaintance might be a better word. Just tell him that Holly Lee Carter would like to speak to him, if he can spare a couple of minutes."

The waitress raised an eyebrow whether in recognition or as big so-what gesture, but said, "Okay," and moved off with drink orders.

The band was pure rock with a Southern fried, bluesy edge. They were a bunch of unknowns but they really knew how to jam. When the waitress brought a second round and another basket of parched peanuts, Eve asked, "What's the name of the band?"

"The Alton Brothers," she said. "No, more like nuts. The Almond Brothers. No! The *All*man Brothers. That's it! I think they're from Georgia."

"Did you bump into Cutter?" asked Holly.

The waitress, who was all of twenty, hesitated. "Yes, Ma'am. I saw him. I told him."

"And?"

"And ... well, a lot of women ask to talk to Cutter. You know?"

Holly felt a warm glow at the base of her neck. "I don't doubt it. But it's nothing like that," Holly assured the young woman. "I just need some information."

The waitress ran her eyes over Holly and the wheelchair. "Okay, look, he was going on break. He's probably over in the pool hall. That's –"

"I know where it is. Thank you," said Holly and handed her a ten.

Eve had to pull Holly backwards up two steps to get her into the long side room where colorful lights hung from the ceiling and low over the tables, perfectly illuminating the green felt surfaces. The rest of the room was deep in shadow except for the bar at the end. Behind the bar was a hidden stairway that led to a poker room.

Cutter was leaning against a wall next to a rack of sticks three tables down. Holly pushed toward him as Eve followed and a number of eyes followed them. Cutter held his cue and pretended not to notice.

"I thought if you didn't have time to come to my table, I'd come to yours," Holly said without preamble.

"My break's just about over," he said taking a short pull on a Miller longneck. "I'm workin' the upstairs. I'll have to get back to it."

"I won't keep you long," she continued as Cutter's opponent paused to check out both women and the conversation.

"Miss Carter, if you haven't noticed, I'm involved in something at the moment," he told her. "Jake, are you gonna shoot or –?"

"Sure," said the man in the John Deere cap. "I'm just linin' up my shot so I put you away."

"Look, Cutter, I only a need a few minutes," she persisted as one ball clicked against the other and moved silently off a cushion near a side pocket. The man straightened and sighed, almost groaned. With cat-like smoothness, Cutter moved around the table. He sank the nine and the fourteen together. A tough shot. The eight was a gimme.

Cutter lifted a small blue cube of chalk and pocketed the ten that had been beneath it. "Thank you, Jake. Come again."

At first the man looked angry as Cutter chalked the tip of his cue, then he laughed. "You just wait till next week. I'm gonna nail your cocky ass."

Cutter smiled an easy, comfortable smile that certainly had its share of cocky in it. "I'll be here," he told the man before the fellow shook his head and waddled toward the bar.

"So, you hustle," said Holly, reaching into a pocket on her brown skirt.

"I wouldn't call it that."

"Why not?"

"Because hustlers take advantage of people they know they can beat. I only play people who can compete with me. And if I happen to win a little something on the side, then I do."

"But you win a lot more than you lose?"

"Mostly."

Holly lay a twenty on the end of the table.

"You rack 'em," she said.

Cutter didn't move but he could feel all the eyes in the room turning toward him and the woman in the chair, her hair a bright flame under the billiard lights. Eve was trying to melt into a wall. The room was quiet as Holly laid another twenty on the rail. "Forty dollars against ten minutes of your time," she said.

"Go ahead, Cutter!" someone called.

"Teach her a lesson," said someone else.

"I told you, Miss Carter. I play for the competition. I don't hustle people."

Holly put two more twenties on the end of the table and thought she knew which button to push. "There's eighty dollars that says I take you. Even from a wheelchair."

Now a circle was forming around the table. "Do it, Cutter!" urged one voice, then another. Someone grabbed the rack and began arranging the balls.

"There you go," said the man. "You two're all set."

Holly dug in her pocket one more time. She found a five, two ones, a quarter, a nickel and two pennies. "All right, that's it," she said. "That's all I've got. Are we going to shoot or not?"

Cutter studied her. "Against ten minutes of my time?" he asked, his smile gone. "Yes."

"Find yourself a cue."

Cutter won the break and slammed the cue ball hard just right of center as Holly rubbed white chalk onto her hands from a round next to the wall. He sank the eleven and the four giving him his choice of stripes or solids. He surveyed the table and took stripes, sinking the ten and the fifteen, bang-bang; then gently dropped the thirteen into a side pocket off two rails. He called the twelve in the corner pocket but it hung on the lip.

It was Holly's turn. The crowd, now two and three deep in places, had to back up as she wheeled around the table, checking the angles. She started to shoot the six but then backed off and took the one long down the rail, before putting away an easy three and a hard five-seven combination. She called the two in the side and squeezed it past Cutter's nine ball, leaving her only the six and the eight. But the six was at a tough angle from her chair. If only she could sit on the edge of the table and stretch for it, keeping a foot at the end of one long leg on the floor as the rules required.

"Excuse me, could you pass me that bridge, please?" she asked a man near the cue rack. He handed it over.

Holly placed the tip of her cue into a slot on the bridge and studied the angle. She could hear a murmur among the men surrounding her. Cutter watched her, his face and deep-set blue eyes showing nothing. Holly knew if she missed, Cutter was set up. She adjusted the bridge one last time and called the corner, but she could only stab at the ball. Without smooth follow-through, it kissed the rail just before it got the pocket and spun away.

Cutter dropped the nine and twelve in the same shot, then put the fourteen in past Holly's six in the corner. That left only an easy eight, straight in. Instead, he crossed to the opposite side of the table and called it off the rail and into the side pocket. His eyes met Holly's for an instant as he took aim. Then, with a perfect, gentle touch, banked it off the rail and in.

A shout went up around the table and several of the onlookers slapped him on the back. Cutter picked up the money from the end of the table, folded it and shoved it into the pocket of his jeans.

He laid the cue on the table. "Break time's over. I've got to get back to work. Nice doin' business with you," he said and walked away.

CHAPTER 5

Late Sunday afternoon I was returning to the house from a church softball game. I never was a big guy, but I had good speed and covered a lot of ground in center field. The First Denomination Crusaders had won 12-9 and Patti had been there to cheer us on, so I was feeling good as my truck rattled east on Pleasant Ridge Road. I had time for a good shower and a sandwich before heading back to First Denomination for choir practice. I already was thinking about how good Patti would smell standing in front of me in the big choir loft – the fine blonde hairs on the back of her neck shining like a golden pathway leading down the neck of her blouse.

After Sheriff Johnson's funeral, we'd driven to a remote, willow-shaded spot out by Gillard's Lake. There'd been some yelling and cussing, a few tears, some promises and then a lot of necking. She even opened her knees a little and let me rub her through the crotch of the damn girdle she always wore. So, things were patched up between us. It was a cycle I knew well.

I was maybe a quarter of a mile away from my house when I saw two black four-door sedans pull out of our driveway and turn right, toward the eastern hills and away from me. I parked by the barn and walked up to the house.

Daddy was sitting on the porch swing in a pair of freshly washed khaki work britches and a clean white shirt. His hair was neatly combed, his chin clean-shaven and he appeared to be sober for the fourth or maybe fifth straight day. A modern record.

"Who were those men?" I asked.

"Government men. Federal men."

"What did they want? Are you in some kind of trouble?"

Billy Wallace chuckled. "Trouble? Yeah, you could say that."

I was starting to get nervous. Maybe Daddy had been so drunk the last couple of years he hadn't paid his taxes. That was the only reason I could imagine for the feds wanting my father. But on Sunday afternoon?

Billy Wallace extended his arm, a glass in his hand. It was steady or near about. "Son, why don't you get us both some tea and we'll talk."

I was hot and tired and wanted a shower; and I wanted to get back to Patti … and the fine blonde hairs on her neck. "Maybe later. I'm in hurry."

My father sighed. "Nate, I know I haven't done a lot lately to deserve your respect, but don't take that tone with me again," he said firmly. "I've got something to say that you need to hear, because it's gonna affect you, too.

"Now go on, boy. Get us some tea."

I took the jelly glass from my father's big hand. His voice and eyes, and the set of his jaw left no room for discussion.

* * *

It was 8:30 that night when the doorbell rang at Wolf's Run.

Holly was in the library working at the desk and watching the latest on the Apollo 11 mission. The Eagle lander had settled onto the lunar surface a few minutes after three o'clock our time. Now two American astronauts were getting ready to leave the module. Holly already had changed for bed into an extra-long Doors T-shirt that was faded from so many washings and soft from so many nights between her skin and the sheets. Eve was taking a bath, so Holly pushed up the long hall and into the foyer as Charlie skittered behind her.

Through the windows framing the door, Holly saw Cutter Carlucci leaning against a porch post – his shoulders broad, his waist narrow and his hips cocked under the tight fit of his Levis. No one else seemed to be around. Holly looked at herself. She surely wasn't dressed for company – braless in nothing but a long t-shirt. The memory of the way his father Tony Carlucci had pawed her backstage at The Gin welled up again and caught in her throat, but she did not want to pass up a chance that Cutter might be willing to talk about her father's death. Holly swallowed the memory as she tried to pull the hem of the T-shirt a bit lower on her thighs, but her breasts and nipples were clearly defined. Telling herself that Cutter was not Tony, she removed the chain and dead bolt and cracked opened the door.

"Hey," he said.

"Hey, yourself," she responded as Charlie peeked out from behind Holly's chair, sniffing the air.

Except for the sing-song of crickets, there was a long silence. Finally Cutter said, "I know it's late to be visitin', but Mr. Gil sent me to Memphis first thing this morning to pick up some supplies down at the rail yard. The train was late. Then there was a hassle about – well, you don't want to hear all that." Holly decided to simply let him talk. "The point is, I didn't get back until a couple of hours ago, and then had to unload the truck. So, this is the first chance I've had to come by." She said nothing. Cutter dug into the front pocket of his jeans. "Eighty-seven dollars. And thirty-two cents. I told you, I don't hustle people."

As Holly and Charlie watched from the cracked door, Cutter put the money on the arm of a white wicker sofa that sat on the porch. "If you hadn't had to use that bridge, you'd have made that shot."

It was a surprising gesture from a guy who'd been nothing but antagonistic toward her since the moment she'd returned to DeLong. Was he being kind or friendly? Or was this simply a sort of late-realized pity?

"I put my money down and took my chances. You don't owe me anything," she told him through the crack. "Except perhaps a rematch one of these days."

"You got it," he said, but made no move to pick the money up from the porch railing where he'd placed it. "Well, then I better take off. Good-night, Miss Carter."

"Wait," said Holly. Whether friendliness, kindness or pity had brought him to her door, Holly knew this might be the only and perhaps best chance she'd have to question Cutter about what Rose Marie saw. "It sounds like you've had a long day. Would you like something to eat?"

"Thanks, but I stopped at a barbecue place in Memphis. Besides, it's late. And the truth is, the astronauts – Apollo 11, you know? – they're about to step out on the moon. It's kind of exciting. I was listening to it on the radio."

"Then you have to come in," said Holly, backing into the foyer. "I'm watching it on television. Wouldn't you rather see it than just hear it?"

"Well, I –," he considered.

"Let me go throw on a robe, and we'll watch it together."

"Okay, sure. That'd be good," he said. "I'm kind of a nut about the moon shots. I'd like to actually see it."

When Holly returned and opened the door she was wrapped in a soft and well-worn white cotton robe bearing the crest of the Hotel BelAir. A gift, not a theft. The robe was cinched at the waist and Cutter saw that a discreet safety pin held it together over her crossed legs. White ballet flats covered her feet.

Cutter stepped inside the foyer beneath a small chandelier. He looked around, not with awe or envy, but with interest. "I've never been in Wolf's Run," he said.

"There's a lot history to it," said Holly mildly. "I'd give you the grand tour, but we weren't expecting company. Besides, I think it's close to time for our astronauts to make some real history. Or more history, I should say."

As Cutter and Charlie followed Holly to the right and then down to the hall, she was saying, "The TV is in the library, which is the only really, well, grand room in the house."

When Cutter stepped through the double doors, he gave a small whistle as he took in the room. "Grand is right," he said. His eyes settled on the billiard table at one end of the room. "Is that where you learned to play?"

"Yes, my grandmother taught me, and she was a shark – at least when she wanted to be," Holly told him. "Come on in."

The grainy black-and-white image of the lunar surface glowed from a 24-inch set fitted into one of the floor-to-ceiling book cases. CBS News anchor Walter Cronkite was talking with experts from NASA as they waited for the hatch to open.

"Make yourself comfortable," said Holly indicating a long, leather sofa. Cutter sat and stretched an arm across the sofa back. "This could be a bed."

"It has been, quite a few times," said Holly. "I used to lay there and look out at the lights of the valley and up at the stars. And sometimes a big ol' full moon. I never imagined just ten years later men would be about to walk on it."

"Yeah, it's somethin'."

Holly motioned to the coffee table in front of the sofa. "I made popcorn earlier. Please."

Cutter took a handful from the large bowl and put a few kernels in his mouth. He coughed. "You think you've got enough salt and butter on this batch?" he asked, clearing his throat.

"Oh, my gosh! I'm so sorry!" Holly told him. "I forget not everyone likes it that way. Can I get you something to drink? Water? A Coke?"

"Have you got a beer?" he asked. Holly considered him for a moment. Clearly the teenager already drank, but – well, in another life Holly would not have thought twice about handing a cold brew to one of The Gin's bouncers of whatever age. But if it got out that the editor-in-chief of *The Current-Leader* giving gave beer to a high school senior, that would be an added problem she didn't need. Of course, if it got out that the first female editor-in-chief of the local paper was entertaining a high school senior boy in her bathrobe, beer might be the least of the talk.

Cutter sensed her dilemma and stood, clearing his throat again. "Look, Miss Carter, maybe it's better if I just go. I appreciate the invite."

Holly knew she was not wrong to consider the consequences that came with the role she had accepted, no matter how reluctantly, but she also knew she was being hypocritical. She'd had no problem shooting beer-hall pool with Cutter the night before. Plus, this might be her one and only chance to find out what he knew about her father's death. "You are eighteen?"

Eighteen was the legal age to drink in Mississippi, in the places it was legal at all to drink. "I'll be nineteen in September," he said. "The coaches held me back a year in sixth grade for football."

Holly had met and photographed G.I.s younger than Cutter in Vietnam. They'd spilled blood by the liter and lost some of their own. Hard-faced and war-hardened. Cutter had been hardened a different way, living under Tony Carlucci's roof and, no doubt, his fist. And now living his own life and making his own way. She pivoted her chair, saying, "Sit down and enjoy the show."

Wheeling behind a wet bar in the corner next to the billiard table she reached in for two beers. Cutter's attention was fixed on the television and his back was to the door in which Eve Howard appeared wearing only a T-shirt and panties. Her hair was glistening from the bath. Eve's face shifted quickly from curiosity to recognition to shock before she mouthed, "What the hell?"

"Later!" Holly replied urgently, silently and motioned for Eve to retreat.

Holly returned with two Rolling Rocks. "Sorry it's not Miller," she said.

Cutter took a quick swig to clear the popcorn from husks from his throat. "You've got a good memory. This'll do just fine."

"Oh, look," said Holly shifting her attention to the television and the grainy black-and-white images being transmitted across a quarter-million miles of space. "It's about to happen."

It was 9:17 and astronaut Neil Armstrong was on the steps of the lunar lander. Holly and Cutter listened along with whole world as Armstrong spoke: "This is one small step for man, one giant leap for mankind." An instant later, he was standing on the surface of the moon. Holly applauded as Cutter smiled, nodded. For a few moments his face was open and unguarded, she noticed. His long arms and legs were relaxed and all the icy walls behind his blue eyes seemed to melt away.

For another five minutes, they sipped their beers and watched with little comment. Cutter even ate more of the popcorn. Then without preamble he turned his attention away from the TV and to Holly. "You said you needed ten minutes of my time. What do you want to know?"

This was what Holly had been hoping for, but now she had to decide how much she wanted to reveal, and the answer was not much. She told him that as executor of T.L. Carter's estate, she was trying to "wrap up some loose ends," but with Sheriff Johnson dead and her father's file probably destroyed, she had to reconstruct the events herself. In attempting to do so, she'd discovered Rose Marie had witnessed the accident, she told him. "I went to the house thinking Tony wasn't home but he was. Rose got pretty upset. She told me I should talk to you."

With each word Cutter stiffened a bit more and another layer of ice formed at the back of his blue eyes. "Yeah, I heard," he told her, his tone flat. "Don't be goin' around there again, Miss Carter. You might get hurt. Besides, my sister is carrying enough weight on her shoulders. I'd appreciate it if you'd not add to it."

Holly straightened in her chair in the face of Cutter's sudden hardness. "All right. I'll try not," she said. "But I do need to get a better understanding of what happened that night."

Cutter drew in a breath, collecting his memories of that night. "People think Rose is stupid, but she's not. She just tangles up her words," he started.

"I know."

He went on. "Rose was worried about a history test the next day. She knew I'd be camped under the overhang at The Well. Daddy was off someplace, as usual. After she got Momma to bed, she put on her raincoat and started walking over so I could help her study for it.

"Anyway, a light rain was falling. It was cold. The clouds were thick so there was no moonlight. Suddenly Rose came runnin' up to my fire, all excited. After a few tries, she managed to get out the words 'car' and 'river.' I pulled my boots on and grabbed my slicker, and we hopped in the Jeep. By the time we got back to the bridge, there was no sign of a car, but I could see where it had gone over the edge."

Holly considered all Cutter was telling her. "How much time was there between when Rose saw the car go into the river and you two got back to the bridge?"

"Well, let's see," he began to figure, then – "Now you know, Rose wasn't right at the bridge when it happened?"

"No. I didn't know. I was just told she saw it happen."

"She did. But Rose was probably seventy-five yards east of the bridge. She saw headlights coming down the switchback. She expected the headlights to turn onto the bridge but they didn't. They just went right into the river, which was running as high and fast as I've ever seen it."

"Did she say whether the car was going unusually fast? Or if Daddy tried to brake but couldn't get it stopped?"

"I was there when Sheriff Johnson asked Rose about that. She said no. She said the lights came down the last part of the grade like you'd expect, but your Daddy just kept goin' straight," Cutter explained. "By the time she ran to the bridge, there was no sign of the car."

Holly closed her eyes, picturing it. She thought about how terrified her father must have been as the car dived toward the roaring freight train of water, knowing he couldn't swim. Her chin quivered unexpectedly, her heart filled with more emotion than she expected. More than she would have imagined possible just a few weeks earlier.

"Miss Carter, I'm sorry if I was too –"

The words snapped Holly back into the moment. "Don't be. You weren't too anything," she said, shaking off a quick sniffle. "I asked you to tell me what happened out there that night, and you did." She was processing the information as quickly as she could. Cutter started to rise. "No, please. A couple more questions."

Cutter reluctantly settled himself again.

"Tell me the rest of it. What happened next?"

"Not a lot more to tell," he said. "She ran to The Well to fetch me. We got in my Jeep and came back to the bridge. I grabbed a flashlight and length of rope, and searched down river as far as I could go. That wasn't far. Maybe a hundred-and-fifty yards. To that spot where the river bends back west at the foot of the mountain. It was way out of the banks. So, I hustled back to the Jeep and we high-tailed it to the Landry house at the intersection of Highway 27. I asked them to call the sheriff's office. It was the closest phone. Rose was cold and shiverin'. So, I took her to the house then went back to the bridge to wait on the deputies. That's about it."

Holly nodded. "And when you were checking the riverbanks you didn't see anything unusual?"

"Such as?"

"Such as a raincoat or a suit coat, maybe caught up on a limb?"

"Nope. Sorry."

"And from the time Daddy's car went in until you and Rose got back to the bridge, how long was it?"

Cutter looked toward the big south-facing window. He could see headlights in the distance on the highway. "I'd calculate about eight to ten minutes."

"Did you see any other cars on the road from the time Daddy's car went in until the sheriff's cars showed up?"

"No. Not a one."

"You sound pretty sure."

"I am. I was hoping someone would come along to help. Someone with a stronger light. But no one did."

"What about while you were still at The Well?"

Cutter was studying Holly now. "No. From where I was camped, no vehicle could have crossed the bottom between the bridge and the railroad tracks without me seeing it," he told her. Then, "Mr. Carter must have had a funny kind of insurance for you to be asking these questions. Do you want to tell me what this is really about?"

Holly considered her response. "Cutter, you've been a big help. And I appreciate it. I appreciate you coming here tonight. But I'm not comfortable saying anything else at the moment. Mostly because it's probably a lot of nothing. Just a daughter's curiosity."

"All right, then. I guess I'll be going."

Holly and Charlie walked Cutter to the front door, then onto the screened porch. "Could I ask one more favor?" she said. "Could you talk to Rose and see if there is anything else she remembers? Even something small could be important."

At the screen door he said, "I'll try, but if I see it's upsetting her, then that's it."

"I understand. That's all I can ask," she said, knowing she should leave it at that, but couldn't, remembering the encounter with Cutter's father at the Old Ambrose Place. "I can only imagine what you and Rose and Miss Jenny have gone through. And I –"

"Don't," Cutter interrupted. "Don't try to imagine. Don't think about it. Don't –" He looked away then back. "Don't try to crawl inside somebody else's nightmare."

"Cutter, I –"

"Look, Miss Carter, I appreciate whatever you're trying to say. But we've all got our struggles. I've got mine. And ..." He looked her up and down in the wheelchair. "And you've got yours. Let's leave it at that."

"All right, Cutter," agreed Holly as he went down the steps and climbed into his Jeep. To her surprise, he didn't instantly turn the key. Instead, he rested his arms on the steering wheel and looked up through the pecan trees and past the crest of the house.

"Do you remember where you were when President Kennedy was killed?" he asked.

The question caught Holly off guard, but she quickly replied, "Of course. I remember exactly."

"Me, too. I'm guessin' this moon landing is going to be the same way. Thirty, forty, fifty years from now when someone asks, we'll remember exactly where we were and who we were with when Armstrong stepped off that ladder."

Strange, she'd had the same thought earlier, but hadn't voiced it. Now, "Yes, I think you're right," she said.

"Thanks for the hospitality. And for the popcorn," he said, his smile brief but bright against his dusky features and moon-cast shadows. "Good-night, Miss Carter."

"You're welcome, Cutter. Good-night."

* * *

W here have you been?" I demanded as Cutter stepped out of his Jeep at The Well. "I've been waiting here since the end of choir practice." He tugged at the front of my shirt. "What are you doing?" I asked, my voice sounding shrill, as if it was coming from somewhere outside myself.

"I was checkin' to see if you'd grown tits. 'Cause otherwise you don't look like my mamma."

"You think this is a joke?"

"Nate, I don't know what it is," he said, starting to take some of his gear out of the Jeep. "You're not makin' any sense."

Cutter was right, and I knew it, but I was so shaken I could barely steady myself. "I left the house, and Daddy. All my gear is in my truck. I, I, I want to rough it with you until we get out of school, and me and Patti can get away to college."

He eyed me without a word as he propped his shotgun against a boulder and dropped his sleeping bag next to the blackened fire pit. He lit a kerosene lantern and put if off to the side so only a light, yellow glow touched us. "All right, Nate. Sit down and tell me what's happened."

I wanted to tell him but I didn't want to sit. I felt like a cat in a cage with griddle for a floor. "It's Daddy. He's gone crazy. He's lost his mind!"

"What? Did he go back on the 'shine?"

"No! He's sober as a judge," I said, pacing. "But that's not a bad idea. I swear I'd buy him a year's supply if he'd crawl back in his bottle. I mean, havin' a drunk for a daddy is an embarrassment, but at least people kinda understood. With Steve and Momma and everything. Even Brother Mac cut him a little slack. But this? Nobody is gonna understand this."

"Nate, stop prowling. Stand still and tell me what happened."

"Daddy swore me to secrecy."

Cutter looked at me as if he wanted to toss me in The Well or the river. I couldn't

113

blame him. "Then you ought to honor your word to your daddy," he said and began unrolling his sleeping bag.

"Daddy's gonna be the new sheriff," I blurted. Cutter said nothing but he stopped what he was doing. I had his full attention. "It's true! I came home this afternoon and that Burke guy – the U.S. attorney – and a bunch of FBI men were leavin'. The governor is gonna appoint Daddy sheriff to fill out Mr. Johnson's term."

"I thought the county board of supervisors already picked Tony's runnin' buddy, Benoit."

"According to Daddy, the supervisors can't appoint, they can only recommend. It's all up to the governor."

Cutter laughed as big and long as I'd ever heard him laugh. It made me want to punch him, but even at that high level of agitation, I had better sense than to try. "I'd give a week's wages to see Tony's face when word gets out. Him and Benoit and Weathers! They'll be kickin' and cussin' and spittin' brimstone."

"This may be funny to you, but it's not to me. Not even a little bit."

"Your daddy used to be a Memphis police detective, right? So, it's not so far-fetched. A lot of people would be proud for their daddy to be appointed sheriff."

"Proud?" I gasped. "Don't you understand what this means? Everybody will know Daddy's sidin' with the race-mixers. Brother Mac could split me and Patti up over this. That's why I knew I had to move out. To show I'm not part of this."

Cutter's smile was gone now. He knelt by The Well and splashed cold water on his face, then around the back of his neck and shook the remaining droplets off his hands. "It could be, Nate, your daddy needs you more than ever now. You're all he's got. You're his son."

"Yeah, well, he should have thought of that before he went into the bottle the last two years. And before he got mixed up with integrationists."

"Do me a favor. Stop talking like Preacher MacAllister. Integrationists? Racemixers? I never heard you use those words in your life until you started datin' Patti."

"That don't make it wrong."

"It don't make it right either," he said, then considered. "Look, my advice is you sleep here under the stars for a few nights until things cool off. Then go on home."

"And what if I don't want to? What if I want to stay here?"

Cutter blew out his breath and walked to the ledge overhanging the river.

"It's a free country, Nate. My people don't own this land. Not anymore. I've got no right to run you off. But just so you understand – I go my own way and keep my own schedule. This ain't Boy Scouts. This ain't 'Camp Cutter,' either, with three hots and a cot, and a counselor to tuck you in. This is a hard, rough way to live for more than a few days," he told me as we stared across the bean and cotton stalks to the Old Ambrose Place. The light was on, as always, in Rose's room at the northwest corner of the house. "I know if I could go home and trust that Tony wouldn't blow my brains out in the middle of the night, or that I might have to do same to him, I wouldn't be sleepin' here."

I didn't know what to say to that, so after a moment I just said, "I guess I better unload my truck."

I thought maybe Cutter would help, but he didn't. Instead, he simply stood there on the ledge, looking up at the moon.

CHAPTER 6

As it turned out, I didn't have to find a way to tell Patti and her father about Daddy's new job. On Tuesday morning, someone in Governor Broderick's office leaked it in time for the noon news on the Jackson, Tupelo and Memphis TV stations. To say that the information sent Weathers, Benoit, Mr. Wellingham, Milton Handley, Walter Kamp, Tom Carter and three of the five county commissioners – and, of course, Brother Mac – scurrying about like decapitated chickens would be a tremendous understatement. They were more like rabid dogs with their tails on fire as they climbed into a trio of big cars and headed for Jackson to confront the current head of state before the reported Wednesday swearing-in. But U.S. Attorney J.L. Burke outflanked them.

"Governor Broderick is in the air now," Burke told Holly Lee Carter in a late afternoon phone call. "He'll be landing at Cattahatchie International Airport at about five o'clock."

"You mean that cow pasture west of town that the crop dusters use?"

"That would be the one," he said. "The governor will swear Billy Wallace in right there, then fly on to St. Louis. His daughter is about to have a baby. So, he has a family emergency and probably will be unavailable to the press, and everyone else, for several days."

"Ahhh," sighed Holly. "The all-purpose family emergency."

"Yes. But if you hustle a photographer out to that airstrip, you'll be the only paper with pictures of the swearing in," he said. "I'd hoped to give you another exclusive, like the McBride thing, but Weathers still has a lot of friends in the state capital."

"Yes. And Broderick is supposed to be one of them," said Holly.

"You must have something pretty nasty on him to get him to publicly embarrass his mentor this way."

"We do our homework, and we buy the best photographic equipment there is," was all Burke would say.

It was enough, and Holly knew she'd get no more from the U.S. attorney who seemed comfortable in the role of Machiavelli. Maybe too much so. She moved on. "Speaking of McBride, is there anything new?"

116

Burke paused, then, "Off the record?"

"If that's how it has to be."

"It is."

"All right, off the record."

"He's definitely in Cattahatchie County," Burke told her. "We had a confirmed sighting on Sunday."

"Where?"

"Sorry, Holly. I can't say. But it gets worse. A sergeant at Fort Hood, Texas, went AWOL last week. When he left, he took fifty pounds of military grade C-4 plastic explosive with him."

"I saw that stuff work in Vietnam," said Holly. "With fifty pounds of it, he could – he could –?"

"Level most of a city block, I'm told."

"My God," she sighed. "But what makes you think this has any connection to McBride."

"The sergeant is McBride's nephew, but on his sister's side and by her second marriage. No one ever made the connection," explained Burke. "The FBI and Army CID now think Sergeant Rudolph has been buying or stealing weapons, ammunition and explosives for years – maybe more than a decade, and passing them on to Uncle Bob and his buddies with the pointy hats. We're fairly certain he was involved in two of the four recent armory break-ins."

"Why did Rudolph take off now?"

"With our, shall we say, reinvigorated interest in McBride, we were turning over rocks we'd never looked under before. I think he was feeling the heat. Now he's gone under, and he's runnin' to Uncle Bob."

"What makes you so sure?"

"In the first place, he's not a demolition man," said Burke. "So, he has no real use for C-4 himself. And you can't just set up a roadside stand and sell the stuff. Second, McBride's nickname is Dynamite Bob, but C-4 is his weapon of choice when he can lay his hands on it.

"And also, well –" he started then reconsidered.

"And also what?"

"This is way off the record."

Holly paused a beat. "Okay."

"A young police officer in Eudora, Arkansas – not far from the Mississippi River bridge at Greenville – stopped an eastbound car Saturday night with Texas plates stolen from near Fort Hood. The driver came out of the car shooting. Though wounded, the officer returned fire. He told his chief he's pretty sure he put at least one in the shooter before he got away."

"How's the officer?"

"He died on the operating table."

* * *

As soon as the news broke on TV about my father's appointment, I made myself scarce from *The Current-Leader* office. I was afraid Miss Carter would be mad that I hadn't told her, and either way, I didn't want to answer questions or be quoted for the story. I read about Daddy's swearing-in like everyone else in the Wednesday morning edition of the paper. Even as angry with him as I was, I had to admit that in the front page picture of the governor pinning the badge on his shirt, William Tice Wallace looked handsome and steady, and more full of spirit than I'd seen in ten years or more. But for me, I had narrowly avoided a personal disaster.

When I rang the bell at the parsonage Tuesday afternoon, Brother Mac was in his study filled with what he called "righteous wrath" as he prepared a radio editorial condemning the "demons of deceit who have corrupted the godly decisions of Cattahatchie County's duly elected public officials."

It would have been the end for me and Patti had I not been able to tell him that my father had made me give him my word not to tell *anyone*. There wasn't a lot of "righteous wrath" he could lay on me for honoring my word to my father. Even though I had broken it to tell Cutter. A fact I omitted from my narrative. And when I told him I'd moved out in order to distance myself from Billy Wallace's misguided deeds, C.E. MacAllister was appeased, or at least stymied.

CHAPTER 7

Wednesday afternoon was rainy as Holly drove through the wet streets of New Albany, twenty miles south of DeLong, and headed west on Highway 30 toward Lafayette County. She had a 3 p.m. appointment in Oxford with Dr. Ferguson Phelps, the county medical examiner.

The rain was drumming on the convertible's canvas roof and Otis Redding was on the eight-track player singing about *Sittin' on the Dock of the Bay*. Charlie was curled next to Holly's hip, sleeping. Eve Howard stared out the window at the rolling hills covered in thick pine woods and the long fertile bottoms alive with cotton, soybeans and corn. Cattle stood in pastures on the low hillsides, chewing their cud, oblivious to the rain. Holly had stopped trying to make casual small talk with Eve; it only seemed to make her angrier. Had Holly not feared she would need Eve to get her over curbs or up a step here or there, she would have left her in DeLong.

Eve lifted her camera and focused out the rain-streaked window. She pushed the shutter release and the motor-drive click-click-clicked.

"I told you my grandparents grew up near some little shit-hole-in-the-road called Skuna, Mississippi, didn't I?" Eve asked without looking at Holly. "Before they scraped together the money for train tickets to Chicago. I guess that was in the 1920s."

"Yes. You told me," Holly said carefully.

"Where is that from here? Skuna?"

"About fifty miles to the southwest. Down in Calhoun County, I think."

"When my mother brought them out to visit out in California, they'd get to cooking their ribs and collard greens and cornbread, and talking about old times 'down home in Mississippi,'" Eve remembered. "They'd laugh, and Grandpa DeRitter would slap his knee over some crazy story about a mule. He'd reminisce about sleeping in a cotton wagon or growing watermelons or tomatoes.

"Then Grandma would talk about how beautiful the hills were. How they smelled of pine sap. And how magical winter's first frost always seemed. 'Like a white satin wedding dress,' she'd say.

"And I'd think, 'This can't be the same Mississippi where they lynch black teenagers for just whistling at a white woman ... where they burn our churches with no more thought than lighting a campfire … where the Klan kills civil rights workers and buries them in the woods.'"

The wet black pavement rolled on across the Cattahatchie River bottom ten miles east of Oxford then rose back into the hills. "Eve, we all have a choice about what we carry forward with us in this life," Holly finally said. "Your grandparents chose to leave the ugliness behind and carry in their hearts only the good times. It doesn't mean they've forgotten, but it sounds like they've forgiven."

The windshield wipers churned back and forth. "I suppose," said Eve. "But I don't have that kind of forgiveness in my heart. I don't know that I ever will. I feel more angry by the day. Angry at myself, too.

"Holly, I don't know how much longer I can justify to myself living in a mansion built by slaves while lots of my people are still using outhouses. Living in the bubble of protection and privilege that your name and family history here creates while regular black folks are being harassed and threatened every day. Simply for wanting to vote and to send their kids to a decent school."

Eve stared out the window as they passed a sign reading: Welcome to the Town of Oxford: Home of THE University of Mississippi Rebels.

"You need to do what your heart tells you," said Holly as they stopped at the light where North Lamar ran into the town square. The red brick courthouse with its tall, white cupola made famous in William Faulkner's novels, stood in front of them. "All I ask is that you give me enough notice that I can find someone else before you leave."

"Okay."

* * *

The clinic was housed in a three-story Victorian on Tyler Avenue. Fortunately, there was a ramp up to the porch for wheelchair-using patients. But Dr. Phelps' office was upstairs, so they met in an examination room on the first floor.

Dr. Ferguson Phelps was bent and balding and leaned heavily on a black cane with a silver handle in the shape of an eagle with its wings folded back. He dropped onto a stool and dismissed Eve with a glance of his milky eyes then carefully looked Holly over. She guessed the man to be close to eighty.

"You're a paraplegic," he said without introduction.

Surprised, Holly responded automatically – "Yes."

"Do you have any use of your legs?"

She hesitated, then, "No. None."

"Can you stand at all?"

"With leg braces and crutches."

"You should do as much of that as you can. It'll help keep your leg bones from getting brittle. Of course, in the long run, nothing will prevent that," he said matter-of-factly. "What about bladder? And your woman functions?"

Holly and Eve shared a look. "Doctor, I'm not here as a patient. I called about my father's autopsy. You are the Lafayette County medical examiner?"

"Oh, yes. Have been for forty-three years."

"T.L. Carter?" Holly prodded. "He was found in the Cattahatchie. Back in March. You ruled his death an accidental drowning."

Dr. Phelps slapped his forehead. "Oh, my goodness! Of course. You're Mr. Carter's daughter. I've read about you. You were a reporter. Got yourself shot in Vietnam."

"I was ... I am a photographer."

"A woman has no business in a place like that," he went on. "Perhaps that's the lesson God wants others to learn through your suffering."

Holly bit her lip then let go of it and her irritation. He was an old man born in another and very different century, and she needed his help. "Doctor, what can you tell me about my father's death?"

"Nothing without the report."

"Is that it there in your lap?" asked Eve.

The old doctor looked down and grumbled something. Eve and Holly shared a look. He opened the file without response. "Let's see," he sighed as he studied the papers. "Yes. ... Uh-hum. ... Yes. ... Yes. ... Well, Mr. Carter drowned."

"May I see the report?"

Dr. Phelps gave Holly the folder and she quickly read through it, forcing herself not to react to detailed descriptions of numerous injuries to her father's body. There was an inventory of the items found with the body. No suit coat or rain coat was mentioned, nor was there anything about glasses or a gold pocket watch. The autopsy photos were in a brown manila envelope tucked into a flap at the back of the folder. Holly did not, could not open it.

"Doctor, how did you determine how my father died?"

"Young lady, your father is not the first drowning victim I've autopsied by a long shot. I've seen more –"

"Doctor, I'm not questioning your competence," Holly assured him. "I'm merely asking a question."

"Well, as long as that's understood. Some people around here think it's time for me to be put out to pasture. But I've still got it up here," he said, tapping his skull with a boney finger. "Of course, there were the obvious circumstances."

"Yes."

"But I know my job no matter what you've been told," he said. "I went the extra mile and I examined your father's nasal passages, sinuses and lungs. We took slides and looked at them under the microscope. They contained water, grit and microbes consistent with those found in the Cattahatchie. I've seen it many times."

"So, he was breathing when he went into the river?"

"No doubt. And there's no doubt he drowned in that river."

"All right," agreed Holly, taking a moment to think. "What about all the injuries to my father's body. Broken ribs? A broken leg? A separated shoulder?"

"As you're probably aware, or should be, during the spring rains the Cattahatchie flows hard and fast especially up your way. Those injuries were sustained by being struck with debris, pummeled against rocks, bridge pilings, that sort of thing."

"What about the large gash on his forehead? And the skull fracture?" she asked, handing him the report and pointing to the sentence referencing the injury. "Could you discern whether this injury was pre- or postmortem?"

Doctor Phelps squinted at the report then suspiciously at Holly. "We often can, but the body was in a rather advanced state of decomposition. Moreover, young woman, there was no need to do so. The injury is consistent with someone striking their head on the steering wheel during an automobile crash."

Holly nodded, but said nothing as she considered. "Doctor, did you go to DeLong and examine my father's car? Specifically the steering wheel? To see if it matched the wound to my father's forehead."

"My dear, there was no need," he told her. "DeLong is a long way to haul these old bones. Besides, there was an eyewitness to the accident. A girl walking on the road, I believe. And, sadly, I've seen this sort of impact head injury dozens of times in the last forty years."

"Impact head injury?" asked Holly, having trouble now holding her temper. "Doctor, there was no impact. My father's car could not have been going more than twenty miles an hour. It slid over a soft, earthen bank and into the river."

Dr. Phelps straightened himself as best his bent old spine would allow. "Young woman, I've seen people suffer similar catastrophic head injuries during ten-mile-an-hour automobile mishaps in a grocery store parking lot."

The doctor's hand was gripping the head of his cane so tightly that his knuckles were growing pale. Holly said, "Just one more question, Doctor. Did you know that witness saw my father's car go into the river before or after you issued your report?"

Dr. Phelps huffed and pushed himself up. "I don't see what possible difference that could make."

"Maybe none, maybe a lot," said Holly.

The old doctor stared down at Holly as he might an insufferable child, then turned his glare on the tall young black woman leaning against his examining table. His face colored with anger and his features were stained with contempt as his hand clenched the head of the cane. Then he wheeled with surprising spryness and opened the door.

"I believe I've said all I have to say," he told them as he stepped into the hall. "I'm not sure what your purpose is in coming here and attempting to impugn my professional abilities, or who sent you, but I won't have it."

Patients and staff paused at the check-in window and necks craned in the nearby waiting room. "Miss Carter, your father succumbed to an accidental drowning. Period. I'd stake my professional reputation on it."

"That's fine," said Holly. "Because that's exactly what you've done. As T.L. Carter's daughter and the executor of his will, I'll need a copy of the autopsy and the photos. I hope I won't need a court order to get them."

The old doctor seethed, then barked down the hall. "Emma!" A middle-aged woman with a beehive hairdo the size of a hornet's nest stepped out of a door by the front office. "Give this woman whatever she is legally due. Then make sure she and her girl leave the premises."

CHAPTER 8

It didn't take long for the Klan to react to Billy Wallace becoming sheriff, or for my father to flex his muscle as the county's chief law enforcement officer.

On Wednesday night in a community east of town known as Chester, the devout of a congregation of a small African-Methodist-Episcopal church were meeting for mid-week services at Clement Turner's Country Grocery. Their church had been burned two months earlier.

Twenty minutes into the services and just on the back side of a misty twilight, hooded men in the back of a pickup opened fire with automatic weapons on a nearby transformer, casting the gravel crossroads into darkness. A moment later another truckload of men pulled up in front of the grocery and unleashed a fusillade of lead that tore the store apart as the little congregation hugged the floor or crawled out the back door and ran for the woods, where slugs were snapping off limbs and smacking into tree trunks. Inside, cans of beans and peaches exploded and twenty-pound sacks of flour were eviscerated, their con- tents filling the air with a white fog. Display cases shattered and the antique cash register rang and chimed as it was hit again and again.

The attack lasted less than a minute, but next morning Sheriff Wallace, his deputies and the feds found more than two hundred 5.56 millimeter shell casings of the type used by M16s – the same weapons our military was using in Vietnam. There also were more than a dozen spent shotgun shells, and that didn't count what they found down the road near the electrical transformer.

Swinging from a hangman's noose hooked to the power pole was a scarecrow with a sign around its neck. The name Billy Wallace was written, then struck through with red paint. Under it was the word "Judas," in black.

"I want every shell casing dusted for fingerprints," Sheriff Wallace told Deputy Leonard Young.

"Mr. Wallace – err, I mean, Sheriff Wallace, we've done that in the other shootings and never got anything. It takes forever to –"

"I don't care how long it takes," the sheriff told him. "Maybe we'll get lucky."

Then to Ridge Bellafont, who was the department's semi-official photographer during major investigations, such as they were in Cattahatchie County – "Ridge,

I want a picture of that scarecrow and ten prints. We'll hit the farmers' co-ops and country stores. Maybe somebody'll recognize it.

"It's probably stolen," said Hugh McGregor, the FBI agent overseeing operations in the county. "Surely, no one would be so stupid as to use a scarecrow from their own field."

"With the arrogance of these people, who knows?" said the sheriff, shaking his head. "But what I do know is that this little display was planned. They didn't just happen across a scarecrow and decide to do this. That means that at least one of them probably was familiar with our well-stuffed friend."

"Meaning that at least one of the perps probably lives nearby to wherever the scarecrow came from," said McGregor. "It's thin."

"Yep, but we have to start somewhere," said the sheriff.

The only good thing about Wednesday night's attack was that no one was seriously injured. Four of the people in the store received cuts from flying glass or minor flesh wounds to the thigh or buttocks, probably from ricochets off the black iron skillets hanging from pegs above the counter. One woman who ran off into the woods went into premature labor and gave birth beside a quick-flowing stream as the moon broke through the clouds. She and the baby were fine.

When Reverend Clemmer arrived to comfort the folks in Chester, he shook his head. Not one pane of glass was intact. The front doors were literally shot to pieces.

"God must have been with them," he said to the sheriff.

Billy Wallace worked his jaw, adjusted his fedora. "That's as good an explanation as any," he agreed. "It sure as hell wasn't because these Kluckers were bein' careful. Pardon my language, Reverend."

"Hell is, indeed, a sure thing for the men who did this unless they find God and change their ways," he said.

"The men who did this aren't lookin' for God," said the sheriff. "They're just lookin' for more meanness to do and hurt to cause. You and your people need to be careful. Canvassin' for votes on these back roads." He shook his head. One of Burke's men had briefed him on all they knew about "Dynamite Bob" McBride and what they suspected about Sgt. Charles Rudolph. "The boys who did this ain't into sendin' messages with burning crosses. They mean business. They're ready to go to war."

"Can you stop them?"

Billy Wallace glanced down at the new badge on his chest then looked Ronald Clemmer in the eye. "I have no idea, Reverend. But I will try."

At *The Current-Leader*, the tension between Miss Carter and her brother was as palpable as hickory – no, coal smoke. There was nothing sweet or woodsy about it. It was just hot and nasty, and loaded with a long-buried history and the promise of flaring at any moment.

Meanwhile, the angry flame between Miss Carter and Eve Howard was as open and obvious as a torch in a midnight hayloft. One misstep and it all might go up.

Miss Howard and Ridge Bellafont were pressing Miss Carter to at least run some of the photos they'd taken at the Turner's Grocery. Ridge's urgings were subtle; Miss Howard's were loud and angry. At the same time, Miss Carter was getting phone calls from Milton Handley, Walter Kamp and several other major advertisers over the large front-page photo and story about my father's swearing-in.

"We may be just plain ol' country folk," Milton Handley told her, "but we're not fools. First, frightening everyone with that ridiculous McBride story, and now you're the only one who knew where and when Broderick was swearing in that washed-up drunk, Billy Wallace.

"Miss Carter, we were willing to give you a chance, but it is becoming increasingly clear that you have returned here with ulterior and pernicious motives. That you may well be in cahoots with Burke, Mulberry and the race-mixers.

"You've got two strikes against you now," he said. "One more and your newspaper is out. Handley's Department Store will pull all of its advertising. Others, I'm sure, will follow."

By the time I left the newspaper late Friday afternoon, the decision had been made not to run anything regarding the attack out in Chester. Miss Howard was so upset that she stormed out of the building with tears streaming down her cheeks. When I was leaving, I saw her striding across the Theodore J. Bilbo Bridge that connected DeLong to all the bright petals and painful thorns of Roseville. I braked my truck at the stop sign beside the jail and watched her turn left next to a cotton warehouse and disappear down a dirt street into the town's only black neighborhood, squeezed as it was between the river and the steep hills that rose around it like high green walls.

F ive minutes later, I was picking up Patti for supper and a movie. We were going to New Albany to see the new John Wayne picture, *True Grit*, playing there at the Cine'. Patti told Brother Daddy that we probably were going to eat at Nicholls, a family steakhouse on Gandy Lake south of DeLong. Words like "probably," and phrases like "I think," "I believe," "I suppose" and "we plan to," were always the operative parts of Patti's speech. No matter what statement of dubious truth she delivered to her parents, teachers or anyone else, she always left herself enough wiggle room within her sentence structure so that she could never be caught in an out-and-out lie.

Before we'd backed out of the driveway, she pecked me on the cheek and said, "I've changed my mind. I don't want to go to Nicholls. I'm in the mood for catfish. I want to go to Ripples."

So off we went, south on Highway 27, past the fairgrounds and the cutoff to Nicholls Steakhouse while Patti rolled a joint in the lap of her pleated skirt and sang along with Jerry Garcia and the Grateful Dead. Had Patti told Brother Daddy that we "probably," or even "possibly" were going to Ripples, he'd have never let her out of the parsonage. Ripples did, indeed, have some of the best fried catfish around and hush puppies loaded with onion and spiced to perfection, but it also was a backwoods hangout for fishermen, roughnecks, loose women, errant husbands and reprobates of all sorts. Though illegal, there was plenty of cold beer to be had, and in the off-season rooms in the motel across the gravel parking lot could be rented by the half day or even the hour.

From my perspective, the most uncomfortable aspect was that it was owned by J.D. Benoit's kin. All the Benoits, Hugheses and Gabbersons were from the swampy low country at the south end of the county where the Cattahatchie overflowed its banks most every spring. The unpredictability of the big river tended to make their lives and personalities hard-bitten and chancy, at best.

As we sat on a narrow, sandy cut beside an algae-streaked backwater smoking Patti's joint, I started to mention the fact that Billy Wallace's son might not be all that welcome in Ripples right now. I even wondered for a moment if Patti was trying to instigate something, just to see the sparks fly. But I forced myself to dismiss the notion, blaming it on pot-inspired paranoia. Besides, any mention of such concerns would only draw Patti's ridicule. She could used adolescent hurt words such as "wimp" and "pussy" with the cold, quick brutality of a fencing master.

By the time we went up the steep steps to Ripples' front door, I had convinced myself that I could be as tough as any of the regulars. In any case, all I could think about was Patti's bare legs scissoring up-down, up-down, up-down as she climbed the wooden stairs in front of me.

W e got some hard looks when we came through the door and found our way to one of the picnic tables inside the big hall of a room. A Confederate flag the size of a bed sheet hung amid the open rafters. It was still early and the crowd was thin for a Friday night. That was fine by me.

The waiter took so long coming over for our order that I wondered if they would serve us at all. I recognized him behind a dirty apron as one of J.D. Benoit's young cousins, Ronnie Gabberson. He had a pinch of tobacco between his cheek and gum, and his sparse brown mustache squirmed on his upper lip like a night-crawler exposed to the light.

Ten minutes later, we didn't have our food. "You should complain," Patti told me, but I sat tight. Finally, the waiter returned with our food sandwiched between the thick paper plates Ripples served everything on. He dropped them in front of us and walked away. When we flipped the top plate, there were our meals with several thick streams of tobacco juice spit across them.

Patti pushed the plate away as if it held live snakes. I thought she was going to be sick, and I didn't blame her. Once her stomach settled a tad, she looked at me.

"Nate Wallace, you march right up there to that counter and tell them we want fresh meals!" she told me.

"Patti, let's just get out of here," I said reasonably. "I've kind of lost my appetite anyway."

She cursed me and them. "I don't care if we throw it in the fucking garbage!" she growled through tight lips and clenched teeth. "If you're any kind of a man, you'll make them give us fresh meals. And apologize!"

"Patti, I don't think that's –"

"Nate, I swear! Sometimes I think you should be the one wearing the skirt," she snarled. "Now get up there!"

I rose on knees that felt soft from the inside out. "And take those disgusting plates with you."

I picked up the defiled meals and walked toward the counter. Ronnie was wiping his hands on the apron, his worm of a mustache twitching. One of his uncles was at the register and another was monitoring a row of deep fryers. Several other employees, mostly consisting of inbred cousins, stopped what they were doing. The stillness and quiet were contagious. Other diners stopped their talk. The only sound I was aware of was a jukebox playing in the back room and men sitting on the outdoor deck telling fish stories over cold beers.

Ronnie Gabberson stared at me across the counter as I put the plates down, then withdrew my hands so the men would not see that they were trembling. He was at least two or three inches taller and thirty or so pounds heavier. He'd played linebacker for New Albany High before he'd been expelled for something or other.

"Excuse me," I said, clearing my throat. "It looks like someone – someone spilled something on our food."

Ronnie leaned on the counter and grinned at me, the same tobacco juice staining his crooked teeth as colored our meals. The tune on the jukebox had ended and the room was silent except for the hiss of the deep fryers and the turning of ceiling fans. My fists tightened at my sides. The groan of the rusty spring on the screen door was as attention-grabbing as fingernails on a blackboard. The squeal seemed to go on for minutes, but in the time it took to cross a threshold, my father was standing in the doorway – his silver badge shining nearly as brightly as the black leather of his gun belt. He had a wad of fliers in one hand
and he crossed the silence to the counter.

Daddy surely had noticed my truck in the parking lot and thus was not surprised to see me there. I, on the other hand, could not have been more surprised if he'd dropped out of the rafters. But I did my best to hide it, along with the strange mix of relief and anger that was sizzling through my bloodstream. Daddy looked at the ruined meals in front of me. Ronnie stepped back from the counter.

"Nate," he said, by way of acknowledgement. "Daddy," was all I said.

"Looks like we're infested with Wallaces tonight," said Ricky Hughes, who owned the place and ran the cash register. "What do you want?"

My father was calm and made no mention of the plates. "Ricky, I'd like to put up a couple of these fliers in the restaurant and a few more at the dock and around the lodge."

Hughes studied a sheet that bore mug shots and a description of Robert Bedford "Dynamite Bob" McBride of Jasper, Alabama. State Trooper Sergeant J.B. Benoit chose that moment to emerge from the deep shadows of Ripples' back room. Ricky Hughes handed the flier to his cousin.

"The only R.B. McBride I know of was a decorated Army Ranger and demolitions expert during World War II," Benoit said loudly enough to be heard throughout the quiet room. "He's a hero and a patriot, as far as I'm concerned."

"He's a murderer who does his work in the middle of the night like the coward he is," Sheriff Wallace told Benoit in an equally firm voice. "He probably killed Floyd Johnson, and I intend to see him in Parchman Prison or in hell for it. Which one is up to him. Now where can I put these up?"

Benoit told my father exactly where he could put them.

"That's right!" said Ricky Hughes, laughing. "You tell him, J.D." The silence was long. I felt like I was in a movie and wanted to turn around and look at the room to see how the scene was playing out, but I couldn't move.

All Daddy said was "Excuse me" as he stepped around the younger, bulkier man and went behind the counter. "I'm feelin' a tad dry."

The sheriff's coolness only seemed to make Benoit hotter. "I heard you've already had three out of your fifteen deputies quit on you," he prodded. "And there's more resignation's comin'. You'll see!"

The sheriff reached into a long cooler and set aside some sodas. He lifted a case of longneck beers onto the counter. "Well now, I've always said nothing washes down a mess of catfish and hush puppies like a cold brew.

"That's a big fine cooler you've got there, Ricky," he was saying. "How many cases will that thing hold?" Ricky Hughes stared at his cousin J.D. "Don't look at him," said the sheriff. "I asked you a question, Ricky."

Ripples' owner swallowed, answered – "Forty-two."

"Well, let's see, according to Cattahatchie County Code, each bottle carries with it a twenty-five dollar fine." Daddy did some figuring on his fingers. "That's $150 a six-pack or $600 a case. Times that by forty-two, and you're talking about $25,000 – give or take.

"Add on however many more cases you've got in your storage rooms, and you're lookin' at bootleggin' charges. And if I find one person to testify that your underage nephew there served them a beer, then you can count on state time."

"J.D.?" whimpered Ricky Hughes.

"He's bluffin'," said Benoit.

"Do you want to bet your livelihood? Maybe prison time?" said the sheriff. "How about if I station a deputy out there on the road to write down the tags of everybody who drops by your motel to enjoy the businessman's special?"

Ricky Hughes eyes went back and forth between his cousin and the sheriff. He and I could see that my father wasn't bluffing. "Now, Ricky, this is your place of business. So, I'll just leave you a stack of these flyers, and let you put 'em up where you see fit. Me or a deputy will be around every day to make sure you don't run out. Do you understand?"

"Yeah," grunted Hughes as Benoit fumed.

"Good. The Cattahatchie County Sheriff's Office appreciates your cooperation," he said. Then to me, "Nate, I think it's time for you and Patti to be leavin'."

CHAPTER 9

On Saturdays the offices of *The Current-Leader* were open only to receive classified ads and allow people to step in from the hustle and bustle of the town square and pay for their subscriptions or purchase a copy of the weekend edition. Vendors hawked their fresh vegetables, fruit, beans, corn and watermelons from their trucks parked around the courthouse. Children were running and laughing along the sidewalks.

Through the big open windows of her office Holly could smell the salty-butter-rich scent of popcorn being sold in front of The Rebel Theater. She looked at her watch. The kids' matinee of *Chitty-Chitty Bang-Bang* and *Heidi* was about to start. She hadn't left the office until nearly midnight when Eve Howard returned from Roseville more than a little stoned. The tension burned between them now in an ever-widening chasm of silence and allowed Holly to sleep little. There was no point in simply laying there, and over breakfast she didn't want to deal with Eve or her own guilt about continuing the newspaper's segregated news policy. So she dressed and returned to town. She'd been at the newspaper's account ledgers for almost four hours as the busy weekend of local commerce built outside her window.

The phone on Holly's desk buzzed. Christine Wright, who worked the front desk on the weekends, said, "Cutter Carlucci is here. He'd like to see you."

This is a surprise, thought Holly, and chided herself when she realized how pleasant the surprise felt. "Send him up," she said.

There was a pause. "Uhm, Miss Carter, he asked if you could meet him around back on the loading dock?"

"Well … all right. Tell him I'll be down in five minutes."

Cutter was at an old picnic table where the pressmen and other employees sometimes sat for lunch. Charlie came scampering over. Cutter extended his hand and let the small white dog sniff it.

"Do you remember me, girl?" he asked. "I was at your house the night when men landed on the moon."

Charlie yapped and pranced as Holly pushed onto the dock. "And our astronauts are safely home."

"Yep. Pretty amazing," said Cutter, standing as Charlie sniffed around his work boots. Holly liked that Cutter wasn't muscle-bound like most football players she'd known. He was stout and sturdy, but he was strong in the way a coiled spring is strong. On this day his boots, his hands and big forearms were speckled with green paint. His gray T-shirt was dark with sweat from neck to waist and he smelled like turpentine. "I apologize for showing up looking like this. Smelling like this. That's why I didn't want to come upstairs. I figure I'm better in the open air right now."

"You're fine. I needed the break anyway," said Holly. "It looks like you have yourself a painting job."

"I'm helping Scotty Thompson and his boys with a couple of the warehouses they're converting for classroom buildings for the new academy."

"Is that where you're going this fall? To Riverview?"

She was not the first to ask. Cutter offered his standard response – "I'm going wherever they're playing football. Just mark off the field and turn on the lights and I'll be there."

"A diplomat in the making," said Holly. Then, "You look hot. There's a Coke box inside the door."

"No thanks. I'm about to head up to The Well and get cleaned up before I go to The Gin. But I was passing by and saw your car and thought you'd want to know, I talked to Rose."

"Oh, good. What did she say?"

"Mostly what I already told you. She said Mr. Carter wasn't going very fast. That he just seemed to never even try to make the turn onto the bridge."

Holly nodded, listening.

"I asked Rose if she recalled seeing brake lights. She said she couldn't remember one way or the other. But she did remember the dome light coming on just as it was going over the bank. Like your dad opened the door trying to get out."

"Really? Did she actually see him trying to get out?"

"No. It was only a flash, for a couple of seconds."

Holly reconstructed the scene in her mind. "Did she recognize the man as my father?"

Cutter took a long look at Holly Carter, then -- "She didn't even recognize the car. But it was your father's car and, of course, it was Mr. Carter whose body was found. Why would you wonder if she recognized your father?"

Holly tried to sidestep the question with one of her own. "How long did it take Rose to run to the bridge from where she was when she saw the car go in?"

Cutter calculated. "Well, my sister isn't a world-class sprinter. Especially on a night like that, wearing a raincoat. Maybe a minute, give or take."

Holly was doing her own figuring now. One minute. Sixty seconds. That would be plenty of time for someone to drive her father's Oldsmobile off the road, roll out onto the bank and hide himself among the brush and debris and pilings under the bridge before Rose got to the railing. Then when Rose went to get Cutter he could have simply walked back up the road. But walked to where? There were only a half dozen houses on this side of the mountain, including Wolf's Run.

The whole thing would be damn risky with the river flowing high and hard, she thought, but then murder always is a risky proposition.

"Miss Carter, if there's something you're concerned about in your daddy's death, Mr. Wallace is a good man. Even if he has had his troubles with the bottle the last couple of years," Cutter told her. "I'm sure he'd look into it."

Holly blinked as if coming out of a light sleep. "Yes. Yes, Cutter, I'm sure he would, but with all he has to deal with right now – Sheriff Johnson's murder, this McBride lunatic running around and the local Klan crazies – I don't want to add to it unless I'm sure."

Holly watched Cutter drive away, then sat staring past the parking lot and the street at the green-brown summer river.

If she was going to pursue this, the next step would be locating her father's 1965 Oldsmobile Ninety-Eight. If his spare glasses were in the glove compartment, then T.L. Carter could not possibly have driven himself from Wolf's Run, down the curving mountainside road to the Old Iron Bridge. Either way, Holly knew she needed to get her hands on the steering wheel of that Olds to see if it matched the wound to her father's forehead. That would mean an exhumation and another autopsy. The thought made her queasy, but there probably was no way around it – eventually. And that likely would draw her into still more conflict with Tom and Mary Nell. They would see it as her questioning the management of her father's death, and probably some sort of sacrilege as well. It was one of the reasons Holly had spent all morning going over the company books, looking for the sale of the Olds, which had been an asset of DeLong Newspapers Inc. She had not wanted to ask Tom about it, but there was no notation in the company ledgers that she could find.

"Conflict? That's all my life seems to be about anymore," Holly said to herself as she drove the short distance across town. *Conflict with Tom and Mary Nell. Conflict with Eve. Conflict with the newspaper staff. Conflict with the advertisers. Conflict with white folks who think I'm a traitor, and conflict with the black folks who think I'm a racist. And conflict with ... with? ... with myself.*

Holly stopped at the corner before she turned down the street she'd played on as a child. The yard at the corner of Jackson and Hood streets was large and shaded by elms and magnolias. They looked larger than she remembered as a child and yet the three-story Victorian seemed so much smaller. Holly turned down Hood Street then into the long driveway that wound between the trees and led behind the house. There a boy who looked like a younger, more innocent version of Tom was winding up and throwing baseballs at a target painted on the side of the clapboard garage.

Smack! ... Smack! ...

Thomas Lanier Carter V stopped his pitching and stared at Holly, his red St. Louis Cardinals baseball cap twisted slightly on his sandy brown hair. The sight of him caused Holly to choke up. It reminded her of how much of her life had passed since the last time she was in this yard. The last time she'd seen her nephew, he was only toddling around, taking unsure steps. Now he was at least five-eight with the long, limber limbs of the Carter clan and his mother's sharp nose and jaw.

"Hi, Lanny."

The boy stared, uncertain what to do or say as he picked up another baseball from the bucket and worked it into his glove. "I'm not supposed to talk to strangers," he finally said.

"Lanny, honey, I've been away a long time, but I'm not really a stranger. I'm your Aunt Holly. Your father's sister."

"I'm not supposed to talk to you either."

The response stung Holly as surely as a slap and she felt her cheeks redden, not with anger but with frustration and sadness that what little family she had left was in such a state.

"Lanny!" Mary Nell called as she came through the screen door from the back porch. "Go change into your swimming suit. We're going out to meet your father at the country club and have dinner there."

"Awww, Momma, can't I stay here. I'd rather try to get up a ball game."

Mary Nell was wearing a white tennis outfit. She tossed her racket into the back seat of a big Buick before approaching Holly's paint-scraped Lincoln. "Don't argue with me, young man," she told him. "I have a two o'clock doubles match and I need to warm up."

The boy took a long last look at his aunt then headed for the back door.

"He's a handsome boy," said Holly.

"That's what everyone says."

"Where's Georgette? I'd love to see her. She's what now? Almost fourteen?"

"Yes, but she's not here. She rode out to the club with Tommy earlier. She's quite a little golfer."

Holly looked around at the yard she'd played in as a girl, the trees she'd climbed.

Mary Nell cleared her throat. "As I was telling Lanny, I have a tennis date. Does your visit have some purpose?"

Holly drew herself out of the happy memories and into the unpleasant present. "A purpose? Yes. It does. I've been going over the company books covering the last year or so and I have a question."

Mary Nell Carter's mouth drew itself into a small knot.

"Daddy's Oldsmobile was an asset of DeLong Newspapers. I'm wondering how it was disposed of. I can't find anything in the books about it."

Mary Nell's gray eyes were hard and Holly could see the color rising in her slender neck. "What are you accusing us of?"

"I'm not accusing you of anything," Holly told her sister-in-law, who also was the company's treasurer, absentee as she had been since Holly's return. "Daddy's car was worth several thousand dollars and I want to make sure that it's properly written off our books."

"Several thousand dollars?" grunted Mary Nell. "Maybe before it went in the river. Afterward, it wasn't worth a dollar. In fact, we were going to have to pay to have it towed out of the sheriff's impound lot once the investigation was completed."

"So … ?"

"So, the Kamps, who are personal friends of Tommy and I, offered to haul the vehicle away at no cost."

"The Kamps?"

"That's what I said."

"And what were they going to do with it?"

"Sell it for scrap, I assume. I didn't ask and I didn't care. I just wanted it out of the sight of my husband and T.L.'s grandchildren."

Holly thought about that for a moment. "All right. What about insurance?"

"Tommy decided to wave an insurance claim," she said. "The car was nearly five years old. It wasn't worth it."

"Still, there should be some paperwork. A bill of sale or a transfer of title? Something?"

Mary Nell's jaw shifted under her pale skin. Holly could see blue veins throbbing beside her sister-in-law's ear. "I suppose that is how they do things in California where everyone's a stranger," said Mary Nell. "But here, a person's word and a handshake among friends remain sufficient. The Kamps have an impeccable family line. Colonel Kamp served gallantly under General Nathan Bedford Forrest. They can trace their lineage all the way back to Charleston."

Holly wanted to ask what that had to with anything, but resisted. For Mary Nell, she knew, it had everything to do with everything. Instead, she said, "Whose hand did Tom shake on the deal?"

"Actually, I was the one who made the arrangements. Tommy was far too distraught to deal with such matters."

"All right, then who –?"

Mary Nell paused, appearing to give it some thought. "LeRoy," she said. "Ann Burton Kamp's son. I feel certain you remember him."

"LeRoy Kamp? Yes. I remember him. Unfortunately."

Burton LeRoy Kamp was one of Holly's mistakes. One of many she made, mostly with older men. But LeRoy stood out. Three years older than Holly, he came home on leave from Germany in the winter of '57. She already had a Corvette and a reputation, and he looked good in and out of his Army uniform. Initially, they'd gotten along fine – lots of laughter, dancing and hot, sweaty fun – even though LeRoy had a rough streak in and out of the bedroom. But as he became more possessive of Holly, the streak went from rough to mean and she saw him for what he was, a bully – especially when it came to women and black people. When he was ordered back to Germany, she said good-bye and good riddance. Not long after, Corporal Kamp was sentenced to four years in the stockade for the attempted murder of a sergeant, who was black. He had written to Holly a few times from prison and, feeling sorry for him, she even responded until the letters became too lurid and venomous to open.

"Impeccable family line ...?" she thought as she turned into the Kamp Motors lot and drove around to the service bays in back.

Holly tapped her horn and a man in greasy blue coveralls came out. He glanced at the Lincoln with its missing chrome and scab of green paint down the driver's side. "Our body shop closes at noon on Saturdays," he said. "But if you bring this'un back on Monday, Gilbert and his boys can fix her up good as new."

"Thanks, but I'm not here for body work. Is LeRoy Kamp around?"

The man looked across the lot. "That's his red Firebird over there, so I 'spect he's somewhere on the place."

"Could you track him down for me?"

"I'll have Mary in the office make a P.A. announcement."

Three minutes later a man in work boots, jeans and a T-shirt came around the corner of the building. Holly recognized the walk – the strut. But that was all she recognized. LeRoy's straight brown hair was almost longer than hers. He had a mustache and beard that was haphazardly trimmed. His eyes were shot full of blood and bitterness.

"Holly Lee Carter. Miss Cattahatchie County," he said. "Where's your 'Vette?"

"I traded it in for this big ol' boat, and that," she told him, casting a thumb over her shoulder in the direction of her wheelchair.

"I heard about that. Playin' soldier over in 'Nam. I don't feel sorry for you. You had no business over there."

"I didn't come here for your sympathy, LeRoy. Or to chat about old times," she said. "I'm here as the owner of DeLong Newspapers Incorporated. My father's car was an asset of the company. I need the paperwork on it to clear it from our books."

"Paperwork? There ain't no damn paperwork. I did your family a favor, hauling that waterlogged piece of junk away."

Charlie stirred on the seat and sniffed the air. She growled in LeRoy's direction.

"I know. And I appreciate it, but to clear it from our books I need a bill of sale. Maybe a picture of it to get the insurance people off my back," she lied in service of the larger question.

LeRoy stared at Holly, his gaze a mixture of resentment and curiosity and remembered lust. "Insurance, huh? Well, I'm afraid you're out of luck. I sold that wreck to a wholesale scrap man a few days after we drug it onto the lot."

"Then you have a bill of sale, right?"

LeRoy grunted and stepped closer to the car. Charlie climbed into Holly's lap and yapped up at the big man. "It was a cash-and-carry deal. Neither one of us had any interest in tithing to Uncle Sambo concerning the transaction."

"Okay, then just give me the name of the wholesaler."

LeRoy leaned on the car door and Holly had to hook her hand in Charlie's collar to restrain sixteen pounds of angry bichon. Kamp ignored the dog's tirade. Finally Holly snapped, "*Arrêtez-vous, Charlie. Installez-vous!*"

Charlie grumbled but settled in Holly's lap so that she could think.

"Those guys are like gypsies," LeRoy told her. "They pull in with a long flatbed. If you've got something they want, they load it up and head on down the road."

Holly thought LeRoy might be lying, but why? Maybe to spite her, if nothing else. "And you've never done business with this guy before?"

"I never laid eyes on him until that day," he told her as he straightened beside the car. "But as best I recall, the trailer had Oklahoma plates."

CHAPTER 10

Cattahatchie County's only black school for grades eight through twelve, Roseville High, didn't have a football program, so its best athletes played basketball and baseball and ran track. Moccasin teams typically were lean, tough and blindingly fast, and Tommy Ray Banks was the finest point guard in the school's history. Barely six-feet tall, he could dunk a basketball with both hands or pull up and can a fifteen-foot jumper with the grace and quickness of an ebony hummingbird.

Cutter liked to compete against the best, and on many a winter Sunday afternoon, his Jeep could be found parked behind the time-worn Roseville gym. For hours, Cutter, Dodge McDowell and Jimmy Garner would play pickup games with the Banks brothers, the Prathers, Gathers and Storeys – all legendary names in Moccasin sports. Four, six, even eight or ten hours of basketball was not unusual on gray January days that settled into black wind-bitten nights.

After the games were done, Cutter, Dodge, Jimmy and the others would walk around the corner to a squat, lopsided brick building with a flat roof. In the spitting snow, a man in a long apron and short overcoat stood under an open-sided tin shed tending barbecue smoking over coals glowing red in a brick trough. Inside, Luther Banks' Good Eatin' House, the air was warm from the heat of the griddle and big oven and deep fryer, and the number of bodies packed together. At a big table at the back of the room, the competitors laughed and recalled shocks and bloacks over ribs and beer, iced tea, dirty rice, collard greens, corn and chicken fried St. Julianne style.

Had Marine Lance Corporal Tommy Ray Banks been a little luckier while on patrol in the Mekong Delta of South Vietnam, my plan to put some distance between me and Daddy, and thus appease Brother MacAllister while continuing to write for *The Current-Leader* might have worked, for a time at least. So might Miss Carter's plan to institute incremental integration of the newspapers' pages. But when time ran out for Tommy Ray, it ran out for her as well.

The newsroom was in the midst of a busy production morning when Miss Winona St. Julianne walked with short, stiff steps past my desk hugging to her chest a large, framed photo of a handsome young Marine. The way her arms crisscrossed the portrait, I could not recognize the face, though I was sure it must be one of her many great-grandchildren. Miss St. Julianne's descendants and their cousins were so numerous that they populated one entire section of Roseville.

Small and frail, and slightly stoop-shouldered, Miss St. Julianne was sandwiched between U.S. Attorney J.L. Burke and his bodyguard, Reverend Clemmer of the National Coalition for Justice, Roseville High Principal Harriett Houston, and, to my surprise, Ron Simpson – Paula Simpson's father and owner of The Cotton Café. Jean Baptiste, the preacher at Roseville African-Methodist-Episcopal Church, walked with a Bible in one hand and the other resting on Miss Winona's shoulder.

Tom Carter stood at the door to his small office and watched the group pass without acknowledgement, except for Ron Simpson, who was a frequent advertiser. Miss Carter met them at the door to her office, and when the group had filed in she asked, "Tom, would you like to join us?"

"I have work to do," he said, and stepped back into the tiny office he'd chosen, but did not shut the door.

C harlie got up from the spot on the sofa where she'd been sleeping and scampered over to stand beside Holly's wheelchair. The pooch yapped a time or two, but her master said, "Quiet, baby. These people are our friends. I hope."

"More important," said Harriett Houston, "I hope you are prepared to be a friend to the black community."

"A community that will be sending its children to Cattahatchie High School this fall and voting," said Reverend Clemmer.

"*If* the federal Court of Appeals lifts the stay on Judge Mulberry's integration plan," reminded Holly.

"Oh, it'll be lifted," said J.L. Burke. "The injunction was issued on only the flimsiest legal grounds. A super-technicality."

"Weathers and his bunch are only trying to buy time," said Clemmer.

"Time to garner more funding and support for an all-white private school," said Mrs. Houston, who had been at RHS for nearly 28 years.

"So, Mrs. Houston, is that why you requested this meeting?" asked Holly, who had accepted the appointment only reluctantly under pressure from the U.S. attorney. Burke had called in the chits he'd earned with the scoops he'd given Holly. "You want to talk politics?"

"No, Miss Carter," offered Reverend Baptiste. "We're here on a matter of the spirit, a matter of fairness for a son of DeLong."

Looking at Miss Winona holding fast to the young Marine's portrait, Holly felt what was coming as surely as if her wheelchair was chained to railroad tracks at the end of a long tunnel. The vibration rumbled through her, but there was nothing she could do about it except try to keep her breakfast down.

"Then why don't you all sit," she said, indicating the big conference table.

As if on cue, Miss Winona unwrapped her bony arms from the picture, laid it on the table and edged it close to Holly. The old woman used brown fingers twisted by tens of thousands of biscuits made, years of knuckle-pressed pie crusts and the weight of one black iron skillet after another lifted for six decades in the kitchen of The Cotton Café. She stroked the edge of the cheap, faux wood frame as if it were something alive, something that love could animate, like a little boy's head resting on great-grandma's lap. From a drawn face scarred pink across one cheek by a long-ago splash of cooking grease, she looked up at Holly with eyes bloodshot with age and remorse and too many years in sweat-box kitchens.

"That's my great-grandson, Tommy Ray Banks," she said with a ragged, aged voice. "He's on his way home now, from Veet-nam. He'll be home Sunday."

Reverend Baptiste covered Miss Winona's hand. "Tommy Ray was killed a few days ago. The patrol boat he was on was ambushed."

Holly nodded. "I am sorry."

Mrs. Houston told Holly about Roseville High salutatorian Tommy Ray Banks, about his exploits on the basketball court and baseball diamond, and about the athletic and academic scholarships he'd earned to Alcorn A&M University.

"He was planning to come back to DeLong and teach," she said.

Reverend Baptiste called him a role model for the youth in his church. "Tommy was engaged to another A&M student."

"The daughter of one of Reverend Baptiste's deacons," offered Clemmer.

"She was too broken up to come to this meeting," said Mrs. Houston. "They've kept steady company since eleventh grade."

Holly shook her head. "What was he doing in Vietnam? He couldn't get a deferment?"

"We tried," said Ron Simpson. "I talked to Earl Grisham myself."

"Mr. Grisham owns the supermarket and is head of the local draft board," offered Reverend Clemmer.

"Thank you, Reverend," she said. "I know who he is. I've known Mr. Grisham since – since, well, as long as I can remember. Please go on, Mr. Simpson."

"There's not much else to tell. He said, 'We've got a quota. Somebody has to go.'"

"No, sir. No, sir," Mrs. Winnona she told the group. "No, sir, Mr. Ronnie. You tells her what else Mr. Gisham said."

Ron Simpson studied the polished table top for moment, then met Holly's eyes. "He said, 'Would you rather it be a white boy?'"

Holly straightened in her chair to better catch her breath and control her fury and fear. She wanted to push away from the table. Push out of the room and leave all this behind. She knew where this was headed, and she could feel her stomach writhing. There was nothing to do but face it.

"I truly am sorry for your loss," she said, "but what can I do for you?"

Mrs. Houston reached into her purse and withdrew from it a folded newspaper page. It was *The Current-Leader* front page from Jan. 8, 1969. She unfolded it and laid it on the table in front of the newspaper's new editor-in-chief. The entire top half of the page was framed in black and dedicated to the memory of redheaded, freckle-faced Staff Sgt. Clayton Palmer, who was killed when a mortar shell landed on his barracks at the giant Da Nang Air Force Base. There was a large picture of Sgt. Palmer in uniform and a photo of him from a Cattahatchie High yearbook, a story about his life and family, and funeral information.

This was the traditional way in which *The Current-Leader* had handled the death of local servicemen since the Spanish American War. White servicemen.

Holly stared at the page. Since returning to DeLong, Holly had felt like she was trying to keep her balance on a tightrope while sitting in a wheelchair. Now it was as if the rope was soaked in kerosene – *or is it napalm?* Holly thought – and Clemmer and Burke were encouraging these nice, sincere, hurting people to light a match that could burn it out from under her.

Reverend Baptiste must have sensed a bit of what Holly Lee Carter was feeling. "It doesn't have to be as much as –"

"No," Miss Winona said firmly. "It should be just like that. Just like the one they gave that Palmer boy."

"I have to agree, Reverend," said Principal Houston. "Tommy Ray deserves to be treated with the same respect."

For a moment there was silence around the table. Ron Simpson offered, "I'm prepared to buy a full-page, so you can run it as an advertisement if it gives you some cover to –"

"No. No, thank you, Mr. Simpson," said the editor-in-chief of *The Current-Leader*. She bit her lip in a little-girl habit she'd never been able to lose, then – "Miss Winona is right. It should run at the top of 1A. Story. Funeral arrangements. Pictures. Just like the Palmer story."

Except for the sound of the slow-turning ceiling fan and noise through the open windows out to the square, there was no sound at all in the room for several moments. Everyone seemed to be holding their breath, as if even the slightest change in the atmosphere might cause a retreat. Finally, Reverend Baptiste spoke, "Praise God!"

Miss Winona's tired old eyes widened, brightened and new tears flowed down her cheeks, but now they landed in the corner of a smile as broad as her face. The old woman reached out and grasped Holly's hand with her bent, calloused fingers. "Thank you, child! Thank you," she said as Holly gently returned her grip and felt her own tears warm on her cheeks.

* * *

You've ruined us!" Mary Nell Carter screamed at her sister-in-law.
Everyone in the newsroom froze – everyone who remained – as the general manager's wife shrieked. Down on the sidewalk and even across the street on the

courthouse lawn passersby stopped to listen. Mary Nell Carter's voice sliced through the sticky Tuesday afternoon air like a scythe, and she was using it to cut and wound Holly Carter as deeply as she could. Charlie yapped and growled. Miss Carter tried to quiet her but the feisty little dog wouldn't quit.

On her eighty-nine-year-old legs, Miss Frances covered the steps from the first floor to the second in what seemed like four long strides once Mary Nell Carter began her shouting and cursing.

"Nate, run get Tom," she said to me since I was the nearest and youngest body. "He's probably over at The Jeff Davis, gettin' lunch and gettin' drunk. Now run! And don't take no for an answer."

"Yes, Ma'am," I said and galloped down the stairs, through the front door and right out onto the street as tires squealed and I cut between honking cars and pickups.

Once Miss Carter made the decision to handle Corporal Banks'death in the same way as *The Current-Leader* had traditionally handled the death of a white soldier in combat, word spread fast. Tammy Gilroy, who covered county government, and Clete Rainy, the sports editor, resigned on the spot when Miss Carter announced the decision. Several of our country correspondents who were in the office typing their columns, stopped virtually in mid-sentence – mid-word – and left the building. Circulation Manager "Hap" Medlin and Tom Carter had left together at 11:30 and by the time Mrs. Carter stormed in at 2:45, they had not returned. Neither had Andy Wilbanks, who ran the big camera that created the page-sized negatives that were used to burn the tin plates that went on the press. Randy Sparks, one of the pressmen, had stopped his preparation for the Tuesday night run, rubbed degreaser onto his hands and washed them over a sink stained nearly black with printer's ink.

"No, sir," he said to production manager Shorty Rodgers. "I ain't puttin' out no nigger news."

Advertising Director Frank Hodges had been sitting in his downstairs office for several hours, staring at a wall covered in certificates, commendations and photos. He looked as if he'd been hit by the train that Miss Carter had felt coming down the tracks.

Only Eve Howard expressed enthusiasm for the decision, as I guess we all might have expected. She let out a cheerleader whoop in the middle of the newsroom and hugged Ridge Bellafont's neck with a naive effervescence that demonstrated how little she knew about DeLong, Mississippi. Ridge hugged her back, but the tight seam of his full lips and the worry in his soft brown eyes told the rest of the newsroom how concerned he really was. Mister Ridge made it clear that he thought Miss Carter's decision was morally and ethically correct, but he was not naive enough to believe that being right was always enough; or that it would save the newspaper and its new editor from an avalanche of repercussions.

After the initial whirlwind of resignations passed, C. Michael Morton rallied the newsroom troops and Shorty Rodgers reorganized the production shop so that he could run the page camera. Two pressmen could run the big Goss unit in the printing bay, but preparation would take twice as long, so deadlines were adjusted.

Through it all, Miss Carter had been steady and decisive, even as she wrote the Banks story and an editorial explaining her decision. If she had any doubts, she didn't let them show in the newsroom.

This would wring out of Governor Weathers and, far more important to me, Brother MacAllister whatever little sanity they had remaining. And Patti would go right along with them. I knew I would have to resign from the paper, and the thought made me sick. But for this one historic afternoon in the annals of our little town, I was determined to stay where the action was – at the center of the storm.

B y the time I returned with our well-buzzed general manager, several members of the staff had gathered at the door to the editor's office, and more than one had tried to calm Mary Nell Carter, but she'd have none of it – breaking away from their touch and cursing them, too. C. Michael Morton had threatened to call the police, but his boss shook him off even as she absorbed the ongoing tirade. From what I could see, and by all accounts afterwards, Miss Carter's expression never gave way to anger or fear, only surprise at the level of coarse and vile invective her private-school-raised, Sunday-school-teacher sister-in-law was able to muster and maintain, pointing her finger and pounding sometimes on T.L. Carter's desk and sometimes on her own thigh.

When a winded, sweating Tom Carter dragged his overweight frame up the stairs to the newsroom, his wife still was thundering at his sister.

"Go back to California! Get out of our lives! There's no place here for a race-mixin' fornicator!" yelled Mary Nell Carter, her face, ears and upper neck bright red, her lips pale even under the heavy shellacking of makeup she wore.

"If you think I'm going to let you roll in here and destroy my home, my life, all the plans I've made, you're crazier than fucking daddy! You're not even a woman anymore! If Tom was any kind of a man, he'd have the Klan run you right out of town," she ranted. "You've never been any good. You abandoned your people for trash in California. And see what it got you. You've never been anything but trouble. A tramp! I wish you'd died in Vietnam!"

Tom touched his wife's rigid shoulders as if he were trying to maneuver a hot stove. She wheeled on him and looked up into his wet, jowly face. Then her hand came up, the big diamond on her finger flashing like a comet. The sound of her palm striking Tom Carter's face made us all wince.

"Get rid of her," Mary Nell Carter growled through clenched teeth. "I don't care how. But rid of her!"

CHAPTER 11

The sun was setting on the last day of my part-time career at *The Current-Leader*. As I stood on the fire escape outside the big windows at the back of the production room, I hoped it wasn't setting on the newspaper itself – though whatever feelings I had were mixed with anger, frustration, disappointment, confusion, uncertainty, and an underlying swell of apprehension that bordered on the restless edge of dread. For Miss Carter, for the paper, for our town. Though I felt terribly hemmed in by Cattahatchie County's narrow, stiff-necked attitudes and its inability to see the future beyond next year's crops, everything else was just words in books, pictures on a page or on the TV set. I had been on one four-day vacation with my parents to Panama City, Florida, twice to the Grand Ole Opry in Nashville and to Memphis a handful of times to shop for school clothes. Otherwise, DeLong was the only reality I knew, and it felt as if it were shifting out from under me.

Beyond the parking lot and River Street, the Cattahatchie was flowing from dusk into darkness, the day's last light making the river molten with color, as if someone had melted an enormous box of Crayolas and sent the rainbow mix flowing through town. Over in Roseville, a juke near the river had Jimi Hendrix cranked up. Night fishermen were lighting their lanterns and hanging them from poles affixed to the prows of their small boats. Several were casting lines into eddies south of the bridge while black children splashed and laughed and swam near a big sandbar.

Holly Lee Carter sat on a small, grassy plateau above the river where an old willow tree held fast to the narrow slip of earth, and thus to life itself. The tips of its long, corded tendrils shifted slightly in what little breeze was stirring.

Eve Howard stepped out onto the fire escape. She had been in the sweltering production shop helping its depleted crew put together pages – pasting strips of type onto cardboard dummies. Her blouse was damp with perspiration down her back, and under her arms and breasts. She stretched her neck and drew in a deep breath as she took in the pink twilight.

"How's she holding up?" I asked cocking my chin toward Miss Carter.

"Holly is the strongest woman – the strongest person I've ever known," responded Eve Howard. "She'll do whatever she has to do."

There was a part of me that hoped Eve Howard was right, that Holly Lee Carter would be able to successfully face down Governor Weathers, Brother MacAllister and the Klan – not to mention the many Mary Nell Carters in DeLong. But it was clear to me that I couldn't, and if I tried, I'd lose Patti. I went back inside, through the production room and to my desk and began typing out my resignation.

I t was nearly dark when Scotty Thompson turned his paint truck down River Street, the aluminum ladders rattling in their racks. Scotty, his sons and Cutter had spent twelve long, hot hours on those ladders, rolling green paint onto the big warehouses at the edge of Governor Weathers' Chalmette Plantation. Cutter climbed out of the truck cab across from The Cotton. He'd left his Jeep there after eating one of Miss Winona's ham steaks for breakfast.

Holly was studying the river as she watched it changing colors below her.

"You've never been any good. ... You've never been anything but trouble. ...I wish you'd died in Vietnam ...You're not even a woman anymore..."

Her sister-in-law's voice echoed in her ears and tumbled down inside her with the weight of rocks sheathed in ice. She tried to make herself focus on the here and the now, but the here and the now felt so much like the then and back when. Back before Ia Drang. Children splashing in a warm, twilit river – laughing, unaware, or pretending for the length of a sunset unawareness of the danger looming around them. Vine-covered, shadow-filled banks and a soldier with his transistor radio cranked up to the naive harmonies of *California Girls*.

Now, in the near distance, Jimi Hendrix was wailing the chords of Dylan's painfully beautiful harbinger *All Along the Watchtower*. If there was any way out of the fix she'd gotten herself into – and worse, gotten the paper into – Holly couldn't see it.

"What was it the joker said to the thief?" Holly asked herself. "'There must be some kind of way out of here ...?'" But if there was any way out of the fix she'd gotten herself into – and worse, gotten the paper into – Holly couldn't see it.

"Rough day?"

Holly startled, her hand jumping to her chest. "Oh, Cutter! You nearly scared me right into the river. Although that might not be the worst thing that could happen."

"I guess you're already catchin' hell about the Tommy Ray Banks thing," he said.

Holly laughed softly. "This town doesn't need a newspaper. The clothesline telegraph is faster than anything we can put out. How did you hear about it?"

"Scotty Thompson talked to his oldest girl on the phone at lunch. She worked in your classified ad department. Until about noon," Cutter explained. "She was pretty upset."

As soon as Holly wheeled into the newsroom and informed the staff of her decision, she knew it would travel throughout DeLong and the county as quickly as shoe leather, Firestone tires and telephone lines could carry it. That accounted for the eight-nine subscription cancellations Miss Frances already had received, and some two dozen businesses attempting to cancel their ads – including the paper's biggest client, Handley's Department Store. At four o'clock, Advertising Director Frank Hodges came into her office, sat down on the sofa, put his face in his hands and cried.

Cutter squatted so that they were level with each other. He caught her eyes, and in them saw gold flecks sparkling on green satin. His eyes were so blue-white that they were hard to read.

"Are you okay?" he asked.

Holly arched her spine, relaxed it then rolled her shoulders. "Other than a terrible backache, I think so. I just had to get out of the office for a few minutes."

"I didn't mean that," he said. "Are you going to stick with the story?"

Holly didn't hesitate. "Yes. I am."

Cutter looked off toward the river then back. "You surely are kickin' a hornet's nest. Is that why you came back? To be some big integration crusadin' newspaper lady? Like people are sayin'."

Holly knew she didn't owe Cutter any explanation. It was none of his business. But a strong part of her wanted at least one white person in DeLong to understand. She shook her head. "No. Nothing like that," she said. "There were, are things going on behind the scenes that most people here know nothing about.

"I came back to keep Tom from losing the paper. Or least control of it. To keep everything my family has built for four generations out of the hands of Cecil Weathers, or someone like him," she continued. "I didn't plan any of this. But I also didn't plan on Corporal Banks."

Cutter bounced on the balls of his feet and stood up. "I once heard a preacher say, 'Man makes plans and God laughs.' I guess that's true of women, too."

"Smart preacher," said Holly. Then, thinking of the river memories of Vietnam rushed back in and she suddenly wanted someone, at least one person in DeLong to understand them, too, even if just a little. "In Vietnam. At Ia Drang, I was with a patrol. Photographing them. It was late afternoon and I was getting great stuff. Then before anyone even realized what was happening, we were surrounded by North Vietnamese Army regulars. Cut off from the main body.

"I kept shooting with my Leica until it dawned on me that the NVA didn't know or care if I was a journalist or a woman. They were going to kill everyone on that plateau. That's when I picked up an M-16 from a private who'd already bought it and started shooting with that instead. The jungle was so thick, we felt like if we could stay alive until dark we could hold them off. Maybe Colonel Moore could send help at first light. We did, but just before sunset, I felt two bee stings in my back and a burning pain in my side, and my legs went out from under me."

Cutter listened without comment or question, even though plenty entered his mind.

"A medic bandaged me up, but there wasn't much they could do for me. So they propped me up against a tree and hid me with dirt and branches and palm fronds. A tough old sergeant gave me a .45, cocked and locked, and said, 'If they overrun our position, use this however you think best.'" She wiped a tear from one eye. "The NVA were all around us. We could hear them moving in the jungle. All night. Sometimes just yards away. And we prayed. Lord, how we prayed.

"'Dear Jesus, please! Just save my sorry ass this one time' and I'll – do, be, say, live, act however you want. 'I swear it by all that's holy!'"

Holly sniffled and fell silent, a silence Cutter did not jump in to fill, but after a moment he said, "That's a helluva story. You should write a book."

"I don't have any interest in telling that story to the world. It's ... private."

"But you told it me."

Holly made no reply to that, but said, "The point is, all of this feels like God calling in His marker."

Cutter thought about that for a moment, then nodded.

"Corporal Banks gave his life for his country – for us – just like any white soldier. He deserves no less," she said. "How could I, of all people, deny him that? I can't. I just can't."

The street lights flickered on with a hum and the voices of *The Current-Leader*'s two remaining pressmen cut through the thick air as they prepared the big machine for the printing run. Cutter picked up a stone from the bluff and tossed it out into the water. They watched as the ripples moved downstream with the current and disappeared before they could reach the bank.

"I better be going," said Holly, releasing the brakes on her chair. "I've got a newspaper to put out."

"Yep. I guess you do," he said as Holly pushed from the grass and into the street. She could feel his eyes on her. "Miss Carter?" he said, and she pivoted to face him. His hands were shoved into the front pockets of his jeans. "For whatever it's worth, I think you're doing the right thing."

Holly started to speak but emotion choked off her voice. Why did Cutter's opinion matter to her? Even a little? Why had she told him about Ia Drang or the forces moving behind the scenes that had brought her back to DeLong? Cutter had been helpful at times and downright unfriendly at others. Even cruel. She had no answer, but when she tried to speak again, it was the same. Finally, "Thank you," she mouthed.

* * *

By the time I got to The Well, Cutter had spread his sleeping bag, washed himself and had two big hamburgers cooking over the fire. There were two baking potatoes down in the coals. While I got my gear out of my truck, Cutter walked over to his ice chest. "How many hamburgers do you want?" he asked.

"I'm not too hungry. One'll do."

He tore a good-sized chunk of meat off a big pack of ground beef, patted it out in his hand and dropped it on the grill, then washed his hands in the stream from The Well.

"What are you down in the dumps about now?"

"I resigned from the paper this afternoon."

Cutter stared at me across the fire pit.

"I had to! I told you, Brother Mac was already making noises about not working for a Jezebel like Miss Carter. Now with her stickin' this colored news in the paper, I didn't have a choice."

The irritation in Cutter's gaze was as hot and easy to discern as the sizzle of grease on the fire pit coals. But I was wound up from the events of the day and eager for an ear to spill my story into.

"What a mess," I groaned as I spread my sleeping bag and began recounting in detail the day's events – from the time Miss Winona walked in to Miss Carter's announcement to the staff; from people resigning to just plain walking out; from Mary Nell Carter screaming her lungs out to overhearing Mr. Hodges crying in the editor's office; from subscription and advertising cancellations that already had come in to finding out that the circulation director was urging the route drivers to stay home.

"Some of the carriers called in saying they're not gonna deliver a paper with colored news in it. Others wanted to be paid in advance. Apparently, Mr. Medlin was also telling them that the paper is so broke Miss Carter might not be able to make another payroll."

"So, is Miss Carter going to be able to get the paper delivered?"

"Who knows? I'm out of it. I don't care anymore," I told him. "You know, I'm starting to think Miss Mary Nell is right. Holly Lee Carter ain't nothin' but trouble. Everything was fine until she showed up."

"Fine for who?" asked Cutter.

I pulled a net bag from The Well, took out a cold beer, cracked open the top and pretended not to hear the question.

We ate the hamburgers and baked potatoes in near silence, listening to the song of the crickets and of the river and watching the full moon on the rise. I was worn out and angry with Miss Carter, my daddy, Miss Winona, Clemmer, Baptiste, Burke and their whole bunch. Everyone who was conspiring to screw things up and derail the wonderful life I envisioned with Patti away from this place of contradictions and confrontation.

After recovering from the shock of a cold, quick shower in the waterfall issuing from The Well, I put up my tent. When I finished, Cutter was sitting on the rock ledge above the river.

"Well, there's no TV, so I guess I'll hit the sack."

"I guess you might as well," was all he said. I knew he was still irritated with me, but he couldn't understand. Grades, sports, girls – women! – came so easily to him. I touched two pimples sprouting from the right side of my face, along my jaw. I couldn't lose Patti. I just couldn't. And for damn sure not over this stupid colored business.

Deep after midnight I awoke needing to piss, and I crawled out of my tent. Clouds covered the moon, and the campsite was near pitch black except for the last glow of the cooking fire. Across the dark, mist-tinged fields, the light in Rose Carlucci's room glowed grimy white as usual. As I stepped to the edge of the campsite, I noticed Cutter's Jeep was gone. I walked over and checked his sleeping bag. Empty. After relieving myself against the base of a chinaberry tree, I went back to my tent and pulled my watch out of the cigar box where I stashed it at night with my wallet. I held the watch close to the campfire's coals and tilted it so the pink light caught the face of the Timex – 3:18 a.m.

CHAPTER 12

Annabelle Watson had a morbid fear of tornadoes, and for good reason. While plowing a twelve-acre field with a two-mule team along a Tishomingo County ridge line, her brother, Elijah, was snatched into a swirling sky by a sudden twister in the spring of 1845. She saw it all from the front porch, and would have died standing there – her arms wrapped around a post – had her father not grabbed her and her younger brother and dived into a ditch as the thunderous cyclone devoured their farmhouse.

The house and virtually all of the family's possessions were gone in the heartbeat of time it took the tornado to race through. Only the stubby brick piers upon which the small house rested remained. They found one mule on a rocky outcrop beside the nearby Tombigbee River. Like an egg dropped from a great height, the animal's body was more than broken, it was shattered. One eye was open – wide and wild with terror, a fear so deep that not even death could mask or dilute it.

About a week later, someone discovered their plow embedded deep into the trunk of an ancient oak two miles away. No trace of the other mule or Elijah ever was found.

So when Annabelle Watson married well-to-do planter John Henry Kamp in 1851 and he moved her back to his three-thousand acres in northeastern Cattahatchie County, her only demand was that the home he promised her have a deep basement to serve as a storm cellar. Kamp did her one better. He had carpenters and masons, and more than two dozen slaves, construct their two-story Greek revival mansion next to a large, pine-covered hill. A door from the kitchen led down to a sprawling basement/root cellar that was dug beneath the hill. Floored in brick and walled in fieldstone, it was more bunker than basement, and from it a web of tunnels extended. One opened on the hillside, another beside the nearby Cattahatchie River, another beneath the family's cotton gin.

Mrs. Annabelle Kamp spent hundreds of stormy nights under its twelve-by-twelve heart pine beams until she died in 1926.

In the Great Depression of the 1930s, the farm became unprofitable and the Kamps moved to DeLong and started a successful automobile dealership. Though most of the land had been sold to raise money to pay taxes and start the car lot, the

Kamps had held onto the old home place and a hundred or so acres around it. Now nearly swallowed in kudzu vines, honeysuckle and wild roses, it was almost invisible by day, and at night melted so completely into the moonlit woods that one would almost have to stumble over the carcass of the house, trip over the bones of the front steps to know that a structure existed.

But the Kamp heirs knew, and so the Klan knew.

Thus it was on that late July midnight in 1969 that the Klarogo, Furies, Terrors and Grand Wizard of the Kattahatchie Klavern of the Imperial White Knights of the Ku Klux Klan met by lantern light amid the stone and shadow of the Old Kamp Place basement. There would be no loud speeches or cross burnings. Such spectacles mostly were for public consumption, cameras and reporters welcome, to a point, as long as they were white. The marching and chanting theatrics were staged to reassure "decent white folks" that the Klan still was on guard, to scare "uppity niggahs" and to intimidate any Jews or Catholics who might, like "stray dogs," be wandering through the county. This was a business meeting, and their business was death.

Overhead and along the rarely used dirt road, members of the klavern's outer guard, known as Klexters, patrolled in black coveralls or camouflage hunting gear. Some carried shotguns, others deer rifles, and eight of the most trusted held M-16s. As Kommander of the Klexters and Kaptain of the Klarogo – the klavern's inner guard – Tony Carlucci was well-pleased with the arrangement of his troops. He always had known he possessed excellent military skills, even if the Army officers over him had been too stupid and prejudiced against "I-talians" to see it.

The Kludd, or klavern chaplain, leaned forward in his chair and opened the box at his feet. There was a buzz like the noise made by a cheap doorbell. Tony hated this part and had to fight the urge to reach for the Luger on his black utility belt. "Idiot," Tony whispered to himself as the man bare-handed a three-foot rattlesnake from the box and held it over his head like a scepter. All rose.

"Dear Lord," began the Kludd. "We ask your blessing and protection for this gathering, and these defenders of the ancient laws ...."

Tony wondered if Olin Farber – the preacher from a backwoods snake-handling church out from Challabeate Crossroads – milked his babies before sticking his hand in that vented wooden box he carried. Or maybe they were defanged. Whatever the case, watching the serpent slither between the Kludd's bare hands made Tony's skin crawl.

As Kaptain of the Klarogo, Tony wore black gloves and boots, and a police-style Sam Brown belt on the outside of his black satin robe. A red cross on a white field inside a crimson circle was the only color on his uniform. His dark eyes floated white in the holes cut for them in the black veil. In his meaty fist, Tony held the traditional whip – a cat-o-nine-tails. A Confederate officer's saber that had belonged to Jennifer's great-grandfather, General Manfred Ambrose, hung from one side of the cargo belt while a holster containing the Luger was on the other side. Tony always claimed to have taken the pistol off a Nazi officer after heroically piloting his B-17 bomber to a belly-landing in occupied France. Through his derring-do and with a little help from the French Resistance, he got his entire crew safely back to Britain – though the lack of immediate medical attention cost him his leg. Of course, all of that was a lie, like the rest of Tony Carlucci's military record. He had swapped two bottles of Scotch for the gun while serving as an Army Air Corps mechanic in the south of England. The pilot's wings, lieutenant's bar and bronze star, which he flashed with regularity in the decade after World War II, were stolen from a casket bound for Weema, Iowa while Tony was assigned to graves detail during a stretch in the brig. Several months later when he lost his leg during a German air raid on his base, the zipper-like stitching at the terminus of his thigh and his own Purple Heart made him a hero in his own mind. That's when Tony was shipped back to the States – to a military hospital in Gulfport, Mississippi – and his favorite role was born, that of Wounded Flying Ace.

While the war continued, the nurses and the younger and even more naive aides at the military hospital remained easy picking – like firm fruit hanging pink from a giant peach tree planted beside the Gulf. Their skin covered in the fuzz that passes for hair on a woman's body and a salty dew of perspiration; their juice ready to burst free, warm and tangy. Those hailing from little crossroads like Plainville, Kansas; Iron River, Wisconsin; and DeLong, Mississippi – four hundred miles to the north – seemed particularly susceptible to his dusky charm and sometimes rough-around-the-edges ways. Away from home, most of them for the first time – away from papa, preachers and prying neighbors – they were ready to taste something different, something with a little spice to it and the exotic tang of garlic.

Much to Tony's surprise, being one-legged didn't slow his amorous efforts at all. In fact, with most of his eventual conquests, his wooden leg gave him instant credibility as a war hero and a sympathy card that he could use to trump almost any fault or flaw they found in him. Just pull off his prosthesis, hop around a little and rub the scarred stump. Moan about phantom pain – which sometimes was real, but most often not – and talk about how it was all worth it for God, country and momma. Before he knew it, pretty, compassion-filled nurses and innocent young aides were asking to rub the stump for him. And one rub usually led to another, he smiled – thinking of how patriotic and sincere they had been, while his only allegiance was to the Nation of Tony, the Continent of Carlucci, which sat fortified above a sea of fools.

Tony's acting skills were somewhat overwrought, however, having been learned from his showgirl mother backstage at vaudeville houses from Philly to Buffalo, New York to Carbondale, Illinois, to Scranton, Pennsylvania. They couldn't fool men for long, especially those who had seen a con or two before the war or real air combat during it. That insight, and some checking with the military, had cost Tony

Carlucci a sales job at a Gulfport car lot and a teller position at a small bank in Bay St. Louis. Even these years later Tony's thick neck burned when he remembered how the bank manager had humiliated him in front of the rest of the staff – fired him, called him a liar and a disgrace. Four nights later, Tony and a tire iron made sure the banker would never talk that way to anyone else, at least not through his own teeth. And the banker's plump little wife? Behind his veil Tony's smile changed and he felt another kind of warmth, remembering how she had begged then screamed. But a quick right hook, just like his father had taught him, turned her cries into an indecipherable whimper as her jaw separated from the rest of her face and she crumbled into the corner, spilling blood and slobber down the front of her torn nightgown. That's when he put the steel to her. When he was done, he knew she'd be lucky if she could ever conceive.

Now, despite the cool stones and damp air of the hidden basement, Tony felt himself sweating under his dark robes. Nobody embarrasses Anthony Joseph Carlucci and gets away with it, he told himself with a hidden smile, forcing himself to slow his breathing.

A fter the Kludd finished his prayer and put away the snake, the Grand Wizard ordered the Kaptain of the Klargo to escort forward the "honored Klavaliers, travelers by night, guardians of the light." The Wizard instructed Robert Bedford McBride and Tony Carlucci to kneel at the stone altar in the center of the room. Tony made a show of the effort. Open there was the Klan's holy book, the Kloran, and both men placed their right hand on the book and raised their left. The Wizard drew his sword and held it in front of his face and told them to repeat again their blood oath allegiance to the Klan and the white race.

Tony spoke the words with his full lips, his distinctly Mediterranean features hidden beneath his black veil. There had been a time in the early part of the 20th Century when no one with his features or a last name that ended in a vowel would have been welcome in the Klan. As it was, he'd had to renounce the "Papist church and all its evil minions." That was fine with Tony, since he hated the nuns and detested the priests who'd tried to rein him in as a willful child and later as a teenage street tough. In any case, the post-World War II Ku Klux was interested in only one thing – eliminating or at least controlling the Civil Rights Movement. Nearly anyone who shared that goal was welcome to wear the robes, and the handful who were willing to go beyond rhetoric to direct, and if necessary, deadly action could rise quickly in the post-war Klan. Even a well-known liar, womanizer, wife-beater and hard-drinking barroom brawler with a name that ended in "i."

The Grand Wizard touched each man on the shoulder with the flat of his sword. "Arise brave Klavalier Knights," said Wizard Milton Handley. "And know that we all are here to serve you in your gallant quest for the salvation of the white race."

CHAPTER 13

Cutter's painting job ran out at the end of the day Thursday. Since I'd left Daddy's farm and quit the paper, we both found ourselves temporarily out of work. The start of two-a-day football practices still was a couple of weeks away and the start of school two weeks past that. If it started on time. And who knew what would happen with Cattahatchie High? Governor Weathers' lawyers still were battling Mr. Burke in court.

So, Cutter and I were awakened by the sun in the unusual position of having no place we had to be on a Friday morning.

I crawled out of my sleeping bag and staggered to The Well. The rocky surface was hard on even young joints when it came to sleeping. I stretched out and dipped my face into the cold, clear water, then splashed some in my hair and onto my back.

"Mornin'," I said to Cutter as he rolled over next to the fire pit.

"Mornin'."

Cutter and I had talked little since Tuesday night when I told him I'd resigned from the job I loved at *The Current-Leader*. He thought I gave way too much control of my life to the MacAllisters, and I was sure that the movie-star handsome Cutter Carlucci – a collegiate All-American in waiting – could not possibly understand what it meant for a scrawny, third-team wide receiver and clipboard carrier to land a girl like Patti. Every time we tried to talk the conversation seemed to circle back to some form of that discussion. We both were tired of it.

"You want to go get some breakfast at The Cotton?" I asked.

"Brother Daddy hasn't put The Cotton off limits as a den of race-mixers?"

As a matter of fact, the Reverend Dr. C.E. MacAllister had suggested at Wednesday night's prayer meeting that those who want to "walk in the way of righteousness" should not frequent businesses that continued to advertise in *The Current-Leader*, but I didn't want to get into that with Cutter.

"You think Brother Mac owns me? Well, he don't," I told him.

Cutter sat up and rolled his neck atop his powerful shoulders. "Aw'right then. Let's go eat."

I t was 8:20 when the tires of Cutter's Jeep rolled onto the square. *The Thomas Crown Affair* was on the marquee at The Rebel Theater. As we circled toward Commerce Street, we saw the crowd gathered between the front entrance of the courthouse and *The Current-Leader* building. Several sheriff's cars were sitting on the street, their lights flashing, as a work crew finished bolting plywood over the front windows. Another sheet covered the front door. Broken glass glistened at the curb and black soot stained the bricks where the windows and doors had been.

Cutter wheeled into a parking space. I followed him over to one of the patrol cars where Deputy John-Thomas Hinton was propped.

"Hey, Cutter, Nate."

"Hey, John-Thomas," said Cutter. "What happened?"

"Fire bomb through the front window. About four this mornin'."

"How bad?" asked Cutter.

"Pretty bad in the front offices there on the first floor," he said as Cutter studied the men working while Miss Carter sat to the side. Eve Howard was behind the wheel of the beat-up Lincoln and Ridge Bellafont was shooting pictures. Miss Carter was wearing a Van Morrison T-shirt and overalls she had quickly pulled on when she was called in the middle of the night.

"It could have been a lot worse, though," John-Thomas was saying. "Deputy Belle was workin' the night radio shift at the jail. He was standin' out front smokin' when he heard glass break and tires squeal. So, he jumped in a patrol car and came up here. He called in the fire alarm and did some good with a couple of fire extinguishers from the car before the smoke got him."

"Roy's my third cousin on my momma's side," I said. "Is he aw'right?"

"He swallowed some smoke and got some burns on his right arm and hand," said the young deputy. "They admitted him to the hospital but they ain't sendin' him on to Memphis. So it cain't be too bad."

I nodded, relieved.

About that time, my father walked around the corner with two men in dark suits and sunglasses. They might as well have had FBI stenciled on their foreheads. A knot of men standing on the courthouse square booed, and a few loudly cursed Billy Wallace and the agents. Not far away, Sgt. J.B. Benoit stood on the sidewalk in front of the Cattahatchie Valley Bank building. Behind the front window, Governor Weathers looked like a ghost in the glare shining on the glass.

Sheriff Wallace and the FBI agents spoke briefly to Miss Carter, then she wheeled over to one of the workmen loading up their truck. The man dug around in a tool box and handed her a can of something. She shook it and pushed next to one of the plywood panels and began writing there in large orange letters – then on the panel covering the front door and finally the other window.

OPEN! ... 4 ... BUSINESS!

* * *

That night I rode with Patti and her folks to a revival Brother MacAllister was preaching at about 12 miles northeast of DeLong. By then, anyone who cared knew the names of each and every carrier who had delivered *The Current-Leader* on Tuesday night, and the names of a handful of others who had simply shown up at the loading the dock and pitched in. Several – including Dr. Marvin Gilbert, Mr. and Mrs. George Ragland, C.B. Davis and Ruth-Louise Melbourne – were longtime members of First Denomination. Mr. Davis, who owned a garage east of town, and Doctor Gilbert were deacons.

Remembering what Cutter told me the night I left our farmhouse – about him going his own way and keeping his own schedule, I had resisted asking him directly about where he'd gone in the wee hours of Wednesday morning. But word was out on the clothesline telegraph that he'd been among the volunteers. I wasn't surprised. I knew he and Tommy Ray had played a lot of basketball together at the Roseville High gym, and hoped that was all that had caused him to leave the peace and safety of The Well. Someone told Mrs. MacAllister that their cousin's best friend had seen Cutter having lunch with "that woman" at the picnic table on the loading dock the previous Saturday afternoon. But that seemed to be only a rumor. Still, there was something in the way he looked at Miss Carter as she sprayed those defiant words – OPEN! ... 4 ... BUSINESS! – across the front of her charred storefront. I had seen Cutter turn desirous eyes on other women at The Gin, some older than Miss Carter. But what I saw in his eyes at that moment? It was something different. And it worried me for his sake, and the sake of our friendship.

When we got back to DeLong, I kissed Patti good night in the driveway and climbed into my truck. I started north toward Blue Mountain Road and The Well, but turned around in front of Kamp Motors.

Why? I'm not sure.

Curiosity? Concern? Guilt?

It was 11:25 as I drove onto the courthouse square. A deputy sat in a patrol car in front of the K.L. Eustis Insurance Agency. He was writing in a notebook. I waved to him but couldn't make out his face in the shadows. At the foot of Commerce Street and next to the Bilbo Bridge, the front of the jail was lit up but the cells were all dark. A man's arms protruded from one second-floor window, his hands clasped outside the bars.

I turned south on A Street, past Weathers-McLemore Trucking and into the lot between the tall metal silos of the Emerson Grain Storage Company and the Randleman Cotton Warehouse. Turning out my lights, I parked next to the rail above the river and almost directly across from the back of *The Current-Leader* building. From beneath the seat, I pulled the scope of a deer rifle I'd been meaning to remount and focused on the open bay doors. In the large, brightly lit room, I could see the press still was turning while Miss Carter was leading a line of people inserting advertising flyers into stacks of newspapers. Eve Howard was bundling stacks of thirty papers and Ridge Bellafont was carrying them out to the edge of the loading dock. C.B. Davis was loading several stacks into his truck.

It was then that Cutter's Jeep turned into the parking lot. He shook hands with Mr. Davis and climbed the steps up to the dock.

"You need some help?"

"Oh, Cutter!" said Miss Carter without missing a beat in the inserting line. "Hi! I think we have it covered tonight. But I do want to talk to you."

"Shorty, could you take over my spot for a minute?" she called to her production manager over the clatter of the press. He was catching a breather on a bench beside the massive rolls of paper.

"Sure thing, Miss Holly."

"Let's go out in the parking lot so we can hear ourselves think," she said.

I watched from a distance as Cutter followed Miss Carter down the ramp. Of course, I could not hear the words. But I could easily read the body language, which was way too comfortable for my liking.

"Where's Charlie tonight?"

"She's up in my office. Charlie is a little too small and curious to be turned loose in the pressroom during a run."

Miss Carter pushed nearly to the edge of River Street where the rattle of the presses was a rumble and not a roar. "What's she trying to do?" I asked myself as I watched them. "Get Cutter in trouble on purpose?"

She turned to face the breeze that was moving south above the river, then shook her mane of auburn hair before running her fingers through it. Pulling her blouse out from her chest to let in a bit of the air, she said, "This time I'm the one who smells too rancid to be indoors."

"I doubt that," he said, propping against the fender of someone's GMC pickup.

"Well, you shouldn't. Everything in that building, including me, smells like a campfire somebody put out with sour water."

"But you are open 'four' business," he said slowly, drawing the number in the air.

Holly Lee Carter smiled. "Yes, we are. For the time being. And part of that is thanks to you," she said. "We kept missing each other Tuesday night. Every time I came in for another load of papers, you were out running another route.

"You ran three whole routes on the south end of the county. It made a huge difference. I just wanted to tell you how grateful I am."

Cutter looked at the river and then back at the woman in front of him. "I couldn't sleep. I figured I might as well make myself useful."

"You are lousy at taking a compliment. Do you know that?" she said. Cutter shrugged. "Anyway, Cattahatchie Newspapers Incorporated is happy to pay you for your work. If you'll come in and see Miss Frances on Monday, she'll write you a check."

"I didn't do it for the money."

"I know. You did it for Tommy Ray. But there's no reason you shouldn't be paid. At least enough to cover your gas."

"What about tonight?" he asked. "You have enough carriers?"

"Enough to do what we're going to do," Miss Carter told him. "We're only going to deliver the in-town routes tonight and to the racks at businesses right on Highway 27. We're not going to run the rural routes until in the morning."

"Miss Carter, if you'll give me a load of papers I'll go anywhere you need –"

She shook her head. "I know you would, Cutter. So would some other folks. But it's too dangerous. We caught the Klan off-guard the other night. Tonight, they're out there waiting," she said, hugging her arms across her chest. "I can feel it."

Holly was ready for Cutter to argue with all the vehemence of a testosterone-stoked teenager who is sure he is as indestructible as the limestone shelf holding The Well. But there was none of that.

"I think that's a good decision," he said, demonstrating a level of maturity that surprised her. "There might be something you can help me with, though," she said. "I hear from Mr. Davis that you're a pretty good shade-tree mechanic. That you fixed up that Jeep of yours when you were only fourteen."

"I had some help," he said. Nodding toward Holly's battered convertible, he added, "But I'm not a body man, if that's what you're lookin' for."

"It's not. I'm looking for someone who knows all the backyard, behind-the-barn junkyards around here. I need to find my father's car," she said. He looked at her curiously then listened patiently as she told him about her conversation with LeRoy Kamp. "Eve and I spent Monday and a good bit of yesterday calling every junkyard the phone company has listed between here and Tulsa, Oklahoma. Nothing."

Cutter squatted next to the pickup. "So, you think LeRoy is lying to you? Why?"

"LeRoy and I have some history," she said. "Back when I was running pretty wild at The Gin, and before LeRoy went to prison."

"It didn't end well?"

"It ended just fine for me. He was in jail and I was free of him. But his perception may be somewhat different."

"I'll bet," said Cutter. "I've seen him get rough with women at The Gin. We've had to escort him out a couple of times. There's not much I'd put past him."

"Neither would I."

"So, you think he's just jerkin' you around as payback?"

"Maybe."

"Or?"

"Or … I don't know," she said, still not completely trusting Cutter and still not completely sold on her own guesswork "But I do know I need to find that Oldsmobile."

He stood but kept his eyes on hers. "You'll be lucky if it hasn't already been crushed up for scrap or eaten up for parts. That is, if we can find it at all."

"I know. Will you help me?"

Cutter drew in a breath. "Sure. Why not? I can ask around."

Miss Carter pushed her chair forward and took Cutter's hand. She squeezed it. "Thank you."

Through the scope I saw that the smile Cutter gave Holly Lee Carter was as warm and intimate and unguarded as any I'd ever seen cross his face. Seeing it made me so angry that I tossed the scope on the seat and ground the gears as I shoved my old truck into reverse and gunned it away from the railing. Gravel rattled under my fenders as I whipped the truck around and I caught a glimpse of Cutter and Miss Carter looking my way. I didn't care if they saw me, or if they knew I'd been spying on them.

My best friend was betraying the town, the people who had loved and lauded him. And he was betraying me. For that – that? – that woman, that *cripple!*

* * *

For the next couple of days, I kept my distance from Cutter. I was angry and hurt. Besides, who knew how many more people saw him and Holly Lee Carter holding hands right there next to River Street? I didn't want to be caught in the fallout if their relationship – whatever that meant – was exposed and Brother Mac went off like an atom bomb.

On Friday night, I drove south and turned down Pleasant Ridge Road toward our house, but I knew I couldn't go back under that roof. A quarter-mile from the driveway, I hung a right down a field road and parked near Asher Creek under a large oak – the only tree amid one-hundred and twenty-five acres of cotton. On one side of the tree's massive trunk was the nlack, wrought-iron fence that surrounded the Wallace family cemetery. My mother and brother were buried there, and Wallaces all the way back to the 1820s.

I didn't know where I'd be laid to take my final rest, and was too young and naive to care. That night, I slept in the cab of my truck.

Cutter worked his usual all-nighter at The Gin from Saturday into Sunday, so we didn't run across each other again until Sunday night after choir practice when I went back to The Well. He was propped against a rock with a lantern on one side and his shotgun on the other, reading a book about architecture – *Modernist Interpretations of the Roman Arch.*

"Hey," I said, walking up to the pit where a small, low fire burned.

"Hey."

"Am I still welcome here?"

"I told you, Nate. It's not for me to say who's welcome here and who's not. But there's plenty of room."

It irritated me that he didn't ask where I'd been or what I'd been up to the last couple of days. He didn't even mention my tire-spinning, gravel-throwing exit from the riverside parking lot on Friday night. More by way of trying to stimulate conversation than anything else, I said, "Klansmen have been thick as fleas in DeLong this weekend. Comin' in from all over. Did you see 'em?"

"I haven't been in town much the last couple of days."

"They've been marchin' around the square in their robes, carryin' signs, makin' speeches. Handin' out flyers, too," I said, pulling a piece of folded green paper from my hip pocket. It was announcing what was being billed as a "historic" Klan rally on the Oscar Campbell farm northwest of town at 7:30 Monday night. There was a map to the location deep in the countryside northwest of DeLong and a drawing of a hooded Klansman carrying an automatic rifle. The U.S. stars-and-stripes and the Confederate stars-and-bars were crossed behind him. I unfolded it and handed it to Cutter. He looked it over and gave it back. "It's supposed to be the biggest rally the Klux have held in years. I've never been to one, have you?"

Cutter looked at me like a parent might look at child, or maybe more accurately, like an older brother might look at his much younger and more sheltered sibling.

"A few," he said, and I thought he was going to leave it at that, but he didn't. "Tony used to take me to them before I got smart enough to run for the woods or old enough to look him in the eye and say no."

"Then I guess you're not goin' to the rally?"

"No. I guess not."

"You're gonna be lonesome then, 'cause everybody is going," I told him. "I ran into Dodge this afternoon. He's goin'. So is Jimmy Garner. There's gonna be music and everything. I'm takin' Patti. It's supposed to be a heckuva show, if nothin' else."

For a long moment he looked at me. "I'll pass," he said and went back to reading the textbook in his lap.

CHAPTER 14

A trickle of sweat slid down the back of Ridge Bellafont's neck and beneath the collar of one of the French-cut shirts he had shipped to him from a shop on Magazine Street in New Orleans. Nothing surprising about that, since the old Chevrolet station wagon driven by *The Current-Leader's* longtime photographer didn't have the best air- conditioning. Especially when moving slowly down a dirt road baking in the late afternoon light of a Monday in early August. At 6:30, the temperature was still in the low 90s. What surprised Ridge was that the droplets moving from his perfectly groomed hair and sliding onto his back felt cold.

Cold like winter raindrops. Cold like fear. Cold like, "Eve, I think this was a big mistake. I can't believe I let you talk me into this."

"Calm down, Ridge," Eve said from beneath a tarp spread over her and a gamut of photographic equipment in the back of the station wagon. "I'm the one who's about to melt. Can't we go any faster?"

"No," said Ridge, testy. "We can't. I just hope we don't run out of gas. This old needle is pointing at E-eeek!"

After fifteen minutes of winding northwest of DeLong through dirt lanes and low hills, Ridge was locked into a line of vehicles a quarter of a mile long – cars, pickups, a couple of logging trucks and even a mule-drawn hay wagon were waiting to turn across a cattle guard gate into a large up-sloping pasture. In the distance, a long flatbed truck sat atop a hill in the shadow of an enormous wooden cross, wrapped in burlap. A four-piece country band sounded tinny in the distance.

"I can't believe this," said Eve. "It's like a concert or a fair."

"One put on by the devil," said Ridge. "If Holly ever finds out I did this –"

"Stop worrying about it. She's not going to find out. I told you, this is strictly for my personal portfolio. Besides, what could happen?" she asked. "You said yourself there would be cops and FBI agents all over the place – observing."

"That's what I'm afraid of," he said, "that if something happens, they'll observe and not intervene."

"Ridge, don't be such a ninny. You have as much talent as any photographer I've ever met, but you're still shooting for a small-town paper. What's missing about you is a spirit of adventure," Eve said with all of the certainty of a twenty-four-old raised in the arms of privilege. "Nothing is going to happen, except that I may die of heatstroke under here."

"If some of these old cobs get hold of yo' black bootie, you'll wish you had died of heatstroke."

"Oh, Ridge, you are such a worrier. But I love you."

"Then show your love by shutting up and lying still," he said. "We're getting close to the gate."

Eve Howard ducked her head, her blouse already soaked in the thick, dark air beneath the tarp. After Holly told her that Ridge would be shooting the rally and that, "There is absolutely no way in this world you can be anywhere near that place," Eve had told Holly she was going to stay at the newspaper and develop film. But this was a once-in-a-lifetime opportunity, a chance to photograph the actual KKK in action at what was being billed as the "largest Klan rally in the history of North Mississippi" – which might make it the largest in the history of the universe, thought Eve. Her mouth went into overdrive as she reasoned with, pleaded with and cajoled Ridge into taking her with him. Now her mind raced with possibilities and anticipation. After all, Holly, her mentor, had honed her chops as a photographer by jumping out of airplanes, riding with cops and finally going into battle with the 7th Air-Cav. What a coup it would be for a black female photographer to have shots of a Mississippi Klan rally in her portfolio.

This could be a career-maker, thought Eve, breathing in the heavy air under the tarp. *This is why I came to this god-awful place.*

"We're at the gate, and they've got guards," said Ridge. "So be very still and very quiet."

As Ridge made the turn he felt some reassurance, some comfort seeing Sheriff Wallace leaning against a patrol car a few yards down the road. A man in a dark suit was standing with him and photographing every car entering the rally. Less reassuring – in fact, downright unnerving considering his cargo – were the robed and hooded Klansmen checking cars as they entered. Two Klexters in white robes with red sashes wore pistol belts and sabers in plain view, and a black-robed member of the Klargo sat horseback with a shotgun propped on his thigh like a prison gun bull.

The Klexter looked in. "I'm Ridge –"

"We know who you are. The Klan knows all," said the man behind the veil. His breath smelled of peppermint and gin. "And we know the rag you work for, too. We're gonna put it out of business, one way or another."

"Well," Ridge sighed nervously, "maybe so. But for now we're still printing. And I'm here to take pictures."

"Wasn't this yo' momma's car?" asked the other guard.

"Yes."

"It looks like a growed man could do better than drivin' his dead momma's car. But you always was a momma's boy, weren't you, Ridge-y?" The man waited but

Ridge kept his eyes forward and didn't respond. Eve clenched her fists, showing the anger that Ridge couldn't. Then, "What all you got under that tarp?" the Klexter asked, and Eve's breath caught in her throat.

Ridge cleared his throat. "Photographic equipment. Lights, tripods, cameras. That sort of thing."

"Why don't you open that tailgate and let us take a look?"

Ridge felt his heart skip a beat.

"Yeah," jeered the other Klexter. "Ridge opens his tailgate for ever'body else. Why not us?"

"I bet he's got 'Open 4 Business' written on his ass, just like the paper," laughed the other.

Ridge felt the heat rise in his neck and his face even though his hands suddenly were cold. Eve readied her legs to kick and her hands to scratch as one car horn in the line went off, then another. And another.

"Forget it, Rob," said the first guard. "Sister Ridge is harmless. Go on."

Before the second Klexter could object, Ridge accelerated under the stars-and-bars of a Confederate flag that hung from the top of the gate.

They were in Klan territory now.

* * *

Holly pushed down the ramp from the side porch at Wolf's Run and headed for the car and the Klan rally. If she had to cover this – *this? disgrace!* – she at least wanted to be comfortable. A loose denim skirt, a blousy peasant top with embroidery in front and white sandals fit the bill. During ten years on the West Coast, Holly had become very much a casual California girl. She was tired of tight-fitting heels that made her feet swell, hose, lipstick and made-up eyes – all of the expected trappings of a "proper small-town businesswoman." She loaded her hips onto the bench seat of the Lincoln. Lifting one leg into the car and then the other, she noted that the polish on her toes was faded and smiled at her own vanity, even when it came to limbs paralyzed for nearly four years. But she'd had little time to deal with such superficial details, even if she'd wanted to. She, Eve, Ridge, Shorty Rodgers and a couple of others had slept in *The Current-Leader* building Friday night, both as cursory watchmen and so they could begin delivering papers to the rural routes at first light, which they did. Despite receiving hundreds of cancellation requests in the wake of Wednesday's integrated edition – particularly from the county's most rural areas – Holly had made the decision that she would drop no subscribers. At least for the time being they would continue to deliver to everyone who'd been a subscriber prior to Wednesday, hoping they'd eventually change their mind. Running those long, dusty routes had taken most of Saturday; and she had spent all day Sunday and into that night at the office working on stories to fill the gaps left by her decimated staff. Eve had worked right alongside her, *bless her heart*, thought Holly. Some wounds between them were still there but they're healing, she thought, thankful that Eve hadn't put up a big fight about not going to the Klan rally.

As she drove, Holly realized how exhausted she was – not merely from the events of the last few days, but from everything since she'd returned to DeLong. She tried to keep her mind in the moment. Deal with one issue at a time, but she could not help but worry about the future of the newspaper and her own. So, she had played her guitar deep into Monday's early hours, running the numbers again and again in her mind. Unless things turned around in a hurry, she could keep the paper going for about four more weeks, six at the outside.

A t the foot of Blue Mountain, Holly had to slow the big car to a crawl as she prepared to make the turn onto the bridge. Just as her father should have done that rainy night. Suddenly, Holly's right arm flew forward on the hand control, jamming on the brakes. Cutter dropped his left foot hard onto the Jeep's brake. The two vehicles stopped nose to nose, inches apart. Once an instant of surprise washed out of Holly's face, she laughed. Cutter smiled, laughed, then backed the Jeep onto the narrow cut of road that led to The Well. Holly stopped the Lincoln on the bridge and Cutter walked over as Charlie sniffed the air and wagged.

"Sorry about that. It's a blind turn," Cutter said from behind his aviator shades.

"I know, I made it many times when I was your age," said Holly, lifting Charlie out of her lap. "*Tais-toi, mon amour.*"

The little dog settled on the seat.

"I was headed up to Wolf's Run to see if you were home."

"Don't tell me you've already found Daddy's car."

"Maybe. At least, I think I know where to look."

"How'd you do it so fast?"

"It's a matter of knowing the right back doors to knock on. And knowing which Kamp Motors employees have an axe to grind with LeRoy."

"Ahhh, I see. So, where's the car?"

"The fellow I talked to told me he saw it hauled away by an old, beat-up wrecker with the words 'Conway Tow & Salvage, Moore's Bridge, Alabama' on the door. The driver seemed to know LeRoy pretty well."

"Looks like LeRoy's still the same ol' lyin' son-of-bitch he always was."

"That's not news to anybody around here."

"I guess not," said Holly, giving herself a moment for a flash of temper to cool. She wanted to stick a cattle prod down the front of LeRoy's jeans. Then she refocused on Cutter. "Does this Conway guy still have Daddy's car?"

"I think so. I called over there this afternoon and told him I was lookin' for parts for a '63 Dodge, a '61 Ford and '65 Olds. I didn't want him to get suspicious about the Olds."

"Smart."

"Anyway, he said he had several Fords but only one '65 Olds."

"*Fan*-tastic!" Holly enthused.

Cutter smiled. "I'm glad I was able to find it. But look, I told the guy I wanted the steering column and some other stuff from the Olds, for sure. I asked him to hold 'em for me. But he said he runs a first-come-first-served business."

"So when can we go?"

"We?" Cutter asked, surprised.

"I don't know how to take a steering column apart. You do. I'll be happy to pay you for your time," said Holly.

Cutter propped against the iron bridge railing and said nothing. His shoulders were flat, his chest was carved and his jeans were tight. He reminded her of a young Paul Newman, but a much bigger man.

"Aw'right," he finally said. "I don't have any for-sure work lined up until next week. But I wouldn't wait too long."

"How about Wednesday?"

"That'll work."

"I'd go tomorrow, but with our staff down to the bone as it is, I can't afford to be away from the paper," she told him, looking at her watch. "And speaking of the paper, I've got to go. I don't want to miss any of the *speechifyin'* out at the Campbell place."

Cutter grunted. "You're coverin' the Klan rally? The same people who tried to torch your building?"

"I know. It makes me mad, too," she said, putting the convertible into gear. "But I don't have anyone else to send. And, no matter how repulsive I find it, whenever hundreds of people gather in Cattahatchie County for anything, it's news."

Cutter studied Holly Lee Carter for a moment. "You're not exactly Miss Popularity with the Klux, you know."

She laughed and Cutter found himself liking the sound of it. "I appreciate your concern. But the Klan has been very public about this rally. There are going to be reporters and TV cameras, deputies and FBI men all over that hill tonight. Even by Klan standards, it would be bad P.R. to pull a paralyzed woman out of her car and tar-and-feather her while the cameras roll."

"Yes, ma'am. But there's a lot of empty road between here and the Campbell farm," he said. That thought had crossed Holly's mind as well, but she'd put it aside because she needed to. Cutter spoke again – "If everybody in the county is goin', I guess I might as well go, too. You mind if I ride with you?"

Holly put the car in park and smiled at him.

"You're a good guy, Cutter," she said. "And I appreciate the offer. You know as well as I do, you're already pushing the envelope by helping deliver papers. But this would be pokin' the Klan in the eye with a sharp stick. You could bring a world of trouble on yourself by being seen with me out there."

Cutter liked Holly Carter's smile. It was wide and white between full, bow-shaped lips. It came easily and suited her. He even liked the small lines her smile created at the corners of eyes – those green eyes! – that had been places, seen things, survived things he could barely imagine, though he had tried after hearing her brief, private description of what she'd been through in Vietnam. To see men die all around you … then have to sit there against a tree all through a night … already shot … wondering whether you'd bleed out before help could come, if it came … probably already wondering if your legs would ever work again, *if* you managed to somehow get out of the fix the platoon was in … praying … making promises … trying to hang onto hope … knowing you might be killed at any moment … or need to kill yourself. It was the kind of courage Cutter hoped he had. That most men thought they had. Or told themselves they had. But Cutter was mature enough to know that until you're in the blood and the shit, the bullets are singing, men are screaming and body parts are flying this way and that, you never really know. But Holly Lee Carter had been there. She knew. And she still had that great, genuine, easy smile. And those green eyes!

Holly watched Cutter walk around the front of the Lincoln, open the passenger door and get in.

"Cutter, you shouldn't do this," she told him, no longer smiling.

He closed the door. "Neither should you," he said. "It's just dumb luck – a deputy needin' a smoke – that the whole newspaper didn't burn down the other night. Tony and those crazies he runs with aren't kiddin'."

"I know that," she told him. "But this is my job. I don't have a choice. You do."

"Okay, I've got a choice. And I've made it."

Holly held is gaze. "Are you sure?"

"You want me to drive?"

Holly shook her head, saying, "No," and dropped the shifter into gear as she hit the gas.

CHAPTER 15

R idge Bellafont pulled the station wagon into a long row of cars halfway up the green hill. The sun had slipped down behind a stand of maples, but Ridge and Eve still were sweating as if it were noon.

"That was a little closer than I would have liked," said Ridge.

"Do you think they'd have really hurt us?"

"This isn't a movie, Malibu girl. It's not your momma's TV show. People don't get killed one week and show up again on the next episode," he said, staring up the hill where a large crowd was gathering. "When they shoot you here, you stay dead."

Cecil Weathers was among those already seated on the long flatbed truck. He looked at a pocket watch he pulled from his suit vest. An old man was walking between the rows of cars carrying a wooden box containing straw and mason jars filled with white lightning. Klexters directed traffic into semi-orderly rows like volunteers at a high school football game. Around the edges of the field, the black-clad members of the Klargo sat on black saddles on horses covered in their own shiny black robes. Most of the Klargo propped shotguns or deer rifles on their thighs.

"I've got to admit, those guys in black are a little spooky," said Eve, peeking out from under the tarp.

"They're more than a little spooky. They're the real hard cases. The Klan's version of the Gestapo," he told her. "Now stay down."

H olly turned the Lincoln under the Confederate flag. The Klexter on the driver's side looked into the car. He stared at Cutter then propped on the door frame so he could get a better angle on the opening in Holly's blouse.

"You don't belong here," said the man by her door.

"Thank God for that," said Holly.

"You always did have a smart mouth. Thought you were too good for all of the boys in high school."

"Wrong, Toby," she said, even after all these years recognizing the voice of Toby McLemore, whose family partnered with Weathers in a trucking firm. The same sandpaper voice that asked her for dates throughout her junior year, and had gotten very ugly when she'd declined. "I just thought I was too good for you."

Cutter pushed his sunglasses up the bridge of his nose and fought a smile. "What are you laughin' at?" asked the Klexter by the passenger door.

"Not a thing," said Cutter, recognizing the voice of Noble Russell, a farmer and CHS booster. His son would be a sophomore linebacker in the fall. "I'm just enjoyin' a late ride in the country."

"Yeah, well, you ought to be more choosey about who you ride around with," Russell told him. "You don't want people to start wonderin'?"

"Wonderin' what?"

"Wonderin' if you know which side your bread is buttered on, and who's doin' the butterin'," said McLemore. "This town's done a lot for you."

Cutter looked at McLemore but said nothing. Holly wondered what was going on behind Cutter's Ray-Bans. As they passed through DeLong she had again encouraged him to reconsider. "Let me drop you off at The Cotton," she'd said.

"No, I'm good," he'd told her. "I already ate. But we're gonna miss the opening act if you don't keep drivin'."

Holly had smirked at his at his bravado, which she knew was not false, but perhaps not well thought out. Now, she said to the guard, "Can we go?"

"Yeah, go ahead. Your *fag*-tographer is already here."

Holly did a double take. "You know, Toby, it's good that I know you're only joking since it's impossible to take seriously a man who wears a bed sheet and a dunce cap in broad daylight."

"You're going to take us seriously before we're done," he snarled. "We got somethin' for you."

"Oh, yeah?" said Holly. "I've got something for you, too."

Holly rested her elbow on the door frame and gave the Klexter a one-fingered salute.

"You bit –"

Holly gunned the big convertible out into the field, letting it fishtail, a spray of grass and dirt showering the men. The horse under the Klargo guard reared. Billy Wallace and the FBI agent who'd been watching the exchange from across the road, looked at each other trying to suppress smiles. When the horse settled under the black-robed Klansman, he started to go after Holly. Then, remembering the proximity of the sheriff, he glanced at the lawman through the cutouts in his veil. The sheriff's face was serious now as he shook his head. The Klargo seethed beneath his robes but calmed the horse and stayed put.

Holly swung the car into a parking spot as directed. Behind the towering cross and the flatbed, above the ridgeline and the maples, the sky was lavender and cream. A sweet concoction melting in the dusk. In the sweltering twilight, Ridge Bellafont checked his camera bag.

"Ridge," said Eve from beneath the tarp. "I'm sorry about the way they talked to you back there."

"It's not your fault, sweetie. Besides, I'm used to it. I've lived with it all my life."

"Test … test." Some bozo in a hood was checking the microphone on the flatbed. "Test … one, two."

"Ridge, can I ask you something – personal?"

"Why, sure, sweetie. Like most ever'one else in DeLong, my life's an open book. Sometimes you have to read between the lines to get it, that's all."

Eve felt awkward but – "The Klan hates black people. But I always thought they also hated, well –"

"Ho-mo-sexuals?"

"Yes."

"Well, here's how it is," said Ridge. "The Bellafonts and DeLongs, the Kamps, Carters, Cutters, Ambroses and Wellinghams have roots in this county deeper than all but the oldest oaks. I'm probably kin in one way or another to nearly everyone on this hill. I know where the line is with these people, and I don't cross it."

"What does that mean?"

"It means, I don't hang my lace undies out on the line in DeLong. If I want to do that, I go to Naw'lins or to Greenwich Village enjoy the clubs and the sort of genteel male companionship that is in my nature to prefer," he told her. "Get down! Here comes one of them."

Holly had been a tall, shapely head-turner since she first became a teen, so she was used to people – particularly men – looking her way wherever she went. Now with the wheelchair, she was used to being stared at for another reason. But this was different. Now she was uncomfortably aware of the number of eyes set in hard faces turned toward her – and Cutter. There was a heat in those eyes that made her uneasy, like coals being passed too close to her skin. If Cutter felt it, he said nothing.

Patti and I had gotten to the rally early because she wanted to get good seats for this circus. But she was as interested in the crowd as the flatbed dais, chatting out the window to passersby as if at a church social. She saw Miss Carter's Lincoln pull into a spot farther down the hill and stop.

"Lookee there!" Patti said to me, pointing down the hill. "Holly the Whore is here. And look who's with her."

I did look and saw Cutter seated casually on the passenger side, sunglasses on, one big, tanned arm resting on the door, the other stretched out along the seat back. Not touching Miss Carter, but almost. "Ohhh, *shit!*" I sighed.

"Has that cunt been coming around The Well?" she demanded.

"No," I told her, still sometimes shocked by how vulgar and vicious Patti could be in her condemnation of lesser mortals. "Not that I know of."

"When I heard Cutter was helping her deliver that rag, I knew something had to be going on between them," she said imperiously as if every thought she'd ever had about Miss Carter had been confirmed. "Naturally, she'd go after Cutter. She's probably paying him in blow jobs. I've heard that was her specialty."

"Patti!"

"Of course, I don't know why anyone should be surprised," she kept on. "A whore and the son of an *I*-talian drunkard. Birds of a rotten feather if you ask me."

Before I could throw my brain and mouth into neutral, I blurted, "It's funny you don't call Cutter that to his face. In fact, you're the first one on the field after a game to hug his neck, and tell him how wonderful he was."

"I'm a cheerleader," said Patti, her back stiffening, her perfect little chin jutting out. "It's my duty to support the team."

"Is that why you signed his yearbook 'someone who admires you more than you know! X-O-X-O'? Yeah, I saw it!"

Patti's face flushed. "Nate Wallace, I don't like your tone or your insinuation," she told me and reached for the door handle. She slid out and I knew I'd gone too far, pricking a nerve of hypocrisy that always was just below the surface with Patti, but also dangerously close to the bone. I hopped out on my side and ran around to catch her.

"Honey, stop!" I said, getting in front of her. "I'm sorry."

"You should be," she snapped.

I reached to take her hand but she stepped back as if I were on fire. She whirled and started down the hill to where Brother Mac and several First Denomination deacons were leaning against his car. Though C.E. MacAllister's sympathies ran the same as those of the men on the flatbed, even he wouldn't allow himself to be photographed with Klansmen in their robes. I didn't follow Patti because I didn't want a fight in front of her father. Besides, while Patti's temper often burned white hot, it usually burned fast. I knew it was better to leave her be for a few minutes than try to argue with her.

On cue, all the cars along the front row by the flatbed turned on their headlights, illuminating the politicians and Klan leaders seated on the long trailer. From the microphone, the Kludd of the Cattahatchie Klavern intoned, "Let us pray."

I t's almost dark," said Ridge Bellafont. "I'm going to work the crowd for some photos. You can peek out and shoot some stuff, but stay under that tarp. And promise me you'll stay in the car."

"Will do," said Eve.

"Say it."

"Say what?"

"Say you promise you won't leave this car."

"Okay, Okay, Ridge. I promise."

In the mirror, Ridge Bellafont looked at Eve's smooth ebony face framed in the blackness under the tarp. "I wish I hadn't brought you here," he said and stepped out with his camera bag. "Please, stay down."

On the other side of the field, Holly made notes on a steno pad in her lap. Though for the most part Cutter stared straight ahead without comment, it was as if the air pressure on her right was different than in the surrounding atmosphere. She could feel it against her arm and the side of her face. He had a maturity, a simple morality and sense of loyalty that some men work all their lives to achieve. Cutter's presence on the other side of the bench seat was making concentration difficult, but she forced herself to pay attention even though she could have almost written the story from memory. Other than J.B. Benoit's announcement that he was running for sheriff, and his promise to maintain "the safe, orderly, traditional way of life dear to all real Cattahatchie Countians," the speeches by politicians and the harangues by robed Klansmen were right out of the 1940s.

Twenty years later, as she looked over the long blue hood of the Continental, she could see herself sitting straddle of the hood ornament on her father's '37 Buick. On one side her dad stood, scribbling into a notebook, nearly grinding his pipe stem in two; on the other, Tom, a handsome teenager, stared, transfixed by the ghostly parade and the hate-scalded rhetoric.

Two decades had passed but as in '49, Cecil Weathers' speech was the climax of the evening. Love his *speechifying* or despise it, Mississippi's former governor was an arm-waving, foot-stomping spellbinder in the mold of Bilbo, Huey Long or, some would say, Adolf Hitler. Weathers himself credited the tent revival preachers on whom he was weaned – a barefoot, overall-clad, pig farmer's son in northeast Cattahatchie County. But by the time he was twenty-one he had a cheap seersucker suit and a following for his toxic mix of white populism, race-baiting and Old Testament us-against-the-heathens religion. He learned to use the modulation of his voice to hammer home his points and became a protégé of longtime U.S. Senator Julius DeLong; and he used his corn-fed charm to marry the senator's simple-minded daughter. When the late senator's son died in the crash of his private plane in 1947, Weathers effectively took control of the massive wealth of sprawling Chalmette Plantation. After his wife died four years later in a riding accident, Weathers had complete control – making him one of the wealthiest men in the state, even the whole South.

Sadly almost unbelievably in 1969 Weathers was still using the steel in his powerful voice to pound rusty nails about "segregation ... mud people ... the decline of American morality ... state's rights ... nullification ... (and) the natural order of God's universe."

Idiot," whispered Eve as Weathers went on and she slipped out of the window of the station wagon. Getting any decent shots laying on her belly in the car was going to be impossible. The angle was bad, and besides, the drive in on the dirt road had left the car glass thick with dust. This was a once-in-a-lifetime chance, and Eve Howard was determined not to let it slip away. Besides, it was dark now and the only real light was focused on the flatbed. So was everyone's attention.

Eve crouched beside the car, cradling her Nikon and the long lens. She happened to be wearing dark clothing and, for once in Mississippi, her skin tone was an asset as she kept to the deep shadow between vehicles – popping up for a quick click-click, click-click- click of the camera's rapid-fire shutter. And she wasn't even breaking her promise to Ridge she told herself. She hadn't left the car. She was right there, close enough to touch it. She smiled thinking about Holly's outright refusal to allow her "anywhere near that rally" and Ridge's Nervous Nelly attitude. Well, she was near it now, inside it, in fact. And it hadn't been that difficult.

"The Invisible Empire, my ass," she whispered – marveling that anyone could take seriously these … these? … *Rednecks in drag,* she thought, and had to stifle a laugh.

Yet, Eve reminded herself to stay aware of her surroundings. The moon was on the rise behind her, but by the time it ate into her sanctuary of shadows, she'd be back in the car, back under the tarp. Hot and sweaty, but safe and sound, and in possession of the sort of pictures that could launch a serious career in photo-journalism.

Suddenly, Eve heard someone walking behind the row of cars. She dropped to the ground beside the station wagon, her heart suddenly pounding. Her survival instinct knew more than her intellect would let her deal with. If it was one of those guys in black, the Klargo, she sensed she could be in real trouble. But when she glanced over her shoulder she saw it was only some blonde girl passing by smoking a cigarette. Eve sniffed. No, she realized, the girl was smoking a joint, and almost laughed. Pausing near the back of the station wagon, the girl nervously looked around, but thankfully the girl really didn't look into the deep shadow where Eve had pressed herself. After a moment, the girl walked on and Eve breathed a long sigh of relief.

Eve refocused her camera and her attention to the flatbed truck at the top of the hill and the huge cross beside it.

Sheriff Wallace turned slowly through the rows of cars in his cruiser. He was looking at everything and nothing. Did he expect to spot Dynamite Bob McBride or his nephew leaning against some old Ford. He had no evidence, nothing solid, but he was as sure as sunrise that the sociopath still was in Cattahatchie County. Making his plans. Maybe making his bombs. Billy Wallace had passed out fliers to practically every business in the county where a man like that was likely to show up. Nothing. But McBride was here. The sheriff could feel it. Maybe right on this same hilltop. The truth was, McBride could be five feet away, under his Klan robes, grinning at him. The thought made the sheriff's hand clench on the steering wheel as he kept one ear to the speeches and one to the low buzz of chatter on the police radio.

Cecil Weathers pulled a checkered, five-and-dime handkerchief from the jacket of an off-the-rack suit and mopped his shining face. He checked his pocket watch again before saying, "Now I don't want to keep you hard workin' folks too long. Sunrise comes early for a workin' man. But I do want to you to tell you folks about this ol' coon dog I've got. He's lazy and slow, and he can be a little snarly at times, but I love him nonetheless. I swear before God, I do," Weathers went on, his baritone rising and falling like that of a singer. "But I don't pull up a chair and have him eat at my dinner table!"

"Amen!" Laughter.

"No, sir!" Laughter.

"'Course not!"

"I don't have my ol' coon dog dine with me at The Jeff Davis Hotel. I don't expect him to use public restroom facilities next to me. Drink from the same water fountain. *Or vote!* And sure as kingdom come, I do not expect him to sit next to my two little grandbabies in a public school classroom," Weathers roared. "It would merely distract my grandchildren and bore my dog!"

The crowd whooped and hollered, even though many had heard the string of ugly analogies numerous times. Ridge worked the row of Klansmen in front of the truck, finding the perfect angle to frame Weathers among a sea of pointy hats. Eve fired away from a distance with her motor drive

... click/click/click/click ....

Sheriff Wallace stopped his car behind the Lincoln convertible and got out.

"Miss Carter," he said, tipping his hat.

"Cutter."

They nodded – "Sheriff."

"Is Nate behavin' himself?" asked my father, not the sheriff. "I've caught glimpses of him since he moved out."

"As best I can tell," said Cutter. "We don't check in with each other. I've told him he ought to go on home, but he's bein' pretty stubborn."

"Until we catch that McBride character, it's probably just as well," said Billy Wallace. "We live a good ways out in the country, and I can't afford to station a deputy at my house twenty-four hours a day. If McBride set his mind to it, it'd be easy pickin's."

Then to Holly – "Same thing goes for Wolf's Run. You might consider moving into town until we get through this patch."

"The governor is in fine form tonight," she said.

"He should be. He's been givin' this same speech since 1932. That coon dog he keeps talking about should be six times dead by now. Don't change the subject. I'm serious, Miss Carter. I can't guarantee your safety out at Wolf's Run."

"No one is asking you to," she told him. "I appreciate your concern, but I'm a grown woman. Any luck with the mason jar fragments you found at the paper?"

"No. No prints. But it was strictly amateur hour. Probably some ol' boys who were mad about you running the Banks story. They got liquored up and decided to waste a couple of jars of moonshine."

"Mr. Wallace, how do you know McBride wasn't in on it?" asked Cutter.

"That's easy, son. *The Current-Leader* building is still standing."

Cutter and the sheriff shared concerned gaze, but if the paper's editor-in-chief saw, she gave no acknowledgement, and continued to focus on Weathers and her notes.

N ow folks, as much as I love my ol' coon dog, if he turned up rabid tomorrow, you know what I'd have to do," Weathers asked the crowd.

"Put him down!" someone hollered. "I'd shoot him!" yelled someone else.

"Now then, there is a terrible disease movin' amongst our colored folks these days. It's carried by Jews, common'nists, our own federal gov'ment people and impure hippies come back from Cali-*fornicate*. It's worse than rabies. It's called in-*tee*-gration!

"Taking up the sword should always be the last resort. And while I would never encourage violence by one human being against another, I am saying you must search your heart for the strength to defend the sanctity of your white, Christian home, your community and the way of life our forefathers fought and bled and died to keep. His will be done!"

That was the signal to touch a torch to the cross. A *whoooooosh* roared up into the night sky as a volcano of flame erupted from the ground and leaped up the kerosene-soaked burlap. The Klansman who ignited it had to dive to the ground to keep from being caught up in the flames. Then there it stood, the most sacred symbol of the church, the Christ – a symbol most have been raised to worship and revere, twisted into a symbol of fear and subjugation.

A single bagpiper in Klan robes stepped to the microphone and the instrument's mournful wail sent a long shudder of disgust through Holly. Behind her heart, she felt a tremble of fear, but there was no way she would let it out. Not here, not now anyway. Not for any of these robed monsters to see.

C lick/Click/Click/Click/Click … Eve snapped away as the burning cross cast long yellow light down the hill. It was a fire that made her cold inside, and she noticed her hands were trembling. Things had turned spookier than she expected. Then a horse's bray startled her so badly that she nearly jumped to her feet. She caught herself, but peeked over the car hood and saw one of the black-robed horsemen shining in the fire glow. He was coming up the row in front of her.

The Klargo … they're the Klan's version of the Gestapo … the real hard cases … Eve gasped. She peeked again. Another guard was walking his horse up the row behind her. *Did they see me? No. No! They couldn't have* ... Eve told herself. But there was nowhere to run and no way to get back into the car.

They were coming closer and she was boxed in. Every story about the Klan she had ever heard from her grandparents or mother, seen on television or read in the newspaper rushed into her mind. As did Ridge's warning, *This isn't a movie, Malibu girl.* ... *When they shoot you here, you stay dead.* ... There was only one thing to do. Eve flattened herself on the grass and rolled onto her back. It was a tight fit – her breasts brushing against the car's undercarriage – but she managed to squeeze beneath it.

As the Klargo reached the back of the Chevy, she pulled her camera bag under the car with her.

O ver the piper's amplified wail Holly, Cutter, my father the sheriff – all of us really – heard shouts from the road and engines cranking. FBI agents in dark suits and white shirts were running out of the nearby woods carrying big cameras, directional microphone dishes and sniper rifles as if a platoon of bears or tigers had been turned loose up in the pines. Some people noticed and started pointing. Others started to laugh. Police radios suddenly were alive with chatter. In the background of the urgent radio call Billy Wallace could hear the town's fire alarm going off. Some of the members of DeLong's volunteer fire department already were running to their cars.

Sheriff Wallace reached into his cruiser, snatched up his microphone. "Ten-four, Base. John-Thomas, don't wait. Call in the fire departments from New Albany and Booneville. I'm on my way."

Holly twisted in her seat. "Sheriff, what's happened?" she called over her shoulder as my father got into his car and hit the red lights.

"Sounds like Dynamite Bob just hit the funeral home in Roseville. Most of a block of houses and stores are on fire."

Holly and Cutter stared at each other, their lips parted as if to speak but saying nothing. Then Holly reached for the ignition key.

C ars were spinning their tires as they swung out of the rows and headed down the hill toward the one small gate. But none of the Klansmen broke their Nazi-like salute. As the pine beneath the burlap crackled and hissed, the piper continued to play – the Kluxers making a fine show of ignoring the news vans racing away on the gravel road.

"They knew this was going to happen," said Cutter, disgusted. "They timed it."

"Yes, I suspect they did," said Holly, trying to rein in her own anger and revulsion ... and fear. "There's Ridge!"

She flashed her lights at him, bumped her horn. He jogged over, his shirt and round face slick with perspiration.

"You heard what happened?" she asked.

"Yes. It's awful. I've got to stop at Peterson's Grocery for gas, but I'll be right behind you," he told her. "I got good stuff tonight, Honey Girl. I did us proud."

"You always do, Ridge. I'll see you in town."

"Right-oh," he replied and hurried toward his car on the far side of the pasture.

I n the confusion and noise, no one noticed the pops from the .22 caliber automatic in the hand of a Klargo guard. The little pistol made less noise than a car backfire, hardly as much of a – *crack!* – as a decent firecracker.

Even Eve didn't realize what was happening until she heard the sudden hiss of air from the left rear tire and felt the big station wagon settling onto her foot. She squirmed and twisted the leg away. But then came another pop. When the right rear tire deflated she tried to push herself toward the front of the car and out from under, but the tire col- lapsed almost instantly, trapping her leg – trapping her!

Panic rose in Eve's chest like a red tide. They knew she was there. They had caught her. The Klan!

Another small slug penetrated the left front tire and the weight of the engine came toward her chest, her face. They were going to crush her under the car. "Please!" she begged as best her constricted chest would let her, trying to wedge herself away from the two tons of metal.

"Don't!" she cried but the sound was buried in the hiss of the final tire deflating and hundred cars and trucks scrambling toward the pasture's only exit. *"Noooooo!"*

PART III

CHAPTER 1

At dawn a haze of smoke hung as thick as winter fog above the Cattahatchie as it bent through DeLong. In the still summer air, smoke clung to the dirt lanes of Roseville and along River Street behind *The Current-Leader* building.

As Cutter walked across the Gov. Theodore J. Bilbo Memorial Bridge, the sun was rising red and bloody above the town. A number of black families were streaming back into Roseville carrying suitcases and belongings tied with rope, like refugees from a war zone on the other side of the world. Some nodded or whispered their thanks to Cutter and others who had crossed the river to help the firemen. Behind Cutter were nine burned homes, another seven or eight that were badly damaged, an incinerated beauty shop, dress shop and funeral parlor – the one where Tommy Ray Banks' services were scheduled to be held later that day. Two people who had been in the funeral home were dead, for sure – a funeral home employee and one of Tommy Ray's cousins, who had volunteered to sit with the body through the night, as was tradition. There might be more dead in there or in some of the houses. There probably were, but no one would know until there was good light and time to dig through the charred, smoldering remains.

At the east foot of the bridge, deputies were keeping television crews and reporters at bay. As Cutter slipped though the gaggle – women and men studying their hair and makeup with equal degrees of obsession – Sheriff Wallace stepped off a Corinth Fire Department ladder truck as it slowed. Like Cutter, his face and arms were streaked with soot and his clothes stained with sweat. They both reeked of smoke. Someone in the reporting pool recognized Billy Wallace and the covey surged toward him.

"Keep those people back!" he barked as he caught up with Cutter. They'd both been breathing smoke and oven-like air much of the night and the sheriff had to fight through a coughing spasm before he could speak again. Finally, he wiped his mouth with a sooty handkerchief and said, "Thanks for helpin' out."

"I didn't do much. Dragged some hoses around. That's about it."

"You did a lot more than that," the sheriff said, but said no more.

There was nothing more that needed to be said. "I don't guess you saw Nate anywhere durin' the night?"

Cutter rubbed his eyes, then his face, thinking. "No, sir. Not that I can recall. Last time I saw him was out at the Klan rally with Patti MacAllister."

Billy Wallace nodded. "When you see him, would you ask him to come by the sheriff's office or give me a call? If I'm not handy, ask him to leave a message with whoever answers the phone.

"There was a lot of meanness afoot last night," he told Cutter. "While we were all focused here, the Klan shot up a church and several houses out in the Knox Community. No one was seriously hurt, thank God, but – well – I'd just like to know he's okay. Bein' my son and all –"

"Yes, sir. I understand. I'll tell him, for sure," promised Cutter. Both men stood in silence as reporters shouted questions from where they'd been corralled across the street. Their voices were like echoes in the heads of both men. Finally, Cutter added his own gravelly voice to the chorus. "Mr. Wallace, what is going to happen? Here, I mean. With all this?"

One side of Billy Wallace's face felt sunburned. He hadn't been asleep in nearly twenty-four hours and his eyes stung with smoke, exhaustion, sweat ... and frustration.

"Honestly, Cutter, I don't know," he said, letting his tired eyes roam high on the green hills to the west. "Me and my guys, and the FBI and U.S. Marshals, have been doin' all we know to do. Obviously, it's not enough.

"I talked to Mr. Burke about an hour ago. Governor Broderick is considering sending in the National Guard. If he doesn't, President Nixon probably will send in federal troops. Just like Eisenhower did in Little Rock in '57 and Kennedy in Oxford in '62. Right now, I'm hard-pressed to think of a reason why they shouldn't."

* * *

Out Highway 8 for many miles on both sides of the road, the land and barns and storage sheds, grain elevators and gins mostly were the property of Chalmette Plantation, and thus Cecil Weathers. Holly disliked the feeling of Weathers' wealth and power, and hate, surrounding her, but the country morning was coming up beautiful and clear, and she was glad to be out of DeLong. The town – her town – reminded her of the burned-out villages of Vietnam. And the odor, the lack of food and depth of worry over the whereabouts of Ridge and Eve made Holly's stomach queasy as she turned north onto the weary pavement of County Road 214 – toward Peterson's Grocery and the Campbell farm, where the Klan rally had been held.

Nine hours had passed since she and Cutter pulled into her parking place behind *The Current-Leader* building. "I'm gonna go see if there's anything I can do to help," Cutter had said as soon as the car came to a stop. Then he'd noticed the shattered glass across the back of the building, across the back of nearly every building with windows facing the river. "Will you be okay?"

Holly had given a quick look to the damage, but wasn't worried about broken glass. In the shards, a red-orange light was dancing. Across the river, people's homes, businesses, their livelihoods were being destroyed. Lives probably were being lost.

"I'll be fine," she'd said, "But you be careful."

"Always," he said, but Holly knew better as she watched him hustle up the street, jogging behind a firetruck with Union County markings.

A mid the noise of those first sirens and confused voices and the distraction of flashing lights, Holly had transferred into her chair and pulled her camera bag from the trunk of the Lincoln. She shot what she could from the newspaper's parking lot, then crossed the street and shot more from the spot under the willow where she and Cutter had talked a few days earlier. She didn't bother to try to cross the bridge to Roseville. Too many obstacles, too much confusion. Besides, she knew Eve had stayed at the office to develop film and print photos. So like any good photojournalist, Eve would have grabbed her Nikon, her lenses and as much hand-rolled 35 millimeter film as would fit in her bag, and run toward the fireball.

Holly knew Ridge would be back from the Klan rally any minute and would join Eve in Roseville. So she kept shooting from the east side of the river, and later from the shattered windows of the newspaper building. Over the course of minutes and then during the long hours of the night, many of the remaining *Current-Leader* employees shuffled in – both to get a jump on what would be a very special edition and to congregate on the roof and fire escape for a better view.

Refugees from Roseville began gathering in the parking lots along River Street, including the newspaper's space. About one a.m., Holly told production manager Shorty Rodgers to pass out the sodas, potato chips and other snacks stashed in a storage room off *The Current-Leader*'s small kitchen. He and Jim Boyd, one of the pressmen, and Miss Frances and her husband did so until everything was gone.

As the minutes passed into hours and the fires kept burning, Holly found herself more and more sitting by the third-floor windows at the back of the production room, using her 500 millimeter lens as a telescope to scour the wet, hose-strewn, fire-charred streets of Roseville. She kept looking for Eve and Ridge ... and Cutter. Though she never caught a glimpse of either employee, either friend, she was able to pick up Cutter's image now and then, and the amount of relief she felt each time created a strange sense of unease. She watched him take charge of a group of older men trying to wrestle a snaking firehose in the direction of a burning house. Cutter was eighteen, almost nineteen, Holly reminded herself. Clearly he had a presence and command about himself that belied his age. Besides, younger men than Cutter were fighting and dying in Vietnam every day. Sometimes leading troops when officers were killed or made themselves scarce. Anyone who looked into the eyes of those young soldiers after two or three nights of jungle patrol would never call them "kids." Cutter's eyes had that same forged-in-the-fire maturity even though his battles all had been fought in Cattahatchie County.

Holly leaned the heavy camera away from her on its monopod. "Stop it!" she told herself, knowing that starting to care – really *care* – about Cutter would be a mistake. "The rules are different stateside," she told herself. "This isn't Vietnam." But when she looked up and saw Roseville burning across the river, she wasn't so sure.

By five a.m., when the pumpers finally had spread enough water onto the flames to settle most of one block and part of another into a soggy, smoldering quagmire, Holly was seriously concerned about Eve and Ridge. They had not returned to the office, not even for more film.

When first light began to brighten the smoky sky, Holly had wheeled downstairs and gotten into her car, fighting the nagging fear that was building inside her. She had driven around the square that was crowded with cars and emergency vehicles, and up and down nearby side streets where Ridge might have parked his station wagon. She went by the sagging old Bellafont mansion where Ridge lived on Hill Street. Nothing. And even if she found his car, that wouldn't account for Eve's whereabouts ... unless ... unless she had somehow talked Ridge into sneaking her into the Klan rally. Eve could be so persistent and persuasive, Holly knew, and Ridge was such a pleaser, never wanting to disappoint anyone.

Now Holly lifted her long hair off the back of her neck and let the fresh air blow through it as she drove through the rolling hills. "Please let me be wrong," she whispered as she turned down the narrow gravel road that led to the Campbell farm.

* * *

When Cutter got to the newspaper's lot, he saw the Continental was gone. Shorty Rodgers and some of the other employees already were nailing thick plastic sheeting over the building's shattered rear windows. Miss Frances was sitting at the picnic table on the loading dock. Her husband had his head down on the table, snoring.

"Oh, my goodness, son!" she gasped. "Are you hurt?"

"No, ma'am. Just dirty. Maybe a little scorched around the edges. Is Miss Carter here?"

Miss Frances twisted one arthritic hand over the other. "No, Cutter, she's not. And truth be told, I'm worried. She went to look for Ridge Bellafont and Miss Eve." Cutter felt his pulse quicken. "We haven't seen either one of them since last night."

"Do you know where she went?"

"She was going back out to the Campbell place. She thought maybe Ridge broke down on the side of the road. Or something."

"Thanks, Miss Frances," he said, heading down the ramp built for Miss Carter. At that moment, he looked up and saw me. "Nate!" he called as I eased my truck along River Street.

I heard Cutter's voice before I saw him jogging across the newspaper parking lot. I had spent the night at First Denomination with Patti, her momma and Brother MacAllister and about twenty members of the congregation who had gathered for a prayer vigil for the firefighters. I was getting my first look at the damage. I waved weakly, shocked by what I was seeing.

"Hey, Cutter."

"I left my Jeep up at The Well. I need to borrow your truck," he said immediately.

"Well, I –"

"Or I need you to drive me."

"To The Well?"

"No. Out to the Campbell farm."

I had been up all night, and was grumpy. "Why do you want to go way out there? I haven't even had breakfast."

"Then get out and go eat at The Cotton, and let me have the truck."

Down the street, three of the café's four big front windows were blown out but they were serving. Paula Simpson was pouring coffee for worn-out men, black and white, propped against the front of the building or sitting on the sidewalk.

"No!" I told him. "I mean, what are you –?"

"Nate, I don't have time to explain. Either get out or scoot over."

I threw the shifter into neutral and slid to the passenger side as Cutter climbed in. He hit the clutch and ground the gears with uncharacteristic clumsiness.

We were headed west on Highway 8 before I took stock of my best friend. He looked like he'd taken a bath in dirty water and rubbed himself with charcoal. He reeked of smoke. Seeing him so haggard as a result of his helping throughout the night made me ashamed of the way I had spent the last ten hours. If I really had been earnestly praying for the safety of those fighting the blaze, it would have been one thing. But I hadn't even been that much help. I only was there because Patti was there, and again in a good mood.

My lips moved, starting to form the words to tell Cutter that but the words felt like, well, ashes in my mouth before I even said them. Instead, I asked, "Can't you at least tell me what we're doing? What do you expect to find out at the Campbell place?"

Cutter kept his gaze fixed straight ahead and took the curves as fast as my old pickup would let him – "Nothing. I hope."

CHAPTER 2

O ut at the Oscar Campbell farm, the burned cross stood black and charred and ugly against Tuesday morning's bright sky.

As Holly drove along the fence line, she saw nothing of Ridge's car, nor had she seen any sign of Ridge or Eve on the twenty-five-minute drive from DeLong. She was both relieved and increasingly fearful as she turned across the cattle-guard gate and maneuvered the Lincoln around a small herd of Black Angus grazing among discarded beer bottles and cigarette packs.

As she came over the curve of the hill – "Oh, no! No!" she gasped and shoved the hand control forward. The big car leaped and crossed the hundred yards in seconds, sliding to a stop next to the battered hulk of Ridge Bellafont's station wagon. All the glass was shattered and there were bullet holes in random locations in the sheet metal. The back of the long wagon was burned, as was a semicircle of grass behind it. The tires were flat.

Holly pushed herself up in her seat and forced herself to look inside the car. "Thank God," she whispered as she saw only destroyed photographic equipment. *But if they aren't here?* Holly thought, and the realization of what that meant filled her with a nearly equal fear. Maybe they were hiding in the woods.

"Ridge! Eve!" she called and hit the car horn again and again. "Ridge! ... Eve!"

Nothing. Then she saw it. A hand almost hidden behind the right front wheel rim.

Holly slammed the Lincoln into park and threw open the door. "Eve!" she cried as she tumbled onto the grass. With her elbows, Holly dragged herself to the side of the station wagon. She grasped the bloody hand, held it to her cheek. "Eve, can you hear me?"

There was no response. Holly felt for a pulse. It was so shallow she couldn't count the beats.

"Eve, I've got to get this car off you," she said. In the three years and nine and a half months since Ia Drang, Holly had never felt so helpless, had never hated being paralyzed so much. She rolled onto her back, clenching shut her eyes and her fists. A moment later she opened her eyes and propped up on her elbows. She looked around and knew what she had to do.

In the dew-slick grass, she scooted backwards to the open front door of the Lincoln and stretched her long arm in, snatching the keys from the ignition. She slid herself around the Lincoln and unlocked the trunk. Throwing one arm inside, Holly pulled herself up until she could see into the big space. The contents of the trunk were a jumble. If the jack was at the far side, she'd never reach it. She used her free arm to push a box out of the way, and a raincoat and to throw a set of jumper cables aside.

There it was! The jack.

Holly's right arm felt as if it was about to tear from the socket, but she grabbed the jack with her left hand and tossed it onto the grass. Then the base. Then the tire iron. Then she let go and dropped to the grass as a sudden pain ripped up her side. Holly reached around and felt a long tear in her blouse and when she drew her hand back there was blood on her fingers. As she pushed up onto her hips, she glanced at the sharp edge of the car tag that bent out slightly from the bumper. However bad the cut, she didn't have time to think about it. Eve was dying! Every foot that Holly slid with the heavy jack and tire iron across her thighs seemed to take hours.

"Hang on, Eve," she called. "Hang on!"

Finally Holly reached the front of the car. She secured the jack under the bumper. With all her remaining strength, Holly click-clacked, click-clacked up the jack, notch by notch, as high as she could get it – then fell back, spent.

There was no sound in the pasture except for birds in the nearby trees, and the occasional lowing of the cattle. Holly could see under the car now. The jack had relieved some of the pressure on Eve's abdomen and pelvis. Holly stretched her arms under the unstable weight of the car and grasped Eve Howard beneath her arms. Holly pulled – once, then again – but Eve's legs were trapped. Holly lay with her face in the grass.

"Eve, I'm so sorry," she told her. Then, "I don't know if you can hear me, but – I can't get you out on my own. I don't want to leave you, but I've got to go for help."

Holly pushed up. Pain burned her side, but she didn't let it stop her. She dragged herself to the convertible's door. Just as she grasped the steering wheel to pull herself up, she heard a vehicle coming fast on the gravel road. Hope jumped into her heart, but fell away as quickly. The driver wouldn't see the cars from the road. Holly stretched for the horn. She hit it – once, twice, three, four times – until she saw an old Chevy pickup bouncing across the pasture.

Cutter slid my truck so hard I was sure one of the retread tires would pop. He was out the door before it came to a good stop. When I came around the truck, he already was kneeling beside Holly Lee Carter lifting her blood-stained top. There was an ugly scratch from her waist to up under the side of her bra.

"It's long," said Cutter, "but it's not deep. How'd you –?"

Miss Carter pointed under the station wagon.

"Ohhh, shhh —" I started.

"I think she's been there since last night," Holly told us. "I got the front end up, but I couldn't –"

"This is bad," I said. "Real bad."

"What about Mr. Bellafont?" Cutter asked.

Miss Carter shook her head. "He's not in the car. I don't know."

"We need to go for help," I said.

"Cutter, she's dying," said Miss Carter, her green eyes locked onto his in a way that made me feel as if they were in one place, together, and I was somewhere else.

"I think we should go for help," I said again, the words like an echo in my head.

"She's not dead yet, is she?" Cutter asked softly, gently. It was a voice I'd heard only a time or two when he needed to calm his sister.

Miss Carter shook her head, never taking her eyes off Cutter's. "No, but –"

"Then there's still a chance."

"I can go for help," I offered, but the noise I was making was of no more notice to Cutter and Miss Carter than the grumbling of the nearby cattle or the cry of a curious hawk.

Cutter stood. "Nate, get the jack out of your truck."

"Don't you think we should go for help?"

"I'm not a doctor but I've seen wounded people," said Miss Carter. "I don't think she can wait."

"But we could kill her by moving her," I warned.

"Yeah. We could. There's a good chance we will. But all we can do is the best we can do right this minute," said Cutter, discussion ended. "Nate, are you gonna get your jack? Or do I have to?"

Once we got one side of the big station wagon propped up precariously on the two jacks, Cutter reached under the front of the car and took an unconscious Eve Howard under her arms and drew her gently toward him. Cutter pulled her a little harder, and a little harder still, but it was no use. Her right foot was hung in the undercarriage toward the back of the car.

"Nate, come around here," Cutter said. "I'm going to slide under there and see if I can't get her foot loose."

I looked at the small space, narrowing as it did into what would be a black forever if the car slipped off the jacks.

"Forget it," I heard myself say, as if someone else was speaking. "You'll never fit. I'm the smallest. I should do it."

Cutter didn't try to talk me out of it; he knew I was right. Miss Carter started to say something, but I got on my belly and quickly slid under the engine block before I lost my nerve. With my right arm extended as far is it would go, I wedged myself under two thousand pounds of Chevy. I could smell blood and gasoline, sweat and urine and feces, and some sickeningly sweet odor like overcooked barbecue.

"Nate, you're doing great," Cutter encouraged. "Can you reach her foot?"

My chest felt tight and I could sense every ounce of the mountain of steel on top of me. "Yeah, I can –"

As I grasped Eve Howard's shoe, it crumbled in my hand and I felt the incinerated flesh of her foot slough off in my fingers. I gagged and choked, and would have thrown up had I eaten anything for breakfast. Instead, I spit bile into the scorched grass.

"Nate, are you okay?" Miss Carter asked.

I gagged again. "Yeah. Just another few seconds," I told her, and forced myself to take firm hold of Eve Howard's ruined foot. I twisted it hard, and heard something crack, but the foot turned. "Okay, Cutter. Go ahead!"

The woman's body slid past me as I scrambled backwards into the daylight.

M iss Carter quickly checked the artery in Eve Howard's neck. She shook her head. "I … I don't know."

"She won't get any better layin' here," Cutter said and scooped my former boss into his arms with the ease a smaller man might use with a toddler. "Nate, open the back door."

Miss Carter startled, too – "Cutter, what are you --?" – as he gently sat on the long wide rear bench. Then he went for Eve Howard and Miss Carter understood. She slid over. Cuttter he knelt beside Eve Howard and slid his arms under her back and legs. She'd been bleeding from her nose and mouth, and one ear. Both legs were burned below the knee, but the right was much worse. Much! He lifted her and scraps of charred denim fell to the grass. I helped him arrange her as gently as we could on the back seat with her head resting in Miss Carter's lap. She showed no sign of life.

If she lives, it'll be a miracle, I thought as I closed the Linclon's trunk.

Cutter slid behind the wheel and fired up the big V-8. "Nate, stop at the first house you see with a phone. Call the hospital and tell 'em we're coming," he said. "Then call the sheriff's office and tell 'em what happened. Tell 'em they need to get out here in a hurry with some men to search. And maybe bloodhounds. Mr. Bellafont might be here someplace. He might still be alive."

All I could do was nod, glassy-eyed.

"Did you hear me?"

"Yeah," I managed. "I heard you."

"Nate, you did great," Miss Carter was saying, but it was as if she were talking under water. "Thank you. Thank you so much!"

"Yeah, buddy, you did. You did great," he said, putting the car in gear and starting to move. Over his shoulder, he yelled, "Call your daddy! He's worried about you."

As the convertible disappeared over the ridge of the pasture, I stood waving – stupidly, weakly – as if they were leaving for a vacation. I waved even after they were gone, until the first jack gave way with a snap and a pop, as loud as the crack of a rifle shot. Then the second. I watched as in an instant the big station wagon groaned and crashed down onto the hard ground, pieces of the second jack flying forty feet across the pasture.

I looked at the car and then my right hand. Eve Howard's blood and pus and blistered flesh still clung to my fingers. I fought to keep my bowels together and the bile in my stomach down, but I couldn't keep my knees from giving way. Suddenly I found myself on all fours beside my truck, rubbing my hand in the grass. I started to cry.

How long I stayed there like that with the morning sun rising hot on my back, I'm not sure. Long enough that I rubbed my hand raw and all my tears were gone.

CHAPTER 3

Rose Marie Carlucci was crossing the Old Iron Bridge near the camp when I pulled out of the narrow road that led back to The Well. Wednesday's late afternoon shadows already were on the river.

"Hey, Rose," I said, idling the truck.

"Huh-Huh-Hi, N-Nate."

"If you're looking for Cutter, he's not at The Well."

"Wh-Where is he?"

I looked away and then back. Trying not to sound as agitated as I felt, I said, "Word has it, he's staying up at Wolf's Run. I was headed that way. Climb in."

She did and gave me a nervous smile as she closed the door and sat close to it. I supposed her edginess was natural, merely being in proximity to a boy in the cab of a truck. To the best of my knowledge, Rose Carlucci never had been on a date. Not surprising considering she wore what she always wore – men's work shoes and a loose shirt under baggy overalls. Still, the outfit did not entirely hide her ample figure, the strong, handsome features of her work-tanned face or the luster of the thick brown hair she pulled back into a ponytail tied with a rubber band. But other than for school, she never strayed farther than The Well from the Old Ambrose Place, except under the watchful and usually bloodshot eye of her father. She was allowed to participate in no after-school activities or clubs and never could have friends over or visit others. In fact, if Rose Carlucci had any friends, I didn't know it. All she had was a mother who'd fallen into a nervous breakdown ten years earlier and never recovered, a father who was more jailer than daddy ... and Cutter.

I put the truck in gear and headed up the steep S cut into the face of Blue Mountain.

Though I'd driven past Wolf's Run many times, never before had I turned through the opening in the faded white rail fence or been down the long driveway that sloped to the cleft in the mountainside that held the house. My first impression was that it wasn't as big as I expected. As I wheeled the truck around the pea gravel circle at the front of the house, Cutter emerged from the big carriage house turned garage, which stood separate from the main house. His clothes were clean and so was he, but he held in his hand a wet dish rag stained pink. Miss Carter's little white dog stood next to him.

Cutter looked so at ease, so at home in the moment that a sense of betrayal instantly boiled up in me anew. I made only a halfhearted effort to shove it down as we got out.

"C-C-Cutter, are you o-okay?"

"I'm fine, Rose. You didn't have to come all the way up here."

"I-I-I w-was worried."

"I'm sorry. We didn't get back from Memphis until almost two o'clock. I stayed here last night."

"Everybody already knows you stayed here last night," I told him sharply. "Except for Rose, I guess. People are already talking about you and her."

Cutter turned around and walked back into the garage. The little dog followed and so did we.

"Cutter, are you listenin' to me?"

"I heard you, Nate," he said. "But there's no 'me and her.' If it's anybody's business, I slept on the porch. Miss Carter didn't need to be alone way out here."

"How come this is all of a sudden your problem?" I demanded. "A few weeks ago, you couldn't stand the woman. Now she's brought this on herself."

Cutter bent down and picked up the little dog and placed it on the work bench. He scratched the animal's back while he let me seethe. "Her name is Charlie."

Rose smiled and followed Cutter's example. "H-Hi, Ch-Charlie."

"Cutter?"

"How about the folks who lost their homes, their lives in Roseville? Did they bring it on themselves?" he asked. "What's the count now?"

"Four," I said. "Four dead. And that's a shame. But blacks and whites aren't meant to mix. Sometimes sacrifices have to be made to keep, to keep order in –"

"I guess Miss Howard and Mr. Bellafont brought all that on themselves?"

I felt my neck and face redden. "Of course, they did," I made myself say. "Showin' up at a Klan rally like that. Them!"

"And you think that gave the Klux the right to do what they did?"

"Brother Mac says –"

Cutter snapped his arm up and hurled the rag at me. I caught the damp cloth against my chest, and looked from it to Cutter, who was saying, "Good! You can finish cleaning Eve Howard's blood off the back seat of the car. That's what I was doing when you drove up."

Images of Eve Howard's burned and bloody flesh grabbed hold of me and wouldn't let go. I could see her crushed body lying under the station wagon and across the back seat of Miss Carter's Lincoln. According to the papers, the doctors amputated her right leg below the knee, but managed to save the other and stabilize her. Her mother, the actress Carol Howard, had flown in from Hollywood to be with her, but Eve remained in critical condition. By early Tuesday evening, word had spread throughout DeLong that Mr. Bellafont's chances had run out. He was found by a search party in an abandoned smokehouse about four miles from the station wagon. He was stripped, gagged and hung by his wrists from a rafter. He then had been whipped so brutally that he probably would have died from the beating. But to make sure, his torturers castrated him and left him to bleed out like a pig for slaughter.

"Nate, I've known you since junior high, and we've turned a lot a miles together," Cutter was saying. "I wouldn't do to a mad dog what the Klan did to Miss Howard and Mr. Bellafont. Neither would you. And that's not even counting the damage they did in Roseville."

I dropped the rag beside the car, my stomach queasy.

"Cutter, this is so much bigger than us," I told him, wiping my hands on my jeans. My right hand still was tender from the rubbing I'd given it in the dirt beside Mr. Bellafont's burned-out car. "We're just kids. We haven't even been to our senior prom. You're messin' with stuff that's none of your business. And I can't let you drag me into it any further. I took a room at Mrs. Fletcher's Boarding House. And I got hooked up with a job after school and weekends. A good job."

"Well good for you. Where at?"

"Handley's Department Store. I'll be working in the stock room on Saturdays and after school."

"Brother Mac fix you up with that?"

"He didn't fix me up. Mr. Handley is a deacon. He put in a good word. That's all."

"Mr. Handley is the head of the Klan. The Cyclopian Dragon Wizard. Or whatever idiot fairytale name he's made for himself. Everybody knows it."

"It's not like you think. The Cattahatchie Klavern doesn't sanction things like, like what happened the other day. Those are radicals. Outsiders, come in to make DeLong folks look bad. Heck, it may even have been the coloreds themselves or that NJC bunch, trying to discredit –"

"Shut up, Nate!" Cutter snapped, cutting me off in a way he'd never done before, not once. He scowled for a long hard moment but softened when he saw the surprise and hurt in my eyes. "Just shut up," he said, his voice a tired, smoky rasp as he turned his back to me. He coughed and cleared his throat, then – "I know that's not you talkin'. I know its Patti or Brother Mac or ... some of that crowd. But I don't want to listen to you standin' there, making a fool of yourself."

I swallowed and ignored the insult. "Look, Mr. Handley – he's on the board of the new academy, too. Everybody we know is gonna leave Cattahatchie High and go there, as soon as all the particulars are ironed out. Come September, there won't be anybody at CHS but niggrahs and white trash. Mr. Handley says he can get me a scholarship to Riverview."

Cutter leaned on the workbench, his arms straight, his hands flat atop it, and said nothing.

"All I know is, I can't screw up again. If I do, Patti and I are done. Done for good."

"What do you mean screw up?" he asked.

"You know. What we did out at the Campbell farm. Interferin'!"

As was his nature, Cutter didn't rush to speak and with every passing second it was harder to keep my feet planted. I wanted to run from that place and from my own words. He turned. "Nate, you didn't screw up. You saved someone's life."

"The-The way the p-paper ha-had it," Rose struggled, "you, you, you're a hero, N-Nate."

"Then why doesn't it feel like it?" I said, my eyes roaming around the increasing darkness in the garage. "Why are people treatin' me like I pissed in the lemonade?"

"Maybe 'cause you're hangin' out with the wrong people."

"Maybe you are!" I told him, and felt tears of anger and loss – and fear – burning my eyes. Cutter was my best friend! What had happened to us?

"You're the biggest thing to hit this county in a long time, but you're not bigger than this," I told him. "Why can't you just do what you said at The Well? Why can't you just give 'em what they want until we can all get the hell out of here?"

Cutter simply looked at me as if I were speaking in tongues. After a moment, I whirled, embarrassed, and trod off toward my truck, my jaw moving, my teeth grinding. I slammed the door. Charlie barked and I turned the key. What could I say? How could I make him listen? Make him understand? But there was nothing. Somehow we had stopped speaking the same language and it was all Holly Lee Carter's fault.

"Good luck, Nate," he called as I wheeled the truck around toward the road but I pretended not to hear him. I gunned it up the hill and left Cutter, Rose and Charlie in the twilight shadows already woven purple and deep around Wolf's Run.

* * *

Cutter stood at the bedroom door for a moment studying the womanly curve of Holly Lee Carter's body under the sheet. At some point after he'd laid her onto her pillows and positioned her wheelchair next to the bed, she'd gotten up and tossed off the skirt and blouse she'd been wearing for some forty hours. They reeked of smoke and burned flesh and were stained by Eve's blood and her own. Sleeping on a blanket outside her open windows, Cutter roused for a moment when he heard movement from inside the room. He looked in through the open window and their eyes found each other in the darkness as Holly dropped her ruined blouse onto the floor. She was not surprised to see him there. Somehow she knew he would be nearby, that he would not abandon her to the night fears, real and imagined. For his part, Cutter did not look away. He followed the length of her long legs starting with her feet on the foot pedals, then took in Holly's voluptuous shape, her generous breasts barely contained in the bra, its white cups glowing against her dusky skin. Holly knew she should cover herself, but for a long moment she did not. She wanted to be appreciated by a man again, even if it was in the deep shadows, a distance between them. Even if it was only a single moment in a thousand lonely nights with ten thousand more to come. And she was thankful and grateful to see the manly enjoyment in Cutter's calm, unapologetic gaze without the violent, sadistic lust that had burned in his father's eyes those years ago at The Gin. In Cutter's face she saw something else, and *thank God* it wasn't pity. There was something pleasant and sweet, and even kind, but buried in the blue ice of his eyes there also was an unmistakable heat.

Holly's lips parted and the word "yes" had almost formed on them, but she drew a long breath over her teeth and forced herself to reach for the push-rims on her wheels. She had made herself turn away and push into the bathroom, where she had softly closed the door behind her.

Cutter lay back on his sleeping bag feeling a damp sheen of perspiration against the cloth, his breath coming in long, slow draws. The rapid elongation of his penis did not surprise him as he took in the former, and not-so-long-ago Miss Cattahatchie County. Her body still lean and firm. The bra and panties almost luminous in the dim, shadow-strewn bedroom, but no more so than the green of Holly Carter's cat eyes as they held his. He had wanted to step through the unscreened window and undress her with more than a stare. In that moment, he wanted Holly Carter more than he'd ever wanted any woman. But could she even --? Was she still able to --? He swallowed deeply as she turned away and choked down his desire as she closed the bathroom door. Now he stared at the rafters of the porch and ran his tongue over his lips and his fingers over his shaft. The veins were thick and hard, like lengths of sun-warmed cable, pulsing with tension. The glans so tender, so sensitive that even the soft cotton of his underwear was nearly painful against it. He desperately wanted to, needed to masturbate, but he forced himself to interlace his long fingers at the back his head and think about something else, anything else but Holly Lee Carter.

In the bathroom, Holly stripped off her bra and underwear. She knew she badly needed a bath, her body sour with smoke and sweat and caffeine. She was too tired, though, to do anything but to pee and go to bed. She shifted from her wheelchair to the toilet seat, positioned her legs and reached into a nearby drawer to withdraw a catheter. With practiced skill, she started to insert the slender plastic tube, but she froze, her breath catching in her chest as her fingers relayed to her brain the reality of how very wet she had become under Cutter's shameless study. Then the tangy scent of her long-dormant desire filled her nostrils. Suddenly she felt dizzy. She dropped the catheter, put her hands on her knees and closed her eyes, hoping the room would stop spinning. She squeezed her knees, maddeningly aware that the sensation of her own touch passed through hands but not through her legs. Her breasts felt too ripe and her nipples ached for the lips of a man, for Cutter's lips, and she began to cry.

Now in the daylight Holly heard Charlie's claws clattering on the hardwood floor and saw her settle into her bed beneath the window. She sensed Cutter standing just inside the bedroom door. It wasn't that she heard him, really. He was a guy who, despite his size, had a light step. It was more like a change in the atmosphere, an increase in barometric pressure that she felt in her chest when he came near. She pretended to still be sleeping as Cutter placed a note on her bedside table. Just as she had pretended it often during the day as she allowed Cutter to head off the concerned and merely curious who called, and those who came by with casseroles, hams and platters of fried chicken. She was being treated like a family member of the deceased, and perhaps that was appropriate. The Carters and the other people at the newspaper had been the closest thing to real family Ridge Bellafont had. His aunts and uncles and his many cousins tolerated him, but few embraced him. Ridge had been her father's friend and confidante, and her most patient mentor and enthusiastic cheerleader. He had opened to her the universe of life within her reach and the reach of a 35mm lens. He had taught her how to make magic in the darkroom and helped her to believe she had a magic within herself, no matter how often T.L. Carter told his teenage daughter she was worthless and selfish and no good – just like her mother.

As Holly thought of Ridge, the tears started again on her cheeks and melted into the stains of the hundreds she'd already shed into her pillow. For Ridge, for Eve, for the Banks family and those others in Roseville dead or injured or homeless, for this place that she both loved and loathed, and that no matter what else was home.

Out her window she saw Cutter and Rose get into her car and head up the driveway. She listened to the tires crunching on the gravel until the sound disappeared and she was alone in the big, silent house. The voices returned. Holly still could hear Carol Howard screaming in the surgery waiting room – "This is all your fault! Get out! Away from my daughter! And don't you ever come near her again!"

Then there was Sheriff Wallace's voice on the telephone late Tuesday afternoon – "Miss Carter, I hate to have to tell you this, but we found Mr. Bellafont …"

"Poor, sweet, gentle Ridge," Holly heard herself whisper now. "I'm so sorry."

The shadows in Meemaw Carter's bedroom seemed deeper, darker than Holly had ever known. They seemed to have a comfortable liquid weight to them that offered a dark, welcome hiding place; but they were filled, too, with the danger that they might crush her. That if she let herself remain too long in their cool arms that she might never emerge. She reached for the note on the bed stand. It was printed by a strong hand.

Miss Carter –
I borrowed your car to take Rose home and get some things at The Well. Will be back in less than an hour.

Cutter

Holly rolled onto her back with the note in her hand. She held it against her body just beneath her breasts. Through the worn-sheer fabric of a pink Newport Jazz Festival t shirt she'd pulled on late in the night she could almost feel the warmth of the hand Cutter had rested against the paper, the nimbleness of his fingers as he formed each letter and made each confident yet unpretentious stroke. It was as if a warm circular pool spread from the paper and enveloped her. Her face flushed, but her thoughts hardened with the cold reality of her situation and she growled an animal cry of frustration that rang through the big, empty house. Through what suddenly felt like a very empty life. Empty but for Charlie, who came to the side of bed wanting to comfort her as she had so many, many times above the ocean and the coast road. Holly rolled onto her side and pulled Charlie up and under the sheet and into her arms.

"*Mon amour*," she whispered.

Why was she letting Cutter – *this boy!* – get so inside her head? she wondered. Her mentor, her kind gentle friend Ridge was dead, almost certainly dying in a grotesquery of pain and humiliation. Eve had lost one leg and she still might lose the other. The only family she had left despised her. The town was against her and no doubt there were Klansmen who would be glad to kill her. And the legacy newspaper she came back to salvage and protect was headed for bankruptcy. Her life was in ruins and the only way she could wreck it more, she thought, was to have an affair with a high school jock – even he was a if street-legal eighteen and gorgeous … and bright, and mature, and gentle when he wanted to be.

No, there was one thing worse, Holly told herself. And she knew it would break her, break her completely, if she reached out to Cutter in need and passion and hope, and he rejected her. Too old. Too worn. Too scarred. Too much trouble. Too … crippled. As she held Charlie close in her empty room on her lonely hilltop, her sister-in-law's venomous words --"*you're not even woman anymore!*" – followed her down into a restless sleep like poison in her veins.

Chapter 4

How's M-Miss Carter d-doing?" Rose Carlucci asked as Cutter drove her home.

"She's sick about what happened to Miz Howard. But the news about Mr. Bellafont. What the Klux did to him. It shook her pretty bad," he said. "But she's strong in ways I've never seen before."

"Wh-What do you mean?"

"She got Mr. Ridge's big ol' station wagon up off Miz Howard. At least enough so she could keep breathing until me and Nate showed up. She did it by herself. Without legs."

There was an inflection in her brother's voice that Rose had never heard. Amazement mixed with admiration, she thought, trying to place it. And respect? Respect – not just the perfunctory yes, sirs and no, ma'ams of the South – but real respect was something Cutter granted to few people, she knew. In Cutter's book, they had to earn it; and with Cutter, it was hard earned. He could be hard and judgmental, but he'd had to be to survive Tony. The fact that he seemed to have added Miss Carter to that short list of those whom he respected surprised and somehow frightened Rose.

"But it's not just physical," Cutter went on. "Do you know she ran the newspaper from the waiting room of that Memphis hospital? She wrote her editorial right there, and dictated it back to the paper. She toughed it out during all the questioning from the cops, and even when Miz Howard's mother threw a fit, screaming at her."

A flicker of a smile crossed Cutter's face, though Rose had heard nothing funny in what her brother had said. "W-What's funny?"

"Not funny. Nothing's funny about any of this. Just that, like I say, she toughed it through everything until we got back in the car at the hospital, then she went out," he said, snapping his fingers, "like a light. She was stretched out on the seat, asleep, before we got to the first stoplight."

What Cutter didn't share even with his sister was that Miss Carter's eyes had fluttered, then closed and she'd slumped toward him there on Lamar Avenue, either in a faint or overcome by utter exhaustion. He had laid her head gently on his thigh and reached over and lifted her legs onto the seat. As they passed through the quiet early morning streets of Memphis then out onto the nearly empty two-lane darkness southeast of Collierville, she had slept there. Slept as they moved into the Mississippi night with the radio playing "cool sounds for lonely lovers," and he ran his fingers along Holly Lee Carter's firm right arm and over her strong shoulders and stroked the luxuriant thickness of her auburn hair. Once back at Wolf's Run, he wasn't sure how long he stayed like that in the driveway, not wanting to move, not wanting to give up the closeness with her, no matter how one-sided.

Cutter was exhausted but wired with a low buzz of adrenaline from all that happened in the last thirty-six hours and a not-too-suffused hum of desire generated by the feeling of Holly Lee Carter's head resting on his thigh and against his privates, which were well aware of her presence, especially now that he was not concentrating on the road ahead. He was mostly concentrating on her and feeling ashamed of the things he'd said to her that morning out on the highway when Benoit and Tony ran her and Miss Eve off into the ditch. Nearly killed them. He laughed softly to himself, at himself. The idea that this woman would be interested in him, especially considering his stupid highway speech, well – he shook his head. No, she couldn't use her legs anymore. She had to use a wheelchair. But if there was any self-pity in her, he hadn't seen it. She was nothing like Tony. In fact, Holly Lee Carter was nothing like any woman he'd ever met.

Finally, Cutter had scooped Holly up and carried her inside, her head on his shoulder, and put her to bed like a sleeping child. He wanted to strip off his smoky, blood-stained clothes and slip under the sheet beside her, but she was so out of it that he wasn't sure how she'd react if she woke up and found him next to her. Besides, he was not sure the Klan was finished. So, he grabbed a pillow and blanket from a bed in a guest room and dropped it onto the screened porch. Then he walked out to the garage and looked around for anything that could be used as weapon. In a storage cabinet he found a double-blade axe. He had returned to the porch, made his bed beneath Miss Carter's window, laid the axe next to him and allowed himself to fall into a shallow sleep, trusting that Charlie would be alert enough to warn them both if anyone tried to get close to the house.

C utter and Rose sat at the end of the rough driveway leading to the Old Ambrose Place. Tony's truck wasn't in sight, but that didn't mean he wasn't around.

"How's Momma?" Cutter asked.

"S-Same as she's b-been for t-ten years. Good days, b-bad days," said Rose. "She stayed awake for al-almost f-four straight days finishing a qu-quilt. I think it's the pr-prettiest one she's ever d-done.

"D-D-Daddy took it with him wh-when he left this afternnoon. I expect he'll get a good pr-price."

"Tony was at the house last night?"

Rose nodded. "Cutter, I'm sc-sc-scared for you. He came in l-last night. Drunk.

H-He was so mad about you helpin' M-M-Miss C-Carter, and what happened out at the C-Campbell farm."

Cutter drew in a deep breath and slowly let it out as he thought about his sister's words. "He didn't hit you or Momma, did he?"

Rose shook her head. "N-No. But he s-s-says he's gonna f-f-fix you for good, and M-M-Miss Carter, too. I was coming to warn you."

Cutter stared into Rose's brown, gentle, fearful eyes. "Sister, don't worry about it. You know how Tony likes to talk big, talk tough. That's all it is." Rose grew quiet. "What?"

She looked at her brother, so unlike her in almost every way. Yet, there was no one in the world she felt closer to or loved more. "I know h-how m-mean Daddy is, but you d-don't think he could b-be the one who wh-whipped Mr. Bellafont, d-do you?"

Cutter fought to hold Rose's gaze. It wasn't fear he saw, but a strange mix of dread and of hope – that the blood that flowed through her did not derive from a man capable of such a thing. It was easy for Cutter to recognize because he had the same blood in his veins and the same worries troubling his thoughts. He let his eyes move over the decaying corpse of the old house and at the circle of beautiful roses his sister maintained – hand-carrying the water and love they needed to survive. Then, "As much as I hate Tony, I don't want to believe it."

Rose swallowed and thought about that. "M-Me neither."

It was nearly dark now and there were no lights on in the house. Rose got out and stood next to the Lincoln. She looked at Cutter in the driver's seat. "It l-looks g-good on you."

"It's not mine," he said.

"I know," she said, turning toward the weedy road, the sagging porch and the rusting roof. "I b-better go. Momma never sl-sleeps more than two hours at a t-time."

"I hate to let you go back in that place."

"It's ooo-kay."

"No it's not," he said. "But I don't know what else to do right now. Tony hasn't –?"

Rose swallowed and shook her head. "N-n-no. He's t-too scared of you."

"Good," said Cutter. "He needs to be."

Lightning was glittering around the edges of Blue Mountain as Cutter stopped the Lincoln just before the Old Iron Bridge. His Jeep was parked in the clearing on the other side of the bridge where he'd left it three days earlier. He got out and walked across the heavy, gravel-strewn planks that constituted the flooring of the bridge. He stopped and leaned on the south railing looking at the river, flowing with summer languor, low and steady but with quiet power. Nothing like it had been on the night that Mr. Carter died. It had been a monster. Rolling, roiling, roaring trying to pull in everything close to its banks. He'd read in *The Current-Leader* – Mr. Carter's own newspaper – that he'd drown. Rose had seen the car go into the river. And Mr. Carter's body was pulled out of it down in Lafayette County. So why was Miss Carter chasing the details now? Why was she so interested in finding the ruined car?

Cutter tapped his palms on the bridge railing and walked on. He drove the Jeep over the rutted, sand-cut road and parked it near The Well. He did a quick cleanup of the campsite he'd left three nights earlier then built a fire in the pit he used for cooking. A big fire that would take hours to burn out. He added kerosene to his lantern, lit it and placed it under the rock overhang where he often lay to read and sleep if he thought rain was in the air. Anyone passing on the road would think Cutter was encamped at his usual spot. But Cutter didn't care about anyone passing on the road. He only cared about Tony. Cared that if his father came staggering home drunk with thoughts of further meanness on his mind, he'd make it to the porch and look across the tops of bean plants and cotton stalks and believe that Cutter was at The Well – watching. Ready to do what he'd promised almost four years earlier when he slammed a .12 gauge shell into the chamber and blew Tony's wooden leg right out from under him – splinters spiking into the remainder of his father's thigh like hot, jagged fishhooks as his heavy buttocks crashed hard onto the planks of the back porch. Cutter had jacked another round into the chamber and pressed the hot barrel to the side of Tony's face as the man whimpered and gripped his bloody thigh.

"Now you listen to me," Cutter had told him, his eyes ablaze, his breath smoking out of his nostrils into the January midnight. The moon was bright and the yard was white with frost. Tony Carlucci's blood poured black on the porch planks. "You've already killed my mother. If you ever lay a hand on my sister again, so help me God I'll blow your head completely off. Whatever happens to me later happens, but your brains'll still be scattered all over these walls.

"Don't you even think about touching Rose like that again," he told his father, pressing the gun even harder into his cheek. "If you do, it'll be the last thought you ever have."

Doctors in DeLong sent Tony on to the Veteran's Administration Hospital in Memphis where it took surgeons three hours to pick out the splinters. He was at the V.A. for almost three weeks and couldn't wear his new plastic prosthesis for almost five months. Of course, Tony swore revenge and Cutter had no doubt he'd try to exact it, which made remaining at the Old Ambrose Place untenable once Tony was released from the hospital. So, he installed deadbolts at the top, bottom and side of his sister's bedroom door, and they agreed on a signal. For a while, Rose had been sleeping with her bed pushed into one corner and the light on.

"If Tony ever – gets in, you turn off the light. Break it if you have to," Cutter told Rose. "Do whatever you have to do to get it out. And I'll be there. I'll end it."

Now Cutter looked around the camp, satisfied with his ruse. Then he looked across the long fields to the old house where the light now glowed in Rose's window, worrying that the bare bulb might be as much a deception as his campfire. Worrying that Tony still was after Rose in the way that no father ever should be after his daughter. Worrying that Rose left the light on and never spoke of it not to protect Tony but protect him from carrying out his promise. The idea that his sister might be making that sacrifice, allowing that sacrilege of herself while he played at being a football star and all that meant in a little, pride-starved town like DeLong made Cutter want to kick something, or hit it or kill Tony right now. But Cutter knew, too, that he was Rose's ticket out, and his mother's – what was left of her.

Cutter knew that if he had killed Tony that bitter cold winter night, he would have his set of worries, but whether his father still was raping his sister would not be one of them. In the years since when he awoke in the night, usually several times, to rub his eyes and check that the light remained on in Rose's room, he hated himself each time for the spark of relief he felt when he saw the yellow-white glow.

The fire crackled, adding an even greater circle of heat to an already hot night.

Cutter threw on one more piece of wood from the remains of a cord stacked against the limestone wall and shielded by the overhang. He looked around and at his watch. It was the best he could do. He walked over to his Jeep, unlocked the trunk attached to the bed and took out a small, elegant travel case. The hand-rubbed leather was tan in color, and it was one of the few items of athletic tribute, aside from food, that Cutter kept. He locked the metal trunk then tucked his tightly rolled sleeping bag under his arm left arm. With his right he took a box of .12 gauge shells from the compartment under the driver's seat. He stuffed as many as he could get into the pockets of his jeans and lifted his shotgun from its rack. Then he walked back down the dark road to the Lincoln.

Chapter 5

When Cutter returned to Wolf's Run, only dim, flickering lights showed through the kitchen window and those of Holly's bedroom. Lightning glowed brighter around the mountaintop, and the rumbling footfalls of thunder were close enough to be heard. Music was spilling softly onto the porch from a record player somewhere in the house. Cutter put down his gear outside the bedroom windows. Except for the shotgun. He quietly walked down the porch to the kitchen door and looked in through the glass. Two candles were burning between plates set out on the table.

Cutter knocked as he opened the door and stepped inside. From somewhere Charlie yapped and her paws began scrabbling on the heart pine. The ceiling fan stirred the candle flame on the table and thin shadows moved amid the yellow light cast on the cabinets. The music was full of violins, muted horns and a voice as smooth as good coffee.

"Miss Carter? It's Cutter."

Charlie came skittering into the kitchen and stood in front of Cutter, waiting to be petted. Cutter squatted like a hunter with the butt of the shotgun on the floor and stroked the curly white fur between the dog's ears. He smelled cornbread and saw a small red light glowing on the stove.

"Miss Carter?" he said again.

After several moments, Holly Lee Carter emerged from the hallway. She was wearing the same BelAir Hotel bathrobe she'd been wearing the night man stepped onto the moon. Her hair was still wet and the candlelight set aglow every copper strand in its dark red weave.

"Charlie likes you," she said, the stress and smoke and hours of tears adding to the natural huskiness of her voice. "She doesn't like many people."

"Neither do I," he said, standing. "But Charlie'll do."

Lightning painted the kitchen windows. "A storm is coming," Holly said as if she were observing the phenomenon from a long distance away. Removed from this place and time and the events of the last few days.

"Yep," said Cutter. "It's been so hot. It had to break."

"The power goes out up here even in a mild storm. I decided I might as well get ahead of it and light some candles."

"Good idea," he said, but saw that in that moment she had drifted away. There was a towel and a brush in Holly's lap, and she picked up the brush and began slowly drawing it through the remaining tangles in her hair. Cutter checked the safety and leaned the shotgun against a door frame, then propped himself on a kitchen chair. He watched in silence as Holly Lee Carter brushed her hair, stroke after smooth stroke, after long, slow stroke. She ignored the lightning and his gaze, and the passing of several minutes as if time had no hold on her or this night. When she finished she put the brush on the counter.

"Do you like Sinatra?" she asked.

Cutter's mouth was dry. He said, "I guess I'm more of a Johnny Cash kinda guy."

"Cash? Yes. He's quite a talent. But there's nothing like Sinatra when you're feeling low," said Holly. "That voice. The phrasing. He's the buddy you want sitting next to you at the bar when you find out everything has … has? … has gone to hell." She laughed softly but there was no humor in it. "Or maybe I'm just showing my age. Ohhhh, how I'm showing my age."

"No you're not. You look good."

Holly smiled wanly. "Cutter, you're a terrible liar. But I hope you never get good at it. A lot of people do," she told him, and placed the towel next to the brush. When she did, Cutter saw the snub-nosed .38 between her thigh and the arm of the wheelchair.

"Where did you get that?" he asked, eyeing the gun.

"The gun cabinet in the library," she said. "Most are antiques, but there's a veritable arsenal in there. Do you think I'm nuts for going around my own house with a loaded gun?"

"Considering what's happened the last few days, I'd think you were nuts if you didn't. One of the main reasons I went by the The Well was to get my shotgun out of the Jeep. Just in case."

Holly looked at the window that alternately captured her image and Cutter's framed in black and the pulse of lightning growing more rapid by the minute. "Yes. Just in case," she said as if to the images in the window. Then to Cutter – "Are you hungry?"

"I could eat."

"Good. I put cornbread in the oven to warm," she said, wheeling to the refrigerator. "People brought enough food to feed a family of six for a week."

She opened the door as Cutter came over and squatted beside her. He began reaching for platters of meat and Pyrex dishes and casseroles filled with other treats. She grabbed his wrist, hard – her emotions already raw and barely contained. "Stop it!" she told him with a sudden fierceness in eyes rimmed red by long hours of tears. "I'm not helpless!"

Cutter didn't blush easily, but he felt the heat in his neck and his face flush even as Holly released his wrist, realizing how panicked and desperate and angry she sounded. Cutter took his hands away from the dishes and looked at her.

"I'm sorry about what I said the morning you got here," he told her. "I didn't know you. I only knew Tony and how he uses his – his? – one-leggedness, his crippledness to excuse every ugly, selfish thing he, he –" Holly saw a glistening in Cutter's eyes, then he turned his face away. "Anyway, I shouldn't have said what I did."

Holly didn't know what Cutter's words made her feel. Happiness? Gratitude? Relief? Irritation with herself that she felt a need to prove anything to Cutter? Who the hell was he? She didn't trust anything she felt at this moment, but like it or not Cutter's words vibrated through her veins like a guitar chord, suddenly but gently touched. Her lips trembled then opened ready to speak in a language her body had all but forgotten, ready to – Holly swallowed then forced words from her throat. "Go sit down," she said, "before the cornbread burns."

Holly prepared plates of cold ham, potato salad and green-bean casserole. The storm broke across Blue Mountain as she lifted the pan of cornbread from the oven. The rain came in on a hard wind that rattled the French doors that led to the interior porch. It plunk, plunk, plunked onto the roof in big, wide-spaced drops then more, then more until it was an uninterrupted roar high in the rafters.

They slathered fresh cream butter from a dairy east of DeLong onto the hot cornbread that Ruth Wiggington had delivered at midafternoon. She had been Holly's English teacher through most of high school.

Holly held the cornbread and sweet butter in her mouth, savoring it with her eyes closed before swallowing. "Ummmm," she sighed. "That is so good."

"Miz Wiggington makes a good pan," Cutter said from across red-and-white checks of the vinyl tablecloth.

"Thank you for dealing with the people who came by today. And the phone calls."

"I was up. I wasn't sure if I should answer the phone. I didn't want to take it off the hook because it might be the paper, but I didn't want it to wake you."

"You did the right thing. Even when I was awake, I was in no shape to talk to anyone," she told him. "But you driving me to Memphis and taking care of things here today, it'll create a lot of talk. Me being in this – this? – 'condition' will ease it a little. But I'm afraid my reputation will precede us both."

"I'm not worried about it. You and I know the truth."

She smiled at him. "I wish it were that simple."

Cutter knew that Holly was right, but what was done was done. There was no point worrying at it. A sudden crash of lightning threw Wolf's Run into darkness and the rain started its rattling drumbeat on the tin roof. Through the open kitchen windows storm-cooled air rushed in and tugged at the candle flames, causing them to dance, but they held up and continued to cast warm light and deep shadows.

"I hope Daddy kept up repairs on the roof," said Holly.

"Yep, it's comin' down, all right," Cutter said. Then, "Did you see my note about Miss Davis calling from Los Angeles? She said she was an old friend. That she'd be here tomorrow."

"She is. In fact, Julie was my best friend when I worked at *The Chronicle*. We shared an apartment a few blocks from the office. More of a crash pad, really, for anyone from the paper who needed someplace to sleep and didn't want to drive all the way home. L.A. is so big! Now Julie is their star news features writer."

"I guess little ol' DeLong has turned into quite a story."

"Yes. I'm sure it has. They only send Julie to the big stuff."

"She said she'd like to stay with you while she's in town. That might be a good idea. I mean, with Miz Howard –"

Holly nodded. "Yes. You're right. I admit, I'm not eager to stay out here by myself right now."

"No one could blame you for that," he said. "I knew feelings ran deep around here about black folks going to Cattahatchie High and votin'. But these last few weeks? It's opened up a wide streak of meanness I didn't believe was here. Or I didn't want to believe it." He looked up at the still ceiling fan for a moment as if he couldn't bear to look at the truth square in the face, then – "Anyway, while you were sleeping Governor Broderick sent in the National Guard. But not local guys. He called up some units from the coast. There's a dusk-to-dawn curfew for the whole county. Maybe it'll help cool things off. Along with a good, hard rain."

"Maybe," she said looking out the windows filled with lightning and a darkness that was as deep as any she could remember. "I guess that means you have to stay here again."

"I'd already planned to. Curfew or no curfew."

In the candlelight, Cutter's eyes were like blue-white pearls. Holly felt blood warming her neck and a tingle sliding across her shoulders and down into her chest.

"You don't have to sleep on the porch," Holly heard herself say, and could hear her pulse thudding in her neck above the crash of the rain on the tin roof. "I mean, there are, you know, six bedrooms in this house," she quickly added. "Four aren't occupied. Five now, I guess."

Holly wondered if in the candleglow and lightning Cutter could see the heat in her cheeks. "Tomorrow night I'll be back to sleepin' on rocks. No sense in gettin' acquainted with a bed tonight. Thanks anyway."

Now Holly was happy to change the subject, even if by saying, "I guess you've had it pretty rough, especially since Miss Jenny –"

"Rougher than some, not near as bad as others," said Cutter, immediately deflecting that line of conversation. "This ham sure looks good. Tom-Ed Belle's wife brought it by. Nobody smokes a ham any better than Mr. Belle."

"You're right. Mr. Belle's famous for his hams," agreed Holly and let the subject go. Mostly they said little during the meal. Cutter was not given to small talk in the best of circumstances, and Holly was too worn out and hollowed out by all that had happened to provide the impetus for mealtime chitchat. Instead, the rain drum the roof and tatter at the windows, and they found a strange comfort in their ability to be silent with one another.

After dinner, Holly washed the dishes and Cutter dried them and stacked them on the blue and white tiles of the counter. It was only 8:30 but all she wanted was to be back, safe in Meemaw Carter's bed. She thanked Cutter and excused herself.

"You can take a couple of candles into the library and work on your pool game if you want to."

"No thanks," he said, drying his big hands on a dish towel. "I'll just sack out. It's been a long couple of days."

"Yes. Yes it has. Good night, Cutter."

"Good night, Miss Carter. I'll be close."

"I know you will. And I appreciate it," she said and pivoted toward the hall.

In the bathroom, Holly washed her face and throat with a cool cloth. She lifted her hair and let it rest on the back of her neck for a bit before slipping into one of her favorite sleeping T-shirts. She lay her battered Martin six-string on the big four-poster. She put Charlie up, too, and the little dog quickly found her usual spot and settled in. Holly blew out the candles on her bedside table and lifted herself onto the fresh sheets she'd put on while Cutter was at The Well. She moved her hips and then her long legs, as if they belonged to someone else. She slipped the .38 under a pillow, then propped on two and picked up the guitar. The rain was only a soft purr now and the air from the open windows was cool and fresh and carried the vague scent of Old Spice. A small creek of water filled the gutters and ran down the drain-pipes to where it spewed onto a square of bricks fashioned by slaves more than one-hundred years earlier. Outside on the porch she could hear Cutter move from time to time as she strummed the guitar the way she often did when she was troubled or confused and needed to think.

How had the guy who had greeted her with such contempt that first morning back in DeLong become her most valuable ally? How had be become even something more? Something she could not possibly –

And yet as Holly fingered the strings with unconscious eloquence, her thoughts returned to the previous night. She wasn't sure what had happened once she and Cutter were out of the parking lot of the Memphis hospital and out of her chair. Had she fainted? Collapsed from exhaustion once she was out of the view of cops, news cameras and Eve Howard's hysterical mother? Whatever it was, when a bump in the highway jarred her eyes open, she had realized her head was in Cutter's lap. She glance down and saw her legs were up on the seat, but she had given no sign of awakening even when his fingers began moving over her shoulders and neck, stroking her hair. It had made her skin tingle in all the places where she still owned her skin and she felt her nipples harden inside the soft cups of her bra. There was a strong part of her that wanted to roll over, reach up, caress the front of Cutter's jeans until he hardened, then unzip them and take him into her mouth. They wouldn't even have to slow down. It wouldn't be the first time she'd dug her fingernails into a man's thigh and performed passionate fellatio at seventy miles per hour. She'd always relished satisfying a man with her mouth, which accounted for much of her less-than-chaste reputation as a teen. The number of men she'd actually slept with was, well, not negligible, but not nearly the number that many in DeLong and even friends in L.A. assumed. And she had not been with a man at all since being airlifted out of Vietnam in '65. Four years. There had been a few awkward dates and kisses at her front door, but she never let it go further. Oh, her mouth still worked fine and sometimes wanted what it had first discovered at thirteen, but she always made her lips part only in a smile as she said good-night, fearful that going on would end in miserable unsatisfaction and embarrassment for both of them. Though she had not had the legion of motel conquests many imagined, when she had opened her legs for a man, she knew her taut, athletic body coupled with a natural sense of rhythm often was able to give him more pleasure than he'd ever before had. Maybe more than he'd ever have again. Indeed, she'd been like a drug to some of them. Now she couldn't move her legs or even feel them. So, she had steeled herself to the emotional loneliness and the physical emptiness, deciding she could do without a man and thus without the humiliation she feared any clumsy, leaden attempt at intimacy would bring.

Now as Holly thought more about the ride back from Memphis she realized that for the first time in a very long time, she had not felt lonely. She had felt safe and comforted and appreciated, and even happy – as terrible as that sounded considering all that had happened. Still, the oppressive combination of caution and exhaustion had kept motionless on the Lincoln's wide bench seat, wishing she and Cutter could drive forever through the warm summer air, his fingertips as soft as starlight on her skin while the radio played "cool sounds for lonely lovers."

On the porch, Cutter lay atop his sleeping bag. He could smell the gun oil on the .12 gauge next to him on the planks. The rain was nearly finished and the bright, loud part of the storm had moved off over the mountain to the northeast. He enjoyed the sound of Holly Lee Carter's fingers moving over the strings and sliding up along the frets. She was the most beautiful woman Cutter had ever seen, and he'd already seen quite a few in his eighteen years and almost eleven months. Standing by his Jeep after football practice or a game. Dropping by his campsites unbidden. Especially at The Gin or sashaying through the pool halls and barbecue joints of south Memphis, where he sometimes went to escape not who he was, but who everyone in DeLong expected him to be – everybody's All-American. But none of those girls or women ever had touched him the way Holly Lee Carter had. And she doesn't even know it, he thought.

"Cutter? Am I keeping you awake?"

He cleared his throat and pulled himself out of the memory he was beginning to cherish in a way that surprised and confused him.

"No. I like it," he said. "Play all night if you want to. I'll be here."

Holly smiled and began again moving her fingers over the strings as Cutter listened and the clouds finally cleared and the moon rose. Listened as a sheer white light filled the yard and painted shadows behind the pines, the old greenhouse and the garage. Listened while Holly held the guitar against her – in the darkness of her bed, like a lover – and played music that was sweet and Spanish and sad until her fingers were too sleepy to find the chords.

CHAPTER 6

As the smell of smoke cleared from DeLong, things seemed to calm down a bit. Funerals were planned and bulldozers were brought in to clear debris in Roseville. Glass installers from Memphis and Tupelo made fast and plenty money plying their trade along River Street and at dozens of houses on the west side of the river. Payment plans were available, but even then some in Roseville could not afford the price. So they covered their broken windows with plywood, plastic sheeting or the cloth saved from twenty-five-pound Dixie Lily Flour sacks.

Really, Klansmen – whether local Kluxers or the unnamed "outside radicals" Brother MacAllister and Governor Weathers were so fond of blaming for the attacks – had little choice but to slip back into their spider holes, or into the supple anonymity of business suits, work khakis and overalls. FBI men were so thick on the roads that a fellow couldn't pull off into a stand of trees to take a leak for fear of exposing himself to a camera lens. Federal marshals, under the direction of U.S. Attorney J.L. Burke, staked out a handful of black churches that had been particularly active in registering congregants to vote.

A gaggle of reporters roamed the streets of town asking over and over the same questions of everyone from lawn men to doctors to dressmakers to mechanics and county officials. They came from as far away as Boston and New York, San Francisco, Miami, Los Angeles and even London. Most encamped at The Jeff Davis Hotel and ate dinner in the Gen. Nathan Bedford Forrest Dining Room or at The Cotton Café, the tragedy creating a strange and unexpected economic boon for local merchants. Several were known to be staying at Wolf's Run. To temporarily augment her staff, Miss Carter exchanged desk space and darkroom privileges at *The Current-Leader* for the right to use their material.

Meanwhile, the National Guardsmen parked Jeeps with mounted machine guns on the town square and set up checkpoints on the main roads in and out of DeLong and at the Bilbo Bridge beside the jail. It was hard to drive more than a mile on Highway 27 without meeting a green National Guard troop transport or seeing a Highway Patrol car on the shoulder of the road.

Throughout the county it was common knowledge that Sheriff Wallace and a couple of deputies he trusted were shaking – sometimes violently – every tree in the county for information about the attacks. Plenty of Klan nuts were falling out but either the rank-and-file Kluxers weren't privy to the information or they really were the work of "outside radicals," I told myself, and did my best to believe it even as my father hauled Milton Handley out of his department store in handcuffs. They questioned him overnight but by Friday morning he was on the local airwaves along with Governor Weathers and Brother MacAllister praying for "the many lost and misled souls in Cattahatchie County doing Satan's work."

Standing in front of the crater that marked the spot where Bryant Funeral Home had been, a network newsman told the nation Thursday night that a "veneer of calm has settled over DeLong, Mississippi." And "veneer" was, indeed, the perfect word because the superficial tranquility was imposed by force and nothing else. Going into the Friday funerals, DeLong was like a fire that had been roughly but carelessly doused. Beneath the surface, the heart of the blaze remained – hot enough to rend skin from bone, I thought with a shudder as I rubbed my hand on the leg of my jeans.

The mirror above the chest of drawers in my room at Mrs. Fletcher's Boarding House vibrated against the flowered wallpaper as a Santa Fe freight picked up speed after slowing for crossings in DeLong. I walked through the screen door and onto the small balcony that came with my room in the sagging, paint-faded Victorian that sat in a wooded V between the railroad tracks and the river south of town. The rooms on the east side of the gabled dwelling were considered the least desirable due to their proximity to the tracks. So, I got a discount, but the truth was I didn't mind the four daily trains – not even the two a.m. express freight that squealed and whistled but slowed little and stopped for nothing – rattling, humming, keeping a hot, bluesy beat as it hurried through the cotton fields toward Oxford, then Vicksburg and all the way down to New Orleans. It reminded me that as sure as steel rails, there was something beyond DeLong. There were other places Patti and I could go, away from here and her daddy and this ugliness. We merely needed to find our train and ride.

With my new job at Handley's I normally would not have been in my room to feel the four p.m. train rumble up through my bones, but on that Friday DeLong was essentially shut down in terms of local commerce. Ridge Bellafont's funeral had been at 10 that morning at the old Episcopal Church at the top of Hill Street. Built in 1831, it was DeLong's first church, and even though it mostly had been abandoned over the decades for more charismatic denominations, it still held for the county's oldest families an emotional connection. They shut their businesses and left their big farms and turned out in their Cadillacs, Lincolns and Chrysler Imperials.

At two p.m., five caskets were lined up in front of the pulpit in the brick sanctuary of Roseville A.M.E. Church. The church was packed and the small window air-conditioning units chugged and groaned and helped little. Outside, several hundred more mourners stood in the scalding August sun listening over loudspeakers as Reverend Baptiste spent two hours preaching the funerals. Holly Lee Carter sweltered across the street in her convertible along with her friend, Julie Davis, from the L.A. Chronicle. Cutter stood out in the crowd of mostly black faces.

Meanwhile, under the watchful eyes of the National Guard, the Klan was holding its own "Funeral for State's Rights" – parading around the town square while shouldering a mock coffin. FBI snipers were on the roofs of the courthouse and hotel, With most of the businesses shut down, the rally drew only a couple dozen Klux and a like number of observers. In fact, the local onlookers were almost outnumbered by reporters, photographers and cameramen shuttling between Roseville and the square as they looked for the best story.

According to the Memphis radio station that was covering the funeral, the five mule-drawn farm wagons that were hauling the caskets the three-quarters of a mile from the church to the Roseville Cemetery now were at the gates.

"It's ninety-six degrees and feels every bit of it," the radio reporter said, and he was right.

I went downstairs and poured myself a glass of tea from the large pitcher Mrs. Fletcher kept in the refrigerator. I drank a bit of it, held the glass to my forehead for a long minute, and drank some more. Then I crossed the back porch and went down the steps into the yard. A worn and uneven brick path led to the river.

Mrs. Fletcher – a big, white-haired woman with breasts that sagged to her waist and a spate of cancerous-looking freckles – and her sister, Mabel Richardson, were sitting in the shade on rusted metal lawn chairs near an old dock. The women had speckled porcelain bowls in their large laps and a bushel of purple-hull peas between them. Their thick fingers were stained blue-black from the dye in the pea shells, but their thumb nails cut through the dark husks of the legumes with the speed and skill of surgeons' scalpels.

"Young Mr. Wallace, you seem to be mighty partial to my ice tea," said Mrs. Fletcher.

"Yes, ma'am. It's as fine as I've ever had," I said, but my mind and eyes were across the river and two hundred or so yards back toward town where Roseville Cemetery poked out into the Cattahatchie like a broken thumb. Because the people of color in DeLong always had been forced to live on the low, swampy land between the river and the Chalmette hills, they had adopted the burial traditions of their south Louisiana cousins – covering graves with slabs of poured concrete or bricking together above-ground crypts where generations of dead were stacked like cordwood. Most years the effort paid off, and did not allow the spring rise of the Cattahatchie to force loved ones from the grave. But every decade or two when the river topped its banks by several feet and temporarily reclaimed most of the soft land next to the hills, caskets could be seen floating downstream, driven by the cold current and spinning in the eddies like ships helmed by blind sailors.

I walked out on the rickety dock and with my hands shaded my eyes against the sun glinting off the water. I could see the caskets – one of them draped in our nation's flag – being borne by pallbearers through the maze of small crypts. They were carried though shafts of light filtering between the oak boughs and placed beside their final resting places as the crowd swelled within the graveyard. Soon a capella voices that were mournful, but hopeful and determined, too, rose in singing *Swing Low, Sweet Chariot*, and the sound swam down-river toward me as pure and beautiful as rose petals strewn in the current. The sound made my chin tremble with emotions I couldn't categorize, and I pursed my lips to get control.

From the end of the dock, I watched the brief graveside service. I saw my father and Miss Carter among the crowd. A petite blonde in a black dress stood beside Miss Carter taking notes. Occasionally, Miss Carter lifted a camera from her lap and snapped a few pictures. Knowing how Cutter felt about Tommy Ray Banks, I figured he was there, too, though I did not see him until the final hymn had been sung and the mourners began to shuffle away on the dusty road that twisted back into Roseville. He stepped from behind a crumbling brick vault and approached the women.

"Cutter Carlucci, this is my friend, Julie Davis, from the *Chronicle*," said Miss Carter.

The reporter extended her hand and Cutter covered it in his grip. "My goodness, you are quite the young Adonis, aren't you?"

Cutter smiled but did not blush or feign false humility. Obviously, this was not the first time he'd heard such.

"Down, girl," said Miss Carter. "I'm sure Cutter has plenty of local sweethearts without borrowing trouble from Los Angeles."

"Trouble? Me?" she asked, her impish brown eyes twinkling. Julie Davis' small frame, features and short haircut made her look like a thirty-year-old pixie.

"Yes, you. And with a capital T," teased her friend.

Cutter asked, "Miss Carter, do you have a minute?"

"Sure," she said. "But not a lot more than that. I've got to get back to the office and wrap up the weekend edition before dark. The curfew is still in effect. We're going to do all the deliveries tomorrow."

"Do you need help?" he asked.

"No. We've reorganized the routes and actually managed to hire a few new carriers. I think we'll be all right," she told him, purposefully trying to distance herself from Cutter and all she had felt lying in her own bed with him sleeping only a few feet away. The more she had thought about that and their candlelit dinner, the more embarrassed and awkward she felt. After all, she was twenty-eight and he was eighteen. For goodness sake! Well, almost nineteen. Still! Then there was the whole wheelchair thing, the paralysis. *What was I thinking?* But knowing that Cutter was little given to casual conversation, she asked, "Julie could you excuse us for a moment."

"Why, of course, Lee," said Julie Davis as she gave Cutter a long look. At six-three, he was at least a foot taller. "It was a pleasure to meet you."

"Yes, ma'am. You, too."

Of course, I did not know until later what was said, but my jaw tensed and my lips tightened at the sight of Cutter and Miss Carter together in public. It made me angry and jealous, and filled me, too, with concern for my friend. My best friend! No matter the rough patch we were going through.

She lifted her hair off her sleeveless black dress and her neck. Even from a distance her shoulders looked beautifully strong. "It's sooo hot," she said. Then, "I'm sure the Banks family and Miss Winona appreciated you coming. I saw you at Ridge's funeral this morning, too."

"He took some of the best football pictures I've ever seen. And he gave me copies of a lot of them," explained Cutter. "I don't keep a scrapbook, but Rose does. He seemed like a nice man."

Miss Carter had to look away. "Yes. He was a very nice man," she said, clearing her throat. "But that's not why –"

"No. Look, I know a lot has happened in the last few days, and you've got an awful lot on your mind, but a '65 Olds is a popular car. Spare parts for them go pretty fast. Every day your daddy's car sits over there in Alabama –"

"The more likely it is we'll find it stripped or just plain gone," said Miss Carter. "Look, I could go by myself, but I'd feel a lot better if I had someone with me."

Cutter looked at her, understanding that her words covered two topics. One of which did not need to be stated. There was a lot of open back road between Delong and Moore's Bridge, Alabama.

"I'm a decent hand with cars," he said.

Holly smiled, hoping Cutter would say that. "I can't go tomorrow."

"And I start a week's worth of work Monday with a surveying crew."

"Do you think that junkyard would be open on Sunday?"

"From talking to the fella, I don't think it's a formal business," Cutter told her. "It's more of a backyard deal. I imagine he'd accommodate us. Especially if we called ahead."

"Do you have plans for Sunday?"

"Nothin' but a trip to Alabama," Cutter said and smiled, and whatever wall of separation Holly was trying to erect between them shook and shuddered.

Behind me and to my left I heard a splash in the river and I startled. A cottonmouth had dropped from a low limb into the water. I checked my watch. When I looked back toward the cemetery, Cutter and Miss Carter had disappeared among the tombs. I needed to go, too, if I was going to have dinner with the MacAllisters and get back to the boarding house before the sundown curfew.

"Ain't nothin' like a colored funeral to make you believe in God," said Mrs. Fletcher as I passed. She was stirring the air around her big face with a spade-shaped fan that depicted Jesus praying in the garden before his betrayal. It was provided by an insurance agency that sold burial policies for two-dollars a month. "If them po'r folks can keep the faith in the Almighty, then surely we can bow our heads to the Creator."

"I don't know, Sister," said Mabel Richardson, lowering a bucket into the river on a rope. She pulled it out, dipped a blue-and-white handkerchief in it and ran it around her wrinkled old neck. "Maybe it's easier for them than we think. All they got in this world is faith. They sho' ain't got nothin' else. Least not in these parts, wouldn't you say, young fella?"

"I guess," was the best I could manage as I watched the water moccasin swim with a poisonous ease across the brown-gold face of the river.

CHAPTER 7

Cutter rolled onto his back and rubbed his sleepy eyes.

"Puffy clouds … blue sky …birds chirpin' and a choir singing," he said from the back seat of Miss Carter's Lincoln. "Am I in heaven?"

"No," she said from the front. "Just Alabama."

Cutter sat up and ran his fingers through his black hair as he looked around. They were parked in the shadow of a maple tree at the edge of a dirt parking lot of the small New Testament Baptist Church. The sanctuary windows were open and *What a Friend We Have in Jesus* filled the air. He stepped out of the car, stretching.

"I thought we were going to stop for breakfast in Tupelo," he said, yawning.

"We were, but you worked all night and this past week's been rough on you, too. I thought I'd let you sleep. We'll stop for a big lunch on the way back."

Cutter opened the ice chest Holly had put in the back floorboard across from her chair. He took out a plastic jug filled with water and unscrewed the lid. "If I was sleeping that good, I imagine I was snoring like a chainsaw."

"For a mile or two I thought we'd lost a tire and we were riding on the rim," she teased. "When I realized it was you, I just turned the radio up. Loud."

Cutter finished washing the pasty taste out of his mouth and spit the water into the dirt. He half coughed, half laughed. Holly smiled. She liked the sound of Cutter's laugh, but tried to keep her mind focused on the purpose of the trip. "Mr. Conway's house is about a mile on down this road," said Holly as Cutter poured water into his hand and ran it over his face and neck. "I drove by, but the gate to his driveway had a chain on it. They're probably at church. So, I thought this would be a good place to wait."

Cutter pulled up his black The Gin STAFF T-shirt, exposing the metal of his belly, and dried his face. Holly made herself look away, mostly. "Yep. This is a pretty place," he said, shoving his shirt back into his jeans. "But it doesn't look much different from Miss'ssippi."

"No, it doesn't."

Cutter came around and propped on the fender near Holly. "You want to hear something sad?"

She groaned. "Not really. I've had about all the sadness I can deal with for one week."

"Not that kind of sad. Just … ridiculous."

"In that case, sure."

"Other than riding the team bus down to Jackson for the state football playoffs the last couple of years, this is probably the farthest I've ever been from DeLong," he said, and took another sip of water. "What do you figure? About a hundred-and-forty miles or so down here."

"Something like that."

"That's farther than Memphis. Even West Memphis, Arkansas. One night I drove across the bridge and parked on the levee just to see what the city looked like from the other side of the mighty Mississippi. And so I could say I'd been to Arkansas, I guess. Now that *is* ridiculous," he said, and chuckled at himself. Holly simply added that to the list of things she liked about him – that despite his often stoic, even stern demeanor, he could laugh at himself. Countless older and supposedly more mature men she had known were not secure enough to manage such casual and unconscious humility mixed with unpretentious confidence. Certainly not Gerry Yards, her former boss at the *Chronicle*, long-ago lover and would-be husband. Yards was among the six out-of-state or international journalists encamped at Wolf's Run, covering the funerals, the Klan and the hunt for McBride. Though she considered Gerry a dear friend, she could do without his pitying eyes following her around the house and the newspaper office.

"I don't know about ridiculous," said Holly. "Everyone can use a change of perspective now and then. A look at things from the other side of the river."

"Now who's being the diplomat?" he asked. "Well, one of these days, I'm gonna get out and see a little of this ol' world. I'd like to see where my mother's people came from in England. And I guess I'd like to see Italy, too. Rome. The Vatican. Florence!"

"Italy is beautiful," said Holly. "It's one of my favorite places."

"I guess you've been all over the world, haven't you?"

"The world is a big place. I wouldn't say I've been all over it, but I've hit some high spots."

"What's your favorite place?"

"Ireland is beautiful, especially by the sea," she told him. "Italy is lovely and filled with so much history and incredible art, but the Greek Isles are … breathtaking. Africa is like a storybook, or a *National Geographic* magazine come alive. Even Vietnam. It's very lush and green, and some of the beaches are incredible. But, honestly, it's hard to beat the U.S.A. for variety and beauty, and the people.

"Where I live in the mountains north of Los Angeles, it's – well, it's almost indescribable. At the right time of the year, you can be swimming in the Pacific in the morning and snow skiing in the mountains in the afternoon. And be back in the city in time for a late dinner at the Beverly Hilton."

"It sounds nice."

"It is. And I'm incredibly blessed to have the home I have. It's not a big place, but it's all mine. Well, mostly. Mine and Charlie's," she said, stroking the side of the little dog who was curled beside her hip.

"Then you're not planning to stay in DeLong?"

"No, Cutter, I'm not," she told him. "I came back to try to keep the paper out of the hands of people like Cecil Weathers. I had planned to stay for six months. A year at the most. But I've botched it so badly that I may get to go back to California a lot sooner than I expected."

Cutter took another sip from the water jug. "Just because things haven't worked out so far, doesn't mean it's your fault."

"Thanks. You're a good guy."

"I try to be. But don't let that get around."

The doors to the church opened and the sweat-dampened congregation began to pour out onto the steps and into the parking area. Cutter looked at his watch – 12:20. "If the Baptists are done, everybody ought to be let out by now," he said, getting in the front seat. "Let's go see how much of your daddy's car is left."

Holly pushed her Wayfarers onto her nose, turned the key and swung the convertible around.

"You know, one of these days when I shake the Miss'ssippi dust off my feet, maybe I'll come knockin' on your door in big ol' Los Angeles," said Cutter. "Maybe you could show me that view."

The words made a dozen images flash through Holly's mind – of dinner at the Malibu Inn, of driving high into the mountains, even laughing at Mickey and Minnie over in Anaheim. And all of them ended up back at her house with the deck and the ocean view and the distant thrumming of the surf mixed with the ever-present hum of vehicles on the Pacific Coast Highway.

Stop it! Holly told herself and forced herself to keep her gaze on the gravel road. "Who knows where any of us will be a few years from now – even a few months from now," she managed evenly. "But I'm sure L.A. will still be there if you get out that way."

* * *

Back in DeLong, 12:20 passed, and 12:25, and Brother C.E. MacAllister still was preaching, though some of the most prominent members of the First Denomination congregation already had departed the sanctuary. But Mrs. MacAllister and her daughters watched, transfixed, as Brother Daddy marched around the dais, mopped his brow with a monogrammed handkerchief and slapped the leather cover of his large Bible.

I've often wondered if Brother Mac planned what he said that day or if he simply went off on a tangent and, like a train picking up too much speed on a steep grade, reached a point where the brakes failed – a point at which he was out of control, the momentum of his own horrendous rhetoric carrying him down. I've wondered, too, whether in their megalomaniacal arrogance Governor Weathers and/or Milton Handley and Walter Kamp put him up to it. In the end, it doesn't matter except as a historical curiosity, because his "sermon" that day broke wide the fissures that separated not so much those who were for or against segregation, but between those who were willing to support brutality, intimidation and even murder to maintain what C.E. MacAllister described as "God's natural social order."

Without rehashing the hour-plus diatribe linking Old Testament battles and Dixiecrat politics, Brother MacAllister attempted to drill deep into unspoken white fear. It was a fear of the perversion and cruelty of our ancestors, and of the legalized social, economic and political repression of our own century. Fear that once freed of Jim Crow laws and the lawlessness of the Klan, blacks would rise up and retaliate with merciless bloodlust against generations of jailers, abusers and oppressors. It was a fear that gained its power from the instinctual knowledge that had the legal and physical leg irons been locked so long above our feet, once many of us were freed, our vengeance would be pitiless and unquenchable. But when Brother MacAllister attempted to sanction the car-bomb murder of Sheriff Johnson and the deaths of four innocent Roseville residents as "regrettable but legitimate casualties in the war to protect white Christian society," a murmur such as I'd never heard passed under the chandeliers in the big sanctuary. It wasn't anything as dramatic as a thunderclap, but it was as clear as the sudden rise of a storm tide to push against a long- standing though ultimately rotten bulwark.

Had C.E. MacAllister stopped there and done his usual altar call and prayer for those listening on WHCI that tide might well have slipped away in a grumbling retreat. At least for a time. But when he went on a harangue about "God's soldiers" rendering their "righteous judgment" in the whipping and mutilation of Ridge Bellafont, more than a few pews emptied. If First Denomination's pastor was perturbed by the sudden exodus, he gave no sign of it. In fact, it seemed to inspire him even more as he talked about God's wheat remaining while "the worthless chaff blows away."

It wasn't that those men and women who left their cushioned seats and guided their children up the long, carpeted aisles and out the doors supported "Sister Ridge's" assumed lifestyle. Most saw it for what the Bible calls it – an "abomination" – but they had the humility and social grace not to cast the first stone. And certainly not at one of their own. Ridge Bellafont was not an outsider, a radical or a black man. He was a cultured, soft-spoken, well-educated Cattahatchie County blue blood, known for the many beautiful and often hand-framed photographs he had gifted to moms, brides, businessmen and proud young athletes over more than thirty-five years.

In the hindsight of history, I wish I could say that the changes that began that day arrived on a surge of broader moral, racial and social enlightenment. But that simply was not the case. In fact, many of those same families continued to fund and enthusiastically support all-white Riverview Academy and pressured others to do the same. But what I can say from my limited Southern white-boy perspective is that the silent, tacit support that allowed the violent resistance of desegregation to flourish in DeLong began to crumble that day, soul by prayerful soul, when key members of several churches turned away from the ugly, twisted demagoguery of Brother MacAllister and his like.

He, and they, had gone too far; but, like the Pharisees, they didn't yet know it.

CHAPTER 8

About a mile from the little Baptist church in Alabama, Holly and Cutter turned through the open cattle gate under a hand-painted sign that read: Conway Salvage & Towing + Cows. A number of beefs of ill-defined lineage grazed on the hillside leading up to the small yellow brick house, but Holly and Cutter saw no junked cars. To the left of the house, though, under a big oak tree was a small, paint-faded 1950s-era wrecker. A far cry from the eighteen-wheeler flatbed with Oklahoma plates that LeRoy Kamp had suggested.

A smallish blond man came out of the kitchen door wearing a white shirt that was whisker-worn around the neck and khakis that had wrinkled in the heat and humidity. Behind a glass door in the carport a pretty redheaded woman looked out, so pregnant she looked as if she might give birth at any moment. A young blond boy in overalls with no shirt stood beside her.

"I'm Ronnie Conway," he said. "Are you the fella who called about parts for the Fords and the '65 Olds?"

"Yes, sir. My name is Carlucci. This is my friend, Holly Lee," said Cutter, offering a handshake. He didn't want to tip their hand by using the Carter name in case there was something going on between Kamp and Conway that didn't meet the eye.

Ronnie Conway allowed himself a good long look at the woman in the driver's seat, at the hand-control mounted beside the steering wheel, and the wheelchair folded in the back floorboard. "Normally, I don't like to do business on the Lord's day," he told them, "but since y'all were comin' all the way from Miss'ssippi. Where'd you say you're from?"

"My goodness, it's so hot out here, I b'lieve I'm just gonna melt," Holly told the men, slathering on her best Southern belle accent. "Honey, can't we get on with this?"

Cutter looked at Mr. Conway. "Ma'am, you can wait inside with my wife and young'un, if you'd like."

"No, thank you," she said. "I'm the one paying for the parts. I want see what I'm buying."

"Aw'right. Come on," he said, and started walking along a field road beside the house. "My salvage yard is over the ridge in back, out of sight, so that the neighbors don't whine."

Holly idled the big V-8 beside the men as they walked. When they topped the ridge, below her on a gently sloping hillside was an old barn that served as a makeshift garage and fifty or so cars in various stages of salvage. Some were nearly new. Others were striped red with rust, and were without glass, upholstery, an engine or one body part or another.

"You want to look at the Fords first, or the Olds?" Conway asked Cutter as they walked.

"Let's see the Olds first."

They turned down a grassy alley between the cars as Holly followed. Cutter helped Ronnie Conway push on a grazing cow until it moved out of the way. They walked on another twenty yards.

"Here's the Olds," he said.

Holly stopped in front of the gold, four-door Oldsmobile Ninety-Eight as Cutter walked around the junked car. There were no wheels on it and it was sitting up on three cinderblocks and a metal milk crate. Holly had wondered what she would feel when she saw the car in which her father died. Really, though, the vehicle itself was purchased years after she left DeLong, so it held no emotional significance for her. No memories of T.L. Carter in the driver's seat. The only thing she felt was relief that it still was mostly intact. The windshield was gone, as were the left fender and the trunk lid. The interior looked moldy but otherwise together. Most important, the dashboard was still in place and the steering wheel remained connected to its mount.

Holly pulled her Nikon out of her camera bag and began shooting, making sure to get Mr. Conway and the Olds in the same frame.

"What are you doing?" he asked.

"Taking a few pictures."

"I see that."

"I'm a photographer. It's what I do," she said. "Cutter, would you please look in the glove box, and tell me what you find."

He opened the passenger door. "The glove compartment is open. It's full of dried mud."

"What is this?" asked Conway. "What are you looking for?"

Cutter opened the big blade of the Swiss Army Knife he carried, poking through the mud then digging it out. "Nothing left in here."

"Who are you people?" demanded Conway.

Holly put down her camera and didn't let her disappointment show. She had rehearsed what she planned to say – "We're the people who can send you to jail for a very long time."

"Jail?"

"That car belonged to my father's company, Cattahatchie Newspapers

219

Incorporated. He died in it. I inherited the company, and there's no bill of sale or title transfer anywhere," she told him. "That means you're in possession of stolen property. Not only that, you transported it across state lines. That makes it a federal crime with federal time."

Cutter kept his face stony but had to suppress a smile. Holly was running a bluff. She knew the circumstances probably wouldn't sustain such a charge, but Ronnie Conway didn't know it. "Whoa! Whoa now! Wait just a dad-gum minute," he said. "I don't know nothin' about no stolen cars."

"Then you better have a good explanation of how this vehicle ended up here," said Cutter, picking up on Holly's rough-and-tough theme.

"An ol' Army buddy of mine, his family, the Kamps, they own a car lot over in DeLong," Conway told them. "He called me up and said he had a junker for me. Said a prominent local man died in it. People were comin' by to gawk at it. That the family just wanted it out of town and out of sight.

"LeRoy Kamp gave me two-hundred to come get it. That's all I know!"

Holly and Cutter shared a look. There was more to this and they both sensed it.

"What about paperwork?" asked Holly.

"Paperwork? Ma'am, look, lots of times with a wrecked car, especially one somebody died in, there's no paperwork," he told her. "People just want it gone."

"Then why did LeRoy lie to me about what he did with this car?" asked Holly.

Ronnie Conway swallowed hard and wet his lips.

"Mr. Conway, you seriously need to consider telling us what we want to know," said Cutter, propping one arm on the car's roof. "Miss Carter, here, owns a newspaper, and she's personal friends with the U.S. Attorney. One phone call from her and FBI men'll be swarmin' over this hill like red ants on a June bug."

"If your conscience is clear, then fine," said Holly. "But if not ..."

Ronnie Conway wiped his mouth. "Okay, Okay. Me'n LeRoy know each other from when we served together in Germany. In the Army. He was always braggin' about how his family owns a big car lot. I told him how I wanted to open my own garage and wrecker service. I did my tour and came back home to Moore's Bridge. I married and opened a shop, but it never took off. Now I do body work for the Ford place in town, and do a little towin' and shade-tree engine work on the side.

"Anyhow, a couple of years after LeRoy got out of the stockade, he called me. He heard I did some pullin' and salvage, and said he me might have some work for me."

The man's eyes darted back and forth from Holly to Cutter.

"Is that it?" she asked.

Conway stood silent but shifted from foot to foot.

"All right. Come on, Cutter. Let's find a phone. We'll see if he has more to say to the FBI."

"No, wait!" pleaded Ronnie Conway. He wiped his sweating hands on his pants legs. "Just wait." He took a breath, then – "Three or four times a year, LeRoy calls me to pick up a car. Sometimes at the car lot, but more often down some dirt road or out in a pasture. All I have to do is haul it back here and leave it sit. Two or three days later, a couple of fellas come by and poke around in it. After they leave, I'm free to sell it off any way I want to."

"The same guys every time?" asked Cutter.

"One's always the same."

"And when they poke around in the cars, what do they find?" asked Holly.

"I don't know," he said and saw the incredulous looks from his visitors. "I swear! When they come around, all I do is point 'em to the car and make myself scarce. I don't know what they're fetchin', and I don't want to know."

Cutter propped against the Olds. "And you do all this for spare parts?"

Conway sighed. "LeRoy pays me five hundred up front."

Holly took a moment to think about all Ronnie Conway had told them, then – "Did those men you spoke of come around to get something out of my father's car?"

"No. No, they didn't." They looked at him. "Hey, you know the whole deal now. I got no reason to lie."

W ith Ronnie Conway's help, Cutter spent the next half hour tearing apart the interior of the Olds. They took out the seats, pulled the dash, tore out the buckled carpet and sliced into the cloth that hung from the interior of the roof looking for a set of glasses – which they did not find. They did, however, find T.L. Carter's gold pocket watch wedged in the crack of the back seat as Holly documented the process on film and Charlie watched. Her heart jumped when Cutter handed the watch to her. As a child she'd played with it many times. She opened the case. The hands were stopped at 8:38. She closed it, the hinges grinding with sand, and held it tight in her hand.

Cutter got his tool box out of the Lincoln's trunk and removed the steering wheel from the Olds. He placed the wheel in the convertible's trunk and shut it as Holly wrote a check for two hundred dollars. She handed it to Ronnie Conway as Cutter got in the passenger seat.

"What's this for?" he asked cautiously as she closed her purse and pushed her sunglasses onto her nose. "For your time and cooperation today, and for what I'll call a storage fee. No more parts get sold off that car. Understood?" He nodded, but Holly thought she saw the gears turning behind his eyes. "Mr. Conway, I believe this car was used in a crime, and I don't mean whatever piddling enterprise LeRoy Kamp is involved in.

"If we come back looking for it and it's gone, or if you tip LeRoy that we were here, so help me, I'll make it my business to see that the FBI turns your life inside out. You'll be lucky to get out of prison in time to see your new baby graduate from high school."

CHAPTER 9

olly and Cutter crossed the Sipsey River and turned north on Alabama 171. Just outside of Fayette they pulled into a burger and barbecue joint that had a paved parking lot. It also had four formidable steps but a sidewalk led around the side of the red clapboard building. In back, five picnic tables were situated on hardpack dirt beneath a large walnut tree. A small lake lay at the bottom of the hill.

Cutter placed their order at a window on the back deck and returned with two large glasses of tea and a basket of sweet potato chips with horseradish dip on the side. Holly was holding her father's watch in her hands, studying it.

"A sweet 'tater chip for your thoughts," he said.

Holly took it from Cutter's fingers and slipped it between her lips. "Those are good," she told him. Then, "I'm wondering how the watch my father carried during almost every waking moment of his life wound up lodged in the crack of the back seat."

"I could say it was because your father's car probably was tumbling in the current like a Matchbox toy in a washing machine. But you already know that," Cutter responded, watching Holly for a reaction. She kept her eyes on the timepiece. "We may never know. Just like we may never know whether your father removed those glasses from the glove box or if it was the work of the river."

Holly nodded as if she was hearing him from a distance. "Of course, you're right."

When it became clear she was going to say no more, Cutter said, "A person's family business is their business, and I try to stay clear of stuff that's none of my business. But it doesn't take a Sherlock Holmes to add up the questions you've been asking and see where you're going with them."

A bell rang beside the pick-up window. While Cutter went to get their food, Holly decided she was going to trust him with all she knew and suspected about her father's death. He'd earned it, more than once. When he returned, they ate and Holly shared everything – from facts to guesswork. Cutter listened and asked smart questions, Holly noted as she sipped her tea. Finally, he said, "When you add it all up? Yeah, I can see it bein' more than possible.

"Somebody hit your father in the head with – well, we don't know with what yet. His glasses flew off and in the killer's panic he didn't notice the lens was missing," said Cutter, thinking out loud. "Then, Mr. Doe, let's call him, loads your father into the back of the Olds. Mr. Carter isn't dead, but since there's no sign that he was tied up – at least not according to the Oxford autopsy – he must have been unconscious. But Mr. Carter was a big man. I'd say he went at least two-fifty. Maybe two-sixty or even seventy. That's a lot of weight to move from the library out to the car. Even if it was parked right in front."

"I've thought of that, too," said Holly.

"So, Mr. Doe would have to be a pretty big man or have help."

"Yes. How big would you say LeRoy Kamp is?" she asked.

"Six-one, two-thirty or so. He's big enough. But what was his motive?" wondered Cutter as he lifted a sweet potato chip to his mouth. "I suppose you've already ruled out plain ol' robbery?"

"Yes. My father never kept large amounts of cash at the house or in his wallet. And everything of real value is still there. There's nothing – well, nothing of real material value missing."

"But something is missing?"

Holly dropped her napkin onto the plate and stared out at the lake. Two little boys were fishing with cane poles from a makeshift raft. "A painting," she said. "A painting of my mother that hung in the library."

"For all these years after your folks split up?"

"Yes. Daddy mentioned it in a letter just a few weeks before he died. No matter how ugly he acted, Daddy never stopped loving her."

"That doesn't mean it had anything to do with your father's death. Or even that it was taken that night," Cutter reasoned. "Maybe Mr. Tom took it for sentimental reasons. Especially after he found out you inherited Wolf's Run."

Holly smiled but there was no humor in it. "I wish I could lay it off on that. But if anyone really loathed my mother more, it was Tom. He never would have taken that painting."

Cutter considered all that he'd been told. "I heard Mr. Tom was out of town at a convention or somethin' when Mr. Carter died. I suppose you've confirmed that?"

"Yes. I talked to the deputy who reached him on the phone in Gulfport."

"So, he couldn't have done it himself."

"Himself?" asked Holly, looking deep into Cutter's eyes, trying to see if he had the audacity to be thinking the same thing she already was considering.

"Maybe Tom got tired of waiting for what he thought was going to be his inheritance," said Cutter. "Mr. Carter's will leaving the paper and the rest to you came as a shock to everybody. Mr. Tom tried to play it off around town like he knew all about it. But –" he shrugged – "I don't know many people who believed it. And I heard Miss Mary Nell took to her bed for several days with one of her sick headaches."

When Holly didn't speak, Cutter went ahead and said it plain, "Tom could have paid LeRoy or someone else to do it and make it look like an accident. But in case there was any suspicion, Gulfport makes for a good alibi."

Holly finally blinked and heard herself swallow. She started to speak, but her mouth was dry. She ran her tongue over her lips. "Tom's my brother, but ... God help me, Cutter, I've thought the same thing."

"If you hadn't, you wouldn't be near as smart as I think you are."

"Sometimes smart's overrated," she said and pushed her plate away. "I think I've lost my appetite."

"I haven't," said Cutter, pulling the plate with the remaining half a cheeseburger to him.

Holly watched the kids fishing from the raft on the lake while Cutter finished. It made her ache to think Tom could somehow be a part of this – if there was any "this" to be a part of. She still had no real proof a crime occurred.

Cutter stood and carried their empty paper plates and other scraps to a black, fifty-gallon drum mounted between two pine four-by-fours. When he returned to the table with his Ray-Bans on his nose and a toothpick at the corner of his mouth, Holly looked up at him. "Maybe I'm stacking one coincidence on another and creating a lot of melodrama over nothing," she said, squeezing T.L. Carter's watch in both hands in front of her. Cutter propped a work boot on the bench seat. "Knowing that Daddy was coming all the way to California to be with me after my surgery, there are so many things I wish I'd had the chance to say to him. And so many I hope he might have said to me. Maybe I'm looking for somebody or something to blame because I never got that chance."

"What's your gut tell you?"

Holly didn't hesitate – "That my very fastidious father did not walk out of Wolf's Run on a cold, rainy night in his shirt sleeves headed for some unscheduled meeting, or whatever, then miss a turn he'd made at least five days a week for most of the last ten years in all kinds of weather," she told him, then drew in a long breath and let it out – "Ohhhh, but it breaks my heart to think Tom might have been ... involved."

"Then prove he wasn't," said Cutter, picking up the keys from the table. "Come on. I'll drive and let you and your gut sort things out."

CHAPTER 10

B
y the middle of the following week, the National Guard still was patrolling the streets of DeLong and major county roads. The word was that the curfew would be lifted for the weekend and the Guard would pull out on Sunday, but no one knew for sure. If any progress had been made on catching McBride or the Klansmen who killed Ridge Bellafont and maimed Eve Howard, no one knew about that either. On page three of *The Current-Leader* was a picture of a scarecrow depicting my father as a Judas. The caption asked for anyone who had seen the scarecrow in some farmer's field to call the sheriff's office. Ironically, the photo bore Mr. Bellafont's credit line.

On Wednesday afternoon Cutter pulled his Jeep into a parking place in front of *The Current-Leader* building. A glazer was finishing the installation of a large piece of plate glass on one side of the new door while a painter was carefully lettering a sign onto the other window.

The Cattahatchie Current-Leader ... Since 1836 ... The Conscience of the Community ...

"Nice," he said to Miss Frances, the octogenarian receptionist/columnist, as he stepped into the rebuilt lobby. The smell of smoke was mixed with the fresh scent of just-cut pine. Most of the new work still needed painting.

"Yes," said Frances Ragland, who had worked behind the newspaper's counter for more than fifty years. "I'd been telling T.L. for years that this place needed to be renovated. I suppose I always knew it would take a fire or tornado it to get it done."

"Yes, ma'am. Is Miss Carter around?"

"No, son. She ran routes all morning, then she and her friend, Miss Julie, were going to Memphis to try to see Miss Eve before her mother takes her back to California. Of course, they'll have to be back in DeLong before dark."

"Yes, ma'am."

"Would you like to leave a message?"

"No thanks," he said and turned for the door. "I'll try to catch her out at Wolf's Run. Or drop by tomorrow."

"Before you go," said Miss Frances, "may I ask, are you a church-goer?"

225

Cutter paused a beat, then said, "My momma did her best to raise me and Rose in the church until –" His words fell away.

"Yes, honey, I understand."

"I haven't been much since, but I've read a good bit of the Bible and I still like the music."

"We're starting a little Sunday morning prayer meeting," said Miss Frances. "I don't want to call it a church service. We don't have a pastor. At least not yet. We're just going to read the Bible and pray, and sing praises to the Lord.

"Miss Holly is letting us hold it here," she said. Cutter could hardly believe what he was hearing from one of the pillars of First Denomination. "Down in the pressroom. It's a big space. We can open the bay door for air and there's plenty of parking. You'd be welcome to come."

Cutter shifted on his feet. "Miss Frances, if you don't mind me asking – I mean, you and Mr. George have been members of First Denomination since … since?"

"My father was a brick mason and he helped lay the foundation for the original sanctuary at First Denomination in 1877," said Miss Frances. "My first date with George – though we didn't call them dates back then – he rented a buggy with the most beautiful bay mare I believe I've ever seen, and we went to services and an all-day singin' and dinner on the grounds." Cutter could see that her eyes were getting misty. "George and I were married there in 1898. And we were blessed to see five of our six children saved in that sanctuary. Along with scads of grandchildren and even great-grands."

Miss Frances wiped a tear from her eye. "I'm sorry," she said. "George and I love First Denomination, but somehow it's lost its way." Cutter nodded thoughtfully, assuming that was all Miss Frances would have to say, but she went on – "Mind you, I don't entirely blame Brother MacAllister. A flock can't be led someplace it doesn't want to go. But Brother Mac has given a lot of otherwise decent folks an excuse for their fear and hatred of nee'gras. And of plain ol' change. He's cloaked it in the robes of Jesus, and that's just wrong.

"George has tried to speak up within the leadership, but they dismiss him. Too old. Not in touch with today's world. But I think it's them that's not in touch with today's world. Jesus was all about people growin' in their spirit and changin', and learnin' to love each other. Not … Not this," she said, opening her arms and look- ing around the room – its high corners still sooty with smoke. After a moment she dropped her arms tiredly to her sides and turned her milky eyes back on Cutter. "Anyways, after what Brother Mac said on Sunday about dear Mr. Ridge and the others, George and I spent a long time in prayer. We just can't be part of it anymore, as much as it pains us. And there are quite a few others who feel the same way."

Cutter wasn't sure what to say, so he said nothing.

"Well now, that's the end of my sermon," said Miss Frances, reaching for a tissue from a box by the cash register and dabbing her eyes. "So sorry. I started out merely wanting to extend an invitation. But … But these are such fragile times."

"Yes, ma'am, I understand," said Cutter. "And I appreciate the invite."

* * *

When Holly turned her convertible into the driveway at Wolf's Run, the shadows were long and deep in the yard. The sun was down behind Blue Mountain and the sky glowed with a halo the color of a robin's egg tied with pink ribbons of cloud.

Cutter sat in his Jeep next to the garage.

"My, my!" said Julie Davis. "This *is* a pleasant surprise."

"Hi," he said.

"Hi," said Holly, happier to see Cutter that she wanted to show. But Charlie didn't bother to hide her delight. Cutter got out and squatted to pet her.

"How's Miss Howard?"

"How did you know we were in Memphis?" asked Holly as she transferred to her chair.

"I dropped by the newspaper this afternoon. Miss Frances told me."

"Eve's mother hired private security guards. We couldn't get in to see her," Holly explained. "But one of the nurses told me her condition had been upgraded from serious to good. But her life? It'll never be the same … because she came here with me."

"No, Holly. It'll never be the same because she made a bad decision," said Julie Davis. "In the end, that decision is what got her hurt and got your Mr. Bellafont killed."

That hard truth hung in the twilight air before Holly broke the silence. "Cutter, what brings you here?"

"I've been giving some thought to what we talked about over in Alabama the other day." He hesitated. "About your dad."

Holly glanced at Julie Davis then back to Cutter. "You can talk in front of Julie," she said. "I've told her everything. She cut her journalism teeth as a night cops reporter in L.A. She may be able to help."

"All right," said Cutter, propping on the front fender of the Lincoln – its paint job still scuffed from Holly's ugly welcome back to DeLong. "Here's what I've been thinking. I can personally vouch for the fact that no cars came down Blue Mountain Road headed to the highway in the two or three hours after Mr. Carter went into the river. Nobody walked it neither. Not that they were likely to on a night like that," he said. "That means that whoever did this had to go out the back way, around the mountain to Pickens' Ferry Road."

"Whoa!" said Holly. "You know that the road all but ends about two miles west of here in Hell Creek Bottom."

"All but ends," he said. "There's still a track through there. It can be done. I've done it."

"On a night like that?"

"No, but –"

"Wait a minute," said Julie. "Why not just hide in the woods until the coast is clear and then be on your way?"

"Whoever did this, didn't walk out here from town – or wherever he came from," said Cutter. "He had to have a vehicle. And between here and Hell Creak Bottom, there's no place to hide one – at least not on a night like that."

"They could have just sat and waited it out," said Julie. "Or abandoned the car and come back once things calmed down."

Holly was nodding more to herself than to something in particular that Cutter or Julie had said. She was beginning to see where Cutter was going. "That's possible," he said. "But there are only two more houses on this road, including one right at the edge of Hell Creek Bottom. Rose didn't know whose car she'd seen. So one of the first things the deputies did was head this way and knock on doors. There's no good spot to hide an out-of-place car. Couple of old, steep logging cuts, but on a night like that they'd be way too slick to climb. Unless we think one of your neighbors did it."

Holly shook her head. "Not hardly. Both couples are pretty elderly and, besides, they loved Meemaw and Daddy."

"So, I think they had to try to cross Hell Creek Bottom," said Cutter.

"Okay," said Julie. "How does that help us in terms of proving who killed Mr. Carter? Or even that he was killed?"

Cutter straightened and took his hands from the front pockets of his jeans. "Not long after me and Rose got back to the bridge, the rain started coming down in buckets. I mean, it poured for a good four or five hours. I'd say it would be nigh on to impossible to cross that bottom in those conditions without getting stuck at least once. So –"

"So!" said Holly. "He would've had to walk out to the other side of the bottom and knock on some ol' farmer's door."

"Yep. And try to hire him to pull the car out with his tractor," said Cutter.

Julie had been listening carefully and Cutter and Holly could see the gears turning behind her reporter's eyes. "That's all good," she said after a moment. "And I hate to throw a monkey wrench in it, but –"

"Go ahead," said Holly. "We don't want to go down the wrong road."

"So to speak," said Julie, flashing a quick smile. Then – "Okay. If that bottom, as you call it, is as bad as you say in that kind of weather, if the car got stuck, why not just leave it? At least for a few days. Then come back and get it pulled out. If questions came up later, you could claim you got stuck the night before Mr. Carter's death, or the night after – or two nights after. With as little traffic as that, that bottom sounds like it gets that time of year, it would be hard to prove otherwise."

"That's a good question, Miss Davis," agreed Cutter, "if we were in a court of law. But we're not. We're just nosin' around. It wouldn't be iron-clad proof, but it'd be mighty interestin' to know who got that vehicle pulled out."

"Yes, it would," said Holly, and they all were quiet for a time, turning over the possibilities in their minds. There was only the sound of cicadas and then the rustle of bat wings emerging from the ramshackle greenhouse as a string of them disappeared over the valley. Then, "There's something else, too," she said. "It's – what would you say Cutter? – twelve to fifteen miles back to Highway 27?"

"Closer to seventeen, I'd say."

"Unless you were dressed for it and used to it, that would be a very long, very cold walk in the middle of a rainy night," she said. "So, even if he left the vehicle, I'd say the odds are good he knocked on someone's door and asked to use their telephone."

"Okay," said Julie. "Sold."

"Cutter, you're brilliant!" enthused Holly.

He laughed, saying, "Thanks, but it's only brilliant if I'm right," and Holly was reminded again how much she liked the sound of his laughter.

Julie caught the look between them. "I'm going to go on in and freshen up," she said, turning for the ramp by the kitchen door. "You two don't do anything I wouldn't."

In the late twilight Cutter's eyes glowed almost like cat's eyes, drawing to them whatever last light of the day remained.

"You said you came by the office today?" asked Holly, mostly to have something to say amid the sing-song cry of the cicadas. "I thought you were working a survey job."

"I went down to Hughestown Monday morning to meet up with them, but Mr. Scott said they had a full crew."

Holly considered that. "Did they? Or is it payback for helping me?"

Cutter shrugged. "All I know is what he told me."

"Either way, you're out a week's wages. Cutter, please, at least let me pay you for the time you put in on our trip to Alabama."

"Nope. No way," he told her. "But I was thinkin', if you have some chores that need doing at the paper or around here. Like, well – I see the grass has gotten pretty deep in the ditches along your fence line. I could sling blade it. And that fence could use a coat of paint. Of course, it'll need to be scraped first."

"And that old greenhouse," said Holly. "There are vines growing wild. No telling what's living in there. Besides bats. The tables and floors are covered with broken pots, broken glass."

"Then how about it?" he asked. "I can take care of all that for you."

Holy looked down the long valley toward Delong. The town was a glow on the south horizon. "All right, Cutter. You're on," she said. "But before you start those projects, how would you like a different job?"

"What's the job?"

"Reporter. Or private detective, if you prefer. Mostly it would mean shaking a few hands and chatting with some farmers."

"On the back side of this mountain?"

"Uh-huh. And I'll be glad to pay you for your time."

"The painting and cleanup around here, I'll be glad get paid for," he said. "The other? I'll put it on your tab."

CHAPTER 11

olly was shooting pool in the library with Gerry Yards on Saturday night when the phone rang. Mickey Dawton of the *London Telegraph*, Tim Holland of *The New York Times* and Julie Davis were playing gin rummy at the card table in the center of the room.

"If that's room service, tell them to send up another bottle of gin, if you please," said Mickey Dawton as Holly wheeled past on her way to the phone on the desk.

"Hello."

"Hello, Miss Carter?" she heard a voice ask over the twang of a country-rock band and the roar of raised voices and clacking glasses.

"Yes. Cutter? Is that you?"

Gerry Yards twisted his pool cue in his hands.

"Yes," he said from a pay phone beside the men's room at The Gin. "I wanted to fill you in on what I found out."

"Is it good news?" she asked, her voice raised.

"Maybe. But, hey, I can barely hear you."

"Same here."

"We're crazy busy tonight. How about I come by tomorrow?"

"Miss Frances told you about the little – well, prayer fellowship, whatever you want to call it – we're holding at the paper in the morning. Right?"

"Yeah."

"Why don't you come?" she tried, nearly shouting into the phone. "We could go for a drive afterwards. I could pack a picnic lunch."

"Me and church ain't on good terms," he said, holding a finger to the ear opposite the phone. "But I'll pick you up at Wolf's Run after your prayer meetin'. And this time, lunch is my treat. You paid over in Alabama. One o'clock?"

"Yes. One is fine!" she told him. "I'll see you then!"

Holly turned, her lips revealing a small, optimistic smile that Julie immediately noticed. She cocked a brow and Holly did her best to wipe the smile from her face but couldn't get rid of it entirely.

"Your break," she said to Gerry Yards as she picked up her stick.

Without a word, he lined up the cue ball and sent it flying against the others so hard that it popped up and jumped off the table. "I'm tired of this game," he said, dropping his stick onto the table.

* * *

On Sunday afternoon, Cutter turned out of the driveway at Wolf's Run onto Blue Mountain Road, then north on Highway 27. It was hot but in his open Jeep, the Sunday afternoon sun was comfortable on his face and on Holly Lee Carter's shoulders. She was wearing a yellow sundress. Her wheelchair was folded and tied down atop Cutter's steel footlocker.

"How did the prayer service go this morning?" he asked.

"Good, I suppose. There were about thirty-five people. And not just people from First Denomination. Miss Frances's husband, Mr. George, led us in reading from the tenth chapter of Matthew where Jesus talks about take up your cross and follow me."

"You don't seem too enthused about it," he commented as they met a trio of National Guard trucks heading south, out of the county. The curfew had been lifted as of sunrise that morning.

"I don't have any doubt that Charles MacAllister and his pals are leading people down a wrong and ugly road," said Holly. "But I grew up in First Denomination, too. Before Charles MacAllister came along. Before the gospel according to Cecil Weathers was being preached. I hate to see First Denomination coming apart. And some other churches around here, too. But that's really what Matthew 10 is about. It's about doing the right thing even when it's hard. But I don't take any satisfaction from what's happening. It just feels very sad."

At the foot of Two-Mile Bridge, which terminated in Tennessee, they turned west onto Pickens' Ferry Road. Ten minutes later, they passed the cutoff to Pickens' Ferry A.M.E. Church where Reverend Clemmer and his National Coalition for Justice volunteers had set up a tent city – or village, at least. Through a thick stand of cypress, they could only glimpse the clapboard church with its tin steeple, and the small circus-like tent that served as headquarters for the voter registration push. Several fire circles were visible and a row of outhouses had been built to one side, the plywood painted green. Two unarmed men sat on folding chairs at the end of the road, ready to check cars before they got close to the encampment. Some good that would do if push came to shove – or to gun shots.

Three miles beyond the church the road bent away from the water and began to wrap southwest around Blue Mountain.

Holly gripped the back of Cutter's seat, for balance, she told herself. But when her thumb slid between the vinyl and the dampness of Cutter's black T-shirt it raised the goose flesh on her arms and she had to fight to keep her breathing even. *What in the world am I doing going out alone for a picnic with this kid?* she asked herself. But in the sunshine and fresh air, and surrounded by the music beaming off of WHBQ's

Memphis tower and through the radio in Cutter's Jeep, she had to admit that at the moment she didn't care. Not even a little bit. But she was curious.

"You still haven't told me where we're going," said Holly. "You found someone who pulled a car out of Hell Creek Bottom that night, didn't you?" Cutter nodded. "Who?"

"A farmer, name of Efram Cole."

"You're taking me to meet him?"

Cutter chuckled. "No. That probably wouldn't be the best idea. He's a pretty rough ol' cob. He doesn't care much for this integratin' stuff or people who are pushing it."

"Like me?"

"Right. But he loves Cattahatchie High football. He played back in the nineteen-thirties when they still folder up their helmets – if you can call 'em that – and stuffed them in their back pockets," Cutter said, smiling as he shook his head. "Anyway, he listens to every game on the radio. Shoot, he remembered things about games I played in my freshman year that I don't even remember."

"Where we're going happens to be in the neighborhood, you might say, but it's a spot I came across a few years ago on a Sunday afternoon kinda like this – just drivin' the backroads. Enjoying the sun shine. By myself. Just listening to radio and thinking."

"Okay, give!" she told him. "What'd this Mr. Cole say?"

Cutter smiled, the Ray-Bans hiding his eyes. "Take it easy. Let's enjoy lunch. That'll be dessert."

Holly wasn't smiling. "Come on, Cutter, this is serious business. We're talking about –"

"Easy there. I know what we're talking about," he said, not angrily but firmly. "The news ain't goin' no place in the next hour. Let's just relax. There'll be time enough to figure on what I found out after we eat."

"Do I have a choice?"

"Not really."

Holly was a woman not used to being told no but this afternoon was afternoon was too beautiful to spoil.

"Okay then," she said. "What's for lunch?"

The gravel lane dipped and rose for another mile or so, then in the middle of a sharp curve was a steep cutback that twisted up the side of the mountain. Cutter rolled the steering wheel under his palm as he shifted into low. Suddenly, the Jeep felt as if it were going straight up. Holly's fingers screwed into the back of Cutter's seat and gripped the frame of the windshield. They climbed on the road and made another sharp turn and emerged in front of the remnants of an old farmhouse surrounded by tall grass and shaded by even older elms. Only the brick piers, part of the floor and a fieldstone chimney framed by the north wall remained.

They drove around to the back of the house to where the elms' high limbs met and tangled to create a frame for the black mirror that was Moccasin Slough, spreading below them for miles to the east and west.

Holly loosened her grip and sighed, "Oh, my goodness, Cutter. What a beautiful spot."

Cutter climbed out of the Jeep and began unlatching his gear in back. He unbucked the straps that had been holding Holly's wheelchair and leaned it, still folded, against the side of the Jeep. He lifted out his ice chest and flipped open his foot locker. He pulled out one of the most ornately designed and perfectly executed quilts Holly had ever seen.

"One of Miss Jenny's?"

"Yes. I took it with me when I left. Otherwise Tony would have sold it like all the rest," said Cutter, spreading it beneath the biggest of the elms. The pattern formed a brilliant orange, brown, gold and green sunflower. Cutter returned to the passenger side of the Jeep. "Okay. I promised to take you to my favorite lunch place. You ready?"

Holly looked at him. "What about my wheelchair?" Holly made herself ask.

"I don't think you're going to need it."

In the blackness of Cutter's sunglasses Holly could see herself reflected. It was the image of a twenty-eight-year-old woman – healthy, whole, even beautiful. Thankfully the need and the fear didn't show. Without the wheelchair there was no sign of how much her life had changed since she last rode these gravel lanes with other handsome young football stars on other days, and on other nights. She looked like the Holly Lee Carter she had expected to be at twenty-eight. Not the one whose legs hung useless under the skirt of her dress. Not the one who slept alone in her Meemaw's bed.

"Put your arms around my neck," Cutter instructed. Holly was tired of demanding explanations, reasoning things out and giving orders. She did as she was told.

For an hour or more they relaxed on the sunflower quilt, eating cold fried chicken, potato salad and baked beans from the Cotton Café. With the blade of his Swiss Army knife he sliced a block of sharp cheddar. He poured big glasses of sweet tea from a gallon jug. As they ate, squirrels performed acrobatics in the limbs overhead and in the clear middle of Moccasin Slough ski boats cut silver lines in the black glass surface. In the distance they looked like small, intricate models. The radio on Cutter's Jeep remained tuned to the Best of The Beatles Weekend.

Having eaten their fill, they sat shoulder to shoulder against the big elm. Holly sighed, "Ohhh, that was delicious. Thank you."

"I didn't make it. I just bought it. Thank Miss Winona."

"Then thank you for bringing me here," she said, very aware of his nearness. Of his deliciously masculine scent. "I'm sure there are any number of young women who would love to be here with you this afternoon."

"I don't bring people here," he said. "This is where I come when I don't want to be bothered. Sometimes I even pitch camp up here when The Well starts feelin' like a cheap motel. People showin' up, usually drunk, at all hours of the day and night wanting to talk about some game I played in two or three years ago." He shook his head. "Sometimes it amazes me how much those games mean to people." His lips tightened and he worked his jaw side to side as if chewing on something, then – "Like they're all livin' inside me."

Holly thought about that and how true that had been much of her life in DeLong. How many of her high school girlfriends had secretly wished they were her? Her looks, her independence. Her Corvette. Some even said so. Now there was the wheelchair folded at the side of the Jeep. *Be careful what you wish for*, she thought, and more than supposed the same could apply to those who fawned over Cutter. How many would trade three hours of Friday night glory for the hell he'd lived through at the Old Ambrose Place? And, to a degree, still was caught up in.

"Anyway," he said, changing his tone, "I guess you could call this my thinkin' spot. I keep it to myself."

"In that case, I'm honored that you brought me here."

The muscles at the corners of his mouth twitched and his lips parted in a small, quick smile. "I'm honored that you came," he said and lay his hand atop hers. Not holding it really, simply resting it there atop her hand, on her leg. Holly straightened a bit. Imperceptibly, she hoped. She knew she should move her hand, or his ... she knew she should ... *she knew!* ... but she didn't. They sat there for several minutes against the elm, listening to *Strawberry Fields Forever* – Holly feeling her heart beating faster than it should under breasts that were starting to tingle. She fought the urge to put her head on Cutter's shoulder, but if the subject didn't change quickly, she knew she'd lose that battle, too. She cleared her throat softly. "You told me that the news from Mr. Cole would be my dessert."

"I did. But the truth is I didn't tell you before we ate because I was afraid it would spoil your appetite," he said, and that changed the rhythm in Holly's chest again. She didn't look at him. She looked straight ahead at the lake –"Okay. So tell me now."

"All right," he said and began. "Efram Cole lives about another two miles or so farther around the mountain with his wife and couple of kids and grandkids. He farms about two hundred acres. Corn mostly.

"One cold, rainy night in late March or early April, he says, a fella came to his door right about when the ten o'clock news was startin'. The fella said he was comin' back from a friend's house, hit a deer and slid off in the ditch. Mr. Cole didn't believe him because he knows everybody who lives between his house and Hell Creek Bottom, and just about all their friends, too. But the man offered him a hundred dollars cash money to pull him out. So, Mr. Cole got his clothes on and got his tractor."

"Damn," Holly sighed, the realization hitting her that her suspicions were correct. Someone had killed her father. She leaned her head back against the tree and took a deep breath. "Damn," she said again on the exhale. Then, "A hundred, huh? It sounds like he wanted out of that ditch pretty bad. What did he look like?"

"Hard to say, according to Mr. Cole. The fella was wearing a black rain slicker. The kind with the built-in hood and a piece that sort of snapped across the front. It hid most of his hair and the lower part of his face. Plus, the night was black as tar and this fella sort of shied away from the light. Stayed out on the porch, in the cold while Mr. Cole got dressed, even though Mrs. Cole tried to get him to come inside for some hot coffee. He took a cup but stayed out on the porch to drink it," Cutter explained. "Mr. Cole said the man was about my size. Dark eyes. Dark hair and mustache."

"A big enough man to drag Daddy out to the car and put him in the back seat," said Holly.

"Yep."

"What about the car?"

"A white, late-model Ford station wagon."

"I don't suppose Mr. Cole remembered a tag number?"

"It didn't have one. But he did remember that the spot where the tag should have been wasn't covered in mud, like the rest of the bumper. Like it had been taken off right before the driver went to look for a farmhouse."

There was a suspicion growing in Holly's mind about the big man in the slicker, but she didn't voice it. "Is he sure this was the night Daddy died? Could he identify the man if he saw him again?"

"He's not sure is the answer to both questions. And I didn't want to press him until I talked to you."

Cutter's hand still was atop Holly's. She turned it and gripped his fingers. "Thanks for not telling me until – lunch was lovely."

"I'm not finished," said Cutter twisting on the blanket so that he could look straight into Holly's eyes. "This could be a coincidence. So, I'm not accusing," he said.

Holly held his eye. "All right."

"Up until right after Mr. Carter's passin', Miss Mary Nell drove a white, late-model Ford station wagon." Holly's mouth parted slightly as if to speak or ask a question, but she didn't. "Miss Mary Nell is a cheerleader sponsor, you know. A lot of times, especially durin' summer two-a-days, the cheerleaders come by after practice with cold drinks and stuff. I've drunk Kool-Aid from the tailgate of her station wagon plenty of times."

The gold flecks in Holly's eyes smoldered. She said, "And Tom was at a press association meeting five or six hours away in Biloxi that week. Of course, there'd be the kids to deal with but Mary Nell's a conniver. She always has been a conniver. She would have found a way around that."

Cutter waited, watching Holly's jaw tighten as she added up the pieces, then went on – "Here's the rest of it. Mr. Cole told me there was damage to the right front fender. Broken headlight, a little crinkle in the sheet metal and a couple of cracks in the windshield. Like I said, the fella told Mr. Cole he hit a deer."

The pleasant buzz in Holly's chest had gone to a grinding of gears in her mind. "You're saying Mary Nell hit Daddy with her car? That doesn't make sense," said Holly. "We know, or think we know, something happened to Daddy in the library."

"I'm not saying anything. I'm just telling you what Mr. Cole told me," said Cutter.

"Did he see a woman in the car?"

"He didn't see anyone else, but it was pitch and black pourin' rain. He didn't exactly search the car. Miss Eve got into that Klan rally layin' under a tarp in the back of Mr. Bellfont's station wagon in broad daylight."

"So she did," said Holly, nodding. "You said Mary Nell drove the station wagon until right after Daddy died. How do you remember –?"

"There was a lot of talk about it," said Cutter. "You know, café talk. About how mean the world, in general, is gettin' and Memphis in particular.

"As best I recall, the story goes that Miss Mary Nell went up there a couple days after your daddy's car went in the river to shop for funeral clothes for her and the kids. They hadn't even found the body, but everybody assumed. Anyway, the way I heard it was she claimed a colored kid jumped her in the parking lot of some department store, beat her up, took her keys and stole the car."

"And you believed that?" asked Holly, a little incredulous.

Cutter shrugged. "I didn't have any reason not to believe. Or give it much thought either way," he said. "But in light of the supposin' we're doing, and what Mr. Cole told me, it's a lot of coincidence. What I can say for a fact is that somebody beat Miss Mary Nell up pretty bad. By the time your daddy's funeral came around about a week later, they were well faded and she wore a lot of makeup, but you could tell she'd had a pair of serious deep purple shiners."

As was his nature, Cutter had said what he needed to say and didn't feel a need to keep on about it. Holly's eyes drifted away as she turned the idea over in her mind. Cutter propped his forearm on his knee, his hand holding the ice tea glass. He sipped from it now and then letting Holly work through it. After a time, her eyes came back to him.

"Do you have any idea who the man might be?" she asked.

Cutter hesitated, then – "Again, I'm not accussin' anybody, but –"

"But?"

"Assumin' the guy's local, there aren't a lot men around Delong with black hair, a black mustache and beard who are that tall, that big. And who might be the kind to get tangled up in something like this."

Holly thought she knew where Cutter was headed but she waited for him to say it. After a breath, he did – "LeRoy Kamp comes to mind."

Holly gave a small, humorless laugh. "Yes, that would describe LeRoy to a T," Holly agreed. "But Miss Prim-and-Proper Sunday School Teacher, Cheerleader Sponsor, Country Club Queen Bee hooked up with a general scumbag, ex-con like LeRoy? It's hard to imagine."

"Work at The Gin for a few a months," said Cutter, "and no kind of hook-up surprises you."

"That's the truth," she said, remembering all she'd seen when singing with this band or that at The Gin or some other state line roadhouse.

"Or it might not have been a hook up at all," said Cutter. "It could have been a straight cash deal."

"It could have been," Holly agreed. "Still, I'd have never thought LeRoy had the gumption for contract murder."

"Maybe," said Cutter. "But we're pretty sure he's involved in runnin' dope, or somethin' illegal, across state lines in those wrecked cars that Ronnie Conway hauls over to Moore's Bridge. Two or three years in a military stockade can harden a man, I expect."

Holly was nodding. "That's true. And he hates me. He could have seen it as a way to get back at me. A bonus, maybe."

Cutter looked at her, the question in his eyes but not on his lips.

"Don't ask," she said. "It's a long, ugly story and not worth telling."

Cutter shrugged. "So what's next?"

Holly already had been thinking about that. She said, "Simple. I have a 500-millimeter telephoto lens, a dark room, and I know how to use both. I'm going to get you a good picture of LeRoy to show to Mr. Cole."

E xcept for the radio, the squirrels and an occasional bird song they sat in silence for a time. Finally, Cutter asked, "You okay?"

"I guess you'd have to define 'okay'," she said. "In spite of her snotty attitude, Daddy always treated Mary Nell very well. At least from what I know and have heard. He made her an officer in the corporation, gave her an office and a salary. Though from what I've learned since I got back, she did precious little except collect a check."

"We could be adding up one and one and gettin' three," he cautioned. "We're still just supposin'."

"I know," Holly agreed, though it felt to both of them like they were past that point. Then – "Cutter I've really enjoyed this. At least the picnic part. But I need to get back. I have three or four hours of office work to do before I put my head on a pillow. And a lot to think about."

Cutter stood. "Sure," he said and began collecting the picnic gear and putting it back in the Jeep. When everything was put away except the quilt, he returned and slipped his right arm under Holly's knees and his left around her back. She put her arms around his neck and inhaled his clean, salty scent. He lifted her with ease, and held her not as if she was fragile or breakable, or perhaps already broken, but like she was precious.

"Thank you for not telling me about Mary Nell before we ate," she said, her face close enough that Cutter could feel her breath on his neck as he carried her the twenty feet to the Jeep. "You were right. It would have spoiled my appetite."

He eased her into the seat. "I do have dessert for you, though."

"Cutter, I'm so full, I couldn't –"

"Just one bite," he said. "It won't take but a minute."

Cutter shook off the sunflower quilt and folded it with military precision, fit it into the footlocker on the Jeep and closed the lid. He lashed Holly's wheelchair to the top of locker then climbed into the driver's seat and wheeled the Jeep around. But instead of heading for the steep road down from the plateau, he drove past what had been the front of the house and through a gap in the split-rail fence. They went over a small rise and down into a flat where an abandoned orchard spread out over several acres. Apple and peach trees gone to frenzy and rot spread away from the rough spit of a road. Blackberries grew wild on a nearby fence put up before Yankees and Confederates scrapped for this land. The air was redolent with the scent of ripening fruit.

"Oh my," Holly sighed.

Cutter stopped the Jeep, tossed his sunglasses onto the seat and walked around to the passenger side where an enormous tangle of strawberries had found its own wild ways, wrapping themselves around a ramshackle old smokehouse. The fruit cascaded from under the eave and was ripe and ready – big and red and bright and plentiful.

"Those are amazing," said Holly, the fragrance of the fresh berries permeating the air like sweet, red sunshine. "Look at the size of them!"

Cutter pulled several berries the size of small apples. "Are they all right to eat?" Holly asked as she took off her sunglasses for a better look.

"I've eaten 'em by the dozen and they haven't killed me yet."

When Cutter stepped next to the Jeep, Holly realized something was different. Something had changed in his posture. In the way he held himself. He was standing very close. Almost looming over her. For instant she had an image of Tony Carlucci wallowing on top of her on a filthy store room floor, forcing her legs apart and ramming his hand up between her thighs. But she had seen nothing in Cutter that would indicate he was even Tony's son, other than his olive complexion and black hair.

Cutter held out an enormous strawberry but when Holly reached for it he gently pushed past her hand until the warm fruit touch her lips and filled her nostrils. Her lips tingled as she looked up into his sky blue eyes. She saw no threat there, no demand, no meanness and best of all no pity, but a very definite offer. An offer of what? *Trouble!* No matter. She opened her lips, her teeth and took the fruit into her mouth as Cutter held it. Her first bite was tentative, but the next was deep, and by then the juice had hit her tongue and was streaming warm down her throat. She keened with pure, sweet pleasure and she wanted it all. She took the third and largest bite and her lips, as full and ripe as the fruit, brushed Cutter's fingertips. He smiled. The fruit's sun-born flavor was overwhelming on her tongue and she laughed lightly as drops of juice escaped the corner of her mouth and fell on the top of her right breast. She reached to wipe it away but Cutter caught her wrist and gently held it as he leaned low into the Jeep and began kissing it away.

Holly's eyes closed as she leaned her head back. "Ohhhh, Cutter," she sighed as her breath went suddenly ragged. His large, powerful hand cupped her left breast, weighing its fullness and instantly her nipples hardened until they felt like heated nails driven rib deep into long untouched flesh now suddenly aching to be caressed and suckled. Cutter kissed her bare collarbone, the strong muscle of her shoulder, her shoulder, again, then the side of her neck as the electric jolt of his lips raced through her upper body. Her hand went instinctively to the hard muscles of his side and stomach, then to the front of his jeans and the long, thick rock of his erection. And with a sudden gasp she knew. She did not feel the warm gush in the way she had before Ia Drang, but she knew. She knew if she ran her fingers up the inside of her thigh she would find the slick, wet, welcoming softness that she thought had been forever stolen from her. Until she met Cutter. Holly moaned with both passion and relief. Her hand began to move up and down from the front of Cutter's jeans, from the fullness of his balls to his belt, as his lips moved onto hers, then their mouths opened. They kissed long and deep and again, and again. When Holly's eyes finally fluttered open, she saw Cutter's hand on her knee starting to push up the yellow fabric of her sundress and her breath caught in her chest. She pulled her hand away from his crotch and grabbed his wrist, and with all the strength she had left to resist him said, "No, Cutter! I – I can't!"

Holly couldn't budge his hand but he didn't try to go farther. He again began to kiss her neck and she wanted to scream. Not with anger but with delight. Instead, she put a hand on his shoulder and pushed gently, then harder. "Stop!" Then harder still. "You've got to stop!"

Cutter relented. He took his hand off of her knee and put at least a bit of space between them. Her lips tingled and she realized they were trembling. Cutter was taking long, slow breaths. "Why do I have to stop?"

Holly looked away and shook her head, fighting what she knew her body craved – the places of ancient instinct and need. She looked at him and said, "Because this is such a terrible idea for so many reasons."

"You want me, don't you?"

"Of course I want you! That's pretty obvious," she said. "You're one of the most gorgeous specimens of male I've ever seen. But – But I'm twenty-eight and you're eighteen."

Cutter smiled, almost maddeningly unruffled. "If you're worried about deflowering me, I hope you won't be shocked if I tell you I'm not a virgin."

Holly put her face in her hands and actually laughed. She realized there were tears on her cheeks. Tears of pleasure? Embarrassment? Regret? She wiped them away then slipped her hands onto her lap and sighed. "No, that does not shock me."

"Then why?"

Holly looked away, gathering her thoughts. She knew the real reasons but she wasn't sure enough of Cutter or herself to share them. Instead, she turned back to him and said, "Because I have responsibilities. I'm the editor of this county's only newspaper. What do you think people in DeLong would say – even the ones who've supported me – would say if they found out you and I were, were –"

Cutter straightened and rested his forearm on the Jeep's windshield frame. "The Holly Lee Carter I've heard about never cared what people thought of her."

The words set off a sudden flare of anger. "Yeah! And look where it's gotten me," she shot back. "I didn't care what anyone said, I was going to Vietnam. I didn't listen when my friends told me I was crazy to come back to Miss'ssippi. I didn't listen when those dressed-up Klan bastards told me they'd break the newspaper if I ran Tommy Ray Banks' obit.

"Well, guess what? I came back to Delong anyway and nearly got killed for my trouble. And now look at Eve! I ran the Banks obit, and the paper my family has owned for 130 years will be broke and bankrupt in just a few weeks. And in case you haven't noticed," she said with a cold glare in her eyes, "I came back from Vietnam without my fucking legs.

"That's what not caring what anyone thought has gotten me. I can't just jump into the sack, now, and screw some teenager whose biggest worry is an algebra test or a football game."

Cutter regarded her. He worked his jaw muscles but said nothing. Holly knew she'd gone too far. Said more than she intended. More than she meant. After all the help Cutter been in trying to discover whatever truth there was to find about her father's death, the risk of serious local disapproval he'd ignored to help deliver the first integrated edition of *The Current-Leader*, the courage he'd shown helping fight the fires in Roseville, and the far-beyond-his-years maturity he'd displayed … and then there was his kiss … his kiss … after all that, in one sentence she'd relegated him to the role of helpful high school kid.

Holly wanted to apologize. Knew she should. But if she tried, what words would she use? How could she possibly explain the tangled emotions and physical longing he brought out in her? And the fear.

Instead, she said, "Would you please take me home now?"

Cutter tapped his palm on the windshield frame and nodded, not in agreement but as if he'd come to a decision about something.

"Sure. Glad to," he said.

CHAPTER 12

utter and Holly said little on the drive back to Wolf's Run, only now the silence was no longer easy or comfortable. When they got to the house Julie Davis was on the porch with Charlie and they both came out to greet them.

"I thought you two had run away together," she joked. Neither Cutter nor Holly reacted. Julie sensed the negative charge in the air. "Ooo-kay."

Cutter released Holly's wheelchair and placed the cushion in its seat. She'd been dreading this moment since they left the old orchard. The moment when Cutter would need to take her into his arms again to lift her out of the Jeep and her heart would start and her skin would tingle ... and ... "If you put the chair right here, close, I think I can transfer myself."

"Holly, are you sure?" asked Julie concerned. "It's kind of a –"

"I'm sure."

Cutter positioned the chair as Holly instructed, and she managed the difficult shift, though her feet remained in the Jeep. "Julie, could you please get my legs?"

"Sure."

Julie Davis took Holly's legs by the ankles and placed them on the foot rests. The right spasmed, becoming almost straight as her foot twitched for what seemed like an hour but in reality was only a few seconds. "Oh, damn!" Holly cursed. Then the muscles relaxed and she positioned the right leg over her left and smoothed her skirt before pivoting the chair and backing up, putting several feet between her and Cutter. He was nineteen – well, almost – and Holly knew she had led him on in all sorts of small ways that had led up to the moment in the strawberry patch. Though he had been mostly silent on the drive back he did not radiate a furnace of hot-blooded anger the way some men might. When he spoke, his voice was cool and measured.

"I'll clean out the ditches tomorrow. Then start on the greenhouse Tuesday. Maybe I can do it in a day. If not, I'll wrap that up Wednesday. Then strip and paint the fence on Thursday and Friday."

Holly was surprised that he still planned to do the work. Another sign of his maturity.

"That's fine, unless you have other –"

"No. Unless you'd rather I –"

243

"No. The work needs doing. I just thought –"

"Then I'll be here in the morning," he said, walking around the Jeep. He got in and turned the key.

"Thank you," she managed. "It was a nice afternoon."

Cutter slowly looked Holly over. "Yeah. Yeah it was," he said then backed the Jeep up, swung it around and drove away. Julie Davis' eyes followed the Jeep then came back to Holly. "What the hell was that all about?"

"Don't ask."

"Seriously. There was enough tension between you two to break glass."

"Julie, please."

"And I'm not talking the good kind."

Holly pivoted away. "I don't want to talk about it."

When she turned to head for the ramp, Gerry Yards was leaning on the porch railing. "I've been waiting on you to go to the office," he told her. "If you're through playing in the sandbox with the local children, we grown-ups have actual work to do."

* * *

By the time Holly was ready for work after a mostly sleepless Sunday night she expected to – or was it hoped to? – look out her bedroom window and see Cutter's Jeep next to the garage. But he wasn't there, nor did she meet him on Blue Mountain Road. She supposed he'd probably changed his mind, and decided to wash his hands of anything to do with her. If so, she couldn't blame him.

As it turned out, Monday was too busy for Holly to give Cutter a lot of thought, though she found herself doing so anyway. Just before noon, the news came across that the 5th U.S. Circuit Court of Appeals, sitting in New Orleans, had lifted the stay of federal Judge Oren Mulberry's integration order. Reorganization of the Cattahatchie County Public School System would take place without delay, as per the plan already approved by Mulberry. That sent county and school officials into a tizzy. Holly had to do much of the reporting herself because of her decimated staff. By three p.m., Cecil Weathers was on WHCI promising that if he had to bring in crews from Birmingham and St. Louis and work them twenty-four hours a day, "Riverview Academy will open on time for the education of any white student of good character."

So it was almost nine o'clock when Holly passed the Old Ambrose Place on her way home. Though bone-tired, she found herself staring across the bean and cotton fields toward The Well. She saw the campfire glow, and wondered if Cutter was reading or listening to the radio? Was he laying there looking up at the stars, his body – his beautiful body! -- glistening with cold, pure droplets from a dive deep into the spring? Was he thinking of her? Or was he laying there, his body shining with feral sweat, as some high school debutante or roadhouse waitress looked up at him with the stars in her eyes?

Holly crossed the Old Iron Bridge and followed the twisting road up the face of Blue Mountain, chiding herself for caring one way or the other. But when she rounded the curve near her house, and the headlights of the Lincoln illuminated a ditch cleared of brush and grass, a sob welled up in her throat and a wave of relief washed over her.

"Stop it!" she told herself and turned down the driveway. "Just stop it."

T uesday was busier and even longer. Holly closed herself in her office for almost three hours in the afternoon writing a front-page column that she knew would set the editorial direction of *The Current-Leader* for as long as it continued to publish – at least under Carter ownership.

"Which won't be long," she reminded herself, "unless something changes."

There was no ambiguity to it. No hedging. No gray areas. It was an impassioned plea for Cattahatchie Countians to accept the court ruling, "continue to support our public schools, and demand equal access to public facilities, especially the polling places, for all of our citizens." It called the actions of the Klan "heinous and cowardly" and said those who support them "overtly, covertly or through careful indifference are complicit in the brutality that the Klux continue to inflict upon those members of our community who are least able to defend themselves. It is repugnant and intolerable, and it goes to the core of what we are as a community."

W hen Holly got home Tuesday night at nearly one a.m., she saw the piles of junk Cutter had pulled out of the greenhouse. She had not seen him since Sunday afternoon, but just knowing he was still around, still nearby, felt almost as good as a hug.

On Wednesday, Holly wasn't ready to leave the house until almost nine, but Cutter still wasn't there. He probably was sitting down at The Well, waiting to see her car on Blue Mountain Road, headed to town. Holly finished a second cup of black coffee and the last of the Spanish omelet Gerry Yards had made. Julie Davis already had left for Oxford and an interview with Judge Mulberry. They were the only two left in the house.

"Thanks, Gerry. That was delicious. I always loved your omelets."

"You know, I wouldn't mind making omelets for you every morning," he said from across the table, his eyes dimmed by the years of alcohol that had made florid the capillaries of his nose and cheeks. Now that his long hair was nearly white, his face always looked sunburned.

"I know, Gerry," she said and tried to find other words. Kinder words. Better words. But she had turned him down so often that she had no new words for him. "I've got to go. I'm running late.

"What are you up to today?"

"Nothing special," he told her. "Just cruising the roads to see what my camera's eye can see."

"Be careful," she said, placing her dishes in the sink. "The Guard and the feds put a scare into the Klan. But they may not stay scared for long."

"After your editorial, I'd think you're in a lot more danger than I am," said Yards. "Do you want me to follow you to town?"

"No," she said, and patted her purse, the .38 inside. "If they want to try to run me off the road again, I'm ready for them."

Gerry Yards chuckled. "You never were afraid of anything. That's one of the reasons I fell in love with you."

"Yes, well, maybe I should have been afriad. If I had been, maybe I wouldn't be in this chair."

"Regrets?"

They had been down this conversational road many times, Holly had no desire to go down it again. "No, Gerry. No regrets. Just a few wishes that things were different. Maybe a little easier. Look, I've got go."

At the door Holly looked over her shoulder at him. She knew he'd mix a Bloody Mary as soon as she left. She wished she had the right words to say so that he would let her go, really let her go. Not for her sake, but for his. She wished he had someone else. "Be careful," she said again, and pushed down the ramp by the kitchen door with Charlie right behind her.

Yards crossed the kitchen and looked out the window as Holly wheeled to her car, then past it; and past the pile of stuff that Cutter kid had excavated from the old greenhouse, where Holly was headed. Holly opened her purse, took out what appeared to be a white, business-size envelope and taped it to a panel of dirty but unbroken glass where it could not be missed.

When Holly turned back toward her car and the house, Yards quickly stepped away from the window. He pulled a bottle of vodka from a lower kitchen cabinet, the tomato juice from the refrigerator and gathered up the rest of the fixings for his morning "steadier," as he called it. He heard the car door close and listened to the tires go up the long driveway as he worked over the glass. When there was no more sound of tires and the drink was ready he took a long swallow, and the heat filled his chest and cheeks and his belly. He drank the rest of it and made a second. Holding it cold in his hand, he walked down the ramp toward the greenhouse.

Three hours later, Gerry Yards stood in the kitchen window watching Cutter working shirtless in the noonday sun. Yards was sipping from a bottle of beer and eating a cold chicken leg and trying to tell himself that he once had had a body like Cutter's, but he wasn't yet buzzed enough to make himself believe it. There had been a time, however, when his hair wasn't receding and was more pepper than salt, and when the paunch around his middle was more like a bicycle tire than a truck spare. That hadn't been so long ago, had it? When he woke up next to Holly instead of on the other side of the house from her? Anyway, what he'd lost in physical attributes was more than made up by the knowledge he'd gained of the ways of the world and how to best manipulate any situation to his benefit, Yards told himself. He studied the handwritten note one last time …

> *Dear Cutter,*
> > *I'm terribly sorry about Sunday afternoon.*
> > *I'll be home by 5:30 and will bring dinner from The Cotton.*
> > *Afterwards, we can talk. I want to explain.*
> > *Please stay, Holly*

…then he tore it into small pieces and dropped them in the kitchen garbage. Now he looked again at the one he'd typed at the desk in his room …

> Cutter,
>
> > As you can imagine, I'm extremely busy this week and will be for the foreseeable future.
> > Please leave an itemized bill and I'll leave a check for you at the newspaper's front desk.
> > If you have any questions, please inquire with Mr. Yards, an old and very dear friend who will be staying with me until this ordeal is over.
> > Thank you for your hard work.
>
> Holly Carter

… and slipped it into the unsealed envelope onto which Holly had written Cutter's name in her own strong script.

Yards finished the beer and chicken leg, washed his hands and dried them on a dish cloth, and headed out the back door. *This is going to be almost too easy,* he thought. "Hey, kid!" he called as he crossed the yard. "I have a note for you from Holly."

* * *

The picture had been there in Holly's *Current-Leader* office all along, but now, knowing what Cutter had told her about the white station wagon, it felt like something hot, always against her back, burning right through her blouse. It sat with a number of other framed photographs on a console behind what had been her father's desk. Now her desk and her office. There were multiple pictures of T.L. Carter's grandchildren, friends in the Mississippi newspaper industry, and a framed magazine cover bearing a picture of her in Marine fatigues, aiming her camera as a battle raged around her. It was the summer 1965 edition of National

Journalism Quarterly, which had printed a feature on her called: "On the Front Lines of Journalism".

But it was none of those photographs that now made Holly's skin crawl. Instead it was a five-by-seven of Tom, Mary Nell, Lanny and Georgette standing beside a white Ford station wagon during a 1967 trip to the Southwest – the vast hollow of the Grand Canyon open behind them.

Holly turned and looked at the photograph for the fiftieth time since Monday morning. She stared at it, as if she could read the intentions behind faces eighteen months in advance of events that transpired on a cold river in Mississippi. That, of course, was impossible but Holly intended to do whatever was possible now. *And what is possible now?* She asked herself. *Right this minute? At nearly noon on an August Wednesday in 1969?*

Turning from the photograph, Holly picked up her phone and dialed the sheriff's office. Five minutes later she was in her car, Charlie beside her and headed north on Highway 27.

* * *

When Deputy John-Thomas Hinton walked out of the Cream Cup cafè north of town holding a vanilla cone, Holly Lee Carter's Lincoln was parked beside his cruiser. His face lit up when he saw her but when the super cold ice cream hit the roof of his mouth it sent a shock of frozen pain into his forehead. He stopped and tilted his head back and held his nose, his mouth open, swallowing the hot August air. Trying to warm his sinuses.

"Ohhh, my goodness," he said, his head still tilted back. "Why do I do that to myself? It looks like I'd learn."

Holly laughed and that made the pain worth it to John-Thomas. "That hurts, doesn't it?" said Holly sympathetically.

"It does," said the deputy. "But I do love their ice cream. Ohh, my!"

"The dispatcher told me I could find you here," she said, stroking Charlie's stomach. The little dog was stretched out on the seat, enjoying Holly's touch and attention.

"Cute," said the young deputy.

"Thanks," said Holly, removing her Wayfarers.

"At least you didn't catch me eatin' donuts," he said and licked the cone. "What's goin' on?"

"I've got a question about the night my dad died."

"Okay."

"How long did it take you – well, meaning the sheriff's office -- to figure out it was my father's car in the river?"

John-Thomas thought about it. "We didn't know for absolute sure until we recovered it the next morning," he said. "But we checked the houses there on Blue

Mountain Road and no one reported a family member or vehicle missing, or a friend who had visited and left around that time. When we checked at Wolf's Run, your father's car was missing and there was no answer at the door. No lights on. So we were just presumin'."

"All right, you were presuming. When did someone decide it was time to notify Tom and Mary Nell?"

"I'd say around ten o'clock," John-Thomas recalled. "Sheriff Johnson knew Mr. Tom was out of town at a newspaper convention – or meetin' or somethin'. Down on the coast. As you know, Miss Mary Nell can be a little, well, high strung. So we didn't want to upset her unless we had to.

"But about nine-forty-five the sheriff decided we had to let 'em know, even if we weren't one-hundred percent sure."

"Who –?"

"In fact, it was me," said John-Thomas, licking ice cream from the cone and his hand. "I stopped at the sheriff's office and called Miss Frances who gave me the name of the hotel in Biloxi that Mr. Tom was staying at. I tried his room but he didn't answer." John-Thomas grunted. "The truth is, I was hopin' if I told Tom I wouldn't have to visit with Mary Nell. But no such luck. So, I drove over to the house."

"Really?" said Holly. "What time was that?"

The deputy thought. "About ten-thirty, I'd say."

Holly calculated. "You're sure?" she asked.

"Give or take five minutes or so."

It couldn't be done. If the knock on the door of Efram Cole's farmhouse came as the ten o'clock news was starting, there was no way the car could have been pulled out and Mary Nell have time to be back in DeLong to answer the deputy's knock. Impossible. Holly knew she should feel relieved that the time line, if correct, seemed to exonerate her sister-in-law – at least in terms of being physically involved in T.L. Carter's death. But there was still the white Ford station wagon. Holly refocused.

"Mary Nell answered the door?"

"After a bit. Yes."

"How did she look?"

"Look?" asked John-Thomas, obviously surprised by the question. He held the cone steady and clearly tried to picture the scene in his mind. He licked the fast-melting cone and said, "She had on a bathrobe. Her hair was wet. She said she'd just got out of the shower."

"And you told her?"

"Yep, I told her what we were presumin'."

"How did she react?"

"She was surprised, of course. Worried. She said she needed to call Tom. I asked if she wanted to come out to the scene, and she said no. That there was nothing she could do there and that she needed to go fetch Lanny and Georgette before they heard about this some other way."

"Fetch them?"

"They were spendin' the night with friends, she said, because she'd been having one of her sick headaches."

Holly thought about that, pictured it in her mind – John-Thomas standing there under the porch light delivering the news to her sister-in-law. "So, Mary Nell was alone at the house?"

"As far as I know. She didn't invite me in, and I didn't blame her. It was pouring and my slicker was drippin' water and my boots were covered in mud."

"What about her car?" asked Holly. "The white Ford station wagon. Did you see it?"

"No. But I was at the front door. The garage is at the back of the house."

"I know," said Holly. "I grew up in that house. I was just wondering." She paused, thinking. "But you did get in contact with Tom, right?"

"If you mean, did I talk to him personally? No, I didn't. Mary Nell said she'd call and keep callin' till she got him. Which she did."

"How do you know that?"

"She must have. He was back in DeLong by eight-thirty the next morning when we recovered your father's car. To do that, he would've had to drive all night. Especially in the kind of weather we were havin' that week."

The deputy bit into the cone and it crunched. "Where're you headed with this?"

Holly dodged the question and asked her own. "Did anyone actually enter Wolf's Run and look around?"

"That's one of the reasons Sheriff Johnson wanted me to get in contact with Tom or Mary Nell. The house was locked up tight. We were gonna have to break in. The sheriff wanted their permission."

"And?"

"And Mary Nell gave it when I talked to her."

"She didn't object?"

"No. Why should she?"

"Did you go into Wolf's Run?"

"No. I radioed Sheriff Johnson to let him known Mary Nell have given her okay. He and, I believe, Deputy Connelly went."

"What did they find?"

"Nothing. Including Mr. Carter. Which was the point."

"But they didn't find anything out of place?"

"Not that I ever heard."

Holly nodded, thinking – Unless someone was familiar with the house and library, they wouldn't have noticed my mother's portrait was missing.

"Look, Holly, what's this about?"

"Just one more question, John-Thomas. I understand that a couple of days after Daddy's accident, Mary Nell was assaulted in Memphis and her car was stolen. The station wagon. Can you get me a copy of the police report?"

The deputy looked her over. "You're not gonna tell me what you're up to, are you?"

"No. Not yet," she said without missing a beat. "If I'm wrong, it'll only add to the bad blood that's already like – like poison between me and Mary Nell. If I'm right, I'll be happy to tell you. And anyone else who'll listen."

John-Thomas Hinton put the last of the ice cream cone in his mouth and licked his fingers. "I guess I can do that for you," he said.

* * *

Holly drove home that afternoon feeling that at least she'd done something. Unfortunately, the something had revived the question of Tom's involvement. If no one from the sheriff's office actually talked to Tom in Biloxi, then they were only taking Mary Nell's word that she reached him there. Of course, there were other ways Tom's alibi might be verified, if it ever came to him needing one. It was a press convention, after all, populated by people who had known Tom Carter since he was old enough to walk into the lobby of the Edgewater Hotel on their mother's hand. Some of them even before then.

Still, Holly was looking forward to sharing what she'd learned with Cutter. But as soon as she turned down the driveway late that afternoon her heart sank. There was no Jeep next to the house. Maybe he had gone down to The Well to clean up, she thought, stopping between the garage and the greenhouse. The old structure now was thoroughly cleaned out and the broken panes of glass removed, the frames made ready for a glazer to come in and fill them. Three piles of debris, about waist high, stood next to the driveway.

Gerry Yards emerged from the kitchen door as Holly turned off the ignition. "Hey, Good-lookin'."

"Hi, Gerry," she said, swinging open the door and lifting her legs out. Charlie scampered onto the grass and began sniffing at the piles of detritus – broken pottery, rotted tables, vines cut and torn loose, an old bicycle and all sorts of odds and ends.

"Julie isn't back yet from Oxford?" she asked, hiding her real disappointment.

"She called. She's got a shot at an interview tomorrow morning with J.L. Burke. So, she's staying down there tonight."

Gerry pulled Holly's wheelchair out of the back floorboard, opened it and positioned it for her. "By the way, that kid you've got doin' the clean-up around here –"

"Yes," she said more enthusiastically than she intended.

"I was talking to him. He said he'll be done by Friday and he'll leave a bill. He asked me to tell you to leave a check at the newspaper's front desk," said Yards. "He wasn't all that friendly about it, either."

Holly stared at the pea gravel under her wheelchair. "Did he say anything about a – well, anything else?"

"Nope. That was it."

Holly knew Cutter was someone adept at holding in his outward feelings, of displaying only what he wanted the world to see – as he seemed to do Sunday afternoon on the drive back to Wolf's Run. But there was no doubt that a deep anger smouldered in him. Now it appeared she had been tossed onto that pyre as well. Having lifted herself from the car seat to her wheelchair, Holly placed her feet on the pedals, then lifted one leg to cross it over the other and smoothed her skirt. She closed the car door, hating the idea that Cutter was so deeply angry with her, and recognizing at the same time that it mattered to her a lot more than it should. So, maybe this is for the best, she thought – or made herself think.

She said, "I brought dinner from the Cotton Café."

Gerry Yards swayed a little as he pulled the paper bags from the back seat. "Smells great! Tell you what, I'll set up dinner on the patio. The light in the valley and on the river this time of day is extraordinary."

"Sure. That'll be fine," she said but didn't move.

"Aren't you coming?"

"You go ahead. I'll be there in a minute," she told him as she pushed around the piles. "I want to take a look at some of this stuff. There are a lot of memories piled up here. That old bicycle? That was my bicycle when I was ten. And that old TV? With the round screen. I watched Elvis on The Ed Sullivan Show on that TV."

There was the footboard to the white canopy bed she'd slept in until she pointed her Corvette toward the West Coast, but she didn't see the rest of it. A water-ruined cardboard box held an old china service. The top layer of plates were broken and she didn't recognize the pattern, but some of it might be worth saving, she thought, and pulled the box away from the pile. When she did, some of the junk shifted. It tumbled and clattered onto the grass as the little dog jumped back, barking her protest.

"Ooops! Sorry, Charlie."

That's when Holly saw it – the L shape of half a gold-leaf frame. She picked it up and studied the ornately carved wood. Looking at the front, then the back, then the front again, there was no doubt. This was the frame that had held the portrait of Veronique Carter, her mother. The portrait that was missing from the library.

Holly looked in the pile. Inside the shoulders of limestone that rolled up around Wolf's Run, the afternoon shadows already were deep. But after a moment, she saw another piece and pulled it free. Along the edge were tatters of canvas, as if someone had ripped the portrait from the frame.

Now she had three-fourths of it. "Come on, where are you?" she said as she moved slowly around the pile. "Yes!"

Holly pulled loose the final piece and stared at it. It was spattered with dry, brown mud or …? She scratched a drop and lifted the frame to her nose. Immediately, she swung it away from her face and gagged. She had smelled that odor plenty of times at murder scenes, fire-blackened homes and in Vietnam. The sweet, coppery tang of dried blood was unmistakable.

CHAPTER 13

All weekend the rumors about the future of the county's public school system and Cattahatchie High's vaunted football team swirled through DeLong like an army of dirt devils, popping up from nowhere out of a hot breeze and picking up grit and trash as they moved from street to street. The Cattahatchie County Fair opened that Saturday night. From the balcony of my room at Mrs. Fletcher's Boarding House, I could see the Ferris wheel and the lights from the rodeo arena, and when the highway and railroad tracks were quiet – which wasn't often – I could even hear the canned organ music coming from the shabby midway.

Really, the fair was like a petri dish in which the virulent and sometimes sickening rumors about Cattahatchie High's future were placed, and given the perfect environment for growth. It brought together the town people, with their baking and cooking competitions, their rose judgings and the Miss Cattahatchie County Pageant, and the rural folk, who brought their pigs, cows and horses to show in the long barns on the west side of the fairgrounds. They mingled, more or less, and talked, and in that August of '69 little of the talk was good.

In a field owned by an unabashed Kluxer across from the fairgrounds, the Klan parked a flatbed truck and set up a loudspeaker system. Those with a bent for angry speechmaking kept up an almost continuous diatribe while men and women, and even children in miniature robes, moved among the cars parked along the highway and in nearby lots placing Klan pamphlets under windshield wipers.

At their spot in the row of public service booths, National Coalition for Justice volunteers passed out their own literature guarded, as always, by two deputies and several federal marshals. Sheriff's cars escorted the NCJ's old school bus back and forth to their encampment at Pickens' Ferry A.M.E. Church. None of that, however, stopped the NCJ workers from being showered with tobacco spit from time to time and needing to duck as eggs or rocks struck their vehicle.

From a distance on Saturday night, I saw Miss Carter with the blonde reporter – her friend from Los Angeles. Miss Davis. They seemed to be enjoying the midway, but mostly they were working. Miss Davis was talking to people – those who would talk to her – and Miss Carter was taking pictures. Rumor had it that after

Wednesday's editorial siding outright with the integrationists, the newspaper had lost several hundred more subscriptions.

Patti, unfortunately, caught my line of sight. "That Jezebel!" she growled. "I can't believe she has the gall to show her face in public. I hate that cunt!"

I started to note that hating people didn't seem all that Christian, not to mention the language, but I had learned better than to challenge the righteous wrath of Brother Daddy or any of his clan. "She may be a cripple, but she is like the prowling lion, picking off and devouring the members of our flock who stray," Patti went on, her cheeks flushed. "Only Satan could have created a woman like her. Even starting her own church!"

"The way I heard it, the Raglands and some others went to Miss Carter," I said before I could put the brakes on my mouth. "They asked her if they could use –"

Patti stared at me, her teeth grinding behind the tight knot of her lips. I knew if I uttered another word on the subject, I'd be leaving the fairgrounds alone.

* * *

On Monday afternoon, the twenty-six veterans of 1968's 13-1 Wolves football team met at the locker room beside Senator Julius C. DeLong Memorial Field. Along with eleven ninth-grade rookies, we were there to get our physicals and receive equipment for the start of two-a-day practices the following morning.

It was the first time I had seen Cutter, except glimpsed from a distance on the road, since the afternoon at Wolf's Run with Rose. As usual, he was surrounded by a knot of people wanting to talk about football or The Gin, girls or The Well or just to be near him.

I sat down in front of a locker on the other side of the room and made no attempt to cross the distance between us. He'd been seen several times since then with Miss Carter. People around town were no longer whispering about their relationship. Many were grumbling out loud. Especially now with Brother MacAllister accusing Miss Carter of "bedazzling vulnerable members of the First Denomination flock," I couldn't afford to be lumped in with her and Cutter.

At four p.m. exactly, Head Coach Gaydon Pearce emerged from his office followed by his three assistants. A big fan in one of the open windows stirred the hot, sticky August air.

"Aw'ight, aw'ight," he said in the booming, nasal baritone that had been the voice of authority in CHS football for fourteen years. "Find a place to park your backsides. We've got some 'nouncements to make. Go on. Grab a chair … and hold on to it."

It wasn't so much that at some level we all hadn't anticipated what we were about to hear, but the timing of it, the swiftness of it, the totality of it caught nearly everyone off guard – like bracing for a slap in the face and getting a punch in the gut instead.

255

"You rookies, listen up," said Coach Pearce. "The first rule on my teams is that when I'm ready to talk, you shut up. Got it?"

Young heads nodded in the coach's direction. He was only five- foot, nine-inches but had the massive upper body and nail-keg thighs of a college fullback, which he had been two decades earlier. Lookng up from his watch, he began, "At this moment, the Cattahatchie County School Board is officially accepting the resignations of one-hundred and fifty-seven of two-hundred and nine white teachers and administrators. Including my resignation, and those of coaches Rutledge, Garrett and Parker, here."

A groan of shock and consternation rumbled across the room.

"I told you, be quiet and listen up!" said the coach. "As soon as that business is officially done, three of the five school board members will resign and leave it to the nigguhs to run it as best they can. If they can.

"A few of the teachers will simply retire, but most will be signing contracts with Riverview Academy. Including this whole coaching staff," he told us. "Men, Cattahatchie football will go on! It will go on just as it always has, except we'll have a new name, a new location and new facilities that are second to none at any private school in Miss'ssippi."

"Coach –?" started Kenny Dillon, but Gaydon Pearce held up his hand. "Now I know y'all probably have lots of questions. The coaches are passing out mimeographed copies of information that should answer most of those questions. Read 'em before you start askin', and take 'em home to your folks. There's information about academic scholarships, athletic scholarships – something most of you boys will qualify for – and low-interest loans at the Valley Bank that can help parents who need it.

"The main things you have to remember are that we'll have our physicals and pass out brand spankin' new equipment a week from today at the Riverview locker room. You all know where that is. You've seen it goin' up. Inside, it's gonna be a beauty. First class. We'll start two-a-days next Tuesday. School will start September 8 and we'll play our first game September 12 against Greenwood Prep."

There were nods, a few smiles, but mostly my blank, stunned look was reflected back at me. I looked at Cutter, as did a lot of others in the room, but as usual, he was infuriatingly unreadable. His icy eyes were fixed on Coach Pearce, his hands folded in his lap. I wondered if someone had given him a heads-up in advance.

Perhaps Coach Pearce was reading many of our thoughts. "And for any of you math-impaired heathens who are wonderin', Cutter's nineteenth birthday is not until September 14. That means he'll still be eighteen when school starts, so he'll be eligible for the entire season."

Many of his teammates sighed with relief. A few clapped and a couple whistled. Cutter probably was the best football player of any color in the state, but in the lily white Academy League, he would be utterly unstoppable. Some of us might have been "math-impaired heathens," but it didn't take anyone more than an instant to calculate that with Cutter onboard, the State Academy League Championship was ours for the taking if we Wolves moved en masse to Riverview.

"One more thing," said Coach Pearce. "There's gonna be a kick-off pep rally for the team and, well, the whole academy, really, at the fairgrounds rodeo arena this comin' Saturday night at 7:30. You're all expected to be there and you'll be up on stage. So wash behind your ears and practice not pickin' your nose."

Many laughed.

"Governor Broderick himself is comin' in to inaugurate things. It's all gonna be on a statewide radio hookup. We're gonna be an example for the whole state that decent white folk don't have to knuckle under to a bunch of race-mixin' judges. We're gonna show folks how to fight back … and win!"

CHAPTER 14

As the locker room emptied and slowly the parking lot, too, Cutter sat in the same folding chair for a long time, unmoving and seemingly unmoved by anything that he'd heard. Coach Pearce didn't bother to make small talk. He and Cutter didn't really get along. Cutter's legs had lifted his coaching career from the doldrums of mediocrity, or worse, to one of the best records in the state over the last three years, but Coach never felt he got enough credit. On the other hand, Gaydon Pearce wasn't foolish enough to express that resentment in obvious ways.

For his part, Cutter had little choice but to tolerate Gaydon Pearce. For better or worse, he was the coach, and football was Cutter's meal ticket for now and, more important, the door to a better future for Rose, his mother and him. So, he mostly kept his mouth shut and led by example.

Cutter stood and crossed the locker room. It was so quiet. No reassuring clatter of cleats on the concrete floor. No whoops of excitement, groans of pain or curses of frustration. He leaned on a locker and stared out at the field. The ghosts of games won there danced behind his eyes. In the three seasons since he'd donned a high school uniform as a freshman, the Wolves had not lost a home game. With his speed, strength and determination, Cutter simply had not permitted it. CHS was 19-0 between those red goal posts. Perfect.

Coach Pearce had asked Cutter to hang around after the announcement. Someone wanted to talk to him. Outside, Coach Rutledge was answering some final questions from players and shooing them out of the parking area. Then he left, and two minutes later, Governor Weathers' silver Rolls-Royce crunched into the gravel lot.

Coach Pearce immediately emerged from his office, stretching his shirt over his belly and stuffing it into his shorts. "Come on, Cutter," he said. "Governor Weathers wants to talk to you."

Cutter said nothing but followed Coach Pearce out to the car. The door opened and Sgt. J.D. Benoit stepped out, the bright late afternoon sun reflecting off his mirrored sunglasses. "Get in."

Gaydon Pearce hustled into the limousine like it was some new and wonderful ride at the fair. But not Cutter. "Go on, kid," said Benoit. "It's hot out here. Get in."

"If y'all got something to say to me, why don't you just say it here?"

"Boy, am I gonna have to handcuff you and put you in this car?"

Cutter flashed a quick smile – "If you can."

"What's got into you, boy?" yelled Coach Pearce. "This is Governor Weathers. He just wants to have a friendly talk."

"And this man is Tony's best friend. Anybody who's that tight with Tony is no friend of mine. And I don't care to ride in the back seat of a car with them."

Benoit balled his fists. "Why, you smart-mouthed –"

"Sergeant!" said Weathers. "Emotions run high concerning family matters. We should tread lightly.

"Please ride in front with Jerome," said the governor, indicating his black chauffeur. "Does that satisfy you, young man?"

Weathers was Tony Carlucci's long-time boss, patron and protector. Friend? Cutter didn't like him either, or his politics, but he thought of the sad scraps of lives Rose and his broken mother lived under Tony's roof. He climbed in as Governor Weathers patted the seat next to him. Gaydon Pearce sat across from them and cringed as Benoit got in the front seat and slammed the door. "What the fuck you waitin' on, Jerome," Benoit told the chauffeur. "You know what the boss wants. Give us the tour."

"Well, now! This is fine, just fine," said Weathers as the car began to move. "What a good-lookin' young man you are. And so much talent! You just don't know how proud this town is of you."

The Silver Cloud seemed to skim over the county roads that led west, through the heart of Weathers' Chalmette Plantation. Even on the north Mississippi clay and rough-quarried gravel of the side roads, it was so quiet and well balanced that it almost floated. The interior of the car was as cool as a refrigerator and smelled of old leather, expensive cigars and fresh talcum powder. Cecil Weathers was making no "common man" pretense this day. He was flexing his muscle, and demonstrating his wealth and power for all to see – especially Cutter. From time to time, Weathers pointed out something about one of the sawmills or cotton gins or warehouses they were passing. About how many laborers it took to work one of his long fields or maintain a row of grain elevators. Cutter said almost nothing. At first, Coach Pearce tried to cajole and interject but finally gave up and simply sat there, sunk in the plush seat looking like he needed to pee. After a time, they stopped on the west side of the river beside the row of cotton warehouses that was quickly being converted to classrooms and a gym. The first home of Riverview Academy while a new brick structure was going up next door to house pre-schoolers to high school seniors.

"It'll be second to none," Weathers enthused. "People will come from all over the state – hell! – all over the South to see what we did and how we did it. It's going to be my legacy, I tell you. My legacy!"

If Cutter was impressed by any of it, he didn't show it. While observing the anthill of work at the new academy, he offered nothing beyond perfunctory "yes" and "no" when asked a direct question. He attached no "sir" to either response. Cutter found no need to speak respectfully to elders he did not respect. That and Cutter's silence was becoming an annoyance to Weathers.

"What about it, boy?" he demanded. "What do you think?"

Cutter considered for a moment, then – "I think it's going to be a grand place."

"Grand! Grand ain't even the word!" Weathers thundered. "It's gonna be magnificint! Nothin' but the best. And you can be a part of it, son. A big part."

After a time, Jerome put the Rolls in gear and moved on. For several minutes, no one said anything as Weathers stared out the tinted window, as if seeing it all – his legacy – come to life in the smoked glass. Then Jerome turned onto a gravel lane known as Convict Road. It climbed and dipped through the hills and eventually led to the county work farm.

As if continuing a conversation that had paused only a moment earlier, Weathers said, "Of course, you now know that Coach Pearce will be the first head coach of the Riverview Raiders, and we already have a full ten-game schedule. We've quietly approached the parents of most of your returning teammates. We have firm commitments from eighteen of twenty-six."

"Now, Cutter, you coming over to Riverview would seal the deal for a lot of folks," offered Coach Pearce.

If this was a negotiation, Cutter intended to get the most out of it he could. "What about my sister?"

"As president of Riverview's board of directors and head of the scholarship committee, I'm certain a way can be found to cover her tuition," Weathers assured him. "And without appearing immodest, I might add that I am a man of some influence with most of the universities in the Mid-South. I have endowed chairs in politics and history. Ministry, too. I sit on any number of boards and committees, and I feel sure I can guarantee you the most complete collegiate athletic scholarship possible under NCAA rules – and then some." Cecil Weathers winked and made a tick-tick sound in the corner of his mouth. "Rose will be taken care of, too, of course."

"And my mother?"

"We can make sure that she and Rose have a nice little house somewhere near campus. In fact, a dear friend owns several well-maintained rent houses only a couple blocks off the Oxford square. I'm sure he'll be happy to give Rose an exceptionally good deal. He might well need some secretarial help in his law office, as well."

Cutter stared at the back of Sergeant Benoit's crew cut head – deciding how far to push. He might as well go for broke. "What about Tony? He's said he'll kill my mother and sister before he'll let them go. That's the only reason I haven't already gotten them away from here. And from him."

"Ahhh, yes. Well, Tony is a passionate man and sometimes impetuous," said Weathers. "But the things he's most passionate about are liquor, women of easy virtue and the affectation of power. He can be supplied with enough of all three to console him for his loss. Isn't that right, Sergeant Benoit?"

"Yes, sir, Governor. Once I'm elected sheriff this fall, I'll need a chief deputy," said Benoit, who was so far running unopposed.

"You see, there's nothing to worry about," said Weathers. Cutter stared at him. The notion of Tony Carlucci with a badge, gun and the backing of the sheriff and the Klan made Cutter's stomach tighten into a knot, but he didn't let on to the men in the car. "In the end, Tony answers to me," the governor added matter-of-factly. "And I assure you, he will not interfere following the completion of your brilliant senior season at Riverview Academy."

The governor reached into a door pocket and held up a silver-gray football jersey with white trim and a gold 13 on the front and back. "Pretty snazzy, huh? I designed it myself. The pants are the same – gray with a gold stripe, like a Confederate officer's trousers."

Gaydon Pearce jumped in. "And the uniforms are just the start of it, Cutter. Governor Weathers and the board are sparin' no expense on Raiders football. We're gonna have our own team bus. But not a school bus. Like a Greyhound, but painted up in school colors. It's gonna be T-top first class."

Said Weathers – "Now, I'm not going to kid you, young fella. It would be a big feather in our cap to have a player of your caliber on the first Raiders team. It would probably bring into the fold a lot of holdouts. But make no mistake, son, Riverview Academy is opening next month with or without you."

"The only thing that's gonna be left at dear ol' CHS is nigguhs and white trash," Benoit added from the front seat.

Cutter drew the car's cold air into his lungs. He couldn't make himself say yes to Weathers' offer, but was afraid to say no. For several minutes they rode in silence while the governor's impatience grew. Finally, Weathers ordered, "Jerome, stop here. I think we've gone far enough."

Benoit got out and opened the back door. Cutter stepped onto the gravel without protest. He didn't like breathing the same air as Weathers and Benoit. The sergeant climbed into the back seat. "But, Governor," said Coach Pearce. "It's a six-mile walk back to town."

"Good!" said Weathers. "It'll give Cutter time to be alone with his thoughts. But just so my position is clear, young man. I love being generous with people who are on my team. Nothing gives me greater pleasure. But so help me, boy, if you screw with me on this, even if I have to endow every major college, small college and piss-ant junior college from here to the Hawaiian Islands, you will never play a down of college football."

Cutter stood still, fighting not to react to the nail of fear Weathers had driven between his ribs. *Without football, I'm just the son of a crazy woman and a one-legged dago drunk!* Benoit added – "And your mother and sister'll rot up there in that shack. With Chief Deputy Carlucci. I'll make sure of it."

Gaydon Pearce looked as if he was trying to get smaller in his seat, sink into the deep leather folds. Even he was surprised and taken aback by the directness, the viciousness of the threats. In the deep blue shadows cast by the surrounding woods, Cutter stood, silent.

"One more thing," said Weathers. "We have a strict morals clause in our scholarships. I'd hate to have to disqualify you and your sister for you associatin' further with a known race-mixer, harlot and purveyor of lies."

"To put a finer point on it – from now on, keep away from that Carter woman and the rag she's printin'," said Benoit as he wadded up the Riverview jersey and threw it out the door. Cutter caught it against his chest.

"Make sure you wear that to the kickoff rally Saturday night," said Governor Weathers before relaxing back into his seat. "Jerome, drive on."

CHAPTER 15

I t was Thursday morning. Holly had three eight-by-ten blow-ups of photographs she'd taken of LeRoy Kamp spread on her desk. It had taken ten days since her conversation with Cutter – their last conversation – because LeRoy supposedly had been out of town on business. Or on vacation. Or no one was really sure. But when she called the family's car dealership on Wednesday afternoon and put on her best sugar baby accent and asked for "Leee-Roy," he came to the phone. Holly hung up. Fifteen minutes later, she and Julie Davis were parked across the highway in Julie's rental car.

Now Holly had the photos, but would Efram Cole talk to her? Emotions were running higher than ever now that Judge Mulberry's integration order had been upheld and she'd opined her support in *The Current-Leader*. The resignation of eighty percent of the county's white teachers and three-of-five school board members had been like tossing gasoline onto a fire. On top of that, no progress – none that the public knew of, at least – had been made in catching Robert Bedford McBride or solving the murder of Ridge Bellafont and the attack on Eve Howard. Holly heard through friends in L.A. that Eve was improving but she'd be in a rehabilitation center for weeks more. Maybe months. The center had refused to put Holly's calls through. She wasn't on the approved list.

The phone on Holly's desk rang. She picked it up. Her mind and eyes still focused on LeRoy Kamp's face, she said, "Hello."

"Holly, this is John-Thomas."

"Oh, yes, John-Thomas. Hi."

"I'm sorry it's taken me so long to get the information from the Memphis P.D. The big city boys don't exactly step and fetch it when the country folk call," he told her. "But I've got it."

"Great! Thank you. Can you drop the reports by the office?"

"I can," said the deputy, letting the pause drag on long after the words were finished. "But I was thinking maybe I'd pass them to you over dinner tonight. Maybe Nicholls Steak House? Or we could go someplace in Tupelo."

Holly pictured the sweet, young deputy sitting at a desk in the sheriff's office, the butterflies beating in his stomach as he waited for her reply. She almost said yes.

If for no other reason than to thank him. Plus, looking at him across a restaurant table would not be difficult. He was a handsome kid. Kid? thought Holly. He's at least three or four years older than ... *Cutter*, Holly sighed inwardly as she held the phone and John-Thomas Hinton waited for an answer. She had found herself thinking of him multiple times in each of the ten days since the picnic behind the old farmhouse. During the week that followed, he had come and gone from Wolf's Run when she was not there, done his work but left no bill. At night, when she lay down with only Charlie, her guitar and a .38 to keep her company, she rolled onto her side and imagined Cutter sleeping outside on the porch beneath her window. Then she tasted again that kiss in the strawberry field, saw his hand on her leg and imagined Cutter sleeping even closer. It was crazy and she knew it, but she missed Cutter in a way that she had never missed any man. And there had been many other men she could have missed.

Dinner with Deputy Hinton was a complication she didn't need. "John-Thomas, that's a very nice offer but with all that's happening, I'm just swamped," she said, then softened – "Can I get a rain check?"

The deputy waited a beat or two. "Sure, Holly. I'll drop the reports by in a few minutes."

* * *

Holly tried to focus on the lead story for Saturday's edition of *The Current-Leader*. It would be a preview of Saturday night's big rally at the fairgrounds' rodeo arena to kick off the opening of Riverview Academy. Like it or not, it was news. Big news. The governor coming to town. A statewide radio hook up. But Holly couldn't concentrate on the story. The pictures of LeRoy Kamp kept staring at her from the side of the desk, and just behind her Tom, Mary Nell and the kids watched her from a photo taken during a 1968 vacation to Arizona. They were standing near the Grand Canyon, trying to smile in the glare of the desert sun that glinted off the white Ford station wagon behind them. She picked up the frame and looked at the photo. Caught in that moment, they looked as if they might be posing for Norman Rockwell. The perfect American family. Except that one or perhaps both of the adults murdered her father.

The intercom line buzzed on her phone. It was Miss Frances telling her that Deputy Hinton had dropped off an envelope for her.

"Thank you, Ma'am."

"Do you want me to bring it up?"

There was much more that she could do on Saturday's edition. Much more that needed doing. But Holly said, "No, thank you, Miss Frances. I'll be down in a moment to pick it up."

"I don't mind."

"No, I'm leaving. I'm taking the afternoon off."

"Good," said Miss Frances. "You deserve it."

Holly turned the frame over on her lap, removed the back and took out the photo of the happy Carter family on vacation. She put it and the photos of LeRoy Kamp into a folder and headed for the county library.

* * *

Two hours later, Holly was lifting herself onto the side of the pool at Wolf's Run. She'd done thirty laps but was not breathing hard. Her shoulders rose and fell evenly as her heart rate slowed beneath her a black, one-piece swimsuit. Julie Davis tossed her a towel and Holly toweled off before lifting her hips onto a low bench next to her wheelchair. The bench was the midway point. Holly checked the brakes on the chair and lifted herself onto the seat. Having watched Holly try to swim her tension away many times at the house in Pacific Palisades, Julie knew better than to ask if she needed help. Holly neither needed the help nor wanted the question. Now she lifted each foot and placed the thong of a flipflop between her toes and then placed her left leg over her right.

Julie watched her friend wheel over to the patio table overlooking the hot, green August valley below and the winding brown cut of the Cattahatchie River. She lifted a glass of white wine to her lips. "Feel better?" she asked.

"I'll feel better when I know who killed my father," Holly said, placing a cube of sharp cheddar onto a cracker. She ate it and took a sip from her own wine glass then tapped a fingernail on the Memphis police reports lying on the glass tabletop. "What do you think?"

"If there's not a tie-in to your father's death, then the whole white Ford station wagon thing is one hell of a coincidence," said Julie Davis, who had put in her share of time covering L.A. cops before moving to major features. "But the report seems to back up the story Mary Nell was telling around town. That she was assaulted in the store parking lot by a large, black male who stole her keys and took the car. If that's not what happened, she took a beating from somebody. According to the emergency room report the police received, this wasn't just a slap in the mouth. She was beat up. Her clothes were torn, too. But she denies there was sexual contact."

Holly nodded, but asked, "Nothing about the report seems strange to you?"

Julie looked at the report for half a minute, thinking. Then, "No. What are you thinking?"

"Mary Nell has expensive tastes in clothing, jewelry and handbags. The kind of stuff you have to go to New Orleans or Dallas to get. Or at least you have to send there for them," said Holly. "I'm thinking that if I was a strong-arm robber who took the time to beat up a woman in a department store parking lot before stealing her car I'd have certainly taken an extra few seconds to steal her expensive purse and jewelry. There's not even a mention of any cash being taken."

Julie nodded. "The only thing stolen was the car."

Holly let that thought rest in the humid air for almost a minute, then said, "I need to talk to Cutter. I need to get him to show Mr. Cole these pictures of LeRoy and the picture of the station wagon."

Julie let those words rest in the air for a time as well before asking, "Is that the only reason you need to see Cutter?"

Holly looked at her friend – her best friend – for a moment and started to speak but when their eyes met, both knew no more needed to be said. Holly placed another cracker and cube of cheese in her mouth and poured each of them a fresh glass of wine.

CHAPTER 16

I t was nearly six-thirty but still terribly hot when Holly began transferring from her chair into the Lincoln. Charlie jumped in ahead of her. Holly put in a picnic basket and a folder with the pictures of LeRoy Kamp and the Tom Carter clan. As she turned the key she heard a vehicle coming down the driveway and instinctively reached inside her purse to reassure herself that the .38 was handy and ready. But when she looked toward the road, she saw it was only Gerry Yards. Her former mentor was not dangerous except to himself.

Yards parked his rental car next to the garage and got out, camera in hand. His clothes looked as if he'd spent the afternoon in a steam bath. When he walked over he smelled like beer and cigarettes. He focused on Holly. She was wearing the coolest pieces of clothing she could put together – a cap-sleeved blouson top with a loose gypsy skirt and strappy sandals over tan, freshly shaved legs. He click-click-clicked the motor drive of his camera.

"You are gorgeous!" he told her.

Holly put her hand in front of her face. "Stop it, Gerry. Please." Click-click-click-click … click-click …"You used to love it when I took your picture. In fact, I think I'm still in possession of some pictures of you that are nothing short of – uhmmm? – breathtaking."

Holly wasn't sure if the comment was meant to be titillating, threatening or just the ramblings of a sad, empty man who now mostly got by reveling in his personal and professional past. "That was a long time ago," she said. "Are you in for the night?"

"I don't know. Are you planning to do a bed check? I hope."

"No. But Julie went to the fair. I was merely going to ask you to be sure to lock up if you go back out."

Gerry Yards threw a casual salute her way. He was clearly drunk. Holly turned the key and put the car in gear.

"Where are you and the vicious guard dog headed?"

"I have an appointment."

"Do you always take a picnic basket to an appointment?"

"It depends on the appointment."

"Come inside and have dinner with me. Just the two of us. Like it used to be."

Holly looked at her watch. "Sorry, Gerry. No can do. I'm booked."

He sneered. "That's an interesting way to put it."

Holly worked to control her temper. "Go on in, Gerry. There's plenty of food in the 'fridge. Eat yourself a good meal, then sleep it off."

"You're going to be with him, aren't you? That Cutter kid?" he asked angrily. "What does he have that I don't have? Never mind. I'm sure the answer to that question would only serve to further humiliate me."

From her wheelchair, Holly often had been the one comforting Gerry Yards as he wallowed in Scotch and self-pity, but with all she'd been through the last few weeks she was in no mood for it. "I've got to go."

Suddenly, he took a long step and grabbed the steering wheel. Charlie growled. "Don't go to that kid. Stay here with me. Please."

"Gerry, let go of the wheel," Holly said as calmly as she could manage.

"You know I still love you, still want you, even though … even though – well, you know. You're just going to embarrass yourself with that kid," he scoffed. "I mean, at your age and in your condition …"

Holly shoved the hand control forward then jerked it backward. The big car bucked, tearing Yards' hand off the wheel. She idled the Lincoln in place and took a deep breath. "Gerry, you were good to me. You gave me a chance when no one else would, and I'll always be grateful," she told him. "But I'm sick of how you constantly find ways to intimate that I'm less of a woman than I was before … before I went to Vietnam. That I'm damaged goods and that I'm lucky the great Gerry Yards would still be interested in poor paralyzed me."

Gerry Yards swallowed hard. Drunk as he was, he knew he'd crossed a line. "Sweetie, I'm sorry. I opened up a six-pack at lunch and –"

"Save your excuses and pack your bags," she said, throwing the car into reverse. "I expect my appointment to take about two hours. When I get back, I don't want to find you in my house.

"And in case you've forgotten, I was only nineteen when you embarrassed yourself with me."

* * *

The sky over the cypress trees was layered with lavender and pink as Holly drove west on the Pickens' Ferry Road. She turned southwest around the backside of Blue Mountain then made the sharp cutback onto the narrow road that wrapped up the hill face. It was barely wider than the tires of the big convertible, but it was cut into solid limestone, so it was firm all the way to the edge. Holly put the car's shifter in low and headed up the hill. By the time she reached the flat where the piers of the old farmhouse overlooked Moccasin Slough her heart was thumping, but she had made it. Holly stopped and took a moment to let her heart calm – at least in terms of the car's steep climb up the hill. Cutter might not even be there. He could be anywhere. But as she drove around the back of the ruins, she saw Cutter's Jeep and then she saw him – and the heart that she had just calmed was racing again.

Cutter was sitting on his sleeping bag which was open atop a camouflage ground tarp. He was reading a book and had another lying next to him, his legs crossed at the ankles above work boots. In the background, Mocassion Slough was mirroring the candy-colored sky. He watched as Holly pulled the car as close as she could and put the shifter into park. She turned off the big engine, but Cutter didn't close the book or get up.

"I thought I might buy you dinner at your favorite place," she said, lifting the picnic basket.

"How did you know I was here?" he asked, his voice even. Not unpleasant but not enthused, either.

"I tried The Well. Then I took a turn through the parking lot at the The Gin. I thought maybe with all that's going on you might need to do some thinking. So, I came to your thinking spot." Cutter picked up a bookmark from the sleeping bag, placed it in the book and closed it. He drew his knees up and rested his forearms on them with the hardback in his hands.

"You drove that big ol' wide-bodied tank up that wagon road? You're crazy."

She smiled. "You're not the first to notice."

Cutter put the book down and stood up. He was seeing the woman he'd kissed with such passion days earlier – the same one who had been on his mind every day since, but he also thinking of Rose and his mother and hearing Cecil Weathers' voice warning him to stay away from her.

"Miss Carter, I told you, this is where I come when I don't want to be bothered. I wish you'd respected that."

The words stung the smile off her face. She said, "You brought me here."

"Yeah. And we both know that was my mistake."

"Oh, Cutter, please don't say that. I had a wonderful day. And I want to explain –"

"There's nothing to explain. Let's just leave it at a wonderful day. Okay?"

Holly understood why Cutter might be confused and frustrated over what had happened in the strawberry patch. So was she, but for different reasons.

"All right," she said after a moment and changed the subject. "You did a great job with the work at the house, but you didn't leave a bill. I want to pay you."

He took a few steps closer and Charlie climbed into Holly's lap and stood on the doorframe. The little dog yapped once and wagged. Cutter gave the dog a small, quick smile. "I'll figure it up and drop it by the office when I get time," he said, his tone a tad less brittle.

Holly heard the change and picked up on it. "Please do. You have no idea how valuable your work was."

Cutter took another step closer, reached out and scratched between Charlie's ears. "How's that?"

Holly told him about finding the broken frame with the tattered canvas and dried blood. "I took it to Doctor Garner," she went on. "You know, he handles simple autopsies for the county and he was Daddy's doctor as well." Cutter said nothing but Holly could see she had his attention. "Doctor Garner said there's no test that can determine with 100 percent certainty that the blood was Daddy's, but he said that the smaller drops on the frame are his type."

"The smaller drops?"

"Yes. Here's the even bigger surprise," said Holly. "On the piece of the frame that would have been at the bottom, there were several large drops that were O-negative. Definitely not Daddy's type."

The possibilities raced through Cutter's mind – questions he wanted to ask, thoughts he wanted to share, but he forced himself to remain silent. "Well, good," he allowed himself to say. "I mean, not good, but it's looking more and more like you were right."

"*We* were right," she said. Then she told him about the Memphis Police reports and what Deputy Hinson had told her about notifying Mary Nell on the night of her father's death. "So, she couldn't have been part of it. Not physically."

"Then why would the killer use her car. Unless –" Cutter started but stopped himself. Holly knew what he was thinking, and said, "Unless it was Tom."

"Have you checked to see if people can place him in Biloxi that night?"

Holly shook her head. "No. The people I'd have to ask would be reporters and editors. Newspaper people. It wouldn't take some of them long to put two and two together. I don't want that until I'm sure."

"How much surer do you need to be?"

This was her chance. She handed Cutter the folder containing the pictures. "I need Efram Cole to look at these pictures," she told him.

Cutter opend the folder and flipped through them.

"Show him the one of the station wagon," she said. "Ask if there was a CHS Wolf's Football Booster sticker on the back glass. Like on Mary Nell's."

Cutter could almost smell the cigar smoke and talcum powder inside Governor Weather's limousine.

"What's this?" he said, looking at a sheet of legal paper. Mostly he was asking only to have something to say while he thought, and tried to fight down a kind of lurking fear that he'd never felt. The fear that he had no control over his future – or that of his mother or Rose. That while no one owned him, someone owned enough of the world to destroy him. He barely heard Holly say, "I went to the library and looked up the Memphis and Tupelo papers for the day before my father died. Those were the top stories.

"If Mr. Cole was watching the news when the man came to the door, this might jog his memory. Maybe we could determine whether it was definitely the night Daddy died."

Cutter nodded though he hadn't really heard. He put the folder on the hood of the Lincoln. "Look, Mr. Cole said it was pitch black. He wasn't sure if he'd recognize the guy again."

"If he doesn't, he doesn't. I'm only asking you to try."

From now on, keep away from that Carter woman and the rag she's printin'... I'd hate to have to disqualify you, and your sister, for you associatin' further with a known race-mixer, harlot and purveyor of lies. Those words flashed behind Cutter's eyes like heat lightning. *And, don't forget, your mother and sister will rot up there in that shack. With Tony.*

"So now that you need me again, you're back."

The words stung, but Holly had to own the truth in them. She tried to think of the words to begin to explain, but Cutter didn't give her the chance.

"Sorry, Miss Carter. The answer is no," he said. "I'm done with all this, and I'm done with you. I'm not sure how we got so tangled up, but it's got to stop right here. Right now."

Holly had expected to have to explain herself, but she was surprised by Cutter's cold dismissal. "If you're still upset about what happened between us. Let me explain –"

"No. No explanations. I don't want to hear it, because I don't care," he told her, stepping back, shaking his head. "Look, I was a jerk that first day when you and Miss Eve got run off in the ditch. I thought about it, and I, I – I felt sorry for you. And I needed to make it up. But it's gone too far and it stops now."

... I felt sorry for you ... The discharge of that phrase was like someone firing a gun next to Holly's ear. It rang there inside her skull. All other sound simply disappeared and all that remained was the echo of the exploding cartridge and Gerry Yards' words – *You're just going to embarrass yourself... In your condition ...*

Holly's face flushed, ablaze with blood and heat and humiliation. She turned the key, and whipped the car around. The folder of photos spilled on the ground and Charlie tumbled onto the passenger floor board as the car fishtailed around in a cloud of dust and nearly hit the Jeep. The big convertible slid around the side of the fallen-down house and disappeared. A few minutes later, Cutter saw it in the distance, its headlights flying east on Pickens' Ferry Road.

Cutter leaned against the ancient elm, his eyes and cheeks silver with tears for the first time since he'd thrown everything he owned into the back of his Jeep and drove away from the Old Ambrose Place.

CHAPTER 17

In my room at Mrs. Fletcher's Boarding House I pulled my number 81 Riverview Raiders jersey over my head. Without shoulder pads, it was long enough to be a dress. I glanced at my watch – 5:03. I was picking Patti up. She and the rest of the new Riverview cheerleading squad had to be at the rodeo arena early to decorate for the big pep rally. A knock at my door startled me as I pulled on my jeans.

"Just a minute," I called, knowing it probably was Mrs. Fletcher with a piece of freshly baked apple pie. The delicious aroma had wound its way up from the kitchen.

I zipped up my pants and opened the door. My father was standing in the hall, turning his hat in his hands. It had been a month since I'd seen him up close. His eyes were shot through with red veins of sleeplessness and I was sure there was more gray in his hair, which needed cutting.

When I said nothing, he asked, "Can I come in?"

"Uh, yeah, sure," I said and stepped out of the way.

Billy Wallace moved slowly around the room with its faded wallpaper and worn drapes. He stopped and looked out the screen door onto the balcony and the railroad tracks and highway beyond. "Nice room," he said with no hint of sarcasm. "The trains don't keep you awake?"

"No, sir. You get used to them."

He nodded and noticed a bookcase on one wall. He bent and studied the volumes that had been in my bedroom for years. "I saw you came and collected some of your stuff from the house."

"You weren't there."

"No, I – I don't spend much time at the house these days," he said. "Mostly I sleep at the jail. Or in my car. But Elmo Washington and his boys are doing a nice job with the farm. The cotton and beans are doin' real good. The corn's aw'right."

"Good."

My father kept his eyes moving around the room until they settled on a picture of the four of us – me and Mom, Steve and him – back when we were a family. Then they came back to the present me in my shabby boarding house room. "That jersey looks real good on you. It's mighty sharp," he said, managing a smile. "In fact, you look real good, Son. Healthy."

"Miz Fletcher's a good cook."

"I heard you found work. How's Mr. Handley treatin' you?"

"Real good. Especially considerin' how you and the feds have been harassing him and his brother," I told him, perhaps looking for a fight. If so, Billy Wallace didn't take the bait, so after a moment, I went on – "He says he could see me bein' an assistant manager in a year to 18 months."

"What about college? I thought you couldn't wait to see what was at the other end of those railroad tracks."

"Oh, I will. You can bet your bottom dollar on that. But me and Patti may go the first two years over at the junior college in Booneville. That way, Patti can keep livin' at home a little longer and I can keep working at Handley's and save some money. That'll let us get a better start when we do go off to college."

"Is that your idea or Patti's? Or maybe Brother Mac's?"

"It was, well – it's not anybody's idea. It's just circumstances. It's just what we need to do," I tried to explain, irritated at how quickly my father had seen the truth of things. "Miz MacAllister's health isn't good. This whole mess has worn her nerves to a frazzle."

"I see."

"Speakin' of Patti, I'm supposed to pick her up in – gee! five minutes – to go to the rally. Is there somethin' you wanted to talk about or –?"

Billy Wallace set his straw Panama on his head and reached for his wallet. "No, I just wanted to see how you were farin' and give you this."

I unfolded the check and couldn't believe my eyes. Fifteen hundred dollars. "Daddy! Where'd you get this kind of money?"

"I sold Ricky Hickerson a few of those acres he's been wantin' over next to his fence line. There's enough there to cover your tuition to Riverview, your books and help out with odds and ends."

"But, Daddy, I got a scholarship. I don't need it."

"Son, take it. Please," he said. "If you're gonna go to Riverview, pay your own way. I don't want you to be any more beholden to those people than you already are."

A bolt of anger shot through me. "Those people are my friends," I told him, pushing the check back into his hand. "And I don't want your money. I'm doin' fine on my own and I like it that way."

"Son, I –"

"Look, Daddy, I gotta go," I said and brushed past him into the hall. "Patti's waitin' on me.

"Shut the door, please, on your way out."

* * *

As the sun set and the lights of the rodeo arena were turned on, me, Mickey Ambrose and Toby Wright propped on a fence rail and watched our cheerleader girlfriends dancing in the center of the arena to Marvin Gaye's *Ain't No Mountain High Enough*, as played by Riverview's new marching band. The smell of animal dung, fried chicken, sawdust, cotton candy and sweat hung in the thick air between the highway and the river. At the north end of the arena, other former Wolves players began filling the tiers of folding chairs. The night before, Janette Wellingham had paraded there on the T-shaped stage on her way to winning Miss Cattahatchie County 1969.

One player who would not be on the stage was our quarterback, Jimmy Garner. After current Governor Broderick essentially refused to appoint a new school board until November's elections, Judge Mulberry stepped in. On Friday, he named Dr. G.P. Garner interim chairman. Mulberry also appointed to the five-member board Reverend Jean Baptiste of Roseville A.M.E. Church, and Ernie Logan, owner of the grocery recently shot up by the Klan. They became the first blacks to hold countywide office since Reconstruction.

Jimmy was a nice guy and a good leader but anyone could take a snap from center and give the ball to Cutter. In fact, if Coach Pearce was smart – and that was debatable – he'd install that new wishbone offense that they were running out in Texas and move Cutter to quarterback. That would require shifting a couple of good athletes to running back, which could open up a wide receiver slot for me. I might even start! Wouldn't that be something?

To be honest, until I saw Cutter emerge from the gap in the north grandstands and step onto the stage wearing the gold 13, I wasn't one-hundred percent sure he'd jump to Riverview. He seemed to have little room to maneuver, but as with the moves he made on the football field, Cutter could be surprising in his decisions and bold to the point of recklessness in his choices. Though Cutter and I had gone through a rough patch amid the agitation by that NCJ bunch and that Yankee judge, and whatever spell Miss Carter had briefly cast over him, he still was my best friend. And now that decisions had been made and the county's social order was being restored, even if in exile, things would be getting back to normal, I told myself.

As I mounted the stage, most of my used-to-be and about-to-be teammates already were seated, as were Senator Wellingham, Milton Handley and Brother MacAllister. Cutter was next to Coach Pearce in the front row. I found a chair in the row behind them as Coach handed Cutter several three-by-five note cards.

"I'll introduce you," Coach Pearce was saying. "Speak clearly into the microphone. Don't mumble."

"I never do. I just don't always have a lot to say."

"Well, stick to the high points I made on the note cards. You'll be fine," said Coach Pearce. "And Cutter, you made the right decision."

"Yeah. I believe I have."

CHAPTER 18

Cutter gave Coach Pearce's three-by-five cards one more look, tapped them on his knee, folded them in half and slipped them into the back pocket of his Levi's. Over the carnival sounds of the midway, the lowing of livestock waiting to be judged and the braying of bucking horses eager to kick their hooves up and their riders off, Headmaster Larry Rhodes was saying something about how exciting it was to have the inauguration of Riverview Academy carried on a statewide radio hook-up. But Cutter wasn't really hearing him, nor seeing the Ferris wheel turning in a big neon circle at the center of the fairgrounds.

His mind was at Wolf's Run with Miss Carter. He'd stopped there on his way to the pep rally. Julie Davis answered the knock at the kitchen door late Saturday afternoon. She looked up at him with eyes that were no longer filled with admiration.

"Hi. I need to see Miss Carter."

"I'm not sure she's going to want to see you, Sport," said Julie. "I don't know what went on between you two the other day, but you hurt her. I mean you really hurt her. And I don't like people who hurt my friends."

Cutter absorbed the reproof without comment. "Would you just tell her I talked to Efram Cole."

"And?"

"And I'll be happy to tell Miss Carter what he said."

Julie grunted. "You are a cocky son-of-bitch, aren't you?"

When Cutter said nothing, she said, "All right. Come in. We were out by the pool. I'll tell her you're here."

Julie Davis went out the French doors that led to the interior porch and courtyard. His eyes followed her out, but he said nothing. He wasn't one to share his personal life with those he did not know well. Often not even those he did. He looked around the kitchen, remembering it warm with candlelight and Sinatra the way it had been the night after the Roseville bombing. Now the kitchen table was covered in newspapers, a ledger, an adding machine and several legal-looking documents, their edges fluttering in the wake from the ceiling fan. When he took a step closer, the seal of the State of California was not hard to read, nor were the words "Deed of Sale" in large black letters. An address on High Ridge Drive, Pacific Palisades, was typed onto a line provided in the form. He flipped a couple of pages and saw Miss Carter's signature on the line for "seller."

The heels of Julie Davis' sandals clattered on the ramp as she returned. Cutter stepped back from the table.

"Go on out," she said.

H olly was sitting next to a black wrought iron patio table. Her long legs were stretched out and her heels were propped on a cushion atop the low fieldstone wall that ran along the edge of the 350-foot precipice. She had a towel covering her thighs and another over her shoulders. Her one-piece suit, wet as it was, was almost as green as her eyes. Almost. She was absently running a brush through her wet copper hair and Cutter thought again of the kitchen and the candlelight. A half empty pitcher of Bloody Marys sat on the table. He stopped on the flagstones 10 feet away. She took a sip of the concoction from a tall glass adorned with celery. Resting against a nearby lounge chair was a large open cardboard box containing a set of waist-to-toe leg braces. With their polished metal frame, multiple leather straps, big buckles and attached ankle-high boots they looked like some Medieval torture device.

Clearly even though he'd brought her news from Efram Cole, Holly was not going to make it easy for him. Looking for someplace to start the conversation, he said, "You wear those?"

Holly pursed her lips and gave him a what-business-of-yours-is-it look, then said, "I'm supposed to. At least twenty hours a week. To keep my leg bones from becoming brittle. They just arrived from California. I didn't have room in the car."

The awkward silence resumed. After a moment, she asked, "Do you want a drink? I mean, you are of legal drinking age in Miss'issippi. Just not in good ol' Cattahatchie County where the consumption of all alcohol is verboten. But you won't tell on me, will you?"

"No."

"No you don't want a drink?" she asked, not looking at him. "Or no you won't tell on me?"

"Both," he said and stepped forward putting the folder on the patio table. "I showed Mr. Cole the pictures. He said he's 90 percent sure LeRoy is the guy, but he couldn't swear to it in court."

Holly nodded. Her eyes remained hard, but they changed, too, like gun sights being redirected. "What about the car?"

"It was definitely Mary Nell's car," he told her. "If you look close at the picture you can see the top part of the H and the S are missing in CHS. He noticed it that night, too."

It was what they had suspected. Still, the growing certainty that her sister-in-law conspired, in one way or another, to kill her father fell on her like a heavy weight that made it hard to breathe. But she took a long breath and then another and asked,

"What about the timing? Did you show him the news stories? Is he sure it was that night?"

"No. Mr. Cole said the knock came just at the moment the news was coming on. He never saw it."

"Did you ask Mrs. Cole?"

"No. She wasn't home. Her sister was sick and she'd gone to nurse her."

Holly nodded absently, as if hearing him from a great distance.

"What are you going to do now?" he asked.

The question seemed to bring her back to the present. "I don't know."

"It seems like it might be time to talk to Sheriff Wallace."

"Cutter, I appreciate you showing those pictures to Mr. Cole. I know you took a risk. But I'll take it from here," she said, shutting a door between them. Cutter felt it but didn't turn to leave. Instead he crossed to the knee-high wall that guarded the edge of the courtyard. Through the kudzu, briars and wild grapevine a narrow path twisted – the wolf's run. He stood there for several moments looking down the long valley, his hands stuffed in his back pockets. Holly just wanted him to leave. Then he turned. "Look, Miss Carter, I wanted to tell you, I didn't mean what I said the other night about feeling sorry for you. I lied. I'm sorry."

Holly studied him. She appreciated what she was hearing, but she was cautious, too. His words had hit her hard, like a punch to the chest, and her heart felt bruised. Gerry Yards was gone back to Los Angeles but his words remained, and Cutter's angry, hurtful tone had amplified them.

"So why did you say it?"

"I just wanted – I mean, I-I needed you to leave," he said, struggling to get the words out with more seemingly stuck in in his throat. Finally -- "The truth of it is, I was scared. And I'm still scared."

Holly's heart felt suddenly lighter, less achy, even if the bruise was still tender. "Ohhh, Cutter," she sighed. "You should have said –"

"I know. I'm sorry."

Holly thought of herself at eighteen and the shock when her surety about her world and the control she assumed she had over it was shattered. It's what Tony Carlucci's attack of her in that storage closet had done. All of her looks, her smarts, her talent, her family position and most of all her confidence had been worthless against his pawing and the putrid, sweaty weight of his body atop hers, splaying her legs against her will. It was only the dumbest of dumb luck that the guys in the band happened by and pulled him off before he could enter her. But in the real sense, the in-her-heart sense, Tony Carlucci had completed the attack. He'd raped her soul. And though she had never said it to anyone, the attack had been the main reason she had fled Delong so quickly after high school. She could not stand to live a moment longer in a place where someone like Tony was protected by someone like Governor

Weathers. Now, she could see, the same men were attempting to rape Cutter – simply by other means. She felt furious and sad, and frightened for him, too.

After a time, Holly said, "I know you're under huge pressure to, well, to be what this town wants you to be. To toe the Cattahatchie line. Believe me, I know that feeling. I ran all the way to the West Coast and crossed an ocean to get away from it. And even then, I never really did."

"I guess I've always –" he stopped and cleared his throat – "thought of myself as a pretty strong person. Or at least, if I was faced with a clear choice between right and wrong, I would choose to do the right thing. At least, the right thing in my eyes. But now?" He shook his head.

"I wish I had a magic answer for you," she said. "God knows, it's hard making those kinds of choices."

"How do you make them?"

She took a deep breath and thought about how to answer, then -- "I look at all my options. If I don't know about my choices, I research them as best I can. On the big stuff, I pray a little. I ask God to guide me. But I don't sit around waiting on a voice from the clouds. I trust that He silently puts the answer in my heart."

"Is that what you did about the Tommy Ray Banks story?"

"No. I didn't have to pray about that," she told him. "After all I saw in Vietnam, and all I went through at Ia Drang – boys, men, black, white dying all around me, some of them dying to protect me – I didn't have to ask anyone what was right. But did ask God for the courage to *do* what was right."

Cutter continued to look south toward Delong, across thousands of acres of fertile green fields, many of which should have been his. Holly lifted her right leg off the wall and positioned her foot on the pedal. She lifted the left, which spasmed for a moment. She settled her left foot then crossed her right leg over her left knee. Cutter tactfully ignored the involuntary twitches and Holly noticed gratefully. After a time, he said, "When Miss Davis came to tell you I was here, she left me in the kitchen. I wasn't meaning to pry, but I saw the bill of sale for your house in California. You once told me that it's the place you love most in the world." When Holly said nothing, Cutter asked, "So you're giving it up? You're planning to stay here?"

In that moment, Holly had to decide how much she would trust him. He had trusted her enough to talk about being afraid of the forces that were swirling around them like a tornado of broken glass. She said, "Without a pretty massive infusion of cash, the paper won't last another three weeks. I've tried banks as far away as Atlanta and St. Louis. But everyone has seen the news. Everyone knows what's going on here. But a screenwriter for Warner Brothers has been wanting to buy the house for over a year. Last week, he called and upped his offer again. It's enough that we can keep the doors of the paper open and presses turning until sometime around Christmas. By then, maybe enough people will have had a change of heart to keep us afloat."

Cutter looked at Holly with real concern in his eyes. "What if they don't?"

Holly didn't answer immediately because she did not really have an answer. "I don't know," she said. "Probably go back to California. See if I can get my teaching job back. I can shoot weddings and birthday parties and such. Maybe I'll start hitting the clubs again. Singing."

"You don't see many club singers in wheelchairs."

"No," she agreed and tried to smile. "I might be quite a novelty act. Maybe if I practice, I can hustle pool on the side."

"But wouldn't you still have this place?"

Holly shook her head. "No, everything is owned by Cattahatchie Newspapers Incorporated. If the newspaper goes, Wolf's Run goes, too."

"Then you don't really have Plan B, do you?"

"My plan is to keep the doors of *The Current-Leader* open for as long as I can, and out of the hands of Weathers and his Klan bunch," she said firmly. "That's what Daddy would want."

"And that's why Mr. Carter left the paper to you and not Tom."

Holly said nothing to that, then – "I believe there are more people in Cattahatchie County like Miss Frances and her husband, and Dr. Garner and Billy Wallace than Weathers and Benoit and –"

"And Tony."

"Yes. And Tony."

"But you don't *know*."

"You're right, I don't. And, if you want to know the truth, it scares the hell out of me. I actually get shaky thinking about it. People I've seen – we've all seen – sitting in a wheelchair at some corner. Begging for change. For a dollar. For anything. The idea that I might be that person someday –" she told him, shaking her head, unable to give words to the image in her head. "I have nightmares about it. That and 'Nam. Pretty often. Sometimes I dread going to sleep. But this is something I did pray about and –" she sighed – "sometimes you just have to step out in faith. Take a chance and believe you'll be okay on the other side of it. Or at least be willing to accept the consequences if you're not."

Cutter said nothing.

After several moments, Holly said, "You seem to have a lot on your mind today."

He grunted. "You might say that."

Holly gave him time to expand on his reply, if he cared to, but she didn't push for more. It was one of the things Cutter liked about her. One of the reasons he was comfortable talking to her. She didn't try to drag out of him more than he was willing to give.

"I want get out of this wet suit and dry my hair," Holly said. "It may not be as good as your spot under the elms, but I've always found this to be a pretty good thinking spot, too. Feel free to use it."

Cutter turned his head, half smiled. "Thanks. Are you going to the fairgrounds tonight? Should be quite a show."

"No. Julie is going to cover it for the Chronicle News Group. I'll pick up her story. But I'm sure I'll be listening on the radio," she said wanting to go to Cutter, take his hand in hers and maybe a lot more, but she still was bruised and unsure. "Good luck," was all she said and pivoted toward the ramp up into the house. By the time Holly had finished changing and wheeled back into the interior hall with its long set of French doors opening onto the big patio, Cutter was gone.

* * *

Three hours later in the library Holly tuned the stereo to WHCI and switched off the lights. A storm front was moving in from the west, creating an early dusk. Cars swam like tiny silver minnows along the course cut by Highway 27. To the south, the lights of town and the fairgrounds mixed into a yellow-white glow. Holly wheeled to the big leather sofa, transferred out of her chair, lifted her legs and stretched out. For a moment she stared at the empty space on the wall where her mother's portrait had hung, then turned her mind to the more immediate. She had checked to make sure all the doors were locked, but with Julie covering the pep rally as the final chapter in her magazine piece, she was alone in the big house. She took the .38 from the pocket of her skirt and placed it within easy reach on the coffee table. Charlie hopped up on the couch and lay against her side as she stroked the little dog's white coat.

WHCI's only real announcer, "Stonewall" Maddox, communicated the pageantry of the rally as if it were a royal coronation. He described the festivities as the newly formed Riverview Academy Band marched, playing several numbers as they tried to avoid piles of horse dung in the rodeo arena. The cheerleaders twirled and chanted in their new butternut, gray and white uniforms near the plank bleachers.

In a way this was it was a coronation, or it could be, thought Holly. She had not needed to ask Cutter what was troubling him. She knew. He did not want to make the jump to Riverview but Weathers and his cronies were pressuring – coercing? blackmailing? leveraging? – him to do so. She remembered how trapped and vulnerable and alone she'd felt when those same men marched into *The Current-Leader* office and threatened the existence of an enterprise her family had poured their lives into for four generations. Now all Cutter had to do was go along with the Riverview crowd, spend the autumn running over and past the slow-footed kids he would face in the Academy League, bring home the championship trophy – and he would own DeLong, Mississippi. At least for a season. One way or another, the town's elite would make sure that Cutter got a scholarship to whichever Mississippi football power he desired.

Heady stuff when you're eighteen – almost nineteen, Holly reminded herself and closed her eyes. "Dear Lord," she began aloud, "I pray that You'll strengthen Cutter's heart tonight. Help him make the decision that leads to the light. And be at peace with it. But whatever he does, please watch over him. He's a good guy." The words caught in her throat. "He really is. Amen."

***

T he sound of his name being called over the public address system seemed distant, like the sound of a bell through water. Then it came again, and Cutter realized it was hard to hear because of all the applause, whoops, whistles and cheers. "Cut-ter! ... Cut-ter! ... Cut-ter!"

The crowd rocked the two syllables of his name back and forth between the bleachers, from one side of the arena to the other as he walked out to the end of the runway where Miss Cattahatchie County had been crowned. TV lights glared and flashbulbs glittered at the front of the stage as Governors Weathers and Broderick took up station beside Cutter, waving to the several thousand locals gathered at the arena.

"Smile, son!" urged Cecil Weathers without disturbing his own grin. "Smile like you mean it."

At the Old Ambrose Place, Rose sat on the front steps holding the transistor radio Cutter had given her. Their mother was pacing the side porch repeating louder and louder the multiplication tables, algebra equations and quadratic formulas until she was almost screaming them. Like a cat smelling smoke inside a burning house, she was yowling at a whiff of something she sensed in the air. How much her mother understood about events around her, Rose was never sure.

The two governors retreated the twenty feet to their seats and Cutter began -- "First, I'd like to thank the folks behind Riverview Academy for thinking enough of me to give me a scholarship. And for offering to give Rose, my sister, a scholarship, too. I'm sure Riverview students will get a good education."

At the far end of the arena, Tony Carlucci leaned on the rail with nine other unrobed Klansmen. One of them jovially clapped Tony on the back. The Kaptain of Klargo managed a brief, crooked smile that hid the disdain he had for the touch of any man and the distrust and contempt he had for Cutter. But mainly the curl of his lips hid a rage of jealousy boiling inside him.

"With, uhm –" Cutter paused looking for the right word, then – "I've been thinking a lot about all the Riverview Academy football team can accomplish this fall in these nice new uniforms. There're a lot of good players, good friends of mine making this move."

"Well, most of you know I kind of live on my own. I've worked construction. Done farm labor. Bussed tables, built fences, painted barns and done more odd jobs than I can name," he said as Weathers gave a hard look to Coach Pearce, who swallowed thickly. This wasn't in the note cards. "And a lot of those jobs I've done next to a colored man – that is, a black man, I guess I'm supposed to say these days. Best I can tell, I'm none the worse for it." A shocked grumble passed through the crowd. Sheriff Wallace, who had been standing behind the stage, started easing up the ramp. He had a feeling about what was about to happen.

"During wintertime when you can't get in the fields or do much of anything else, I played a lot of basketball with Tommy Ray Banks and his friends from the Roseville High gym. I've got to say, as many times as I bumped up against Tommy or one of his cousins, I can't find a smudge of black that ever rubbed off on me."

People were booing now. At first a few here and there, then a chorus.

"That's enough!" shouted Cecil Weathers. Coach Pearce jumped to his feet as if he was ready to tackle Cutter, or try. That's when my daddy and Deputy Hinton stepped in, blocking the runway. "You wanted him to speak, now you're gonna let him," I heard daddy say.

Listening over the statewide radio hookup, Judge Mulberry and U.S. Attorney J.L. Burke clinked their whiskey glasses, shared surprised smiles and sat back in their rocking chairs on the porch of Mulberry's Oxford home as federal marshals patrolled the grounds. Over the clatter of Saturday night's busy supper rush, cooks, waiters and busboys at The Gin listened in the kitchen as they loaded steaks and catfish suppers onto plates. In the big tent outside of Pickens' Ferry A.M.E. Church, Ron Clemmer and a couple of dozen youthful volunteers from the North held their breath as Cutter went on.

"So, I've got to speak from my heart and tell you folks that I don't get it. I don't get why sittin' in a classroom next to a black kid is a big deal."

I leaned forward and held my head in my hands. I thought I was going to throw up. The dream I'd had only a few minutes earlier of Cutter and I starting on the same championship football team was utterly destroyed. Brother MacAllister looked as if he was going to tear his Bible in half and Patti's mouth was twisted as she snarled words her father probably didn't even know. I couldn't pick the words out. They were caught up in the increasing howl, like flames from a fire rising in a chimney – all the heat directed at Cutter.

Miles to the north, Rose Carlucci hugged the little radio to her chest, never more proud of her brother but also never more frightened for him. And for herself and her mother. Tony would be livid, and if he couldn't take it out on Cutter, he'd take it out on them, she knew.

"I figure black kids probably want to learn, just like we do. Maybe more, because they've got some catchin' up to do in this country."

Instead of trying to fight through my father and his deputy, J.D. Benoit jumped down from the front of the stage, swung open the six-inch blade of his pocket knife and grabbed the microphone cord.

"I appreciate everything the people of DeLong have done for me. But my heart tells me I need to stay at Cattahatchie High and –"

The microphone went dead and Cutter's natural voice was drowned in what had become a rage of boos and profanity.

There was no point in trying to continue to talk to the crowd, but Cutter turned, pulling off the Raiders' jersey to expose a black-and-red CHS football T-shirt. He looked into the stunned faces of the would-be Riverview players and spoke. He had to shout to be heard over the jeers. "I'm going to be at the high school field Monday afternoon at 3, ready to practice," he yelled. "The season-opener is in two weeks. We'll have to work our tails off to be ready. If any of y'all are still real Wolves, be there!"

As Cutter walked down the ramp, someone threw a cup of soda that hit him in the shoulder. More than one person spit in his direction, and ugly voices followed him as he walked out of the floodlights and into the shadows behind the stage. He ignored them all.

"You ungrateful dago scum! … You're done in this town! …You're as crazy as your momma! … And as stupid as your idiot s-s-s-sister!"

At the other end of the arena, Tony Carlucci punched the plank fence and heard the wood crack under his rage.

Cutter cranked the Jeep and headed toward the fairgrounds exit. Someone threw a rock that cracked the windshield on the passenger side. My father climbed into his patrol car and followed him. North of town Sheriff Wallace hit his red lights and Cutter pulled over onto the entrance to gravel side road. The sheriff stepped out of his cruiser and walked to the side of the Jeep. He tilted his hat back on his head. "That was a helluva thing you did back there, Son. It took a shitload of guts. But that don't mean people are gonna love you for it."

Cutter dropped his hands into his lap. "I know."

"Where you headed now?"

"There's a little cut off on Blue Mountain Road, just before you get to our place. I figured I'd park there and keep an eye on things."

"Bad idea. You know Tony's gonna be hoppin' mad," said the sheriff. "If you and him tangle tonight, somebody's probably gonna get killed."

"Maybe it's time."

Billy Wallace looked hard at him. "I don't want to be arrestin' you for murder in the mornin'."

"Murder? You'd call it murder?" said Cutter before pausing to gather his words. "Everybody knows what Tony did to momma. And they know what he did to Rose, too. Yeah, they know! They just don't have the gumption to do anything about it as long as Tony's tight with the ol' guv."

The sheriff let Cutter simmer for a bit. "I know. And it's shameful," he said. "If I can ever get things to settle down on this integratin' mess, I'll do my best to do something about Tony. But in the meantime, for the next couple of days and nights

I'm going to station a patrol car in that cutoff. We'll make sure Tony nor none of his runnin' buddies get to your momma or Rose. And you're gonna make yourself scarce."

Cutter shook his head. "I'm sorry, Mr. Wallace. That's not good enough."

"It's gonna have to be," the sheriff told him. "You need to git gone and stay gone for at least the rest of weekend. Let tempers cool a little bit. By Monday, people'll go back to work, to their fields. They'll have more to think about than what happened tonight. I'll have a talk with Tony, if I can find him, and try to put a scare into him."

Cutter grunted. "My daddy may be a lot of things, but he's a hard man. He takes a lot of scarin'. Believe me, I know."

"I don't doubt it," said the sheriff.

"What about after that?"

"I don't know. We'll have to try to figure somethin' out. But my goal right now is just to keep everybody above the dirt for the next 48 hours."

"And if I don't do what you say?"

"I'm going to arrest you and put you in a jail cell. Protective custody."

"You'd really do that?"

"There's no air conditioning and the cots are lumpy, but you're used to livin' rough. Miss Hattie Pyle contracts to cook for the inmates. Her biscuits and gravy are the next best thing to Miss Winona's," said Billy Wallace. Then soberly – "Damn straight, I will. Either point your Jeep out of this county right now, or step out and put your hands behind your back." Cutter still hesitated but Billy Wallace slapped the side of the Jeep like he would a horse he wanted put to run. "Go on," he told Cutter. "Git!"

With a jerk of the shifter and a toss of gravel and dust Cutter pulled back onto the highway and headed toward Tennessee.

PART IV

CHAPTER 1

The parking lot at First Denomination was nearly empty when Patti and I walked out into the searing Sunday afternoon heat. Patti had stayed after the services to support her father in his "righteous trials" as pastor, shaking hands with stalwarts of the diminished flock. We were crossing the parking lot, walking toward the large parsonage where Mrs. MacAllister surely had dinner on the table, when I saw a big blue car moving out from under the shade of two big oaks at the edge of the lot.

"Oh, shit!" I sighed, knowing there wasn't another one like it in the county.

Holly Lee Carter stopped the Lincoln five feet in front of us. She was wearing a white, green and blue floral print dress with a green scarf tied under her chin that matched her eyes, I noticed, as she idled the car and took off her Wayfarers. Without preamble she asked, "Do you know where Cutter might be? I need to find him."

"What are you doing here?" demanded Patti. "This is holy ground. Ground that Reverand MacAllister has prayed over, and that God has –"

Miss Carter ignored Patti.

"Nate, Miss Jenny had a stroke this morning. A bad one," she said evenly. "I've tried The Well and The Gin."

"A stroke!" Patti crowed gleefully, a manic light in her eyes. "You see, Nate, it's just like Daddy says, God's judgment is sure and merciless against the wicked, and it can be swift, too."

"Patti, stop it. Please. This is serious," I said, trying to sort the possibilities. "He has a place he calls his 'thinking spot' but I'm not sure where it is. Except when he goes there he usually brings back a load of strawberries."

"I know. I've already been there," she said. "Where else?"

I suppressed my irritation that Holly Carter knew where Cutter's "thinking spot" was and I did not. There was talk, guessing, rumors and some sniggering, but no one really knew what the relationship was between the newspaper's editor and Cutter. Not even me. I hesitated, then – "Look, it's not unusual for Cutter to, you know, for him to meet someone and go home with her."

"Fornicator," growled Patti and spit, theatrically, on the hot pavement, but if Miss Carter cared about Cutter's late-night habits, she didn't miss a beat – "If he

286

did, then we'll just have to wait for him to show up. But Nate is there anywhere else? Think."

"Nate Wallace, you don't have to answer questions from this whore of Babylon," said Patti, grabbing my arm. "Let's go."

Everything was coming at me so fast. It seemed like the world had started spinning faster and faster this summer, especially since Miss Carter came back. At moments such as when Daddy told me he was going to be sheriff, last night at the fairgrounds and now this, I felt like I might fly right off. Right off into the blackness, alone. And I'd had too much alone time since Steve and momma died and Daddy had crawled into the bottle. It looked like he'd crawled back out, but it seemed Billy Wallace now was concerned about everyone in Cattahatchie County except me. Even if we were on the outs, maybe for good, Cutter still was the best friend I'd ever had. I pulled my arm away from Patti.

"There's an old hotel in Memphis he goes to sometimes when he really wants to get away from here, from everybody," I told her.

"That's probably it!" she enthused. "What's the name of it?"

"That's the thing, Miss Carter. I don't know. He never told me. Or if he did, I don't remember it."

"Think, Nate! This is important."

"I know," I said trying to pull from my memory whatever Cutter had told me. "We were together at The Well the night Martin Luther King was killed at that motel in Memphis. Cutter said, if he'd been at his 'Memphis place,' he could have heard the shot."

"Okay. The Lorraine Motel. Yes. That's good. What else?"

"Damn it, Nate!" said Patti, her face pink with anger. "Stop talking to that woman! You don't have to that bitch anything!"

"It sits on the bluff, overlooking the Miss'ssippi. Cutter said he likes to get a room in back where he can prop and watch the river and the barges, and the bridge at night."

"Good, good," Miss Carter encouraged.

I went on. "It looks like one of those New Orleans apartment buildings. You know, with the balconies and iron work. And, and – right next door there's a colored pool hall and barbecue joint. He said it's got the best dry-cured ribs he ever ate."

"Great. Do you remember the name of the barbecue place?"

I shook my head. "I don't think it's got one. You know, it's just one of those hole-in-wall eats places."

"Okay, Nate. You've been a big help. Thanks," she said and put the car in gear. I nearly told her, *Wait! I'll go with you.* But I didn't. Patti was yelling now, her hands balled into fists -- "Don't ever come back here! You're evil! I hope you die!"

I turned on her, grabbed one arm as Miss Carter drove away. "Patti, stop it! Do you hear what you're saying?"

Brother MacAllister's daughter wrenched her arm away and looked at me with the most undiluted hatred and rage I'd ever seen in anyone's eyes. Then she whirled and stomped off toward the parsonage. Shaking my head, I sighed, but after a few moments I followed her across the scalding blacktop.

* * *

Northbound traffic was unusually heavy on two-lane Highway 78 for a Sunday afternoon in August. It took Holly nearly two hours to cover the 85 miles to the Memphis city limits where it became Vance Avenue. Holly was familiar with the city from many shopping trips there with Meemaw Lois and many debutante balls and fraternity parties she had attended in her youth at the Peabody and King Cotton hotels. Mostly though, she remembered from her early childhood a wonderful birthday party her father had thrown for her mother on the Peabody's Union Avenue rooftop. As she waited at a downtown light she could see the back of the grand dame and the memories rushed in. It was 1947. She was six. World War II was over and so many soldiers were coming home. She remembered men in uniform all over the sidewalks, swaggering in their khaki and olive and Navy blue, and everyone seemed so happy. Like anything was possible. Like the world had begun anew, created just for them. And as her parents danced under the stars to a big band with a sound-alike Sinatra crooner, T.L. Carter in his tux gliding on the boards with his smart, talented, exquisite wife Veronique – they were happy, too.

Soooo happy, she thought and shook her head. "What happened to you?" she asked aloud. "What happened to us?"

Behind her a horn sounded and she looked up to see that the light was green. Her mind returned to the present and to Cutter and she made the turn onto South Main Street, away from the splendor of the Peabody and Goldsmith's Department Store, toward the mostly black neighborhoods that scrabbled among small factories and sprawling warehouses for purchase on the bluff near the big river.

It didn't take Holly long to find The Hobart Hotel & Weekly Apartments. She located it on her second pass. She missed it the first time because the front of the faded old, four-story red brick building had none of the scrolled ironwork of a French Quarter townhouse. But as she slowly crossed Docks Avenue and looked west down the steep hill to the river, she caught a glimpse of the balconies at the back of the building.

There was a parking lot halfway down the block. On Sundays it was free. She put the roof up on the convertible before loading herself into her wheelchair, crossing her right leg over her left and locking the car. She put her .38 in her lap and covered it with a casual white wicker purse. Thankfully the heavy glass doors to the lobby stood open to allow a breeze to blow through from somewhere at the back of the building, and with it the scent of barbecue. There was one 6-inch step but in three years Holly had become confident enough in her balance and strong enough in her upper body to shift her weight, pop the chair's front castors up, then muscle the back wheels over such an impediment.

Once in the shadowy alcove Holly took off her sunglasses and her scarf and shook out her hair. Pushing into a lobby of chipped tile that needed a good and thorough mopping, she saw a staircase to the left and in the corner an old bird-cage elevator. A slender young black man was sitting behind a registration counter staring intently at a magazine, his brow furrowed in concentration. The quiet of her wheels and the squeaking of two large fans turning overhead in the high, arched ceiling hid her approach. When Holly got to counter unnoticed she said, "Hi."

The man jumped up from his stool as if he'd been shocked. "Shit, Mama!" he said. "Where'd you come from?"

"Mississippi."

"No! I mean –" he started and gave up on it. Flustered he closed the magazine, which she saw was *Playboy*, and put it under the counter. "What can I do for you?"

"I'm looking for a guy named Cutter Carlucci."

The man took a toothpick from a small tin dispenser on the counter and pushed it into the corner of his mouth as he studied her. "You are one mighty fine lookin' woman," he said. "What'chu doin' in that chair?"

"None of your business," she told him. "Is Cutter Carlucci here?"

"White boy?"

"Yes, a white boy."

"You his sister? You both got that kinda dago skin," he said. "Almost like a couple'uh high yella's."

"No, I'm not his sister."

"Girlfriend?"

Holly hesitated an instant, then – "No. And I'm not his mother either. I just need to talk to him. Damn it, is here or not?"

The young man stroked his nascent goatee and rubbed together the fingers of his other hand. "I'm havin' a tough time rememberin'," he said. "I mean, we gets so many big, stout, black-haired white boys through here."

Holly opened her purse and unsnapped her wallet. She took out a ten and laid it on the counter. "Does that help your memory?"

"Hit me like that again, Mama, and I'll tell you what he had for breakfast."

"More than I need to know," said Holly. "Can you just call up to his room and ask him to come down."

"Ain't no phones in the hotel rooms, just the 'partments."

"Does that elevator work?"

"If you talk to it right. Stroke its handle a little bit. I bet you can stroke it just fine."

Holly ignored the innuendo. "What room is he in?"

"The one he always gets. Four-oh-six. Top floor. Last room on the right."

"Thank you," she said and pivoted toward the tarnished brass antique of a lift. "Does anyone ever use that thing?"

"Only if they's too drunk to get up the stairs."

Holly opened the outside cage-like door and the inner door, whirled around and backed in, then reversed the process with the doors. Beside the handle were letters and numbers, chipped but readable: L 2 3 4. She slowly pulled the handle to four.

The old elevator jerked suddenly and Holly gasped as machinery above her began to grind and cables rattled. The small, unsteady platform began to groan and creak and rise in its narrow metal silo. Finally, it rattled to a stop and she pushed down the thread-bare runner in the hall, a space lit only by tall uncurtained windows at either end. They were open to catch what breeze there was. The one next to four-oh-six led to a metal fire escape down the south side of the building. She lifted her hand to knock but she heard a radio playing Stevie Wonder's soul hit *My Cherie Amour*. For the first time it occurred to Holly that Cutter might not be alone. She realized her hand was shaking.

So what if he is with someone? she asked herself. *I pushed him away and he did the same to me. We have zero claim on each other*. But that wasn't how it felt. She swallowed and knocked on the door.

A few seconds later Cutter cracked the door open.

"Holly!" he said with surprise but no irritation. Strangely it was the first time she could recall him using her first name. For a frozen moment he looked at her through the narrow opening. Then – "May I come in?" she asked.

He stepped back and swung the door open. "Oh, sure. Of course. Come in," he said and let her wheel past him. He was barefoot and bare-chested. His Levis looked like they were sown onto him with no room to spare. She saw the model 1911 Colt in his hand. He closed the door and thumbed on the gun's safety, then walked over to a gym bag on the floor and pulled on a white t-shirt. He tugged it over his head and chest. It fit him like his jeans. Cutter saw there was nothing happy in Holly Carter's expression or demeanor and immediately he asked, "What's happened?"

Holly told him all that she knew. That she'd been on her way to the Sunday morning prayer meeting at *The Current-Leader* building when she saw an ambulance and sheriff's car pull out of the Old Ambrose Place. That she followed them to the hospital. That Dr. Garner examined Miss Jennifer while she waited with Rose. That Dr. Garner had told them Miss Jenny had suffered a massive stroke. "He took me aside and asked me if I knew where you were," explained Holly. "I told him I didn't. And he said, 'If you can find him, tell him he needs to get here in a hurry. It may be is his last chance to see his mother alive.'"

Cutter swallowed. "It's that bad?"

"I guess so."

Cutter immediately took socks from the chest of drawers and sat down on the neatly made brass bed, on the yellow spread and started pulling them on. "What time did you leave the hospital?"

"About eleven."

Cutter picked up his watch on the bedside table. It was almost four.

He pulled on work boots and reached for the laces, but stood up instead and started digging in a drawer. He came out with some change. "There's a pay phone down the hall. I'm gonna call the hospital," he said and walked out the door without closing it behind him. He left Holly alone in the room, which was surprisingly nice and clean and large for a place that was just a notch above a flop house. The furnishing were old and wear worn but not wrecked. There was no TV or phone, but in the corner was a standup Zenith radio circa 1940s, maybe '30s. It still sounded good, though. Elvis' cousin George Klein was covering someone's weekend slot on WHBQ. He intro-ed The Stones' new single *Honky Tonk Woman* and Holly realized she was more relieved than she should have been that Cutter was by himself in this hotel room. On a table on the balcony was an open beer bottle and a Graham Greene spy novel. She saw the open bathroom door and pushed toward it. Her chair barely fit through the opening, the push rims scraping on the frame before she closed the door behind her. She needed to empty her bladder, which meant transferring onto the toilet seat and inserting one of the catheters she kept in a plastic bag in her purse. She took care of what her injury, her situation, required then paused at the sink to freshen up. She put the .38 in her purse and took out lip stick and a compact. Holly rarely needed or wore much make-up. Just a little powder to accentuate her high cheek bones and gloss to moisturize her full lips.

When Holly emerged from the bathroom she saw Cutter standing at the corner of the wide balcony, leaning against a black iron support post, his boots still unlaced. He was no longer in a hurry. Holly put her purse on the bed as she passed and wheeled to the open French doors. Much of tin-roofed South Memphis spread out before them, a field of silver and rust-colored flowers running down to the brown-green river, awesome in its relentless movement, its implacable might. Beyond it the Arkansas Delta lay flat and green, fertile with cotton and beans and the sweat of generations of sharecropping farmers. Cutter heard Holly's wheels on the balcony's plank flooring.

"She's gone," he said without turning around.

Holly knew it before Cutter uttered the words, but still she said automatically, "I'm sorry."

"Are you?" he asked unexpectedly. "Why?"

Holly was taken aback for an instant. Was Cutter somehow blaming her for Miss Jenny's death? For not reaching him sooner? But then there was nothing in his tone or body language that suggested that such was his intention. She realized

Cutter was asking a real and, under the circumstances, legitimate question. So she answered it honestly – "Miss Jenny had a wonderful heart for her students. For everyone really. For you and Rose. She must have seen something in Tony, back in the day. Some glimmer of kindness she thought she could nurture into something more. I'm sorry that never happened. I'm really sorry about the absolute hell Tony put her through for years." Holly's voice broke, but sniffled and went on. "I'm sorry that such a bright, gentle, loving woman had no place to run to but inside her own mind. But am I sorry she's dead? No, I'm not sorry," Holly told him. "I'm glad she's gone on. I'm glad she's free."

Cutter turned to face Holly. Then, as if some great weight was pressing on his shoulders he slid down the post, until he was sitting on the floor, his big forearms resting on his knees. He sniffed, but there were no tears. "Me, too," he said. "I almost want to dance a jig or shout hallelujah, or something. But I'm her son. Isn't that awful?"

Holly wheeled next to him. On the river a tugboat growled and five stories down a door opened and the sound of a Motown juke box spilled into the ally then was gone. She leaned forward and touched his arm. "It's not awful at all. It's love."

Cutter looked up and their eyes met. Holly's breath caught and she watched as he covered her foot, the straps of her white sandals, with his left hand. She could see he was squeezing gently.

"Can you feel that?" he asked softly but firmly.

Holly swallowed. "No," she told him.

Cutter shifted his weight, leaned and kissed the front of her right leg, which was crossed over her left. "That?" he asked.

"No," she said but that was only superficially true. Her chest was tingling and her nipples were hardening at the sight of Cutter's lips on her skin.

He pushed the hem of Holly's dress over her knees, and he would have taken it farther right then if she hadn't tightly grabbed the fabric. Cutter didn't force it. He kissed her knee. "That?"

"No," she groaned, shaking her head even as heat blossomed into her neck and face. "But when I see you touch me that way, I think I can."

Cutter got to his knees, to where he was eye level with Holly, demanding her gaze. He slipped his hands to either side of her legs under her dress. Her thighs were warm and smooth and the hardness in his jeans felt to Cutter like new-forged steel against his belly, molten at its core.

"How about that?"

Holly shook her head. She knew she should grab the rims of her chair and pull away – now! – before she was embarrassed and before things went so far with this very young man, this beautiful, powerful, magnetic boy, that they could not be undone. Every logical neuron in her brain told her to back away, but every pheromone fogging the sweltering August air around them and years of pent-up need wanted to follow the path Cutter was on. A path to – "You don't understand," she managed. "It's not just my legs. I – scars! There are scars. I can hide them under my clothes, but –"

"I don't care."

"You may."

"I won't," he told her and leaned in to kiss her, long and deep. When their lips parted Holly's eyelids fluttered, and the river seemed to have a new sparkle to it.

With his powerful mixture of agility and strength, Cutter scooped Holly into his arms as he stood. She opened her mouth to make one final, weak protest but – "Don't," said Cutter as he carried her to the bed and laid her down atop the spread. Holly watched with unabashed wonder and immense need as Cutter pulled his t-shirt over his head and tossed it away, then unbuttoned and unzipped his jeans, and in one smooth motion stepped out of them.

* * *

In the bright late afternoon light of August neither Cutter nor Holly could hide anything from the other. Nor did either try. Not an inch of salt moistened skin, not a panted plea for more or an unspoken hand-guided desire. The air in the room seemed afire with the hot, white light of their desire and the stamped tin ceiling shaped and reformed itself in Holly's half-lidded eyes as she wrapped her arms around Cutter's neck and held on. Embracing every need she'd ever had and every desire she'd thought could never again be fulfilled.

When they finished the first time, Cutter remained on top of Holly, resting his weight on his powerful arms as her breasts pressed up against the hard muscles of his chest. He wanted to stay inside her forever. That was right where Holly wanted him to be for now, for another hour or day or week or – *Don't think about that now*, she told herself as she looked up into Cutter's young, unlined face. Holly smiled a slow, dreamy smile. "You're so beautiful," she whispered.

Cutter returned the smile, his face slick with perspiration, his blue-white eyes almost luminous even in the sunlit room. "Funny, I was gettin' ready to say the same thing to you."

"Yes, but in your case it's true," she said loving the sensation of a man's weight pressing her into damp sheets, a sensation she hadn't felt in years.

Cutter looked at her, the palpable sexual energy fading from his face, being replaced by something softer. "Why would you say that? If you can't see that you're an absolutely amazing woman, you need more than reading glasses."

"Okay. I guess I am pretty good looking for almost thirty and stuck sitting on my butt all day long. At least, as long as I keep my clothes on."

"I just saw every inch of you without clothes, and I didn't see anything that turned me off."

A small blossom of embarrassment colored Holly cheeks. "You're sweet.

But – entry wounds, exit wounds. Treated at a field hospital. Major spine surgery twice in the last four years."

Almost seeming not to have heard her, Cutter rested his weight on his left arm and with a gentle finger traced a gray line from under Holly's left arm and beneath her breast. "What's this one?"

"The third time I went in with a team of smoke jumpers, up around Yosemite, I stumbled getting out the plane's door. So I missed the pasture we were supposed to land in and instead went into a stand of pines," she remembered. "I got tangled up in them. A branch got me. It felt like it tore my whole boob off. But it turned out the cut was long but not deep. The team medic bandaged it up, slammed a big glob of penicillin into my butt – all of which he enjoyed far too much -- and I stuck it out with them for three more days. I got my pictures. It's what really launched my career at *The Chronicle*. Short as it was. But it left its mark. As you can see."

Cutter smiled, shook his head. "Dadgum, you are one tough female."

"I used to be," Holly said, her voice wistful. "Or maybe I was just crazy. Now I'm more like a rag doll that's been sewn up too many times."

"That's what you think?"

She looked away. She didn't want to talk anymore about this. Then – "I see my body every day. It's what I know."

Cutter lifted himself off of Holly and lay on his back. She sat up and shook out her flame of hair, then using one arm and then the other, she put legs together. The left spasmed for several seconds but Cutter took no notice, and she rolled over next to him, her hand on his chest, intoxicated with the nearness of him. The solidness of him. Muscles so hard they felt like sun-warmed metal. His fresh, salty scent and the outdoorsy tang of some woodsy cologne. Good stuff, expensive stuff. Not dime store, teenage boy stuff. Probably a gift from some other woman he had bedded. Holly didn't care. She wasn't a virgin either. *At least the woman has good taste*, she thought.

After a time Cutter asked, "Is that why you pushed me away at the strawberry patch?"

Holly nodded against his shoulder. "The scars were part of it. The age difference. But the truth is, you scared the hell out me. You had me feelings things, wanting things that I had told myself for years to forget about. Made myself forget about. Then there it all was, rushing up," she told him. "Oh, God, how I wanted you! But I felt like I was drowning. I was afraid I'd, that I'd be, you know, terrible. That I'd embarrass myself." She swallowed. "I don't want to be anyone's charity fuck. I can't be. That would kill me."

Cutter tightened his arm around Holly's shoulder. "You surely don't have to worry about that, Miss Holly Lee Carter. There was no charity needed, and none given. But I am curious, what changed today?"

"You mean besides the fact I've had a case of the world-class hornies for you since that day?"

Cutter grunted a quick laugh. "Yeah, besides that."

Holly kissed Cutter's chest, his nipple and gentle flexed her hand around his flaccid penis as she thought about it. "I suppose it's because of what you did last night. The kind of character you showed. Away from a battlefield, I haven't seen it in many men," she told him. "When you touched me, and it started happening, I just knew even if I wasn't all that I used to be, or all that some other women have been to you, you wouldn't turn that on me. You wouldn't hurt me with it."

"You can stop worrying about that," he told her, kissing her hair. "I don't know what you used to be, but I can tell you right now, you're still more than plenty."

Holly sighed inwardly with relief.

Cutter said, "I want you to tell me the truth about something, though." He felt Holly stiffen a bit against him. Before she could speak, he said, "Wait. That didn't come out the way I meant it. What I meant was, I want to ask you something and I want you to know you *can* tell me the truth."

"All right," she said against his shoulder.

"Can you feel it when I'm inside you?" he asked -- his voice gentle, his question honest, indeed, Holly thought, and the most natural thing in the world for her lover to wonder. She said, "Okay, truth time then. I can't feel those parts the way I once did. It is different now. I don't exactly feel it when you're inside me, but – it's so hard to explain – I *know* when you're inside me. It's wonderful. It makes my whole body come alive. Like there's this warm glow from down there that radiates up into all the parts I can feel."

"Then you really were able to, to cum?"

"You couldn't tell?"

"Well, women have sometimes been known to –"

"Fake it?" Holly laughed, the sound low and sweet with the lingering afterglow of pleasure. "Not even a little. Different. I mean, from before I was hurt. But very real. And very wonderful."

Cutter nodded, smiled. "Good," he said. "I'm glad."

CHAPTER 2

Cutter and Holly dozed for a while in the damp sheets, in that sun-splashed room, the grayed sheers on the south-facing windows rising and dancing now and then on rogue breeze that had stolen up the bluff from the Mississippi. They had made love in a tumbling frenzy of fast give and take, of playful bites that verged on pain, of scratch and lick and suck, Holly drinking Cutter down like a woman who had been on a near four-year trudge through a very arid, empty and hope-stripped desert. But she had found her oasis in these sheets, among the brass tines of the old hotel bed, and she meant to sate and be sated. This time was different. As the late afternoon light lengthened and softened, so did their kisses. Cutter began again, cupping her breasts, lifting her coppery hair and drawing his tongue along the side and back of her neck. Slowly teasing her nipples until her breasts were filled with a sweet ache. And when he was sure Holly was ready, he entered her slowly, deliberately, moving inside her. She used the strength built up in her arms and shoulders to shift herself beneath him, encouraging Cutter to map every inch of the warm summer river that she sensed was flowing through her, even if she could no longer wholly experience every eddy and surge and nuanced current that swam inside her. They took each other to the edge and back. To the edge and back. And when they finally climaxed again they lay next to each other, spent and comfortable and satisfied. Holly was happy and at ease in a way she had not been in years, maybe ever.

After a time, Cutter sat up and swung his legs off the side of the bed. Holly stretched out her arm and ran her fingers down his back. Holly saw several scratches on his back and a bite mark on his shoulder. They were noticeable but not deep, and she smiled thinking of how feral she'd been in her wanting of him.

"I'm starving," he said. "I didn't eat lunch. Did you?"

"No," she said drowsily.

"There's a barbecue place in the alley right down below. How about I go get us something?" he asked. "We could eat out on the balcony and watch the sun go down."

"You're not going back tonight?" she asked, surprised. "I shouldn't have kept you here this long. It was selfish. Rose was terribly upset. She needs you. Even more than I do. And you'll need to make funeral arrangements."

"That's right. We didn't get past the, the part about momma passin', did we?"

296

"No. What's the rest?"

Cutter turned sideways on the bed so he could look at Holly, who had a sheet wrapped around her now. "You're right, Rose was mighty upset. Blaming herself 'cause Momma slipped out of the house while she was taking a nap. Not that the nap or where Momma was had anything to do with anything," he said. "Anyway, Dr. Garner gave her a shot of something and put her in the hospital overnight. He says she'll probably be out until the middle of the day tomorrow.

"As far as Momma's arrangements, Sheriff Wallace wants to get someone up from the state crime lab, a – what do you call it? – a –"

"A pathologist?"

"Right, a pathologist to see if he can swear Momma's stroke was caused by the beatings Tony gave her over the years. If he can, Sheriff Wallace told Dr. Garner he'll throw Tony under the jail," explained Cutter. "Dr. Garner says there's no sign of recent head injuries, so it's a long shot. But he says it's worth a look. That means Momma's funeral won't be till toward the end of the week, at the earliest."

Holly sighed, taking his hand. "Too many damn funerals lately."

***

A red sun was half-hooded by the flat, green horizon of the Arkansas Delta as Holly wiped her mouth with a paper napkin and drew on the straw tucked into a large Styrofoam cup filled with ice and sweet tea. Desiccated and spice-rubbed, the ribs were delicious.

"These may be not only the best dry ribs in Memphis," Holly was saying. "They may be the best dry ribs I've ever put in my mouth. Just great. What's the name of the place?"

"The fellow who owns it, who does the cookin', is named Mo'rice Robinson. He just calls it Mo Eats. They've got a good jukebox – all Motown and Stax – and a couple of pool tables. Sometimes I go down there and shoot with Mo for my supper."

Holly leaned back in her wheelchair. "That was Heaven on a bone," she said, and saw the smirk on Cutter's lips. "I'm not talking about that kind of bone. And that's a different kind of Heaven."

He smiled and wiped his mouth before tossing the napkin into the empty food container and closing it. It had been filled with double helpings of fried okra and cole slaw, plus a full rack of ribs. "That was sure 'nough good," he agreed. "It always is."

"How often do you come up here?" she asked.

"Not often. Once every two or three months. When I want to be in my own skin, not the one I have to wear in DeLong."

Cutter picked up the containers from the grayed, chipped wicker table and headed for a garbage can that was outside in the hall. Holly watched his hips move under his jeans like twin pistons then focused on the sun, turning low clouds bloody at the edge of the earth. She was wearing a black football jersey with a red 13 front

297

and back. It finished on her about mid-thigh. It smelled like him. That expensive, woodsy smell and she loved being wrapped in it. After taking a quick bath, Cutter had brought it up from the footlocker bolted to his Jeep. While he went out for ribs, Holly found fresh linens in a bathroom closet, changed the sheets, then easily slipped into the old, rust-stained tub. It took her three tries to get out of the tub, but she managed finally to lift herself on the onto the lip and transfer into her wheelchair. After she dried herself and dressed in Cutter's jersey, she dug into her purse for some change and the .38, all of which she put into her lap, and covered it with a towel before pushing down the hall to use the pay phone. She had hoped to catch Julie Davis and she did. After quick hellos Holly had said, "I wanted to let you know, I'm not going to be home tonight. Wolf's Run can be a little spooky when you're alone. If you want to, leave a couple of lights on, lock the doors, go to town and stay at the Jeff Davis. But take Charlie with you, okay?"

"Sure. But where are you?"

"Memphis. Listen, would you also call my M.E., Mike Morton, and tell him I won't be in until about noon tomorrow," Holly had hurried, not wanting to give one of the L.A. *Chronicle*'s top reporters time to think. "His number is by the phone in the kitchen."

But, "What's in Memphis?" she'd asked.

"I don't want to get into that right now."

"I heard you were out looking for the Carlucci kid," she persisted. "Do you know his mother died?"

Holly chose her words carefully. "Yes, I heard. Look –"

"You found him, didn't you? The kid."

"Stop calling him that."

"You're with him, aren't you?" asked Julie, already sensing the answer. "Holly do you really need more trouble --?"

"Please, Julie! Don't! Don't, don't, don't," she almost pleaded. "Tomorrow you can tell me how stupid I am. How crazy it is want him the way I do. But not tonight. Not for this one night."

When Cutter came back onto the balcony dusk was settling on the river and the city, and the day that had been was just an orange line on the horizon reflected off the newer tin roofs and high warehouse windows. He settled on one of the frayed curtains on the old wicker love seat, stretched his long arm across the back of it and looked at Holly. She wheeled over, locked the brakes on the chair and transferred onto the seat. He cupped his arm around her shoulders and she leaned into him, feeling safer and more satisfied than she had since she hopped aboard that helicopter bound for the Ia Drang Valley.

"I don't think I've gotten around to telling you how proud I am of what you did last night," she said.

"Thanks. But as the old saying goes, no good deed goes unpunished. Now Momma's dead, the whole county hates me and I've got to get a place for me and Rose," he said. "She can't stay alone in that house with Tony. Momma was no real protection, but Tony was kind of afraid of her. Like she was a witch or somethin'. Between me and Momma, he mostly kept his distance. But he won't anymore. Not for long. If nothing else, he'll go after Rose to spite me."

A shudder ran through Holly as she flashed to the memory of what Tony Carlucci had done and almost done to her. Now here she was, happily wrapped in his son's embrace. *Could life's ironies run any deeper?* she wondered.

"You okay?" asked Cutter.

"Just a little drafty, I guess. I don't have anything on under this jersey."

"That's good news," he said, dropping his right hand onto her bare thigh.

Holly wrapped her hand around Cutter's and stopped it from moving up. "Before we get to that again, let's talk about Rose."

Cutter looked at her. "Okay. Talk."

Holly began, "I've been thinking. I've got a lot of extra room at Wolf's Run and no one to fill it now that Eve is gone and Julie's heading back to L.A. on Tuesday." Cutter looked at his new lover and Holly saw caution in his eyes. "Look, this has nothing to do with what happened between us today. Or however this, whatever this is, works out. I was thinking about this on the drive up here."

"You didn't even know Momma was dead."

"No, but Dr. Garner told me that if Miss Jenny survived, she'd never be able to go home again. I knew Rose couldn't stay there alone with Tony," she said. "Then after last night, you're right. Tony's likely to hurt her, to get at you. That's the kind of asshole he is. No offense."

Cutter grunted. "There's nothing you could say about Tony that would offend me. But taking Rose in? That's too much."

"Don't take get this wrong. I'm not offering charity. I don't need much help, but Rose could earn her keep and a little more helping me the way Eve did. Plus, I know Rose struggles in school. I could tutor her, or at least be there to help her with her homework. And being around the newspaper office might be good for her. It could begin to open up the world to her after being cooped up in that house all these years." Cutter was nodding slowly, starting to see the possibilities. "The other part of it is, honestly – I'm afraid to stay alone so far out in the country in that big house."

"The way things are right now, you'd be crazy not to be scared," he said. "I don't want you out there by yourself, either. But you could be callin' down more trouble on yourself. Tony would not be happy with that arrangement."

"I don't have blinders on. I know what he's capable of," she said and wondered when, if ever she would tell Cutter about what happened at The Gin. Someday maybe, but not now. Not on this good, sweet Memphis evening. "Honestly, Rose would be doing me a big favor. If she's willing."

Cutter considered for a time, running all sides of it though his mind. Holly didn't press. Finally, he squeezed her hand and kissed her forehead – "I'll talk to her."

After night fell, they undressed and slipped under the fresh, but age-worn sheets and made love again – the room soft with cityglow and the sound of Smoky Robinson and Miracles and Al Green floating upward from the open door of Mo' Eats in the alley below. Now and then a tugboat bellowed on the river as Cutter whispered his needs into Holly's ear and she rolled onto her stomach, whimpering her assent and pleasure. They made love not fast, not slow. They found a rhythm that suited their mood and their bodies until both groaned and gasped and finally uncoupled, Holly's hands relaxing around the tines of the old brass bed. When their breathing finally settled, she rolled over next him and laid her arm across his damp chest. A chain of red lights winked at them from the arches of the Memphis-Arkansas bridge. She relaxed against him, enjoyed a breeze from the open windows on her bare back, and quietly reveled in the way he made her feel right now, this night, in this bed, in this cheap, worn, wonderful little room with the music floating up from the ally to sing them into sleep, a Motown lullaby. Julie was right, of course, this was crazy. It could and probably would end badly, in tears and longings impossible to fulfill, but not tonight. Not for these few hours. There'd be time enough later for heartache, Holly told herself.

* * *

Next morning Holly awoke in Cutter's arms when the first good light cast a yellow-white streamer through the south windows and across the sheets. She rolled over and looked into Cutter's eyes, her breasts pressing against his chest, and kissed him gently on the lips.

"How long have you been awake?" she asked.

"A little while. I'm an early riser."

Holly moved her hand under the sheet and brushed his erection, sighed, then grasped it. "I can see that," she said. "Is that for me? Or do you just need to pee?"

"A little of both."

Holly laughed. "I love your honesty!"

"I hope so, but I've generally found that a little of it goes a long way with most folks."

She smiled with her lips and her green, gold-flecked eyes, her hair a burnished copper halo around her head in the morning light. "That is a fact," she said. "And here's another one, you're just going to have to go pee, because I've got to get dressed and leave. I've got a newspaper to put out, at least for a few more months."

As much as Cutter wanted Holly again, he didn't argue. As awful and wonderful as the last twenty-four hours had been, Monday's reality had come up hot and hard with the sun and the groaning of trucks on Docks Avenue. He propped on his elbow and watched Holly as she sat up, stretched her long arms and arched her back in a way that made her large breasts look even bigger. She lifted one leg and then the other over the side of the bed and with practiced alacrity transferred into her wheelchair. She placed her feet on the pedals and squeezed the chair through the door and into the bathroom where her dress and underwear hung on a line that stretched above the tub. Ten minutes later she returned looking amazingly fresh and energized, one leg crossed over the other, her hair brushed and a fresh layer of gloss making her lips look full and wet.

"Dadgum, you clean up good!" said Cutter, smiling before he rolled out of bed. He pulled on his briefs and jeans and grabbed a t-shirt. "Lemme wash my face and I'll walk you to your car."

"'Kay," she said. The air in the room held the salty tang of their love-making and she happily drew it into her lungs. She could taste him in it and her breathing started to change. She wanted him again, even if only in her mouth, but she shook her head and forced herself to say – "I'll meet you at the elevator."

They turned right out the Hobart and went the half block down South Main, then crossed the street. Holly transferred onto the front seat of the Lincoln and lifted her legs inside. As the roof folded back Cutter put her chair into the floorboard behind her seat.

"You sure you don't want to get some breakfast?" he asked.

"I can't. I wish I could," she said, looking up at him smiling behind her sunglasses. "But I surely will take a raincheck on it."

Cutter leaned down and propped his forearms on the doorframe. "So, where does this leave us?" he asked. "Was this just a nice roll in the hay?"

Holly stared at him for moment, then – "Of course not. Not for me."

"Me neither. So --?"

"Sooooo, we have to be careful. If it got out that you and I are sleeping together, a lot of advertisers and subscribers who've stuck with me, with the paper, would bolt," Holly told him, remembering how hell bent she was as eighteen to have who and what she wanted, when and how she wanted. She was already was readying arguments in her mind to make him understand that they couldn't just – but he said, "That's what I figured. I get it. But the good part of Rose helping you out – and I'm sure she will – is that gives me the perfect excuse to come around. Pick her up for school. Drop her off. Check on her. Hang out and help her with her homework."

Holly smiled. "I like the way your mind works."

"I hope I'm not the only one to think of that."

"Maybe it crossed my mind," said Holly, a smile playing at the corners of her lips. "Around the time I was having my first orgasm."

CHAPTER 3

Cutter didn't see Tony's truck anywhere around the house but he knew that didn't mean anything. One of his running buddies such as Benoit could have dropped him off or his truck could be in the barn. At the end of the driveway he knocked the Jeep into neutral, got out, opened the locker bolted to the back and took out the Colt. He pulled the slide back on the .45 and chambered a round. Just in case. Then he drove down the weedy lane and parked in front of grayed, unpainted house that had been more prison to Rose than anything else. Long ago the rusty nails that held together the weather-worn planks of the Old Ambrose Place had lost their hold on Rose. She stared at the porch. The rusty screens and Jennifer Carlucci's quilting frame. She had never resented taking care of her mother in those increasingly rare hours and moments when some glimmer of that gentle, intelligent, gracious woman was there with her. But increasingly Rose had been alone in every real sense, her mother fled to someplace inside herself leaving her daughter to dread the sound of Tony's truck turning from the road. She had stayed only because of her mother, and because the people in DeLong who were supposed to be their family had turned their backs on her and Cutter years ago.

When at the hospital Cutter had told Rose about Miss Carter's offer, she'd said, amazed – "You, you m-mean I'd *l-live* at Wolf's Run. R-Really live there?"

Cutter smiled. "Yes. You'd live there. You'd have your own room. There's a pool and lots of books. And Holly, err, Miss Carter loves music. She can play the heck out of a guitar. Maybe she can help you with your songs."

She'd looked up from the hospital bed, her eyes wide. "B-But I don't know h-how to live in a place l-like that?"

"You'll be fine."

"D-Do I have to c-clean that whole b-big place?" she'd asked, worried.

Cutter shook his head. "No, Honey," he told her. "You're not going to be her maid. She's got a cleaning woman for that. Just help her with little things at the house and the paper. Like getting' something off a shelf she can't reach. Or runnin' errands. Or helpin' her over a couple of steps if she can't manage. Maybe cookin' a little. You like to cook."

"And I'd l-live at W-Wolf's Run?"

302

"Yes."

Rose had turned her head on the pillow and her eyes welled again.

"What's the matter? Do you not want to do it?" Cutter asked, concerned.

Rose swallowed. "I-I do. M-More than anything," she said. "I-I-I just don't w-want to feel g-glad Momma's dead."

Cutter nodded, thinking of Holly lying next to him in that Memphis hotel room. "I know."

R ose Marie Carlucci was surprised, relieved, frightened, excited, apprehensive, thankful and fretful as she gathered up her belongings from the only home she'd ever known.

Cutter watched Rose open each compartment of an old chest of drawers. She stared into a nearly empty chiffonier. In the end, everything Rose had, or at least everything she wanted to take from that rotting purgatory, fit into three large grocery bags that Cutter carried out to the Jeep. She tucked the scrapbook she'd kept for Cutter under her arm and grabbed her old Gibson B-25 acoustic he'd given her.

"You ready?" Cutter asked as she climbed into the Jeep.

Rose brushed her dark brown hair over her ear, swallowed hard. "Y-Yes. No! W-Wait!" she told him and ran up the steps onto the porch. She quickly stripped her mother's latest quilt from the frame. Rose folded it and ran back to the Jeep, clutching it to her chest.

"Is that it?"

Rose looked over the place, the rust stains cut almost black into the tin roof. They reminded her of a crying woman, her eyes red-rimmed, her mascara running down aged cheeks. "W-We should b-b-burn this place."

Cutter hit the shifter – "One day we will."

***

C utter took Rose to *The Current-Leader* where Holly welcomed her into the publisher's office with hugs and encouragement. Rose was accepting but stiff, unused to any touch that didn't contain the hard back of her father's hand or the grope of his thick fingers.

"Cutter says you write beautiful songs. I can't wait to hear them."

Rose stared as Charlie sniffed at the old, faded high-top Keds sticking out from the cuffs of her overalls. "When you're ready," added Holly, who looked amazingly fresh considering how little sleep they'd allowed each other the night before – waking in the still dark hours to talk and cuddle and finally make love again above the quiet streets and ceaseless river.

"Charlie likes you," said Holly as the little dog stood on its hind legs, pawing the air.

"C-Can I t-touch her?"

"Of course," said Holly.

Rose knelt and began to stroke the dog's soft white fur. Soon Charlie rolled over and offered her belly for scratching. Rose obliged, smiling.

"I put Sister's stuff in the back of your car," said Cutter. "I'll come by Wolf's Run later and check on her. Make sure she's settlin' aw'right. If you don't mind?"

Holly bit her lip, wanting to devour him again right then, right there, right that moment. She said, "I don't mind at all. But somebody held me up this morning. So I got a late start here. It may be dark before we get home."

"All the more reason for me to drop by," he said. "Make sure the two of you are safe and sound."

The smile faded from Holly's lips. "Yes, I guess it is."

Rose lifted her head enough that she could follow the conversation with her eyes as well as her ears. She sensed that her brother and Miss Carter were speaking a language of their own and that every word contained a different twist, an altered weight. She said nothing, and hoped.

***

Later that afternoon, Cutter drove to the Cattahatchie High School locker room. When he turned into the parking lot behind it, Jimmy Garner and Dodge McDowell already were there, sitting on the tailgate of Jimmy's pickup.

Fullback Donnie Thompson was present, as were linebackers Charlie Haygood and Chris Goodlet, defensive back Teddy Renfro and wide receiver Kyle Long. As I sat watching from an old log road cut through the dense woods south of the gym, much to my surprise, Haughton Wellingham IV, and cheerleaders Becky Hardin and Kathy Reed climbed out of Teddy's Camaro.

They surrounded Cutter's Jeep. Becky Hardin touched Cutter's arm. Doctor Garner's son spoke. "We're real sorry about your mom," he said.

Cutter looked away for a moment, wet his lips. "Don't be," he said. "Wherever she is, she's in a better place than she was." He gave Haughton a long look. Wanting to change the subject he said, "I'd be lyin' if I said I expected to see you here. Does your daddy know?"

"Not yet. I'm sure he'll know soon enough," said Haughton. "He and Mother'll kick about it for a few days, but they'll get over it. Ridge Bellafont was my mother's first cousin. Daddy's sticking with the governor, but Momma's mad as hell."

Cutter nodded and began counting. "Nine. Well, if you girls care to suit up, we'll have eleven. We can play football."

Dressed in her usual black shorts and red cheerleader T-shirt Becky Hardin looked at Cutter through her big sunglasses. "I'm all for it. I've had dreams about getting all hot and sweaty, and wallowing around in the grass with you."

"Down girl," said Teddy Renfro.

Cutter reached behind the passenger seat for a football. "Okay. We've got most

304

of the offense here, so we can at least throw the ball around and run through some plays."

Jimmy Garner, whose father was the school board's new president, held up a set of keys that had hung from Coach Pearce's belt. "We can do better than that. I say we suit up just like for a regular practice."

"Yeah," agreed Chris Goodlet. "We need to get the pads on."

"Damn right!" Donnie Thompson enthused.

"Then let's do it," said Cutter, stepping out onto the gravel parking lot.

"We'll go get some ice and fill the big coolers," said Becky Hardin.

Jimmy Garner checked his watch. "I've got five till three. By three-fifteen, let's be under the west goalposts, stretchin'."

Everyone knew that Cutter was the team's real leader, but Jimmy Garner was the quarterback. After all that happened, Cutter was happy to let Jimmy organize practice. Dr. Garner's son stuck his hand out into the middle of the circle that had formed around Cutter. Chris Goodlett covered it and so on until there was a stack of fingers and palms.

"Come on, girls," said Cutter, "get your hands in here. You're part of this team, too."

"One, two, three – Wolves!" I whispered as I watched the knot of my one-time friends moving in pantomime. They broke apart and Jimmy opened the door to the locker room. I watched until they disappeared inside, then I cranked the truck and drove away. I already was late for the first day of practice at Riverview.

B y the time Cutter and the small cadre of players made their way onto the field, two deputies were walking the south side of the practice field. One carried a shotgun, the other a high-powered rifle with a scope. At Sheriff Wallace's instruction they were watching the woods that rose up across a small creek and could provide perfect cover for a sniper. Everyone noticed, but no one mentioned them. Cutter's surprise announcement on Saturday night had sent furious shock waves through Klan Kovens from the Tennessee River to the shrimp docks in Biloxi thanks to the statewide radio hookup. Among the Citizens Committee crowd, Cutter's name now was as infamous as those of Oren Mulberry and J.L. Burke. State and federal law enforcement officials had long known that there was a bounty on the judge and the U.S. attorney. The idea that Cutter Carlucci had been added to that list did not take much of a leap.

As Jimmy orchestrated the little practice, a handful of reporters from as far away as Nashville and Atlanta began to gather under the goal posts. There was even a camera crew from a Memphis station. When drills and wind sprints were completed, the reporters stopped fanning themselves with their notebooks and surrounded Cutter like fading, mismatched flowers wilting in the August sun. Questions were coming quickly and from all directions.

Cutter wiped his face on his white practice jersey and held up his hands. "Folks, I appreciate you bein' here, but I'm not going to answer any questions about Saturday night. I did what I did for my own reasons, and it's enough that I know what they are," he told them. "But I do want to say I'm really proud of the guys who came out today. Jimmy Garner, our quarterback, did a great job gettin' us goin'. And of Kathy Reed and Becky Hardin. Our cheerleaders. We'd have never made it without the cold drinks they brought. We're hoping this is just a start."

"Cutter, the faces out here are still all white," noted one reporter. "Do you expect this to remain a segregated team?"

"That'll be up to the, uh, the black kids who'll be coming over here from Roseville. We've got about twenty-five more uniforms hanging in the locker room. We need ballplayers to fill 'em."

"How about a coach?" asked another.

"We need one. What are you doing for the next three months?" he asked the reporter. The press corps laughed. Julie Davis stood back, scribbling in one of the narrow reporter's notebooks they all favored. She smiled. For all of his strong, silent ways, Cutter was a natural in front of the cameras.

"Can you tell us –?"

"Hey, Cutter, over here!"

Cutter looked as a flashbulb went off close to his face. He tried to politely push through the circle of reporters but they moved with him. "Cutter, Governor Weathers told the AP today that you're a 'turncoat against your community and your race'," said a small balding man with a sunburned pate. "He also promised that – quoting here – 'if I have to endow every school in the Continental United States, Cutter Carlucci will never play a down of college football.' What do you say to that?"

Cutter stared at the man but forced a smile to hide the bolt of apprehension that shot through him. "I, uhm, well, I guess that leaves Alaska and Hawaii. I think I'll try the place with the hula skirts."

Everyone laughed. "Is that it?" he asked, but knew it would not be.

Several members of the group looked at each other. Julie Davis prepared to asked the question that had to be asked but a fat, sweating man in red-and-white slacks, sweat-soaked white shirt and red suspenders spoke up. "Cutter, we heard your momma died Sunday. Is that true?"

"Yes. She passed yesterday afternoon," he acknowledged.

"Were you with her?" asked another.

"No. I was out of town," he said evenly. "It was sudden. My sister was with her."

"When's the funeral?"

"Later this week, or the weekend. Sheriff Wallace wants an autopsy."

"So there was foul play?"

"No. Not that I know of."

"Then why does the sheriff want an autopsy. She died at the hospital, didn't she?"

"She did. You'll have to ask Mr. Wallace."

The rapid-fire questions ceased for a moment and Cutter started to move but the man in the red suspenders caught his eye again. "So, your momma died less than twenty-four hours ago and you're already out here practicin' football for a team that may or may not even exist."

"Oh, we exist. We're a team, and we're going to stay a team," he told the reporters, allowing a quick flash of anger to cross his face but impressively refusing to take the ugly bait Mr. Suspenders had tossed out, thought Julie. He pointed to the yellow brick school building up the north hill from the field. "The happiest days of Jennifer Ambrose's life were spent right up there. She loved teaching. And she loved her students. She loved me and Rose. And she did the best she could for all of us, for as long as she could. That's why I'm here.

"I'm not going to give up on Cattahatchie High and all it's meant to this town. And all it meant to my mother," he added. Then – "Excuse me, folks. I need a shower."

Chapter 4

That afternoon Holly had introduced Rose to those *Current-Leader* employees handy, showed her the offices and found her a desk, which was not difficult, considering how depleted her staff remained. Julie came into the stifling newsroom and wrote a story based on Cutter's comments. Outside the tall front windows a pink dusk was settling over the courthouse and the square. As Holly finished reading the piece at the publisher's desk, Julie said, "That's kid's got it. Whatever 'it' is. Like you."

Holly pulled off her reading glasses, smiled wanly. "Wheelchairs don't make for much charisma."

"Some people can transcend things that others know deep down would crush them. Utterly destroy them. You know," Julie went on, "I've always found that those sorts of people are drawn to each other by some sort of gravitational pull. They can't help it. You do realize you're glowing like a hundred-watt light bulb?"

"That's just an extra layer of 'dew,' as we say down South," Holly tried. "It's hot as Hell in here. Daddy should have invested in air conditioning instead of that new press. The paper would be solvent and this building would be comfortable."

Julie lifted her hands in mock surrender. "Okay. Clearly you do not want to talk about it," she said. "I just -- this could go bad in so many ways."

"That didn't seem to worry you when you came on to Cutter."

Julie snorted. "Is that jealousy I hear? Already." Holly felt her cheeks redden. "I just wanted to taste the candy. I wasn't hoping to own the store. Or let it own me."

Holly looked out the window onto the town square, the many East-facing buildings now in deep shadow. Seeing her past, her present and as far into her future as those shadows allowed. "All I know, all I care about right now is that I feel more alive, more ... more *whole* than I have since I jumped out of that helicopter with those guys in the Seventh Cav," she told her best friend. "But I don't have any illusions about owning the 'candy store,' as you put it. By January or February, I'll most likely be back in L.A. with nothing but my cameras, my guitar and a scraped up old convertible. And my wheelchair, of course. And Cutter will be – he'll be on to, well, the rest of his life. But for now – for a week or a month, or until the paper goes broke -- I'm going to keep a level head, but I'm going to enjoy the way he makes me feel. Okay?"

"Just be careful," Julie told her. "Sometimes it's harder to walk away from things than you think."

Holly nodded then, wanting to change the subject, said, "Look, it's been a long few days for everyone. Especially Rose Marie. Why don't you take her on out to the house, give her some dinner and get her settled. She can use the room Tim Holland was in."

"Has your cleaning lady had a chance to disinfect it?"

"Yes, I saw her in there the other day."

"Sounds like a plan."

"By the way, Cutter may drop by. To check on Rose."

Julie smiled. "Uh-huh."

"Be nice. Tell him I'll be home –" Holly looked at her watch – "about 10 if he wants to wait."

Julie laughed. "I'm sure he will. Till Hell freezes over, if necessary."

Holly laughed. "Go on, girl. Get out of here!"

* * *

Though Julie Davis was only in her early thirties, she was an only child who had grown up in a world of books and her own writing. She had never really learned to talk with teenagers even when she had been one. Rose was shy by nature and had become more so as her stuttering worsened. She often had been shamed by others because she could not get her words out properly. Other than with Cutter, she used as few as possible, and never spoke to strangers unless she had no other choice. So, after moving all of Rose's scanty belongings into Julie's rented sedan, they drove north on Highway 27 and made the turn west onto Blue Mountain Road in silence. Even though it was dark, when they got close to the Old Ambrose Place Rose slid down in the seat so that there was no possibility of being seen from the house.

Julie gave Rose the quick tour of Wolf's Run and saw that the teenager almost seemed in a daze. When they went into the library, Rose walked to the large mullioned window and looked out at the valley spread before her. "I can't, can't … can't …" Rose closed her eyes and shook her head in frustration, then tried again. "I c-can't be-believe I'm going to l-live here. It's l-like a castle in a f-fairytale."

"Well it's your castle, too, chickadee, at least until Holly goes broke."

Rose turned, her face shadowed with sudden anxiety.

"I'm sorry, Rose. I shouldn't have said that. I'm sure everything will work out fine," she lied. "Come on, I'll show you where you're going to sleep."

The room, which The Times correspondent had occupied, had been Eve's. Her things were boxed up in the closet but Holly had not found the time yet to ship them to L.A. The room was not large, but it was neat and comfortable with a four-poster double bed of burnished walnut. There was a window unit air conditioner and the room shared a bath with what had been T.L. Carter's bedroom closest to the library.

Rose ran her hand along the fine dark chest of drawers. The things at Wolf's Run were old but they weren't shabby and threadbare like at the house she'd lived in all her life; they were well-cared-for antiques, treasures. Julie had seen Tony Carlucci with Sgt. Benoit several times during her stay. She watched Rose, thinking how the Klansman's genetic influence was much more visible in his daughter than in his son. But even in bib overalls and without makeup, Rose was a pretty girl with dark eyes and lips full enough that they balanced the considerable width of her nose and offset the roundness of her face.

"I bet you could use a nice, hot bath," Julie said. "Why don't you relax, and I'll put something together for dinner. Holly won't be home until later."

Rose nodded but she didn't budge. She seemed frozen at the foot of the bed. After several moments, Julie asked, "Are you okay?"

"Yes'um," she said "I-I'm just afraid to move. That I'll br-break the trance and none of this w-will be real."

***

Down the mountain and across the Old Iron Bridge above the river Tony Carlucci stood on the porch of the house now empty amid the bean fields. Alone but for cotton stalks and chickens. He had parked in the barn and turned on no lights in the house when the shadows settled in. He stood in the dark alley at the center of the dog-trot dwelling, invisible to the occasional car going to or from the mountain top.

In most ways it had been a bad weekend, he thought. The only good news was that the weak, crazy, frigid old hag he'd been married to was dead. Her mumbling and pacing for hour after hour and writing numbers and all sorts of mathematical mumbo jumbo on the walls of the house had nearly driven him as crazy as she was. Good riddance. Of course, she could quilt like nobody's business. He'd have to replace that income somehow, but he wasn't worried. Once he was Benoit's chief deputy, there would be no end to scams he could run, the out-and-out shakedowns he could get away with. He would never understand why his kids sided against him with that worthless bag of bones that had done nothing but rattle around the place for years talking to herself and accusing with her wild, almost feral eyes. But it didn't matter. He didn't really care about understanding. Attempting to understand was wasted time and effort, Tony told himself. What he *knew* was that for years Cutter had been quietly showing him up by living on his own as if he was too good to dwell under his father's roof, refusing to even own up to his last name unless he had to. And now he and the Carter bitch had stolen his daughter. *His* daughter! It was already all over town, and he knew people who would never dare laugh at him to his face were cackling behind his back. Making sport of him. Saying he wasn't good enough, tough enough, smart enough, man enough to hang on to his children. *His own children!* Without the work of his seed they would not even exist. The sense of humiliation that had scalded him Saturday night as his arrogant, two-faced spawn spoke into that microphone continued to burn with the ferocity of cooking grease thrown smoking onto his genitalia. It clung to him and smoldered.

The Mexican whore Tony had bedded and beaten Sunday night in a motel near Selmer, Tennessee had taken none of the edge off his anger. He didn't think there was enough pussy – willing or otherwise – in the world to absorb the blood rage that coursed through his veins and instantly stiffened him whenever he thought of finally reclaiming Rose, every soft, pink petal of her. And he would take her back one way or another. He was as certain of it as he was the coming of September cotton. Now that everyone he knew, everyone that mattered, everyone with any real say so in Cattahatchie County had turned against Cutter, he could be dealt with without interference. He thought of simply walking out to the end of the road with his shotgun, waiting there in the ditch by the mailbox in the shadow of the willows then just stepping out when the boy's Jeep got close. Or maybe he'd do Miss-Too-Good-To-Spread-'Em first. Or maybe it didn't matter. It would be like Russian roulette. Only they wouldn't know the game until it was too late. Whoever came by first. Two, three, four loads of double-aught buckshot into Cutter's open Jeep or that big convertible with the top down. He imagined the spray of blood and skin and brains on the seats and across the dashboards in a red flume. He would be the last thing they ever saw and they would know that he had won, that he was taking back what was his, and there was nothing they could do to stop him.

That's what he wanted to do. He knew that ol' Cecil, Mr. Money-Bags, would protect him. Had to with all he knew. And, of course, the hidden hand of the Invisible Empire would do the same. But with that drunken, self-righteous turd Billy Wallace sitting in the sheriff's office, that route could lead to more trouble than he wanted to bring down on himself. It was a shame, but a roadside ambush wouldn't do. He'd have to be more cunning.

"If that Carter bitch and her nigger girlfriend had died up against that bridge railing," he mused aloud and shook his big head. "It's all her fault. Mine, too, I guess, for not finishing what I started."

Tony remembered the fight Holly Lee Carter put up when he'd had her down there on that floor in the back hall of The Gin. Kicking and clawing at him. Biting his hand and this lip, tasting his own blood mixed with her saliva. The pure rage and disbelief in her eyes, those green, green eyes as he grabbed hold of those big, luscious, melon-sized tits. *How dare he touch her!* Breathing hard now, Tony remember with malignant glee how her rage had turned to fear, and finally something like pleading when his fingers nudged the soft flesh between her legs.

Blinking as if coming out of a dream, Tony looked down at himself and saw he'd ejaculated in his pants. A warm, wet circle colored the front of his greasy work khakis and ran down the insides of both legs. His stump throbbed inside its plastic socket as it always did when he finished the act. But he did not move to clean himself or change. Instead he stood, staring out at the road where he knew Holly Lee Carter would pass with her big car and haughty ways. A tobacco-stained grin spread across his face, his features inhuman and malevolent as those of a rotting jack-o-lantern left on the porch of the empty house.

CHAPTER 5

It was 10:20. Holly and Julie startled badly when a knock rattled the kitchen door. "Cutter?" Holly called out even as she reached for the pistol next to her leg.

"Yeah, it's me."

"Shee-it," groaned Julie and unlocked the door. "You scared the crap out of us."

"I thought you were expecting me."

Holly still was letting out a sigh of relief. "We were, but we didn't hear your Jeep."

"I walked."

"From The Well?" asked Holly.

"No. I've moved camp," he said. "There's an outcrop a little ways up the mountain. It's got some natural cover for when it rains. Gives a pretty clean view of your fence line and driveway. I want to keep an eye on, on Rose."

"Uh-huh," grunted Julie.

"We were just watching you on the ten o'clock news," said Holly by way of changing the subject.

"What I said, did I sound aw'right?"

"It was perfect," said Holly.

"Yes, almost like it was scripted," said Julie. "Yet the way you delivered, you made it sounded spontaneous. Was it scripted?"

"I didn't write anything down," he said. "But did I figure I'd get a question like that? Yeah. And did I think about how I wanted to answer it? Yeah, I thought about it. Is there something wrong with that?"

"No, nothing. I'm impressed," said Julie. "Young man, you are wise beyond your years, it appears. And the camera loves you. You might have an acting career waiting, if you were to, somehow, end up in L.A."

Cutter looked to Holly, a question in his eyes. But Julie said, "I'm headed to bed. Gotta get my beauty sleep. I'll leave you two to dine alone."

They said their good nights and listened as Julie's footfalls on the hardwood floor receded toward the west wing. When they could be heard no more, neither rushed toward the other. They sensed they had embarked on something that was rare and not to be hurried. They knew they needed to steer a careful course.

"Are you hungry?" Holly asked.

"Starving. I didn't get to eat supper," Cutter told her.

"Me, too. Sit down. Julie fixed us both plates. I'll just heat the cornbread."

Cutter sat. "I'm fine with it cold," he said, as he pulled the Colt from the back of his jeans and laid it on the table.

Only when Holly finished putting out the food and glasses of milk and joined Cutter at the table, did they lean toward each other and exchange a long, soft kiss.

They ate cold pork chops with their fingers, and Miss Winona's potato salad and green bean casserole brought home at some point from The Cotton Café. Miss Annie, Holly's housekeeper, had made two big pans of cornbread between the washing, ironing, dusting and mopping on Friday. Holly pealed back the plastic wrap and they ate it right out of the black iron skillet. They said little, not because they were anxious about the words they might say to each other, but because they had quickly come to share an intimacy that did not require the continuous sound of voices, the movement of vowels, the coupling of consonants to make it real or give it sparkle. Cutter loved the throaty sound of Holly's voice, especially during their love-making, but loved even more the fact that she did not find the need to use it during every waking moment.

When they finished eating and put the plates in the sink, they went out onto the front porch and Holly transferred from her wheelchair to the green seat cushion in the swing so that she could sit next to Cutter. Charlie settled near the screen for a better view of the teeming fireflies. Cutter put his arm around Holly's shoulders and she leaned into him. After a time, Cutter asked, "How's Rose?"

"She wanted to stay up to see you, but she couldn't keep her eyes open. She seems to love her room, but she won't turn out the lights."

Cutter nodded against the top of Holly's head, enjoying the lush, fresh scent of her hair. "I know. I'm hopin' when she's been away from Tony awhile, she will. He's the thing in the dark that every kid's afraid of."

Holly remember that night in the supply room at The Gin and a quick shudder ran through her shoulders and down her back. "You okay?"

"I'm fine. A cat must have walked over my grave."

Cutter sensed there was more to it than that, but he held to a wordless pact that was already developing between them – an unspoken promise not to delve, not to dig, not to drag skeletons into the light that the other was not ready to unearth. Instead, he said, "Miss Davis knows about us."

It wasn't really a question, but Holly answered as if it were. "Yes. She'll keep it a secret."

"It won't be a secret long from Rose," said her brother. "She stutters but she's not stupid."

"I know. Does that bother you?"

"Of course not," he said. "It's just – all Rose has ever known is that shack.

Dodgin' Tony and taking care of Momma the best she could. Her life's just way up in the air right now. I want to be – I don't know -- careful with her. Not hit her with any more than I have to at once."

"I know," she said. "And you're right. I just want you so much. When I'm around you, I feel like Jello inside."

"I think of you more like warm ice cream," he said slipping his hand onto her breast.

"Damn!" she sighed, trying to straighten but Cutter held her firmly, gently in the crook of his arm. "If we don't quit right now, I'll be dragging you out of this swing and scaring Charlie."

"Charlie's little but I bet she's brave," teased Cutter. "I bet it'll take a lot to scare her."

Holly felt her breathing change, felt her lips starting to tingle -- "It's a big house and Julie and Rose are asleep."

"Looks like it's just me and you and the lightnin' bugs way out here in the country."

"And Charlie."

"And Charlie," Cutter agreed as he slid off the seat and onto his knees. He slipped his hands under Holly's arms and lifted her gently off the swing and onto the porch next to him.

W hen they had finished quietly pleasing each other, Holly let Cutter help her into her chair. She felt lightheaded. They softly kissed good-night, and Cutter went down the steps and onto the turnaround that circled the big, unrejuvenated planting circle.

"This flower bed could use fresh roses," said Cutter, his voice strong but not much above a whisper. "I'll bring some next time I come. Clean that bed out and plant them for you. Sister knows how to take care of them."

"I know," said Holly, dropping the thumb latch back into place and touching the screen. "Good-night."

Cutter walked up the long gravel driveway, overhung with the dark branches of oaks and elms and pecan trees. He didn't have far to go. Just turn left on Blue Mountain Road and go west two-hundred or so yards, then up a derelict logging trail that now could barely be called a road. So steep near the plateau where he'd made camp that he needed to run out a length of steel cable, hook it around a century-old pine and use the winch to help the Jeep up the final twenty yards to the top. It was an act of faith going down.

The way he and Rose had grown up at the Old Ambrose Place, he wasn't entirely sure how happiness was supposed to feel outside the lines of a football field or a locker room. But the calm and peace and trust – and the physical satisfaction -- he felt with

Holly seemed like maybe this could be it. For the first time in perhaps his entire life he thought, and then said aloud to the owls and fireflies, "I'm happy. ... I'm happy."

As he got to the top of the driveway, Cutter laughed at his silliness. When the sound died away, it was then that he heard the crunch of gravel close behind him, too heavy to be any kind of animal in these woods. Too clumsy and night blind to step carefully. He realized that someone must have been hiding behind a tree as he passed, his mind on Holly, his eyes clouded with the memory of her awestruck face when her body let go around him. Someone who must have been watching them on the porch. Cutter froze, every muscle as tense and hard as new-strung barbed wire. He felt the big Colt at the small of his back, but if it was Tony behind him, or Benoit, or some other Klan psycho out for the mean Koven glory of killing him, he was a dead man.

"It's me," said a woman's small voice.

Cutter turned and stared at Julie Davis, shards of tree-broken moonlight shining off her blond hair and the blue silk dressing gown she wore. He made himself take long, slow pulls of air like after a set of wind sprints. He was utterly relieved and close to furious at the same time.

"The way things stand around here, that's a mighty chancy thing to do," he told her, his voice even but hard.

Julie ignored him and marched all five-foot-nothing of herself within inches of him, looking up without apology into his stern, bewildered face. Her brown eyes blazed at him, unconcerned with his obvious irritation.

"I hate this damn place," she told him with enough anger to match his own. "This backward, asshole-of-the-universe town. And after I leave on Wednesday, I hope I never set foot in it again. But so help me God, if you hurt Holly, I'll come back and scratch your fucking eyes out." She poked him in the chest with two small but resolute fingers. "You got that, Sport?"

They held each other's eyes until Cutter dipped his chin just enough for her to see. "Yeah, I got it."

"Good," she said, then crossed her arms beneath her small breasts, whirled and tramped back down the moon-shadowed driveway without another word.

CHAPTER 6

Two-a-day football practices continued that week at both CHS and Riverview. I actually was working out with the first-team offense, though I had to admit our efforts looked slow and pedestrian without Cutter and Jimmy Garner in the backfield. Our defensive line seemed anemic minus big Dodge McDowell. By the middle of the week the word around town was that at least five black kids now were practicing in Wolves uniforms. That gave "Cutter's Team," as people were referring to it, enough bodies to kick off a football game and play – assuming nearly everyone played both offense and defense and very few got hurt. But for me, the biggest difference continued to be that we Raiders were not practicing under threat. Armed deputies remained watchful at every CHS practice, and FBI men could be regularly seen on the hill above the field, scanning for potential shooters.

Despite all that had happened, Cutter and I had covered a lot of dirt-road miles together, and I was scared for his sake. As it turned out, the shots fired that week were not at Cutter but at my father, among others.

Reverend Clemmer and 11 young NCJ volunteers were returning from the fair on Wednesday after manning a voter registration booth there. Escorted by a sheriff's cruiser in front and back, they left the fairgrounds without incident in their old white school bus. All was well until they reached a hairpin turn in the unlit dirt of Pickens' Ferry Road. There the vast swamp pressed itself within a few yards of the rising hills. As the bus started across the plank bridge it exploded, bucking the front end of the bus a good 10 feet into the air. It came down hard, nose-diving into the smoking, watery hole where the bridge had been – sending the occupants flailing and tumbling. Almost before the front bumper dug into the muck, the bus and the police cars came under automatic weapons fire from boats hidden among the cypress knees in the black morass of the swamp.

Slugs stitched the side of his patrol car but my father snatched his shotgun from the rack beside the radio, rolled out next to the cruiser and returned fire across the hood. Newly hired Deputy Clint Conroy emptied his .357 twice. In the midst of all this, gas from the bus's ruptured fuel tank found the hot exhaust manifold and caught fire, sending a hot serpent of orange flame slithering across the water. At the edge of the spreading light, the sheriff saw four black-hooded men in two small boats disappearing into the deeper darkness of Moccasin Slough.

Billy Wallace grabbed the microphone on his police radio and called for assistance, "Shots fired! Shots fired!" And, "Send as many ambulances as you can to my location," he told the dispatcher. "And fire trucks, too."

My father then climbed onto the burning bus and helped get everyone off before it was consumed.

The whole attack had lasted less than ninety seconds and the men who committed it were gone, like ghosts into the swampy darkness.

H olly's bedside phone rang about 11:20. The woman on the other end was a girl with whom Holly had gone to high school. Her husband was a volunteer fireman, and his wife gave Holly all the information she had.

"Good luck, and God bless you. Not everyone supports this Klan meanness," said Clara Franks. "But, Holly, please don't tell anyone I called you. Okay?"

"Of course, Clara," Holly said, as she held the phone between her shoulder and ear as she transferred into her wheelchair. "I won't. Thanks."

Holly roused Rose. They threw on whatever was handy and were in the car in under five minutes. Holly checked her camera bag and made sure the .38 was in her purse. "Are you okay with this?" Holly asked her new helper.

"L-Let's go."

T wo ambulances already had arrived at the emergency room when Holly turned into the parking lot. They got out as a stretcher rolled through the doors heading for a waiting ambulance. The young redheaded man's leg was splinted from ankle to hip and an IV line was running into his arm. Holly could see at least a dozen stitches along his jaw line. Doctor Garner had walked with the stretcher to the ambulance and Holly and Rose followed him back inside.

"How bad?" asked Holly.

"Compound fractures of the right leg," said the doctor. "We stabilized him. They'll have to do surgery in Memphis. Put pins in it. But he should be all right. Eventually."

"Good, but I meant –"

"Oh, you mean overall," said the doctor. "Well, from what I was told, Reverend Clemmer missed a gear as they went around the curve so the bus came almost to a stop. It must have thrown off Mr. McBride's timing because the bomb went off in front of the bus instead of directly under it. The engine block shielded the occupants from the worst of the blast, according to Sheriff Wallace.

"Reverend Clemmer has a concussion and nasty head wound, but no one is dead at the scene. It looks like mostly broken bones and minor burns."

"Thank God," said Holly.

"Yes, indeed."

Cutter came in through the emergency room doors and approached them. "I saw you tear out of the drive way," he said to Holly. "I guess that wasn't thunder I heard from the backside of the mountain."

Dr. Garner had the good grace or good sense not to ask what Cutter was doing out near Wolf's Run at 11 o'clock at night. Holly told him what happened. "Guess Miss Davis left too soon" was all he said.

"This is awful, but I'm glad you're both here," the doctor told them, as if Rose was not present. "There's a little break in the action it looks like, and I've got good news. Some of it bad. Some – well, don't know how to classify it. Let's talk over here."

Dr. Garner led them to an examining area as Rose followed. He reached for the heavy curtain but hesitated. "Anything you can say in front of us, you can say in front of my sister," Cutter told him. Gerry Garner shrugged in his white coat and drew the curtain around them.

"Okay, I'll give you the bad news first," he said. "The autopsy report on Miss Jenny came back as natural causes."

"There was nothing natural about them," Cutter shot back with unusual rancor. "He killed her by degrees over years."

"I have no doubt you are correct," said Dr. Garner. "The report notes that there certainly had been head trauma and much more over the years, but linking her death to a specific recent injury that can be shown as the 'proximate cause' of the stroke? No. I'm sorry. It's just not there. If it was, Steve Andrews would have found it. And from his reaction to what he saw, he'd have been happy to do so."

Rose stood and listened blankly but said nothing as Cutter asked about how to move forward with the funeral. The doctor explained the formalities then to Holly said, "Now, I don't know if you'll think this is good news or bad, but I think there is clear evidence to prove that violence was committed within close proximity of the picture frame you gave me to examine. I can't say with certainty when or exactly how it happened, but ..."

"But?" Holly pressed.

"All right, let me explain. When you gave me that picture frame and asked me to check if the blood was human and if it was your father's type, that's what I did," he said. "I tested several drops, and as you know found two types of blood."

"Yes."

"As I also told you, there were more than twenty drops of blood on the frame and several smears. I didn't test every drop or the smears because I'd answered your questions and then some, but something about it bothered me."

Holly was nodding now. "You have my attention."

"I was actually in my lab at the office tonight, working on the frame when I got the call to come the hospital."

"Don't tell me you found a third blood type?"

"Sort of," he said. "I tested the smear and it was a combination of your father's blood type and the O-negative." Holly knew what the doctor would say next before he said it and it chilled her to the bone and made the heat in her neck rise at the same time. "I'm not a criminologist, but what that would indicate to me is that your father's blood and this other person's blood was put on the frame at the same time. Otherwise, they wouldn't be commingled in the way they are. So two people were bleeding in that room at the same time. Your father and –"

"Whoever killed him," she finished for the doctor.

"I'd say that's a reasonable supposition."

Holly's eyes drifted away for a moment, seeing with chilling clarity her father being attacked in the library near where her mother's portrait had hung. Then they came back to focus on the present and the doctor. "What do you think our next steps should be?"

The doctor considered. "I know this would be painful, but if I were in your shoes, I would want another autopsy by a trained pathologist with up-to-date knowledge of forensic science. Of course, that would involve an exhumation."

This was not the first time Holly had considered the possibility, but it still gave her pause. "Daddy's body was in the river for so long, and it's been almost four months since the accident. Do you think Dr. Andrews could really find anything?"

"Every corp – Every case is different, but Steve Andrews is excellent."

Holly took only another quick moment to consider. "Then let's do it. What do I need to do?"

"You need to file for a request for exhumation with the chancery clerk's office," Dr. Garner told her. "Then you take it over to the funeral home and they'll do the rest. Of course, this is a private exhumation and autopsy so there will be some fees involved."

"No doubt," said Holly. "But I'm not broke. Not yet. Just send me the bill."

The sudden clatter of a metal hospital chart rattling against the floor just outside the cubicle startled the group. Rose gasped. Doctor Garner snatched open the curtain. Nurse Rhonda Hines was squatting, hurriedly gathering the chart back into her arms. She stood, flustered. "I'm, I'm sorry, Doctor. I didn't want to, to interrupt. I have the chart for the male Negro in Exam Four. You need to approve –"

"Yes, yes. I know," said Dr. Garner, taking the chart from the nurse and scribbling some notes. Rhonda Hines small gray eyes were darting back and forth between Cutter and Holly, not bothering to hide her disdain. The doctor handed the chart back. "One last thing, Miss Carter – Holly. I know you want to be as sure as you can be before going to the sheriff. But Billy Wallace is a good man. I think it's time you let him in on all this shade-tree private-detecting you and Cutter have been doing."

CHAPTER 7

On Friday morning, Sheriff Wallace drove out to Wolf's Run. The first long light of another hot summer day was only beginning to paint the Cattahatchie Valley when Rose brought onto the patio a platter of biscuits, eggs, bacon and sausage. For years she had been the only cook in the Old Ambrose Place, and she'd gotten good at it. At first it was by necessity, then she came to enjoy it – singing to herself as she worked, her hands white with flour ahead of scrambling eggs, squeezing fresh orange juice and making coffee. She sat with Holly, Cutter and the sheriff at the poolside table still cool with the shadow of the mountain's eastern ridge, as it would be until almost ten o'clock.

My father looked about as haggard as a man can look and still be moving around. His eyes were red-rimmed and sunken under heavy brows. Wrinkles cut deep at the corners and his mouth was drawn as he ate and listened as Holly and Cutter shared all they knew and all they suspected. Holly had typed up a step-by-step timeline of their inquiries and another narrative form outlining what they thought happened the night T.L. Carter's car went into the river. At the end of it, my father wiped his mouth, put the linen napkin from his lap and said, "I wish you two were working for me."

Holly and Cutter smiled politely, then – "So, Sheriff, you don't think this is simply a daughter's paranoia? Especially directed at a woman with whom – well, clearly there is no love lost between me and Mary Nell."

"Miss Carter, I have more to do than I can shake even the biggest stick at right now," said Billy Wallace. "If I thought this was a wild goose chase, I'd be the first to tell you so. At the moment, I don't have the time or patience for fool's errands.

"Now, you've laid out a good case here, though it's all circumstantial and a lot of it is speculative. So, I'm not prepared to say I definitely believe T.L. was murdered, or who may or may not have been involved. But I can say with 100-percent certainty, based on what you've presented, that your father's death merits further investigation."

Holly sat back in her wheelchair, crossed her arms beneath her breasts and stared out in to the valley, filling quickly now with August light. No one spoke. Rose listened carefully but said nothing. "I guess there was some small part of me that hoped you'd say, 'Holly, you're just letting a few stray facts and your imagination run away with you.' The wounds are already so deep between me and Tom. And Mary Nell." Holly shook her head. "But I knew. I knew."

"If you keep pushin' this, the wounds are only gonna get deeper from here on out," said the sheriff. "Are you prepared for that?"

Holly didn't hesitate. "Yes. I am," she said, all business again, and took another piece of paper from a folder beside her plate. "This is a formal request to exhume my father's body. I plan to file this was the chancery clerk this afternoon since it has to be filed forty-hours in advance. Dr. Andrews is coming up from Jackson to do the autopsy Monday morning."

The sheriff looked over the standard request form. "It seems to be in order. You know if Tom and Mary Nell are involved in T.L.'s death, they'll fight tooth and nail to keep his body in the ground."

"Can they?" asked Cutter.

"With Miss Holly here being T.L.'s majority heir and executor of his estate, I don't see how. Not legally. Not for long. But Tom and Mary Nell have a lot of friends in this county, including one who lives out at Chalmette Plantation. So, I wouldn't put anything past them."

"On that score, gentlemen, it looks as if we finally have a little luck running our way," said Holly. "I've heard through the clothesline telegraph that Tom and Mary Nell left yesterday for a wedding in Mobile. They won't be back until Sunday night.

"That's why I don't intend to file the request until late this afternoon," she went on. "And I'm paying the funeral home extra to have their people out at the cemetery at first light on Monday."

Both men smiled, admiring Holly's guile.

The sheriff tapped the folder on the table that Holly had created for him. "I'm not going to take this with me," he said. "I don't have any place to lock it up that I know for sure can't be got at by people not loyal to my – well, to me. I suggest that you put this and any other copies you have in a very safe place. Or put it in a safe deposit box in a bank, but not around here. Memphis. Or Tupelo, at the very least."

"I understand," said Holly. "I'm taking Rose to Tupelo tomorrow to buy some new clothes. I'll do it then."

Billy Wallace stood. "Good. Cutter, would you mind walking me out?"

***

Daddy and Cutter stood by the unmarked sheriff's cruiser. Cutter eyed the bullet holes in the right front fender and both doors. The glass on the right back window was missing.

"I'm glad you made it through aw'right the other night," my best friend told my father. "You saved some lives."

I had not spoken to either since the bridge bombing, adhering to Rev. MacAllister's credo that daddy had put himself in that dangerous position by "defying the will of God and the church community and siding with those who wish to dilute white Christian blood until it flows poisonously through the veins of a Mud Race." Even then I knew that closer to the truth was that Patti was letting me feel her up on a regular basis now that I was a starting wide receiver for the Riverview Academy Confederates. In fact, out behind Reilly Jamison's hay barn one twilight, just ahead of full dark, she'd lain back against the passenger door of my truck cab and opened her legs to reveal she had on no Spandex chastity girdle, not even patties under denim skirt. For the first time she actually let me let me see the neat blond bush at the intersection of her thighs and I stopped breathing, mesmerized. Then we came as close to having actual sex as we ever had. I wasn't about to screw that up over a voting rights squabble.

"I'm glad nobody got killed, but if Reverend Clemmer hadn't missed a gear, ever'body in that bus would have died," the sheriff told him. "Call it divine intervention or just dumb luck. I didn't have anything to do with it."

They stood in silence enjoying the mountain's cool shadow ahead of two-a-day football practice for Cutter and God knew what for Billy Wallace. Finally, "I hear your plannin' to bury Miss Jenny way out at Fount Springs Church on Sunday afternoon. No visitation, no funeral."

"There'll be words at the grave," said Cutter. "Brother Childers will preach the service. He was one of Momma's students. He offered a free plot, too. Free's good right now. Rose and Holly are gonna sing."

"Miss Jenny was a well-loved teacher from two old families. I'm sure there are a lot of people who would like to pay their respects."

Cutter tightened his jaw, moved as if he was chewing some bitter root, then loosened enough to speak. "Those students who supposedly loved her so. The other teachers and people at First Denomination. Those uncles and aunts and cousins of mine, livin' up there in their big houses at the top of Hill Street – where have they been?" he growled. "Where were they when Tony was beatin' Momma into the crazy house? When he was beatin' me and doin' –" Cutter shook his head at the memory – "doin' worse to Rose? No. They wanted nothin' do with any of us for the last ten years or better. Let 'em stay at home and soothe their consciences some other way. I don't want them anywhere near Momma's grave, or me and Rose."

Billy Wallace waited for the unusual burst of anger to sizzle away before saying, "Technically you're not Miss Jenny's next of kin. Tony could try to intervene or show up out there at Fount Springs."

"If he does, I'll kill him," Cutter said matter-of-factly.

"That's what I'm afraid of. Or vice versa. Or both," said the sheriff. "Now listen to me. There's some stuff goin' on behind te scenes with the feds that I can't talk about. But it'll probably keep Tony, McBride and his Rudolph kin, and some of the worst of the Klux backed down into their snake holes for a time. But Fount

Springs, way out there at the end of that gravel road, woods right up to the edge of the cemetery. It's a perfect spot for an ambush."

Cutter said nothing but didn't disagree.

"I'd like to come out to Fount Springs Sunday afternoon. Bring a couple of deputies just to make sure everything stays quiet. If that's aw'right with you."

Cutter shrugged. "It's aw'right by me," he said, then – "If Nate wanted to come, to stand with us, with me, that'd be aw'right, too. Will you tell him?"

My father nodded. "If I see him, I sure will."

***

That Friday afternoon I saw my father's unmarked cruiser fall in behind my pickup when I left practice at Riverview's new field near the fairgrounds south of town. He hit his red dashboard light. I ignored it for a half mile but I pulled over when he whooped his siren. I didn't get out. With my Confederates teammates passing by in their vehicles, I felt unreasonably angry and embarrassed as he stood by my door.

"Isn't there some law against using official cars for personal stuff?" I asked acidly.

"These days I guess Brother MacAllister isn't hitting that part of the Bible very hard where it talks about honoring thy father and thy mother," he said.

After a long silence during which I stared through the windshield at the road ahead and Daddy stared off into the woods to let his quiet but considerable temper cool, he made no attempt at small talk. He told me about the funeral plans for Jennifer Ambrose Carlucci and Cutter's invitation.

"They're keepin' it private. Real private," he said. "Just him, Rose, Miss Carter and the preacher. Plus me and some deputies to make sure nothin' goes sideways."

"Why's she gonna be there?"

Daddy knew who I meant. "Miss Carter has put a decent roof over Rose's head for the first time in her life. I imagine that earns an invite."

"If you think that's all there is to it, then you aren't much of a detective."

Daddy's big hand gripped the window frame while the other rested on the butt of the .357 that hung from his utility belt. He wanted to hit me, and I wanted him to take a swing to justify my unjustified anger. Before my teen years, I had endured a few hand spankings and even a couple of belt whippings from Billy Wallace, but he had never struck me. Not even when he was drinking. Now I was trying to goad him into it, but he wouldn't take the bait. After a time he said, "Whatever you've got goin' with Patti, or whatever you think of Miss Carter, whatever Brother Mac has schooled you to think about her, your best friend is asking you to stand beside him when he buries his mother. You need to think hard about that, Son."

Again Cutter and my own father were putting me in a terrible bind. Couldn't they see that? If Cutter had just done things the normal way I'd have been only one of maybe hundreds passing through the funeral home visitation and maybe dozens at the graveside. But like this? Just me and Miss Carter. Brother MacAllister would pitch a blue fit and Patti squeeze her very fine ass back into a girdle and recross her legs. Or worse.

"Aw'right. I'll think about it," I told him. "Can I go?"

Daddy took his hand off the truck door. "Yeah, go on."

Hitting the shifter, I pulled out. Down the road I looked in my side mirror and saw Daddy still standing there, hands on his hips, disappointment written all over his tough, tired face.

CHAPTER 8

Because of the way the two limestone walls cupped Wolf's Run in the green hollow between them, on clear nights the stars seemed to flow over the mountaintop and cascade above the house before spilling out silver-white across the valley. Holly lay next to Cutter on the double chaise lounge by the low patio wall. Though they had stolen a kiss here and a caress there, they had not been intimate since Monday night and both had felt the tension of it like a knot tightening in the middle while the rope frayed and frazzled at both ends. Once sure that Rose had gone to her room, gone to bed, Holly reached for the zipper of his cut-off jeans, still damp from a late afternoon swim. He was ready and together they broke the knot, or at least loosened it to the point that they no longer felt as if they were being suffocated by their mutual desire. Charlie had lain next to the chaise, keeping quiet watch.

"Where'd you get these?" asked Holly as she moved her hand over Cutter's bare chest, mapping with her fingertips the narrow column of black hair that flourished at the center, then exploring the smooth plateaus of his hard pecs. "Do you lift weights?"

"Not a day in my life," he told her. "Just hard work and lots of it. And any kind I could get. Plus about a million push-ups and sit-ups."

Despite the upset and melancholy of the funeral, it had been a good weekend.

On Saturday, Holly and Rose had driven the fifty miles to Tupelo – birthplace of Elvis Presley and the biggest city between Memphis and Birmingham. After renting a safe deposit box and placing in it a copy of the report she and Cutter had prepared for Sheriff Wallace, she'd taken Rose on a shopping spree at Reed Brothers Department Store. Other than hand-me-downs that Tony brought home from time to time and she refused to wear, Rose hadn't had a new dress since her mother was sent to the state mental hospital at Whitfield. Eleven years, during which time Rose had gone from being child to a rather shapely young woman. They bought everything from a couple of new dresses, including a black one appropriate for a funeral, to jeans, several skirts and blouses, three pairs of shoes, a nightgown, underwear and even a swimsuit.

At first Rose was resistant – "M-M-Miss Holly, I-I don't have any m-money. I sh-shouldn't let you –"

Holly shushed her. "Stop. I'm enjoying this. Besides, these aren't gifts. Well, maybe a couple. But I expect you to pay me back out of your salary for the rest."

They ate a late lunch at Johnnie's Drive-In before making it to a 2:30 appointment at the nicest beauty parlor in town. The only one in the phone book that advertised "Dallas-trained stylists" instead of beauticians. Holly treated Rose to the works – a cut and style of her overlong, frowzy brown hair, a facial, manicure and pedicure – and treated herself to much of the same.

When Cutter came into the kitchen that night after working all day helping prep The Gin for the Saturday night crowd, he saw the young woman, her back to him, in jeans and t-shirt making salad at the long counter by the sink and nearly asked Holly, "Who's this?" Even when Rose turned, for an instant Cutter was unsure. Her olive skin looked as clean and bright and fresh-scrubbed as a new penny and her hair, now shoulder length, had a new gloss and bounce and some sass, too, in the way it hung on her forehead. Then she spoke, "Do I l-look o-okay?"

Cutter took half a step back as if pushed and dipped his chin as he turned his face away and drew in a breath. When he look back, his eyes were glistening and he had clear his throat before he could speak. "You're ... beautiful!"

***

On Sunday morning Cutter went back to The Gin to help with clean-up from Saturday night and set-up for the after-church restaurant crowd. He showered in the band dressing room and met Holly and Rose at the turnoff to Highway 2. They had spent the morning practicing several songs for the graveside service, including one that Rose had written. It wasn't bad. In fact, it was amazingly good for a girl who had taught herself to read and write music and play the guitar. Better than a number of songs friends had managed to record in L.A., thought Holly. Rose's voice was limited and untrained, but magically when she sang, her stutter disappeared.

Sheriff Wallace led the Cadillac hearse through the turn off from Highway 27. Holly's Lincoln and Cutter's Jeep fell in behind. Another sheriff's car brought up the rear. At Fount Springs, the sheriff opened the back door of the car of his cruiser and quietly chambered a round into a scoped rifle. Then he took up a pair of powerful binoculars and began scanning the woods that surrounded the cemetery on three sides while Deputy Glenn Stubbs walked the tree line with a similar rifle over his shoulder. The mid-afternoon temperature was near 100 degrees and the air was as still as the dead, but Cutter leaned against the black body of the hearse in his pressed jeans, white button-down and a dark blue tie with a small stitched pattern of crop-duster aircraft. Holly and Rose waited in the car in the shadow cast by the clapboard walls and tin roof of the church. Under a nearby tree, two funeral home employees stood sweating copiously in their black suits and ties.

At ten after two, the shorter of the two men waddled toward Cutter across the hard-packed dirt lot, the collar of his shirt soaked with perspiration from the overhanging folds of his neck. "Cutter, I hate to push a family, but we've got another funeral over in Kossuth at four o'clock," said Mickey Teal, who wore a name tag identifying him as associate funeral director. "Is there anything you need us to do before we proceed?"

Cutter straightened and looked down the gravel road. There was no rooster tail of dust in the distance. No sound of gravel rattling off the undercarriage of an old pickup. No sign of me. My father looked in the same direction, then spit in the gravel.

"Sorry, Mickey. No, no reason to wait. Let's get it done," Cutter told the young man. Then to my father, "Mr. Wallace, we need one more man. Would you mind?"

My father reset his hat. "No, Son. Of course not. I'd be honored."

Two employees of the DeLong Funeral Home carried the front end the coffin, part of the mortuary's "Modesty Collection." Meaning modestly priced. Thus it was lightweight, almost to the point of being flimsy, and since Jennifer Carlucci had weighed only ninety-three pounds at time of her death, it wasn't much of a carry for four good-sized men. They placed it gently onto the green straps of the frame that was fitted above the open grave cut into red clay soil.

Holly's voice smoothly cleaved the thick layers of humidity. With perfect a cappella pitch, she sang the gospel hymn *In The Garden,* which had been Cutter's request. He remembered his mother singing it to herself on Sunday mornings as she got them and herself ready for church at First Denomination, before all the music left her and all she had left in her head were the numbers. Brother Bruce Childers, who had been two years ahead of Holly at Cattahatchie High, went light on the theology and instead shared reminiscences of Jennifer Carlucci, the teacher, and mathematics and quilting clubs sponsor. He talked about her gifting families in need, including his one Christmas, with beautiful, handmade quilts.

"Your mother's quilts were made with such precise care and eye to detail that they were mathematics perfectly rendered into soft, comforting squares," he told them. "But they were made with so much more than that. Every stitch was an act of love, and they were given in kindness from a loving and gentle heart. Even as Miss Jenny was bearing uncounted struggles, she never ceased to serve and love others. And because of her generosity, my brothers and sisters and me slept warmer many a winter night when the wind blew cold down Hatchie Bottom."

Cutter had his sunglasses on, but Holly saw his chin quiver as he fought his emotions. She wanted to go to him. Embrace him. At least take his hand. But of course she did not. Could not. When Brother Childers had finished, Rose had to take a moment to compose herself before placing the strap of her guitar over her shoulder. Her fingers trembled on the neck of the instrument. Her fingers were clumsy on the strings. She stopped, closed her eyes for a beat.

"You can do this?" Holly encouraged. Rose swallowed, nodded. "Okay then. One, two, three ..."

Together they performed *Blue Mountain Angel,* which Rose had written for her mother after her death. Like Rose's voice, the song was sweet and mellow, both sad and wistful, and in the end hopeful. Holly's harmonies on the chorus were understated and haunting.

"Wow," said Cutter who had not heard it. No one had, except Holly. Up the hill, Billy Wallace's reaction was the same. Even the deputy over by the tree line stopped and clapped his hands together twice before remembering he was at a funeral and quickly turned and went back to watching the trees.

Brother Childers ended the services with the 23rd Psalm:

The Lord is my shepherd; I shall not want. He maketh me to lie down in green pastures: he leadeth me beside the still waters. He restoreth my soul ... Surely goodness and mercy shall follow me all the days of my life: and I will dwell in the house of the Lord forever.

"And today, Lord, we commend to the earth the mortal of remains of Jennifer Ambrose Cutter Carlucci, in the sure and certain hope of resurrection," finished Brother Childers. "And we commend her soul to Your care, to Your loving embrace, in the belief that she will dwell with You in the house of the Lord forever and ever. Amen."

When they got back to Blue Mountain, Cutter winched his Jeep up onto the rock shelf where he was sleeping, changed clothes then walked back down to Wolf's Run, as had become his practice. It was so hot, they all three went for a swim, though Rose mostly kept to herself, swaddled in beach towels. Her one-piece swimsuit was not immodest, but she felt almost naked, vulnerable, having spent so many years hiding herself inside baggy overalls and loose work shirts, in work boots and under big straw hats, giving Tony as few places possible to rest his bloodshot eyes and iniquitous thoughts. Cutter figured he could outswim Holly, but he dropped out after twenty-eight laps of the big pool. He sat on the edge and watched as she did thirty, then thirty-five. He loved watching the strong, fluid muscles in her shoulders, and the way she smoothly cut through the water. When Holly finally finished, she turned to Cutter and pumped her fist in triumph, and he liked that even more – the fire that burned in her even in regard to little things.

While Holly changed from her swimsuit, Rose took Cutter to her room and showed him a small ledger – much like a funeral guest book -- that had been in the bottom of a box of her mother's few belongings brought from the Old Ambrose Place. On the cover was embossed in white letters: State Hospital, Whitfield, Mississippi. The pages were almost empty, but not quite. There were a handful dates and names. Rose shrugged in question, not dismissal. Cutter nodded. After dinner, Rose went to the library. On the dark patio, Holly lifted herself onto the plump cushions of the double chaise lounge next to Cutter. She ran her hand under his black pullover, pushed it up and began to kiss his chest, his hard belly, then unbuttoned his cutoffs. When Holly had finished, they lay on their backs merely holding hands and letting the spill of stars fill their eyes. When their breathing had settled Cutter said, "You visited my mother six times in the 10 months she was in Whitfield. That's a three-hour drive each way."

"I owned a Corvette. I liked driving it. And I got to Whitfield way under three hours."

"I'm serious," said Cutter, his voice flat.

Holly propped on her elbow and looked quizzically at him. "You make it sound like an accusation. Where'd this come from?"

Cutter explained about the guest book.

"Does that bother you?" she asked.

"No, of course not, but you never mentioned it."

"There was no reason to mention it. It was a sad time," she said. "I wasn't the only one who went."

"You're the only one who went six times."

Holly rolled onto her back and put one hand behind her head as she took Cutter's hand with the other. "It's all because I was lousy at math," she said to the stars and to him. "I would never have gotten through algebra or geometry if Miss Jenny hadn't tutored me after school. Along the way, we started talking about other things. Things I couldn't even talk with Meemaw Lois about, or at least not in the same way."

"Like?"

"Like I had daddy problems of my own back then. Nothing of the sort you and Rose experienced, thank God. Momma problems, too. I already felt abandoned by my mother. Hell, I didn't feel abandoned, I was abandoned by my mother. We all were. Daddy and Tom and me. And Meemaw Lois, too. She loved my mother," Holly explained. "And as I grew into my – my womanhood, I looked so much like her that Daddy couldn't stand to be in the same room with me. That's what he told me. And other people, too. Lots of other people – 'I can't stand to look at her.' At fourteen, fifteen, sixteen – that hurt. A lot. So, really, I lost him, too."

Cutter said nothing but gently tightened his grip on Holly's hand.

"Anyway, I was there in Miss Jenny's homeroom that morning. When she took off her coat and I saw the damage Tony had done to her poor body, it broke my heart. All the times she had let me go on about my insecurities, my high school soap opera nonsense and the whole time Tony was –" Holly shook her head, bit her lip, then – "but she never said a thing. She was always encouraging. Always smiling. Ready to laugh. When they sent her to Whitfield, I didn't want her to feel abandoned, because I knew how much that hurt. For the people you love most to, to simply throw you away."

Cutter rolled onto his side, propped on his elbow and looked down at her. "I wanted to go. I wanted to see her. But no one would take us. Me and Rose. What did you do when you went?"

"We'd sit in the big sun room or outside on a bench. It's actually quite pretty there if you put aside the locks on the doors and the mesh in the window glass," Holly told him. "I usually brought a magazine or two, or a book, and read to her. Or I simply babbled about whatever silly thing was going on in my life."

"Did she talk or – anything?"

"No," said Holly. "She rarely even looked at me. Just stared into space, whispering numbers like she was working on a formula but could never get it to come out right. The only time she ever reacted to anything was when I – on the second visit, I think – brought her a box of quilting scraps. She took out two big handfuls and held them to her. To her chest like they were a treasure."

"But you kept going back."

"Yes."

Cutter leaned down and kissed Holly's forehead, then each eyelid, then the tip of her nose, and finally her lips as she shuddered and sighed and put her arms around him. They felt their passion rise again as Cutter pressed his body to Holly's, so close that not even the moonlight could pass between, not even starlight could separate them.

CHAPTER 9

M onday morning started out bad and the week got worse from there.
The phone rang in the kitchen while Holly and Rose were eating
breakfast. No one was calling with good news at seven-twenty, Holly
knew before she picked up the phone. It was Doctor Garner. "Some busybody saw
the gravediggers at work out at the cemetery and told Mary Nell. She went out there
and pitched a fit."

"Did they stop?"

"Until Tom showed up and got her under control, and away from there," said
Gerry Garner. "She was spittin' mad. Talking about desecration and lawyers and
court orders and so forth. But they finished. We have T.L.'s remains here in the
hospital morgue."

"Okay. Then tell Dr. Andrews to do the autopsy as quickly as he can. Before she
can run to one of Governor Weather's crony judges."

"Sorry, Holly, that's not all of it."

She waited.

"There was a quadruple homicide down in Natchez last night. The state police
called Steve Andrews in. He says with the backlog of cases he already has, he can't
get up here for a 'do-over' – his words, not mine – until at least the end of the week."

"Damn it!" she cursed, rubbing her forehead, a headache starting. "You're the
county pathologist. Can't you do it?"

"Holly, pathology is just a sideline for me," said the doctor. "I'm not qualified
to do this sort of in-depth forensic autopsy."

"There's no one else?" she asked.

"There's Dr. Nabors in Nashville and a couple of good people in Atlanta. But
who knows what their schedules look like? And they'll charge a premium fee if you
want them to rush down here."

"I don't care," she told him, though she felt as if she was hemorrhaging money at
every turn. "Would you reach out to them? See if one can come sooner. Meantime,
I expect I need to get a lawyer."

"Unfortunately, I expect you do."

***

On Tuesday night as Holly and *The Current-Leader* staff were working to ready the midweek edition for the presses, Cutter brought dinner to his sister from the Cotton Café. There happened to be enough for the publisher, too, so they ate at the conference table in Holly's office, the windows open at both ends of the building as fans stirred the mix of sweat and cigarette smoke that roiled in the rafters of the news and composing rooms. It was almost nine-fifteen. Rose wiped clinging pieces of wax from her fingers. She'd been learning fast and helping Shorty Rodgers and two others paste newsprint onto the lined cardboard pages before they went to the camera room on their way to engraving and then the presses.

In her reading glasses studying page A7 as they ate, Holly was beautiful – she was always beautiful, thought Cutter, but she did look hot, tired and careworn, and for good reason. On Monday afternoon, County Judge Otis Fairbanks, who owed everything in his life to Cecil Weathers, had issued a restraining order enjoining "any form of autopsy" on the remains of T.L. Carter III. The Tupelo attorney Holly hired – she didn't trust anyone in DeLong – assured her there was no legal justification for the injunction but she wasn't so sure that would matter. A lot of Mississippi judges owed their careers to Weathers, and she had no doubt that the influence of the "Invisible Empire" would be brought to bear as well. In the end, none of the pathologists Gerry Garner contacted could come sooner than Dr. Andrews so everything was on hold anyway. Holly hated to think of her father's body pulled from the grave, waiting in cold storage to be cut apart, again. She closed her eyes. She wanted it over with.

"How're you doing?" Cutter asked after a long pull on a big glass of iced tea.

With her fingers Holly tore off a piece of sweet white, perfectly spiced chicken breast the size of her thumb and gave it to Charlie, who was eagerly waiting beside her right wheel. Charlie yapped and wagged the tail that curled over her back. "No more, baby. We've got to watch your figure," said Holly, smiling. Then her smile faded and to Cutter she said, "I'm as okay as I can be, I suppose. From here on out, I guess it'll be open warfare between me and Tom and Mary Nell. Until I either prove Daddy's death was no accident. Or they prove I'm nuts. How was practice?"

"Hot. But we had three more guys from Roseville come out today."

"How many is that?"

"Eleven blacks and the nine of us," he said. "We almost have enough players to have a full offense and defense in practice. But things are getting' ragged. We need a coach to keep things organized and keep people payin' attention, if nothing else."

"I know Doctor Garner is trying to find someone. Do you have any candidates?"

"Not anybody who'd take it," he said.

* * *

About the time the presses started turning at ten-forty-five a light rain began to fall but it did little to cool the sticky night. It was a thick, warm drizzle. The big door on the loading dock was rolled up and papers were flowing off the press. Sorters and carriers – some longtime hands but most of them new – were stuffing advertising inserts and sections together on a long table and creating stacks for delivery. Holly opened the paper and flipped from page to page, checking every headline, every photo caption one more time. It was after eleven by the time she was satisfied.

"What now?" asked Cutter.

"Rose and I are going to deliver the Madison Street route," said Holly. "It's only one-hundred-twenty papers right off the square. It won't take long. Then we go home. It's been a very long day."

"I'll follow you."

Holly smiled a tired but appreciative smile and let her hand brush Cutter's without taking it. "Thanks. I'll get the car and you load us up. Four bundles. Okay?"

"You got it."

Holly pushed quickly across the parking lot with Charlie running alongside. She swung open the front door of the Continental. Charlie hopped in and Holly lifted her hips onto the bench seat. She grunted with effort and for an instant didn't notice Charlie's low growl. But as Holly lifted her right leg and settled her foot onto the floor mat, she saw that Charlie's lips were pulled back and her teeth were bared. Holly felt a chill race up her spine as the little dog barked and snapped at something under the passenger seat, then watched in horror as a bolt of black lightning emerged and struck the little dog.

"*Charlie!*" Holly screamed and reached for her companion, her very best little friend. But from another angle beneath the seat a second water moccasin sprang – this one a mottled brown and as thick as her wrist, but there was no mistaking its cotton-white mouth as it opened and plunged its fangs into the dog.

Charlie yelped and jumped but held her ground as Cutter and Rose looked toward the Lincoln.

Instinct and fear took hold of Holly and she pushed herself out of the car and across her wheelchair, both tumbling over onto the wet pavement. She landed hard. "Charlie, *viens! Viens!*" she shouted, her husky voice shrill with terror. "Come, Charlie!"

Cutter leaped from the loading dock and ran toward the car.

Finally, Charlie obeyed and hurried toward the open door but yelped again as she took another hit that knocked her off her feet. But she got up and hopped out of the car as the large black-and-tan moccasin slithered over the hump in the front floorboard. Holly pulled her leg out of the car as the viper's thick V-shaped head dropped down toward the pavement. Cutter saw it and never slowed down. He slammed his hip into the door, sending it crashing shut and cutting the moccasin in two about five inches behind its head.

Rose came up, breathing hard from her run down the ramp and across the lot, and watched as the remainder of the snake writhed and opened its cotton mouth trying to strike. Cutter stomped the head and ground it under the heel of his work boot as Rose grabbed Holly under her arms and dragged her several feet away.

Now others noticed the commotion and came running from the loading dock and press room. Cutter knelt beside Holly and snatched off her remaining shoe. He tossed it aside and began checking her feet then her legs, front and back.

"Ch-Ch-Check her knee," said Rose.

"Just a cut. From the fall," he said, sighing with relief as Holly propped on her hands. "Charlie?" she sobbed. "Where's Charlie?"

A gap opened in the circle of workers who'd surrounded her. Charlie was sitting a few feet away, panting as if she had run a two-hundred-yard dash. She looked dazed, confused. Cutter guessed she already was blind. Through her tears Holly saw there were at least four distinct streaks of blood on her coat. "Ohhhh, Charlie."

Shorty Rodgers, the production manager, saw the remains of the snake and said, "I'm callin' the law. This was no accident."

"Call an ambulance, too," said Cutter. "Just in case."

Now one of the carriers was shining a big flashlight inside the Lincoln. "Holy shit! There's another one in there. No! Two!"

Holly watched as Charlie tried to stand up, but she stumbled then fell over.

"Charlie? Ohhh, Charlie! Bring her to me," Holly pleaded.

Rose picked up the little dog and put her in Holly's arms. Charlie was like a rag doll even though her breathing was very fast. Holly held the bundle of red-streaked white fur to her chest. "Oh, Charlie, you were so brave," she whispered, her lips trembling. "You saved me. Do you know you saved me?"

Charlie's eyes blinked and her breathing slowed as if she heard and understood the words, and was comforted by them. Then as Holly slowly, gently stroked her white coat – "You did good. ... You did so good, *mon chéri* ... I love you. ... I'll never forget you."

The little dog convulsed once, then again, then Holly felt Charlie's heart go still beneath her fingers.

Three minutes later two sheriff's cars pulled into the newspaper lot. Not far behind were the sheriff, the ambulance and Doctor Garner, who lived off Hill Street, not far from the square.

"I heard the call out on my scanner," said the doctor as he knelt beside Holly and began examining her legs. After a couple of minutes, he allowed himself a deep swallow of relief. "No puncture wounds. But I don't like the looks of that knee. We need to clean it up. You may need a couple of stitches. And there's a little swelling in your ankle."

Doctor Garner motioned for the ambulance attendants.

"No," she said, her whole body trembling. "No ambulance."

"Miss Carter, I want to keep your leg as stable as possible until we can get X-rays and see what's what," the doctor told her. "The stretcher will let us do that."

"But Charlie?" she asked, her eyes full of pain and pleading.

"I'll take care of Charlie," said Cutter, lifting the little dog from Holly's arms and cradling her like a baby.

"I want to keep her leg as straight as possible," said Doc Garner, motioning to one of the attendants. "Jack, get under her arms. I'll keep her legs steady. On three. ... One. Two. Three."

They lifted her onto the stretcher and quickly wrapped a blanket around her. Cutter walked with her to the ambulance, holding Charlie. "I-I'll ride with H-Holly," said Rose, climbing in without being asked.

Once the ambulance pulled away, Cutter went to the footlocker in his Jeep and took out a towel and gently placed Charlie on it in the passenger seat. He stroked the dog's blood-speckled side. "Thank you, Charlie," he mouthed.

Sheriff Wallace was standing by the back passenger door of the Lincoln when Cutter walked over. "Look here," said my father, pointing to a small, neat three-inch cut in the car's canvas roof. "That's how he got 'em in the car."

Cutter studied the small hole.

"This was somebody who knows how to handle snakes," said Billy Wallace. "Somebody who's not afraid of 'em. And look at this."

The sheriff shined his flashlight onto the backseat. A sheet of paper torn from a spiral notebook had unfolded there. Cutter had to tilt his head to read it – "Death to the hore of Babylon and the deseever of men."

Cutter said, "From what I know there are at least three snake-handlin' churches in the county. One out in the low country, among the moonshiners down in Hughestown. Another one somewhere in the deep woods between Pleasant Ridge and Dumas."

"And another one off Challabeete Road on the north end," said the sheriff. "Just a couple of miles from the field where the Klux picked up that scarecrow."

"The 'Judas Wallace' scarecrow?"

"That'd be the one," said my father.

***

At two-fifteen, John-Thomas Hinton turned his cruiser down the driveway at Wolf's Run. Cutter followed in his Jeep. The house was big and dark except for a single light in the kitchen. When Cutter stepped out, he had the .45 in his hand.

"John-Thomas, you mind walkin' through the house with me?"

The deputy looked at Holly transferring from the front seat of his patrol car to her wheelchair with help from Rose. Her left knee was wrapped in white gauze covering the three butterfly bandages Doctor Garner had used to close the cut. Her ankle was snug in inside an Ace bandage.

"Sure, Cutter," he said, unsnapping his holster. "Let's go."

Once they had checked the kitchen and Holly's bedroom, she and Rose came inside. The women went directly to the bedroom and closed the door without a word. Ten minutes later Cutter and Hinton had checked every room and closet, under beds and beneath the steep eves of the sprawling attic. He and Cutter walked outside. The showers had passed and the moon shone here and there as a tatter of clouds drifted across the sky.

The young deputy propped on his cruiser. "She was my first big crush, you know? And even now. Even in that wheelchair ..." He shook his head, smiled for a moment as he looked at Cutter, as if he was appraising him for the first time. As if he was about to say something then let it go along with the smile. "I've spent my whole life in this town except for the four years I went off to school, and that wasn't but sixty miles away. I've seen so many acts of genuine kindness and love among people in this county. I've always been proud of where I come from. But when I see something like this, or the other meanness that's gone on this summer –" he sighed and shook his head. "What's the matter with people?"

Cutter let the question float in the air like the scraps of cloud passing the moon.

"Well, I better get back on patrol," said the deputy, opening the car door. "But I want to make sure you and Miss Holly understand, this wasn't a message, this was attempted murder. Those crazy Klan mother-fuckers meant for her to die tonight. They've upped the ante from scare her off to kill her off."

Cutter nodded. "I know."

"Aw'right then," he said settling into the front seat of the cruiser, the radio crackling. "Take good care of her. And be careful yourself. You're one helluva football player. The best I've ever seen up close. But you ain't bulletproof."

***

Cutter carried Charlie's corpse into the garage and placed her in the tool locker so that no fox or bobcat would get at her during the night, then went inside. Rose was alone in the kitchen drinking a glass of milk and looking shaken. He crossed to the sink, squirted some dish liquid and washed his hands and forearms and splashed water on his face and neck. Rose handed him a dish towel from a drawer.

"You all right, Sister?"

Rose nodded and took another sip from the tall glass.

"What about Holly?"

Rose looked out the dark kitchen window then back to her brother. "She's pretty m-m-messed up. H-Here. And here," said Rose, touching her head then her heart. "She's sh-shaking like it's t-ten degrees in her room. You n-need to stay."

"I planned to. I'll spread my sleeping bag –"

"No!" Rose told him sharply as she grabbed his wrist. "You n-need to stay w-*with* her tonight. Sh-She needs you."

Cutter considered all the meaning behind Rose's words, all the knowledge in her brown eyes, then – "Can I have some of that milk?"

Rose got a glass down from a cabinet and poured for her brother. The milk was cold and good and they drank it in silence as they stood there at the kitchen counter of Wolf's Run, so different from the Old Ambrose Place and the rock outcrops that mostly had been Cutter's home for the last four years. Finishing her milk, Rose washed her glass and put it in the drain board.

"So, you're okay with me and Holly being together?"

Rose nodded, reached out and squeezed her brother's hand. "I'll s-see you in the m-morning," she said and disappeared down the long hall of French doors toward the west wing.

After washing his glass, Cutter put it beside his sister's, then went down the hall to Holly's bedroom. He didn't knock, but slipped quietly inside. There was no moonlight and the rain had started to pick up, a steady hum now on the tin roof. Holly was on her side, her back to him with a blanket pulled up over her shoulder and around her neck. He crossed the room quietly in the dark and sat on the edge of the big bed.

"Rose?" she asked in a voice barely above a shaky whisper, empty of her usual energy and spunk.

"No. It's me," said Cutter and waited for her to say something more but she didn't.

He unlaced his boots in silence, then stepped out of his jeans and tossed them with his T-shirt onto a nearby chair. He placed the .45 on the bedside table then slipped under the covers and slid next to Holly. He ran his hand gently down her arm and then her leg. They were cold. Even her back felt cooler than it should. Some sort of delayed shock, he figured. Gently he enfolded himself around her, pressing his bare chest to her back, his pelvis to her hips. He slipped his arm around under breasts, full and firm through the gauzy t-shirt she wore for sleep.

"Ohhh, thank God!" Holly gasped into the pillow, her voice shaking with cold or with cold fear. Her teeth chattering. "I'm cold. I'm so cold!"

"I know," he whispered pressing himself against her, letting the heat of his body start to warm her. "It's all right. I'm here."

"Hold me tight," she asked, her voice fragile with anxiety and exhaustion. "I feel like I'm about to fall off something. Into something dark and cold and, and full of, full of fucking snakes! Don't let me go, Cutter. Please don't let me go."

He lightly kissed her neck and her cheek and brushed his lips across the pinna of her ear as he softly told her, "I'll never let you go."

CHAPTER 10

When dawn came it was gray and what fell Holly's grandmother would have called a "sleeping rain" – just enough to keep the world quiet and still and perfect for dozing into the morning – and that's what Holly and Cutter did. They were emotionally and physically exhausted and the opportunity to snuggle together in bed was a joy.

They made love gently, slowly. They let each other find their way, inventing the techniques to flawlessly map the geography of their connection. For Holly it was like finding the perfect chords on her guitar or the flawless note in a song. When it came up through her fingertips and across her lips she knew it was right without thinking about it or being told. Just when Holly was ready to let go, Cutter smoothly rolled onto his back. He deftly helped Holly position her legs and sit up so that she straddled him. She looked down at their coupling and shuddered with pleasure, unable to speak even if her mind could have formed a coherent thought. Cutter used the powerful muscles of his hips and legs to drive deep inside her, deep enough that Holly thought she actually could feel him in the warm, wet nadir of her sex. And maybe she did. Either way, she rode him as he bucked under her until together they came and she collapsed onto him, one heart pounding against the other.

After a time they lay next to each other under the sheets watching the soft, steady rain through the big windows onto the porch. Cutter had held and kissed and loved the cold out of her. Holly said, "If we keep this up, I'm going to have to see a doctor."

"If?"

She laughed softly. "Okay. I'll make an appointment."

After a moment, he said, "So you can have babies."

Cutter didn't intend it as a question but Holly answered as if it were – "I think so. All the plumbing still works, cramps and all. It can be risky, but other women in wheelchairs have done it."

"Good. I'm glad."

"Me, too," she told him, then rolled onto her side and put her arm across his chest, thinking of the beautiful babies she and Cutter could make together, then quickly pushed the thought from her mind. *Ridiculous!* Holly drew her mind back to the present and changed the subject. "I can't get back in that car. I'd always be afraid a cottonmouth was going to crawl out from under the seat or drop from behind the dashboard."

"I figured. I wouldn't want to drive it either," he said. "There's a guy who owns a car lot up in Jackson, Tennessee. He comes in The Gin all the time. Always wants to talk football and play pool. He's lousy, but I let him win now and then. Good customer relations, you know? He'd probably cut you a deal. We could go this afternoon."

"Okay. I want a hardtop."

"I don't blame you."

A fter Rose prepared a late breakfast Cutter went out to the garage and found enough scrap wood to hammer together a box. Holly came out with a blanket and several of Charlie's favorite toys. Together they placed Charlie's body among them and Holly said her good-byes, but there were no more tears. She had cried herself out in Cutter's arms. He said, "I was thinking a good place would be under that first big pecan tree by the driveway. If you want, we could nail up a little marker on the tree."

Holly and Rose watched from the porch as Cutter worked in the light rain to dig the grave. He worked in a t-shirt and jeans without a rain coat. He dug until the hole was three feet deep. He picked up the box and looked to the porch. Holly hugged herself beneath her breasts and nodded. Cutter placed it in the earth and shoveled the dirt over it then walked down the driveway and stood with the shovel in front of the porch. His hair and clothes were sodden and water dripped from his nose.

"This much rain sure won't do the farmers any good," he said. Then, "I buried her deep. Nothing'll get at her."

"Thank you. But you're soaked," said Holly. "Come on in and get out of those wet clothes. We'll put on some soup."

T he rain quit just after noon. In jeans still warm from the dryer Cutter drove to the sheriff's office in DeLong and asked to be let into the impound lot where the Lincoln had been taken. "I need to get the hand controls off of it," he told Billy Wallace. "She's never getting back in that car."

"Neither would I," said the sheriff. "I'll have a deputy meet you there."

"Any news? Fingerprints or anything?"

"Rain washed away whatever fingerprints might have been on the car, but we lifted some from the paper," the sheriff told him. "Now all we need is somebody to match 'em to."

"Start with those snake-handlin' preachers."

"I intend to, but I've got to a have a reason to take their prints," he said. Cutter started to speak but before he could the sheriff added, "I'm workin' on it. You take care of what you need to and I'll take care of what I need to."

On the way out of town, Cutter stopped at a pay phone and called Bobby Garner to tell him that he wouldn't be at practice that afternoon. "Don't worry about it," said the Wolves' quarterback. "The field's under water. Nobody's gonna practice there today, but it should be aw'right by mornin'."

"Okay."

"Cutter, everybody's heard about what happened. The ol' gov's keepin' it off the radio, but everybody knows," said Bobby. "It's all anybody's talkin' about. What the Klux did, that's pretty damn sorry. Is Miss Carter aw'right?"

"Good as she can be under the circumstances."

"So are you two --?"

"I gotta go, Bobby. If nothing else happens, I'll see you in the morning."

By the time Cutter and Holly drove north on Mississippi 27 the sun was out and the Cattahatchie Valley seemed trimmed in silver, the bright afternoon light glinting off the water standing between row after thousands of rows of cotton, soybeans and corn grown tall into late summer. They crossed Two-Mile Bridge that separated Moccasin Slough from the Cattahatchie River and connected Mississippi and Tennesee, and passed The Gin and several other roadhouses before stopping at the single red light in Middletown. They continued north for another thirty minutes listening to George Klein's afternoon show on WHBQ.

Ned Pickens of Ned's Nice & Clean Used Cars was, indeed, happy to see Cutter. Almost before he could get out of the Jeep Mr. Pickens was asking if the Wolves really were going to be able to play in September. "We sure are," he said. "This is my … friend Holly Lee Carter. She needs a car. I told her you might give a pool hall discount."

"Miss Carter, it's a pleasure to actually meet you," said Ned Pickens and nodded to her. "I've got a sister livin' in DeLong. We've heard about what happened. I'm not sure how I feel about all that intergratin' mess goin' on down there in Cattahatchie, but I know how I feel about puttin' water moccasins in somebody's car. I wouldn't do a dog that way."

Cutter saw Holly wince but Ned Pickens' wasn't being intentionally cruel, and she said nothing.

"Lemme show you what I got."

Holly tried transferring in and out of three cars, folding her wheelchair and getting it behind the front seat. She settled on a two-door red 1966 Plymouth Fury with a black interior, wide bucket seats, the automatic shifter in the middle console, four-barrel carburetor and dual exhausts. Definitely a hard top.

"This baby'll run like a niggah with his ass on fire," said Ned Pickens.

Holly glanced at Cutter but neither commented. Racism was so ingrained that people didn't even hear the echo of it in their own words. Or if they did, they didn't care. They were white, and thus in the club that ran the world, at least that part of it. All of it really, but here along the Tennessee-Mississippi line and in most of the old Confederacy there was no pretense. In some ways it was more honest than the myriad forms of subtle racism Holly had witnessed in California and in other places in the U.S. she'd traveled to before Vietnam. After all that happened in the last few weeks she no longer felt angry about it, just sad. And tired.

"It's got the muscle-car package," Ned Pickens went on. "A four-twenty-eight V-8 Hemi. It's barely street legal."

Holly turned the key and the big engine growled then settled into a smooth purr.

"How many miles?" asked Cutter as he knelt beside the open door.

"Just twenty-three thousand," he said. "It's cherry. This was a fella's weekend car. He only drove it when he was showin' off. Cruisin', you know. He traded up for a brand new Mustang Super Cobra."

Cutter reached across Holly's shins and pressed the accelerator. The four-twenty-eight roared as she sat, her hands on the wheel, the car trembling with power. He stood. "What do you think?" she asked.

"It's a lotta car," said Cutter. "But I think it suits you."

She looked up at him and smiled. "I think so, too. I'll take it."

CHAPTER 11

On Thursday Holly went back to *The Current Leader* and Cutter returned to football practice. Friday evening, Sheriff Wallace ambled through the newspaper's pressroom and up the back stairs. He crossed through the second floor composing room and saw Rose Carlucci working with Shorty Rodgers at a paste-up table. He smiled to himself. The sudden change in Rose was nothing short of amazing. *Neesie would have called it 'a miracle,' and maybe it is,* he thought, wanting to believe the way his wife once had, that such things happened. "God touched," she had called it.

The double doors to the publisher's office were open, but he took off his hat and tapped on one of them before entering.

"Sheriff, hello," said Holly, taking off her reading glasses and laying them atop a page proof on her desk. "I wasn't expecting you. Do you have news? Good I hope."

"Not for the newspaper," he said. "May I sit?"

"Of course. I'm sorry. Would you like coffee? Or maybe iced tea? I have a pitcher in the refrigerator."

"No thanks," he said, crossing his legs and placing his Panama hat on his knee. "I wanted to let you know that we're finished with your car. The Lincoln."

"Good," she said. "I'm going to sell it for whatever I can get. I never want to see it again. Besides, I can use the money."

"I've seen you in your new car. I think it looks good on you, but it was hard to tell. You were just kind of a blur as fast as you were going when you went by Clyde Simpson's Grocery this morning."

"Ahhhh," sighed Holly. "I was late getting to the office. Guilty, Sheriff. Sorry. I'll try to slow it down. I know I have a bit of a lead foot. Hand, actually."

She held up her left and waggled it.

Billy Wallace smiled. "I'd appreciate it," he said reaching into his shirt pocket. He handed a card across the desk. "I also wanted to give you this."

Holly looked at it: Memphis Electric Gate Company.

"Thank you, Sheriff, but I can't afford an electric gate," she told him. "I just had to buy a car. Every dollar I spend takes away a dollar from keeping the paper's doors open."

Sheriff Wallace's eyes had bored into Holly. "Those dollars won't do you any good if you're dead," he told her. "The way things are now, somebody could drive a carload of dynamite practically onto the porch at Wolf's Run."

"Then catch them, Sheriff. Catch them!" Holly told him a bit too loudly, her frustration and the strain of living under constant threat erupting through her usually smooth exterior. "Then I won't have to worry about it."

"Look, Miss Carter, we think we have a good solid lead on the person who put those snakes in your car the other night," he said. "We have the individual under surveillance. But we're waiting to make an arrest hoping he'll lead us to bigger fish. Maybe McBride."

Holly was shaking her head. Billy Wallace stood.

"The fella who owns this company is a retired police officer. I worked with him when I was on the Memphis P.D. I've already talked to him about your situation. He'll do it for you at just above cost," the sheriff told her. "I can't station a car out at the end of your driveway twenty-four hours a day."

"No one is asking you to," Holly told him.

"Please consider it. If not for you, then for Rose. And maybe even Cutter," the sheriff told her. Their eyes met and they exchanged a knowing look. *There really are no secrets here, only lies we live with*, thought Holly. She blew out a breath, leaned back in her chair and put her hands behind her head. "Shit! It feels like giving in to those bastards."

"That's not giving in," said Billy Wallace. "It's just being smart."

***

The weekend was mercifully quiet and peaceful. Holly spent some time at the newspaper Saturday catching up on paperwork. On Sunday morning she led the singing at the growing prayer meeting, as it was being called, on *The Current-Leader*'s loading dock. Cutter had moved to the day shift at The Gin so that he could be close to Wolf's Run when dark came. Like a busy family, they ate dinner together when time allowed, and sometimes breakfast. As much as Holly and Cutter longed for it, both knew he could not spend the night in her bed on a regular basis. If it became common knowledge, that would be "a lie" many of those who were sticking with the newspaper and pushing back against Weathers and the Klux could not live with. To give them time alone, Rose diplomatically excused herself after dinner and went to read or to work on a song in her room or the library, or watch TV, but by midnight Cutter was back on his rocky perch above the road and Wolf's Run.

On Monday morning, Holly made two calls. The first was to make an appointment with a gynecologist in Tupelo. The second was to the Memphis

Electric Gate Company. Kirkwood Ahern, the owner, said they could have the gate up before the end of the week.

As Holly hung up, her private line rang. It was Dan Freeman, the Tupelo attorney she'd hired to ensure the second autopsy of T.L. Carter took place. District Judge Omar Autrey, who could lift the injunction, had become a very hard man to get in to see, he told her.

"Isn't there another judge you can go to?" asked Holly.

"No. Not unless Autry asks for help with his docket," Freeman told her from a phone outside of District Court in New Albany. "Autrey's the next step of the ladder."

"Is he tied to Weathers?"

"Not on the surface," said Freeman. "But you know Weathers has his hooks in a lot of people in a lot of ways that can't be easily seen."

"I know. Keep trying and keep me informed."

***

A t dusk, three men stepped out of the hidden opening to a cave that sat about a dozen feet above a tributary to the Cattahatchie River. It had been turned into a tunnel by Colonel John Henry Kamp, C.S.A., before the War for Southern Independence, as it still was frequently referred to locally. The tunnel led to basement storage rooms beneath the main plantation house. Over the years, more tunnels had been dug until the sprawling basement was like the hub of a wheel. From 1861 to 1865, it had been used as everything from a Confederate hospital to field headquarters for General Nathan Bedford Forrest, before and after the Battle of Shiloh.

Robert Bedford McBride liked very much the notion of treading the same ground as one of his namesakes. Sleeping in the same small room that was used by the great cavalry general and founder of the Ku Klux Klan. It made him feel even more a part of history. He hoped it would not have to be destroyed. But better that than have the Federals seize the Klavern's armory contained behind a heavy steel door in a side room.

Dressed as a fishermen out for a night on the river, LeRoy Kamp led the men down an almost invisible path to where a sleek, high-powered speedboat and two small fishing skiffs were hidden under an overhang of low branches and camouflage netting. LeRoy knew the foot trail and creeks by heart and in the dark. It was the way he brought in uppers, downers, pot and LSD by the thousands of doses in a compartment hidden under the floor of the speedboat. It was then distributed in various ways, including in derelict cars towed to Moore Bridge, Alabama from time to time.

Tony Carlucci sat in front of one flatboat, next to two 5-gallon cans of gasoline. Kamp got into the other skiff. No hot speed boat tonight. Too showy. He untied the boat from a tree trunk, pulled the starter rope on the small Mercury outdoor and throttled quietly down the creek. McBride sat in the middle. Under the fishing rods and a tarp were three Army-issued M16 combat rifles.

Ten minutes later they were on the main river, drifting slowly south, trolling their lines like the night fishermen they pretended to be. At the entrance to Henderson Creek, Kamp turned the boat east. When they'd gone as far as the shallow creek would allow, he nosed the boat into the bank. It was 10:25. Olin Farber was a farmer when he wasn't acting as chaplain for the Kattahatchie Klavern or preaching to a small, uneducated, fundamentalist flock with a Bible in one hand and a snake in the other. He worked his kids as hard on the land as he did his tractors, and even his wife – a registered nurse in DeLong – would be asleep by now.

"The back of Farber's house and his half-ass church are about a mile over that ridge," said Tony Carlucci. He and Kamp slung the M-16s over their shoulders and each took a gas can. "It's not a hard walk, if you've got two good legs."

McBride looked into Tony Carlucci's round, sweating face. He did not like the man's swarthy skin, his remnant of a Yankee accent, or the fact that he probably was a closet Papist – if he believed in anything at all beyond satisfying his low cravings for liquor and whores. It was important to believe in something. He believed in "The Cause" – segregation then, segregation now, segregation forever – as the Klan referred to it. People had the wrong idea about him. He didn't hate niggers. Like children or dogs, most were pretty docile. But from time to time they needed to be taught lessons. And that was his calling in life. The people he truly hated were whites who encouraged mostly harmless coloreds with uppity ideas about voting and race-mixin'. Even marrying among whites and blacks. The very thought made him shudder.

Without sympathy, McBride said, "You're not gonna grow another good leg standin' on this creek bank." Even in the dark he could see Carlucci's face color, but he didn't care. How could he have any respect for man who could not manage his own family? Control his own children? That boy of his had embarrassed the whole white race of Mississippi with that traitorous speech he'd made on the radio and now he'd gone and organized a mixed-race football team. *Damn!* To top it off, Carlucci's daughter had run off to live with that crippled newspaperwoman. That haughty bitch was a race agitator if there ever was one. But she was going to get hers. They wouldn't even find pieces of her when he was finished.

LeRoy Kamp knelt in the thick woods a hundred yards from the back porch of the Farber farmhouse and the squat cinderblock structure off to the side. Entirely whitewashed – even the roof – the church building practically glowed in the dark. "Are you sure about this?" he asked McBride.

To the right and down the slope of a hill was the barn where Sergeant Charles Rudolph had died from the gunshot wounds delivered by a Eudora, Arkansas police officer. The one Rudolph had killed on his way to joining his revered Uncle Bob. Charles had seemed much better, seemed to be regaining his strength, nearly ready to rejoin him in the fight, thought McBride as he studied the barn. The long fight. For The Cause. Then bam, just like that. His eyes rolled back in his head and he dropped dead while eating oatmeal for breakfast. Probably a blood clot broke loose somewhere near the wound, Mrs. Farber had said. Not that it mattered. Dead is dead.

McBride waited so long to reply that Kamp thought the famous Klan bomber had not heard him. Then, "Am I sure about what?"

"Look, I understand why we have to kill Farber," said Kamp. "Putting those snakes in Holly Carter's car was stupid. It's turned a lot of people against us, but --"

"He's out of control," said McBride. "Your Mr. Handley went to see him Saturday. He told your own Grand Wizard to his face that he no longer answers to the Klan. He says God's voice told him to put snakes on that woman."

Tony had to stifle a smile. It was only God's voice if He talked like a dago from Philly. It has been Tony who came by three times to fire up Farber and egg him on. He wanted Holly Carter dead, but he wanted the cunt to know she was dying, not merely disappear in one of McBride's fireballs. More than that now, Tony wanted his children to see her suffer. Especially Cutter.

"I know, but --"

"Worse than that," continued McBride, "he's talkin' about not carin' if he gets caught. About if that's God's will, then so be it. He means to proclaim the truth and let God be his judge."

"Yeah, but --"

"Mr. Kamp, I've dedicated my life to The Cause. To saving this country for the white race. And because of what I have done here in the last few weeks and will do in the coming days, I probably will spend the rest of this life on the run," he explained without rancor or emotion. "But one thing I will not do is live out my days in a 5-by-8 concrete box because some brain-dead religious zealot gets himself caught by the feds. You spent four years in a cell. I'd think you'd appreciate my position."

"I do!" Kamp told him. "But the whole family?"

"Who knows what he babbles about to them?" asked McBride. "And who knows what my nephew may have revealed in his delirium that some of them heard? I don't want any loose ends and I don't want any witnesses. Do you?"

On a ridge on the opposite side of the Farber property, Deputy John-Thomas Hinton was sitting in his police cruiser. It was just after 10:30 and he'd put down his night-vision binoculars only long enough to pour a cup of strong, black coffee from his thermos. He had another ten hours to go on his 12-hour shift. He hated stakeouts. In fact, there wasn't much he liked anymore about being a deputy. Oh, Sheriff Wallace was a good man, but John-Thomas had just about decided that he wasn't cut out for dealing firsthand with the sort of ugliness he'd seen over the last few weeks. He was thinking more and more about what Dr. Garner had said to him as interim president of the county school board, about taking a teaching job at the high school and coaching the football team.

The popping sound he heard was so distant he nearly didn't pick it out of the low static from his police radio. He turned down the volume and the sound came again in a short burst. John-Thomas tossed his coffee cup out the window and grabbed the big binoculars. The deputy watched as one room of the Farber house after another was lit up as if by a quick series of flash bulbs.

He grabbed the radio mike. "Base, Base! This is Unit Five. Is Sheriff Wallace there? Over."

"Unit Five. Ten-four, but he's catchin' some shut-eye in his office. Over."

"Wake him! Now! Over."

Thirty seconds later, the sheriff was on the radio. "Unit Five, what's happening? Over."

The deputy told him as he held the binoculars to his eyes. Then, "Oh, geez! Sheriff, the house is on fire. The barn, too!"

"All units, respond to a fire distress call at the Olin Farber farm on Henderson Creek Road, one-point-seven miles past Challabete Crossing," the sheriff said into his mike as the dispatcher hit the switch that called out the county volunteer fire department. "But, all units, be aware – there could be armed suspects on site. Approach with extreme caution. Over."

"Sheriff, the whole place is goin' up like dry newspaper. What should I – Oh, geez! Oh, God! – someone just jumped out the second-floor window. They're on fire! I gotta go! I gotta help 'em!"

"Unit Five! John-Thomas! Damn it! Listen to me!" Billy Wallace shouted into the mike. "It could be an ambush. Wait for backup. We're on the way. John-Thomas? … John-Thomas!"

CHAPTER 12

T he headline at the top of Wednesday morning's *Current-Leader* read: Farber Family Killed in Fire ... Mr. and Mrs. Olin Farber and their five children die in Monday night blaze.

There were pictures, shot by Holly from a distance, of the scant and blackened remains of the two-story house, the big barn and the cinderblock structure Olin Farber called a church. Fire had shattered the small windows and burned through the roof of the utilitarian structure, but most of the building remained standing. The story made no direct connection between Farber, "a farmer, self-ordained minister and the leader of a small, ultra-conservative flock in the Challabete area," and the attack on the newspaper's editor; but it did note that "law enforcement officials and firemen encountered an inordinate number of poisonous snakes on the property during their investigation. ... The cause of the fire remains under investigation."

By Saturday, the Labor Day weekend edition of *The Current- Leader* was filled with stories about Tuesday's opening of schools – Cattahatchie High and Riverview Academy. Governor Weathers would cut the ribbon for Riverview at 7:30 a.m. Across town, the Klan was calling on "all right-minded white citizens to line the streets of DeLong in protest of the illegal usurpation of our public school system by the federal courts." Speeches were planned all morning on the town square.

Also in the paper that weekend was a follow-up to the fire story, saying that arson was suspected, but little else. Several family members expressed frustration in the story that the bodies had not been released for burial. When questioned about it, County Medical Examiner Dr. G.P. Garner sent a written statement to the newspaper saying that the "press of doing medicine for the living" had caused the autopsies to be delayed. He promised the bodies would be released by Monday.

Leading the sports page was the news that John-Thomas Hinton, a three-year starter for the Wolves from '61-'63, had resigned from the sheriff's department to become football coach at Cattahatchie High. He'd also would be teaching civics and American history, replacing Nancy Magee who had been named assistant principal.

By Sunday night, Holly, Cutter and Rose had slipped into a comfortable routine. Really, they had miraculously and without intentionality created a new family from the broken shards of two.

On the nights when *The Current-Leader* was in production, Cutter brought supper from the Cotton Café – ostensibly for his sister, but there was always enough for Holly. They ate together and read page proofs. The act fooled no one at the paper, but many of Holly's remaining employees had become fiercely loyal and they said nothing. Then Cutter followed Holly and Rose on their short, in-town delivery route and on to Wolf's Run – the .45 on the passenger seat, his shotgun ready on its rack. On other nights he drove out Blue Mountain Road after football practice and winched his Jeep up the narrow, disused logging path to the outcrop above the gravel lane then walked back, hopped the fence and went down the long slope of the yard past the pecan tree where Charlie was buried. The three of them ate dinner together then went their ways. Rose was fascinated by television, which she'd seen only occasionally during her first 17 years. There had never been a set at the Old Ambrose Place, and the only one at Wolf's Run was in the library, so Holly and Cutter mostly spent time together in the kitchen, on the chaise lounge by the pool, the front porch swing or in her bedroom. She often played her guitar while Cutter, a fast and rapacious reader, settled into something he'd borrowed from the shelves in the west wing. Their passion for each other had not cooled, but their actual sex life had, by necessity. They had to be careful. No gynecologist in Tupelo or Memphis wanted to see Holly for the purposes of prescribing birth control or insertion of an IUD. They weren't familiar enough with young women with spinal cord injuries to feel comfortable with the risk, they all said, and suggested seeing someone at a top-flight teaching hospital such as Vanderbilt in Nashville or Emory in Atlanta. Or maybe the Ochsner Clinic in New Orleans. Of course, that did not preclude love-making to a point or with the use of a condom, but neither enjoyed the final act as they did when the full length of him was rigid and thick and bare in the warm depths of her. Still, a journey to Nashville or elsewhere would have to wait. Holly had neither the time nor money for such a trip. *The Current-Leader* was barely scraping by. Making payroll every two weeks had become a dicey thing without scouring away ever larger sums of the cash she'd gotten for the sale of her home in California.

That Sunday night, however, Rose was watching *Bonanza* on TV while Holly and Cutter played one cut-throat game of eight-ball after another. "That's four out of seven," said Cutter, a devilish smirk twisting his smile.

"Rack 'em again," Holly told him, her competitive streak on full display, when they all jumped at the sound of the buzzer for the new electric gate. The crew from Memphis had finished the installation on Thursday. Holly had one speaker placed in the library, one in the kitchen and one on the patio, but this was their first visitor. They certainly weren't expecting company at 8:45 in the evening.

Holly wheeled to the box on a side credenza and pressed the button. "Yes?"

"Miss Carter, this is Sheriff Wallace. Glad to see you did this," the voice said over the intercom. "Can I have a few minutes of your time?"

"Of course," she said and buzzed him in through the metal gate.

Cutter and Holly greeted the sheriff on the front porch. The men nodded respectfully to each other.

"Have you had dinner?" asked Holly. "We grilled pork chops. Would you like one?"

"I've eaten. Thank you."

"Come inside, then."

He glanced at his watch. It was almost nine. "I'd be pleased to but I don't have much time, and this isn't a social call. I'm glad to see you're both here. Cutter, this saves me trackin' you down," he said, turning his hat in his hand. "I wanted to let you two in on a couple of things before you found out on your own. Understanding that this is strictly between us until it all goes down."

Cutter propped against a porch post. "All right, Sheriff. We're listening."

My father stopped turning his hat. "I like to consider myself a fairly honest man, so I'm loathe to lie to people I respect," he said, looking at Cutter then Holly. "But in this case, I suppose I have to use the greater good argument.

"There were two survivors of the attack at the Farber farm. The 16-year-old daughter, Ruth, and her youngest sister, Naomi. She's four. That night we – that is to say me and Deputy Hinton with the help of a couple of FBI men – spirited them off to a Memphis hospital. We've had them under guard there, under fictitious names ever since," the sheriff began, and spent the next several minutes explaining the events of early Tuesday morning. "The little girl has a broken arm and some minor burns, but she's still scared out of her wits and hasn't said a word since that night. The older girl was shot in the shoulder and another slug grazed her head, knocking her unconscious for several minutes. The shooters left her for dead. By the time she roused and found her little sister hiding in a closet, they had to jump out a second floor window. Ruth's nightgown was on fire. Some of the burns are pretty bad, but she's conscious and talking."

"How much she been able to tell you?" asked Holly.

"Ohhh, quite a lot. It's the break we've been waiting for, been needing, sad as it is to come by it this way," Billy Wallace told them. "She says there were three or four men in the house that night. She can't name them all, but she can absolutely identify her shooter. He was one of two men who came to take the body away when McBride's nephew – the AWOL Army sergeant, Charles Rudolph – died out in their barn. Mrs. Farber was an R.N., as you know. She had been taking care of his gunshot wounds."

"Okay, so don't keep us in suspense," nudged Holly. "Who was it?"

Cutter braced for the possibility it was his father, but the sheriff said, "LeRoy Kamp."

Holly and Cutter looked at each other, and she saw a small relief in his eyes.

"Even more important," the sheriff went on, "Ruth told us where to find her father's diary."

"It didn't burn up in the house?" asked Cutter.

"No, he kept it in a metal strongbox in a hole crawlin' with snakes in the concrete floor of that cinderblock building. He called it the 'Book of Olin' and it's all laid out in chapter and verse like the Bible. Well, the Bible if Satan wrote it. Farber has been keeping it for more than twenty years. Aside from his own lunatic ramblings about religion and the end times, it's a history of the Kattahatchie Klavern going back even before World War II. His father was neck deep in it. His grandfather, too."

Holly and Cutter were speechless for a moment. Both understood how important this could be in breaking the back of the local Klan and maybe beyond.

"Does Farber name names?" asked Holly.

"Oh, yes, in many cases," said Billy Wallace. "Like the biblical Book of Numbers, there's practically org chart. Others have only coded references, like 'The Benefactor.' Pretty obvious who he's referring to — Weathers, of course — but he's never actually named."

"Damn," said Holly.

"I will tell you this — Farber makes no mention of your father's death in his book, diary, whatever we're gonna call it. So, it probably was not Klan related. Or at least not something ordered by the Klan hierarchy. But we may be able to use these charges to squeeze information out of Leroy Kamp and others."

"Thank you, Sheriff. I appreciate you letting me know."

"Here's the other part," Billy Wallace went on. "Starting about one a.m. me and three deputies I trust, the FBI and U.S. marshals will be serving 11 arrest warrants for the leaders of the Kattahachie Klavern and another seven search warrants that we hope will give us McBride. Or at least flush him out."

Holly thought about Tuesday's start of schools. "I have a feeling the timing of this is not coincidental."

"Well, here's how it is," said the sheriff. "All the men listed in the warrants will face various state charges up to and including murder, but they're also being charged with violations of the Civil Rights Act. That makes it a federal matter and puts them in the hands of Mr. Burke and Judge Mulberry. They'll be transported immediately to the federal lockup in Memphis. By the time anyone even figures out where they are, lawyers get involved and bail hearings get scheduled, it'll be the middle of or late this week. Maybe even early the week after if Burke and Mulberry can drag it out long enough."

"In the meantime," said Holly, "school gets started with the Klan leadership behind bars and out of the way. Well done, Sheriff."

"It's yet to be seen how well done it is. There's a lot that could go wrong. In any case, it wasn't all my idea. But, yes, we're hoping that without their leaders, the rank-and-file Klansmen'll be like — like chickens with their pointy heads cut off when the school buses roll Tuesday morning," said Billy Wallace, allowing himself a quick smile. "We'll see."

"Good plan," said Cutter, then – "I'm guessing Tony's name is in Farber's book. He's probably got a whole chapter."

Sheriff Wallace turned his Panama in his big hands. "Not quite," he said. "But it's prominent. That's the other reason I came out. I wanted you to hear it from me. And so maybe you could prepare Miss Rose a bit. Along with Gary and Claude Knowles from out Dumas way and Frank Gandy from Ashland, Tony will be charged with the capital murder of Ridge Bellafont and with the attempted murder of Eve Howard."

All relief disappeared from Cutter's face as his jaw tightened and he swallowed dryly. Remembering the cat-o-nine he'd seen swinging from the Sam Brown rig Tony wore over his black Klan robes, Cutter had sensed this coming, feared this coming since word got out that Mr. Ridge had been whipped to death. But he had refused to acknowledge it to anyone. Not to Rose. Not even to himself, not fully. Now he swayed on his feet as if suddenly assaulted by a blast of cold wind. As much as Holly despised Tony Carlucci, her heart ached for Cutter. And for Rose.

After a moment, Cutter steadied himself and said, "All right. Thank you, Sheriff. I appreciate you lettin' us know ahead of time."

Holly and Cutter watched the sheriff's cruiser head up the long driveway, the brake lights glowing, the car pausing as it ran over the buried cable. The sheriff waited as the gate swung open, then he drove through. Holly moved next to Cutter and took his hand.

"I'm sorry, for your sake," she said. "And Rose's."

Cutter squeezed her hand but didn't answer immediately. After a moment, he said, "Don't be. I hope they catch him and fry his sorry ass. For Mr. Ridge, and God only knows what else. For all he did to Rose and to my mother. Good riddance." He slapped the porch post hard and gripped it with his long, powerful fingers. "It's just that – that the thought that Tony's blood flows through me makes me want to tear off my own skin!"

Cutter gently tried to pull his hand away, but Holly held on, held on tight until he relented. She already had considered the ugly and immense irony that if she and Cutter ever had a child, the baby would be Tony's grandchild. The blood of the man who tried to rape her, almost surely raped his daughter, had terrorized his wife into an insane asylum and now had killed the sweet, gentle man had been her mentor would be passed through Cutter, through her body and into that baby. She knew what Cutter meant about wanting to tear off his skin, but she said, "You've got Miss Jenny's blood, too. Kind. Gentle. Smart. Artistic. Her beautiful, beautiful quilts. All of that. That's the part I see in you. And in Rose."

All That The River Holds

"You are *nothing* like your father," she told him, her voice strong and steady and insistent. "If you were, you and I certainly would not be sharing a bed."

"When we can," he said, then gratefully squeezed Holly's hand as he straightened. "I guess I better get to it. Hard to know how Rose'll take this deep down. Sorry as Tony is, a person's still only got one daddy."

"Do you want me to be with you?" asked Holly. "I will."

"No. I think I best do this alone. But then I've got to get on up to the camp. I've got to be up at first light. We've got the last of two-a-day practices tomorrow," he said releasing Holly's hand. "But if she needs to talk it out later –"

"I'll make sure she knows my door is open."

355

CHAPTER 13

I n the parking lot behind the North County Farmers' Cooperative building on the Kossuth Road, my father was standing over a diagram of the old Kamp Plantation property. He, three his deputies, and four FBI agents were studying it in the glow of their flashlights. Off to one side were the members of an Army demolitions team that had choppered in from Fort Polk, Louisiana.

The Book of Olin described the Kamp place as the "alter and arsonul for the knights of the Empire." This part of the sweep Billy Wallace would handle himself. The FBI didn't like it, but the sheriff had the blessing of the U.S. Attorney.

"LeRoy Kamp's house is here but there's no direct access from the road. We have to go down this dirt road here, then into his yard. The ruins of the old main house are back here, two hundred yards or so, against this hill," my father was pointing out. "There are several outbuildings down through here. A barn and an old gin. A tractor shed. A sizable creek runs behind the whole place. Deep enough to float a boat most of the year.

"According to Farber's diary, they've been using that creek and the tunnels that run all under this place for years to bring in illegal weapons, ammo and explosives. So, our goal is to go in hard and fast, take the small house here and LeRoy, then bring in the Army team.

"If LeRoy gets down into those tunnels, my guess is he'll pop out back here on this creek somewhere. I flew over the area yesterday with Jack Yancy in his crop duster. I didn't see a boat. Still, I'd bet there's one there. That's why I want you two on this bridge," he said to deputies Ingram and Cauthon. "LeRoy has to pass under it to get to the river. Now, I want him alive, if possible. So, don't go blastin' away at the boat if you don't have to. String you a line or two of that half-inch cable across the creek to stop a boat if it comes through."

"Question, Sheriff," said one of the FBI agents. "There's only one road in. It's going to be awfully difficult to get close without being heard or seen. Don't you think it would be smarter to work our way up through these woods and take him by surprise? It looks like only a quarter mile, maybe, from the road here to the house."

"Well, Agent, uh –?"

"Martin."

"Agent Martin, from what we've learned, Robert Bedford McBride has been around this place, on and off, for more than a month. With time on his hands and plenty of supplies, there's no telling what's in those woods. Trip wires? Homemade land mines? Bouncing Betties? If you'd care to lead the way, I'll be happy to follow – at a distance."

Everyone laughed except the young FBI agent.

LeRoy Kamp was asleep – that is to say, passed out – in his bedroom when the roar of car tires coming hard over gravel jarred him from his stupor. He rolled over, snatched the M-16 from beneath his bed and flipped the safety off as he ran to the living room. Through the bay window he saw two sheriff's cars sliding to a halt in the front yard, their lights flashing. He glanced over his shoulder and saw more out back.

Even though LeRoy had been in the Army, he'd never seen combat. Everything was happening so fast. He had to – to? – set the timer! The timer!

When Kamp started to swing around toward the kitchen his nervous hand clamped on the trigger of the automatic rifle. Before he was even conscious of it he was spraying 5.56 millimeter slugs through the front window and door. He stared at his hand and the gun jumping as if they both belonged to someone else. In the next instant the small house was alive with the rip of bullets and the buzz and tear of shotgun pellets. Dozens of holes opening up filled with flashing light the color of blood. The sudden pain in his leg snapped him from his half-dream and the jolt of his shoulder blades slamming onto the floor nearly knocked the breath out of him but he groaned and managed to roll over. He lay there trying to dig his fingers into the linoleum in desperation.

After a few moments the sheriff yelled, "Cease fire! Cease fire!"

As suddenly as the shooting had started, it stopped and things were terribly quiet. Everyone's ears were ringing and the rank scent of cordite and the sweetness of night-blooming jasmine mixed into a noxious brew in the hot still air. LeRoy started crawling, broken glass gnawing at his hands and knees. Outside, he heard the sound of fresh rounds being chambered.

"LeRoy!" a voice called. "This is Billy Wallace. There's no way out. No place to run. If you give it up, I promise no one will hurt you."

Keeping low, LeRoy reached onto the kitchen counter for a simple egg timer. He and McBride had timed it. Two minutes was enough to get through the trapdoor in the hall closet and through the tunnel to the main basement and down the side tunnel to the boat. Plenty on a dead run. But the pain in LeRoy's leg was awful. In the flash of the red lights he could see a large hole ripped in his thigh and something that looked like black paint oozing from it.

"I cain't do that, Sheriff," he called back. "No surrender!"

"LeRoy, don't be a fool. Don't make us fight our way in there."

Kamp was sweating more than he ever had in his life. His shirt was soaked and he was disgusted by his own rank odor. Two minutes? Two minutes was enough on two good legs, running hard. But now? LeRoy wiped the heavy sheen of sweat from his face. No. He'd need four – no five.

"If you try to bust through that front door, this whole place is gonna go up like an atom bomb," LeRoy yelled, lied. "Bob McBride does good work."

"If we go up, so do you."

"I'm ready to die for The Cause," LeRoy lied as he twisted the timer and scuttled as quickly as he could toward the closet, his leg on fire. He pulled open the trap door and headed down the steps, firing one final blast from the M-16 as he descended. Falling the final few steps, LeRoy landed on his back, but got to his feet and began limping down the dimly lit tunnel, hearing the muffled sound of gunfire above and behind him.

A fter a fusillade of return fire, silence descended again. The sheriff sat against the front wheel of his cruiser and pushed eight more rounds into the shotgun. Agent Martin asked, "What do you want to do? Do you think the place is really wired?"

"I don't know, but I'm not eager to kick the door and find out," he said. "Let's ease up close and see if we can't slip in through that bay window." Motioning to the men behind the other car, he said, "Cover us."

The sheriff and Agent Martin quickly worked their way up to the shattered front window. The exchange of gunfire had exploded all the glass and most of the woodwork.

For a few moments they listened as the seconds ticked silently away on the timer. …3:39 … 3:38 … 3:37 …

"I don't hear anything," said Agent Martin. "Do you think he got down in the tunnels?"

"Maybe. I'm gonna try to ease in. Keep your eyes on that hall."

My father stepped inside, onto the crunch of broken glass. He could feel his hand sweating on the shotgun's slide. He secured a position behind a large recliner and told Agent Martin, "Come on in."

Once both men were inside and had cover, the sheriff flipped on the light switch behind him. Lamps were smashed but one or two ceiling lights were intact. The room lit up and they could see the blood trail leading to the hall closet. The sheriff motioned the other team inside and they quickly went from room to room, securing the scene before snatching open the closet door. The blood trail stopped at the big trap door.

Agent Martin reached for the handle. "No!" said the sheriff. "Let's wait until the demolitions boys can check this whole area."

"But Sheriff, he's a suspect in three murders –"

"I know what he is. I also know who he is and that he's wounded," said Billy

Wallace. "LeRoy'll turn up. I'm more interested in preserving the evidence than catching him right now."

"It's your show," snapped Martin, "as per the U.S. Attorney. But I have orders to call Mr. Burke and give him a full report on what went down here."

"Go ahead, if the phone is still workin'. But don't mess up any fingerprints."

The FBI agent gave Billy Wallace an arrogant smirk and walked off toward the kitchen.

"I'll radio for the demolitions team," said Deputy Jackson.

After a moment, Billy Wallace strolled into the kitchen, careful to step over the large splotches of blood on the linoleum floor. The smell of liquor was all in the house and he badly wanted a drink – a stiff one that would dull his senses. Instead, he looked in the refrigerator and saw a plate of cornbread and a bottle of milk. He took both out as the young FBI agent donned gloves and picked up the phone from the wall cradle. He began his report to J.L. Burke. It wasn't very flattering, emphasizing that LeRoy Kamp had escaped. The agent stared, incredulous as the sheriff leaned against the sink eating a wedge of cornbread. As he lowered the milk carton from his lips, he saw the egg timer behind the agent, counting down under a minute. Way under a minute!

Billy Wallace put down the milk and pushed aside the startled agent. "Hey! What are you doing?"

The sheriff took a quick look behind the timer then pulled his pocket knife from his trousers. He fingered out a rounded blade and turned the timer over in his hand. Quickly but without rushing, he unscrewed the two electrical leads from the back. He slowly let out a breath then laid the wires on the counter and used his knife to cut off the frayed ends so that they could not make contact.

As the stunned agent held the phone in one hand, my father slapped the timer into the other. "You can thank me later," said Billy Wallace.

The agent looked at it. There were seven seconds left.

Agent Martin stared silently at the device, his mouth slightly agape as J.L. Burke hung on the other end of the line. In that instant they all heard a blast in the distance, in the direction of the creek behind the old plantation house. Out the back window they saw a fireball roiling up into the night sky.

CHAPTER 14

Had the stakes not been so high, it would have been comical to see robed Klansmen marching on the town square carrying signs complaining that the civil rights of their leaders were being violated. Their civil rights? But as Holly watched from her office, that's what she saw early Tuesday morning – the first day of school, 1969. Mercifully, the Klux were outnumbered by reporters and FBI agents. Down on the highway, almost no one turned out to harass black youngsters and poor whites as the buses turned onto the road up to Cattahatchie High School. It was soon obvious that a larger-than-expected group of white students had stuck with the school. Much of it thanks to Cutter and the football program.

Even out in the most rural parts of the county, the buses rolled with only minor incidents here and there – rocks or eggs being thrown, trees cut down on a couple of roads to block the buses. Of course, the fact that each bus traveling the country roads had some sort of law enforcement escort was part of it. That couldn't go on forever, but it would continue for at least the first two weeks of school, the newspaper told us.

The strategy that my father and J.L. Burke put together, and that Judge Mulberry quietly approved, worked almost to a T. With the major leaders of the local Klavern either hauled away to the federal stockade or in hiding, members of the Klan's rank-and-file were confused and frightened. Most hunkered down and stayed out of sight, hoping FBI agents or sheriff's deputies didn't come to their door next with a warrant to search or arrest.

For the most part, "The Sunday Night Massacre," as Klansmen were calling it, was bloodless. The only fatality was LeRoy Kamp. He made it to his hidden speedboat, fired it up and raced toward the river. He saw the two sheriff's cars sitting on the bridge, red lights flashing, but instead of easing back on the throttle, he stood tall at the controls and slammed the throttle to the max – which gave him no time to react to the cables strung across the creek, if he ever saw them. Tied off two large, deep-rooted trees on either side of the creek, the bottom cable cut through the boat's fiberglass hull like a bandsaw and the upper strand sliced through LeRoy's neck like a scythe. In the scream of tearing fiberglass a severed fuel line found a spark and the deputies dove for cover. Later they would say they saw LeRoy's head spinning in mid-air, "like a flipped coin," before it splashed into the creek. It had not been recovered.

The only other injury was to an FBI agent named Martin, who got too eager to explore a barn on the Kamp property before it was thoroughly checked by the Army demolitions team. He hung his foot on a trip wire and the place went up. Fortunately, his injuries were minor.

E ven though three of its board members were in the federal stockade in Memphis dressed in prison uniforms, Riverview Academy opened Tuesday morning as planned, but with a much smaller turnout than anticipated. Cecil Weathers drove up in his pristine white pickup followed by J.D. Benoit in an unmarked state police car. After Brother MacAllister gave the invocation to open the first-day celebration for Riverview, Weathers led the ribbon-cutting ceremony but due to another sudden family illness the current governor did not attend. Apparently the Brodericks were a sickly lot. Weathers grinned fixedly for the reporters and photographers who had swooped back in from as far away as Atlanta as the FBI raids and arrests added a new chapter to our small town melodrama. In the early sunlight Weathers already was sweating so copiously in his cheap man-of-the-people suit, that I almost felt sorry for him, but then he took the mike and launched into a speech so vicious and venomous that even some mommas and daddies who were true-blue believers in segregation now and forever were taken aback.

* * *

A t a few minutes after seven Tuesday night, Sheriff Wallace entered *The Current-Leader* building through the loading dock and went upstairs to Holly's office. She, Cutter and Rose were eating fried chicken at the conference table.

"You're just in time," said Holly. "Won't you join us? Or is this not a social call, either?"

"It's not, but if you've got enough I'll join you anyway," said my father and pulled up a chair. "I haven't had a chance to eat today."

"How was school?" the sheriff asked.

"Tense," Cutter told him. "I asked guys on the team to step in if they saw anything starting. There was some pushin' and shovin' here and there, but nothing serious that I heard about."

"Good."

"Did all the afternoon bus routes go all right?" asked Holly.

"Yes. Thankfully."

"Sheriff, what you and Mr. Burke cooked up, it was brilliant," she said, "and it probably saved many injuries and maybe even some lives. This county owes you a huge debt of gratitude, and I'm saying so in tomorrow's editorial."

Billy Wallace finished a crispy thigh and wiped his mouth with a paper napkin. "Well, that's kind of you, but we're not out of the woods yet," he told her, scooping some mashed potatoes onto a paper plate. He picked up a plastic fork. "We missed three of our main targets."

Rose was following the conversation with her large brown eyes but said nothing. "McBride, Gandy and Tony," said Cutter, who'd already heard talk around town.

"Maybe they're on the run," said Holly, more for Rose's sake than because she really believed it.

"Maybe," said the sheriff. "Anyway, that's not why I came by."

"Then –?"

"When we searched the Kamp property, we found something – interesting, let's say, for lack of a better understanding of what it means," the sheriff told them. "We found a 1968 Ford station wagon. When we ran the plates, it came back to a set stolen at a grocery parking lot in Holly Springs. But when we ran the VIN number the car it came back to your brother."

Holly and Cutter looked at each other.

"Does the right front fender have damage?" asked Cutter.

"Yes. Just like Mr. Cole described."

"I knew it!" said Holly. "What about fingerprints or blood?"

"I'm afraid that's the bad news," the sheriff told them. "You probably heard about an FBI boy settin' off one of McBride's booby traps and burning down a barn out there." Holly, Cutter and Rose looked at him. "The car was in it. So anything like that is gone." Holly groaned and slumped back in her chair. "The FBI techs are still going through things, starting with LeRoy's house, the basement and tunnels, and then working their way out as the Army demolitions guys clear the way. Maybe they'll turn up something else when they fully process the wagon."

Holly pushed back from the table, staring at the pictures on the table behind what had been T.L. Carter's desk. Most were of Tom, Mary Nell and the grandchildren in some combination. The more certain she became that Mary Nell, at least, was involved in her father's death, the more she wished it was not so.

"There's one more thing," said the sheriff. "We only found a few sets of fingerprints in LeRoy's house. Apparently he didn't have a lot of friends."

"Were McBride's among them?" asked Cutter.

"Off the record, yes. But as it relates to our discussion, the techs found several sets of fingerprints that probably belong to a small-framed female because of the size and shape," Billy Wallace told them. "Including on the laminated wooden slats in the headboard of LeRoy's bed."

There was a pause, and everyone got the picture.

"And you're suggesting Mary Nell and LeRoy were lovers?" asked Holly. "I can't see it."

Billy Wallace cocked his head to one side. "Wife, mom, Sunday school teacher gets bored with the PTA and running Daughters of the Confederacy bake sales? Mary Nell wouldn't be the first woman like that to go for a walk on the wild side."

"All right, Sheriff, assumin' that's true, it still doesn't explain why they would kill Mr. Carter," Cutter pointed out.

"Could be plain old greed," he said. "If Mary Nell thought Tom stood to inherit. Maybe she promised LeRoy –"

"Wait a minute. We're getting ahead of ourselves," Holly interrupted. "Can any of the fingerprints in the house be matched to Mary Nell?"

"As far as we can tell, Mary Nell has never been fingerprinted. And we don't have enough for a judge to compel her to give them to us. Especially in this county," the sheriff explained. "Speaking of judges, what's happening with that exhumation order? I'm sorry, I've lost track."

"You've been a little busy. I understand," said Holly. "Judge Autry finally ruled for us on the law last Wednesday, but stayed his order until Tom and Mary Nell could take it to the State Court of Appeal. They could rule any time. I just hate thinking of Daddy up there in that damn meat locker at the hospital all this time."

Billy Wallace wiped his mouth and said, "I've never been much of a church-goer, but I've read my Bible and I do believe in the words in written red. According to them, T.L. Carter's done gone on. All that's up there at the hospital now is, evidence. Or possible evidence. Just keep your mind tight on that."

***

And that is what Holly Lee Carter did. On Thursday morning her determination paid off when the private line on her desk rang. It was her Tupelo lawyer telling her the Mississippi Court of Appeal had ruled in her favor.

"Hallelujah!" said Holly, pulling off her reading glasses and tossing them onto the desk.

"But I'm sure Haughton Wellingham is scrambling to find one of three Supreme Court justices Weathers has in his hip pocket," said Dan Freeman. "Unless you want another delay and maybe have to take this thing to federal court, I'd get that autopsy done as soon as possible."

"Of course," she said and called Gerry Garner as soon as she hung up.

"Great!" said Dr. Garner when he was told. "It looks like the stars may be finally lining up for us. Steve Andrews is only forty miles away, right over in Alcorn County doing a consult. We had dinner in Corinth last night. I'll call now and see if he can get over here this afternoon or tonight."

***

Late Thursday afternoon while Cutter still was at football practice, Holly and Rose sat outside of the morgue at DeLong Memorial Hospital. Holly had copies of several stories in her lap that she had brought from the office to edit, to keep her mind occupied while she waited. The sheriff and one of his new deputies came in through the emergency room doors and spotted the pair down the hall. He stopped across from them. "How're you doin'?" he asked gently.

"I'm okay," she said, rubbing the bridge of her nose. "Part of me wants Dr. Andrews to find evidence of a murder. Another part wants him to come out here and say, 'Miss Carter, this was a big waste of time.' The thing is, if Mary Nell is involved, I don't see how she could have covered it up without Tom knowing. Or at least suspecting. I'd hate for –"

"There she is! There's that woman!" Mary Nell Carter yelled as she strode toward Holly from the main hall, her 4-inch heels pinging off the tile floor like two tack hammers. Her attorney, Senator Haughton Wellingham, was on her heels and Tom was trundling unsteadily in their wake. "This is all your doing," she hissed, suddenly bending down and grabbing the frame of Holly's chair. She shook it and tried to tilt it.

Billy Wallace grabbed Mary Nell around the waist and lifted her off her feet with no more effort than he'd need for a rag doll. She flailed her arms as he put her down, keeping himself between her and Holly.

"How dare you lay hands on me!" yelled Mary Nell. "You fuckin' worthless drunk!"

"Mary Nell, you need to calm yourself," said the senator, speaking as her attorney. Doctors, nurses, patients and aides were peeking around corners and out of examining rooms. "You're causing a scene."

"You think I care what these hillbillies think?" spat the one-time Delta debutante. "Don't talk to me like I'm a child! Do your job. Have them stop this, this – this desecration. Now!"

Senator Wellingham pulled a document from the jacket of his tailored seersucker suit. "Sheriff, I have a stay here issued by State Supreme Court Justice Miller, ordering you and Dr. Garner and Dr. Andrews to cease and desist from any autopsy procedure until plaintiff's position can be heard by the full body of the State Supreme Court."

Sheriff Wallace held out his hand. "Let me see that," he said. He flipped the three-page order. "Dadgum, it's hell to get old. I can't read this worth a nickle without my glasses." He turned to the young deputy. "Pete, go out to my cruiser and find my glasses, please. You may have to look hard. I'm all the time losing the things. Could be under the seats, in the glove box, trunk, anywhere."

"Yes, Sheriff," said Pete Barkley. "I –"

"Now, Pete, this is important. I don't care if it takes you an hour, don't you come back in here without those glasses," the sheriff told him. "I want you to search that whole cruiser. The trunk. Everywhere."

"Yes, sir, Sheriff," said Deputy Barkley, a twinkle of understanding in his eye. "I sure will."

"Damn it, Billy, you think I don't know what you're pullin'," said Wellingham.

The sheriff shrugged elaborately. "I have no idea what you mean, Senator. I can't enforce a court order I can't read. So just hold your horses."

As the legal back and forth continued Holly looked sadly at her brother. He leaned heavily on the counter of a nearby nurses' station and seemed to be trying to form a feeble smile, but couldn't manage it. Holly could see that Tom had lost a tremendous amount of weight – maybe 25 or 30 pounds – as if he'd been on a liquid diet of sour mash and barley malt. So much so that his skin had a jaundiced cast. His tie was askew and his disheveled suit hung on him. His eyes were sunken under his prominent brow, yet red and swollen. His shoulders sagged and sweat rings wrapped from under the arms of his cream-colored linen jacket. No matter what he'd done, Tom still was her brother, and seeing him looking so brittle and broken made Holly want to cry and curse and pray, all at the same time.

Mary Nell stomped one high-heeled foot. "Don't just stand there," she told her attorney through gritted teeth. "Make them stop!"

"I'm sure that Sheriff Wallace will –"

In one sudden movement, Mary Nell stepped around the sheriff, her manicured nails balled into the palm of her small fist, and swung her arm at her sister-in-law's face. Focused on Tom, Holly didn't see the blow coming until the last instant. She tried to turn away but Mary Nell's small knuckles caught her on the cheek, just under her left eye. Holly reached for her face more shocked than hurt. Before anyone else could react Rose, who was six inches taller and twenty-five pounds heavier than Mary Nell, stood and grabbed the woman's blond bouffant and flung her across the hall. Mary Nell smacked against the wall without one of her high heels.

"That's it!" barked Billy Wallace with more relish than anyone else understood at that moment. He spun Mary Nell around and grabbed one small wrist as he jerked a set of handcuffs from his belt and began to ratchet them on. Mary Nell began to wriggle and try to kick.

"What are you doing, you redneck idiot? Get your hands off me!" she was yelling. "I'm the victim here! I'm the victim!"

Rose and Haughton Wellingham were squatting in front of Holly's wheelchair.

"Are you all right, Miss Carter?" the senator asked with real solicitude.

"H-H-Holly --?"

"I, I'm okay. I think. She just surprised me. I had no idea she could move that fast in those heels," said Holly, managing a wan smile.

Visitors, staff members and any patient who could make it into the hall now were ogling the scene, the ugly family drama with unabashed eyes, frozen in place.

"Mary Nell Carter, you are under arrest for assault," Sheriff Wallace was saying. "You will be fingerprinted and booked into the Cattahatchie County jail until such time as you can make bail."

"Don't be absurd!" Mary Nell told him, her face pressed to the wall. "That little bitch! That dago cow! She assaulted me! She's crazy! Just like her momma. Just like all those Carluccis. They all ought to be the locked up at Whitfield!"

Haughton Wellingham stood quickly and turned on his hand-tooled wingtips. "For your own good, Mary Nell, shut up," he told her.

A nurse now was kneeling in front of Holly, examining her cheek. Seeing she was getting no support from anyone, not even her attorney, Mary Nell finally settled her tearing eyes on her husband. "Ohhh, Tom," she gasped, her voice a plea. "They're hurting me. Help me. Tom, darling, please help me."

With great effort, it seemed, Thomas Lanier Carter IV pushed himself away from the nurses' station and toward his wife, his gate unsteady. When he got close, Holly smelled beer and nicotine, and maybe urine.

"Billy, let her go. Please," Tom managed, his voice an exhausted rasp. "She's not well."

"Tom, don't step into this," the sheriff told him. "I don't want to have to arrest you, too."

Haughton Wellingham stepped in front of Tom and gently but firmly put his hands on both shoulders. "Billy won't hurt her. You know that," the attorney told him. "There's nothing you can do for her right now."

Holly's heart ached seeing her brother's once handsome face so gaunt, his eyes so distorted and staring imploringly into the face of his perfectly groomed attorney. "You don't understand, Haughton," he said, his voice a pathetic plea. "She's my wife."

"I do understand, Tom. I do," Wellingham assured. "We'll go straight from here to Judge Autrey and get her bailed out."

CHAPTER 15

Holly barely slept Thursday night. During the long dark hours from midnight until dawn she'd wished a hundred times that Cutter was sleeping next to her. Being in his arms was like being in the cleft of a mountain. He was so solid. Not just physically, but in his head, his reactions to things. His intuitive filling of her needs, in and out of bed.

By the time Cutter had walked through the kitchen door that previous night he'd already heard through the clothesline telegraph about what happened at the hospital. At least the high – or was it low? – points. She was sitting at the table with a tall glass of white wine mostly consumed and an icepack pressed to the left side of her face. He crossed to the table and sat in the chair to Holly's left. He touched the hand holding the icepack – "Let me see."

There was definite purpling along her cheek and under her eye. "Whooo-wee," he sighed with a small smile creasing his lips, trying to ease the situation. "You definitely have the makings of a decent shiner. I hope you kicked Mary Nell's ass."

Holly laughed in spite of herself. "No, she was too quick for wheelchair girl. It was one and done. Except for Billy Wallace hauling her off in handcuffs."

"I sure hate I missed that," he said, smiling. "Are you all right?"

Holly put her elbows on the table and rested her forehead in her hands, massaging her temples with her thumbs. "I don't know. I mean, physically? Yes," she told him. "I've just been sitting here wondering how did my family get to this point? You should have seen us. It was like some sordid thing out of a hillbilly circus act."

"Every family has a story, and a lot of them aren't pretty when you tear the cover off," said Cutter. "That's what's happened with all this integration stuff. It's torn the cover off a lot this county's been hidin' and denyin' since before me and you were ever born. You want more wine?"

Holly looked at her glass as Cutter crossed to the refrigerator. "Sure. Why not?" she said. "How'd you get so wise so young?"

He brought the cold bottle of chardonnay and poured Holly's glass half full and sat down with a Miller long neck in front him. "Talk about ugly family stories," he groaned. "I had to get wise – or smart or savvy, or whatever you want to call it – or let Tony kill me. What about the autopsy?"

"With all that was happening with Mary Nell, that got a little lost in the shuffle," she said. "Well, not really. Doctor Garner came out of the autopsy room after the fracas was all over and found me with an icepack on my cheek and – long story short, Doctor Andrews wanted time this evening to write up the report and talk to Sheriff Wallace again before telling us. I have a meeting with them at eleven o'clock at the jail. The good news is, we now have Mary Nell's fingerprints to compare to the ones on LeRoy's headboard."

Cutter lifted his bottle in a small toast and Holly did the same with her wine glass.

"So maybe it'll be worth a shiner."

"May-be," she agreed. "I don't suppose you could slip out of class –"

"And meet you at the Sheriff's Office?"

"Yes."

He nodded. "I wouldn't miss it."

They sat in comfortable silence. From down the hall they heard the sound of Rose playing her guitar. Holly said, "There was some good news today."

"What's that?"

"I got my period," she said. "Right on schedule."

They looked at each and smiled with more relief than either wanted to admit.

* * *

At just before eleven Holly pulled her red Plymouth into the parking lot next to the jail. Cutter walked over from his Jeep parked across the street under a large shade tree. He steadied her wheelchair while Holly lifted herself from the car and into it. He had learned better than to offer more help than that. She was wearing her biggest, blackest sunglasses.

"Does it show?" she asked.

"A little. Around the edge. But you're still the prettiest Miss Cattahatchie County there's ever been."

"God! I needed that! Thanks," she told him with a tired smile, wanting badly to kiss him but instead -- "Let's get this over with."

The four of them squeezed into the sheriff's private office, which was not large – most of the space taken up with filing cabinets, a cheap utilitarian desk and gun racks, the weapons secured by chains and padlocks. One barred window held a small air conditioner unit that was working hard and with limited success in the late August heat.

Holly pulled off her sunglasses and dropped them into the purse on her lap before placing it on the edge of the sheriff's desk. "It looks like the icepack may have helped some," said Dr. Garner.

"Some," agreed Holly, but her nerves were jangled and she immediately got down to the business she had paid for. "So Dr. Andrews, what can you tell us?"

Steve Andrews had played left tackle for Tulane before med school and a stint in a M*A*S*H unit during Korea. With brown hair that fell over his collar and ears, he was a big man. Broader and heavier than Cutter but not quite as tall.

"Of course, Miss Carter, I have a typed formal report prepared for you in triplicate in case you want to or need to share it with the sheriff or someone else," he began.

"Thank you. I'm sure it's very professionally done. But can you simply give me the CliffsNotes version?"

"Certainly, but with a corpse, that is to say a body, that is and was as badly decomposed as Mr. Carter's, it's difficult to –"

"Dr. Andrews, please! I understand all the disclaimers," said Holly, who was exhausted. Plus Friday was the busiest production day of the week at the newspaper. "Could you please get on with it?"

"Yes, yes. Of course," said Andrews. "Bottom line, your father was alive when he went into the river. He did, in fact, drown. That would be my official opinion as to cause of death. However, prior to his drowning, Mr. Carter received a severe blow to his forehead that resulted in a skull fracture and sudden and intense bruising of the brain that was not the result of striking his forehead on the steering wheel."

Holly straightened in her chair, nodding slightly. That was the news that Holly had been both wanting to hear and dreading.

The doctor continued – "We attempted to match the wound to the steering wheel from the automobile that you two cleverly acquired. But it's not even close. Moreover, from the amount of bruising to the brain, it should have been easy for any competent pathologist to see that the injury occurred at least two hours prior to Mr. Carter's death.

"Also, Mr. Carter suffered a compound fracture of the left femur and a severe dislocation of the left shoulder that certainly was pre-mortem. Therefore, with the head injury and the rest it would have been virtually impossible for Mr. Carter to have driven himself to the bridge or off of it that night," said Andrews. "My report will list the manner of death as homicide."

To Holly's surprise, the words gave her no satisfaction. She was hot and achy from her period, and now the room was spinning. She drew in a deep breath, hoping it would stop and praying she did not throw up as she thought of her father, his body so broken, the pain he must have been in. The cold night rain, the churning, debris-filled river as dark in its depths as a mine shaft. Just hours before he was to come back to her. To surprise her with the love and caring he must have still felt for her, even after all the years and all the hurt between them. Cutter almost reached for Holly's shoulder to steady her, but she took another long breath and the room stopped moving.

"All right then," she said, her mouth and throat dry. "What do we do now?"

"There's more," said Sheriff Wallace reaching for something on the floor behind his chair. "We believe we have the weapon that delivered the blow to T.L.'s head." He placed on his desk a bronze fireplace poker wrapped in clear plastic and labeled. It was blackened in places but Holly instantly saw that it bore a unique wolf's head handle.

"Do you recognize this?" asked the sheriff.

"Yes," she said, nodding. "It's from the set in the library at Wolf's Run. We haven't had need of a fire since I've been back, so I hadn't noticed it was missing."

"About noon yesterday, FBI technicians processing the scene at the Old Kamp Place found this inside of the spare-tire well of the Ford station wagon registered to Tom and driven by Mary Nell Carter as her personal car," the sheriff said. "The one that was allegedly stolen in Memphis."

"The head of the poker, shaped like a wolf's head, is a perfect match for the wound to Mr. Carter's forehead," said Dr. Andrews.

"Then we have the murder weapon," said Holly.

It was not a question. It was a statement which the doctors were loathed to contradict. But the sheriff knew he had to tell her, "Not exactly. You see the autopsy and evidence cuts both ways. Someone struck T.L. a hard blow to the head."

"Which he survived short term," offered Dr. Garner. "And was theoretically survivable in the longer term."

"Right," said the sheriff. "We believe he made it outside. Maybe trying in a disoriented fashion to get to his car and drive for help. Maybe chasing his assailant. At which point he was struck by the station wagon, and that's when the other injuries occurred."

Holly was tapping the palm of her hand on her knee, not looking at any of the men. "So you're telling me my father – what? – lay out there in the driveway in that cold rain –" her chin quivered but she did not cry – "for two hours while Mary Nell and, and somebody – LeRoy! – decided to put him in the river."

Billy Wallace nodded – "That's how it appears."

Holly's head snapped toward Dr. Andrews. "Did Daddy know? I mean, would he have been conscious? Did he suffer?"

Steve Andrews wrestled with the answer. "The kindest thing, I suppose, would be to simply say no. But you don't strike me as a woman who wants to be deceived. The truth is, after this length of time with that type of injury, it's impossible to tell."

Cutter ached for Holly. She was being hit by an avalanche.

"Thank you, Doctor, for your honesty," she said. "So, Sheriff, when are you going to arrest Mary Nell?"

Billy Wallace clasped his big hands on the desk in front of him and bounced them up and down, then stilled them. "Last night when I hauled Mary Nell in, I'd barely taken her fingerprints and closed the cell door before the Senator was here with a bail warrant signed by Judge Autry and a check for 500 dollars."

"Yes! But we're not talking about some bullshit assault charge here," said Holly. "We're talking about murdering my father."

"That's why it is so important to get it right," he said. "Look, Holly, I'm with you. I'm on your side. But right now it's all circumstantial. My own deputy – well, former deputy John-Thomas – would testify Mary Nell was at home when he came to tell her about the, the alleged accident. If there were fingerprints on that poker or blood on the station wagon, it's gone now."

"Because of the stupidity and clumsiness of the FBI," said Dr. Garner irritably.

Sheriff Wallace nodded – "It certainly was a setback. So was LeRoy getting killed. We might have been able to squeeze him and work a deal. Take the death penalty off the table if he gave up Mary Nell and whatever happened at Wolf's Run." Holly was shaking her head. "But on the good news side of the ledger, the FBI matched Mary Nell's prints to some of those that were found in the house. Including some on the headboard."

"So they were having an affair," she said. "There's some irony for you."

Dr. Garner and the sheriff glanced at each other. The fact that Holly and LeRoy had once dated was well known.

"Apparently," said Billy Wallace. "And it's another piece of the puzzle, but that's all it is. For now."

"How many damn pieces do you need?" Holly snapped.

Sheriff Wallace waited a beat then – "More than what we've got right now. It's a lot of circumstantial evidence. A lot. But at the moment, we have nothing that actually places Mary Nell at Wolf's Run that night. With the kind of lawyers her parents, the Poindexters, can afford, not to mention the influence Wellingham and Weathers could bring to bear, if we don't have her cold, she'll walk. None of us want that."

Holly was shaking her head.

"You know she did it."

"Yes, Holly, I believe she did. And I promise I'm going to do my best to put her in prison, but we need more than we've got now."

Holly was still shaking her head. The room was so hot and small. "I've got to get out of here," she said. "Get some air. I can't breathe."

Cutter opened the door as Holly pivoted around. Dr. Garner started to follow but Cutter put out his hand. "Thanks, Doc, but she'll be okay," he told the older man. "Just let her be."

Cutter took his time walking out to the Fury, not wanting Holly to feel he was on top of her. She already was inside firing up the four-twenty-eight four-barrel. He reached down and picked up the white flat she'd left on the pavement.

"I think you forgot this," he said handing it to her through the window.

She took it and threw it hard into the passenger floorboard. "I've got to get out of here! Out of this town. Out of this fucking county!" she told him. "I can't stand it another minute. That awful Mary Nell is going to get away with it!"

"You don't know that. Mr. Wallace'll do his best."

"And what if that's not good enough?"

Cutter could not answer that. No one could. "Let me drive," he said.

"No. Get in if you're coming with me."

"Where're you going?"

"I don't know. Does it matter?"

He looked at Holly, the flecks in her green eyes ablaze with golden fire.

"No," he said and walked around to the passenger door. Almost before he could get in and get the door closed Holly slammed the shifter into reverse and hauled down on the hand control. The big rear tires barked. The sheriff looked out his window to see white smoke pour from the rear wheel wells as she put the Plymouth in drive and shot north on River Street.

CHAPTER 16

From her kitchen window Mary Nell Piondexter Carter watched her husband of almost fifteen years walking behind the big, red low-slung Yazoo mower in the late Tuesday afternoon sun. The thermometer on the patio registered ninety-four. That was in the shade. Guiding the mower, Tom was only in the shade now and then as he passed under the big trees that surrounded the three-story Victorian on Jackson Street. After much cajoling and then demanding on Mary Nell's part, Tom had trudged out of the house whining about the stomach flu he'd picked up probably in that damn hospital. The kids were down with it, too.

"You can't lay around the house forever," she had told him. "Fresh air will do you good. Otherwise, I'll hire the yard done and you know how tight money is at the moment."

Both of them had resigned their positions at Cattahatchie Newspaper Inc., and what little savings they'd had was gone, thanks to Mary Nell's pretentious and unabated spending habits.

"We still have forty-nine percent of the paper," he reminded her. "We can borrow against that if we need to."

"Borrow? Borrow from whom?" Mary Nell scoffed. "Everyone in the state knows your idiot sister is running the paper to the ground. That stock is worthless. And the way she's carrying on with the Carlucci boy. It's shameful! It's disgusting! I've never loathed anyone so much as her."

"Stop it," Tom had protested weakly as he pulled an ankle over a knee to tie the laces of a tennis shoe. "Whatever Holly is, she's my sister. My blood."

"Yes, she is that," agreed Mary Nell and quit the argument. "I'll bring you a big glass of lemonade in a bit, and take some up to the kids, too. Maybe it will settle their stomachs and they'll feel up to eating later."

"That would be nice," he said, putting on an old straw hat with a sweat stained band.

"I'll talk to Holly about what happened the other day. I don't think she'll press charges."

Mary Nell had stared at him as if he were referring to some half-remembered incident that involved only an acquaintance. Then, "That'll be fine, Dear," she'd said blandly. "Don't miss that spot behind the garage. The whole yard needs a good tidying."

Now she stood at the sink washing the lemonade glasses and pitcher and watching as Tom trudged through the side yard next to Wilcox Street. He certainly had enjoyed the lemonade. The kids, too. It was one of her specialties. Tom's white legs were exposed by shorts cut too high. His UM Athletics t-shirt was soaked dark with copious sweat, his arms flaccid from too many years of lifting nothing but beer bottles and whiskey glasses. How she hated him. The way he smelled. The way he walked. When he touched her, she wanted to scream. Not that he touched her often now. He treated her like some snappish little dog, and all the while it was his weakness that had put her in this untenable position.

Mary Nell watched Tom pause beside one of the big oaks that was lifting the sidewalk on Wilcox. Not so bad that anyone was complaining, but its roots were going far and getting bigger. He propped himself against it with one hand, took off his old hat and wiped his forehead with a handkerchief from the back pocket of his shorts. And then, without bending his knees he simply toppled forward, landing hard on his chest and face.

How long Mary Nell stood at the window, gripping the sink edge she was not sure. It was as if she was looking at a movie, waiting for the scene to change but a static image remained and remained. She knew that there were things that needed to be done, that she needed to break out of whatever trance held her, but she couldn't manage it, couldn't move until a neighbor returning from shopping on the square walked by on the uneven sidewalk, saw Tom and went to him.

"Mary Nell! Mary Nell!" cried Hannah Overton, dropping her purse and fresh vegetable purchase on the grass. The big lawnmower was still idling. "Come quick! It's Tom! I think he's had a heart attack."

That's when Mary Nell finally unrooted herself from the kitchen, and ran through the backyard and across the lawn to her stricken husband.

* * *

A few minutes after 4 p.m. the phone on Holly's desk rang. She pushed away from the conference table where proofs for Wednesday's edition were spread. She wheeled by the open windows that allowed in the occasional stirring of air from the square and past Charlie's little bed which still was tucked into a corner near her desk. She answered.

"Holly, this Gerry Garner," said the voice she recognized. "I wanted to let you know before you heard this through the grapevine. Kudzu vine."

"What is it?" she asked anxiously, her first thought of Cutter, then Rose. She glanced at her watch. Both should still be at the high school for football and cheerleader practice. "What's happened?"

"It's Tom. He's had a heart attack."

"Ohhh, good Lord," she sighed, hating the flash of relief that passed through her. "How bad?"

"Pretty bad," said the doctor. "And to make matters worse, he and the kids have some sort of miserable stomach virus that has really drained all three of them. Mary Nell told us it hit them all Saturday, but she shook it off. Then Tom insisted on going out and cutting the grass this afternoon. In this damn heat. Crazy."

"He looked terrible on Thursday," remembered Holly. "I thought he was going to collapse then."

"I think he's been hitting the bottle pretty hard of late. Then the virus. Then out in that heat. A guy who hasn't been doing a lot of exercising," said Dr. Garner. "It was almost predictable."

Holly dreaded asking the question because she feared the answer. "Will he live?"

"Honestly, I don't know. We're doing the best we can. I'd love to send him on to Memphis, but he's too unstable. He'd never survive the ambulance ride."

"Crap!"

The doctor waited to let Holly absorb what he had told her, then -- "And so you know, we've got the kids up here, too."

"What? They're that bad?"

"They're two pretty sick kiddos," he told her. "Mostly just dehydrated, I think. We've got them on IV fluids and starting some antibiotics. I might not have admitted them, but Mary Nell wanted them close. And it won't hurt for them to sleep here overnight where we can monitor them."

"Thank you for letting me know. As soon as I can hand off the paper to my managing editor. I'll be up there."

"Whoa, Holly."

"What?"

"That's the other thing I called to tell you," said Garner, turning to his role as the hospital's chief of staff. "I don't want you walking into another sucker punch. And I don't want any more scenes in the hospital."

"What does that mean?"

"Mary Nell has given explicit instructions that you are not to be allowed anywhere near Tom or the kids."

Holly was too anxious about Tom to be angry. "But he's my brother."

"I know, but Mary Nell is his wife. She says she's asked Mr. Wellingham to get a restraining order barring you from coming within 50 feet of any of any of them."

Holly rested her elbow on the corner of the desk and put her forehead in her hand. She sighed. "All right, Doctor. Will you let me know how Tom's doing?"

"Mary Nell doesn't even want me to do that," he said. "But, here I am. Yes. I will. Quietly."

"Thank you."

* * *

That night deep in the shallow backwaters of the Cattahatchie River along the uncertain border where Union, Lafayette and Cattahatchie counties meet without notice, a flashlight winked one long then two short, again and a third time. "KKK" in Morse Code. "Mailman's here," said Frank Gandy, lowering his night-scoped sniper rifle and poking his head inside the cabin.

Robert McBride was standing at a camp stove, the flame alight beneath a coffee pot even though it was only 4 a.m. Tony Carlucci sat up on the edge of a cot and held his head. "That son-of-bitch better have brought some whiskey this time or I'm going to feed his sorry ass to the gators," he said.

McBride, who valued steady hands over a drink, said nothing. Instead, he poured himself a cup of coffee into a tin cup and walked toward the screened door carrying it and an Army standard M-16. He propped the rifle beside a chair and sat looking out on the forest of cypress that screen the river-fed lake. The cabin was at the far end and accessible only by boat with someone at the tiller who intimately knew the area. It was one of three Klan safe houses the trio had been moving between every few days since the FBI swarmed over the Kamp property. Carlucci and Gandy had warrants out against them for the murder of Ridge Bellafont and the attempted murder of Eve Howard. McBride was wanted in the deaths of the four people who died in the Roseville bombing and the murder of Sheriff Johnson. All described and attributed in the Book of Olin.

Instead of coming directly across the lake, the boatman kept to edges using only a small, quiet trolling motor as he closely skirted the cypress knees. He'd been listening for the throp-throp of an FBI helicopter since leaving Benoit Landing 35 minutes earlier, but except for the constant groaning of frogs, the occasional growling of alligators and the constant buzz of mosquitoes against the netting covering his face, he heard nothing outside of the natural world he loved. He pulled up alongside the dock as close to the porch as he could get. Gandy propped his rifle next to McBride's weapon and went out onto the plank dock. Keeping their voices low, the man in the boat said, "Howdy, Frank."

"Howdy Coach."

Gayden Pearce, who'd left Cattahatchie High to coach the Riverview Confederates, quietly stacked several cartons, three cases of beer and three large bags of groceries on the dock then said, "Frank, reach down here and help me with this."

Gandy, who was wiry but not a particularly big man, squatted and stretched to get hold of one handle of a 20-gallon chest loaded with ice, soft drinks and a gallon of milk. Together, the men heaved it onto the dock.

"Tony, you might humble yourself to come out here and give us a hand," said Gandy.

"I might but I'm not," said Tony. "I'm Kaptain of the Klargo. You're just a foot soldier doin' what foot soldiers do."

"Well in case you haven't noticed, there ain't no fuckin' Klargo around here no more," said Gandy irritably as he passed by with two armloads of groceries. "Billy Wallace and the federal boys have seen to that. My ass is in the shit just as deep as yours -- Kaptain."

Leaning back against the cabin wall in a straight-back chair – "Tony, go help Coach Pearce," said McBride without looking up.

Tony grit his teeth but headed out through the screen door. The mosquitoes immediately swarmed and he cursed and swatted. Tony hated McBride – *the arrogant prick!* – but had to put up with him for now. McBride was the big name, the Klan prince who everyone was bustin' their butt to get out of the country, plus those loyal Klansman with him. Without McBride, Mexico then safety and maybe even honor in Paraguay might slip through their fingers no matter what Weathers had promised. But he knew one damn thing, he wasn't going anywhere until he got what he wanted. At least he and McBride agreed on that, but for different reasons. McBride wanted to leave this county, state and country – the FBI and every soft, worthless liberal do-gooder -- with a final fuck-you. He'd done his best to keep the USA from descending into a swamp of degenerate mud people. They could have it. Meanwhile, Tony did not intend to go into exile alone or leave Holly Lee Carter alive. That would be his final *coup de grace* to his traitorous son. And if he had to kill the boy in the process – well, maybe he should have done it a long time ago. Cutter always had too much of his momma in him, thought Tony. Figured he was better than his old man. But he was going to find out different. Ohhh, yeah. Pappa Tony was going to settle the score good and proper.

"Let's go inside," McBride said after the men had finished bringing the supplies from the boat. He closed the wood door and said to Gandy, "Close those shutters."

McBride struck a match with his thumbnail and lit a kerosene lantern that filled the front room with yellow light. He looked into a box on the corner of the picnic table that sat in the middle of the room then pulled out a garment and held it up.

"It's a Kramer Ballistic Vest," Pearce proudly announced. "They're the latest thing. I slipped four of them right out of the National Guard Armory last weekend when we did some training. They're supposed to stop any kind of pistol round or shotgun pellets. Mixed results versus Kalashnikovs but I don't figure y'all will be facing many of those around here."

McBride felt the weight. "Well done, Mr. Pearce," he said. "It's always wise to be prepared for any contingency. Fill us in on what's been going on in the outside world that we couldn't hear about on the local radio station."

Pearce put a stack of newspapers on the plank table then filled them in on all the local gossip, much of which had to do with Cutter and the Carters. "Your girl's on the cheer squad at CHS," Pearce told Tony. "She looks fine now that she's finally shucked her overalls and took herself to a beauty parlor." Her father grunted. "Of course, it's her and a couple of hold-over sluts from last year's squad and four niggers."

"I don't care anything about that shit," said Gandy. "What about my wife and kids? With me gone they're –"

"With you gone, they're taken care of just fine," Pearce told the nervous little man. "Weathers brought her in at the bank. All she's gotta do is set by the front door, look pretty and say, 'Can I help you?' Then point. Your boys and your girl are on scholarship to Riverview. So calm yourself, Frank."

Placated but not satisfied, Gandy sat heavily onto an animal chewed recliner in the corner that doubled as his bed. "So what's the timeline?" asked McBride. "When's our flight?"

"Yeah, when are we gettin' out of here?" demanded Gandy, still agitated. "I'm goin' stir crazy cooped up in this or some other furnace all day. Only comin' out at night like some damn bat."

Pearce shook his head. "Hard to say. Between the FBI and the Army, they've got two choppers up just about all the time."

"The Army?" squawked Gandy.

"Yep. Looks like they want their C4 back," said Pearce.

Tony grunted and rubbed the stubble on his big chin and round jowls. "They got most of that when that numb-nuts Kamp didn't blow the tunnels," he said.

"Not quite," noted McBride without having to glance into a corner where a black duffel rested. "That's what I meant about always having a contingency plan."

Pearce unscrewed the top from a pint of whiskey, took a big pull and offered it to McBride. Dynamite Bob shook his head almost imperceptibly but it was enough. Frank Gandy pushed himself up from the chair. "I'll take a hit'uh that," he said. "I need me some nerve medicine."

Gandy took two long pulls, capped the bottle and tossed it almost too hard to Tony, who was not happy with how little remained. "You little termite!"

"Don't worry," said Pearce. "There's two fifths in one of those grocery sacks."

"Good man, Coach. Good man," said Tony before hitting the pint bottle hard.

McBride asked, "So what do you think? How long before extraction?"

"I talked to our friends in New Orleans. They won't chance bringin' a float plane in until the feds get tired of flyin' those choppers," said Pearce. "The shine's gotta wear off lookin' for y'all soon. They'll get tired of it or figure y'all slipped out some other way."

"Why don't we?" asked Gandy. "Why don't we just pick up a couple cars and skedaddle. The cops can't be watchin' every road every minute."

"Then what, Mr. Gandy?" asked McBride. "It's a long drive from here to Grand Isle, Louisiana for three of the most wanted men in America."

"Besides," said Tony. "I told you, I ain't leavin' here without what's rightly mine."

"Pervert," Gandy grumbled, shaking his head.

"What'd you say?" demanded Tony, his eyes bright with whiskey and sudden anger.

"Nothin'. I didn't say nothin'. I just cain't take much more of this."

"We'll take what we've got to take to complete our mission," said McBride.

CHAPTER 17

Cutter and Holly hung next to each other on the edge of the big pool at Wolf's Run, the lights embedded in three walls causing the water to glow turquoise around them in the dusk.

"Is this nightmare ever going to end?" Holly asked as her breath slowly calmed. His black hair glistening with droplets and the glow from the pool light, he said nothing, which was what she wanted to hear. She didn't want platitudes or hollow reassurance. She liked that about Cutter. Respected it. He was a realist far beyond his years and saw things and situations for what they were. He didn't pretend that they were something else, or predict that everything would be just fine – knowing there was a damn good chance it would be otherwise. He'd learned under Tony Carlucci's roof that life had to be seen for what it was. Doing otherwise likely would have gotten him killed.

They had swam lap after lap together, Holly trying to wear some of the tension out of her. Some of the anger and anxiety. Cutter kept up as long as he could before dropping out and swimming over to hang on the side, to watch and admire and appreciate. And to worry. Sixteen laps later, she swam over to him. Next to each other they were mostly quiet. Proximity gave each of them a calm that they did not otherwise experience, but even that was of little comfort at the moment.

"I, I never would have imagined such a thing," Holly quietly said, resting her head on her arms. "Not even of Mary Nell."

"Yeah. It's, I don't know," said Cutter. "I don't have a word for it."

"I don't think there is a word for it," she told him.

***

Holly began feeling the tremors, like a ripple in the earth, in a phone call from Jane Wommack, who lived on Wilcox Street three houses in back of the Victorian occupied by Tom's family. The house she had lived in and loved as a little girl. Mrs. Wommack had a daughter about Holly's age, and they'd been good friends until they drifted apart in high school when Holly moved out to Wolf's

Run. However, Jane Wommack now was part of the contingent sticking solidly with Brother MacAllister at First Denomination.

"We have different points of view on the politics of, of all that's been going on," said Mrs. Wommack, "but with Tom in the hospital here and Mary Nell up in Memphis with the children, I thought you should know – there are sheriff's cars and some FBI people at the house. They aren't letting anyone even in the yard to ask questions. Lord knows what they're doing in there. Or since you're in cahoots with those people, perhaps you're already aware."

Holly once spent hundreds of happy hours in and out of Jane Wommack's kitchen and yard. Playing with dolls and reading story books through too hot or too rainy afternoons in Bridget Wommack's room. It was like that. After Holly's mother left and her father distanced himself from his young daughter, she had been adopted by several families, almost as the neighborhood orphan. Though she later would learn how they had whispered cruelly about her parents – about how Veri Carter had been too pretty, too vivacious, too exotic, or maybe just too much woman for T.L. – they could not have been nicer to Holly to her face. That had meant a lot back then.

"No, Mrs. Wommack, I don't know anything about it," said Holly. "I appreciate you letting me know. I'll call over to the Sheriff's Office and see if I can find out what's going on."

T he Sheriff's Office dispatcher refused to give her any information but said she would relay a message to Sheriff Wallace and ask him to call. Thirty minutes later when he had not done so, Holly wheeled to her car and drove the few blocks to Jackson Street. Indeed, the yard was swarming with police cars. Three sheriff's cars, two unmarked black Fords, a white Chevy with a bubble light on the dashboard and Tennessee plates, and a black van with the door open exposing supplies for a forensic investigation. Perhaps 100 people were gathered on shaded sections of sidewalk. Some she recognized as neighborhood people. Others in overalls and cheap farm dresses probably had been drawn from the square by the commotion.

Holly tried to turn into the driveway off Wilcox, but a deputy stepped in front of her. Before Holly had time to explain, cajole or demand, Billy Wallace called from near the back steps where he'd been talking with a technician in white coveralls -- "Let her though."

The sheriff walked over to a shady spot near the garage beside an oak from which a child's swing hung in the hot still air. She put the car in park next to him.

"What's going on?" she asked. "Is this about Daddy?"

Billy Wallace sighed, shook his head. "I wish it was. I'm sorry. I should have come and told you. Or called, at least. I guess I was just puttin' off facin' you with this."

Incredulous, Holly asked, "What the hell?"

"It's Mary Nell. She's under arrest in Memphis."

"For what?"

The sheriff looked at her with tired, sad eyes. "The attempted murder of Lanny and Georgette. In my back pocket I have an arrest warrant on the same charge related to Tom's condition."

Holly's lips parted but for a time no words came out. She wondered if she was dreaming, if her loathing for Mary Nell had manifested into some crazy fantasy. If all the pressure she'd been under finally had broken her and she'd had crossed the line from reality into a dark, squalid Gehenna of waking nightmares. Involuntarily her hand went to her cheek where the last coloring of a bruise lingered under a light dusting of powder.

"How?"

"Arsenic," said the sheriff, turning his Panama in his hands. "Apparently, she'd been poisoning them all for at least several months. Small daily doses so it wouldn't be obvious. Tom was the most affected because of all his drinking. Arsenic builds up in the liver, and his was already compromised by too much of it. That's why he looked jaundiced when we saw him at the hospital." Holly drew in a long breath and swallowed but said nothing and the sheriff went on. "Something caused her to change over the weekend. Georgette – she's the only one of the three who can talk now – says their eggs tasted funny on Saturday morning. After that, they all started getting sicker and sicker. Mary Nell acted like she was sick, too. The three of them couldn't hold down much food but she told them that Doc Garner wanted them to drink plenty of fluids. Doc says she never called. Anyway, she kept pushing her lemonade on them. It was loaded with the stuff."

Holly was more stunned than if they found a home movie of Mary Nell bashing in T.L. Carter's skull with the fireplace poker. In fact, when she had turned it over again and again in her mind, she'd assumed Mary Nell had struck her father in the midst of some sort of argument. In a fit of the sort of rage of which she was obviously capable. But this? … President of the PTA … CHS Cheerleader sponsor, and now the same at Riverview … Vice President of the DeLong Garden Club … First Denomination Sunday School teacher and regular in the shimmering golden robes of the choir … It was incomprehensible.

"You're sure?"

"No doubt about it," said Billy Wallace.

"Why didn't Gerry Garner --?" her voice trailed off.

"He feels terrible about it, but from what the FBI experts tell me, arsenic poisoning is very hard to detect unless you're specifically looking for it," he explained. "Regular blood tests don't pick it up. And it can mimic all sorts of things. Like a severe stomach virus."

"How'd they discover it in Memphis?"

"Maybe there's an angel looking out for the kids. One of the nurses up there was readin' a mystery novel where the killer was using arsenic. She recognized the symptoms. And she'd seen Mary Nell giving Lanny lemonade from a Thermos. It took going to three doctors before one would listen to her, but when they tested for it, it was right there at lethal levels. They called the Memphis P.D. and she was arrested on suspicion. When they tested the lemonade that was left in the Thermos, it was conclusive, and they charged her."

"Good Lord," grasped Holly. "Those poor children. How are they?"

"Georgette seems to be holding her own. Lanny? He's touch and go."

"And Tom?"

Billy Wallace shook his head. "He's alive. In a coma. But Doc Garner isn't hopeful."

"Has Mary Nell said anything? I mean –"

"You mean, tried to explain herself?" asked the sheriff. "How could anyone explain something like that? No. Her parents, the Poindexters, and one of her sisters was there with her when she was arrested. She denied everything. They immediately hired the top defense attorney in Memphis, and she lawyered up. Won't say a word. But they've got her cold. We're just trying to find the arsenic she used. Nail it down."

"None of this proves she killed my father."

"No it doesn't. But the search warrant I've got allows us to go through every inch of that house from basement to attic. Who knows what we might turn up?"

Even though Holly had not lived in the Jackson Street house for fifteen years, she hated the idea of strangers pawing through it, touching so many things that once had been precious to her. She shook her head slowly, smiling a humorless smile. "I want to cry, but I don't have any tears."

"I know. There've been so many this summer," said my father. "I think we're all just worn out. Cried out."

Holly was quiet, then – "You know this will never be over until you catch Tony Carlucci and the rest of those – those? – monsters."

"I know," said the sheriff. "We're doing our best."

"Then, damn it, do better."

CHAPTER 18

That Friday night from the balcony of my rented room, I watched the Cattahatchie High team bus pass by, headed south on Highway 27 to the Wolves' opener against New Albany. John-Thomas Hinton – Coach Hinton now – was driving, and black faces outnumbered white in the windows. I had heard that there were 28 players, including freshmen and Roseville kids who never had participated in organized football.

Instead of the two or three spirit buses and dozens of vehicles that usually followed the CHS team bus, there were only a handful of cars. Including Miss Carter's red Plymouth Fury carrying Rose Carlucci and several other cheerleaders, a couple of them black. As big a mess as this all was, I was glad for Rose. To my knowledge, she never had been to a high school football game. Never seen her magnificent brother play.

Riverview didn't open its season for another week, and it looked like I would start at wide receiver. Start in my white-and-gold uniform with my pretty cheerleader girlfriend shaking her pompoms and high kicking to encourage me. So I turned my back and stepped inside as the old screen door squawked its rusty call. I needed to get ready for my date with Patti.

* * *

If cheering loud and hard from the sidelines could earn a football team a victory, then the efforts of Rose Marie Carlucci and the other five teenagers on the squad would have given the Wolves a three-touchdown win. Rose was determined to make up for all the games she had missed.

TV stations from Memphis and Tupelo, along with at least ten print reporters, including Holly, were there to capture the moment in history when the Cattahatchie Wolves kicked off their first-ever season as an integrated team. To be sure, many who had been following the story of the Wolves hoped for a fairytale season. But it quickly became evident that such was not to be. The Bulldogs scored on their first five possessions and CHS was down 34-6 at the half.

Cutter ended up rushing for 281 yards and four touchdowns, but it wasn't nearly enough. New Albany exploited the inexperienced CHS defense for 675 yards and a 64-31 win, as Holly Lee Carter told Managing Editor C. Michael Morton when she phoned in her story. Next morning when Cutter when he awoke in his sleeping bag on the rock precipice where he made camp across from Wolf's Run, he could barely sit up. Since early in his junior year when he dislocated his right shoulder – the shoulder he lowered and led with when he bowled over linebackers, often two or three at time – it was always tender after a game to the point of being painful. But he talked to no one about it except me. He didn't want the coaches to know. Certainly not our opponents. And surely not the handful of mostly small college scouts who showed up at the rough, often nearly cow-pasture fields we played on in our league. Such had been our friendship that he had let me see him in pain. Acknowledged that he was hurting. It was no small thing.

Against New Albany, Cutter had played every down on offense and defense, plus returned kickoffs and punts. Now he rolled over onto his left side and pushed himself up onto his knees. He stood and tried to stretch but couldn't lift his right arm above his shoulders. He worked the fingers in his right hand and finally got the tingling to stop. A half hour later, he was sitting at the kitchen table with Holly and Rose tucking in a large second helping of bacon, scrambled eggs with cheddar cheese, sausage patties and biscuits with white sawmill gravy.

"Labor Day Weekend," he said. "I've got three good days of work at The Gin. Mr. Clanton's got a spool of barbed wire in one the storage rooms he told me I could have."

"Barbed wire?" asked Holly. "What are you going to do with that?"

"I don't like the idea that somebody could pull a boat up at the bottom of this hill and walk up that path from the river and right onto the patio."

Rose looked up from her plate, the concern, almost fear, plain on her face. Holly said, "Do you really think that's necessary? They'd have to be mountain goats."

Cutter looked at his sister. "Probably," he said. "But rather be safe than a long time sorry."

What he didn't say was that he'd walked that path down to the river a couple of days earlier and back up. It was narrow in places and would be tricky in the dark, but it could be done. Even by a man with a prosthetic leg, if he was tough enough and determined enough.

"I think you're being a little silly," said Holly, more for Rose's benefit than because she believed it. But Cutter, his shoulder aching and short on sleep, didn't pick up on her concern.

"Well, I don't," he said sharply. "I can't watch both sides of the house at once. It's your house but it's my sister's life."

Holly looked at him. "Are we about to have our first fight?"

"Not unless you want to."

"M-M-Mister Grumpy!" Rose interjected.

The three of them looked at each other, then Cutter laughed out loud – unusual for him – and Rose and Holly shared in it. "Go ahead and put the barbed wire on the trail if you want to," she said and everyone smiled and turned back to finishing breakfast. "But don't make the place look like a prison camp."

"Don't worry," he said. "I'll cover it with brush. Nobody'll even know it's there."

* * *

On the Sunday morning of Labor Day Weekend 1969, my father pulled his unmarked police cruiser into the lot between the Randleman Cotton Warehouse and the Emerson Grain Storage elevators on the west side of the river. The lot was directly across from the rear of *The Current-Leader* building where more than 120 people were gathered for the Sunday morning "downtown prayer meeting," as the service was coming to be known. Cars filled the newspaper lot and spread out down River Street and up the hill toward the town square.

Daddy parked next to Cutter and got out. Cutter was sitting on the hood of his Jeep wearing his black-and-red letter jacket. The sun was beaming warm from a perfectly clear sky, but in the shadow cast by the warehouse the air was unseasonably cool and free of humidity. Holly and Rose were part of a quartet of musicians providing the backdrop for the service, playing mostly old gospel standards that all the worshipers knew, since there were no hymnals. She was leading those gathered in a rendition of *Blessed Assurance*, her voice so pure and sweet that it seemed to travel not on waves of sound but on pathways of sunlight.

"Mornin', Cutter."

"Mornin', Sheriff."

"Dadgum, it's turned off cool all of a sudden for this time of year."

"Yes, sir."

"Supposed to get even colder later this week. Almanac says it's gonna be an early winter."

"Looks like it's right again."

"How come you're not on the other side of the river?"

"I guess me and Jesus still have some things to work out," Cutter told him. "But I'm close enough to feel the Spirit."

"And to hear Miss Holly sing? She has an amazing voice."

"Yes she does."

"I think any man would be lucky to have her, and luckier still if he can handle her," said Billy Wallace.

Cutter kept his eyes fixed across the river. "I expect you're right."

Then Sheriff Wallace got to it. "Mary Nell wants to see Holly."

Cutter looked at him in with those blue-white eyes. "For what?"

"She says she'll tell what happened at Wolf's Run and give up why she poisoned Tom and the kids, but only to Holly."

Cutter thought about that for a moment. "Are you sure it's not just some game to – I don't know – to get at Holly?"

"Honestly, I don't know what it is," said the sheriff. "I'm sure that's probably part of it. But don't worry. Mary Nell'll be shackled. There's no way we'll let her hurt Holly."

"I'm not thinking about physically."

"I knew what you meant, but this may be our best chance, our only chance to find out what happened to Mr. Carter and why she tried to kill her family."

Cutter was quiet for a time, listening to Holly sing, her face open and happy and at ease. "Isn't there some other way?"

"If there was, I wouldn't be asking."

Cutter drew in a breath. "When and where?"

"The sooner the better, before Mary Nell's lawyer or parents or both can talk her out of it," said Billy Wallace. "I thought maybe you two could drive up to Memphis this afternoon. There's an interview room at the Shelby County Jail. It's got a two-way mirror, microphones and cameras. The whole nine-yards. If she gives it up, we'll have it all on film."

Cutter shook his head, studied the gravel on the ground in front of him, pursed his lips and watched the river flow past for a bit then looked at the sheriff. "You know, even somebody as strong as Holly has a breaking point. I think she's pretty close to hers."

There was nothing to say to that, so my father didn't try.

"All right," Cutter said after a time. "I'll talk to her."

CHAPTER 19

With five good-sized men crammed into the interview room across the table from Holly the space felt hot and claustrophobic, like a phone booth in an open lot. Cutter leaned in one corner and Sheriff Wallace stood next to him beside the large two-way mirror. Two crew-cut detectives were trying to fill the air with reassurance when all Holly wanted was some space and air. In the open doorway was Mary Nell's attorney, the venerable and regionally famous John G. "Happy" Belmont.

"I want it on the record and in writing that I strongly object to this whole interview," he was saying.

"Not happy, huh, Happy?" said Sgt. Lance Brown, the bigger of the two detectives. "Tell it to your client. She requested this meeting and signed off on it in writing."

"My client is a sick woman," Belmont told the room. "Very sick."

"You'll be free to argue that at trial," said Officer Dave Russell. "But for now, you need to be quiet and get out of the way. Go in the observation room. Or go outside and smoke that fancy pipe of yours. I don't care which. But quit yappin'."

"Now Miss Carter, this table is bolted to the floor. And you see this O-ring screwed into the table?" asked Brown.

Holly, taking deep breaths, looked straight ahead but nodded.

"There's another just like it on the floor," Brown went on. "Mrs. Carter will be shackled hand and foot. So you don't have worry about any kind of assault." Holly nodded. "We'll also be right behind that glass. If anything goes sideways, we'll be in here in three seconds flat."

She swallowed. "I get it. I'm fine with all this. I just need all you big men to back out of here so I can breathe. You're sucking up all of the oxygen. And all of the air conditioning, too. Could you turn it down, please? It's like an oven in here."

"Okay, men. You heard the lady," said Russell. "Let's back out of here and give her some air."

"I'll turn down the air," agreed Brown.

Cutter and Holly held each other's gaze a long instant, then he nodded and slipped out of the room behind Sheriff Wallace. "Everything is going to be fine," said Russell as the detectives exited. As soon as they left, a new figure appeared in the doorway.

"Mr. Burke," said Holly.

"Miss Carter," he said and stepped inside. He leaned against the wall with his hands in the pants pockets of his expensive blue pinstripe suit. He looked tired and older than when they first met less than six months ago. *Of course, I probably do, too,* thought Holly.

"Aren't you out of your jurisdiction?" she asked.

"Technically, yes," he told her. "But this dovetails into a larger, multi-state investigation. So, the Shelby County D.A. kindly offered me a window seat, you might say."

"Any word on McBride or the rest?"

"On the record or off?"

"Whichever way you want it."

"Off, then," he said. "We think we have them bottled up in the south end of the county. Down in the Three Corners area. But there's enough swamp out there to hide a regiment on horseback. We're watching, listening, patrolling the roads and in the air. We'll get them."

Holly looked at him, not very convinced, especially since the U.S. Attorney didn't seem all that convinced himself.

"We appreciate you doing this," he said. "For whatever reason, I believe your sister-in-law wants to tell you her story. She wants to justify her actions at least in her own mind. So, it's important for you not to be too confrontational with her no matter what comes out of her mouth. Control is very important to that woman. I realize it will be extraordinarily difficult under the circumstances, but try to disconnect from the emotions and step back. Talk to her like you would during a newspaper interview. Draw her out as much as you can. Let her talk, no matter what she says. The more she talks, the better the chance she'll hang herself or give us something we can use in another context."

In the observation room, someone tapped on the back of the two-way mirror.

"Okay, that's the signal that they're bringing her up," said Burke. "If it gets too bad, just say, 'I want out of here,' and we'll be here in a flash."

At exactly 4 p.m., two Shelby County Corrections Officers – one male, one female – marched Mary Nell into the small, gray-green interview room. As soon as she shuffled in on ankles that were shackled, her blue eyes fixed on Holly's, reflecting a gleam of manic energy and something like merriment. The female guard knelt beside the chair and hooked the ankle chain into the O-ring clamp as Mary Nell primly held her legs together beneath the dark blue prison-issue skirt with the wide gray stripe down the side. The male guard hooked the short wrist chain into the ring on the table and stepped back.

"We'll be right outside the door if you need us," the female officer told Holly.

"Thank you so much, Hilda," Mary Nell responded as if the officer had been addressing her. "I doubt a woman in my sister-in-law's ruined state is dangerous. You may go about your other duties."

The guards looked at each other and stepped into the hall, closing the metal door behind them.

Holly was shocked that Mary Nell's hair was nicely coiffed and her makeup was perfect. From talking to plenty of cops during her years with the *L.A. Chronicle* Holly knew that almost any kind of contraband could be had in jail or prison for the right price. With the Poindexter money still at her disposal apparently lipstick and eyeliner weren't hard to come by, even in a Tennessee lockup. Still, it was disconcerting. Mary Nell looked a lot more confident, secure and happy than logic would dictate she had any right to be.

"You asked to see me."

"Yes, well, I thought you should hear it from me before I make your family's filth public to the entire community."

"All right, Mary Nell. I'm listening."

The small knot of a woman drew back and focused her hard, gray-blue eyes down her perfect nose. "You will please address me as Miss Poindexter. Or if you prefer, Miss Mary Nell."

Holly wet her lips and felt a trickle of perspiration slide down between her breasts. "Mary… Miss Mary Nell, what is it you want to tell me?"

"Filth, filth, filth," Mary Nell repeated. Holly stared at her and said nothing, remembering Burke's instructions. After almost a minute, Mary Nell finally spoke again. "You know, of course, your mother, Veronique Dupre, was born and reared in New Orleans – a place of decadence and fornication."

"I'm aware my mother was from New Orleans, yes."

"What do you know of your mother's blood?"

"My mother's 'blood'? Not much," admitted Holly. "She was an only child. Her parents died in the Great '27 Flood. The rest of the family was scattered."

"So your mother wanted her poor husband and children to believe."

Holly felt her breathing become shallow, growing more uneasy by the moment. "What does that mean?"

"In a safe deposit box in my name at First United Bank of Vicksburg you'll find a file gathered by a private investigator in 1949 outlining your mother's complete genealogy – and thus that of you and your brother."

"And why is this important?"

"Oh, it's terribly important. It's, it's – well, it's all that matters, really. Your blood. The sum of all the generations that came before you," Miss Poindexter told her. "You see, you and your brother were tainted from the womb. If it weren't so disgusting, I could feel sorry for you. Like idiot children born to some syphilitic whore. It's not really the fault of such children, but that fact makes them no less idiots."

Holly fought to control both her temper and her dread. "I'm sorry, Mary … Miss Poindexter, I don't understand."

"Then let me clarify it for you. Your grandfather, a respected New Orleans businessman, rutted with a colored maid to produce your mulatto mother – a high yell'er who could pass. And she did pass. Passed well enough to hook your daddy. But that don't change the fact half the blood flowin' through her veins was Negroid. Makin' Veronique Dupre all nigger in the eyes of decent society." Holly felt herself stop breathing. In the other room Cutter stiffened, and he and Burke and my father looked at each other. None of them had seen this coming. "That means Thomas Lanier Carter the third and his negress were guilty of the crime of miscegenation. That means their offspring – you and the individual who stuck himself inside me to produce two offspring – are quadroons. One-quarter colored. Under the natural laws of genetics and the state of Mississippi, you and the man who impregnated me are as much Negroes as the naked savages who came babbling their African gibberish off a slave ship two hundred years ago."

Suddenly, Mary Nell leaned back in the chair in a guffaw of a laugh as she smacked her hands on the table top and stomped her feet to the extent her shackles would allow, the chains rattling. Other than swallowing slowly Holly sat frozen until suddenly Mary Nell stopped laughing and leaned forward, grinning.

"Look on the bright side, Holly dear. Just think of all of the firsts you will have accomplished for your, your people. The first Negro to graduate from Cattahatchie High School. The first to own a newspaper in these parts. Oh, and lest we forget, the first colored Miss Cattahatchie County!" crowed Mary Nell. "You'll go down in history!"

The woman settled back in the chair, a satisfied smirk on her lips. "You don't believe me?"

Holly thought of the dusky complexion she had inherited from her mother while Tom got their father's creamy English coloring. She remembered some of the vile things T.L. Carter had said to her when she was a teenager. Things that bordered on what she now sensed was the truth. "Actually, I do believe you," she said. "How long have you known?"

"Since the weekend prior to T.L.'s demise."

"That's why you killed my father?"

"Why, yes. Of course," she replied without hesitation or emotion or the slightest concern for who might be watching and listening behind the mirror. "T.L. showed Tom and I the detective's report. He told us that Mr. Weathers commissioned the inquiry in the late 1940s after hearing rumors from business associates in New Orleans. To his credit, when Mr. Weathers showed T.L. the evidence, he immediately dealt with the problem."

Holly was trying to fight through myriad confused emotions – remembering the terrible day she came home from school, to the house on Jackson Street and her mother was gone. No note, no explanation, simply gone.

"Some of Mr. Weathers' associates made sure she never returned," Mary Nell added. "Oh, and it might interest you to know, considering your current living and rumored, shall we say, sleeping arrangements, that I believe chief among those associates was that awful Carlucci man. He's always been Mr. Weathers' chief – what would you call him? – fixer?"

Cutter realized his mouth was open but no sound came out. He covered it with his hand almost as shocked as Holly.

"What did they do to my mother?"

"That, I cannot say. T.L. did not share those details. But I will say, since that conversation I have stood at the kitchen window of the house I shared with your brother and looked out at that big back yard and – well, wondered."

Cutter shook his head. "This is cruel. She already admitted to killing Mr. Carter."

Burke looked over his shoulder at Cutter, saying, "We need more. Besides, this is what Holly came for."

Inside the small, hot room Holly fought to control her breathing and focus her mind as she thought of how her father despised Cecil Weathers and yet refused to openly challenge him in the pages of *The Current-Leader*. Now she knew the reason. What she did not understand was – "Why did Daddy show you and Tom the report after all these years? Twenty years."

"Because he said he was going to Los Angeles to, among other things, tell you all about it. To cleanse his soul and beg your forgiveness. And when he returned he planned to integrate the pages of *The Current-Leader* and change its editorial policy concerning the race-mixers," Mary Nell explained. "Worse than any of that, he planned to publicly disclose the truth about your mother, so that Mr. Weathers could no longer hold it over his head. Of course, that was entirely out of the question."

Holly understood the impact that series of events would have on the people of Cattahatchie County, but especially on Tom and Mary Nell, who made their home in DeLong, Mississippi where old times are far from forgotten.

"So when did you and Tom decided to kill him?"

Mary Nell looked at Holly with what appeared to be real surprise.

"There was no plan. Truly," Mary Nell insisted. "Tom fell into a useless state of drunkenness and denial, and drove off to that convention in Gulfport. I went to Wolf's Run to reason with T.L. privately. Though I suppose I was prepared to do whatever was necessary to prevent such utter humiliation from befalling my family."

"Georgette and Lanny …" whispered Holly, almost to herself, sympathetic to how cruel kids could be, and surely would be once their mixed-race blood became common knowledge. Mary Nell heard and said incredulous -- "Georgette and Lanny?

Heavens no! They're Carters. Octoroons. They carry the same tainted blood as you and your brother. I'm talking about my parents, Mr. and Mrs. Poindexter. And siblings. We'd be the laughingstock of the state, of the entire South, if it were disclosed that I, Mary Nell Poindexter, had been impregnated by a Negro."

Holly stared at Mary Nell, aware her mouth was open but unable to find words. Then, "What happened at Wolf's Run?"

The chains rattled on the floor as Mary Nell tried to cross her legs but could not. She sighed and settled. "I had slept very little since T.L. told us of his plans on Saturday afternoon. Not even the strongest of my nerve pills had any effect," she remembered. "I was crazed. Desperate.

"When I arrived at Wolf's Run the electricity was out. T.L. showed me to the library where he had a fire going. I tried to talk to him, to reason with him. But he wouldn't listen. He just wouldn't listen. He crossed the room to fix me a drink. To calm my nerves, as if my nerves were the problem. And there was your mother's portrait. I saw her smiling at me in the firelight. Her eyes dancing. Mocking me! That lying Negress!

"T.L. had been cutting some stories from the Memphis paper. I grabbed the scissors from the coffee table and began slashing the portrait. T.L. ran across the room, tore the scissors from my hand and threw me down. He just stood there staring at the painting, mumbling something.

"I looked at my hand and I was bleeding. It was all so wrong! I, I simply – exploded. I grabbed the first thing I could put my hands on and I swung it. He turned just as I did. It took only one blow. He went down hard. Blood went everywhere."

For once, Holly was glad she was sitting. She felt physically and emotionally ill, but she swallowed and pressed on. "Daddy wasn't dead, though."

"Oh, I thought he was. I couldn't hear a heartbeat. I was sure I'd killed him."

"How did LeRoy Kamp get involved?"

Mary Nell smiled demurely at first then cocked her head and ran her small tongue slowly around her lips. "Well, you see, Mr. Kamp, who is, err, was from a very fine old Miss'ssippi family, excellent bloodlines – was an acquaintance. I thought that he might be wise in such matters. I started to use the phone, but thought better of it. So I drove to his house for counsel. I felt that it would be imprudent to allow T.L. to be discovered in such a state. A thorough investigation might lead to the discovery of his wife's true nature."

"I see," was all Holly could manage.

"Out of, uhm, friendship, Mr. Kamp followed me back to Wolf's Run. But as we were going down the driveway in the pitch-black night, there was T.L. staggering toward the garage. I was horrified. It was like seeing a zombie come to life."

"And you hit him?"

"Yes."

"On purpose?"

"Why, yes. I'm quite a good driver. He had to be stopped. In any case, he went onto the hood and hit the windshield. The damage to my car wasn't terribly serious, but it was a shock to my system. To our utter astonishment, the old fool was still breathing," Mary Nell went on, shaking her head. Holly wanted to reach across the table and slap her or choke the life out of her. Instead, she asked, "Whose idea was it to put Daddy in the car and drive it into the river?"

"Mr. Kamp suggested that it might be a workable scenario," she explained matter-of-factly. "I went inside and tidied up. I cleaned the blood from the floor. I tore the rest of that woman's portrait from the frame and burned it in the fire. I discarded the frame in the old greenhouse, with the rest of the trash. Where it belonged.

"It all would have worked perfectly if that demented Carlucci girl had not been traipsing through the rain." Holly bristled, but told herself, *It's nearly over.* "With T.L. scheduled to leave for Memphis and then California first thing the next morning, he might not have been missed for days. Who could say when the car went in the river?"

Holly nodded. "But Rose did see it, and you knew that she would get to a phone as quickly as she could."

Mary Nell studied not so much Holly but a space in the air beside Holly as if she could see it all playing out again in some vaporous TV monitor. Grudgingly she conceded, "Yes. Just a piece of bad luck. By the time LeRoy returned to Wolf's Run and told me, the police already were at the bridge."

"So, you and LeRoy had to go around the back side of Blue Mountain."

"I was following Mr. Kamp in the station wagon but my wheel slipped off into a flooded ditch. Mr. Kamp was so kind. He understood that I needed to be home in case visitors came to call. So he gallantly allowed me to take his truck," she said. "When we discussed the matter later, he told me about the need to employ a local rube to extricate my station wagon from the ditch. We decided it might be best if the vehicle disappeared. Mr. Kamp suggested a ruse involving an out-of-state theft could help in that regard. He surreptitiously drove me to Memphis a few days later."

"It was LeRoy who beat you."

"Yes. We had to make the theft appear genuine. But I must ask you to cease calling Mr. Kamp by his Christian name. Please show the proper respect for the departed. And for your betters," said Mary Nell, a sneer crossing her lips, but Holly pressed on.

"Where was Tom during all this? Did he know?"

"Who knows what a drunken Negro knows? Or can comprehend? But he certainly could not be trusted in this matter."

Holly realized she was breathing through her mouth. Trying to get enough air into her chest. Her ribs felt as heavy as ironwork, pressing on her lungs. All the oxygen was being sucked from the room. "If the purpose of all this was to keep my mother's ancestry hidden, why are you disclosing it now?"

"Sadly, I've undergone an unfortunate change of circumstances. Mr. and Mrs. Poindexter feel it appropriate to maintain a certain, uhm, distance in this matter. Allowing myself to be deceived by the Negro Tom Carter has put our family in a sordid and scandalous position. So, it is up to me to clean up my own mess," she explained. "Once I tell a jury of white men how I was duped into becoming a Negro's wife, they won't send me to prison for any of it. They'll give me a parade down Main Street."

Holly had only one more question. "When did you decide to kill Tom and the children?"

"Why, as soon as T.L. revealed the report to us. You see, T.L.'s death really was an unfortunate moment of circumstance. Of his refusal to listen to reason," explained Mary Nell, straightening her shoulders. "But the notion that I would continue to share my bed with a Negro and raise his pickaninnies – well, such a thing was simply out of the question."

Holly was shaking her head. "Why not divorce Tom? Leave them?"

Mary Nell looked at Holly as if she'd suggested she walked naked through the lobby of the Peabody Hotel. "Divorce?" she said, shaking her head. "Poindexters do not allow themselves to become involved in that sort of sordid legal adventure."

That was it! That was all Holly could listen to. "I've got to get out of here," she said to the mirror as she pushed away from the table. Mary Nell's eyes widened and she got to her feet, the chains rattling. "Stop! How dare you leave without my permission!" she screamed. "I didn't dismiss you! You filthy –"

Burke stepped through the door with Cutter right behind him. As Holly wheeled toward the door, Mary Nell drew her head back then spit in Holly's face. The shocked caused Holly to pause, the spittle running down her cheek. Cutter whirled, drawing his arm to backhand the women but Burke stepped between them. Holly pushed through the door and Burke shoved Cutter back. They stared at each other, then Cutter followed Holly out. She was wiping her face on a monogramed handkerchief proffered by J.G. Belmont.

"Plainly, Mrs. Carter is a sick woman," her attorney was saying.

"Will that be your defense?" she asked.

"It's certainly a viable one from what I saw."

Holly tossed the soiled handkerchief into the lawyer's round, sweating face. He let it drop to the floor as she pushed toward a bank of elevators at the end of the hall.

CHAPTER 20

I n the jail parking lot Holly handed Cutter the keys saying, "Would you mind driving? I'm too shaky."

Those were the last words that passed between them for 40 miles, until they reached the old antebellum town of Holly Springs. As they were going around the town square with the big white courthouse at its center, Holly said, "I feel sick. I need to put something in my stomach. Can we stop at that little drive-in by the railroad tracks?"

They parked in front of the place, which was in a copse of live oaks across from several cotton warehouses. The sign on the small, cinderblock building read Cup & Cone, with likeness of both painted on the white tin and a Confederate flag between them. Holly watched Cutter get out and walk to an order window, his Levis tight on his powerful hips. On the side was another window with a sign that said: Colored. Holly stared at it and wondered if she would have even noticed it two hours earlier.

Cutter came back with milkshakes – strawberry for her, chocolate for him. Neither of them were eager to push on to DeLong. Holly sucked on the long straw and her stomach settled. She stared quietly at the "Colored" sign as a young black man and woman approached the window. They ordered, waited in the unusually cool Sunday afternoon light, dressed in their church finery.

"Guess that's the window I need to use from now on," Holly said without looking at Cutter. "Did you ever think you'd be with a black woman?"

"How do you know I haven't been already?"

"Touché."

"Holly, the whole thing is ridiculous. It's stupid."

She laid back on the seat. "Yes, but it is the law. In this state and most states in the South, legally I'm as black as those happy young people there, as black as anyone in Roseville. The 'one-drop rule,' you know?" When Cutter said nothing, Holly told him, "Anyone who has even one drop of black blood is considered a Negro by the great state of Mississippi, and I far exceed that quota. I'm what's known in race-conscious circles as a 'quadroon.' One quarter black. I might as well be a charter member of the NAACP."

"If Mary Nell is telling the truth," said Cutter.

"I'm sure Mr. Burke will get a court order to open her safe deposit box in Vicksburg," said Holly. "But that's pro forma. As soon as the words came out of Mary Nell's mouth, I knew it was true. It explains everything. Why my mother suddenly disappeared. Why she never contacted us. Why my own father could barely stand to look at me." She studied Cutter, suddenly and awkwardly aware of the years that were between them. "You're too young. You weren't even born. You think we're dealing with some racial shit now? I remember Miss'ssippi just after the war. The big war. World War II. I'm that old. I remember how strict the lines were between black and white back then. I remember grown black men and women stepping off the sidewalk to let me and my mother pass, as if the happenstance of our light skin bestowed royal privilege on us. And all the while, my mother knew." Holly shook her head. "If it had come out then, it would have ruined the paper, my family. We'd have had to leave the state. Probably leave the South. It would have killed Tom. Who knows what it would have done to me, meant to me at seven. It certainly would have changed everything about how I was seen growing up and how I saw myself. What I was allowed to be and become."

Cutter didn't rush to speak, but after a moment asked, "Then you're okay with what your daddy did?"

"It's not that simple. I don't know what I am with it. I remember my parents as being very much in love. But if she really did deceive him –" Holly shook her head – "at that time, in this state, it would have been a terrible betrayal. But to simply dismiss from your life someone you seemed to love so deeply." Holly looked away, biting her lip. "What I don't believe is that he killed her or had her killed. If he had, there's no way he would have been coming to L.A. to tell me the truth or reveal her race in the paper."

"Then you don't think Tony was involved?" asked Cutter. "That Mary Nell made that up to, I guess, to hurt us – me and you."

"I didn't say that," Holly told him. "I wouldn't put anything past Tony. He may well have helped spirit her out of town on Weathers' orders without knowing the reasons why. Otherwise, I think he'd have used it against Daddy or me by now." She paused and closed her eyes. When she reopened them she said, "I have to tell you something about your father because it may well come out now, too. It happened at The Gin when I was singing there. When I was a senior in high school, like you are now."

Holly proceeded to tell him about Tony's brutally and nearly successful attempt to rape her. Cutter said nothing, asked nothing as she shared every detail. Every fear and smell and grimy sensation that she felt pinned to that storage room floor, and all the physical and emotional ache that came after. How it was one of the main reasons she ran to California.

"I couldn't stay someplace that let men like Tony get away with things like that," she said. "I had to leave. And I planned to never come back. Then all this."

Cutter opened the car door and got out. He looked around as if lost then started away from the car and toward Highway 78.

"Come back!" Holly called. "Cutter!"

He kept walking and started south on the shoulder of the two-lane road.

Holly groaned with effort and exhaustion as she slid her hips across the console and then lifted one leg over and then the other until she was behind the wheel. She cranked the big four-barrel, turned the car around in the gravel lot and headed for the stop light down the hill from the railroad tracks. Cutter was walking hands in pockets as eighteen-wheelers, family cars and pickups passed him by, grit stinging the back of his neck as they did so. Holly got into the line of traffic and slowed to a crawl as she got beside him, horns blaring behind her. "What are doing?" she called through the open passenger window. But he kept walking.

The line of angry drivers lengthened behind the Fury as did the noise of horns. She pulled past him and whipped the Plymouth into the pitted parking lot for an auto parts dealer. In a couple of minutes Cutter walked past the car, his eyes straight ahead. She stared at him as he passed.

"Cutter, stop! Do you hear me? You know I can't chase you down," she called after him. Then, exasperated, she pressed her palm onto the horn, long and loud. As the sound died away, "Damn you!" she yelled. "Don't make me feel like a cripple!"

He froze, as still and hard as a bronze statue. Then he turned and walked back to the driver's door. He looked down at Holly. She asked, "Are you angry with me for telling you what happened at The Gin?"

Cutter's face registered real surprise, almost hurt.

"Angry? With you? No!" he told her. "I'm just mad at everything, I guess. I'm crazy mad that Tony did that to you. I'm ashamed he's my daddy. I'm mad at myself for being a coward. For not killin' Tony when I've had the chance. I'm mad that, that –" he fought to find the words – "that I'm eighteen and you're twenty-eight, and that I wasn't there to protect you."

Gripping the door frame he squatted on his haunches, staring at the gravel as if he could no longer bear all the weight. Holly stroked his black hair and ran her nails gently down his neck and drew her fingers across the hard, flat mantle of his shoulders.

"Come on. Get in," she said, and he did.

W hen they got back to DeLong the sun was low behind Blue Mountain and Wolf's Run was deep in shadow. Rose was sitting in the well-lit kitchen with her guitar on her lap and what she called her "song journal" open on the table. A butcher knife beside it.

Holly said a polite, distant hello but answered none of the questions that were in Rose's eyes.

"Could you please pour me a glass of wine and bring it into my bedroom?" Holly asked. "I'm not feeling very well."

"Sh-Sure."

Cutter was standing by the sink, looking out on the lighted patio and glowing pool when Rose returned to the room and stood beside her brother. He decided he wouldn't tell Rose about what Tony had done to Holly at The Gin unless he had to, and right now he didn't have to. But without being asked, he told her what had transpired at the Memphis jail, knowing it was likely to come out one way or another in the next few days.

"H-H-Holly a Negro?" Rose asked, disbelieving. "That's st-st-stupid."

"It is stupid," said Cutter. "But I'm afraid it's the law."

"And you c-care about that?"

"Of course not, Sister. But there'll be a lot of people around here who do."

Rose looked up into her brother's eyes, her face defiant. "F-Fuck them!"

In spite of himself, Cutter laughed and impulsively put his arms around her. Rose stiffened. He could feel that she actually had stopped breathing and quickly stepped back.

"I'm sorry," he said. "I know you don't like being touched."

Rose looked down, shook her head. Then she turned and gathered up her guitar and song journal. "I'm going to m-my room and w-w-work on my songs," she said, her back to him. "G-G-Good night."

"Good night, Rose," he said, and noticed that the butcher knife was no longer on the table.

Cutter turned out most of the lights and sat down on the hall floor, leaning back against the wall beside Holly's door. He listened to the quiet of the big house. He heard nothing from inside the bedroom. Not a Sinatra album on the record player. Not the radio playing cool sounds for lonely lovers. Not Holly expertly fingering the frets of her guitar. Only the soft keening of an insistent breeze in the eves. There was no light coming from under the door. After a long while he went into the kitchen and got the open bottle of California rose' from the refrigerator and tapped on the bedroom door. There was no response. He turned the inlaid porcelain knob and the weak light from the patio spilled into the bedroom. Holly was in a t-shirt sitting at the antique Deco vanity looking at her reflection in the large round mirror, the light of one candle playing over her features. She said nothing. She was touching her face as if her skin's dusky pigment might rub off onto her fingers. Her wine glass was empty. Cutter crossed the room, refilled it and placed the bottle next to the candle. She stopped inspecting herself and reached for the glass. She'd obviously been crying. Without looking up, she sighed and said, "Thank you."

"Do you want me to stay tonight?" he asked.

"No," Holly said immediately, then reached out and grasped Cutter's hand.

"I mean yes, but no." Cutter said nothing. Holly half-smiled at her own confused response. "I want you in my bed every night but not tonight." She looked at him, candlelit in the mirror. "It seems like the only times we actually sleep together is when there's been some sort of disaster. I'm starting to associate the two things. When I think about making love with you, I want it to, you know, be joyful. I want to think about happiness. Satisfaction, of course, but – I know I sound crazy. Maybe I'm drunk or too tired to think straight. But I want to laugh when I'm in bed with you. I want to feel loved, all the way through without thinking, 'God! That was wonderful, but ....' I don't want it all tangled up with tears and bad feelings. Can you understand?"

"Yeah, actually I can. I'm feeling a little of that myself."

Holly looked up at him, relieved. "Are we okay?"

"You mean about your momma or my daddy?"

"Both."

Cutter thought for a moment. "I am if you are."

"It'll get out, you know? About my mother. Me. Mary Nell will make sure of that," Holly told him. "I'll probably have to deal with in the paper at some point. It could get pretty embarrassing."

"Why?"

"Why what?"

"Why will it be embarrassing?"

"Come on, Cutter. You've lived here your whole life. You know why."

Cutter sat down on a dressing table bench that went unused by Holly. "Look, I get that no one wants their family's laundry aired in public," he said. "But in the case of you Carters, that horse has pretty well cleared the barn."

Holly lifted her glass in a mock toast and took a long sip. "Yes, indeed. Thanks for reminding me."

"It's the same with me and mine," he told her. "My daddy's wanted for murder. Maybe you read about it. It's been in all the papers."

Holly nodded, not looking at him but appreciating the fact that he was unafraid to challenge her with some sarcasm of his own. "Yes, I believe I did read that somewhere."

"All I'm sayin' is, nobody can embarrass you about having a streak of colored blood unless deep down you really are ashamed of it. If you are, you are," he told her with a shrug. "Most people around here would be. But you're not 'most people'."

Holly raised the wine glass again but instead of taking another swallow, leaned forward and put the cold crystal to her pounding forehead. "Ohhh, Cutter," she sighed. "You give me far too much credit."

"And you don't give yourself enough," he told her, standing and putting his big hands lightly on the firm muscles of Holly's shoulders, gently kneading them, fighting the urge to let them slide down onto her chest. That was what he wanted, but not what she, what either of them needed in this moment on this night. After a couple of minutes, he kissed her on top of her head and turned to the door. When she heard it open, Holly said, "Thank you for being there today. It helped."

"Glad I could be," he told her. "Now try to get some sleep. I'll be just up the hill."

"I know."

CHAPTER 21

Once Mary Nell Carter achieved the ugly satisfaction of looking into her sister-in-law's eyes when she told her of Veronique Dupre Carter's lineage, she began a public relations onslaught that would have impressed a team of Madison Avenue ad men. She used a pay phone in the common area of the Shelby County Jail to place collect calls to anyone in Cattahatchie County who would accept them, and that included almost everyone she dialed. The list was long but began with Governor Weathers, followed by Brother MacAllister, then the wives of the deacons and spouses of influential men with obvious and not-so-obvious ties to the Klan. Despite conversations that often contradicted each other, the loyalists at First Denomination were willing to tangle themselves in any fable that extricated Mary Nell.

"It's no wonder she can't think straight, locked up in that awful place," said Edith Reed, whose husband, Proctor, owned the only real shoe store in town. "It's more than a white, Christian woman should have to bear."

Mary Nell told various lurid stories, often in detail, related to the death of T.L. Carter and the poisoning of her husband, children and, she claimed, of herself. In all versions Mary Nell was the victim and the central character in the drama. In one fashion or another, she declared that she was being framed so that Holly Lee Carter could steal the other 49 percent of *The Current-Leader* from her and Tom. She'd merely gone to Wolf's Run that rainy March night to help her much-loved father-in-law pack for his trip to Los Angeles when he'd attempted to sexually assault her. She fought back to defend herself and accidentally struck him with her car while trying to get away. She had enlisted the help of LeRoy Kamp – "a member in good standing of the Cattahatchie Chapter of the Sons of the Confederacy," she pointed out – in an effort to spare Tom and T.L.'s grandchildren the humiliation of the truth. As for the poisoning, that was Tom's doing. Why, she had deathly ill herself only to fight her way through via the "miracle of constant prayer." Mary Nell now realized poor Tom had been so distraught about the "awful revelation" that his mother was "nothing more than a bright mulatto, that he began poisoning all of us out of abject shame. It was an awful and demonic deception that Veronique Dupre played on everyone, even T.L. Now it's easy to see why Tom's sister is conspiring with the awful Mr. Burke and that colored preacher, that agitator Clemmer and all those vile integrationists because she is, in fact, a Negro. Her blood is calling her to betray us all. Blood well tell. It always does."

By Wednesday night's prayer meeting, talk about Holly Lee Carter was so vicious and hateful that I half-expected the sanctuary roof to collapse from the weight of all the invective. And I almost wished it would. The attendance for Sunday morning services had been dwindling for weeks and the drop-off was even more pronounced at practice for the youth choir and prayer meetings. Thus those who attended now were the staunchest in their commitment to The Cause of racial separation. The notion that a "quadroon" – legally a black woman in the state of Mississippi – was running the local newspaper infuriated them almost beyond measure and Mary Nell was happy to stoke that fire.

"How are those poor children?" asked Gladys Cole, who ran a sandwich shop a block off the square. "And Tom?"

Brother MacCallister, who was standing in the space between the front pew and the pulpit, said, "Latest report is that Tom was transported to Memphis Labor Day night, but Dr. Garner is not hopeful. Of course, there are much better doctors in Memphis, so we shall see. Georgette is showing improvement, but it's still touch and go with Lanny."

Much headshaking and sighing followed, including from Patti, who sat beside me in a fuzzy white sweater that fit her like spilled milk.

For my part, I still was angry with Miss Carter for stealing Cutter's friendship and attention from me and endangering his college football career. That's how I saw it. And I still blamed her for much of the mess that had happened since Cutter and I pulled her and Eve Howard out of that ditch a little more than two months earlier, but some of the stuff being said by thirty-five or so otherwise sane grown-ups I'd lived around and worshiped with all my life was simply – nuts. Crazy talk.

"I don't believe it," Claire Newby said firmly and I thought, *Thank goodness, somebody's going to talk sense.* Mrs. Newby, who worked in the Chancery Clerk's office, went on, "You mark my words, Tom Carter may be a lot of things. He might even be half colored, but he loved those children. There's no way he fed arsenic to those precious babies. Mary Nell's got that part wrong. But I'll tell you something I do know, that house is owned by the newspaper company. That means that Carter girl most surely has a key to every door in the place. This all started, all our real trouble started when she came back. She could have sneaked herself in there any time and put poison in the sugar bowl, in food, in drinks. In the very lemonade they claim Mary Nell was usin' to make them sick."

My hand went up as if I were in second period English and people stopped talking and started looking at me before I had time to reconsider. "You know," I said as inoffensively as I could, "Miss Carter is in a wheelchair. She's paralyzed. She can't walk." People were staring at me. I saw Patti's grip tighten on the hymnal she was holding.

"So-o?" said someone, dragging that small word out into two syllables.

I should have stopped there, but I said, "So-o, there are five or six steps up to every porch and outside door at Tom Carter's house. That would be pretty tough for a woman in a wheelchair to pull off."

There were several long seconds of silence. People stared at me as they chewed over that thought. Leo Jamison, a local constable, spoke first, "Well, listen to the junior G-Man."

Everyone who wasn't simply scowling laughed at me, including Patti. I felt my face burning.

"Maybe he wants the sheriff job once we kick his daddy's butt out of office," said Randle Kilmer, a farmer in the Mount Zion Community.

"The office ain't really his anyway," said Jamison. "He stole it from J.D. Benoit, 'cause J.D. wouldn't kiss nigger ass."

"Please!" intoned the pastor. "I understand your righteous anger, but let us remember we're in a house of worship."

"Amen, preacher," said Mrs. Farrell Hughes, speaking from beneath her jet black beehive. "We need to put this in God's hands. We need to organize a prayer group for Mary Nell."

"That's right, sister!" said another woman.

"And we need to be praying for Cutter, too," said Margery Wingwood, a thirty-something mother of three who I knew for a fact had slipped up to The Gin more than once when her lawyer husband was out of town. I'd seen her sidling up to Cutter at the end of his shift one cold January Saturday night. Her arm around his waist, leaning into him, leading with her ample and amply exposed cleavage. "He's not a bad kid, but he's been bewitched by that Carter woman. It shows the power of demons surrounding her that she's able to do that even though she's, she's – she's not even whole. Powerful, dark forces surround that woman! Whatever color she is."

"Sister Margery speaks the truth!" agreed Mrs. Hughes. "Who's in? We can meet for lunch at Rowdy's barbecue. I'll tell Rowdy we want to use the side room for some privacy."

Several hands went up as I hung my head, slowly shook it, quietly mumbling, "This is craziness … just pure craziness … they're all nuts." Still, Patti heard and pinched the back of my arm so hard I yelped, but no one was paying attention to me.

CHAPTER 22

The almanac was right again. It continued unseasonably cool that early September of 1969, and in the mornings a column of fog rose from the river and settled into the low spots of the land in white drifts, like snow. On Thursday night, pep rallies were held around bonfires at CHS and Riverview. The Wolves' home opener was scheduled for Friday and the Raiders were set to play their first-ever game on the road at Greenwood. When the team was introduced by Coach Pearce at the pep rally, I stepped forward as one of the starting wide receivers. Me!

It's hard to put into words how big that moment was for me, how much it meant. I wasn't just an afterthought, a scrawny guy inserted late into games that already were long-since won by Cutter and Dodge and Jimmy Garner. For the first time ever, it let me step out of the long, deep shadow that Cutter had cast over me, unintentional though that was. And Patti seemed to look at me with different eyes. Eyes only slightly glazed by pot and probably pills she did not let me see. Out in the middle of the new Riverview Field under the new Riverview stadium lights, the new Riverview band was playing fight songs and finally *Dixie*, I felt myself stiffening in the front of my jeans thinking about my hand sliding beneath the short gold skirt of Patti's cheerleader uniform.

In that moment, before things changed, I couldn't imagine life being any better. Except, of course, it would be when Patti and I were off at Ole Miss, away from Brother Daddy, who was crazier by the day. And then when we got married and moved away to New Orleans, or maybe Atlanta or, hell, even New York, this place and all this meanness and insanity would be behind us. So would Cutter, I supposed. But he'd chosen his path, and he'd have to live with it.

Across the river, Coach Hinton and Jimmy Garner made brief speeches while Cutter stayed out of the limelight as much as he could. On Friday the Wolves were going to lose and badly to a very good Baldwin team, and Cutter knew it, but it didn't matter as much as seeing Rose clapping and cheering, wearing the spirit T-shirt that she and Holly had enjoyed making together – adding glue and glitter. Just as the fire radiated light and heat, Rose's face radiated a joy and a hope that made the blood run warmer through Cutter's heart.

Washed in the warm, moving light of the bonfire, Cutter wished his mother could see her children now. Away from Tony, and happy for the first time in years. Yet, the ugly force of Tony's hate pressed in around them, held at bay by deputies cradling shotguns at the edge of the light – the flames glowing on the black, oiled steel of the gun barrels. Out beyond them in the dark were FBI agents and U.S. Marshals scattered in the hills that rose to the south of the high school, on the lookout for Klansmen with deer rifles – including McBride, Gandy and Tony. Cutter wasn't unaware of the dangers. The big red C on his black letter jacket might as well have been a bullseye. Holly knew it, too. She had parked the Plymouth at the edge of the road next to the field behind the high school where the bonfire blazed. She was resting her elbows on the door, clicking away with her camera for the Saturday edition of *The Current-Leader*. Now and then she and Cutter caught each other's eye and shared a private smile, neither one of them allowing themselves to dwell on the ugliness or the danger. Instead, almost like proud parents they were committed to supporting and encouraging Rose, and to simply enjoying the moment, wondering if this was what normal could feel like, be like for them.

Sitting together on the porch swing at Wolf's Run afterwards, a blanket wrapped around their shoulders against the surprising chill, Holly said, "I've missed you."

"Yeah, me, too, you."

"You're not angry about the other night?"

"Nope," he said. "We've both lived pretty much alone for a long time. I enjoy being with you in, well, in a way I've never enjoyed being with anyone else. But there are times when I need to be off by myself. I think you're like that, too."

"Yes, you're right," she said. "I'm glad you understand. A lot of men wouldn't."

"There's not a lot men sittin' here on your front porch," he said. "Just me."

"I'm glad. Being with you has beocme the best part of my day. Or night," she told him with a smile that was knowing and yet somehow shy. "And I don't want to spoil it. But I have something I want to show you. With the phone-call campaign Mary Nell has going, and the innuendo Weathers has his announcers spouting over the radio station, I have to address it. I want your opinion, before it goes in the paper Saturday."

Holly took two sheets of paper from a pocket in her denim skirt. Cutter unfolded them and stared at the type. "Too dark out here," he said and stood, stepping around her wheelchair and walking to the front door. He stood in the front hall where a lamp was on. He read it twice and returned in about three minutes, sat next to Holly and handed back to her the "From the Publisher's Desk" column that was to run in less than two days – the day before his nineteenth birthday.

"There's a misspelling in the first sentence of the second paragraph," he said, slipping his arm around her shoulders under the blanket. "Distraction. It's missing the second i."

Holly stared at him. "That's all you have to say?"

"You told me Mr. Burke got a court order and got into Mary Nell's box at that Vickburg bank, right? And found that detective's report?"

"Yes."

"And you're sure it's true?"

Holly thought about it. "I'm as sure as I can be without hiring a private detective to reinvestigate it all. Something I clearly can't afford at the moment," she said after a bit. "I certainly believe it to be true. It answers questions I've had most of my life."

"In that case, you said it good."

Holly waited. When it became clear Cutter had no more to add, she said, "Okay then. It runs Saturday on page one."

Cutter pulled the blanket tighter around them as Holly leaned into him. "Out of curiosity," he said, "if I had hated your column, pitched a fit and told you not to run it, what would you have done?"

Holly drew in a deep breath and let it out. "I'd run it anyway," she told him.

Cutter laughed softly. "That's what I thought," he told her.

Chapter 23

The twisty-turny road to where Cutter was now making his camp up the slope from Wolf's Run was barely that, a road. It was more like an overgrown wagon path. There was no way my truck could have negotiated the steep parts, so I was glad that I had left it around the curve and out of the way. Even on foot it was a difficult walk, especially in the dark, and I felt like I was carrying 60 pounds of sharp glass in my chest. My shoulders sagged and my feet barely found enough lift to take the next step. When my shin hit a tripwire I heard the rattle of rocks inside tin cans. The sudden clack-clack of Cutter chambering a round into his .12 gauge froze me in the moonlight.

"It's me!" I called up the hill.

"Nate?"

"Yeah, yeah. Take it easy."

"Are you alone?"

"Yeah."

"All right. Come on up." I climbed the last 30 feet onto the plateau. Through a natural gap in the trees, the precipice offered an almost unobstructed view of Miss Carter's property – the newly painted fence and the new electric gate. Farther down the slope, glimpses of Wolf's Run were visible behind a screen of pecan, walnuts, pines and oaks.

"That's a good way to get yourself killed," said Cutter.

"It used to be a fella could drop by your camp for a beer or conversation without worrying about getting his head blowed off."

"It used to be a lot things around here," he said, testy. "But things have changed a good deal, in case it's escaped your attention."

Cutter reached into an ice chest sitting next to the Jeep, which held a precarious perch on the edge of the plateau. "Coke's the best I got. You want one?"

"Sure."

Cutter popped the top on an opener attached to the ice chest and handed a bottle to me, walked over and sat on his sleeping bag. The clearing was small, much smaller than the area around The Well. He propped the shotgun on a large rock and leaned back next to it. I sat down across from the coals of a low fire. It wasn't chilly enough to see my breath, but it would be before morning. Fall was rushing into the Cattahatchie Valley.

"What time is it?" he asked.

I tilted my wrist in the light of the half moon until it glinted off my watch. "1:52."

"Dadgum it, Nate! I've got a football game to play tomorrow night, and so do you. What are you doing here? In fact, how'd you know where to find me?"

"I called Miss Carter from the pay phone outside Gibson's Grocery."

"When?"

"About thirty minutes ago."

"At one-thirty in the morning?"

"Yeah. I thought you might be – I mean, well, I told her I had to see you."

"What? Did Miz Fletcher throw you out?"

I had wondered how I was going to tell it, but I opened my mouth and it just came out. "Patti was in on what happened to Miss Howard and Ridge Bellafont."

Cutter stared at me through the moonlight. I'm sure I must have looked ghostly in the sheer white glow from the cold heavens. I felt like all the blood had been drained out of me. I went on before I lost my nerve.

"We had a pep rally tonight. The band was there and the cheerleaders. I took Patti. She never looked prettier or sweeter. Like an angel," I told him, and looked away for a moment, seeing her in that moment before I knew. "Afterwards we went parking out in Clark Creek bottom. But she was poppin' some of her momma's nerve pills, and smokin' pot, too, but instead of calming her down, she was strung as tight as a cat in a room full of rocking chairs. She was all worked up about Miss Carter. She said, 'At least my conscience is clear. I'm a good girl. I did my part to stamp out her kind'."

"I asked her what she meant. She reminded me about our fight at the Klan rally and how she'd walked off. It turns out she spied Eve Howard beside Mr. Bellafont's car. Patti turned her in. She told the Klargo."

To my consternation, Cutter didn't show any surprise. He merely stared at me across the embers. He always had understood what Patti was capable of in a way that I had not, or at least would not allow myself to believe until that night. Cutter understood fundamental evil, because he had lived with it. When he said nothing, I went on – "She told it like she'd tell about how she did on a, a, history test or, or what she had for lunch. Like it was nothing. I tried to make her see what she'd done. What I saw under that car the next morning. About how Miss Howard's skin was so cooked it came off in, in –" I stared at my hand but I couldn't say the word. "Patti just looked at me like I wasn't – I don't know – getting it?

"Then she said, 'Nate, you make me sick. I swear, I think sometimes you ought to wear panties. We're just talkin' about an out-of-town nigger and fat old fag.'"

In the woods and not far away a bobcat squalled. A shiver crawled up my spine like a six-inch centipede, and I drew my knees to the gold 81 on my jersey and wrapped my arms around them. I felt my chest heave with a deep sob. When I'd forced my own emotion back into my chest, I said, "Right that minute, I took her home, opened the door and told her to get out. She sashayed up the driveway. Then turned around and said, 'You'll be back.'"

The quiet of the night settled around us for a time. Then, "Will you? Go back?" Cutter asked.

I thought about it for a bit. "I hope not," was the best I could do. "Can I keep camp with you for – I don't know, a few nights until I can kinda, kinda …?" I didn't have the words to finish the thought or the strength to consider my future, but I did know something about my past. "Cutter, I'm sorry about all that's happened between us the last few weeks. I've been a sorry excuse for a friend. If you don't want me around, I'd understand."

He used a stick to stir at the fire coals and threw on another log. Sparks flew up red and disappeared among the tree limbs. "You're gonna be a might chilly before mornin' without a sleepin' bag."

"I got one. I left it down the hill a piece."

"Then go fetch it and settle in," he said, sliding down into his bag. "I don't want to be up all night."

* * *

Next morning a small, wind-up alarm clock began to rattle at 5:50 a.m. I had slept on the rocks near Cutter's Jeep and felt as if they'd worked their way inside my skin. It was still dark, only the slightest hint of pink in the eastern sky. But Cutter rousted me up and within 10 minutes had his camp area cleared, the fire embers doused and was ready to roll. That was his way of doing things.

"Let's get some breakfast," he said, his breath coming out white in the brisk air, and I climbed into the Jeep's passenger seat. When he cranked the vehicle and downed the clutch I nearly dove out. The Jeep looked as if it would go right over the edge of the outcrop. After that, there would be almost nothing but a steep slope between the front bumper and the front porch of Wolf's Run. But he backed up, maneuvered and headed us down the narrow lane.

"Pretty fancy," I said when he took something from under his seat that looked like a television remote and pointed it at the metal gate that had been built into two new brick pillars.

The lights already were on in the kitchen at Wolf's Run and what I guessed were a couple of bedrooms. We parked behind the wreck of the old greenhouse where the Jeep would be mostly out of sight. Cutter tapped on the back door and walked in without waiting. Rose was frying bacon and scrambling eggs at the stove.

"G-Good morning," she said as Cutter passed by. I hung back in the shadows of the mud room that was lined with shelves and glass jars filled with fruit preserves and locally canned vegetables as both colorful art and a second pantry. "Are you r-ready to w-win tonight?"

"Oh, yeah. I'm ready. What about the coffee?"

"A little gr-grumpy this morning?"

"I sleep on rocks. I'm grumpy every morning."

"N-N-No you're not."

Cutter grunted noncommittally over the sound of a radio from up the hall. The Memphis news was on. He walked over to a corner of the counter near the hall and started pouring a cup from the coffeemaker. It was just then that Holly Lee Carter wheeled in from the hall. Her long hair was up and wrapped in a towel above a white terrycloth bathrobe. She hooked the long fingers of her left hand into one of Cutter's hip pockets and left them there.

"Hey you. How about pouring me a cup?"

It wasn't what Holly Carter said, but the husky tone she used and the easy familiarity with which she was dressed, or undressed, and how she approached Cutter and touched him, that told me all I needed to know. I suppose I already had known, but I still did not know how to feel about it.

"We have company," he said, and Holly withdrew her hand from his pocket.

I cleared my throat and stepped into the light of the kitchen -- "Miss Carter."

"Nate, well – hi!"

"I'm sorry I woke you up last night."

"That's all right. I see you found Cutter."

"Yes, Ma'am."

"Have a seat, Nate," said Cutter. "Rose makes a fine breakfast."

I was starving but said, "Maybe I should just walk on back to my truck. I don't want to –"

"You're here," said Cutter. "Sit."

Rose, whom I would have barely recognized in other circumstances, smiled and said, "There's pl-plenty."

I looked at Miss Carter, who did not look as enthusiastic as Rose sounded, but said, "Of course, Nate. Please join us." And I did.

* * *

After we ate, Cutter excused himself to the west wing and took a quick bath. I was in the courtyard by the pool when he came out. The light in the valley floor was moving from gold to white as the sun fully cleared a thin ribbon of silver-tipped clouds that feathered above the eastern hills. At the bottom of the steep bluff that fell away from Wolf's Run, the Cattahatchie was flowing south, its brown skin veiled in mist. In the distance traffic hummed its busy Friday song on Highway 27. Pickups, cars, tractor-trailer rigs and yellow school buses moved along the faded blacktop as if on gray rails.

Cutter approached. "Great view, huh?"

"Yeah. It's somethin'," I said. "Is this where you call home now?"

"I don't have any place to call home. I haven't for a long while. You know that better than most," he said. "But I'm grateful Holly's taken Rose in and worked a miracle. Or maybe Rose has always been a miracle waiting to happen. She just needed a chance."

Cutter allowed himself to admire the valley for a time, then – "We're all gonna have to hustle to get to school before first bell. Let's go."

"I'm not goin'."

"You've got a game tonight. You're gonna start."

"To hell with it, I'm not goin' back to Riverview. I don't want to be anywhere near Patti or those people."

Cutter sat down on the knee-high stone wall that guarded the patio's edge and regarded me. "Nate, you've been through a lot in the last few hours. Heck, the last few weeks. Don't make a snap decision you'll regret."

"This isn't a snap decision. It's been building up, one of Patti's lies on top of one of her meannesses for a long time," I told him. "Now this with Miss Howard and Mr. Bellafont? It's too much."

"Nate, Patti couldn't have known what they were going to do. She shouldn't have done what she did but –"

"But what? She helped the Klan kill somebody, like you'd slaughter a hog. Worse! Nobody'd whip a hog to death. That's sick! Almost past any way to measure it. And they meant to kill Miss Howard. Crushed her to death or burn her alive. They didn't care which. And Patti still don't care. She's as pleased as pink lemonade with herself. Thinks she struck some blow for the white Christian race," I told him. "It's fucked-up, man. They're all fucked-up! I'm sick to death of it!"

Cutter stood, his hands stuffed into the pockets of his jeans. And it was at that instant I realized I had been talking about Tony Carlucci, about his father. His blood. "Cutter, I'm sorry. I didn't mean to go off like that about –"

"Don't be. It's all true," he said with no noticeable emotion. "Look, if you're not going to school, why don't you stay here and get some sleep. Things may look different to you after you've had some real shut-eye. There're three or four spare bedrooms down the west hall."

Under the circumstances that sounded like an offer to ascend to heaven and sleep among the clouds, but I said, "I'm not sure Miss Carter would be very happy about that."

"Don't worry about that. I'll fix it," he told me and headed for the ramp up to the kitchen. At the top of the slope he turned and called, "Hey, Nate! If you don't go to the Riverview game, come see the Wolves play. But I warn you, it may not be pretty. We're still mighty ragged."

I waved to him. "Maybe I'll do that," I told him across the pool and big patio. And that's how we left it that Friday morning.

* * *

As it turned out, I never left Wolf's Run that day. I didn't want to be any place where Patti or Coach Pearce or anyone else from Riverview might find me. I hadn't slept more than a couple of hours the previous night, so the jolt of morning coffee quickly wore off. About ten o'clock I found an empty bedroom, threw off my clothes and crawled under the covers. I was out almost before the sheets settled and slept until mid-afternoon. I awoke around 3:30, took a quick bath and, starving, ate two cold pork chops I found in the refrigerator before walking back to my truck. For an hour or more I simply drove around. I slowed at the boarding house and at our farm on Pleasant Ridge Road, but didn't stop. The sweet yellow light of late afternoon was spreading across every road and field. The cotton and beans and corn were standing high now in neat rows. Soon it would be harvest time. The sides of nearly every bottomland road in the county would be so white with cotton fiber blown from full-to-the-brim wagons that it would look like snowfall. The county's eight gins would start running 24 hours a day, their gears and lint cleaners resting only on the Sabbath – like the farmers and field hands and bale press operators who tore their livelihood from the land and the cotton bolls it fed.

The Riverview buses, carrying the team, cheerleaders and band, had left on the 150 trip to Greenwood hours earlier. But I had to fight the urge to turn my truck south and race toward Leflore County, to somehow beg forgiveness from Coach Pearce and my Raider teammates, and most of all Patti. Finally, I turned my wheels onto the pavement of Highway 27 and pointed my old truck toward CHS stadium. It was only fifteen minutes until game time, and I drove north expecting to hit traffic as soon as I passed the fairgrounds. Often late-arriving fans had to park on the shoulder of the highway and walk nearly three-quarters of a mile to get to the grandstands. But not on this night. Not for this team. A sheriff's deputy stood beside his car, his red strobe vibrating in the dusk, but he had little traffic to direct. I turned up the drive toward the school, circled around the side and parked close enough that I could have stepped out and hit the back of the press box with a thrown baseball.

At the main gate a black deputy – one of my father's new hires – stood next to another black man, whom I did not recognize, and collected my two dollars. I ambled inside. During the "Cutter Era," in which the Wolves had gone 33-6, spectators often ringed CHS field and gate receipts showed crowds in excess of 5,000 – more than twice the population of DeLong. On the opening night of the Wolves' 1969 home season, there were perhaps 350 people occupying the plank bleachers that usually overflowed with 1,500 or more. In fact, Baldwin fans on the opposite side of the field nearly outnumbered those in the home stands.

I spotted Miss Carter's Plymouth parked outside the west end zone. When the

Wolves jogged back to the locker room for final instructions and a prayer, I walked down. Rose and the other cheerleaders were waiting to run onto the field in front of the team.

"H-Hi, Nate. I'm gl-glad you came," Rose told me. She looked like a different person from the one who, in overalls and a slouch hat, had ridden up Blue Mountain in my truck only a few weeks ago. Her transformation did, indeed, seem a miracle.

Moments later we heard the shout from the locker room. The door opened and the reincarnated Cattahatchie High School Wolves charged out for their first-ever home game. They all wore green and gold patches on their black jerseys, honoring Roseville High's traditional colors. That had been Jimmy Garner's idea. Cutter smiled at me and Rose as he went by, running toward the sideline where Miss Carter had positioned herself with her camera and notebook.

"Nate!" Jimmy Garner called as he went by. "You better have your skinny ass out here for practice Monday."

"Or I'm gonna kick it clean to Tennessee," added Dodge McDowell and playfully smacked me in the back of the head with his huge open hand.

I smiled and gave them a little wave, but at that moment I didn't know where I'd be on Monday.

* * *

Cutter was right. It was ugly. Baldwin had a senior quarterback name of Ramsey who would go on to start two years at Auburn, and he feasted on the inexperienced Cattahatchie defensive backs. From his linebacker spot, Cutter knocked Ramsey out of the game late in the third quarter with a clean but vicious hit that sent the quarterback's helmet flying, but the scoreboard damage was done. Baldwin was up 45-18 going into the final period, and won it 58-31.

When the game was over, I didn't wait around, not wanting to talk further to Dodge or Jimmy or to anyone, fearful I would be asked to explain myself. In my truck I headed back toward Blue Mountain Road. I caught the after-game comments from Coach Pearce on WHCI, which had abandoned the Wolves in favor of the Confederates. Fielding a team including about seventy percent of the players from the 1968 CHS team, Riverview Academy had won its first-ever game 35-27. I'd known most of the guys on the team since I was in kindergarten. I was glad for them, but more sad to see Cutter return to his – our – camp so beaten down. He always played hard but he now was trying to carry the whole CHS team, and it showed on him as he unrolled his sleeping bag using only his left arm. He opened and closed his right hand again and again. I knew he was trying to get feeling back into it.

"How's the shoulder?" I asked as I put another small log on the fire. It was nearly 1:15.

"It's a little dinged," he said. "I'll be alright tomorrow. But takin' a butt-kickin' like that don't help."

"Where'd you go after the game?"

"Up to the paper. I just wanted to make sure Lee and Rose got home safe."

"Lee?"

Cutter didn't respond.

"I heard on the Memphis radio that McBride is a suspect in bombing two black churches near Stone Mountain, Georgia. They say the bombings have his – what do they call it? – signature. You think it was really McBride? You think your daddy's with him?"

"I don't know what to think. But I'm not taking any chances," he said propping his shotgun within reach and laying down on the sleeping bag. "Besides, sad as it is, they're not the only crazies in these woods."

* * *

The Riverview team and spirit buses did not get back from Greenwood until 2 a.m. Parents grumbled awake in their cars and took in cheerleaders, pep squad members and players who were without their own vehicles. Those with them climbed into cars and trucks and mostly headed home. A few went north to The Gin or down some narrow gravel road to bang on the back door of their favorite bootlegger. But Coach Pearce did not go to any of those places and did not go home. At the end of a narrow, disused lane that stopped at a small and ragged boat house, he loaded supplies from his truck and edged a skiff into the current of the Cattahatchie. Twenty-five minutes later he was unloading on the muddy bank near the most hidden of the Klan safe houses in the Three Corners. Bob McBride materialized out of the ground fog as quiet and cool as a corpse cradling an M16. Moments later Tony Carlucci and Frank Gandy came rattling through the underbrush.

"Did it work?" asked McBride without preamble.

"Weathers' sources say yep. Most of the feds and even the Army demolitions guys lit out for Georgia Thursday afternoon," replied Pearce.

Tony chuckled. "The Gov! I knew he'd come through for us, even if it's just to save his own ass."

"Halle-fuckin'lujah!" said Gandy. "When's the plane comin'?"

"Crack'uh'dawn Monday morning. Right out there," Pearce told him. "That wide spot in the river. He'll light as soon as there's enough mornin' to see where the cypress knees ain't. Be ready, 'cause this fella ain't the kind to wait."

McBride nodded thoughtfully. "That means we've just got two nights to get our business done."

"Damn it, Bob! Why don't y'all let that shit go?" asked Gandy. "Let's just get the hell outta here."

"Mr. Gandy, we've had this discussion several times, and I do not intend to have it again," said McBride. "The decision has been made. The plan is in place and we will execute it. Do I make myself clear?"

Frank Gandy hung his head, shook it, but said, "Yeah, yeah, yeah, yeah. You make yourself clear. I got it."

"Do you have the needed personnel lined up?" McBride ask.

"Yep. Benoit'll stay on the road with Gandy and the vehicles," he said. "The three of us'll go in and get the girl, run the charges and take care of whatever other business you need to. If anything goes wrong, we'll take the girl and go down that mountain-goat trail to the river. Buddy Epps'll have a boat waitin'. Nobody knows the river better than Buddy."

McBride nodded.

"If you have to," Pearce said to Gandy, "take the cars down into Hell Creek Bottom. There's a road that runs down to within 30 yards of the river. This time of year, it's dry enough to get through. There'll be gas cans in both vehicles. Torch the cars and get down to the water. There's a big sandbar. We'll pick you up there."

Everyone waited for McBride to pronounce his approval – or not. "Good work, Mr. Pearce," he said. "That sounds nicely workable."

Gandy was unsatisfied and worried. "Where's Cutter keepin' himself these days?"

"Some say he's sleepin' with that Carter bitch," said Pearce. "Some say he's still at The Well. People have seen his fire burnin'. Others say he's beddin' down on a cot at The Gin. Most don't really know."

"Shit!" said Gandy. "I hope to hell he ain't at Wolf's Run. He may take a lotta killin'."

"You scared of a little boy?" teased Tony.

"I notice you ain't killed that 'boy' yet," snapped Gandy.

Tony Carlucci glared at the smaller man. "Yeah, well, if he's there I'm about to," said Cutter's father. "And if he's not, he'll wish he was dead when he sees that place blown right off the side of that mountain along with that Carter cunt. There won't be enough left of her to put in a spit can."

All four men were silent for a moment, gleefully picturing the flaming nightmare that would be the end result after "Dynamite Bob" McBride did his work. Then Tony Carlucci began to smile, then grin wide enough that the whites of his stained teeth were visible in the dark, and an ugly laugh started low in this throat.

"What's so damn funny?" asked Gandy.

"I think luck is finally starting to run our way," said Tony. "I just remembered, Sunday is my boy's birthday. He'll turn nineteen."

The other three men looked at Cutter's father, his eyes hooded and black in the shadows cast by the moonlight. The irony of it gripped even McBride, who allowed himself a rare smile. "Well then, we're gonna throw your boy a helluva party. Fireworks and all."

CHAPTER 24

O n Saturday morning we let Rose and Miss Carter sleep in. Cutter and I
would be heading to The Gin and the girls were going to Tupelo to finalize
plans for Cutter's Sunday night birthday party at Wolf's Run. Cutter was
resistant to a big party, especially one as formal as Miss Carter was planning, catered
with a three-piece band. He relented only when she told them that the gathering was
about more than him. It was about holding onto the paper and maybe his college
football career. That was all she was willing to say, and Cutter didn't press. He
trusted her.

At first light we stirred and began packing up the camp. He said I could stay
there or go with him to The Gin.

"Mr. Clanton probably has a man's day of work for you, too," he said. "If you
think you can handle it."

"I'll work your sorry ass under the table," I said, both of us knowing that was
a lie. But Cutter had lain down a challenge, knowing I'd accept it. Mostly, I think
he wanted to keep me close, fearing otherwise I'd slink back to Patti. He was right,
of course, as only a best friend can be. I was, in fact, mulling ways to get past what
she'd done. Going to talk to her would be the first step.

"Let's go," said Cutter, dousing the camp fire.

I suggested we go to The Cotton Café for breakfast like we used to, but Cutter
said, "No. Let's go to Sally's Biscuits in Middleton. I don't want to have to go over
every play and screw-up from last night. It was hard enough to live through once."

We turned into Sally's graveled lot off Tennessee 57 thirsty for coffee and
hungry for bacon. There were newspaper boxes out front from Memphis, Jackson
and Bolivar, Tennessee and from DeLong. A nice black-and-white picture of Jimmy
Garner making a cut along the sideline was the centerpiece on the front page of *The
Current-Leader*. I pushed a quarter into the slot, opened the door and took out a copy.
The machine spit out my dime change and I followed Cutter through the door. The
waitress nodded to him and smiled with recognition but didn't say his name. He
found a back booth and we slipped into it.

While we waited for our breakfast we enjoyed the first jolt of coffee that was the
color of axle grease and I flipped through the paper. "Holy *fuck!*" I said loud enough

that an older couple gave me a hard look, but I didn't care. I flattened the paper on the table. "Have you seen this?"

Cutter looked down at *The Current-Leader*'s editorial page. The publisher's column was stripped across the top with Holly Lee Carter's picture and a headline that read: Blood Will Tell – Mine Tells the Story of Shared Mississippi Heritage. In the editorial she acknowledged the decades-old report from the New Orleans detective agency and said that while the claims in the report are at this time unverified, she assumes them to be true. And went on to say, "If so, just as I am proud to claim the English part of my heritage, which provided this nation with its concept of law and justice; and the French in my blood line that turned the Louisiana frontier into one of the great Colonial empires of the New World; I am proud, too, to claim the blood of the strong black men and women upon whose scarred backs was built most of what we treasure today as the physical heritage of the Old South – from Chalmette Plantation to my own home, Wolf's Run."

"Did you know about this?" I persisted with consternation.

"I caught a misspelled word after she finished it."

"And you didn't talk her out of this?"

"I don't talk Lee in or out of stuff."

"Geeeez-us!" I groaned. "She admits to being half colored!"

"A quarter."

"What?"

"If that report is true, then she's a quarter black."

"A quarter? A half? What the hell difference does that make?" I went on. "In Miss'ssippi that makes her all black!"

"And?"

"And ... and ..."

It was then that the waitress brought our breakfast. We fell silent while she put down our plates and poured our cups full again. Cutter thanked her and asked for more pancake syrup. As it often did, Cutter's coolness only made me more anxious.

"Don't you understand how people will see this?" I said as Cutter forked scrambled eggs into his mouth. "It's kickin' a hornet's nest that's already buzzin' mad! Geez! I mean you and her. It's –"

Cutter fixed me with his hypnotic eyes.

"It's what?" he said, his face suddenly hard as stone. "With Mary Nell on the phone to anybody in Cattahatchie County who'll take her crazy calls and the whole town talkin', Holly did what she had to do. And she did the right thing. She owned up to the truth about who she is and what made her. Some other folks around DeLong might consider bein' as honest. There's been a nigger in many'uh woodpile in these parts. Lee's just honest enough to tell the truth. There's some others who might want to give that a shot, just for the novelty of it."

I was angry, though not sure why, and snapped, "And what about you and her. What about honesty there? I notice y'all are keepin' that news item pretty close."

Cutter started to raise a forkful of eggs to his mouth then put it down, clinking onto the plate. "Dadgum it, Nate, grow up," he told me. "While you've spinnin' your high school confidential bullcrap with Patti, Lee's got responsibilities and pressures you can't even imagine."

My cheeks burned at the rebuke, but never one to leave well enough alone, I swallowed and asked, "Just tell me one thing. Are you in love with her?"

Sighing, he leaned back in the booth and looked at me at me for a long time like a grown man might look at willful child. Finally, "I don't know, Nate," he said wiping his mouth with a paper napkin. "I don't even know what love looks like. I've never seen it up close. You know, between a man and woman. I never saw it at my house. What's it supposed to be?"

I thought of my father and my mother, his 'Neesie. I thought of the way they seemed to brighten around each other. But I didn't have words for that, and I wasn't even close to figuring out what I had felt or still felt for Patti. So I said nothing.

"Look, Nate, me'n Lee, we're not exchangin' class rings. We're not slobberin' on each other in the backseat out behind the gym. We aren't makin' each other any promises and we don't talk about next year. Shoot, we don't even talk about next month," he told me. "What I do know is that I feel easier in my mind when I'm around her, and it's the same for her. I'm comfortable with her in a way I've never been with any other woman. With anyone. Period. I trust her to do the right thing, even when it's hard. Like today's newspaper column. I respect that, and I respect her. And she does me. Maybe that's where real love starts. With respect. I don't know. But it's what we've got, and so far it's plenty."

* * *

C utter and I put in 10 hours, mostly helping with a new section Mr. Clanton was adding to the pool hall part of The Gin to allow for more tables. We both earned a decent wage as we worked and listened to the Ole Miss game on the radio, but even Cutter was mortal. After a hot bath and several aspirin, at supper with Rose and Miss Carter he could barely use his right arm and his face was tight with discomfort.

"You're going to have to have that shoulder fixed, you know," said Holly.

"After the season."

"If you make it that far."

"I'll make it. It'll be better tomorrow."

When tomorrow came, Cutter's shoulder was better, a little, I noticed as we packed up the camp, the sun streaming coolly through the overhang of pine boughs. His nineteenth birthday was starting out clear and beautiful and crisp, but not as unusually cold as the previous couple of sunrises.

"If you want to let the girls sleep, we could get baths and eat at Mrs. Fletcher's," I said. "Breakfast and supper comes with my room."

"Aw'right," he said, used to living vagabond style, sleeping and showering wherever was handy. "But I want to be at the prayer meetin' early. Things could get ugly."

Thinking again about Saturday's newspaper column, I agreed.

At the boarding house south of DeLong, we ate big breakfasts of pancakes, bacon and spicy sausage washed down with coffee and fresh squeezed orange juice. Most of the other borders were pensioners who could not afford their own homes and the occasional frugal traveling salesman who did not want to pay the twenty a night demanded at the Jeff Davis. The reception for Cutter was cool but country polite.

After we both bathed and changed, Mrs. Fletcher stopped us in the kitchen. She waddled over on her short, thick legs, handing each of us a paper bag. "For your lunch," she said.

"Thank you," we both said, but she was looking only at Cutter, looking up at him with blue eyes going gray with age. As she handed him the bag, she squeezed his hand. "I was real sorry to hear about, Miss Jenny," she said. "She taught my youngest girl. I wish life had treated her better."

"It wasn't life that treated her bad, it was Tony Carlucci," said Cutter.

Mrs. Fletcher nodded thoughtfully, sadly. "I know, Son, I know," she told him. "Look here, I'm an old woman. I've lived all my life one way. What all's goin on with our coloreds, I just don't know. But I know it took a lot of gumption for you to do what you did at the fairgrounds."

Cutter didn't know what to say. He looked for words and when he didn't find them quickly, she said, "Now bend down here and give this old woman a hug. It's surely the last one I'll ever git from a man as good lookin' as you."

Smiling he enfolded the old woman in his much larger frame and she hugged him tight. She stepped back and said, "Now you boys git on. I've got to get ready for church."

* * *

Cutter had planned to park close to the loading dock where Holly and Rose would be leading the singing, but when we arrived we saw that River Street was blocked by two sheriff's cars and a couple of unmarked black sedans were in the lot behind the newspaper. My father was standing beside his unmarked cruiser talking on the radio when Cutter pulled up next to him. This was the last thing I expected or wanted.

When he finished the radio transmission, Billy Wallace turned to us.

"Cutter," he nodded, then looked me over. "Son, I'm glad to see you here." I knew he wanted to added, *and not with Patti and the MacAllister clan at First Denomination*, but had the good grace not to say it. I flailed around in my mind, looking for almost anything to say and came up with only, "Looks like you're the man in charge. What's goin' on?"

"Nothin'," he said. "And we want to keep it that way. Miss Carter's column stirred things up a bit."

"You brought in the FBI for that?" said Cutter, pointing with his chin toward the sedans. "Is there a threat?"

"Nothing in particular," he said. "They're not FBI cars. They're federal marshals. Protection detail. We'll have some distinguished guests this morning in the crowd. Judge Mulberry, Mr. Burke and a fella by the name of Ralph McCloy. He's the deputy U.S. attorney general for civil rights. All the way from D.C. There's some big newspaper guy from North Carolina, too. A friend of Mr. Burke's, apparently."

"When did they get here?" I asked irritably, still stumbling along some crazy line between how Brother Daddy had been schooling me for almost a year and half and what I knew in my heart to be the truth of things, even if I couldn't yet fully admit it. "What do they want in DeLong?"

Daddy looked at me, his eyes hard – not so much angry at my insolent tone, merely tired of it. "They got in last night after dark," he said. "Stayed at the Jeff Davis. Held some meetings there with me and the school board and some of the colored pastors. Reverend Clemmer was there, too, along with some other folks from the National Coalition for Justice."

"Sounds like quite a powwow," said Cutter. "I'm surprised Holly wasn't invited."

"Her man Morton was there," said my father.

Then the newspaper's publisher surely knew about the conclave, thought Cutter, and was surprised she had not mentioned it over dinner or later as they lay together on the chaise lounge by the pool watching the ribbon of headlights moving along Highway 27. Then he thought about what she had said concerning the party tonight being about more than celebrating his birthday.

"Aw'right then," said Cutter. "Looks like y'all have it under control. Guess I'll go to my usual pew."

"Good deal," said my father. "But, listen, don't be flashin' any of that firepower you keep handy. The marshals have snipers out on a couple of roofs. They don't know you like I do."

Cutter and I automatically glanced around at roof lines along both sides of the river. "Ten-four, Sheriff. I'll keep that in mind."

Cutter drove across the Bilbo Bridge and parked in a sunny spot overlooking the river between the grain silos and a big, clapboard cotton warehouse. There was a cool breeze coming out of the northwest and thus blowing across Roseville. It carried on it the scent of burned timber that was yet to be cleared from many lots alongside the dirt roads that crisscrossed that section of DeLong until they butted up against the steep incline of the Chalmette Hills.

We had been intentionally early, so we sat mostly without talking, watching people coming down from the square where they were forced to park since River Street was blocked off. As a crowd gathered in the newspaper's parking lot, Holly and Rose arrived in the red Fury and were allowed to park near the ramp. She pushed up it followed by Rose carrying two guitar cases. The meetings had gotten more sophisticated over the weeks and she had to skirt a couple of microphone stands. Holly waved to several people as some called out encouragement – "We're with you, girl!" She smiled and stopped her chair at the edge of the dock, reached down and shook hands with a woman in a homemade dress holding a child on her hip.

With the eerie feeling that I was being watched, and perhaps not by friendly eyes, I glanced over my shoulder and saw a number of black people filling the gap behind us, between the warehouse and grain silos. I smacked Cutter's arm. He glanced in the rearview mirror attached to the Jeep's fender. He nodded and casually pointed down along the river and to the Bilbo Bridge where Roseville residents were gathering, some in their Sunday finery, others in work clothes and younger men in CHS football jerseys. Several dozen were gathering at the river's edge in the spaces between other warehouses. After a time, as the all-white crowd began to gather behind the newspaper building, a huge black teenager wearing a number 72 Wolves jersey stepped up next to Cutter as the group behind us moved closer. He made Cutter look small, which was no easy thing. I was as nervous, anxious. It was well known that I dated Patti and was tight with the First Denomination crowd, or at least had been.

"John Henry," acknowledged Cutter.

"Mornin'," said John Henry Reese in a baritone that started at the core of his three-hundred-and-forty-pound frame and rumbled its way up.

A couple of more young black men appeared beside me. One wearing a CHS jersey, the other in a starched white shirt, black pants and wide red tie. I knew their faces from around town, but not their names. We nodded to each other but did not speak.

"Roseville A.M.E. not having services this morning?" asked Cutter.

"Oh, yeah. We havin' 'em," said John Henry. "We just stopped by to pay our respects along the way."

That caused even Cutter to skip a beat. "Your respects? Who died now?"

John Henry chuckled, and it sounded like a slow freight chugging through a tunnel. "Nobody, praise Jesus," he said. "They's a lot of us – from grannies down to young folks – who want to let Miss Carter know we appreciate her and all she's done since she come back."

Cutter started to speak but John Henry Reese went on in his deliberate way. "Tell you somethin', Cutter'man. I could walk up onto the square any day, march into Kilmer Hardware Store and clap my ol' white granddaddy on the shoulder. After he finished shittin' in his doors, he'd call me a lyin' nigger sum'bitch and spit in my face. Even if it's his face, too. Just a darker shade of it. Miss Carter didn't have to say what she said in the paper. She could have lied and denied likes been done 'round here forever. Like my granddaddy does every time he passes me on the street and looks straight ahead. But Miss Carter owned it. That's why we're here."

The slender young man in the red tie and goatee standing next to me whose name I still could not place said with an angry edge, "Uh'course, she don't look black, and I guarantee she ain't never thought black or lived black. In the real world she ain't no more black than Mr. Patti MacAllister here." I flinched and reddened under his hard stare before he went on. "But at least she didn't hide from what's in her blood, the way most do that can pass. It ain't much, but it's somethin'."

Cutter gave the young man a withering glare, knowing all that Holly already had put at risk for something that did not have to be her fight, long before the revelation about her mother. Cutter knew all that but the cocky young man in the red tie did not. He let it pass, but only barely.

"Thank you, John Henry," said Cutter, turning back to the huge lineman who was now his teammate. "I'll let her know. She'll appreciate it."

It was then that we saw four well-dressed white men round the corner from Water Street loosely surrounded by six men in dark suits, ties and sunglasses. J.L. Burke and Judge Mulberry, with his shock of longish white hair, were easy to recognize by anyone who'd been paying attention to the news in north Mississippi over the last two years. There was a tall blonde man and a short, stocky, balding fellow. One must have been the man from D.C. and the other the newspaperman from North Carolina. But we didn't know who was who. The group made their way into the middle of the crowd, which was about a third smaller than it had been the previous week. No doubt due to Mary Nell's ongoing phone-a-thon and Saturday's column. Burke waved to Holly and she returned the gesture with a smile, not appearing surprised to see him there or the others.

A couple of minutes later a young seminary student from Berryhill College in Holly Springs who'd been coming down to lead the services called all within his amplified voice to prayer. Then he turned to the two women with guitars and three singers surrounding one other mike. He said, "Now we're going to ask Sister Rose Carlucci and Miss Holly Lee Carter, who –"

The clapping began along the Bilbo Bridge with black women in their Sunday hats, then flowed downstream with the current until it jumped the Cattahatchie and gathered in the crowd near the loading dock. The young black men and women surrounding the Jeep were clapping and hesitantly I did so as well. Cutter stepped out of the Jeep and stood in front of it, clapping slowly, almost a pantomime of applause, and I saw Holly lock eyes for a moment with his then smile, raising her hands in a please-stop gesture.

"Thank you," she said into the microphone "You're very kind. I appreciate this. It means a lot to see *all* of you here. Thank you. Thank you so much. But let's focus on the real reason we're here this clear, beautiful morning -- to praise and worship the Lord our God as each of understand Him. And maybe know that this river no longer has to separate us." She paused, cleared her throat. "It is the warm, flowing, moving heart of Cattahatchie County and it touches each bank equally. It can be the thing that unites us."

Shouts of "Amen!" and "Tell it, Sister!" and "Praise God!" echoed from both sides of the river as Holly turned to Rose and the ad hoc choir. When she turned back, they led both sides of the Cattahatchie in the gospel standard "Shall We Gather At The River."

Everyone knew the 100-year-old hymn and followed Holly and Rose in singing it, even the edgy young man in the red tie and the out-of-towners in the expensive sports coats. Even Cutter. Only the men in sunglasses and dark suits did not join in. Instead they kept their backs to the men they surrounded and watched the crowd.

CHAPTER 25

That night was a night of firsts for me. It was the first party I ever attended that called for a jacket, though I did not wear a tie. It was the first event I attended that was catered and had more silverware at my place setting than I knew what to do with. It was the first gathering for me that began with a cocktail hour and uniformed waitresses circulating with plates of hors d'oeuvres. One tray had smoked salmon on a fancy cracker with black caviar on top. To my surprise I found I liked the salty tang it delivered once I got over the idea of eating fish eggs. Washing it down with free beer from a staffed bar at the edge of patio helped, though I likely would have drunk a lot more if I'd had any idea what was coming before sunrise.

During a quick lunch at The Cotton Café, Miss Carter had told Cutter and me to make ourselves scarce for the afternoon. "Rose and I have a lot to do, and I don't want you two under foot," she'd told us. "But be back at the house by 5:30 to get ready. Guests should start arriving about seven."

"Holly, I appreciate all this," said Cutter. "But don' you think you're going a little overboard? Especially as tight as money is."

"As much as I'd like to pretend this is all about you, it isn't," she replied. "One thing I learned in L.A. is you have to look successful to be successful. People with substantial resources want to invest in and with people whom they see as on the rise." She looked away for a moment, her lovely face suddenly washed with concern. "They do not want to invest with people who appear to be sliding toward -- oblivion."

Oblivion? How bad are things with the paper? I wondered but did not voice the question. Suddenly I was a Cutter insider again, and I was both elated by the notion and vaguely frightened by the torrent of very adult energy and even danger that seemed to swirl around him and Holly Lee Carter. I felt as if I was being pulled too quickly, at least much more quickly than I wanted, out of my small town boyhood and into something much bigger.

"Will the men who were at the prayer meeting be there?" Cutter asked.

"Yes," said Holly. "And another special guest as well. But I'll leave that as a surprise."

"Surprises haven't turned out to be a good thing lately."

"This one will be," she assured him. "The men coming tonight can change your life. Rose's life. And mine, too."

Cutter sliced a piece of roast beef, put it in his mouth and chewed. "I'll keep it in mind," he told her and drank from a glass of sweet tea.

W e followed the red Fury as far as Blue Mountain Road, waved and stayed on Highway 27 until we crossed Two-Mile Bridge and turned into the graveled lot at The Gin. Parking around back, we went in through the screened door to the large, steamy kitchen. The Gin did a big after church lunch business, despite its roadhouse reputation. Cutter was looking for an afternoon of work. He needed every hour he could get, he told me, because Miss Jenny's funeral had taken everything he'd been depositing for almost four years in a savings account at a Jackson, Tennessee bank. And then some.

"Wouldn't Miss Carter help?" I asked.

Cutter's head snapped around. "She offered. But that's not how things are with us. Or ever will be," he told me. "I pay my own freight."

He stared at me as if I was, again, someone he barely knew, or perhaps more accurately, someone who did not really know him. I thought he was about to say something about my cowardly absence from his mother's funeral, but the moment passed when the kitchen manager came up and said, "Sorry, Cutter. We've got a full wait crew. Bartenders, too. One dishwasher didn't show, but you don't wanna –"

"I'll take it," he said.

"Aw'right," said the man. "Grab an apron. You know where the sinks are."

A t 5:20 we rounded the bend in Blue Mountain Road until it straightened as it ran past Wolf's Run. Cutter had taken me to the boarding house because I wanted my truck, my wheels – at that age, in that part of the world, my freedom. I was not sure what to make of the fancy party to which I had been of late invited, and I wanted to be able to leave if I decided to, and not just the house. There already were a half dozen cars parked beside the old greenhouse and big catering van parked near the kitchen. At the top of the driveway were two black, government-issued Fords. One inside the gate, one outside it. Two men, one black, one white, in dark suits and sunglasses were standing beside the outside car and the electric gate. One held a walkie-talkie.

"What the hell?" I said aloud in my truck cab as the men tracked our dusty movement.

Cutter drove the Jeep up the log cut, winching it the final few yards onto the rock shelf, as usual, then walked back down to my truck where I retrieved the clothes I'd also picked up at the boarding house. Cutter carried nothing, explaining that he now kept most of his clothes in the closet of a spare bedroom. I had my belongs in a gym bag. At the gate, the men, both whom were as big as Cutter, eyed us through their sunglasses.

Cutter started, "I'm –"

"We know who you are," said the taller of the men. He stepped forward and extended his hand. Cutter shook it. "Happy Birthday. I'm Deputy United States Marshal John Renfro. That's my partner, Deputy Marshal Rothman. A lot us heard you or heard about what you did on the radio. That took some balls."

"Thanks. It just kind of happened," said Cutter.

Then to me. "I need to look inside your bag, please, Mr. Wallace."

I almost looked over my shoulder for my father then realized the marshal was talking to me.

"If you please," he said more firmly.

"Oh, sure," I said and handed over the bag. The marshal took a quick but thorough look through it and handed it back.

"Say, where did you young men put your vehicles?" asked Marshal Rothman. "You can park down by the house as long as we check them first."

"That's aw'right," Cutter told him. "We left them on a side road around the bend. I make camp in a clearing up the hill."

"That's where you sleep?" the first marshal asked, incredulous.

"Most nights."

Marshals Renfro and Rothman looked at each other, shrugged. "All right, then. You gentleman have an enjoyable evening," he said as the gate swung open and we started down the long, tree-shaded driveway to the house.

In the room at Wolf's Run where I had slept off the emotional hangover from my last conversation with Patti, Cutter sat on the bed in pressed Levis and the only white button-down he owned. Holly sat in her wheelchair next to him, rubbing Ivory lotion into his hands left red by four hours of dishwashing in scalding water.

"I love your hands," she said. "You have the most beautiful hands I've ever seen on a man."

He grunted. "Not so pretty this afternoon."

Holly lifted his right hand to her face and laid her cheek against it. "They're beautiful to me," she said.

Cutter gently let his fingertips slide down the side of Holly's neck. She lifted her chin, her eyelids fluttering until his hand settled on her breast. She closed her eyes and let out a sound that started as a sigh but ended as a breathy moan. With enormous effort Holly took hold of the chair's push-rims and propelled herself backwards several feet, forced herself to say, "Ohhhh, Cutter, we can't start this now."

"I think we already have," he told her.

Holly looked at the clock on the bedside table. "It's almost six and I still have to finish dressing," she said. "But tonight. Later. I want you to stay."

"Is that my birthday present?"

A small laugh came up from her throat. "No, silly. It's mine," she said, calming her breathing as she wheeled to an antique chifforobe and opened one of the walnut doors. She took out two beautifully and meticulously wrapped boxes, put them on her lap and returned to Cutter. "There are some little things, too, but we wanted to give you these before the party," she told him. "The top box is from Rose. The bottom from me."

He took the first box and opened it with care. Inside was a pair of black-and-tan deck shoes with leather laces, something hardly ever seen in DeLong, where patent leather penny loafers were considered the height of fashion. "Rose has good taste. She picked them out herself," said Holly. "They'll look great with those jeans."

"I should have asked. Are jeans alright for tonight? I've got a pair of black pants, I could –"

"No, jeans are perfect on you. I don't want you to look or feel overdressed. Some of the men coming tonight will be sizing you up," she told him. "I want you to be comfortable. But there is something in that box that may dress up the look a little."

Cutter turned to the large flat box wrapped in embossed gold paper. "I hate to tear into it. It's done so pretty," he said.

"It's no good unless you open it," she said. "Go ahead."

And he did, pulling from the box a black cashmere sport coat with silver-blue lining. "Oh, geez, Lee, this is beautiful."

"What did you call me?"

Cutter paused, momentarily sidetracked, thinking. "Lee. That is your middle name, isn't it?"

"Yes, of course. But no one ever called me that except Meemaw Lois," she told him. "It was like this love word between us."

"I'm sorry if I –"

"No, no. I like it. I always liked it better than Holly," she said feeling odd, as if something otherworldly had just happened, almost a message from another time. Still, she wondered, "Why start -- I mean, why Lee now instead of Holly?"

He shrugged. "I don't know. I said it out loud once and it just sounded right, I guess."

She nodded, thinking about the special gift she had for him after the party, but quickly shook off the sensation. "Try on the jacket. I want to see how it fits. I had to guess a little at your size." Cutter stood and slipped it on, the blue silk sliding over his arms. "I had Morty make it a little large. We can always have it taken in a little if we need to."

"Morty?"

"A tailor I know in Los Angeles," she said. "I did a photo spread on his store once for *The Chronicle*. Mortimer & Sneed on Wiltshire. They've made suits and jackets for everyone from Clark Gable to Cary Grant to Paul Newman. Morty's been in love with me ever since. Or at least in love with the story. Morty is very gay. But he cuts a beautiful suit. Turn."

Cutter turned in front of the full-length mirror. Holly said she thought it looked great, almost perfect, and even Cutter was impressed. With his black hair, pearl blue eyes and Mediterranean bone structure, he was aware of the effect he had on many women, but what he saw in the mirror and in Holly's face was something different, something new.

He ran his hand over the smooth surface of one sleeve. "This is the nicest thing I've ever had. By a long shot," he told her. "I don't know what to say."

Holly rolled up beside him, appreciating the way in which the tailored jacket gave Cutter a look of sophistication and maturity and insouciant elegance that he instantly wore as comfortably, as easily as a t-shirt and cutoffs.

Holly smiled to herself.

"Is something wrong?" he asked. "My fly open or something?"

She shook her head, as she drew in a deep, appreciative breath. "No. I simply should have known," she said. "You wear that jacket like you were born for it. And you probably were."

Even to my sartorially untrained eye, I could see there were several men milling and chatting beside the pool in suits that cost more than my truck. More than everything I owned. The four men who had attended the morning prayer meeting – Mulberry, Burke and DUSAG McCloy plus the newspaper man from North Carolina -- came in together with a like number of security men who spread out around the perimeter of the big patio. The four men quickly surrounded Cutter at the wet bar, where he was getting a Coke. He smiled, nodded, chatted as if he went to parties such as this three times a week. At one point, as I hung near the group but not in it, I heard Cutter talking with the McCloy fellow about architecture, which was one of his favorite subjects. Meanwhile, I felt like a knotty frog at a homecoming dance, especially having been with Patti on the segregationist side of things all summer. It was only 7:20 but I was getting ready to bolt and would have had Rose not approached me and began talking with me, even though it was a struggle for her. She was lovely, if not quite beautiful, in a long-sleeved red dress with a gathered collar. I got a second beer and relaxed a little.

"If I d-don't g-g-get too sc-scared after d-dinner, I'm g-going to sing s-s-some songs I wrote," Rose told me in her halting way. "One I wrote f-for Cutter. I w-want you to h-hear it, too."

"Then I guess I have to stay, don't I?" I told her. "I want to hear you sing."

A blaze of color rose in her cheeks and she smiled.

Coach Hinton was there in a brown off-the-JCPenney-rack number with his wife and a black man who he quickly introduced to Cutter. "This is Harold 'Night Train' Nesbit. He played five years for Chicago. Now he's head coach of the College of Maine Mariners in the All-New England Conference. He flew all night to get here and to meet you."

"Well, wow," said Cutter. "I'm honored, but I don't understand. How'd did Maine get wind of me?"

"It's really pretty simple," said Nesbit, who had been an all-pro linebacker three times. "Judge Mulberry is a Maine alumni – as was his father and grandfather -- and he sits on our board of trustees. He also was a pretty darn good lineman back in his day. He knows his football and football players. When he told me the best running back prospect in the country was hiding down here in a small Mississippi town, what was I going to do? I had to come."

Coach Hinton said, "We've been at the school all afternoon watching film of you."

"All I can say is, I think the judge might be right," Nesbit told him.

"That's a mighty big compliment," said Cutter.

"It's deserved," the coach went on as I listened nearby. "And you've got something else. You've got character. The kind that doesn't break when it's tested. Even before Judge Mulberry reached out, a lot us have been following what's been going on down here. Cattahatchie County, 'the last of its kind,' praise Jesus! It took guts to do what you did, to stick with your high school. I want players with that kind of guts and commitment."

Maine! I walked away. *Who ever heard of Maine?*

There also was a contingent of local people. Dr. Marvin Gilbert, the optometrist; Dr. Garner; Gil Clanton, owner of The Gin; *The Current-Leader's* Managing Editor Michael Morton and the paper's production chief Shorty Rodgers, and their wives or girlfriends. Reverend Clemmer was there with his daughter, who was taking a semester off from some up-north college to help with the NCJ's voter registration drive. It was the first time I had seen the black preacher/"agitator" up close. After months of being around Brother MacAllister in and out of First Denomination I was somewhat surprised to find that Clemmer did not have horns and a tail. Of course my father had been invited, but short of deputies he declined, opting to stay out on patrol, especially with so many important people visiting. Miz Frances Ragland was there in a beaded white dress that she proudly said she'd been saving since 1927. Mr. Ragland had not felt well and stayed home.

"Thank goodness Holly gave me one more chance to wear it again in this house before I pass," she said to Mrs. Gilbert as they both sipped from chilled martini glasses and listened to the three-piece band. "Miss Lois, and before that, her mother Miss Annie, threw wonderful parties at Wolf's Run. Anyone who was anyone in Mid-South society was here. Anyone who wanted to be anyone in Mississippi politics came."

One of the earliest and biggest surprises was when Holly Lee Carter came down the ramp to the patio upright, on her feet. Of course, that required aluminum crutches that clamped to her forearms and twenty-pounds of metal beneath the flowing, flower-print peasant skirt that almost hid the metal bolts and black boots, but not quite. She wore a simple white silk wrap top that was small town modest but left no doubt about her figure. Besides her curves, the main thing that struck me was her height. Right at six-feet. Though by agreement they mostly kept their distance, when she and Cutter came close it was like a jolt of silent lightning passing through the flagstones. The air near them changed and the hair on your arm almost stood up. You felt a tingle there, or someplace a lot more private.

"Is *this* my present?" he asked later handing Holly a glass of white wine while giving her a quick once-over.

"I told you, that comes later. This is for Mr. Garland and his checkbook," she said quietly, smiling. "No one wants to loan three-quarters-of-a-million dollars to someone they may worry isn't healthy enough to repay it. Being on my feet may help salve Mr. Garland's anxieties. But I do love being able to look you in right in those beautiful eyes."

Cutter nodded. "You're tall."

"Yes. I'm glad you're not a shrimp."

Cutter laughed.

"Now we better mingle, mingle," she said, "before I shuck all this metal and drag you into my bedroom and take advantage of your youth. I mean, I should be ashamed. You're only eighteen."

"Nineteen," he reminded.

"Oh, yes. That's right," she agreed playfully. "Now I feel so much better about my cradle-robbing."

"Rob away," he said, smiling and moving away, already wishing this gathering was over so that the real party could begin.

At a long, linen-covered table set up beside the pool, we dined by the light of tiki torches and the glow from the nearly continuous wall of French doors that wrapped the patio on three sides, casting a warm yellow light on the flagstones. Miss Carter sat at one end of the table with Mr. Garland to her right and the other dignitaries close by. Cutter sat at the other end with coaches Nesbit and Hinton to his right. To his left sat Rose and me.

Before the meal began Miss Carter levered herself upright with the crutches and the braces locked at her knees and hips. She asked Dr. Gilbert to offer a prayer of blessing, which he did eloquently, then introduced each of the out-of-town guests.

"Now as much as we are honored to have these visitors with us, with apologies, this night is not about any of you," she went on. "It is about a young man who through his courage, talent and maturity has changed the course of Cattahatchie

County life for the better, for all our citizens. Happy Birthday to number 13, Cutter Carlucci."

As one those at the table stood and enthusiastically applauded. After a moment Cutter stood, his white shirt glowing against his skin and the black jacket. "Thank you. Thank you very much," he acknowledged.

As seats were retaken, uniformed waiters began to arrive. Miss Carter continued to stand – "Let me tell you, especially our visitors, about our meal tonight. It is a testament to the bounty of Cattahatchie County and our hopes for it," she said in her best chamber-of-commerce delivery, well aware that a possible investor might be measuring each word. "Everything you will enjoy in this dinner tonight was caught, grown or raised right here in Cattahatchie County. From the lettuce in our salads to the crawfish bisque, from the vegetables and fried green tomatoes, from the filets and the bacon in which they are wrapped, to the berries for the crème brulee. The only thing imported at this table is the wine. But please don't tell anyone. This is still a dry county, and not even the last of its kind in Mississippi." There was laughter around the table. "Perhaps that will be my next editorial campaign."

"Please, no!" Gil Clanton called. "You'll kill my business."

More laughter and Miss Carter let it fade way.

"Seriously, though, despite the struggles we've been through this summer, I have nothing but faith in the long-term goodness, kindness and common sense of the people with whom I grew up. And I stand – yes, stand!" – more applause – "here tonight with nothing but hope for the bright future that awaits Cattahatchie County once we've put this difficult chapter behind us. Now, no more talk. Let's enjoy this celebration."

There was a vigorous round of applause, then dinner was served. All of us at our end of the table, including Coach Hinton, surreptitiously watched "Night Train" Nesbit, who was the only person in our vicinity who knew what all of the appropriate uses for the multitude of forks spoons and knives arrayed before us. When dinner was finished Cutter sliced a large birthday cake adorned with a running football player wearing number thirteen. While guests enjoyed cake and coffee, Rose walked on trembling knees to the corner of the patio occupied by the trio and climbed onto a stool. She crossed her legs and put Miss Carter's perfectly tuned Martin on her thigh and sang two covers – *Me and Bobby McGee* and *Four Strong Winds* – then four of her own compositions including, "Th-this one, I-I-I –" she paused, frustrated and embarrassed, but took a breath and went on, "I wrote for, for the b-best brother any g-girl every h-had. It's c-called, *Kind Survivor.*"

The song was a beautiful and sweet and honest ode to a boy living alone in the elements and by his wits, watching over others, and never being made cruel even by a "river of meanness and hurt" that flowed around him. When I glanced at Cutter, his eyes were wet and silver, and Holly Lee Carter was not the only person with tears on her cheeks both for the raw honesty of the lyrics and the soulful depth of the delivery. Even "Night Train" Nesbit took a sip from the china coffee cup and cleared his throat.

After coffee, guests began saying their good-nights and, to my amazement, Rose started supervising the kitchen clean-up. When she struggled to speak, she wrote in a spiral notebook and firmly showed it to the catering crew. The trio packed up their instruments and speakers. The tables, torches and other gear were torn down and packed into the catering truck. By 12:15 only four of us remained upright at Wolf's Run. I was helping Rose put away some things in the kitchen. Cutter and Miss Carter were on the patio. From the window above the sink we could see them together, shoulder to shoulder on the double chaise, holding hands, talking.

Cutter shook his head, laughing softly at the irony. "So why did Miss Frances end up in your bed?"

"When she went in the kitchen and told the chief caterer that her head was spinning and she needed to lay down, they just walked her to the first bedroom they found. Mine," Holly was explaining. "She's sound asleep."

"Do you mean passed out?"

"A lady such as Miss Frances never passes out. She merely becomes desperately in need of a nap."

"Is she alive?"

"Yes!" said Holly gently punching Cutter's arm. "She's snoring like a southbound train."

"Why couldn't she fall desperately into a nap in one of the guest rooms?"

"I wish she had, but that's not the case."

"I could carry her."

"Even if you did, I've known Miss Frances since, since before I can remember. It would be like, well, making love with your grandmother next door," said Holly.

"It's a big house."

"What if she gets up in the middle of the night and comes looking for me and catches us – *in flagrante*, you might say?"

"I don't speak Spanish."

"It's Latin."

Cutter sighed. "Whatever. This was almost a perfect evening."

"Don't be cross," said Holly. "She's a lovely old lady. Besides, it's just one more night. Tomorrow night we'll retire to my boudoir before the dishes are even washed, and not come out until we're sated or blind."

"That may take some time. How about I play hooky on Tuesday and we can have the whole place to ourselves? I'll get Nate to pick Rose up for school."

Holly sighed. "God, that's tempting. But I have a newspaper to put out."

"Let Mister I-Should-Be-at-*The Times* Morton deal with it."

"You're a corrupting influence."

"I hope so."

Holly had been pushing herself almost nonstop for nearly three months. "There are no big stories breaking Monday or Tuesday. That I know of. I can write my column tomorrow. All right, we'll both play hooky on Tuesday."

"For real?"

"For real," she told him. "So you better get up to your rock and get some sleep, because you're not going to get any tomorrow night."

"You promise?"

"Yes, sir. Cross my heart," she said as Cutter sat up and she let her hand drift down his back. "Oh, wait. I do have one more present for you before you go."

Holly slipped her hand in the hidden pocket of the peasant skirt. From it she withdrew a small gold box with a red ribbon. Cutter held the box in his hand. "The jacket, this party and everything – gettin' Coach Nesbit here – that's plenty."

"I didn't do that. That was Judge Mulberry."

"Yeah, but I bet you gave him a nudge about it. But Maine! Geez, that's a long way off. And cold!"

Holly nodded. "I know."

"Would you come visit?"

"If you want me to."

Cutter looked at her quizzically. "Of course I'd want you to."

"Open your present."

Cutter pulled the ribbon loose, then the foil paper and took the lid off the box. He stared at the object for a moment, surprised. "It's your father's pocket watch," he said. "I can't take this."

"If it wasn't for you, it still be in a junk yard in Alabama. Or crushed into scrap metal."

"It's a keepsake of your father. I –"

"Stop. I want you to have it," she told him. "Besides, it's too late. I already had it cleaned and repaired, and engraved for you. Open the back cover."

Cutter fumbled then found the sliver of a button that popped open the back. He tilted it to catch the light. It read:

To Cutter:
Be Strong. Be Bold.
Be Kind. Love Well.
Lee Carter
1969

He looked into her eyes. "Lee Carter. Lee. The love word between you and your grandmother."

Even during the passion of sex, neither of them had ever uttered the word "love."

By unspoken agreement they mutually understood it to be taboo. A word that once said would create so many entanglements that it might well trip up and then strangle whatever special thing was going in between them.

Finally Cutter said, "This is an amazing gift. I don't know what to say."

"Thank you usually works."

"Then thank you," he said, and Rose and I watched him lean in for a long kiss, though of course we could not hear the words they were speaking. "I'll always keep it close."

A wistful smile crossed Holly's lips. "I hope so. I hope twenty or thirty years from now, when all the pain that's been wrapped up in this summer is way behind you, you'll open that back cover up and only good memories will be inside."

Cutter straightened on the seat and looked at Holly with unease. "That almost sounds like some kind of good-bye."

"No," she said, reaching for his hand. "Not at all. It's just that life will look a lot different to you after high school, and you leave DeLong and go off to college. I know it did to me. I had no idea how big the world is, and how much is in it."

"And you think I'll forget you?"

"I hope not. But in time you may see all that's happened this summer in a different light."

"Including you?"

Holly looked away for moment, then back. "Yes, including me."

"I don't think so."

Holly sighed. "Cutter, sweetheart, it's been a wonderful day, but a long one. Let's not talk about this now."

"I think this is a fine time to talk about it," he persisted. "I've been wondering how things really are between us."

Holly's green eyes darkened. The gold flecks in them flashed but not with anger, with something sadder and more tender. "Okay, here's how it is – I think you are one of the most gorgeous, intelligent, gentle and brave men I have ever met. Anywhere of any age. I think I am inexpressibly lucky, blessed, fortunate – however you want to say it – to have you come into my life. Not to mention into my bed. But, Cutter, I'm twenty-eight and you're nineteen, as of today. You've never been farther from DeLong than Moore's Bridge, Alabama. And like you said, it's not much different from here. There is a big, big world waiting for you out there, one way or another. Full of adventures and possibilities. Whether it's football or something else, you're going to be a star. Anyone can see that. Mulberry saw it tonight. Burke. Even McCloy. All those very powerful, successful men told me how impressed they were with you. And the women? Lord, they'll be lined up around the corner. They'll be climbing through your windows." Cutter started to speak but she squeezed his hand – "No. You asked. You're right. You need to know how it is." She took a breath. "Even if we put all that aside, here's what we'll never be able put aside – I'm never going to walk again. I'm always going to be in that fucking wheelchair. And that is not the life I want for you."

"Not the life you want for me?" he asked, incredulous. "Don't you think that's a decision for me to make?"

Holly looked away, considering how to respond. Finally, slowly she said, "I think it's the only decision in the world you may not be mature enough to make."

* * *

Thirty minutes later, Cutter had a low fire going on the small outcrop of rocks above Wolf's Run. In the courtyard hidden in the U-embrace of the house, Rose spread a blanket over Holly.

"It's g-getting ch-chilly. I thought you might w-want this."

"Yes. Thank you."

"You're not c-coming to bed?"

"Not yet. It's such a beautiful night," she said, looking up at the amazing glitter of stars in the black silk sky. "I don't want to let it go."

"I-I know. It's been a w-wonderful day."

Holly reached out, took Rose's hand, said, "I'm so proud of you. You were wonderful. Everyone loved *Kind Survivor*."

"Th-Thank you. Once I st-started singing, I wasn't sc-scared at all. D-Did you get the l-l-loan thing worked out?"

"I don't know. But at least Mr. Garland didn't turn me down flat. So there's hope," said Holly. "Say a prayer."

"I pr-pray for you and C-Cutter every night," said Rose. Holly smiled, grateful. "W-Will you need help with your br-braces?"

"No. They're a lot easier to get out of than into, and I've had lots of practice," said Holly. "Go on to bed. I'll be in soon. Is Miss Frances still asleep in my room?" Rose nodded. "Then I'll sleep in one of the guest rooms."

Up at our camp, I was fighting sleep, watching Cutter, who was laying on his back studying the stars and from time to time the gold pocket watch that Miss Carter had given him. He had the Jeep's radio on, the volume low – "cool sounds for lonely lovers." As always, his shotgun was propped within arm's reach.

There was never going to be a good time, but on this special and unusual day I wanted to clear the air between Cutter and I of all the poison I could, knowing that given my actions over the last weeks it might never be enough. I fixed my eyes on a star hanging like a Christmas tree ornament off the end of a long branch and said, "I'm sorry I didn't come to Miss Jenny's funeral. Daddy told me you asked. There's no good excuse for it. I was scared of what Patti and her bunch would say."

Cutter was silent for so long I thought perhaps he fallen asleep and not heard me, but when I looked across the low fire I could see his eyes were open. I waited.

"Don't worry about it, Nate," he finally said. "Momma didn't know the difference."

"But you did."

I suppose I'd hoped for, maybe even expected further absolution but Cutter didn't give it. Though not unkindly, he firmly told me, "Nate, there're some decisions we make that, well, they can't be unmade. You did what you did. I'm not mad at you about it, but I'm not going to take it off your shoulders. It's your weight, and you need to carry it."

I swallowed, rolled my lips, tried to find words, more words that would – would what?

After a time, Cutter sat up, stretched and turned off the radio. "Good night, Nate," he said and rolled over onto his good shoulder, turning his back to the fire and to me.

CHAPTER 26

When Rose awoke in the quiet darkness of her room, panic flared in her chest. For years she had slept with a light on by her bed at the Old Ambrose Place signaling Cutter, warding off her father and the demons he left in the corners of her room and her heart. With the help of Cutter and Holly she had left the Old Ambrose Place behind but the terrors had moved up the hill with her. Once night fell, they hung in every unlit corner of this house, too, like laughing bats. Only the light kept their screeching and feral gaze at bay.

She lay motionless on her stomach. Still as could be. *The bulb burned out,* she told herself. *That's all.* But she lay still, eyes squeezed shut, listening. Boards creaked in the hallway. It was Holly going to bed in one of guest rooms, she told herself. Tried to make herself believe. But it was not the thump-thump, thump-thump of Holly crutching forward then swinging her braced legs and repeating the process.

She listened, the muscles in her face so tight her jaw hurt, begging the wind to move in the trees, causing limbs to tap-tap on the tin roof. That would explain the sounds. Or maybe rain. She listened hard for rain. But there was none of that. And yet the house seemed to be moving, something applying pressure to planks, creating a whisper of movement in the air. Then she smelled him. The dried sweat and stale clothes, motor oil, testosterone and dirty hair.

Rose's eyes flew open, wild with fear. Her hand shot toward the butcher knife under the pillow next to her, but thick, hard fingers wrapped around her wrist like cable, paralyzing her hand. Her mouth opened to scream, but it was too late. Before she could empty the sound from her lungs, her father's other hand shoved her face down into the pillow. Deep. She flailed, but Tony's weight was on top her. She felt the wire stubble of his beard against her shoulder and the side of her neck. His fingers – the nails always overlong and dirty – were calloused claws that threatened to crush her skull.

"Stop wigglin'," Tony Carlucci growled into Rose's ear, so close she could feel his lips against her ear, but she fought through the pain and paid him no heed. "Stop!" he told her again. Rose couldn't breathe but she kept swinging her arms, kicking her legs. "Stop! Be quiet and go with me, and the Carter woman lives. Otherwise, she dies. I'll slice her open from her pussy to the top of her head."

438

Rose's lungs felt as if someone had dumped hot coals down her throat, and her head would implode in the crush of her father's hand, but she thought of Holly and let her limbs go limp.

"That's Daddy's girl," Tony Carlucci whispered then stuck his thick, rancid tongue inside her ear. Rose's body convulsed and bile churned hot in her throat before falling back into her stomach liked poisoned water. "You didn't think I was gonna leave you behind, did you? Noooo. We're goin' south. Way south. Start a whole new life. Just me and you." Rose clenched her fists, wanted to fight but stilled herself, hoping Tony would leave Holly alone, as unlikely as that hope might be. "You need a daddy, and I need a wife," he told her. "This is all gonna work out just fine."

A chilly breeze on my face and neck brought me awake. I slipped my hand from my sleeping bag and used a stick to poke at the coals where our little fire had collapsed to embers, and barely even those. That's when I heard them. Men. Grown men. Trying to talk in whispers. But tension and adrenaline caused their voices to become brittle and crack like ice on a winter lake. I eased up onto my elbows, my ears straining to hear.

Silence.

Was I mistaken? Or maybe dreaming?

Then I heard the door of a vehicle open and softly close, and the rattle of a tailgate being gently lowered. I bolted up, scuttling on my hands and knees toward the edge of the rock. I got there just in time to see three men going over the white plank fence in front of Wolf's Run. My heart was pounding so hard against my ribs that I was certain that the two men standing by the truck and a four-door Oldsmobile sedan could not help but hear them rattle. Yet neither looked up the steep hill to the promontory. They continued to look one way on the road then the other, floppy fishing hats hiding their faces. One cradled a deer rifle, but I couldn't place either one. Whoever these men were, I knew as sure as my soul they were there to do no telling what to Rose and Miss Carter.

I pushed away from the edge and crawled to where Cutter lay, pouncing on his sleeping bag with my hand covering his mouth. His body bucked and nearly threw me off, but I held fast until his eyes focused on my face.

"They're here!" I whispered. "Five, I think."

He blinked once, twice, then I saw the comprehension in his eyes as surely as moonlight.

T ony Carlucci grabbed Rose's wrists, pulled them together then yanked a strip of black duct tape applied to the front of his camouflage coveralls. He roughly turned her over and covered her mouth with another strip. When he pulled her from the bed in only a t-shirt and panties, her bare legs were shaking.

He stepped behind her and ran his rough hands over her shoulders and down her arms. She was crying quietly now. "My goodness, you sure do look good now that you're out of those baggy-ass overalls you always wore around me. You sure do."

Robert Bedford McBride appeared silhouetted in the bedroom door cradling an M-16. "All right, Mr. Carlucci. I've set the charges and you've got what you want," said McBride. "Now let's collect Mr. Pearce and wrap this up. We've got a plane to catch."

Tony said nothing but pushed Rose barefoot into the hall, forcing her to duck under what looked like a white clothesline. She looked in both directions – toward the library, then to where the hall turned right past the dining room and sitting room/music room then right again past Holly's bedroom and on to the kitchen. The cord was suspended from globs of pinkish putty stuck to the walls about every twenty feet. Rose looked at McBride and knew. Knew what it meant. She began to struggle again but Tony dug his brawny fingers into her upper arm and shook her hard. She grimaced with the pain and stilled.

Gaydon Pearce came around the corner from the other side of the house.

"Did you get her?" asked McBride.

"Where'd you put her?" asked Carlucci.

"She wasn't in there," said Pearce. "Neither was Cutter. Old Miz Ragland from the paper was sleepin' in her bed."

Tony cursed.

"What'd you do with the old woman?" asked McBride.

"I did what I had to do," said Pearce whose eyes were wide and almost glowing with adrenaline. "I slit her throat."

Rose moaned and her knees went weak but Tony held her up. "The bitch must be here somewhere!" said Tony and instantly Rose thought of Holly earlier on the chaise lounge staring up at the stars. She must have fallen asleep out there, Rose realized. *Ohhh, stay asleep! … stay asleep! … stay asleep*! she thought. *Please God, let her stay asleep.*

"Her car's out there in the garage," Tony was saying now.

"Yeah, but your boy's Jeep isn't," said McBride. "After the Fancy Dan birthday party they threw here tonight, they probably lit out for one of those Tennessee roadhouses to keep the party goin'."

"Did you see her wheelchair?" asked Tony.

"Yeah, it's in her bedroom," Pearce told him.

Tony drew in a long breath, his wide nostrils of his thick, flat boxer's nose dilated. "Then she's here," he said. "I'm gonna see that bitch dead if we have to search every inch of this fuckin' place. She's here!"

Bob McBride shifted his weight on his feet and his hand on the rifle, just a little. "No, we are not," he said. "We've gotten two-thirds of what we came for. You've got the girl, and I've got the house wired. We're going out the front door, right now, trailing demolition wire. Just like we planned. When we get to the top of that driveway, and I hit my plunger, anything that is in or near this place is going to be plenty dead."

Tony seethed – "It ain't the same as killin' her by hand. Her lookin' in my eyes when I choke the life out of her."

"It'll have to do," McBride told him. "I'm not hangin' around here chancin' the electric chair because some crippled woman escaped your pecker 10 years ago. Now let's go."

In an instant, Cutter was out of his sleeping bag, pulling on his jeans, then his boots, and tying them tight around his ankles, getting ready to run on rough ground. From where he sat, he could see the vehicles and the men resting against them, one smoking a cigarette.

"All right, Nate. I need you to do exactly what I tell you," he whispered as he got to his feet, shotgun in hand, and hustled to his Jeep. He reached into a compartment under the seat and pulled out the .45 and stuffed it down the back of his jeans. Then he took out a box of .12 gauge buckshot, stuffed a fistful into the front pockets of his jeans and quietly poured the rest into the little fire pit.

Cutter reached in and knocked the Jeep out of gear.

"Get on the other side," he told me. "Help me push it over." I stared at him for a second then understood. We were about to launch a ground-to-ground missile. I took hold of the cold metal. "I'm going down right behind it," he whispered. "You get to your truck and haul ass to the nearest phone. Call the law and tell 'em to hurry."

"But –?"

"Push!"

Down below, the man with the deer rifle crouched beside the truck, focused on the house. The other man leaned against the back quarter panel of the sedan trimming his fingernails with a pocket knife. They heard the groan of metal but no engine sound. As J.D. Benoit looked up the hill, I recognized him. He got the impression of something large and solid and heavy speeding down the steep slope. He dove away from the car, but long before the man behind the truck could react, the Jeep slammed into the pickup, knocking it onto its side in the ditch.

Cutter reached the road less than three seconds after the Jeep. Benoit was on his feet, reaching for a pistol in a shoulder holster but Cutter had the pump aimed at his chest from 10 feet away.

"Whoa! Okay, boy. Okay. Easy," said Benoit, slowly moving his hands away from his body, palms open. "You know me. Let's just go easy and talk this over."

"Too late for that," said Cutter, his voice cold as ancient ice. The blast knocked Benoit backward into the ditch and out of one boot. His chest was a mangled red mess and his eyes were open, seeming to stare in wonderment at his own blood spattered across the white fence rails. An instant later he was dead.

Cutter chambered another round and wheeled on the smallish man pinned under the truck – Frank Gandy. His mouth was opening and closing in a small O, like a fish gasping its last on a river dock. No sound was coming out. Only bubbles of blood. Cutter turned again and blew out the back tire of the sedan, jacked another round and blew out the front, then hopped the fence and ran toward the house.

T he Jeep slammed into the truck just as McBride, Pearce and Tony Carlucci stepped onto the front porch of Wolf's Run with Rose. A moment later they heard the bellow of the shotgun and saw the muzzle flashes and a tall, lean figured bounding over the fence and disappearing behind a screen of trees near the driveway.

"What the --?" started Tony.

"Looks like we found your boy," said McBride. "Or more precisely he found us. You've told me how much you want to see him dead. Here's your chance."

Tony looked up the hill to where Cutter surely was moving fast in darkness, then from McBride to Pearce. "I-I got enough of what I came for," he said. "I want to make sure I live to enjoy her. Let's get out of here."

McBride smiled. "That's what I thought," he said, and all three men stepped back inside the front hall and shut the door. "Mr. Pearce you need to lay down suppressing fire and give us two minutes to get over the wall with the girl. Then you come to us. We'll cover you. Once we're all safely over, I'll blow the house. Carlucci, if your boy or the Carter woman are near, then its happy trails for everybody. One way or the other."

O n the patio, Holly had, indeed, dozed off on the chaise, cozy under the blanket, but the sound of crashing, groaning metal punctuated by the shotgun's thunder jerked her awake. She twisted so that she could see the house behind her. The light was on in her bedroom. At first, that was all she could see. Then her eyes widened, her heart raged as she saw a man – Tony Carlucci! – drag Rose through the light spilling into the long hall of French doors. Instinctively, she felt in her pocket for the pistol she'd been keeping close. "Oh, no!" she gasped, remembering that with federal marshals and FBI protection agents all over the place she'd left it locked in her nightstand drawer.

Holly knew she had to do something. She used her arms to swing her braced legs off the chaise and plant her booted feet on the flagstones. She grabbed the forearm crutches and leveraged herself upright.

I stood beside my pickup staring at the shattered chest of Mississippi Highway Patrol Sergeant J.D. Benoit. One boot still was planted at the spot where the buckshot hit him. Frank Gandy's eyes were open and blinked from time to time but they didn't really seem to see. I thought about doing what Cutter had told me. About hauling ass to the nearest phone. But everything was happening too fast. Depending on where they were on patrol, it could take ten to fifteen minutes for a cruiser to get here. No!

I looked down the hill toward Wolf's Run and remembered what Cutter had told me only an hour or so earlier -- *Nate, there're some decisions we make that, well, they can't be unmade.* Already that summer I had let down Cutter and Miss Carter and the newspaper – and my daddy and myself – in so many ways, but leaving Cutter to fight this battle alone was one weight I could never carry. If Cutter and Miss Carter and Rose were killed while I ran – ran! – for help, I knew it would crush me. I stepped down in the ditch and pushed Benoit's camo jacket aside and pulled the .357 Smith & Wesson from its holster. It had blood on the grips and I wiped it with my t-shirt. Before I could reconsider, I went over the fence, my bladder feeling tight and my asshole feeling loose.

Moving from walnut to pecan to pine, I saw the light in Miss Carter's bedroom go out. The house was now dark except for a blue-ish glow over the arched roof cast by the pool light. I wondered if she was dead. I wondered if it would kill Cutter. But I didn't have time to think about much of anything. I reached the last row of trees in front of the house and saw Cutter stumble then roll inside the old greenhouse as a fusillade of 5.56 millimeter slugs poured from the M16 and into the waist-high brick wall, filling the air nearby with red powder.

"I think I hit him!" Pearce yelled over his shoulder.

"I hope he hit something, as much ammo as he blew though," said McBride as he quickly backed down the ramp to the patio, spooling out demolition wire.

It was then that the first shotgun shell exploded up the hill. I ducked, forgetting for a moment about the ammo Cutter had tossed into the coals. Another boomed, then another.

Coach Pearce cursed, fired another long burst from the M16 then hunkered down as Cutter popped up and pumped three blasts of buckshot into the kitchen. I fired two shots through the front door to announce my presence to them and Cutter.

"Damn! He's not alone," Pearce yelled, his voice high and sharp with fear.

Holly was trying to get to the porch steps near the library. If she could get there, she could she drop to her butt, lift her hips one step at a time and scoot into the library. In there was a phone and the gun case, but trying to hurry in the heavy braces was like trying to run in lead boots. Tony saw Holly and threw Rose down hard. He ran toward Holly as fast as the swinging gait of his prosthesis would allow, and he was almost on her when she saw him. Holly brought her right crutch up hard and fast, the metal slamming into the side of his head. Carlucci went down on his hands and knees, blood dripping from his left ear. She lifted the crutch again and hit him hard across the back, but he reached out and grabbed the brace-frame running down the outside of her calf and jerked her leg out from under her. She crashed onto her right shoulder, the pain burning through her neck and arm.

C utter was as startled as anyone when he heard the reports from the .357 come from the tree line near the front of the house. If it was friendly fire, good. Or maybe one of the bastards had somehow circled back around. Either way, he knew he couldn't worry about it.

"Let us pass, Cutter!" Coach Pearce shouted from the kitchen window, trying to buy time. Cutter could feel the drum beat of his pulse change in his neck. We both recognized the voice. We'd heard shouted orders coming from that throat a thousand times over the last three years. But this time Gaydon Pearce wasn't ordering, he was almost pleading.

"No way, Coach!" Cutter told him. "We settle this here. Tonight."

"Your sister's blood'll be on your hands! The woman's, too!"

"If you hurt either one, I'll cut you up an inch at a time. I swear!"

More shells blew up on the plateau and Pearce ducked.

I didn't know what I was going to do but I knew I was doing no good where I was. With their vehicles out of commission, there was only one way off this mountain for them and it was down that little trail below the patio. I ran to the west side of the house, opposite of the kitchen where Pearce was keeping Cutter pinned down. The boards came so close to the kudzu and the limestone wall that a man much bigger than me could not have fit. I had to duck under two window-unit air conditioners to get by. But I hustled through the narrow gap thinking I might be able to get behind the men in the house. Then suddenly I found myself staring almost straight down at 350 fifty feet of nearly nothing all the way to river. My stomach did a flip and stepped back into the narrow alley.

M cBride grabbed Rose by the arm and tried to lift her off the flagstones but she made herself dead weight. That only angered him. He kicked her hard in the back with a black combat boot then whipped the belt from his pants and in one quick move cinched it around her neck. "Now, girlie, you're going to get up and move or I'm gonna strangle you to death draggin' you," he told her. "What's it gonna be?"

There was nothing in McBride's look or history that would make Rose doubt him, and she didn't. She got to her knees and then stood. "Carlucci!" he called across the patio. "I've got your girl. Now kill that woman, and let's get gone."

When I steadied my stomach and nerves, and leaned back out over the edge of the drop and around the corner of the library, I saw "Dynamite Bob" stepping over the wall leading a bound-up Rose Marie Carlucci by what looked like some sort of leash. I thought about the dead man's gun in my hand, even raised it, but knew I was not nearly a good enough shot with a pistol from 75 feet away to guarantee I'd hit McBride. Or guarantee I wouldn't hit Rose.

G aydon Pearce stared down at his watch, disbelieving. It felt like the gunfight had been going on for hours but had been only a minute and half or so, yet all the glass in the kitchen windows was shattered, cabinets blown apart, shards of dishes and light bulbs and anything else breakable littering the floor.

One-minute-forty-seconds.

Two minutes? thought Pearce. *To hell with that!*

Glass crunched as he reset his feet and got ready to fire one more blast from the M16 before running for the patio and path down to the river. Cutter was ready, standing tall, the shotgun aimed on the window. As soon as Pearce swung out to fire, Cutter squeeze the shotgun's trigger. With arms strong enough to hold the barrel steady against the recoil fired twice more in rapid succession. The first array of pellets tore into Pearce's face like a swarm of flaming hornets. The second one caught him in the left shoulder and the armored vest he had on under his camo. The third round missed as he went down with a crash and rattle on the debris-strewn floor.

Cutter did not hesitate. As soon as the third blast had left the barrel, he ran toward the kitchen, hit the door hard with his shoulder and landed, sprawled on the kitchen floor next to the man he'd shot. Gaydon Pearce held one hand over a neck wound, blood pulsing through his fingers with every waning heartbeat. One eye was blown out. He stared at Cutter, panic filling his remaining eye, and reached for the teenager who'd been the coach's wet dream.

"Help me, boy," he begged, his voice already weak. "Help me!"

In those moments, Cutter felt nothing. Not pity, not sorrow, not judgment, not anger, and not fear. Not anything except an all-consuming need to keep moving, knowing any second could be the last for Holly or Rose. He stood and groaned as he pulled a shard of glass from his upper arm before digging the final three shotgun shells from his jeans and loading them into the magazine. There was nothing for it now but to go. He darted onto the courtyard porch and a three-slug burst tore into the wall behind his head. He dove over the railing and landed hard but rolled behind the big stone fountain as three more slugs from McBride's M-16 sparked on the flagstone where he'd been.

From my perch I watched as with four quick, practiced strokes from a utility knife, McBride cut, split and skinned the end of the detonation cord in less than fifteen seconds. He twisted the wire around the two small metal posts on the detonator and screwed the caps down on top of them. He released the handle of the plunger from its safety position and pulled it up. I didn't have to be a demolitions expert to realize it was ready.

"Let's go, Carlucci!"

Cutter crouched behind the fountain, the barrel of the shotgun steady on his father but he couldn't fire. Tony was laying behind Holly, who was on her side.

"Now or I leave you!" shouted McBride.

"I can't!" Tony told him. "He'll cut me down with that shotgun."

McBride fired another three-shot burst, then another, and another that sent Cutter to his belly and stone chips flying from the fountain. "Come on!"

Instead, Tony Carlucci wrapped his big forearm around Holly's neck and used the stiff leg braces as a way to leverage her up into a standing position, keeping her between him and Cutter. He pulled a Luger from a pocket of his coveralls and pressed it to the side of Holly's head.

"What are doing?" demanded McBride.

"Unfinished business," Tony told him. "Between me and the boy and her."

McBride shook his head. This was why he hated working with amateurs. They never could leave the emotion out of the equation and simply do the job. He looked at the detonator. He could grab it, duck behind the wall and blow the whole house to kingdom come, and everyone on that patio with it. He looked at the girl who now was almost unnaturally calm. She was crying silently, snot dripping from her nose and down the duct tape to her chin, but they were no longer big, scared tears. They were angry tears. Cold tears. Tears of hate and loathing. She'd be a handful.

"I'm out!" called McBride.

"You son-of-a-bitch!" yelled Tony.

"My mother thanks you for the kind words," said McBride. "If you make it off that patio, hit this plunger on the way by. It'll be a helluva show!"

With that, I watched Dynamite Bob pull a small flashlight from a utility pocket and start down the narrow path, leading Rose behind him like a dog on a leash.

"Your daddy ain't the only one who could use a sweet young wife," he said. "Let's go, girlie. We're gonna take a trip."

Above them I looked down as they moved along the steep path. I set my feet and aimed the pistol straight down. *Damn!* Benoit's gun felt like it weighed 20 pounds. Like it was going to pull me over the edge. I hurriedly got down on my stomach so that my body stretched back into the narrow gap between the house and rock wall. I could just drop arms and fire straight down. In seconds they were almost directly below me. I had to shoot now or let him take Rose away to who knew where and who knew what horrors. Then they stopped.

McBride was shining his flashlight over some brush piled up in the first switchback on the trail. Rose was several feet behind him. This was the best chance I'd ever have. I took in a breath and closed my eyes for a second, planning to pull the trigger as soon as I opened them, but in that instant Rose squatted then uncoiled her legs, coming up with all the force that her expanding muscles and adrenaline could deliver, driving her shoulder up under the arm holding the flashlight. McBride was caught entirely off guard and the impact catapulted him off the path. The old Klan bomber did not scream, did not call out, but I heard his body crash through brush then smash into a rock outcrop two-hundred feet below.

He looked like a little boy's military doll that had been smashed with a hammer. I stared at McBride for seconds, more seconds until I heard Rose groaning.

"Shit!" the collision with McBride had sent her tumbling into the barbed wire beneath the brush Cutter had used for camouflage. There was a grapevine as thick as my arm running down the limestone face of the mountain. I stood, shoved the pistol into the waist of my jeans, grabbed hold of the vine and started down before I could think about the fact that if I fell I'd be down there with McBride or beyond. As soon as I set foot on the dirt path I went to Rose. The stuff was all around her and a trickle of blood was seeping from several places on her legs and stomach and face where the barbs were digging in. I squatted and pulled at a loop of the wire but it only tightened around her and she closed her eyes grimacing in pain.

"Damn! Rose I'm sorry," I quietly told her. "It's gonna take wire cutters to get you loose, and I don't even have a pocket knife with me." But I did work my hand through the loops and manage to pull the tape down from her mouth. She swallowed and ran her tongue around her lips, tasting the blood and snot at the corners of her mouth.

"Help Cutter!" she told me with absolute clarity.

"But –"

"G-Go!"

Rose was right, I knew. There was nothing I could do for her now. I stood and pulled the big pistol from my pants and started up the narrow trail.

Tony Carlucci kept his left arm locked around Holly's shoulders dragging her a little at a time toward the east side of the patio where the path began just across the low wall. With the other hand, he kept the barrel of the Luger to her head.

"So, it's come down to this, huh, boy? You and me," yelled Tony. "Just like it ought to be."

I crouched, easing up the path, gripping the Smith with both hands until I could peek over the stone wall. Tony Carlucci had his back to me as he edged Holly Carter alongside the pool.

"Tony, there's no way out," said Cutter. "Let her go, and I let you go."

"'Tony?' You smart-mouthed, know-it-all brat. You call me Daddy or Papa or Dad or Blessed Fucking Father, but don't you dare call me Tony again," he snarled, pressing the gun to Holly's temple. "You acknowledge me right this mother-fucking second as your father, or so help me God I'll –"

"All right ... Dad ... Take it easy."

"That's better, Son," he said, his voice calm, cold. "I don't care much for your idea. With my gimp leg, you'd be on me with that scatter gun like a duck on a June bug."

Cutter let things settle for a moment. He held the shotgun close and reached for the .45 but realized it was gone.

"If you hurt her, I'll blow you in two," he told him. "I swear to God! You know I will."

"Ohhh, I don't doubt it a bit … Sonny Boy," said Tony as he continued to pull Holly toward the east end of the pool a half step at a time. I rested my forearms atop the wall. Tony's broad back was twelve feet directly in front of me. Even with an unfamiliar gun, it was a can't-miss shot. I saw Cutter peek around the edge of the fountain and for just an instant I caught his eye, and he saw the big revolver locked on his father's back. Tony quickly snapped his gun arm out and fired a shot that sparked off the flagstone near Cutter, driving him back. I adjusted my grip, my hands slick with sweat. It was can't miss. Holly was digging her nails into Tony's forearm, trying to free herself or at least get a breath of air into her lungs. She felt lightheaded and realized darkness was closing like black water begging to fill her eyes.

"Nope, tell you what we're gonna do instead, Sonny Boy," he was saying as my arms began to buck atop the wall. "We're gonna up the ante and see how much you love this crippled bitch! Better hope she's part fish and not just part nigger!"

With that Tony Carlucci shoved Holly forward, hard, and into the middle of the deep, 8-foot end of the pool. I heard her gulp air an instant before hitting the water and being immediately dragged to the bottom, feet first by the heavy boots and 20 pounds of steel encasing her legs. Immediately she began to try to unbuckle the straps of her braces but they were all tangled in her long, flowing skirt. She understood that with every frantic pull at her skirt she was burning through whatever oxygen was in her lungs, but she couldn't help herself.

Cutter immediately popped out from behind the fountain and fired a quick blast at his father, who was already on the move for cover behind the stone barbecue grill. I ducked as the spread of pellets from Cutter's shotgun popped against the wall where I'd been hiding. My feet tangled as I got out of the way, and I went down hard on my back and the back of my skull. My head below ended up my feet on the trail, the gun tumbling out of my slick hand as flashing balls of yellow light ping-ponged before my eyes.

Two more shots from Tony's semi-auto sent Cutter diving into the bushes at the far side of the patio's U. Beneath the water Holly desperately tried to reach the side or shallow end of the big pool, but the braces and boots might as well have been made of concrete. She felt panic rising. With one, then two enormous swims of her arms she drove herself to the surface, gasped and gulped down as much air as she could in the instant before the dead weight of her legs dragged her back to the bottom.

For a moment I thought it was my ears ringing, but then I realized I was hearing the sound of approaching police sirens. Even in this remote and well-hunted part of the county, there had been enough gunfire to get people out of bed and to their telephones. The police cars still were several minutes distant at best, but they were coming. Thank God they were coming! I hoped to sweet Jesus my daddy was coming!

As I tried to clear the bright ping-pong balls from my eyes Tony ejected the

Lugar's spent magazine, sending it clattering onto the flagstones, then expertly smacked another into the pistol's grip causing the slide to snap down into firing position as he taunted – "What's it gonna be, Mr. Football Star? Mr. All-America? You just gonna hide in the bushes while your woman drowns?"

Cutter had no more time to think, to consider, to strategize. His father was right. He had to act now or Holly was surely going to die.

"God! Help me!" he said as he rolled from the bushes and onto his feet, the shotgun rising to his shoulder as a slug from the Lugar buzzed past his ear. He fired at the side of the stone barbecue, pumped the gun as he ran to eject the spent, smoking shell and to chamber another. His last. He fired his final round to keep Tony pinned down for one more second, tossed the pump gun away and dove for the pool.

Pop! Pop! Pop! I heard as Tony swung around from behind the grill's chimney, went into a two-handed shooter's stance and followed his son's flight, his eyes and lips widening with satisfaction as he saw the impact of at least one bullet turn Cutter in midair.

Tony rushed to the edge of the pool as the police sirens grew close enough to be loud and distinct. The disturbed water in the pool had a sudden pink patina, a shroud of blood forming around Cutter who floated motionless at the bottom nearly at Holly's feet. She was standing upright locked in place by the braces, her long, loose hair a veil around her head, her arms floating beside her.

Tony smiled his jack-o-lantern smile and spit on the water with a sneer, then turned for the stone wall. Down on the dark trail I got to my feet, staggered and picked up the big Smith & Wesson. Tony threw his prosthetic leg over the wall and sat, putting the Lugar down next to the detonator McBride had readied. Tony was ready to grab it, duck behind the wall and set off the fourteen C4 charges running from the library all the way around the U of Wolf's Run to the kitchen. Approaching officers not killed outright would be both too shocked and too blocked by fire and debris to follow down the trail that would take him away, away from five capital murders and to freedom in Paraguay with his new young wife, who also was his daughter. As he straddled the wall he saw me, 20 feet below on the trail as I turned sideways and lifted the Smith.

I felt like I needed to say something like *halt!* But in that crazy moment the thing I was struggling with was what do I call him – I mean, he was Cutter's father. Did I call him Mr. Carlucci? Tony seemed too familiar for my engrained Southern manners. I didn't really know him beyond the way everyone knows everyone in a small town. Sir? Well, I wasn't going to give him that moniker of respect. Asshole? That was closer to right than anything else, but I had been brought up to respect my elders, especially my friends' parents. An instant later I just said, "Hey, you! You! Don't move!"

For a short moment surprise showed on his large, round face then his look turned to something like amusement. I saw his eyes stop for a second on where Rose lay pinned in the barbed wire. Then his hand shot forward. I should have pulled the trigger then, but I didn't. Instead of going for the gun he grabbed the small detonator.

"I ain't goin' to jail," he told me. "Now throw that gun off this mountain and get outtta my way, or I'll blow me and this whole place to Hell, and you and Rosie down there can come along for the ride."

My hand was shaking, visibly shaking and my mouth was so dry I couldn't get out a word. "Night's a wastin', boy!" he told me, his big hands and thick fingers wrapping easily around the small firing box, no fear in his eyes. I knew he would do it. I knew there was probably enough fear in my eyes for both of us. I had not seen what happened up on the patio, but I had not heard Miss Carter make a sound since she had fought her way up for one more desperate gulp of air. Her last? Now Cutter was quiet, too. No splashing. No yelling or even crying. No nothing. The police sirens had stopped, meaning they had arrived. Deputies – maybe even my father – were likely working their way down the driveway. Tree to tree. The air was as silent and still as death except for my tremulous breathing.

"What's it gonna be, boy?" he demanded with a sneer. "Show me what'cha got."

My Adam's apple bobbed so hard I thought it would tear through the flesh of my neck. "*Fuck you!*" I yelled long and loud, up from the gut, and felt the twelve pounds of trigger weight collapse under the angry demand if my finger. Once, twice – the gun bucking with each exploding magnum load – again and again, until my best friend's father disappeared behind a blinding wall of white flame.

EPILOGUE

Christmas 1973

'Fate is a funny thing. But most of its humor
is black and ironic; and the joke is usually on you.'
▪ *John Bastrop*

T he night was overcast and cold, and a frost-filled northwest wind went through my lightweight Class A Uniform. I had forgotten how cold north Mississippi can be deep in December. Through the fog of my own breath, I hustled up to the ticket window at the Rebel Theater, bored and a little buzzed after sitting around my room at the Jeff Davis Hotel for much of the afternoon eating cheeseburgers, drinking bourbon and Coke and watching the AFC Championship Game on the old black-and-white TV bolted inside a chest-of-drawers. The Dolphins defeated the Raiders 27-10 to go on to Super Bowl VIII. Damn fish! I had twenty on Oakland with a fellow in my platoon from Fort Lauderdale.

I glanced at the prices behind the glass and said to the heavyset young woman making change, "A dollar, huh? Last time I was here, it was 75 cents for adults and a quarter for kids."

She looked me over in my Marine greens and asked, "You from DeLong?"

"I used to be. But I haven't been home for a while."

She didn't pursue my history, my reasons for leaving or coming back, and I was glad.

"I reckon it costs more now to get the movies. You know, to show," she said pleasantly, her dumpling-shaped cheeks red from the cold seeping in from the half oval hole at the bottom of the glass. "But you're late. You've done missed the cartoons and the movie's already started. I'll just charge you fifty cents." She slid two quarters back through the slot.

"No, no. Please. I wasn't complaining," I said and pushed them back to her. "Just commenting on how things change."

"I guess they do," she said. "But they sure take their time about it around here. Tell you what. Come on in, I'll get you a hot popcorn on the house."

451

"All right. That'd be top notch."

I entered the small lobby, which, thankfully, was warm. It smelled of salt and butter, Coke syrup and pine-scented cleaner as it always had but was completely remodeled since the last time I was there in the late spring of 1970. The lobby carpet was new, the concession area had been rebuilt and expanded and there was a fresh coat of paint on the walls.

"Things certainly have changed here," I said, looking around.

"Yeah?" she asked, looking around now, too. "Been like this since we been in DeLong. But that's only a year. Moved down from Selmer, Tenn'see when daddy got a job at the new furniture factory north of town."

I nodded, finishing my once-over of the lobby. "The movie any good?" I asked, waving a hand toward a poster for *The Last Picture Show*.

"It's aw'right," she said as she scooped popcorn into a big square cardboard cup. "Kinda slow in places. And it's in black-and-white. Don't know why they done that. Ain't no movies in black-and-white no more."

I put fifty cents on the counter. "Could I get a Co-Cola, too, please?" She filled a large cup for me instead of the medium I'd paid for, fitted a plastic lid on top and slid a straw through the hole. "You see, it goes in easy as pie. You in town long?" she asked, her smile making her cheeks blow up like pink balloons.

"No. I'm catchin' the bus for New Orleans at 0-700 hours, then on to Diego," I told her. "In fact, I'm shippin' out overseas at the end of next week. Vietnam."

"Well, that's a shame. That you're leavin' so soon," she said, another small disappointment in a life already full of them. "I had a cousin from Alabama who went. He got killed. I didn't know him much, though. Hey, I thought President Nixon said the war was over?"

"We don't officially have combat troops there anymore. But there are still a lot of Marines on the ground and a lot of fightin' to do," I told her. "Thanks for the popcorn."

"Sure. Be careful over there."

* * *

I t had been a long 39-hour bus ride from the Marine barracks at Camp Pendleton near San Diego by way of Tucson, San Antonio and New Orleans, and a disappointing eight hours since I'd stepped off at the Greyhound stop next to The Cotton Café. I had quickly turned away from the restaurant's windows so no one in the late Sunday morning breakfast crowd would recognize me, walked up to the square and checked into the Jeff Davis. I took a shower and redressed in a fresh uniform I pressed with an iron from the closet. I wanted to look top notch for inspection by a pretty damn good soldier, my father, William Tice Wallace – still sheriff of Cattahatchie County, and likely would be now for life, or until he got tired of it. In the fall of 1969, he'd been elected to a four-year term by 27 votes. In the recent November elections, "Sheriff

Billy" had been reelected with 73 percent of the ballots as the county's African-American voters finally were able to fully exercise the franchise in large numbers. They had not forgotten his fairness or heroism during that long, arduous summer.

Calling over to the jail, I held my breath hoping the deputy who picked up wouldn't – "Sheriff's Office. Deputy Overby here," said the voice.

"Marvin, hey," I said, having known the man on dispatcher duty a bit at Cattahatchie High, though he'd been three years ahead of me. "This is Nate. Is my daddy handy?"

"Howdy, Nate. No, he's sure not. In fact, he's not in these parts right now. Miss Nancy's oldest sister got killed in a car wreck on Friday night. Up in Knoxville, Tennessee. She and her husband was teachin' at the University. You know? Go Vols. Your dad and Nancy left Saturday around noon, even though she's about pop with them twins she's carryin'. Don't expect 'em back until late Tuesday."

Part of me wanted to laugh. Not about the death of my step-mother's sister, of course, but I had ridden a bus fifteen-hundred miles to say my farewells – though hopefully not my good-byes – before going off to war. I hadn't called to let Daddy know I was coming. I told myself that it was because I wanted it to be a big, happy surprise, but now the surprise was on me. Closer to the truth was that until my Marine shoe leather landed on the DeLong sidewalk, I wasn't sure I'd get all the way here. That in Tempe or Houston I wouldn't turn in what was left of my eastbound ticket and head back to California. Arrogantly, I supposed Billy Wallace simply would be at work in his jailhouse office or sitting on the front porch down at the house waiting on his prodigal and mostly profligate son to return. Instead, his life had moved on without me, but that was no one's fault but mine.

"You there, Nate?" the deputy was saying on the line.

"Yeah, I'm here, Marvin."

"Sheriff calls in pretty regular. You want me have him call you? What number you at?"

I thought of telling him I was in town, but what would be the point? Knoxville was eight hours away in good weather and there was sleet then snow moving in from the hard, gunmetal clouds to the northwest.

"No, Marvin. Don't bother him," I said. "Sounds like him and, uhm, Nancy have enough on their plate. I'll call him next week after he gets back."

"Aw'right, Nate," said the deputy. "Kiss a few of them suntanned Californicate beach bunnies for me."

I pretended a laugh and told him, "Ten-four." Then I hung up, loosened my tie and sat down heavily on the old bed. Suddenly I was exhausted, weary of myself and embarrassed. I blew out a breath and unlaced my high-gloss Oxfords before putting my feet up, crossing my ankles and staring up at the ceiling through the gray winter light that found its way in via the two tall windows overlooking the square. I closed my eyes and in two minutes I was asleep.

When I awoke at 1:45 I was a ravenous with hunger and filled with some clarity of direction. I pulled the county phone directory out of a drawer in the bedside table looking for Teddy's Taxi Service. Theodore J. Joyner ran the only such service in the area, and the book wasn't much thicker than a beefed-up comic so the search took only a moment. Teddy Joyner had made a modest living for 40 years driving old folks to do their grocery shopping and to church. He had a regular route that ran more like a bus schedule than a taxi for hire, and I knew my timing was good – his "church people," as he called them, would be back home by now, warming old bones against the winter chill. Teddy was out in front of the Jeff Davis in five minutes in his two-tone 1953 Chevrolet Belair sedan. Both it and Teddy had seen better days. He told me the Chevy's heater didn't work so good and that I better sit up front if I didn't want my feet to freeze. So I did. I told him where I wanted to go and he headed the vehicle south, immediately beginning to fill me on every important event in the town's history since I left in the summer of 1970. He talked almost nonstop. I half-listened, feeling disconnected from most of it, and merely grunted now and then, but all I really wanted was for him to be quiet and drive.

At the farmhouse I got out and walked and around the place, hands stuffed in my uniform pockets, like someone who might be interested in buying it. The house had been painted since I left, and a new swing hung from fresh chains above porch planks the same forest green as the shutters. Toward the back I saw the new much larger master bedroom that had been added when in early 1972 Daddy wed Nancy Collins Magee, despite her being almost twenty years his junior. She'd returned to DeLong in 1964 after her young husband, an Army sergeant, became one of the early casualties of the Vietnam War and had taught me civics and history at CHS. When all that mess happened in '69, Miz Magee was one of the few white teachers to stick with the public high school, earning her what we in the military would call a "battlefield promotion" to assistant principal. She and Daddy got close when they worked together on the busing plan for the county schools. Her promotion stuck and so did their respect and affection for each other. Now they were a power couple in the small universe of Cattahatchie County. Things do change. In the ninth grade I had a pimply crush on the shapely Miz Magee and had, on quite a few nights, lain in bed in this very house and chanced blindness fanaticizing about her as my hand moved under the covers. To think that she was now sleeping under the same roof but in my father's bed, and pregnant with twins was, well, irony personified. Daddy had wanted me to be his best man, I would later know, but at the time I was unfindable, lost to him and myself, among the shrimp boats, 24-four-hour juke joints and cribs of South Louisiana.

Continuing around the house I saw the large deck that had been added, and further back a swimming pool, now covered with a tarp. My father was leasing out virtually all of the Wallace farm land, thus reaping rents and often a share of the profits and taking none of the risk. Add in the salaries and perks from their jobs and

454

Mr. and Mrs. Wallace could well afford such accoutrement. Hard to believe that just over four years ago, Daddy had been held mostly in ill repute, too drunk to mount a tractor. Purpose, I now realized, could do amazing things for a man, and I hoped I'd found mine in The Corps.

Outside the windows of my old bedroom, the one shared with Steve, I stood on tiptoes, trying to see in. Wondering if they'd cleared things out and turned it into a guest room or sewing room or some such. Though I had grown a couple of inches, I still was not tall enough. But when I looked up at an angle between the sill and the half-drawn shade I could see that the bookcases that Steve had made for me still were in place. So were my books, just as I had left them. I swallowed. From the ceiling flew the spacecraft models I had hung there during my NASA phase. I thought of the night of the moon landing, and remembered where I was, and who I was then, and was ashamed of my stupidity and selfishness. Instead of being proud and excited that my father was going to be sheriff, I ran whining to Cutter, and was angry at him for not being right there at The Well, on duty to play camp counselor and holy confessor to me in all my insecurities. I had not known then that he had been with Holly Lee Carter, or that the night men walked on the moon was the night my best friend fell in love with a woman who could not walk.

At the front of the house I gave the fresh, well-cared-for home one more good look, then got back into the cab. "You not goin' in?" asked Teddy.

"Nope," I told him. "Can't even if I wanted to. I lost my key to this place a long time ago."

"Where to then? Back to the hotel?"

"You know the Wallace buryin' place? Under the big oak. Take me there."

Teddy Joyner babied the old Belair down the mostly disused farm road as far as he could without it getting stuck but we still were a hundred yards from the graves. "I'll walk it," I said opening the door onto the cold wind.

"Aw'right, Nate, but I've got to be back in town by three-thirty to pick up Miz Kilmer for her Sunday bridge game," said Teddy. "She's a regular."

"I'll just be a minute," I told him and shut the door. It closed with a solid thump that you didn't get with cars coming out of Detroit these days, and sure as hell not from rice burners that were starting to infest California roads.

Dodging and hopping over a couple of deep puddles, I hunched against the wind and a starting of sleet.

In summer this was a pleasant place, almost beautiful – green and sun-warmed, the massive old oak providing shade when the days turned hot and the field work was hard. With hundreds of acres sending new sprouts, then striving stalks up toward a bright blue sky it did not feel like a place of death or regret. But in winter, it was an ugly, cold place. The grass over the graves was gray-white and hundreds of black, stubbly acres ran away from it in all directions – the shallow furrows ripe only with rain water. And the oak, leafless and stark. It looked like a gnarled hand, bones black with age, that had clawed its way out of the earth and was reaching for – for what? The open air? The cold sky? The warm promise of Heaven? Or just any fucking place that wasn't eternity under the ground?

Whatever it was, it was ours. That tree, these graves, this land -- we'd earned it. My Wallace forbearers had fought the British and Indians alongside Andy Jackson to gain it. And for five generations we'd battled Yankees, carpetbaggers, the boll weevil and asshole bankers like Cecil Weathers to keep it. I grasped the black wrought iron that that was planted in this soil, outlining this cemetery and the cold that it held shot through me. Corporal Steven Lamar Wallace 1946-1965 was buried next to our mother Denise Lamar Wallace "Neesie" 1925-1967. I spoke to each one in turn.

"Momma, I know this isn't what you'd want for me," I told her. "But there are things I need to know about myself, and that place, in this uniform is the only way I know to find out. I love you. No boy ever had a better mother. I wish I'd known how to help you. But I didn't. Neither did Daddy. He loved you so. Losin' Steve, it just about killed all of us. Somehow me and Daddy got through it. I'm so sorry you didn't. Couldn't."

To Steve's gray granite headstone, I said, "Shippin' out next week, Big Brother. The Nam. The shit ain't as thick as it was when you were there. But I hear there's still some operations over near Cambodia that could get pretty hairy. I won't embarrass you. I'll make you proud. I miss you. I wish you could've come back. You sure could've done something with this place."

The sleet was falling harder. It would be snow soon. Teddy Joyner gently tapped his horn. It was time to go. I stepped back from the rail, brought myself to attention and snapped off a perfect Marine salute to my Army bother, my brother in arms.

* * *

Nodding, I smiled at the chubby girl behind the candy counter at The Rebel and stepped through the curtain into the nearly empty theater. That's when fate stepped in.

On the screen Jeff Bridges and Cybill Shepherd were 20 feet tall and their moving images lit everything in front of me in silhouette – including a sleek, low-backed wheelchair about halfway down the aisle. A couple sat next to it, he with his arm around her, she with her head on his shoulder.

My heart thudded and I cocked my foot as if preparing to execute a classic military about-face, but instead I just stood there, staring. This was exactly what I had told myself I wanted to avoid, why I'd told no one of my visit home and arranged it to be as brief as possible. Drop in, drop by to see Daddy and take the first bus out the next morning.

Someone in the back corner cleared his throat in complaint. I looked around for where to sit, as if I didn't have my choice of most of 400 seats. I slipped into the closest row to my right and hunkered down next to the wall.

456

So much had happened since the summer of 1969, since men landed on the moon and Holly Lee Carter returned to DeLong. As I sat there in the flickering semi-darkness, ignoring the movie and staring at Cutter and Holly, my mind again began to catalogue it all.

That night at Wolf's Run, when Cutter and I sent his Jeep crashing down the hillside, marked the end of the most violent and ugly period in our county's history since the Civil War. That September night at Wolf's Run, I emptied a dead man's revolver into or at least at Tony Carlucci. From 20 feet away the impact of one of the 158 grain bullets traveling at over 1,200 feet per second knocked the detonator from his hands and he tumbled or threw himself from the stone wall and down the steep face of the mountain. His prosthesis – with a bullet hole through the calf -- was discovered several weeks later, half-buried in a sandbar about four miles south of the Old Iron Bridge. It was an area patrolled by old gators and notorious for undertows and water moccasins.

Of course, J.D. Benoit was as dead. The close range blast from Cutter's shotgun had blown a hole through his chest and out his back wide enough that a small man could literally stick his arm through, if such a man cared to do so. Rose had bravely ended the career and life of the infamous "Dynamite Bob" McBride, though parts of her body and face were scarred by deep cuts from the barbed wire. And Coach Pearce bled out on the kitchen floor from his neck wound. Good riddance to all of them. I believe God made the hottest parts of Hell for people like them and Mary Nell.

Frank Gandy survived being pinned under the truck but was left a total quadriplegic, needing a ventilator to help him breathe. In his early telling of that night's events, it was rumored that he claimed Cutter killed Beniot in cold blood while he was trying to surrender. Later, after Gandy cut a deal with prosecutors, that was never mentioned in his official statement. Gandy testified in two state conspiracy trials against Grand Wizard Milton Handley, Walter Kamp and former Governor Cecil Weathers. Both ended in hung juries. J.L. Burke, who by then had been named a Deputy U.S. Attorney General, was going to have a go at them in federal court on civil rights charges, but before the prosecution could be mounted, Gandy died.

The good news, however, was that Gaydon Pearce was as incompetent an assassin as he was a football coach. Miz Frances Ragland survived his attack and – now in her mid-90s – still wrote her once-a-week newspaper column, though nowadays she did so from home. Meanwhile, two weeks after the attack at Wolf's Run, Brother Dr. Charles Everett MacAllister was ousted from the pulpit at First Denomination.

In the end, not a single Klansman ever did prison time for the violence of that summer. Multiple investigations, prosecutions and finally a wave of public outrage encouraged on the editorial pages of *The Current-Leader* broke the back of the Kattahatchie Klavern, though many of the Kluckers continued to be a significant, if diminished economic force in the county. Miss H.L. Carter remained editor and publisher of *The Current-Leader*, which received a raft of awards, many national in scope, for its coverage of and role in the desegregation of the Cattahatchie County School System and the voter registration drives that followed.

Mary Nell Poindexter Carter never stood trial. Tennessee relinquished custody and while undergoing evaluation at the Mississippi state mental hospital at Whitfield, she hanged herself. Others claimed it was murder, bought and paid for by either the Poindexters because of their shame at having a homicidal daughter who'd been involved with "the colored Carters," or by Holly Lee Carter as payback for the murder of her father and brother. Tom Carter never came out of his arsenic-induced coma and died the first week of October 1969. Tom's children – Lanny and Georgette – survived the poisoning, and Holly tried to get custody of them, but she was no match for their wealthy, well-connected Poindexter grandparents. Last I heard, they'd shipped Georgette off to a boarding school in Switzerland, and Lanny was at some military academy in New Mexico that specialized in out-of-control teens.

Then there was Cutter.

One of Tony Carlucci's bullets hit Cutter's leg and another grazed his head, knocking him momentarily unconscious. But as Tony straddled the stone wall and grabbed the detonator, Cutter shook off the blackness long enough to pop to the surface, gulp air then go back under for Holly. As I emptied the S&W at his father, Cutter pulled her into the shallow end of the pool, up the steps and onto the deck. She wasn't breathing. Despite having a shattered left knee, he began giving her mouth-to-mouth and doing chest compressions while I stood stunned on the path staring dumbly at nothing but the space where Tony Carlucci had been, my ears ringing almost to the point of deafness and my shooting hand feeling as bruised and hurt as if a mule had stepped on it. Within a minute, Daddy and two of his deputies were on the patio and at Cutter's side. They took over and after another thirty seconds that seemed like three hours, Holly coughed up a great spew of pool water and opened her eyes and breathed. Cutter remained conscious on the flagstones long enough to take her into his arms. Both of them lay soaked, shivering with cold and onrushing shock, clinging to each other for dear life as my father applied a life-saving tourniquet to my best friend's leg.

Cutter was in a cast from hip to foot for almost three months. When he got out of the Memphis hospital after 10 days he needed help with almost everything, so he moved into Wolf's Run with Holly and his sister. From that day forward, Holly and Cutter had been "a couple," and no longer gave a damn who knew it. They weren't showy about it in public, but life was too short and could too easily be snatched away to wait and pretend. Together they attended every remaining CHS game that fall. Cutter cheered in the stands and was the team's biggest booster in the halls of CHS. He offered tips or suggestions when asked over beers at The Gin or barbecue at Wolf's Run but otherwise pretty much kept clear, understanding that it was no longer his team, and humble enough to let go. In the end, the Wolves finished 2-8, but the best, quickest, toughest, fastest player anyone in that part of Mississippi had ever seen would never play another down of football. If Cutter was bitter about the loss of a scholarship, the fame that a college football career could have brought and the money that might have awaited him as a professional, he hid it from everyone – especially me.

Despite much encouragement from Cutter, Jimmy, Dodge and others I never went back to the team though I did quit Riverview and returned home. I finished high school at CHS, but my friendship with Cutter was never the same after that night at Wolf's Run. Or said more fairly, after I turned my back on Cutter, and what I knew was right, multiple times that summer for the sake of a cheerleader's flounce. I could not look into Cutter's eyes without seeing my own guilt and weakness reflected back, even when he turned a genuine and open smile my way. So mostly I kept my distance and kept things casual when I could not. And like many before – notably an 18-year-old Holly Lee Carter – I got the hell out of DeLong practically before my graduation mortarboard had hit the ground.

Almost before I realized it, another Hank Williams tune was playing over the movie credits. The lights came halfway up as Holly stretched then deftly transferred back to her wheelchair with a strong, practiced movement. Cutter stood straight, his shoulders as flat and broad and hard as they'd ever been, his waist narrow. I felt something like panic race into my muscles and I hustled down the row and into the lobby. I heard Holly laugh, her voice as mellow and mature and weightless as autumn leaves. Was she laughing at me? No. That was stupid. She hadn't even noticed me. I shifted on my feet in the lobby, the concession stand closed and dark behind me, feeling my old nemesis, uncertainty, rise. I pushed through the front door into the alcove holding the ticket booth and a trio of Coming Attractions movie posters. Snow was falling now, carried on a light, frigid wind. Why I did not keep walking I don't know, but I stood there, my hands stuffed into my pants pockets. A minute later, Cutter held open the theater door and Holly pushed through. She had on jeans, fur-lined boots and a Navy pea coat cut short, the black wool making her copper hair seem almost ablaze. Cutter wore Levis, work boots and a short down-filled nylon jacket bearing the Cattahatchie County Sheriff's Office six-pointed gold star logo. From beneath the elastic gather of the jacket I could see near his left hip the leather of a cross-draw holster. Even deep in winter their tawny pallor made them both look tan and healthy and, well, beautiful.

They were almost past me when Cutter turned and gave the soldier boy a once over. His eyes lit up and he yelled, "Nate! Nate Wallace!"

I turned. "Hey, Cutter."

Before I could say more, he had his big arms around me in a bear hug, lifting me off my feet. He put me down and looked me over again in my uniform, which I was straightening along with my cap. "Gosh! It's good to see you!" he said. "Lee, look who's here. Doesn't he look fine in his uniform? All filled out. The Marines put some muscle on you, I see. And you're a couple inches taller."

Holly Lee Carter looked me over. "Hello, Nate. You look wonderful. It's good to see you," she said, but her voice held none of Cutter's excitement.

"When did you get here? How come you didn't let me know you were coming?" he asked, the questions spilling out. "Didn't you see us inside? Why didn't you come say hello?"

Dodging the first two questions, I said, "You two looked so – comfortable, I didn't want to interrupt."

"Interrupt?" he said, but didn't chase an answer. "So we've got to get together. Catch up. I want to hear everything. Are you stayin' down at the farm. Terrible thing about Nancy's sister."

"No, I've got a room at the Jeff Davis," I told him. "I'm only in town a few hours. I came in on the 9 a.m. bus. I'm goin' out at 0-700. I meant to surprise Daddy. But I'm the one who got the surprise."

Cutter pretended confusion to hide hurt and perhaps a little anger, but it was readable on Holly's face. His breath clouding in the air, he said, "Well, dadgum, Nate. You haven't been home in three-and-a-half years. I'd love to catch up. Hear how things are with you."

"Things are – well, I'm shippin' out to Vietnam at the end of the week. That's kinda how things are," I said and half laughed. "I thought I should see Daddy before I left."

Cutter looked for words and finally said, "I see."

At that point, I thought they might say their goodnights, which I could see Holly wanted to do. But Cutter said, "Look, Wolf's Run was too big for us to keep open year 'round. Besides, it's too far out in the woods with me down at Ole Miss three nights a week and Rose gone to L.A. We bought a little house about three blocks from here on Calhoun Street. A fixer-upper, and we fixed it pretty nice if I do say so. This woman took to power tools like you wouldn't believe. She can run a miter saw as good as I can now." Holly smiled politely. "We tore out a wall and added French doors in back, a deck and even a hot tub." He laughed. "And Lee can get at everything. I'd love for you to see it. We could catch up."

Before I could answer, Holly said, "Whoa, fellas. I can see this turning into all-night gab session. I have to be up at five. Remember, I'm doing that presentation for the New Albany Chamber of Commerce breakfast."

"That's probably going to be snowed out," said Cutter.

"Maybe, but I won't know until sunrise."

Why I didn't remain silent, I'm not sure, but I cleared my throat, which was starting to feel raw in the cold air. "Like I said, I've got a room at the Jeff Davis. We could talk there."

"Then that's perfect," he said, looking from me to Holly. "I'll just make sure Lee gets home aw'right and be over in about 15 minutes."

Holly cocked her head. "The car's only around the corner. You don't have to see me to the house. I go home by myself three nights a week."

"Don't remind me," he said. "But there's no need to make it four. Me and Nate haven't talked in a long time. It'll keep another fifteen minutes."

Holly sighed, but all of the annoyance was pretend. As was much of her warm embrace when she invited me into a long good-bye hug, saying aloud, "It's good see you, Nate. Come back safe." But into my ear she whispered, "Don't you dare blame Cutter for whatever mess you've made of your life."

When I straightened and she sat back, her eyes were as cold and beautiful as the falling snow.

Twenty minutes later, a '65 blue Ford pickup laid new tracks in the snow, fresh fallen on the square, and pulled into a spot in front of the hotel. A minute later Cutter was knocking on the door of my third-floor room. I opened it with a drink in my hand, said, "Come on in. I hope you won't have to arrest me for this, Deputy Carlucci."

"I expect I can let it pass if pour me one," he said, taking off his jacket and putting it next to my Marine uniform coat on the bed. The big .45 rested on his hip but on him it did not seem over-large. I had forgotten how big a man he was. He was a little thicker around the middle but he still carried his size with extraordinary ease despite a rebuilt left knee.

We sat on opposite sides of a table by the windows, sipping our whiskey and watching the snow fall. The wind had calmed but big, dime-sized flakes still were coming down, painting the townscape white. Through a handful of letters from Daddy and Nancy, plus the stream-of-consciousness gab of Teddy Joyner, I already knew much about what was happening in the openly co-habitational lives of Miss H.L. Carter and part-time Deputy Carlucci. He would finish his bachelor's at Ole Miss in early June. Two weeks later, he and Holly would wed. In the fall, he'd begin law school and finance all of it playing "semi-professional golf," as my father described it in one letter.

"Miss Carter, err, Holly looks good," I said.

"Yep," he nodded. "She's pretty amazing. It's like that hair color commercial on TV goes, she's not getting older, she's getting better. Though sometimes I have to work a little at convincing her of it." He smiled. "But it's good work."

I returned the smile. "I hear congratulations are in order."

"If I had all the say-so, we'd have been married as soon as I got out of Cattahatchie High," he told me. "But Lee's as stubborn as she is good lookin' and smart. Our deal was, even if we lived like man and wife – 'wallowing in hedonistic sin,' as one preacher told me -- I wouldn't pester her about getting married until I finished college. She wanted me to know I had the freedom to leave if I ran across some little sorority cutie that I liked better."

"One who's not in a wheelchair?"

"That's right. And younger. I told her that wasn't going to happen, but she wouldn't have it any other way. Say, I was planning to write and ask you to be in the wedding. Suppose Uncle Sam would turn you loose for such a thing?"

By then I figured I'd be waist deep in blood-spattered elephant grass and dead gooks. "I kinda doubt it."

We sipped our bourbon. I changed the subject. "So, what's this I hear about you becomin' a golf sharp?"

He leaned his head back and laughed a little at the notion. Then – "Crazy, huh?"

"Yeah. As far as I ever knew, you never even had a golf club in your hands. Thought the game was way too slow."

"In case you haven't noticed, I'm a lot slower than I used to be," he said, but there was no rancor or irony in it. "I needed something I could really compete in. I tried to play softball in the county men's league, but I spent more time on the bench icing my knee than I did on the field. Pool's okay, but I get tired of hangin' around bars workin' up games. Besides, that's only pocket money. Gas and beer money. There's no high-rollin' shooters in this part of the country.

"So for our second Christmas together, Lee got me a set of second-hand clubs. Told me our house here in town was too small for me to be hangin' around all the time under foot. That I was drivin' her crazy and Rose, too. Sister was living with us at the time, goin' over to Booneville to the junior college. Lee told me to take the clubs and learn to play. So I did. I guess I got pretty good pretty fast," he said, something that did not surprise me considering his long arms and legs, and his always extraordinary strength and hand-eye coordination, not to mention an even-keel personality that masked a ferociously competitive nature. "I started bettin' a little here and there, hole to hole, then round to round, then in little tournaments. Before I knew it people – rich, important people – were wanting to pay me to play on their scramble team or back me, like a horse, in some club tournament. Pay all the expenses for me and Lee to come. Put us up in nice places."

"Wow."

"There's a sort of an unofficial Mississippi country club tour from about April through the middle of August," he explained. "Big Delta money gets bet in what're called Calcuttas or Nassaus. We came home from Greenwood last summer with six thousand dollars cash money."

"You're shittin' me?"

"Not a bit," he told me. "Paid for a whole year at Ole Miss. Meant I didn't have to bartend or wait tables at night in Oxford. I could concentrate on my studies. And more than that, I could be more help to Lee with house bills. Between us, Nate, things may look great on the surface – 'cause that's how we want them to look – but behind the scenes, Weathers and his bunch are still trying to sink the paper. There've been many weeks when we wondered if we'd make payroll. Or, shoot, even be able to buy groceries." Then, "Enough about us. Gimme a couple more fingers of Grandad and tell me what's been happening with you these last three years."

So I did, realizing that this was the real reason I'd come home, as much as I had tried to avoid it. Before I shipped out to a place I might never come back from, I needed to tell someone, and the only one whom I could tell, who might understand and not judge me, was sipping bourbon across the table.

I told him that I loved New Orleans – the wonderful food, people, music, the arts scene – and Tulane, and appreciated the help Holly had been in getting me a journalism scholarship there; that I even got a part-time job with the New Orleans paper, which was a dream come true; and another part-time gig tending bar at a club on Decatur; that I was living in a basement apartment on Montegut Street when late one night in the middle of my sophomore year someone knocked on my door.

"It was Patti," I said. Cutter's lips parted as if he might say something but he didn't, so I went on. "She told me Brother Daddy had lost it after he was dismissed from First Denomination. He moved them up into the mountains in north Alabama onto a, a 'compound' she called it, with a bunch of people that were half holy-rollers and half drug-dealin' bikers or worse. A lot of them were ex-cons who claimed they found 'the truth' inside. They were all white, of course, and they flew a Confederate flag and a Nazi flag at the entrance to the place." I took a long sip of the whiskey and went on. "About six months in, four of them gang raped Patti and her little sister. You remember Colleen? She was in the ninth grade when we were seniors."

"Sure," said Cutter, his face stony.

"They went to Brother Daddy but that fuckhead called them whores and harlots and accuaed them of leading on 'righteous warriors of our blood.' Couple of months later when Colleen realized she was pregnant, she and Patti lit out. They lived on the streets in Birmingham and Atlanta for a few months before Colleen miscarried." I paused and readied the words. "She bled out in some rent-it-by-the-hour motel room. That's when Patti caught a ride to New Orleans with some Dixie Mafia asshole. He dumped her but she found work at a club on Bourbon Street. A strip joint. She said she was walkin' by the bar where I was workin' and saw me. She followed me home."

As was Cutter's way, he said nothing, made no judgment with his words or even his eyes. Just opened himself up to hear whatever I wanted to say, needed to say.

"She told me her roommates had kicked her out 'cause she couldn't make her share of the rent and that she needed a place to crash for a couple of days. A couple of days turned into a couple of weeks then a couple months. And they were mostly a real good couple of months. Patti had broke loose from all of Brother Daddy's bat-shit craziness. When it was just me and her, she was the Patti I always thought she was. Or could be. She was smart and funny. Thoughtful. She didn't hate black people or anybody else. She loves listenin' to Bob Dylan and reading poetry in bed, and sleepin' late on rainy days." Cutter waited. I cleared my throat, went on. "Together we were kinda fixin' up the place, shabby as it was. The only problem was she had a hundred-dollar-a-day habit and was turnin' tricks to feed it. She said those men she laid with for money didn't have anything to do with us, but I couldn't – I mean the thought of her with – well, I tried to get her into a drug treatment program. I tried to get her to stop, and tried to help her find a real job. But I guess I pushed too hard, too fast. Asked too much of her, maybe. One afternoon I came in from class and there was a note that said, 'Nate, you're a good guy. Too good for me. Maybe we'll meet again someday. When I'm better. Love, Patti.'"

Cutter waited to see if I was finished, then, "That's pretty rough. All the way around."

"Yeah, it was kind of a shitty day," I agreed. "And I let it turn into a shitty week, then a shitty month. I knew the city pretty well by then and looked for her every place I could think of. I finally found one of her stripper friends who told me she'd split for parts unknown with some guy in a new Cadillac. Pretty soon I stopped goin' to class and lost my job at the paper. I started drinkin' about as much as I was pourin' at the bar I worked at. The owner was a nice guy, but he told me I had to get my shit together or get out. Number one didn't seem like a viable option. So, I got out."

Cutter picked up the open bottle of Old Grandad and poured a bit more in my glass and his. No ice. After a time he asked, "How'd you land with the Marines?"

"I kicked around the Oil Patch down in Terrebonne and St. Mary's parishes, catchin' a day of work here and week of work there. Sleepin' in flop houses and hot pillow joints when I had some dough. Under bridges when I didn't. One night I went out drinkin' in a little wide-spot-in-the-road place called Galliano and woke up about a hundred miles away down the Mississippi in Plaquemines Parish. How I got there, I still don't know. But one place was as good as another, so I found and lost two or three jobs workin' the shrimp boats out of Delacroix when I hooked on with a long-haul trawler called the Blessed Day. The captain – a fellow by the name of Byron Boudreaux – turned out to be a salty old ex-Martine who'd done his share of fightin' and killin' on Iwo Jima and later in Korea. Bein' out on the deep blue for 10 days to two weeks at a stretch, runnin' all the way down to the Yucatan under that Gulf sun started cookin' some of the alcohol out of me, and maybe bakin' some sense in. Over the months I stayed aboard, me'n Captain Buck had some long talks."

"He suggested the Marines?" Cutter asked.

"No, he didn't have to. He just said that the military – the training and discipline and sense of connection to something larger than yourself – had made him the man he was. After five months crewin' for him I knew that was the kind man I wanted to be."

"Your daddy is that kind of man," said Cutter. "I wish you and him could patch it up better."

I nodded slowly. "Me, too. Maybe when I get back," I said, then, "You're the same. You did your share of killin' when you had to."

Cutter looked at me and something passed between us. I had never told him that I had hesitated on the rock outcrop above Wolf's Run long enough to see Benoit open his hands in surrender an instant before Cutter blew a fist-size hole through his chest. But in that moment I felt sure he knew.

"When I had to ..." he almost whispered, then blinked the thought away. His voice regaining its oak-solid resonance, he grunted and said, "My share of killing? I suppose I did. But I didn't like it much. I hope you don't get to likin' it either. Some men do."

I thought about that, then shifted – "You don't think Tony's dead, do you? That's why you became a deputy. So you can be out there on the roads. Watchin' for him. Waiting on him. Lookin' for sign. That's why you carry that big ol' pistol all the time."

After several moments, he said, "Tony was the hardest man I've ever known. But you emptied a .357 at him at close range."

"McBride and Coach Pearce were wearing vests," I reminded him. Then, with a small quaver slipping into my voice, my eyes downcast I told him, "Cutter, my hand was shakin' so bad! After the first shot I just closed my eyes and kept squeezin' the trigger."

"Nate," he said, his voice suddenly soft, wrapping around my name, "let it go. Whatever happened, Tony wasn't your demon to kill." Then he forced a quick, mirthless laugh. "Anyway, if nothing else, the fall down the side of that mountain would've killed him."

I looked up, meeting his eyes. "You really believe that?"

He considered. "I sure would like to."

At six o'clock, I walked back into the bedroom after taking another piss and said, "Damn, we talked the whole night away. I'm starvin'. Let's get breakfast at The Cotton."

We put on our jackets and I quickly repacked the small duffel I'd brought with me and we went downstairs, out through the silent lobby, into the silent town. We got in the cab of his truck and cranked up the heater and he used the windshield wipers to brush the inch or so of snow off the glass.

"I hope they call off that chamber breakfast down in New Albany," he said. "I don't want Lee out on the road in this if she can help it."

"Why don't you drive her?"

"Can't. I've got to go home and take a shower. I go back on duty at eight."

"Shit!" I groaned. "Why didn't you say somethin'? I wouldn't have kept you up all night with my ramblin'."

Cutter waved that away. "Forget about it. My best friend doesn't come home every night."

Looking out the window, I cleared my throat of the emotion that suddenly swelled there – *my best friend* – and asked, "You mind takin' a loop around the square?"

"No. Not a bit," he said and started the truck around the courthouse. DeLong looked as if it were covered in soft, white linen. The streets were as beautiful and serene as I had ever seen them. We went past the town's granite memorial to its war dead, which now held in its stone cold embrace the names of all the young men from Cattahatchie County – black and white – who had given their lives in service to their country. Of course, it included Steve's name and now that of Army Pvt. 1st Class Wesley Dodge McDowell. Dodge enlisted about two weeks after graduation. He lasted about two months in Nam. He never saw twenty.

There was a new awning over the second floor balcony outside of Holly's office and a metal table with several chairs. At the top of the red brick front the sign had been repainted not long ago. It was fresh and bright under two lights that extended from the roof:

CATTAHACTHIE CURRENT-LEADER
'The Conscience of the Community'
Since 1836 * H.L. Carter, Publisher

Cutter eased down the snow-slick hill toward the river and the Bilbo Bridge over to Roseville. Businesses had been rebuilt in the place of those wrecked in the bombing, and *The Current-Leader* had led a civic push to create a memorial park on much of the block destroyed by fire. But I won't attempt to calculate or pretend to comprehend the pain and anger that lingered behind the long row of cotton warehouses. That wasn't the life I lived. It wasn't my part of the drama. But I hoped someday someone from that side of Cattahatchie would tell it.

We parked across the street from The Cotton. Paula Simpson was away at college and her mother no longer waited tables on the early shift, so the girl chewing gum behind the counter was new. An acne-pocked blonde, she didn't fill out her pink uniform nearly as well as her predecessor. But Miss Winona came out of the kitchen and gave me the once-over with her milky eyes and welcomed me home as if I'd already been to war.

"Why, Nate Wallace! You've just growed up to make the handsomest young man!" she crowed, resting her strong old hand on my forearm. "And look at you in your uniform. Nothin's too good for our soldier boys. Breakfast with all the trimmin's be on the house. Cutter, you pay."

He laughed -- "Yes, Ma'am." And I realized I had heard Cutter laugh more in the last eight hours than maybe all of high school.

We sat at the same spot at the end of the counter that we had on so many

Sundays, including the morning on which Cutter and Holly had met on such unfriendly terms four years ago.

"Guess Miss Winona doesn't remember the side I took that summer," I said.

"There's nothing wrong with Miss Winona's memory," he said, warming his hands around the steaming coffee cup. "But like a lot of people, she'd rather live today in forgiveness than dwell on four-year-old upsets and ugliness."

I didn't know what to say to that, so I said nothing.

Miss Winona's pancakes, sausage, bacon and hash browns were delicious, and the snowy morning made The Cotton's coffee taste even better, but after a third cup it was time to go. I excused myself to the men's room and when I came back I said, "Guess I better get outside. If I'm not there to flag down that old gray dog, the driver's liable not to stop on a mornin' like this."

Cutter walked out with me. He was wearing his green Sheriff's Office jacket. The wind was light but still out of the northwest and as sharp as razor blades. The sky gave little hint that dawn was only minutes away. We shifted and waited and stuffed our hands into the pockets of our pants as we huddled behind the corner of the café, using it for a windbreak. The green-and-white neon glow of a blooming cotton stalk lit us and the snow around our feet.

"I hate you're not going to be here for the wedding," he said. But before I could speak, he told me, "Nate, don't go gettin' yourself killed to prove something that don't need provin'. You're not a coward, and you never were." The flakes touched my face like lost tears. He went on – "You saved us. If you hadn't grabbed Benoit's gun and followed me down that hill, me and Holly, Miz Ragland. We'd be dead. God only knows where Rose would be or what she'd be goin' through."

My chin shook. "But I could have killed Tony the first time I had him in my sights. If I had, he –"

"Yeah, or you could have hit Lee," he interrupted firmly. "Or Tony could have squeezed that Lugar's trigger on reflex, or out of plain meanness, and killed her."

"But your leg!" I gasped. "You were the best football player I ever saw. The best anybody around here ever saw! You could be a star!"

Cutter grabbed my shoulders. "Nate, stop it! That was your dream. That was this town's dream. But it was never mine. I wouldn't trade the life I have with Lee for a hundred Heismans and twenty Super Bowls." He shook me a little. "Do you hear me? I didn't lose anything. I found Lee. I gained *everything* that matters."

Stepping back from him, I wiped my face as the bus rumbled down River Street, the driver shifting gears, the snow sliding away from the big tires. I stuck my arm up and waved. The airbrakes on the Greyhound hissed.

"Nate, we all did the best we could," he told me. "Don't throw your life away trying to prove something that don't need proving. Come home to the people who love you."

The door to the bus swung open. I threw my arms around Cutter and we embraced until the driver bumped his horn. "Let's go soldier boy," he said. "Daylight's comin' and I need to put this burg in my rearview."

I rubbed more tears from my cheeks, grabbed my duffle, climbed aboard and found a seat where I could see Cutter. He stood there in the cold and the snow next to the neon bloom of The Cotton Café sign waving until the bus was out of sight.

The driver geared the bus up onto the square and pointed south toward Highway 27. I'd been awake for more than 24 hours and my mind was giving way to fatigue, and relief and the endearments of Old Grandad. My hands were cold but my belly was full, and my eyelids suddenly felt as heavy as tent canvas.

As we passed Mrs. Fletcher's boarding house and the fairgrounds, the sun was breaking through small cracks in the leaden clouds. To our right, the Cattahatchie looked like a wide black ribbon lain on a white tablecloth. To the left, the east, the fallow fields of winter were glistening like cake frosting laced with diamond dust. As we approached the short bridge where Holly and Cutter met, a shaft of light as defined as a glass tube and as pure and golden as liquid platinum painted the creek, the ditch and part of the nearby field. I smiled as it glittered on the bus and through the windows and onto the souls wrapped in blankets, snuggled on small pillows and sleeping around me. Unaware. Though we quickly passed out of that sunbeam's singular radiance, it hung there on that spot for as long as I could see.

The bus picked up speed and quickly put the quiet acres and snow-frosted miles of Cattahatchie County behind it, until there were no more. My long road to New Orleans and California and Southeast Asia lay ahead. I settled down in my seat to sleep, certain that such a perfect stream of golden light was what the finger of God looked like when He chose to touch the earth.

THE END

ACKNOWLEDGMENTS

The first fragment of the idea that became Wolf 's Run was scribbled into a reporter's notebook while covering a Bolivar County (Ms.) Board of Supervisors meeting in Rosedale about 1980. Since then I have sought and been blessed with the input of countless people. Many deserve a mention here and will not get it because of my poor memory, note-keeping and the confines of space. To each of you I want to say a heartfelt thank you and offer a heartfelt apology if your name is not mentioned.

However, there are a handful of people who were invaluable in this multi-decade process and I am pleased to acknowledge them.

First and foremost, I want to again thank my wife, Joyce, for her incredible patience, support and encouragement throughout the thirty years of our marriage; plus some darn good editing.

Also I want to thank:

Greg Akins, my best friend, for his consistent encouragement and faith in me even when I lost faith in myself.

Maureen Rung Simonson, Milita Dolan, Liz Winkelaar, Lenore Castro and numerous other spinal cord injured individuals who shared with honesty and openness about their lives in wheelchairs; and, of course, my wife, Joyce, who did the same.

David L. Maxwell of Everest & Jennings wheelchairs.

Bill Bowen, Sarah Peters and Jodi McNeal for their editing skills; and my very best and most dedicated editor and most honest critic, my wife, Joyce.

Thanks to photographer John Sizemore for the book jacket photo that does not do me justice (in a good way).

My mother, Louise Park, and Mrs. Valerie Boyd Howell, who instilled and nurtured in me a love for the written word.

The Pickens, Akins and Reno clans of north Mississippi who, at one time or another, took me in as one of their own and gave me a sense of family that I would not otherwise have had.

And finally, Mrs. Allie Gaddis, her daughter Paula and girls everywhere in Tuff-Nut overalls.

CPSIA information can be obtained
at www.ICGtesting.com
Printed in the USA
LVHW030848221119
638065LV00001B/37/P